Praise for Gilbert Sorrentino's trilogy

Odd Number

"*Odd Number* extends and expands the exploration of the impossible limits of experience and language. . . . Works that venture into this strange territory that eludes language inevitably are difficult and complex. *Odd Number* is no exception. Few authors now writing are as demanding as Gilbert Sorrentino—and few are as important."—*Los Angeles Times*

"In *Odd Number* . . . Sorrentino investigates yet another formal problem—the disintegration inherent in the investigative process. By calling into question the whole notion of truth, and trust, he manipulates the very nature of facts. Reality is always suspect. [He] is a master of artifice."—*Washington Post*

"The work of a sophisticated, meticulous artist with a gift for comedy, a perfect-pitch ear for American speech. . . . Sorrentino surpasses even Flaubert in the contempt he lavishes upon a world portrayed with extraordinary craft. This is an easy book to put down, but worth not putting down in order to watch the writer's infinite invention."—*Hudson Review*

Rose Theatre

"*[Rose Theatre]*, this novel, this exercise, this hilarious, infuriating book. . . . Sorrentino has long been one of our most intelligent and daring writers. . . . He is also one of our funniest writers."—*New York Times*

"*Rose Theatre* is a torrent, a furious and often obscene account . . . it washes over you, the language soaks in. . . ."—*Washington Post*

"A refreshing and rewarding visit with one of the most creative writers publishing today."—*Library Journal*

"In a darkly comic metamorphosis, the characters and scenario of [*Odd Number*] are reshuffled and redeployed as Sorrentino continues his rigorous investigation of the fictional mode of narrative . . . resulting in a work that is both demanding and rewarding."—*Booklist*

"Sorrentino's fiction does not reveal a world of sense, of reason, but portrays with equal brilliance our fall into nonsense, into the Babel of our everyday lives."—*Los Angeles Times*

Misterioso

"With this closing volume, Sorrentino's trilogy . . . reaches its postmodern climax."—*Booklist*

"Rich in voice, devastating in its satiric impulses and startling in its formal ingenuity, *Misterioso* is a literary game which not only imitates, parodies, satirizes and elaborates upon the fantasies, pleasures, surprises, and disappointments of American life, it also most tellingly *invents* specific possibilities of which American life is incapable. In this sense, reading *Misterioso* is a liberating experience all too rare in a culture that values art which reassures—and restricts—our imaginations."—*Los Angeles Times*

"Sorrentino has shown himself a perfect mimic of the information age, an era when all is revealed and no one can quite remember who appeared on the cover of last week's issue of *People*."—*Washington Post*

"Because of Sorrentino's great talent for mimicry, the novel's lure isn't its narrative pull but its hilarious and savage catalog of American usage."
—*San Francisco Chronicle*

Gilbert Sorrentino

pacK
of
Lies

 Dalkey Archive Press

Sorrentino, Gilbert.
    Pack of lies / Gilbert Sorrentino.
        p.   cm.
    Contents: Odd number — Rose theatre — Misterioso.
    1. Detective and mystery stories, American.
PS3569.07P33   1997   813'.54—dc21   96-51793
    ISBN 1-56478-154-2

This publication is partially supported by grants from the Lannan
Foundation, the National Endowment for the Arts, a federal agency,
and the Illinois Arts Council, a state agency.

Dalkey Archive Press
Illinois State University
Campus Box 4241
Normal, IL 61790-4241

Odd Number

Thus we have characters who are to be considered identical because they look alike. This relation is accented by mental processes leaping from one of these characters to another—by what we should call telepathy—, so that the one possesses knowledge, feelings and experience in common with the other. Or it is marked by the fact that the subject identifies himself with someone else, so that he is in doubt as to which his self is, or substitutes the extraneous self for his own. In other words, there is a doubling, dividing and interchanging of the self. And finally there is the constant recurrence of the same thing—the repetition of the same features or character-traits or vicissitudes, of the same crimes, or even the same names through several consecutive generations.

SIGMUND FREUD (The "Uncanny")

Was it still twilight, or had it already grown dark?

If you'll again permit me to get my notes in order, I'll according to my data, what there is of it, it was not yet quite dark, yet it was
just past what is usually called twilight certainly it was not yet dark
enough not to be able to see, since it is clear that the three of them were
seen in the street, beneath a plane tree it was a soft evening late
spring

The seating arrangement in the car?

Mr. Lewis was driving although the car was owned by Mr. Henry
owned more or less it was Mr. Henry's car he owned the car,
but not exactly outright, as these reports make clear Mr. Lewis was
driving, Mrs. Henry was seated next to him, and Mr. Henry was in the
back seat no one else was in the car

Earlier you mentioned, in passing, that there had been a lot of
drinking. What sort of drinking?

I did? I don't remember saying that was there a memo on that?
they had been drinking all afternoon but I have no evidence that they
were drunk perhaps a little high would be the word, the expression
after all, Mr. Lewis was driving, quite competently all right, all right!

Mr. Lewis had thrown up earlier in the day and Mrs. Henry had
modeled a new bathing suit for her husband and Mr. Lewis
somebody took some her husband had taken some photographs of her
I have two of them here, supposedly not a very good likeness but would
you like to see them? whatever information I have is yours

What was Sheila wearing?

Mrs. Henry was wearing a sleeveless shift of off-white raw silk,
the hemline coming to just above the knees, a black-and-white-figured
rayon scarf knotted loosely about her neck, sheer nylon stockings of the
shade called just a moment the shade called Smoke and black

9

sling high-heeled shoes   I have an addendum on her underclothing but surely   good   yes, that would do it, standard   standard feminine underclothing, fine   you can use your imagination   I don't mean you you

There have been persistent rumors that Lou Henry owed something to Guy Lewis and that this debt was the reason that Guy was tolerated as a more or less permanent guest in Lou's home. What, if anything, did Lou owe Guy?

It wasn't exactly a debt, as you put it, but more like   gratitude it's well documented that Mr. Lewis did a series of linoleum cuts for Mr. Henry's first book, which was either   *Sheila Sleeping* or *The Orange*   no   or *Lobster Lays*   and that, further, he had arranged for its publication with a friend of his, Saul Blanche, who owned a small press at the time in New England   Vermont   so it was   gratitude and they were also good friends

What was the occasion for the party to which they were going?

I have no information on that   an occasion?   no, I don't seem to have   an occasion, you say   the folder I have is labeled simply "The Party"   nothing about an occasion   that I can find

What were you doing in the car?

I wasn't in the car!   why would you think that I was in the car?

I have a photograph of the car taken as it passed under a streetlamp and it's obvious that the car has only   three   people in it, Mr. and Mrs. Henry and Mr. Lewis   would you like to see for yourself?   take a look?

Did Guy make indecent advances to Sheila in the car?

Well, indecent   I don't know about indecent   I think that's the sort of thing that's in the eye of   all right, fine, the memo   it's rather sketchy   Mr. Lewis did a few   minor things   the memo never once uses   does it?   no   the word indecent, by the way Mr. Lewis did a few small things in a spirit of   fun, it seems   the memo isn't explicit but they seem to have been bawdy or   ribald? ribald   the memo, yes   at occasional stops for red lights Mr. Lewis touched Mrs. Henry on her breasts and on her   thighs and knees and once put his hand   let me see now   put his hand under her skirt and here an interesting note states that he even told Mr. Henry that his wife had the most beautiful legs he'd ever seen   I think there was a lot

of horseplay   no it doesn't say that but I'm   Mr. Lewis was quite
candid   it seems   I don't think a man announces really indecent, as
you say, acts   advances, pardon me   that would seem to be it   Mr.
Lewis touched Mrs. Henry a few times and made a remark about her thighs
    about her legs

Was Guy Lewis married?

He was indeed, for almost ten years, to a woman named   Joanne
    I haven't got   yes I have   her maiden name was Harlan, Joanne
Harlan   all her friends called her Bunny   at this time they'd been
separated for   a while   I have a large envelope of materials on Mrs.
Lewis here, all sort of things   letters   diaries   a few drawings
and some   other things   not much of interest   just things I said
they're photographs that's all   of course, if you wish, it's just that I
don't understand you, you had no interest in the photograph of Mrs. Henry
nor the pair of photographs of the car but you're interested in   I don't
agree, I don't think you can prove anything from these photo   and what
else?   odds and ends, knick-knacks, souvenirs, private things that
wouldn't make sense to anybody but   here's for instance a little amber
glass ashtray that says Welcome To Kansas City   and   here's a
book of matches from Mama Gatto's Restaurant and a menu from
Imbriale's Clam House   thank you   I still don't think that these photo
    it's not my business to think   all right   but to jump to conclusions
doesn't seem

Why were you invited to this party?

I wasn't invited to the party   first you have me in the car, now
you have me at the party   soon you'll be saying that I was friendly with
everyone   look, I mind my business and do my best   I don't get any
pleasure out of all this   these folders and envelopes and cartons full of
old junk and stuff it's better to leave dead and buried   I can't imagine
who'd want to know this, some sort of sick mind prodding and poking
into people's lives   this one, "The Party"   you can look through it,
every scrap and   what you'll find out is what I found   Horace Rosette?   yes, but that's right here too   that doesn't mean that I knew
him or that I knew anything about any new book of his   these are pieces
and scraps   if you want to make connections   go ahead   I certainly can't help it   I gathered these things together   believe me I
don't get any pleasure out of all this   and worked hard to get them in

some kind of order because I knew that you'd want   no I was not there   why would I be invited to Mr. Rosette's?   I say it again   I didn't know these people   not at all   and when I say didn't know I don't mean know at a distance   I mean I didn't know them   at all   what I know is what all this   all these papers and things   know   if they know anything either

Who was at the party?

I'll just read the names off if that's   Horace Rosette, of course, and you know that Mr. and Mrs. Henry and Guy Lewis were there   then there were Lucy Taylor, Lena Schmidt, Harlan Pungoe, Duke Washington, Karen Ostrom, Buffie Tate, Vance Whitestone, Craig Garf, Joanne Lewis, Leo Kaufman, Anne Kaufman, Ellen Kaufman, Biff Page, Lee Jefferson, Chico Zeek, Anton Harley, Antonia Harley, Page Moses, Baylor Freeq, Bart Kahane, Conchita Kahane, Lolita Kahane, Lincoln Gom, Roger Whytte-Blorenge, Dick Detective, April Detective, Luba Checks, Sister Rose Zeppole, Ted Buckie-Moeller and   that's it   that's the complete list

It is?

It is as far as I have it   I have another list here   of people in the same folder   "The Party" folder?   but it must be a mistake because they seem to be people who were involved with some film that was being made   or being discussed   with the title   and here's where the confusion comes in   the mistake   with the title *The Party* certainly I'll give you their names   but I don't think they were all at the party necessarily even though they're in "The Party" folder   fine as long as all this is kept in mind so that things don't get really confused   no   I don't have any idea why these people should be in this folder   unless   you know the old saying about it's a small world unless some of the people at the party   "The Party" people   knew some of the people who were involved with *The Party*   the film   yes I said I'd give you their   Tania Crosse, Lorna Flambeaux, John Hicks, Jackson Towne, Léonie Aubois, Biggs Richard, Marcella Butler, Cecil Tyrell, Sol Blanc, Annette Lorpailleur

What were Bart Kahane's motives in following Sheila into the bathroom?

Motives is a strange word to use   I don't think that I'd use that word   I have a few   three   accounts here but they're of necessity secondhand, even thirdhand   it was a bathroom after all, it wasn't exactly crowded with people was it?   the truth?   you talk as if I was in the bathroom with   I understand   the consensus   that's a good word, almost as good as motives   the consensus then   is that Mr. Kahane's motives in following Mrs. Henry into the bathroom were simply   he had to relieve himself and he had no idea that Mrs. Henry was already in the bathroom   or that anybody at all was in   yes, she was when he walked in on her   that's why she was in the bathroom   the what?   the scene?   what else would the scene be?   it was embarrassing for both Mrs. Henry and Mr. Kahane   all right, as clearly as I can, anybody who'd want to know all these things is   I'm not judging anybody   Mr. Kahane entered the bathroom because he had to   relieve himself   and he had no idea that anybody   let alone a woman   let alone Mrs. Henry was   sitting   relieving herself   and Mr. Kahane saw her and she saw him and there was a moment of   surprise   and embarrassment and then Mr. Kahane   I don't know if they said anything   Mr. Kahane left the bathroom as quickly as he had entered and a few moments later Mrs. Henry emerged from   no there are no comments or reports or anything else that say anything about laughter or remarks of any kind being made by either   quickly means what it says   quickly   maybe a minute, less than a minute, a half a minute, a few seconds, a split second, a fraction of a split   no I'm not being arrogant and uncooperative   you're making me feel like a voyeur and believe me   I don't get any pleasure out of all this   anybody who'd want to know all these things is pretty   what?   as modestly as possible, I'd assume, from these statements   three, I said   I don't know how they knew, all I did was get this stuff, these statements and diaries and photographs   this material   together   Mrs. Kahane, Miss Lorpailleur, and Miss Jefferson   just a moment, let me see what   no, not exactly that word   all right, not that word   I said modestly because the statements are more or less in agreement as to it all being an accident and embarrassing and   innocent in nature   of course she knew Mr. Kahane   I'd have to check on that, it was   Mrs. Detective who introduced them   no, Mrs. Detective didn't make any statement at all about this incident   no   nothing   yes, I have a remark of Mrs. Detective's here but you said about this particular bathroom incid   it's to the effect that Miss Lorpailleur told her that Mr. Lewis had said in Miss

Lorpailleur's hearing that he was really angry with Mr. Kahane because
Mr. Kahane had said that he had Mrs. Henry's   an undergarment of
Mrs. Henry's in   her panties   in his pocket   why would it be odd
for Mr. Lewis to be angry?   he was a good friend of the Henrys   to
whom?   Mr. Kahane said this   according to Mr. Lewis   to Sister
Rose Zeppole   what?   I don't know what time Miss Lorpailleur arrived   I don't know, but she and Miss Ostrom shared an   that's right,
as an editorial assistant   they shared an apartment and probably arrived
together   of course I'm sure that Miss Lorpailleur was at the party!
the color of the?   black   anyone who'd want to   no not plain
trimmed with black lace   my God, anyone who'd

      Why did Lolita Kahane slap Conchita?

      Now we're really getting involved in the past here   I've got to
go into a lot of old things here, diaries, letters   here's even a book   a
novel about these things   a roman à   what do they call that?
roman à?   I can't remember   hold your horses!   I want to give you
the reasons and the background   no, I don't mistake the novel for fact

     I just mentioned the novel to show   *Isolate Flecks*   mentioned it
to show you that these events were thought interesting enough to write
about in this roman à whatever it's called   all right, here it   when Mr.
Kahane was a young man he was in the Navy for awhile   four years, I
think, but I don't know what importance that   four years   he married
Conchita, a Mexican girl   couldn't speak a word of English   then
they got divorced and Mr. Kahane married Lolita Schiller   I don't know,
some machinist or lathe operator   by this time Mr. Kahane was beginning to get a reputation and beginning to sell pretty well   a sculptor
although he had been for many years a painter   through the Gom Gallery   yes, Lincoln Gom, I mentioned that he was at the party
Schiller? Richard   Richard Schiller   I don't know, the latest information here is that he was last seen in Flint   he may have paid him off
as you put it   I don't know   Mr. Kahane married Lolita Schiller and
his career started to really   as they say   take off   well, the testimony I have, which is all anonymous so as to protect the innocent
that's a good one   the innocent   I'm sorry, right, no comments   I
thought that it might help to relieve the boredom, I don't get any pleasure
out of all this you know   the testimony maintains that the present Mrs.
Kahane, Lolita Kahane, really set Mr. Kahane irrevocably   as they say

irrevocably on the golden road to success   no I'm not being funny, what's the matter with the phrase golden road to   all right   his career really took off when a very important collector   Barnett Tete   bought a large piece, *Gin City*   stainless steel and   wait a minute, some kind of plastic   styrofoam   a piece that's now considered a milestone in the movement   the movement called   I can't find it right now but it's here somewhere   lyrical expressionism?   did you ever hear of that?

    abstract lyricism?   anyway, Mr. Tete bought the piece and because he was such an important collector and connoisseur of the arts   especially contemporary art   Mr. Kahane's reputation was pretty well made and he began to   I'm getting to why Mrs. Kahane slapped   the testimony   the anonymous testimony says that Mr. Tete would never have bought the piece if Mrs. Kahane hadn't   yes, the present Mrs. Kahane

    Lolita Kahane   if she hadn't   one says   if she hadn't granted certain   sexual favors   to Mr. Tete   another, if she hadn't prostituted herself to Mr. Tete   another, if she hadn't given herself to Mr. Tete   another   well, they all go on in the same vein   they're really all the same, what's the use of   all right, another says if she hadn't blown Mr. Tete   another, if she hadn't   gone down on Mr. Tete while Mr. Kahane was   my God   in the next room fixing drinks   satisfied?   the slap, right   Conchita Kahane meanwhile had learned to speak perfect English and went to work for Lincstone Productions as executive secretary to Mr.   I didn't mention this earlier?   Lincstone Productions was involved in developing properties   inexpensive properties   for television   mostly television movies according to my reports from   here's a prospectus if you want to   you'll take my word for it?   that's a surprise   anyway, Mrs. Kahane, Conchita Kahane, became executive secretary to Mr. Whitestone and was deeply involved in the property called *The Party*   which is perhaps why she was at the party at Mr. Rosette's   that's right   exactly   Lincoln Gom and Vance Whitestone, Lincstone   so Mrs. Kahane   Conchita Kahane

    was at the party with her boss and when she was introduced to the present Mrs. Kahane she made a crack about her   indiscretions   supposed indiscretions   and the present Mrs. Kahane slapped her

    Is it possible that Conchita had learned of Lolita's indiscretions with Mr. Tete through Bart?

    Supposed indiscretions   I said that these were mostly anonymous declarations   no, impossible   Mr. Kahane hadn't seen the first Mrs. Kahane for many years and didn't even know that she was working for Lincstone Productions   didn't even know she'd learned to speak English for that matter   although a note here says that he knew that she'd left Mexico   who?   Miss Ostrom, who was, I've already told you, an ex-editorial assistant to Mr. Whitestone   when he was in publishing, of course   when he went into partnership with Mr. Gom he took Miss Ostrom along with him   no not as an editorial assistant, as   an acquisitions   to be in charge of acquisitions   I think that she may have acquired *The Party* property   or the rights to the novel   is that the same thing?   the novel?   I'm sure I mentioned this   the novel was *La Soirée intime* by Léonie Aubois   yes very modern   no I haven't read it   I can barely read French and even if a translation were available I don't think that I'd care to read it   this modern   so-called modern   fiction is confusing   you can't keep anything straight bad as life   yes, well a reader's report says   this is a novel in which what we think of as reality is seen to be, because of a fractured and multiple mirror image of self-reflective, as well as self-reflexive events, not at all the   the gist?   well it seems to be a novel about a group of people who go to a party in order to talk about making a film about the very party that they're attending   you don't know after a while if what is going on at the party is really going on at the party   or will go on in the movie that they're supposed to be talking about making   and in the novel, the movie that they're talking about making will also be called *La Soirée intime*   it seems very self-conscious and   artificial   to me   for whatever my opinion's

      Why did Bart Kahane tell Leo Kaufman that he had surprised Anne Kaufman and Biff Page on Horace Rosette's bed?

      You'll pardon me if I say   I hope you'll forgive me if I tell you that this is a ridiculous question?   I have this excerpt, the same one that you've probably already seen   right here   and I was wondering if you'd be asking about anything that Miss Schmidt had   well perhaps I don't have the same excerpt   but all my data point to the fact that this was simply slander, this   is supposed to have come from Miss Schmidt who supposedly made a tape recording of her views as to what supposedly went on at the party   this and that   everything from what was on the buffet table to the drinks available at the bar to what books were discussed

to various indiscretions and who said what to whom   about whatever
    acute observations   reasoned opinions   sage judgments   no I
wouldn't call it sarcasm, I don't know of course Miss Schmidt   but I do
have a thorough medical report here   glance at it yourself   you'll see
that it would have been quite impossible for Miss Schmidt to have made a
tape recording because she was a deaf mute   beyond that   it's also
the fact that she had a very imperfect   command of the English language   so that even had she managed to sputter and   stammer   or
whatever they   it's unlikely that she would have been able to make a
statement of any value   then there's all this other material, a matter of
record, public knowledge, what have you   I mean to say that Mr. and
Mrs. Kaufman, Anne Kaufman, had been divorced for years   so that
why Mr. Kahane would think that Mr. Kaufman would care if Mrs.
Kaufman, the first Mrs. Kaufman, was in bed   my mistake   on the
bed   with Mr. Page is beyond   what? impossible   it couldn't have
been the second Mrs. Kaufman   Ellen Kaufman   all my notes state
that she was seen all evening long circulating among the other guests and
never   disappeared for any length   of course I assume that she went
to the bathroom but that's not what I would call disappearing   now, if I
may further squash   quash   this so-called eyewitness indictment
no one states flatly in any of these reports that Mrs. Kaufman, Anne
Kaufman, was even at this party   the guest list?   that's a list that's all
    but her name   as far as I can see   doesn't come up again   and
the clincher that contradicts this   these supposed   alleged   remarks by Miss Schmidt is that Mr. Page   although he might have been
as you say   as Miss Schmidt allegedly said   on the bed with either
one Mrs. Kaufman or the other Mrs. Kaufman he might as well have been
there with a good book as the saying goes because Mr. Page was a fa
homosexual   so the whole thing is a   what do they call that?   a
tissue of lies   that somebody came up with to denigrate people, these
people supposedly involved in   Mr. Page?   he did this and that
wrote theater and film reviews for a couple of weekly newspapers   the
arty-radical-one-step-ahead papers   you know   did some acting in
little-theater groups   took courses in modern dance and poetry and that
sort of thing   his living?   he was Mr. Zeek's   I don't know what
you'd call it   a sort of housekeeper and secretary and valet   a sort of
paid companion I suppose   Mr. Pungoe had got him the job   Mr.

Pungoe?   he owned some sort of plant that manufactured some kind of
   let me check   oh yes   meat-cutting machines   no not an old
friend of Mr. Zeek's, they'd become friends when Mr. Zeek was involved
in avant-garde films and Mr. Pungoe had patronized   been the patron
for a film that Mr. Zeek had made   I'll check   *Hellions in Hosiery*
I have no idea, I have a clipping here   of course I'll read it   Annie
Flammard brings new meaning to the tired words erotic imagination
from *Compost*   Annie Flammard?   I have nothing on her
   What does the phrase "metallic constructions" mean?
   Metallic constructions? I have no idea. Would you mind telling
me where you got that one? I can't imagine what it is you're
   Who was Annette Lorpailleur?
   If I knew who Miss Lorpailleur was   she seems to be   at the
center of everything   but the information on her is   what can I call it?
   indecisive   inconclusive   all bits and pieces   she's not quite
   there   one note says she taught school in France   some little town
called either   Fanapa   or   Antoine   another says she wrote
novels under the name Sylvie Lacruseille   here's a publicity photograph of Miss Lacruseille and if that's an author   I'll eat my hat
looks more like a starlet   and here's another photograph   of Miss
Lorpailleur   supposedly   you can see that Miss Lorpailleur is surely
not Miss Lacruseille   then there's a brief entry on a page that looks as if
it was torn from a diary that mentions that there was a scandal of some
sort involving Miss Lorpailleur and Mr. Harley   Harley, yes   that's
Mr. Anton Harley, not Mr. Harlan   there's no Mr. Harlan, there's a Mr.
Harlan Pungoe   and you remember that I said that Mrs. Lewis's maiden
name was Harlan   Joanne Harlan   but this is Mr. Harley   I don't
know, some kind of a farmer or something   raised hogs or cows or
whatever   yes, his wife's name was Antonia, but I gave you the list of
guests   people at the   what?   that's all it says   some sort of
scandal involving Miss Lorpailleur and Mr. Harley   at Mr. Marowitz's
house   I'm sure I told you about Mr. Marowitz already   I know
you're being patient as   Mr. Marowitz was Ellen Kaufman's father
the unknown   what do they call that?   the silent partner   in the
Gom Gallery, according to these financial records   the one with the
money   the real money   I don't know exactly, some sort of businessman, quite wealthy   there's an investigative report here that links him

with Mr. Tete but it doesn't say how or when or for how long they were associated   I don't know whose diary   it just mentions some sort of scandalous behavior   the exact phrase   the verbatim phrase Annette and Anton Harley's behavior was so shameless that no one had the courage to admit that it was actually happening   that's all it says and it earlier mentions that this gathering was a Christmas party at Mr. Marowitz's house   what?   I don't pretend to know why there's a similar scene in *La Soirée intime*   I have these notes and records and files and   folders and diaries   and bits and pieces of reports and testimonies and   God knows what else and   believe me I don't get any pleasure out of all this   I'm doing it because I   for certain? for certain, Miss Lorpailleur shared an apartment with Miss Ostrom and was somehow   I suppose   involved with *The Party*   I mean the movie that was being   all right   she was it appears also a guest at the party   and if she's not on the party list in the folder   I simply cannot help that   if you think other people have better information   please go ahead and ask them   ask anybody   you won't hurt my feelings   far from it, I assure you   you certainly must realize how hard it is to answer   to try and answer   these questions when all I have are these folders and files and   and all these papers

But if what you've said about April Detective is true, how do you explain these photographs of her?

What I've said about is good   really good   I don't know where you get the idea that I've said   anything   over and over again this is a bore   I've told you that I'm telling you what I've got here in all these   Mrs. Detective had   for some years   been living quietly in   New England with her husband   taking care of the house, giving quiet parties   Vermont   I told you that earlier   giving quiet parties as I say   while Mr. Detective was working on a novel   he'd always wanted to write a novel and   no I didn't say *Blackout*   I said *Black-jack*   I don't know whether you realize it or not but it's not easy trying to answer new questions and then go back and answer   all over again questions that I've already answered   trying to keep all these papers in some kind of reasonable order and if I make a small mistake now and then   yes I'm sure it's *Blackjack*   yes, here's the dust jacket *Blackjack* is right   Blanche Neige Press, in a limited edition   Blanche Neige?   that's right, they also published *Sheila Sleeping* and   or

Lobster Lays, Mr. Henry's book   or books   I'm not certain   oh
thanks, I'm glad that it's not important   now that I've dropped this stuff
all over the   yes, I am a little piqued, as you put it   do this and do that
and do the other thing and then all of a sudden it's not important   anymore   yes, Mr. Blanche was the   he was, so to speak, Blanche Neige
Press   money?   he made enough I suppose to survive   led a simple
life   the books were all   what do they call that?   they were all
letterpress?   hand set   a labor of love   he had no regular assistants, once in a while he'd put a   someone   up for a while   a few
weeks   or months   and they'd assist him in the work, he didn't have
a large operation, you understand   this was deluxe publishing for collectors   bibliophiles   well, Miss Crosse was there for a time   and
Miss Flambeaux   Miss Butler   Mrs. Checks   no, I don't know
why they were all women   besides   they weren't all women because
here   a letter shows that Mr. Harley would go over to Mr. Blanche's
house to help once in a   go over?   Mr. Harley was a neighbor, he had
a farm of some kind, I'm sure I've noted that   raised chickens and pigs
or something and lived about fifteen miles   no, I never thought about it
being a strange coincidence that they all lived so close to each other
what exactly does all mean?   Mr. Harley   Mr. Blanche   and the
Detectives is not exactly a crowd is it?   well is it?   I know that you
ask the   I'm not digressing   you're the one who keeps elaborating
these questions   about books and assistants   and how come all these
people lived so close to each   I haven't forgotten your question   the
simple truth is that, as I told you, I can't explain these photographs of Mrs.
Detective   I agree that they're   erotic   as far as pornographic
I wouldn't say that   we've been through that, no, they weren't taken by
Mr. Detective   because they were mailed to Mr. Detective at a time
when he and Mrs. Detective were   temporarily separated and Mr. Detective had taken an apartment   the apartment's not important either
wonderful   well, if that is Mr. Harley it doesn't look like this other
snapshot of him taken just a couple of years   apparently a couple of
years before   I agree that this other woman appears to be Miss
Lacruseille   but it's hard to tell because her face is   you can't really
compare it to the publicity photo of her because the lighting is   use?
I don't know of any use that they were put to   Lorna Flambeaux?
her book was called   *The Sweet* or *The Sweat of Love*   I can't quite

make out this handwriting   and it was   it says here   illustrated
with photographs   but I don't think that evidence of any use   as you
put it   of these photographs of Mrs. Detective   and other people
all right then   pornographic   I'm perfectly willing to call a spade a
spade   I just don't get any pleasure out   the book was also published
by Blanche Neige Press   sure   I can give you a list but it's not, as far
as I can tell, complete   let's see now   *Sheila Sleeping* and or *Lobster
Lays* by Louis Henry   *The Orange Dress* by Sheila Henry   *Blackjack* by Richard Detective   I'm reading these right off the list   *The
Sweet of Love*   it is *Sweet*   by Lorna Flambeaux   *Les Constructions métalliques* by Henri Kink   that's all I have   oh, I'd guess there
were more books but this is far from complete   I think   no, he had no
other income and these statements show that he probably couldn't have
supported himself very well with the income from the press   earlier?
     earlier he had been involved with Mr. Tete and Mr. Pungoe in some
sort of real-estate   real-estate   thing   partly real-estate   and
there are legal papers here   I can't understand a word of them   about
some legal   action or suit concerning   let me see   concerning
some sort of   suit or action concerning   it's something about
forgeries of   prints   the defendants were Mr. Blanche   Mr. Tete
     Mr. Harley   and   Mr. Gom   I imagine   yes   that you can
make a lot of money that way   yes   enough to buy a house and land
almost anywhere   yes   Vermont included   Sol Blanc?   he was
one of the people   I mentioned him   involved with *The Party* project
     this report says that he was   a photographer   and that he had been
engaged for a time to   Miss Crosse who was   don't tell me I beat you
to it?   Miss Crosse was a photographer too   fashion photography
what?   it doesn't say but I suppose that she could have done   any
kind of photography   there's nothing here but certainly she could have
known Mrs. Detective but I don't see that that   implies anything
anybody can know anybody   right?   right?
     Do I understand you to mean that Joanne Lewis—Bunny—had
known Harlan Pungoe long before she met Guy?
     That's what everything seems to point to   but I don't know
why you're making a federal case out of it   she was still single and had
a perfect right to do whatever she   in some small town   Boonton
or   Katydid Glade   ashamed of her father?   I don't think so

yes a high school teacher   automotive trades   but Bunny had what
they call a good relationship   no, not my tired phrase   as you put it
    I'm reading it right off this sheet   I don't know what the signifi-
cance of the Indian corn being hung up by Mrs. Lewis's mother has to
there's nothing here about anything like Indian corn   yes she'd had
some affairs   yes   one was with a young English novelist   I don't
know what Mr. Ward's reaction to his daughter's taking up, as you say,
with Mr. Lewis   as I said   she was single and   Mr. Ward?   Mrs.
Lewis's father of course   you remember him   the automotive trades
    Ward?   yes   Mrs. Lewis's maiden name was Joanne Ward
I've already   Harlan?   no   not Harlan   you're thinking about
Mr. Pungoe   I said Joanne Harlan?   impossible   it's right here
I jotted   Joanne   Joanne   well   I can't imagine why I said
Harlan   it's definitely Ward   Joanne Ward   no I'm not trying to
confuse you   God knows that I'm the one who's confused with this one
and that one and ex-wives and ex-husbands and everything else that I
protect people?   that's really   that's really an insulting remark after
I've done my best to   Mr. Pungoe, yes   came between the English
novelist and Mr. Lewis   but it was brief and more like a   friendship
    than anything else   he was quite a bit older than   friendship is
what I said   yes   I called her Harlan because her relationship with
Mr. Pungoe was what?   an indelible experience?   indelible is quite a
mouthful   after all   Mrs. Lewis was not exactly Bo-Peep when she
met Mr. Pungoe   and even though he was a mature and   experienced
man   she wouldn't exactly be so impressed by this brief   relationship   so as for it to be indel   I don't think strange tastes could be
applied to Mr.   what book?   now this is the sort of thing that it's
unlikely I can find in   yes   I said a large envelope but that doesn't
mean that everything in the world will necessarily be in the envel   but
    well   so it is   how lucky we are, now we can really get to the
bottom of this mysterious and   profound   and really   sinister
well I'm tired of your insinuations   particularly when I have very little
choice   I'd be happy if you talked to somebody who knew these people
firsthand   believe me   I don't get any pleasure out   all right so
I've said that already   it seems to me that I can't say it too often because your insinuations are really getting to   the book?   the title isn't
given, it only says   in its entirety   she told Guy about it once and he

started to read to her from Stekel   I don't have any idea what she might
have   these photographs   again?   I told you that I don't think you
can prove a thing from these   I say that because it's obvious to me that
these are posed   some sort of a   joke   all right   that's not the
right word   I admit   maybe a   or maybe this was a modeling job
     something like that   Mrs. Lewis had to eat   as they say   and
you know those bizarre fashion photographs that they   bizarre   you
know what I mean   bizarre   strange   a suggestion of   perver-
sion   fetishism   bondage   whatever they think is   I mean maybe
she was simply making a few dollars   it's an adobe house but what's
wrong with that?   you see all kinds of things   locations   adobe
houses and townhouses and penthouses   lawns and construction sites
     bridges and vacant lots the subway   even art galleries and saloons
     they use any damn stupid background that they   the man?   could
be anybody at all   some model or   some sort of model   I think he
looks very much like a model, yes   I can't give you any idea at all why
Mr. Lewis would read from Hegel to   Stekel   from Stekel to Mrs.
Lewis   I never heard of Stekel   I don't know if they met before Mr.
Pungoe got involved with Mr. Zeek   no I've never seen it and I've
never even seen a picture of   this other woman is Annie Flammard?
absolutely   there's no doubt that she's Miss Lacruseille or   as they
say   her double   do I find what else odd?   no I don't think there's
anything else particularly odd   it's a still   obviously   from a movie
     I suppose it's *Hellions in Hosiery* but I wouldn't be able   you don't
mean that?   how am I supposed to know exactly what you're driving
     oh   yes   it looks like the same adobe house but it seems to me
that all adobe houses look   where in both of them?   yes I see   it's
a drawing on the wall   it's the same drawing   all right   it is odd
but then it's very easy to make all kinds of assumptions about all kinds of
things when you don't have all the information   there is probably a
perfectly good   a perfectly plausible reason as to why   Baylor Freeq?
     I mentioned him when I told you   I didn't mention him?   it seems
as if I did but anyhow   he was Miss Flammard's co-star in *Hellions in
Hosiery*   just a moment, I have to find   Mr. Freeq was an actor who
worked in small experimental theaters and experimental repertory groups
     had been in a number of plays   some of them?   some of them
were   this can't be right   it says that he was in *The Party*   a one-

act play by Craig Garf   that can't be right unless   I mean it's too
strange a coincidence   that's what it says   *The Party*   and the
other vehicles   I love that word   it always makes me think of a bunch
of actors   I'm sorry   I don't mean to waste time   Mr. Freeq
was also in *Ten Eyck Walk* and *The Caliph* and *Black Ladder*   it was a
stage name   his real name was   just a   his real name was Barry
Gatto   no there's no mention of him having anything to do with
Lincstone Productions or *The Party*   the movie   the projected movie
I   all right, I just wanted to keep things as straight as   Mr. Henry?
yes   he knew Mr. Henry, not very well   they had a kind of   I don't
know   business arrangement having to do with Mr. Henry's car   Mr.
Freeq was paying off Mr. Henry's car for him   there's no clue here as to
why so I don't know   they were friends   maybe they had come to
some sort of arrangement   Mr. Freeq was an old friend of Mrs.   Mr.
and Mrs. Henry   he'd known the Henrys years before when Mr. Henry
was a graduate student   there was some sort of help he'd given Mr.
Henry especially   something that could have been a tragic   yes he'd
helped both of them   Mrs. Henry tried to   she put her head in the
oven because she was so unhappy at being   feeling   left out of her
husband's   Mr. Freeq had been a very good friend at the time   well,
he'd found her   so I imagine that Mr. Henry felt that he owed   and
Mrs. Henry too of course   they felt that they owed him a great deal and
     I don't know why he'd pay off his car if it was Mr. Henry who was
indebted to   what?   more than meets the eye?   oh please, this is
just   yes I am tired   sick and tired   maybe Mrs. Henry   the
Henrys   had somehow given Mr. Freeq more than he expected and he
found himself in debt then   to them   I don't know what Mrs. Henry
     the Henrys gave him   I said maybe gave him   yes, Mr. Freeq
knew Mrs. Lewis when she was still Miss Har   Miss Ward   as a
matter of fact she first met Mr. Lewis at a little café that Mr. Freeq had a
part interest in   Mama Gatto's   just a name, there was no Mama
Gatto   it was apparently a kind of private joke because only a few
people knew that Mr. Freeq's real name was   right   it says that it
closed within a year or so   fire violations or health violations about
something about storing   paints and dyes   no   for fine-arts use
storing them   in the basement   I have no idea why he would store
such things in   a passing acquaintance with Mr. Tete, yes   through

Mr. Kahane who knew the Henrys   no there's no record of legally fighting   anything   he closed the café and that was   I don't know what
happened to the materials in the base   what?   well, that would depend, wouldn't it, on whether or not Miss Lorpailleur was   I mean
yes   Mr. Freeq knew Miss Lorpailleur only if Miss Lorpailleur was also
Miss Lacruseille   which I doubt because of the photographs that we
looked at a   and whether then Miss Lacruseille was also or actually
Miss Flammard   which might be so because this still from the movie
looks like the   you get what I mean?   he knew Miss Flammard whoever she was   of course   because he was her co-star in   right   I
don't think that he knew Mr. Pungoe   despite the fact that Mr. Pungoe
was the   what do they call   the angel   he was the angel for *Hellions in*   what?   because he knew Mrs. Lewis and Mrs. Lewis knew
Mr. Pungoe it doesn't follow that   people can know people who know
people that they don't know, you know what I   what? I don't have any
record of that as far as I can see   except for one brief note that you can
take   again   with a grain of salt because it is supposedly by Miss
Schmidt who as we know   fine, for what it's worth   a good way to
put it   it states that Mr. Pungoe took Mrs. Lewis to one of the shooting
locations   one afternoon   *Hellions in Hosiery*!   what other film
could I be talking about?   *The Party* wasn't a film, it was a one-act
you've confused it yourself with the film that was just being talked about
at the party   I'm expected to keep everything straight when you
with your information as well as mine   and God knows who else has
told you whatever comes into their heads   you have as much trouble as
I   these papers and files and ex-whatevers and friendships and   who
knows exactly when this   I mean it's not as if all this is dated   and in
order   no wonder that   I'm just getting it off my chest   let's go on
by all means

What did April Detective see when she entered Mr. Rosette's
study?

Mrs. Detective has written   in passing   in a letter to Mr.
Kahane about that   it's a very   distraught   letter that falls
maybe   in the category of the woman scorned   I suppose jealous
it seems to me accusatory   of Mr. Kahane   exactly?   your behavior was so shameless that I didn't have the courage to admit to myself that
what I saw was actually happening   I don't know what she means by

behavior   after the bathroom?   I don't know if this was after or before   it could well have been compromising   certainly   that I can't
tell you   but it's fairly obvious that it was   that Mrs. Detective and
Mrs. Kahane   Lolita Kahane   were very good friends and perhaps
Mrs. Detective felt that it was   unwise   for Mr. Kahane to be alone
with Mrs. Henry because of what it might have looked like to the other
guests   Mr. Rosette?   most of the evening he was at the   tending
bar   he enjoyed tending bar when he gave a party even though   I was
about to say   even though he had a bartender who was   I imagine
perfectly competent   Mr. Towne I believe   I know nothing about
him except that Mr. Rosette often employed him to tend   he may have
been living with Mr. Rosette at the time, I don't know   no I didn't know
that he'd reviewed *The Orange Dress*   qualifications? do you need
qualifications to review a book?   it seems to me that any fool who can
write   you'll pardon the expression   English can review a   also in
Compost?   isn't that   sinister and mysterious, isn't that really
well you have this   faculty?   faculty   this faculty for making all of
this   these things   into a kind of complicated web of   certainly
Mr. Rosette could have gone into his study, after all it was his study and it
certainly doesn't seem out of the ordinary for him to   with Mrs. Detective?   he may well have   perhaps for some privacy to talk about Mr.
Detective's novel, *Blackjack*   which he wanted very badly to use   to
take some sections or chapters from for an anthology that he was   I told
you that he was an editor and an anthologist   well-known   oh many
books   just a minute, some of the better known   some of them
used in freshman English courses in a lot of   here it is   *Tableaux
Vivants: Selected Poems of Pamela Ann Clairwil*   Mr. Rosette edited
and introduced that   also *Gusty*   I mean *Gutsy*   *Gutsy Ghetto
Tales*   and the best-known   an anthology   *Bridges: Poets Express
Their Love*   yes he made a very good living   he also acted as a kind
of   literary consultant   did editing and proofreading and wrote jacket
     what do they call that?   blurbs?   no   jacket copy   and
reader's reports for various publishers   and did essays and reviews as
well   all in all a   man of letters   no I'm not jok   Mrs. Detective
instead of Mr. Detective?   that's a good question to which I don't have
the   I see you're waving those photographs again in my   we've been
through this before and I admitted that they're a little   that they're

risqué   we seem to be drowning in photographs   as if a photograph
could tell us   I am looking   well if you say that this is Mr. Rosette's
couch in Mr. Rosette's study then you know better than I do and if you
know better than I do then aren't we wasting our   he might well have
taken the photographs   he also might well have sent them to Mr. Detective   but for what reason I   yes I told you that the Detectives knew
Mr. Blanche   that they were neighbors in Ver   Mr. Rosette wanted to
get in on the what?   the print   scheme?   I'm not following you
I told you that that involved   it was never   what's the word?
litigated?   prosecuted?   there was a lack of evidence that   again?
again   Mr. Blanche   Mr. Tete   Mr. Harley   Mr. Gom   Mr.
Detective might well have known something about it because he was
as I said and said and said   a neighbor of Mr. Blanche's and Mr. Blanche
was his publisher so there was a good possibility that he'd heard something about it   you know small communities   the pictures might
have been a kind of blackjack?   I mean blackmail?   so that Mr. Detective would what?   his friendship with Mr. Blanche to   that seems
to me a lot of trouble to go to for a well-off man who was profitably involved in the arts   and letters   and   no it's not incomprehensible
it just seems to me to be   you're once again digressing, not I   I
told you about Mrs. Detective's letter to Mr. Kahane and that seems to me
to be clear enough   I mean exactly that   clear enough   she doesn't
mention in the letter anything about what she saw in Mr. Rosette's study
there's one small note on the back of an envelope here   I don't
know who wrote it   it says   April pale and trembling after seeing
Sheila doing B   it seems to me the pale and trembling is pretty
overwrought   purple   doesn't it to you?   I wouldn't know who
or what   B is   depositions?   that's a pretty fancy word for what
people thought they saw   or knew   but if that's what you want to call
them   I do have some other   depositions   here   here's one from
Miss Schmidt   and anything she says is as I've already told you to be
taken with a grain   a very large grain of   she says that Mrs. Henry
was performing a sex act with Mr. Kahane   here's one from   this
can't be be right   it's supposedly made by Miss Lacruseille   impossible   that says that   this is very vulgar indeed   verbatim?
verbatim then   Sheila was deliriously sucking Bart Kahane's   this is
really too much, it might be a description of a scene from *Hell*   a hell of

a filthy blue movie   I'll read it   yes   God, anyone who'd want to know this stuff is really   Sheila was deliriously sucking Bart Kahane's   my God   enormous rigid cock   you know I don't mind giving you the gist of this garbage but when you get something filthy supposedly said by someone who wasn't even at   as far as I know from the list wasn't even at   the party then I really feel as if things are going   one more yes   there's one more   this is a statement by Mr. Rosette   so it says   I tried to shield Mrs. Detective from the surprising and disgusting scene that greeted our eyes as we entered my study, but I was too late and fear that she saw every detail of the licentious behavior of this, what word can I use? this shameless couple   no   he nowhere mentions what couple it is   so much for your   depositions   I don't think at all that it follows that the bathroom incident was arranged   as you say   after all you'll remember   speaking of depositions   that I gave you the deposition of Mrs. Kahane and the deposition of Miss Jefferson and the deposition of Miss Lorpailleur   Mrs. Henry's panties?   just a minute   I'm confused here   let me dig out   oh yes you'll remember that that was something that Mrs. Detective said that Miss Lorpailleur told her and that Miss Lorpailleur had overheard Mr. Lewis saying that he had been told this by Mr. Kahane   I mean   this was hearsay   in spades   Miss Jefferson?   she'd been an editorial assistant to Mr. Whitestone before he and Mr. Gom became partners in Lincstone Pro yes she was an editorial assistant along with Miss Ostrom   how do I know?   I don't know how many assistants a senior editor needs but I imagine a   well whether I said so or not he was a senior editor   at Crescent and Chattaway   he may have had three or four or ten assistants   it doesn't seem to me to   thank you   I'd be delighted to continue   Miss Jefferson didn't go with Miss Ostrom and Mrs. Kahane, Conchita Kahane   to Lincstone   she opened a little boutique with Lucy Taylor   very chic and expensive   it's right here   Lorzu Fashions   Lorzu Fashions for the Woman of Punctilious Dash is what their card says   Lorzu?   that's lor from Taylor and zu from ZuZu which was Miss Jefferson's nickname   Miss Taylor?   she'd been a sweetheart of Mr. Lewis's   an old flame as they say   no not his childhood sweetheart   I think that's carrying mockery and cynicism a little   you accuse me of making cracks about this and   as a matter of fact he did have a childhood sweetheart   Ann Taylor Redding   no I don't think they were sisters, Taylor is a name like Smith or Brown isn't it? there's a million Taylors   you think that there are too many coincidences?   what can I say?   you get ten or twenty or   fifty people who know each other and you're bound to get coincidences   and all sorts of odd   what's the word I'm looking for?   alliances   no not alliances though alliances is all right but   I can't seem to   say   call them   configurations   it seems to me that with your questions and doubts and going back over the same ground you're complicating things more than   it is a maze   I agree   but I'm trying to give you what I have   as objectively and cogently as   well all right   an occasional opinion but based on materials that I   I have no interest in protecting anyone   why would I want to   what?   lies?   look I can give you all this   all these papers   everything   I don't get any pleasure out of this   as I suggested   ask somebody else   somebody who personally knew these people   it's all right with   my God   I mention two Taylors and immediately it's a significant   it's significant   you wouldn't think this was strange if you read it in a novel   like the one by Mademoiselle Aubois   *La Soirée intime*   where you don't know if what's happening is happening or   something   which reminds you of *The Party*? oh   it reminds you of the *party*   the question   right which was?   all right, to answer as precisely as possible   from the evidence to hand   the depositions   Mrs. Detective saw   in Mr. Rosette's study   Mrs. Henry performing a sexual act   fellatio   on Mr. Kahane   that's all you wanted to know?   fine   then why you got into all the other things I'll never   of course   let's continue we've only been here about a hundred years   at this rate

Tell me some more about Annette Lorpailleur—for instance, what did she do at this party?

Well as I said before, she seems to be at the core of so many things   and nobody knew precisely where she came from   Gapoine or something   Fagapa   it's spelled so many different   God knows what the name of   yes I understand that you want details of the party   I'm coming to   you have to realize that she seemed to be everywhere and that the reports on her are   to say the least   contradictory   I suppose I can start any   fine   just as the material is arranged arranged is a great word to use for this   this   all right   to start she was involved in some kind of quarrel with Mr. Whitestone as well as a real

shouting match with Mademoiselle Aubois but for   I think   yes
different reasons but they had something to do with each other   probably   apparently she was doing some pretty heavy   petting   in full
view of   with Miss Ostrom   and Mr. Whitestone somehow objected
and there was   as I say   there was a quarrel about   no I don't know
anything about Miss Ostrom and Mr. White   the acquisitions coordina-
tor or something   other than that I   they indeed shared an apartment
     she may have   they may have been lesbians   I have no idea about
that   Mademoiselle Aubois?   that was perhaps more serious since it
had to do with something   I don't know what happened first   you
said to reel this goss   this stuff off as   Mademoiselle Aubois?
there's no evidence as to her sexual preferences and   I am trying to tell
you about   Miss Lorpailleur is said to have been trying to persuade Mr.
Whitestone to give her a part in *The Party* since Lincstone was   you
know all this   fine   as long as you know it God forbid that I should
repeat any   what?   if I said that Miss Ostrom was involved in acquiring the rights to *The Party*   or to *La Soirée intime* precisely   then
that's what I said but I   oh   you mean if Miss Ostrom was the one in
charge of this deal for Lincstone then Miss Lorpailleur   it's rather crude
and obvious   isn't it?   oh   I see   why the sudden passion when
she and Miss Ostrom were always together as   oh   you mean   I
see what you're driving at   for the benefit of Mr. Whitestone   so that
he would maybe give her   if she'd stop with Miss Ostrom   the part
     that would presuppose   of course I can see the possibility of Mr.
Whitestone and Miss Ostrom being lovers   and if not then   then I
don't know why he was so upset   maybe he thought that it wasn't too
good for the Lincstone image for its acquisitions   person   to be writhing around with her skirt all up around her   I don't know what Mr.
Whitestone said about any part for Miss Lorpailleur   no I didn't say
that Miss Flammard was at the party   only that Mr.   Mr.   who the
hell was it now?   Mr. Freeq had been her co-star   right   Miss
Lorpailleur had no acting experience but she had a kind of   obscure
background as I've   I told you about the novelist   business
Lacruseille?   I did   well God knows she may well have had acting
experience   I never thought of that   yes   she might well have been
Miss Flammard   which would make her Miss Lorpailleur as well as
Miss Lacruseille and Miss Flammard and a lesbian a novelist an actress

maybe she was also a maid a nurse a nun a policewoman a corporation
executive a doctor   fine!   she may well have been Annie Flammard
except that you seem to be forgetting the photographs that   faked?
fine   faked   whatever you say   Mademoiselle Aubois?   at
some point Mademoiselle Aubois and Miss Lorpailleur got into a terrible
quarrel maybe because Miss Ostrom's skirt was up   I'm sorry   I'm
thinking of Mr. Whitestone   pretty soon I won't know what I'm
they had a terrible quarrel because Miss Lorpailleur claimed that *La Soirée
intime* was a case of plagiary   that Mademoiselle Aubois had read a
manuscript of Miss Lorpailleur's only it was signed by Miss Lacruseille
it's so stated   and stolen almost everything from it for her own book
I don't know anything about the truth of this   only that there are
fragments here from I guess letters   about publishing a novel by a Miss
Lacruseille   Sylvie Lacruseille   from Crescent and Chattaway
yes as a matter of fact   signed by Mr. Whitestone   some five years
ago   or is it?   I can't tell, it might be   fifteen or   twenty-five?
what?   Miss Ostrom may well have been employed at the time by
Crescent and Chattaway but I don't think there's anything on it   no
not as far as I   it was titled   let me see   it was going to have the
English title of *Mouth of Steel*, in French it was   *La Bouche métallique*
no, apparently it wasn't published as *Mouth of Steel*   and it wasn't
published as   it wasn't published in France either   it wasn't published period   doesn't say a thing about any reason, just that the deal
was off   yes there were other incidents involving Miss Lorpailleur
here's another set of memos stapled together   how official   about
Miss Lorpailleur approaching Mr. Gom about a part in *The Party* and
depending on what you want to believe   if anything   all this seems
as if it comes out of   talk about fiction   out of a novel by some
obsessed   all right   Miss Lorpailleur, as I said, and Mr. Gom   she
either   offered him Miss Ostrom   or as I say   depending on what
you want to   I know that you can   or Miss Lorpailleur suggested that
she had certain   records and other proofs   concerning Mr. Gom's
finances   the monies that had enabled him to go into partnership with
Mr. Whitestone while still holding on to the gallery   I'm getting to
the records had to do with certain large amounts of money that came from
Mr. Gom's involvement with the   situation?   whatever   the business with the faked   the forged prints that I mentioned earlier?   I'm

getting to that   if you'll just take it   I'm getting there   Miss
Lorpailleur allegedly told Mr. Gom that she knew all about his financial
dealings because of Mr. Marowitz who was   you'll remember   the
money man   what a disgusting phrase   the money behind the Gom
Gallery, so she knew all about the money that had been made through the
sale of the prints and how much had come to Mr. Gom   how?   well
that's an interesting question   for a change   because Miss Lorpailleur
swears up and down in about half a dozen different places   here, see?
and here   and here   and here   she swears that it wasn't true,
but Mr. Marowitz and Mr. Harley and Mrs. Kaufman   Ellen Kaufman
and Mr. Kaufman   all swore on a stack of Bibles as they say   that
Miss Lorpailleur was Mr. Marowitz's maid   and for some time   it's
really too much   isn't it?   what do I mean? I mean   a French
maid!   my God   it's just like that Annie Flammard movie, *Silk Thighs*
what?   I never implied that I never saw a film starring Miss
Flammard   I distinctly remember saying that I never saw *Hellions*
fine, let's let it pass   and also   here it is   also   in addition to this
sworn testimony, if that's what it is   sworn or testimony   there's an
interesting note that says   an anonymous note   that says   that
Miss Lorpailleur wasn't really Mr. Marowitz's maid   only that she was
his friend   it says friend   someone who would come and visit regularly and dress up for him like a maid   yes, this little piece of notepad
paper   the little note in red ink at the bottom is a little list   it says
French maid   nurse   nun   policewoman   corporation executrix
doctor   what?   yes of course I'm thinking what you're   it's a
list of roles   that somebody wanted somebody to play for   or that
somebody played for   maybe Mr. Marowitz   maybe not   I don't
know   she may well have been   yes   the maid   so to speak
when she was involved   allegedly   in the alleged scandalous behavior with Mr. Harley but if you'll recall that was mentioned briefly in a
diary entry and   I hold no brief, as you put it, for anybody   can't we
get off this party?   you talk as if you've never been to a party   I mean
any party   at any party the things that are liable to go on   the old
friends and new friends and husbands and wives and exes and lovers and
the unspoken   I'm not trying to educate anybody   yes, yes, and yes
again   Miss Lorpailleur   or Lacruseille or Flammard   whoever she was   whatever her name   might have been a maid at the

time of the incident with Mr. Harley   or the nun   how should I know?
what?   why?   because it's on the list here   I happened to think
of a nun, I could just as well have thought of   Sister Rose Zeppole was
according to this and that and the other thing   all these papers and
I'm sick of this, I might as well just make it all   invent the whole
thing since whatever I tell you you insinuate that   I was about to say
that   according to these unimpeachable sources   these sources that
glow with golden shining truth, Sister   I wouldn't call it sneering
Sister Rose Zeppole was a real nun   about thirty-two according to these
unim   all that this brief note says   and oddly enough   or maybe
not oddly at all   this note is in the folder labeled *The Party*   the film
right   not "The Party" folder with the list of   right   of course
I told you that *The Party*   the film   has a folder all to itself?   more
like a small carton in fact   I'm getting on with it   the note says that
Miss Lorpailleur spoke for about ten minutes to Sister Rose Zeppole and
that Sister Rose Zeppole   I can't quite make it out   she either blushed
or flushed   I grant you that it's strange that a nun should be involved
with such a group of   I don't know how or why   there's absolutely
nothing about   well there is one little scrawl here on the report on the
Detectives   it seems that   read it?   all right   it reads   Sister
Rose of great help to D.D. in marital troubles in spirit of SIS   not sis,
it's all in capitals   S I S   no, that's all   I have no idea   I wouldn't
even attempt to venture a guess   pretty?   I suppose you could call
her pretty   here's a snapshot taken of her when she was a   what do
they call that?   an apprentice nun?   a novice, right   I'd say about
twenty or twenty-one   no I don't think she looks like Mrs. Detective, as
a matter of fact   nothing   nothing   I was only going to say that she
looks a little bit like Miss Lorpailleur but in the light of the conversation
that Miss Lorpailleur had with her it can't be possible can it?   can it?

I know that you ask the

Can you give me a brief synopsis of *La Bouche métallique* or
Mouth of Steel?

Certainly   I have a translator's   or reader's   or something
report right here   are we actually off this party?   here's the   O.K.

La Bouche métallique is   it's signed   Roger Whytte-Blorenge
La Bouche métallique is an ingenious novel of worlds within worlds   it
concerns a young man, Antoine, whose best friend, Octave, is asking him

persistent questions about a dinner party that Antoine has not only not attended but most of whose guests he has never met   Antoine soon discovers that Octave is trying to find out whether his wife, Roberte, who is Antoine's lover and who was a guest at the dinner party, permitted herself to be seduced by an offficer of the Guards   Antoine gallantly attempts to protect Roberte's reputation by inventing the incidents of the dinner party   he decides that painting too innocent or ingenuous a picture of Roberte will only serve further to excite Octave's suspicions, and so tells him that Roberte was accidentally instrumental in saving the honor of her old school friend, Jeannette, by stumbling into the bathroom at precisely the moment at which   what?   yes   stumbling into the bathroom but I don't think that it means that she actually stumbled but that if you'll let me go on   fine   at precisely the moment at which the officer of the Guards and Jeannette were about to satisfy their carnal desires   so you see he means stumbled on   fine   carnal desires Antoine further tells Octave that Roberte confided to him that she was shocked at Jeannette's licentiousness, but not surprised by it, because her husband, unlike Octave, had for years been cold and inattentive toward her   at this moment Roberte enters the room carrying a book and tells Octave and Antoine that she has just finished it   it is, she says, a fascinating new novel set at a dinner party during the course of which a beautiful young wife whose husband is out of town on business is tempted to be unfaithful to him with a handsome actor   just at the moment when she feels herself yielding she remembers her husband's kindness, wisdom, and quiet, strong love and she rejects temptation   the actor then reveals that he has been hired by her husband to test her chastity at which moment the husband himself steps out of the room into which the actor was about to lead the young wife   Roberte then smiles at Octave and kisses him tenderly, meanwhile looking knowingly and lecherously at Antoine, who is leafing through the novel which is in reality an erotic *récit* entitled *La Soirée intime*   Miss Lacruseille's novel is witty, dry, delicately ironic, and reverberant with suggestion   all in all a wonderfully controlled piece of writing   that's it   the entire report   I don't know if Miss Aubois had got hold of the manuscript or if she did whether or not she plagiarized it or   of course there are a number of similarities given the information we have on the novels   but I haven't read either of   well yes   the title of the novel in Miss Lacruseille's   Miss

Lorpailleur's novel   that's suspicious

Why did John Hicks visit Horace Rosette some time after the party had broken up?

John   Hicks?   I don't think I mentioned any John   oh I see   yes, he's in *The Party*   the movie   group   if that's what you want to call it   I don't know why   I don't have anything of any value at   maybe he was just a friend   even Horace Rosette had friends I'm sure   I don't mean even   I mean that anybody has friends that other people might not know anything ab   two little lines that's all one says   this must be somebody's idea of a joke   it says that he was some sort of city official   the Buildings Department   well I think it's a joke   or a mistake because what would a city   a Buildings official be doing with people who were all involved   more or less   with the arts   theater and film and what have you?   yes that's all it says, some sort of city official involved with   in   the Buildings   the other line?   just as brief   it says that he was a recent acquaintance of Mrs. Henry   that's all   no, not what kind of an acquaintance   no, Mr. Henry isn't mentioned   no   it doesn't say a word about this Mr. Mr. Hicks   knowing Mr. Tete or Mr. Pungoe   look for your   me?

I don't have any opinion, as I told you, I   well if you want to call that an opinion but   to me   it seems obvious that a man involved in real   ordinary   work   you know   a regular nine to five job would seem out of place with people like the people involved with *The Party*   the film   and the party itself   don't you think so?   don't you?   again   a city official in the Buildings Department   that's one   two   a recent acquaintance of Mrs. Henry   how should I know how he managed to meet Mrs. Henry?   my God   Mrs. Henry probably met a million   where?   what do you mean where?   any- where, everywhere, how the   I am tired and confused, if you'd just stick with one line of   I don't know why Mr. Hicks went to see Mr. Rosette   Mr. Rosette may have been alone   why wouldn't he be alone if the party was over?   look at what?   this?   of course I can

it shows four men sitting around a table, one is looking at a   loose- leaf book?   one is looking at the one who is looking at the loose-leaf one is smoking a   you asked me what it   on the back?   yes   four names   Rosette, Pungoe, Tete, Hicks   so?   so Mr. Hicks did know Mr. Pungoe and Mr. Tete   maybe   I still don't know what he was

doing at   under the lamp?   under what lamp?   I see   it   it
looks like it could be   anything   it looks like a woman's   things
a scarf I think and   and   could be anything   I suppose   a
scarf and   under   underthings   under   a slip and   I guess
panties   yes, black   no, with black lace   why anyone would want
to   I don't know!   they could be Mrs. Henry's and they could be the
Queen of Sheba's   how should I know whose   or why?   what?
wait a minute   you're the one who said that the party had broken up
well, whether you're interested or not you said that the   no I can't imagine a woman forgetting them   unless she was   well, drunk   or
maybe for a prank?   I take it back, you're right   it's not much of a
all right   let's assume that they're Mrs. Henry's   now what?
what?   I still don't know what Mr. Hicks was doing at Mr. Rosette's
God knows, Mrs. Henry's   assuming they're Mrs. Henry's things
don't answer the question   neither does this photograph   does it?
I mean, what do you think this photograph has in it to   right   I do the
answering   but I can't hear   can I?   what a photograph is saying
    I mean   what these men are saying   can we get off the Mr. Hicks
business for now?
        And what did Lolita have to say to Sheila on the telephone?
        The transcription of the tape is   spotty   a lot of blank spaces,
apparently the tape was   it's unintelligible in a lot of   in effect, Mrs.
Kahane told Mrs. Henry that her husband   Mr. Kahane that is   her
husband had confessed all   a little melodramatic I'd say, wouldn't you
agree?   you wouldn't agree   I thought you shook your   pardon me
    it doesn't have any information about what it all means, no   there's
a deletion noted   no I don't think anybody, as you say, did it   I told
you that the tape apparently was faulty   yes there's some more   Mrs.
Kahane insisted   it seems over and over again   seems?   all right,
she did insist   over and over again that Mrs. Henry do the same with
Mr. Henry   right   the same   meaning that Mrs. Henry should tell
Mr. Henry what she did with Mr. Kahane   if you will   yes   confess all   no there's no mention here of where   if it was true, of course
it would have had to be   I suppose   at the party   I don't know
the bathroom   or the study   I don't know why you're making a mountain out of a molehill   I don't care what I said!   it's not what I said
anyway   it's what this   and this   this and this   these

goddamned papers and files and God knows what else   I'm so confused
with who did what and with whom   and when and where   I don't
care who said anything to   all right, I hope   I do hope that we're
almost finished and done with all this   this mess   yes   I suppose
you might say that Mrs. Kahane called because   as you say   misery
loves company   afterward?   you mean after the phone call?   the
testimony is that of Mr. Lewis who told   somebody   that   I don't
know who he told, it's not here   he told somebody that   what?   I
took it for granted that you knew that Mr. Lewis was with the Henrys at
their apartment   we've been through all   yes, he lived with the Henrys and had been   freeloader is kind of a harsh   I told you that Mr.
Henry was obligated to him because he had arranged for the publication
of   fine   I thought for a minute that maybe you'd forgotten but you
    God forbid   you don't forget anything   only I tend to forget
things, right?   right?   all right   Mr. Lewis said   it says   that
Mrs. Henry did tell Mrs. Kahane that she and Mr. Kahane had   they'd
succumbed to temptation and that she was truly   deeply sorry   she
begged for forgiveness   it all reads like a lot of baloney to   right
she got down on her knees and begged her husband to   I don't know if
that's figurative or what it is   it was Mr. Lewis who said this   she got
down on her hands and knees and wept   oh boy   and wept bitterly as
she told Mr. Henry what had   Mr. Lewis says that she told her husband
that Mr. Kahane had   taken advantage of her in the   clothes closet
    it says   right here   the clothes closet   that's a new twist and it
seems to me there's something wrong about it   because it's where
supposedly   Miss Lorpailleur and Mr. Harley at the Christmas party
did something that was, you remember   said to be scandalous   I did!
Jesus   I specifically recall telling you that Miss Lorpailleur   fine
fine   as long as we don't start in again on things we've already   and
then what?   you mean at the Henrys   oh   it goes on   Mr. Lewis
goes on   to say   that Mr. Henry wept and then began to shout and
threw some papers around and some other objects   an ashtray   a
book or two   a lamp   and so on   and then he demanded that his
wife do for him what   what she did for Mr. Kahane   what?   Mr.
Lewis said that he retired   left the room   so he didn't see whether or
not Mrs. Henry   yes there's one more thing   Mr. Lewis said that he
heard Mr. Henry say that he was damned if his wife was going to be a

whore for Mr. Kahane   too   I don't know who he   it might have
been   yes   Mr. Lewis that he   Mr. Henry was referring to   I've
told you at least ten times   Mr. Lewis had done Mr. Henry a favor with
Mr. Blanche   Blanche Neige Press   in getting Mr. Henry's book
The Orange Dress?   yes there's some evidence that Mr. Lewis inter-
ceded with Mr. Blanche concerning *The Orange Dress* too   it could
have been   could have   that Mrs. Henry was willing to   and Mr.
Henry too   yes   willing to do favors   as you put it   for Mr.
Lewis in return for   who?   Cecil Tyrell?   he was   he was   let
me see, he was   he was somehow involved with *The Party*   the film
project   that's all I know about   no   no mention of him at the party
in any way   any way at all   why do you mention   why do you
bring him up?

You referred to some paper of agreement or contract that Lou
signed with or for Saul Blanche—what was that all about?

I was waiting for you to bring that up   I'm surprised that you
didn't ask about it earlier   it's just the sort of thing that you'd find really
yes I have all the answers   what a word   I have them all here
clipped together so that   here they are   if you'll bear with me since
this is complicated   what?   I can't understand it and I don't want to
I don't get any pleasure out   I know you know   I just thought I'd
all right   it appears that Mr. Henry signed a paper   or contract
whatever you want to call it   with Mr. Blanche   that implicated him,
Mr. Henry, in the business concerning the forgeries of the prints   the
forged prints that I told you about?   fine   I wanted to make sure that
you remem   anyway, Mr. Henry signed this contract or whatever
that said   that made it clear   that he, Mr. Henry   was instrumental
in arranging for the purchase and storage of paints and dyes and such
it says the prints themselves here too   for the storage of these things in
the basement of Mama Gatto's and that he   Mr. Henry   was in on
that he was in on this   scheme   concerning the forgeries with the rest
of   once again?   Mr. Blanche, Mr. Tete, Mr. Harley, and Mr. Gom
but   but it appears that Mr. Henry was actually not and that he was
duped   tricked   into signing this contract or what   contract, fine
signing it for Mr. Blanche by   Mr. Lewis   it's not especially clear
but it would seem that this contract   that it was then used by Mr. Blanche
as a kind of   used to   blackmail is the word   yes   I think the

word used in this report is   wait a minute   pressure   I'd accept
blackmail   yes   so it would seem   the reasons are   this is all
in the papers here we seem to have everything but the   the contract
itself is missing   I don't know if by design or acci   what?   I was
going to say that the reasons given are all   what's the word?   conjecture   conjectural   as a matter of fact they look so farfetched that
of course I'll give them to   to the bitter end   after all, we have so
much proof of everything   built on sand   if I may say so   that we
might as well build a little   I have no intention of wasting your time
right   the reasons given   right   the rock-solid   brass-bound
unimpeachable reasons   right   Mr. Blanche was angry and annoyed
at Mr. Henry and at Mr. Lewis   and at Mrs. Lewis too, I'd imagine
because   as you know   Blanche Neige Press had published *The Orange Dress*   Mrs. Henry's   what was it?   it was   it was described as a   poetic novel about a doomed artist   a poet   a doomed
poet   in any event it turned out that Mr. Henry   and Mr. Lewis
who had done, you'll recall, a group of linoleum cuts for the book   it
turned out that they knew that Mrs. Henry had not actually   it wasn't
actually her work   her book   I mean that Mrs. Henry had   it would
appear that *The Orange Dress* had been written by someone else   who
had left it with Mrs. Henry and that she had   no   there's no name
mentioned but whoever it was   committed suicide   I have no idea
who it was   why would I know who it   yes   Mrs. Henry had
discussed this manuscript with Mr. Henry and they had   perhaps with
Mr. Lewis too, it doesn't make it clear precisely who   they discussed it
and what with one thing and another and given the quality of the manuscript and that the author had been   a good friend   well   with this
that and the other thing it was decided that it would be a good idea to get
in touch   with Mr. Blanche   to see if he would be interested in publishing *The Orange Dress*   as a novel by Mrs. Henry   and so they
what?   it notes that this was   well, not notes   there's a little note
    a sort of diagram here   that says   Sheila   and then there's an
arrow that points to the name   April   that would be Mrs. Detective
    and then another arrow that points to the name   Saul   right
Mrs. Henry got in touch with Mrs. Detective because she   Mrs. Detective was a neighbor of   you remember   I'm glad that you remember
something because I   I don't remember any   I mean   talk about

convoluted   certainly I am going on   ever onward   well, to make
a long story short   ha ha and ha   Mr. Blanche published *The Orange
Dress* as a   as being by Sheila Henry and it made a considerable stir in
publishing circles   literary circles   and was given raves in   let me
see   *Bookwatchers PreViews* and *Big Apple* and did   as they say
very nicely for Blanche Neige   it went into a third printing   within
the year   and there was some talk about a movie option   so   right
there is of course more to it   it then happened somehow that Blanche
Neige   the very next season   published Mr. Henry's poems   *Sheila
Sleeping* or   *Lobster Lays*   perhaps both, it's not clear   somehow?
it looks as if   there's some evidence   hearsay evidence   that
Mr. Henry threatened   he told Mr. Blanche that *The Orange Dress* was
by   someone other than Mrs. Henry   and that if Mr. Blanche would
publish Mr. Henry's poems then   exactly   you might say that
what people don't know won't hurt them or something like   Mr. Lewis
was   forced   I suppose is a fair enough word   by Mr. Blanche to
act as the agent   so to speak   in reference to the agreement   the
contract   concerning the prints   and so on and so forth   I suppose
so, yes   the blackmailer was blackmailed   so it seems   well he
must have had something   as you put it   on Mr. Lewis to recruit him
as the   what did I call him?   the agent   who got Mr. Henry to sign
the   what?   I suppose that Mr. Blanche might have had   I mean
anything is possible   have had those photographs of Mrs. Lewis   I
don't see what you're driving   anything is possible but I don't know
anything about   other photo   who?   Tania Crosse?   the way
you suddenly   the way these names pop up out of   you must think
that I'm some kind of a human computer or   Tania Crosse   all right
Miss Crosse was   she was a photographer and she was   for a time
Mr.   Mr. Blanc's fiancée   and she also knew   right   she also
knew Mr. Blanche and assisted him at Blanche Neige   I remember that
I told you all this   definitely   and Mr. Blanc was also a photographer
no   no   nowhere does it say that Mr. Blanc knew   or had even
met Mr. Blanche   of course it's possible!   that good old possible
if Miss Crosse was in Vermont with Mr. Blanche and Mr. Blanc was her
fiancé then   what?   once again and I hope that it's the last time   I
hope that it's the   Mr. Blanc was a photographer   Mr. Blanc was at
one time Miss Crosse's fiancé   Mr. Blanc was involved with *The Party*

the film   period
    What other people at Horace Rosette's?
    Other people, that's all   just other people   I mean a few
people stayed   apparently   at Mr. Rosette's after the party ended to
    I suppose   to talk and have a few laughs   maybe a nightcap
just other people outside of Mr. Pungoe and Mr. Tete   so far as our
I like that our   so far as our   I'm sorry, and Mr. Hicks, of course
the world-famous Inspector of Buildings, known in song and   all right
    so far as our information goes   outside of Mr. Pungoe and Mr.
I'm only trying to be as precise as   there were Mr. Moses, Mr. Buckie-
Moeller, Mr. Towne, Mrs. Lewis, and   either   Miss Lorpailleur or
Sister Rose Zeppole   or maybe both of them   I don't know   I
mean I don't know!   look for yourself   see?   it says Lorpailleur
and under that Sister Rose and then there's a   what do they call this?
I don't know   a little sort of   parenthesis   anyway, this little
bracket   that's it   bracket   and then a question mark   that would
seem to mean that it could be either one or   fine, you agree   will
wonders never   what were they what?   up to?   I know what this
junk tells me   and it doesn't tell me much   if you ask me they were
hanging around to have a nightcap and sort of wind down after the
wind down, wind down   God   you know what I mean   you'd
think that we don't speak the same language or something like   I mean
    to be specific   relax a little the way people will tend to   I don't
have any idea what they talked about   I don't have any idea what they
did   what?   no   I don't have any idea why the people who stayed
stayed   oh fine   fine   that's a little nasty   I think maybe this is
getting on your nerves as much as   all right, not   I repeat   not
to answer in kind, I do know what my name is but what I know about this
after-party   gathering   is exactly what I have here and it is very
sketchy   incomplete   of course   as a matter of fact you can have it
framed if you like   in precious metals   I'll read it   I said I'd   I
thought that we were almost finished with this   I don't even know what
to call what we're doing   I   will   read   it   in all its blinding
clarity   Page Moses slash Chico Zeek colon Moses Z's name when
doing comms   comms   that's what it says   c o m m s   I don't
know   and if you're going to ask me what this   shorthand   means
I really don't think that we ought to even bother about this because   it's

all that way   little stupid scratches and abbreviations and   all right
Page Moses slash Chico Zeek colon Moses Z's name when doing
comms Z slash belt slash Pungoe all he likes for more film dollar sign
Bunny too w Pungoe and Z via Ted's suggest also Pungoe dollar sign here
in re slash So West Devel Co Jackson in Annie's uniform and she as mother
sup Hicks will prob sign o.k. anything Rosette bustles as host slash ess
and Barn voyeur and shifts Annie slash tux Jack slash wimple and ling
dollar sign to Z and Ted and Bunny to b slash r w Annie var phone calls
April slash Sheila slash Lo K somebody lost und question mark refresh
for all scene of LA work in prog question mark   and then it's signed
Sylvie   that is   as they say   that   Annie?   I suppose Annie
Flammard, I don't know of any other Annie   no she's not named as
being there   not named as being anywhere for that matter   I told you
    Miss Lorpailleur and Sister Rose   or Sister Rose   with the little
bracket next to their   who?   it would seem that Sylvie is Miss
Lacruseille   Sylvie Lacruseille   who is also not named   leads me
to believe?   leads me to believe nothing   since I can't make heads or
tails out of who is who or who was who or who is liable to be who   or
when   or why   I told you   a few laughs   a nightcap maybe
a kind of relax   I didn't tell you what?   oh   I see   I didn't really
notice that   it says   *The Party* like a   heading, a title   like the
title we've talked   that's all   there's nothing about anybody discuss-
ing or doing anything insofar as making a   Duke who?   oh, Duke
Washington   yes, he was at the party   at least he's on the list but I
don't have any idea who he is   what do you mean   real?   I have no
idea   as a matter of fact as far as I'm concerned they're all just names
    as far as any of them being real or   *Hellions in Hosiery*?   oh God,
are we going back to   no I don't care what I do or don't do   it's
immaterial to me but I thought that we were going to wind this whole
thing   I've got it   I've got it here   *Hellions in Hosiery*   the stars
    what a laugh that is   stars   the stars were Annie Flammard and
Baylor Freeq   you'll forgive me if I mention   if I whisper   if I
dare to suggest that we've been over this so many   what do you mean
what else?   oh   Annie Flammard played a schoolteacher named
Marcella Butler and Baylor Freeq was a repairman   this was certainly a
really profound movie   named   well   Duke Washington   I
didn't say so before because you didn't ask   it must be obvious to you

that the more information I give you the more you confuse and involve
and mix up the   it's in a   you'll pardon the expression   press kit
     a few mimeographed sheets is more like it   this was not exactly
a mammoth production   an extravaganza   Marcella Butler?   I
don't recall mentioning that name at all   I say I don't recall it   I don't
know why Duke Washington is on the party guest list   I thought we
were through with the damn party   maybe it was some kind of a mistake   maybe it had something to do with *The Party*   the film project
     or whatever it was   maybe it was   I don't know   you know I'm
about   I'm really fed up   Miss Butler?   fine!   if you say that I
said that she was on the other   then that's fine   that's absolutely fine
     Miss Butler was a world-renowned molecular biologist   a Nobel
laureate   and a distinguished professor   also a loving wife a devoted
mother and a pillar of the community who had round heels   yes   it is
my little joke   can we wrap this up?   just get it over and done with?
     Miss Butler and Mr. Washington were   apparently   not real
they were characters   names   that's two down and the rest to   I
mean if we play our cards right maybe we can turn the whole bunch of
them into just   make all of them unreal   then maybe we can wrap the
whole   I don't get any pleasure out of all   Biggs Richard?   I never
heard of him   no   never   a blank   fine   I told you   if you
say so then it's fine with me   yes   cooperate?   of course   it's
just that the more we find out about these char   I was going to say
characters   these people   the more we realize that we don't know
any   hardly anything about them, they just get more and more un
sure, we can talk about anybody you like   Miss Tate?   right   here
     on the party list   I mean the people who attended the   right
there's nothing about any activity of hers at the party   and only one
other thing   she was apparently a neighbor of Mr. Detective's at one
time   I have two old leases with her name and Mr. Detective's   you
can see for   you can see   the same address   same place   Mr.
Detective in Cottage 33 and Miss Tate in Cottage   I can't make it out
     but there doesn't seem to be anything   no, it's as you can see
Tate with an a not an e   in *Isolate Flecks*?   I don't know that book
but I'm sure I mentioned something   no I didn't know that Buffie Tate
is a character in   I agree that Grey Crimson sounds like a nom de
nom   a pen name   no   nowhere   not a mention

Why did Leo Kaufman leave Rosette's with Anne instead of Ellen?

There are conflicting accounts here if you'll bear with me   for
a moment   as if you haven't been or is it that I'm bearing with   yes
here are a number of accounts   again   oh Christ   again one
from Miss Schmidt who seems to have been everywhere   she says that
she   wait a minute   this is all post-party material   it says
she says   that Mr. Kaufman was in a rear booth in some bar with Mrs.
Kaufman   Anne Kaufman   and he was crying   he was crying and
telling her   Mrs. Kaufman   his ex   all right, I want to be sure you
know exactly   telling her that he was sorry   that he should never
have allowed   Duke   Duke?   he should never have allowed Duke
to move in with them when they were so happy together   it says
Duke   I can only guess that he means Mr. Washington so it looks like
this information   press kit   about *Hellions in Hosiery* is so much hog
what?   it could have been Mr. Freeq but why would Miss Schmidt
call   well I know, Miss Schmidt   I know what I said!   but it's
possible she could write   don't you think so?   you don't have to be
able to talk to know how to   I don't know how she could have heard
right   I never thought of that   I don't know how   all right   he
was crying and saying that he had been a fool to let Duke whoever move
in with them   he didn't care what this Duke had on him   he shouldn't
have let him do it because he knew   the account goes on   he knew
that she   his ex-wife   Anne Kaufman   he knew that she'd fall for
his line and that   things   would happen   and then his ex-wife said
that she didn't   she wouldn't have done anything   wouldn't have
been such a   I can't make this out   wouldn't have been such a something   if   he   Mr. Kaufman   hadn't insisted on it being a nightly
thing and did he   Mr. Kaufman   think that she was happy doing all
those things   with him   watching?   and sometimes other people
too?   then Mr. Kaufman cried some more and   sat next to her in the
booth and said that if Mr. Washington hadn't had the snapshots would she
have   wait a minute   I have to find the rest   would she have
would she have   that's all I have here   there must be something miss
oh here it is   would she have   wait a minute   there must be
I think a sheet is missing because this starts   I'll read it   but Anne
said that it was better just to take off with Duke than put up with this

degradation so that he could get some flunky job with that bastard
Whitestone   what?   he?   I guess   Mr. Kaufman but   it's not
clear   then Mr. Kaufman started to cry harder and they left the bar and
Mrs. Kaufman   Anne Kaufman   took him to her apartment in
wait a minute   in a taxi   don't ask me!   I don't know what any of
this means   here's another account by   Mademoiselle Aubois
very brief   drunk as usual Leo stumbled out with the whore   that's
one and here's another   the whore?   well this is supposed to be about
Mr. Kaufman and his first wife   and his second   present wife   so
it might be that the whore is Mrs. Anne   I'm telling you that's all it says
    and then one more by Miss Ostrom   that says that   Mr. Kaufman
was very drunk as was Mrs. Kaufman   Anne Kaufman   and that the
present Mrs. Kaufman   Ellen Kaufman   what?   I do like to be as
you say formal   I think it's better to stay as objective as poss   fine
Mr. Kaufman and his first wife were drunk and his present wife   as far
as Miss Ostrom knew   his present wife surprised them making love
the account says out   making out   in Mr. Rosette's study for   an
audience   then?   how should I know?   oh, Miss Ostrom's
then, Miss Ostrom says   that that would probably finish Mr. Kaufman
as far as sponging off his wife   I would guess, yes, his present wife
Ellen Kaufman   I suppose   when I say present I don't mean present
present   now   you know what I mean   fine   those are the accounts   if you'll pardon the   like all of these   accounts and depositions   testimony   eyewitness this and that   and the notes and
the photographs   none of this seems to jell no matter   none of it
seems to paint a   Mr. Kaufman?   he was   he was   hm   he
had been a poet   had a small reputation as a poet when he married for
the first time   and then he   wrote reviews and gave readings and
let's see   here's a contract   two contracts   to teach somewhere
some writing workshop   then   then   he did some free-lance work
for   Crescent and Chattaway, some   publishers   I told you they
were publishers   I don't know why I bother to keep going through all
this junk when you forget   maybe you don't forget   all right   but
it certainly seems as if   all right   all right!   Crescent and
Chattaway when Mr. Whitestone was there   but he   it was only
freelance   he   Mr. Kaufman   never got on the payroll   then
here's a photostat of a final divorce decree   then it looks like   it's a

wedding invitation   Mr. and Mrs. Jack Marowitz and so forth and so on   it just warms your heart   a real all-American story   everything in such nice order   I am getting crazy   then   then   Jesus!   there's just so much crap here   can I cut it short?   can I just sort of   all right   the essentials   thank you   Mr. Kaufman started drinking   heavy drinking   and Mr. Marowitz supported   no   Mrs. Marow   I mean Mrs. Kaufman   Ellen Kaufman   had an allowance from her father and she supported her husband because she thought that he was a great artist and decided to   she supported him because she thought that he was a great poet   that's what it says   a great poet   but he just kept   he was a hopeless drunk   so Mrs. Kaufman would cut him off   his allowance   what?   there's a copy of a page here   from a   diary?   no   an account book I guess   not a diary   it   could be I guess   yes   but this page is a page of accounts   I fail to understand why you blow the smallest things out of all   who cares   whether it could be a diary or an account book or a notebook or an address   right   it says   it shows   God forbid that I should say says   it   shows that Mrs. Kaufman gave Mr. Kaufman   let's see   twelve and   two-fifty and ten and   let's see   she gave him thirty dollars a week?   I guess a week   but she would sometimes increase   according to   a deposition   another deposition   by Miss Lorpailleur who at the   time   it says that she was a maid at the Marowitz house   but I seem   to recall that she wasn't?   or it was said   sworn   that she wasn't a   real maid?   is that right?   is that the fact?   or am I   fine   Miss   Lorpailleur   the trustworthy Miss Lorpailleur said that Mrs. Kaufman   told her father that she would cut Mr. Kaufman off   so he wouldn't   drink I suppose   and   no Miss Lorpailleur doesn't say that   I say   that   I have a right I think to an occasional opinion   what else?   that's about all   what?   that's all   what?   this? oh, I didn't see it   on the back of the wedding announce   of course I'll read it   we   aim to please   ask and you shall receive   I know you're tired   at   the top of the card   typed   it says   Leo's Last Poem   then   underneath   in a very clear handwriting by the way   it doesn't look   at all like what you'd expect Mr. Kaufman's   it says   first line   I   love   second line   your can   third line   did tits   I'm not   making it up   look for your   see?   I love   your can   did tits   I don't know much about poetry but if this is poetry   no wonder he

became a drunk   Ellen Kaufman?   there's absolutely nothing here
but I don't think that she would have any   trouble, as you put it
getting home from Mr. Rosette's   why? Mr. Gom   you remember
that Mr. Marowitz had the money that   for Christ sake he probably
would have been happy to carry her   piggyback   I don't know how
Lincstone was doing   but a bird in the hand

What's that about Lucy Taylor at Lou and Sheila's?

I mentioned this already when I told you about the phone call
from Mrs. Kahane to Mrs. Henry   what did I tell you?   this is really
too much for   I told you that Mr. Henry and Mrs. Henry and Mr. Lewis
had left the party   and etcetera   and that Miss Taylor had left with
them   because she'd been on the outs with Miss Jefferson   you recall
Miss Jefferson?   Lorzu?   do you recall Miss   right   you ask
I answer   anyway   Miss Taylor and Miss Jefferson had had   let
me see   they'd had a business disagreement over some bill   wait a
here's the bill   made out to Harlan Pungoe   and according to a
letter written by Miss Taylor Mr. Pungoe had never paid the   in the
amount of twelve hundred and sixty-seven dollars and forty-nine cents
and Mr. Pungoe had never   for lingerie   lingerie and undergarments
and some specialty items   lingerie, lingerie   of course I can give
you a general   camisoles, teddies, panties, bras, corsets, garter belts, a
bustier?   whatever that may be   nylon hosiery   the usual
the other items are   a maid's uniform   a nurse's uniform   a habit
it says   I guess a nun's habit   yes, well   here is   according
to a preliminary statement   Miss Taylor wanted Mr. Pungoe to pay this
bill and Miss Jefferson wanted to write it off   I don't know   yes
that was the cause of the disagreement according to   yes   Miss
Jefferson went her way and Miss Taylor   I told you this   Miss Taylor
went with the Henrys and Mr. Lewis to the Henrys' apartment   what
makes me think I did?   because I know I did!   certainly I can
surely I can   back into the boxes   back to the trusty files where everything true and good is recorded for   I am annoyed   Miss Taylor
was   had been   an art student   a water colorist of   it says
limited talents   this appraisal   appraisal?   whatever   it says
from a teacher   it says   possible talent for undemanding communal
no   commercial art   then   just a second   then she met Mr.
Lewis and they had lived together for a   well, he   Mr. Lewis   had

lived with Miss Taylor   it was her apartment   what?   well   I
don't know if living off other people was   as you say   his chief talent
     she also lived with a painter or a sculptor   I don't know his name
he worked with   chicken wire and rags?   that's what it says
maybe after   maybe before   these documents   these scraps of
paper I should say   don't have any dates on   I don't know if she was
     back together with Mr. Lewis   all it says is that she accompanied
him to the Henrys' apartment   after the party at Mr. Rosette's had broken   Mr. Lewis was driving and Miss Taylor sat next to him and the
Henrys were in the back   what?   according to   it says that Mr.
Lewis had his hand on Miss Taylor's thigh   it doesn't say whether his
hand was under   this is Mrs. Henry's statement   I don't know what
they were doing in the back   looking up at the mysterious stars
contemplating the swift passage of time   reciting deathless poetry to
     of course it says   Mrs. Henry says   that it was indeed Miss Taylor
     why wouldn't it be Miss   wearing?   now how am I   yes, now
that you mention it I   this is a   it looks like a clipping   Miss Taylor
modeled, and quite beautifully   a sleeveless shift of   off-white raw
silk in the new shorter length designed to reveal the patterned stockings
that promise to be the season's hottest item   no it's not   necessarily
     necessarily strange   as you put it   that Miss Taylor might have
been wearing the same   on the other hand   what leads you to believe
that Miss Taylor was wearing this clothing   on this particular night?
I mean   why would you think that Miss Taylor would wear something
that she apparently model   I said that Mrs. Henry stated that it was Miss
Taylor that accomp   what?   they had a drink   and then the phone
call from Mrs. Kahane   and then Mr. Henry   do we have to go
through   and then the business with Mr. Henry and Mrs. Henry begging
him to   Mr. Lewis had gone into another room   that's what it   as
I recall   said   this account?   this account is by   it's anonymous
     I don't know   maybe somebody was looking in the window   how
should I know who knew what   maybe it's a lie   maybe all of this is
a lie   I'm doing my   I went to a lot of trouble to   this account says
that   Mr. Lewis went into   wait a minute   I have to find the other
     that Mr. Lewis went into the bathroom with Miss Taylor   when Mr.
and Mrs. Henry began their private   discussion   and that Mrs. Henry
     stumbled on them when she went to use the bathroom   she stumbled

on them at precisely the moment at which Mr. Lewis was about to   I
can't read it   Miss Taylor   and that she was shocked at Miss Taylor's
abandon   abandoned position   that's it in its entire   yes there is
    not a photograph but   I guess it's a copy of   a xerox copy of
yes   it looks like a shift   no I can't see the woman's face   I mean
I can see it but   it's blurred because the copy   like who?   Mrs.
Lewis?   I wouldn't say that   besides we have evidence   evidence
is some mouthful   we have evidence that Mrs. Lewis stayed at Mr.
Rosette's so that   how should I know when it was taken   or copied?
    it's with this stuff   this crap   this   about what happened
maybe   at the Henrys' apartment   an effort to what?   it was
believe me   hard enough to get it all together   what I could of it
without verifying any   what?   Mr. Lewis is referred to as   let me
check   he's referred to as L in this statement   I suppose it's possible
that L   could stand for Lou   why not?   it's also possible that Mrs.
Henry could have been with Mr. Lewis in the living room   you know
    there's nothing   absolutely nothing   nothing that I've told you
that hasn't been made into   made into some kind of a   what's that
thing you do with a strip of paper where you twist it and then   you put
the ends together?   so that you can't tell where   you can't tell one
side from another?   what do they call that?   that's how you twist
things   everything I say   you twist
        What did Whitestone, Gom, and Miss Ostrom talk about in the
bar to which they went afterward?
        Oh God   I have a   what do they   a dossier an inch thick on
    I don't know   maybe a waiter   or bartender   I really don't
know   all right   not quite an inch   but if you want me   really
    to really read this then we'll be here for a   what?   oh the sheets
stapled together   all right   that's better   I'll start   yes, at the
beginning   beginning is a hell of a word to use don't you think?   I
mean   beginning!   why don't we start going back into their child-
hoods so that we can see what happened to them   like they do in those
big fat novels   those what do they call them?   good reads   then we
can understand everything   you know   like somebody saw his mother
putting a present under the Christmas tree   not Santa   his mother so
that the kid knows that there's no Santa   some pathetic little thing   a
windup toy or something   a little soldier   or a tin   yes   sorry

Mr. Whitestone said that it was a hell of a   what?   I don't have to
read   general statements?   fine   the core is what you'll get   the
really deep and important   the gold!   Mr. Whitestone said that   he
thought that maybe they should seriously consider giving Miss Lorpailleur
a role   settle things peaceably with   it doesn't say what   *The Party*
I guess   the film business   settle things   and Mr. Gom thought that
was a good idea   something here   a rather garbled note   about
how he   or they   agreed that she   Miss Lorpailleur   had no
no something   to make trouble over the plagiarism thing   and there's
the name Léonie Aubois in a little box   a box drawn around it   and
then   let me see, a new page   she mentioned that Miss Lorpailleur
had told her that   I would guess Miss Ostrom?   she   it only says
she   that Miss Lorpailleur had told her that Miss Lacruseille was a very
powerful figure   a friend   and   chair?   what this is I   oh
she chaired some international authors' organization that looked into these
situations in order to pro   that's what I thought too   that she was
so to speak   Miss Lacruseille   that Miss Lacruseille wasn't real
just a name   why did I tell   for Christ sake?   I told you what these
    dossiers   say   I can't help it if they don't say what you want them
to say   maybe if you asked different questions we'd get to the bottom
of   whatever it is   whatever it is you're trying to find out   what?
    see?   you're doing this again   hopping around from this to that in
no order at   all right!   material on Miss Ostrom material on Miss
Ostrom material on Miss Ostrom material on   yes   first of all   no
mention here of her activities with Miss Lorpailleur at Mr. Rosette's
that's number one   a remark by Mr. Gom to the effect that she   that
he   Mr. Gom   thought that she   Miss Ostrom   had the most
beautiful legs that he'd ever seen and that he'd really like   I suppose so
    yes   that he'd seen plenty of them at the party   and then
number   number three   Mr. Whitestone suggested that Miss Ostrom
do her best to please her while they figured out what to do about her threat
    a veiled threat?   I suppose so   concerning the   concerning
Miss Lacruseille and so forth and so on   no   please her is not spelled
out   yes, right   that's all on Miss Ostrom   three little   what?
what would who really like?   Mr. Gom?   I don't know what you
oh yes   I'm sorry   you   as usual   interrupted me   you know
if we could just follow one line of   Mr. Gom said that he'd really like to

see the rest of them   legs   Miss Ostrom's legs!   God   that's it
   one no mention of party scene two legs three please Miss Lorpailleur
and that's that for   trusty faithful hardworking and bright Miss Os
yes yes yes   to the stars!   Mr. Whitestone and Mr. Gom were most
concerned though that Miss Lorpailleur   because she was Mr.
Marowitz's maid   there are little quote marks around that word and
then   in a   in parentheses   the word laughter   because she was
   she definitely   there was a definite possibility that she knew a lot
about the   stock deal   and this was a problem that they couldn't
it says stock deal   no   I've never heard of anything like it   I mean
   you know   come across anything that   anyway they couldn't
afford such a problem because   if Mr. Marowitz thought that he'd be
implemented   implicated   he'd drop the gallery   pull out his
money   then a note in the margin   here   see?   says   Tete
pressure certain   and then   Mr. Whitestone notes   if Mr. Marowitz
for whatever reason blacks out?   oh   backs   backs out   there
goes Lincstone   Mr. Gom added here that if he   himself   were
involved in any public   publicity concerning the stocks   that too
would mean the end of Lincstone   they might as well fold and take a
   take a something   it's illegible   then one of the men   it doesn't
say which   one of them said they might as well give the fucking bitch a
part in the thing   or else it might all go down the drain   Miss Ostrom?
   I guess she was just listening   there's nothing   I told you
nothing other than the three   and   fine   and the other man agreed
and said   maybe they could give Miss Lorpailleur a part and also make
an   agreement?   yes   an agreement with Miss Aubois on credits
   whatever that means   now   there's a page or two here about
possible screenplays   people to write   yes   I'll read the water-
mark if you want   I am tired, yes   it's a goddam list   it says
Dick D, Whytte-Blorenge, Lorna, Léonie A   then   here's some more
on what seems to be   yes   the last page thank Jesus   Mr.
Whitestone says   or   yes   Mr. Whitestone says that there is still a
problem with Mr. Pungoe whom they   Mr. Pungoe was more or less
promised that Annie Flammard would be very seriously considered for
the   for a role   because she'd been so good   had   it says
made a splash with hip people   in *Hellions in Hosiery* and Mr. Gom
added don't forget *Silk Thighs* and *Sisters in Satin*   then they talked

about   grosses and earnings   what?   no figures are included
then   let me see   then Mr. Whitestone says that that   would be a
problem   the Annie Flammard thing   and Mr. Gom says that Mr.
Pungoe admired her a great deal and thought she had a lot of talent   and
talent is   it's got quote marks around it   like the word before that I
   right   Mr. Whitestone says that that   plus the fact   that?   I
suppose that refers to the fact that Mr. Pungoe wanted Miss Flammard to
have a role in *The Party*   anyway   he says that that plus the fact that
Mr. Pungoe and Mr. Tete were also involved in business together could
mean that they couldn't even defend on   depend on   Mr. Pungoe's
share of the backing   then someone says   whoever   says that Mr.
Pungoe might not be a problem after all because Mr. Lewis seemed
persuaded?   persuaded that it would be wise to ask his wife   who
else?   of course   to ask her to entertain Mr. Pungoe and that she
might be doing that right now   it says   as we speak   entertain?
that's all it says   it doesn't say how or where   I don't know   why
would I have an opinion about Mrs. Lewis?   no   there's nothing
more   just that they left   they stiffed the waiter
         Well, what was the substance of April and Dick's conversation?
         Well   the substance   why don't I give you   it would be
easier to give you the important   so to speak   the important information   I have a transcript from the tape here and   no   I won't with-
hold any pertinent data   just drop the hums and the ohs and the ahs the
   well   personal relations because it appears that about   about halfway through their talk they had an   interlude   they   it appears that
they made love and they say   a lot of   well   intimate things
they speak rather intimately to   they say sexual things   they ask each
other to   do things   I don't think it's important   as a matter of fact
anybody who'd want to know this sort of thing is   it's not something
that anybody would want to know   it's bad enough that we're   yes I
will   they were talking over the party and   the real party they were
just at   and Mr. Detective said   that was some scene with good old
Bart and Sheila in the bathroom what a surprise to me and I guess everyone because I thought that it was Guy who was getting into Sheila's pants
         and Mrs. Detective said that   she said   you're really terrible
besides it wasn't the bathroom scene that was so bad it was later when
Horace and I walked in on them in Horace's bedroom and Sheila was at it

really hot and heavy   and Mr. Detective said   if I didn't know that
Horace mine host was as queer as a three-dollar bill I'd be a little annoyed
with you going into his bedroom like that   what by the way did you
want to do there?   and Mrs. Detective said   I wanted to talk to him or
rather he wanted to talk to you but you were as usual making a fool of
yourself with Rose so he decided to talk to me   it was about I think
because we never did talk at any length because of the wild scene but I
think it was about asking you to contribute something to a new anthology
of his something about cities a collection of pieces on cities?   and Mr.
Detective   Horace can go fuck himself with his dollar fifty a page I'm
sick of him with his cheap shit and his poor mouth   but what exactly
was Sheila   what were Sheila and Bart up to?   and Mrs. Detective
   well Sheila was on her hands and knees with half her clothes off and
Bart was behind her giving it to her in her backside but the worst part is
that and I think we ought to keep this really quiet the worst part is that that
poor sick bastard Lou was sitting in a chair watching them and jerking
himself off and groaning   my God they were all so stoned out of their
minds that they didn't even see us or hear us   and Mr. Detective
Jesus Christ!   and Mrs. Detective   I was so embarrassed that I
couldn't even look at any of them later   and Mr. Detective   you've
gotten pretty modest in your old age haven't you?   and Mrs. Detective
   exactly what does that mean?   you're going to bring up those
goddam pictures again after all these years?   and Mr. Detective   no
I'm sorry but when I think about how that son of a bitch rube Pungoe used
those pictures to get us to persuade persuade is some word for it persuade
those poor ignorant bastards to sign away that acreage that son of a bitch!
   and Mrs. Detective   well it's all water under the bridge and the best
thing is to forget all about it don't you think so?   and Mr. Detective
I suppose you're right but when I think of that bastard leering at those
pictures and my God!   that good wonderful true blue old pal from
school days Tania conning you with how the pictures would get us back
together again Jesus!   I could just   and I still can't figure out why
you didn't think something was funny when she laid out all that for Christ
sake a thousand dollars' worth of fancy underwear and those costumes I
mean I still can't figure out why you didn't realize that something was
fishy   and Mrs. Detective   I thought we weren't going to bring this
up?   and Mr. Detective   I'm sorry   then there's this   as I said

interlude   Mr. and Mrs. Detective make love   what?   no not as I recall   no mention earlier at all of Mr. Henry in   well you have it all down there   don't you?   no   there's no mention of Mrs. Detective writing to him   I told you I wouldn't leave   of course   Mr. Detective said   you know the whole thing reminds me of the time we went to that party that dinner party when Roberte Flambeaux got caught in the clothes closet with some dirty old lecher by Lorna do you remember that?   and Mrs. Detective   oh God yes and Roberte said God she was drunk Roberte said that she was just doing what Lorna only wrote about remember?   and Mr. Detective   the old bastard said he thought she was only a maid hired for the night for the party I'll never forget Roberte's fiancé's face what was his name?   and Mrs. Detective   I don't remember but he'd just about gotten over Lorna's book when that had to happen I wonder whatever happened to Roberte?   and Mr. Detective

I heard that she was working as a buyer for ZuZu and what's her name but I can't see how a little shop like that can afford a buyer   and Mrs. Detective   I don't even know how they can afford the rent at that location let alone a buyer   and Mr. Detective   speaking of money I heard a rumor from Karen that Whitestone might ask me to do a treatment for *The Party*, which would be great if it's true and also if I knew what a fucking treatment is and how to write one   and Mrs. Detective   that seems strange to me when they can get Craig Garf probably I wonder where Karen got that idea?   and Mr. Detective   I was thinking about it myself and all I could figure is that the author of the novel that French writer I don't remember her name or the name of the book for that matter thinks that maybe it's a way of getting me in between her and Annette because you know that big scene at the party about who really wrote the book or whatever the hell they were screaming about and she figures that I'm a good friend of Annette's wherever she got that idea   and Mrs. Detective   well let's not count our chickens God I'd like to be a fly on the wall when Sheila or I should say when Lou starts crying tonight about what a whore she is in front of Guy and probably asking Guy's advice my God!   and Mr. Detective   that's their problem why don't we go to sleep?   and Mrs. Detective   uh-huh   and that's the end of the transcript   Mademoiselle Aubois?   I don't know why she'd think they were good friends   except   well   except that if Miss Lorpailleur and Sister Rose Zeppole were the same woman   we had

some testimony?   or some kind of   possibility or something? if you'll
recall   something about it anyway   if Mademoiselle Aubois knew
    or thought   that Miss Lorpailleur and Sister Rose were the same
person   then she might think that because   she might know that Mr.
Detective and Sister Rose   that is maybe Miss Lorpailleur   knew
each other because of what somebody   or some paper or witness or
something had said   about Sister Rose and Mr. Detective when he and
Mrs. Detective were separated   what?   I can't remember exactly but
    it was something about Sister Rose being of some help to him   you
might remember the ref   S I what?   S I S?   no   no   I can't
recall that at all   I said I can't!   I'd really like   very much like
to wrap this up now   do you think that we
        And to whom was Léonie Aubois saying all this?
        Well   I was about to tell you   that's the trouble with this sh
    this data here in this blue folder   it not only doesn't make clear who
was involved   it mentions a number of names but there's no absolute
    no specific   well Mademoiselle Aubois of course   then maybe
Mr. and Mrs. Harley and Mr. Freeq   or   Mr. Harley and Miss Schmidt
    or Miss Schmidt and Mrs. Harley   or maybe all of them   what
was I   oh yes   it not only doesn't make clear who exactly was involved   but it doesn't indicate who said what   only just what was
said   fine   sure   God knows, it can't be any more impossible than
the rest of   yes I will!   somebody said   I'll just say   it was said
    all right?   it was said that Miss Lorpailleur's book was not a book at
all and that Mademoiselle Aubois took the junk   all the scraps and un-
finished scenes   the anecdotes and such   and made a real   a beautiful work of art   and that Miss Lorpailleur's book anyway   outside
of it being just a kind of notebook   a kind of journal   wasn't even
fiction   wasn't shared   shaped   wasn't shaped at all but was based
on things she did when she was working as a maid   a so-called maid
for some neurotic couple because she'd do anything for a dollar   and
she kept a kind of diary there   that's all *Mouth of Steel* was   just a
title on a jumble of diary entries   a diary of this couple's very strange
pastimes   this couple would write little plays   weird and perverse
plays and have friends over to act them out it must have been like   La
Coste?   yes   it says La Coste   whatever that means   and
and   right   and Miss Lorpailleur thought she could cash in on this

with some self-styled fearless publisher   lucky for that   no   lucky
for the world that Mr. Harley saw the possibilities and that the mass
the mess   the mess found its way to Mademoiselle Aubois   and all
this pretentious planted   these pretentious planted rumors that Miss
Lorpailleur is a known writer who works under the name of Sylvie
Lacruseille   what an incredible nerve   it's well known that Miss
Lorpailleur's real name is Sylvie Lacruseille and that Annette Lorpailleur
   strictly confidentially but it wouldn't hurt if everyone somehow found
out   Annette Lorpailleur   according to someone who should know
   Annie Flammard   Annette Lorpailleur is a name that she got out of
some novel   so you see the brazen   the unbelievable nerve of the
woman   and to make it worse   to threaten Mademoiselle Aubois
with a suit   it is too vulgar   as if *La Soirée intime* owes really anything   anything at all to that almost illiterate pile of scrawls   to treat
Mademoiselle Aubois as if she were no better than Mrs. Henry   and
what about Mrs. Henry?   well   one thought by now that everybody
   it's almost public knowledge   in any event   an open secret
Mrs. Henry simply put her name on somebody else's completed manuscript   *The Orange Dress*   some poor man who took those disgusting Henrys into his confidence   can't recall his name   something
like Cedric   or Charles something   Cedric Try   Cecil Tyrell!
of course   for Miss Lorpailleur to suggest that what   or even to imply that what Mademoiselle Aubois did is in any remote way the same as
what Mrs. Henry   well   he committed suicide is what people say
he'd given the manuscript to his dear oh very dear friends the Henrys
and she lost no time in having it retyped   was that a Crescent and
Chattaway book?   it seems as if it should have been what with Mr.
Whitestone with his eye for the daring and   adventurous?   adventurous new writer if you'll pardon the expression   good old Mr. Whitestone
   loved   absolutely loved daring and exciting fiction   fiction that
employed the greatest daring and freedom and experimentation but the
kind of judicious experimentation that doesn't look with contempt on the
reader of good will the common reader   the sort of fiction that is extremely daring and experimental and free but that has a strong moral purpose and a message of hope and humanity for all humankind and so on
and so forth   what good old Mr. Whitestone would say   oh yes   of

course it should have been but even Mr. Whitestone smelled a rat   apparently   how could Sheila Henry have written a book like *The Orange Dress* after those years and years   and years   of the most idiotic little poems   let's not forget her little experimental   oh God   paragraphs full of her utterly pedest   pedest   oh   pedestrian and vulgar erotic fantasies   she called them bursts of energy didn't she?   oh Jesus   she should have said busts   so then if it wasn't Mr. Whitestone who   oh of course   Blanche Neige   what else?   and what is so amusing   if it doesn't make you sick   what is so amusing is that Mr. Henry then published some dull collection of poems   Blanche Neige again   the Henrys were becoming a cottage industry   and Saul Blanche also published that dreary *Blackjack* by Mr. Detective   or his wife?   who knows?   isn't that the one about the stealing?   that's the book about someone   yes   someone stealing somebody else's book and becoming famous   and the fame   oh it's too ghastly   a Connecticut soap opera   it's too ridiculous   the fame ruins him God it's too fucking precious for   you don't know the book? oh God it's literally   quite literally beyond   that scene in front of the fire when the hero rhapsodies   rhapsodizes   on his first year of marriage and his wife's plaid skirt   from Peck and Peck   sweet bleeding and suffering Jesus   it turns out that he wants her to leave the skirt on while he screws her   right   but he's ashamed to ask because of what he knows   oh brother   what he knows turns out to be that she is innocence don't forget the capital I   she is innocence and he is corruption perversity   one can't even be that hilarious intentionally   well all right   but it's hard not to be hilarious writing about the suburbs what a book   it must have been very weird for Mrs. Henry though given   right   but to get back to Miss Lorpailleur   Mademoiselle Aubois thought it best to make some kind of peace with her   after all, Lincstone was about to start looking for a screenwriter and legal difficulties and so on would simply delay things   Miss Lorpailleur might accept a credit and she could even perhaps   collaborate   not really but act as a consultant   give her some kind of a title   money money of course would have to be offered and be right   that's all she really cares about   and perhaps a dinner party   some kind of a party to make her feel   right   but the guest list will not   not   include

Mrs. Henry   not after that awkward scene that night at   where was
it?   oh yes   at Mr. Rosette's publication party when she was locked
in the bathroom with   well   some say it was with Mrs. Kaufman
God knows which one   and others say it was Mr. Kahane   who has
     it's well known   no taste at all   if you look at his work over the
past few years   anyone can see that he's lost   maybe washed   and
that's it   it breaks off right there   no questions? you're actually not
going to ask any questions?   this has got to be some kind of a
     Why is it that so much of what you've told me also happens, more
or less, in *Isolate Flecks*?
     That's really   really too much   for the last   I hope I dearly
hope   for the last time I   right here   see?   I haven't told you
anything that's a n y t h i n g   this   these all these papers   this
testimony and data and reports   eyewitness reports anonymous reports
     these transcripts and depositions   and   God!   diaries   this
crap   this shit   you ask and I answer and always   almost always
     before I can finish you ask some more and some more and some more
     and I find   or try to find   something that will do   that will
answer   if you think that what all this   all this is   is just some
from some fucking novel   why don't you read the novel and get all the
answers right there?   read it and get everything   get all of it   and
if the names are different in the novel just put the right ones in   substitute the right ones   they don't matter anyway   all these people might
as well be   all these people are just names anyway   as far as I'm
concerned   don't ask me   ask the novel   what?   I have   as
far as I'm concerned I have answered the question   I've answered the
     as a matter of   I've answered all the questions I'm going to
enough is enough   if you're so   if you're still interested   why
don't you take a shot at answering your questions yourself? or get somebody who knows these things   firsthand   with experience   don't
ask me   just don't ask me   enough is enough   I am not   absolutely not going to   what?   I told you   it had already grown dark
     not quite dark

Why is it that so much of what you've told me also happens, more or less, in *Isolate Flecks*?

Isolate Flecks? My God, I haven't thought about that book in years! I remember poor old Leo when it was first published rushing around trying to look as if he wasn't concerned *what* they said about him, the poor unfortunate bastard, as if anybody would have anything at all to say about that wreck, that, I might say *desperate* wreck of a novel. He got *one* review, a terrible one in some rag, I think by that asshole, Vance Whitestone —not that he was wrong about the book—who said something really nasty about the novel being Kaufman's lunge for the main chance. The only thing Leo ever lunged at was somebody's wife's ass—God knows he never got much of his own wife's. Either one. But your question, if you'll forgive me, I think it springs from ignorance—what I mean is you've got it backward. What happens in *Isolate Flecks* is based on what I've told you, it's a *roman à clef,* all the characters in the book are really people Leo knew for years, people I knew for years. A lot of them really blew up when that book was published, you know, the way people do when they think they discover themselves in some book, as if their miserable lives weren't an open book anyway. Pardon the pun. Leo's novel tried to make them look *good,* as a matter of fact. He turned a lot of those deadbeats into artists and poets and such, which Christ knows they weren't. Oh they scribbled and daubed away, dance classes and all the rest of that stupid shit, but they were really concerned with what they used to call making the scene. Even the slang in those days was putrid. There were a few decent ones, by decent I mean somewhat connected to reality, you'll pardon the expression, in some tenuous way. Lou and Sheila Henry, as I've told you already, weren't too bad, nice people really. They were kind of enthralled by that phony bastard Lincoln Gom for a while, with his ecopolitics, and the story goes that he had an affair with Sheila that really ruined Lou for a while, he tried to commit suicide, pills, booze, lost his job, roamed around freeloading, weeping all over his friends, oh Sheila, Sheila, how could you do this to me? You know, really fell apart while Linc was popping the old lady and believe me, Sheila was a luscious piece—Christ, she still looks good now, put on a few pounds with the years but she's still got the most beautiful legs I've ever seen. And a few more were O.K. Lena Schmidt was one—she was engaged for a long time to Anton Harley before he married his wife, Antonia—that's a beauty isn't it? Antonia. Anton and Antonia. That's what's known as a match made in heaven. God what a dummy *she* was! Perfect mate for Anton, sitting around in his corduroys and tweeds with his fucking briars and corncobs and meerschaums spieling away about Proust and Joyce and Christ knows who else, didn't know a damn thing except what he read in the papers, Joe Schmuck's review of the latest novel by one of our ga-rate writers and of course Joe Schmuck is an assistant professor of English at Northeast Boise A and M, talks a lot about characters we care about and moral authority and the artist's obligation to everything and then some. Anyway, how he got hooked up with Lena I'm damned if I know, she was a very nice girl, I think at the time an editorial assistant, she had a slight limp but she was very pretty and sharp. You know that scene in *Isolate Flecks* where the elastic on the girl's panties snaps while she's dancing and they fall down around her ankles? That sort of happened, the girl was Lena and there was a party at Biff Page's house, some rich jerk whose father made Venetian blinds or something, designer shower curtains, I don't know, some great contribution to culture, only Lena didn't *lose* her panties, she was dancing with Anton, I think she'd just met him then and already he was giving her some editorial about the artist's responsibility to communicate and speak to the people and Jack Towne, Jesus, this must have been just about a month or less before he died, Jack Towne, who was drunk, and Lena was in the bag herself a little, Jack yells out, give me a garter of thy love!—I'll always remember that, I think it's from Heine, Rilke maybe, and Lena reached under her skirt and pulled her panties off with a kind of fantastic, I don't know, *elegance,* and threw them across the room. She was absolutely beautiful! Old Anton really got pissed off, he *already* thought that she was his property, you know the type, he probably felt her up and figured that was it. What a pain in the ass he was! Biff, I think, or maybe Chico Zeek, he and Biff worked together in some ad agency or public relations agency or something, but Biff worked for the hell of it, he had an allowance from his old man, anyway, Biff or Chico draped Lena's panties over a lamp in the corner, these tiny little black panties, nothing to them, with a black lace trim. That wasn't a bad party now that I think of it. It went on into the next day, a whole bunch of us after it broke up went to have breakfast in an all-night diner and then we went to the beach, brought a lot of vodka and orange juice and sat around till the sun came up, then we all went back again sloshed to the city to Bunny Lewis's place, Guy, her so-called husband, I think I told you this, he was back again, he and Bunny were always splitting up because Guy had this little business going, a direct-mail business with some grim yokel named Harlan Pungoe and he'd work seven days a week till all hours and was never home. I think he might have been carrying on with a girl who worked for them part-time too, Lorna Flambeaux, she wanted to be a poet, or said she was a poet, some really homely girl she was too, compared to Bunny. But, you know, she must have figured that Guy was going places, as they say, because she worked right alongside him, like a slave, all those horrible hours, and of course Harlan was there too, this hayseed, a good ole boy with a clubfoot from some damn farm somewhere, I never really liked the guy, there were a lot of creepy stories about him too. Anyway we all, or most of us that had been at Biff's party, got to Bunny's house, wait a minute. Maybe Guy *wasn't* back because Lucy Taylor was there when we all arrived, she'd been there the whole time, I mean she didn't go to the party, and I know that Lucy and Bunny were having a lesbian, let's say, relationship. Lucy was all right, a little mousey, you know how some of those women are, a perfect stereotype really, thick glasses, straight thin hair, stringy you know? and big shapeless breasts, piano legs, and she wore those sweaters, cardigans, and tweed or plaid skirts that came to, you know, mid-calf, the perfect length to make her legs look even worse, flat shoes. A catastrophe. But she was all right and she was pretty good to Bunny, Bunny looked better than ever as a matter of fact, anyway, what the hell was I driving at? Oh right, oh yeah, that was the clincher when it came to Lena and Jack Towne breaking up because Léonie Aubois, *Madame* Aubois, started talking to all kinds of people, oh Christ, she'd been talking all night but she went into high gear that day, swilling down the vodka, what a winner she was, you know the type, she worked at some little boutique that catered to rich women, dumbo celebrities, actresses, so she got to think that this made her important. Anyway, she started to talk to a lot of people and because she hated Lena because Lena wouldn't put up with her pompous crap, she started saying that Lena's taking her panties off was no surprise to *her* because she'd seen some *very* compromising photographs of Lena and two men taken at Horace Rosette's house, pictures that left, as dear Léonie said, nothing to the imagination. So Jack got wind of this and they later, I heard, had a talk about it, and there were harsh words and so on, and Lena refused to deny this picture business, saying that if Jack could even bring it up that was too bad for them both and then good old arts-and-letters Anton moved right in in spades. But it started that day with Léonie talking to anybody who would listen and even those who didn't want to—she was everywhere, lushing up the vodka and buttonholing people, telling them all about these pictures. I remember it as if it happened last week, for Christ sake. I went into the goddam bathroom with Tania Crosse and we smoked a little marijuana to allay the boredom. You could hear Léonie scratching at the door. Pictures! Pictures! Did I tell you about the pictures?

And to whom was Léonie Aubois saying all this?

I told you. To anybody who'd listen to her, when she was into the sauce she'd talk nonstop for hours, days sometimes, and she really developed a kind of mean streak as time went on and by the time she was Madame Aubois, she was a certified bitch. See, she'd worked at this boutique for years, maybe ten, twelve years, and she was still not the manager, the manager was a woman named Sylvie, Sylvie Lacruseille, she was supposed to be French, sure, like my ass is French, the truth of the matter is that Sylvie was the mistress of a very wealthy man, Barnett Tete, who owned boutiques and chic little restaurants and bars and those little stores that sell those little novelties, paper things, you know, you want to buy some goddam napkins for a party and they have these napkins that say Bon Jour or have little notes on them, music, the first couple of bars of a Mozart quartet, all kinds of cutesy things, strictly for the parvenu trade, two-fifty a box of six, you know, and the box is a production as well. Anyway, he had a lot of these places all over as well as, as I said, a few bars, cocktail lounges, authentic English pubs, lots of wood, heavy chairs and tables tastefully scarred, sawdust on the floor for Christ sake, and one place even had brass spittoons, only God forbid that anybody should actually spit in one, they'd call the National Guard. Anyway, Sylvie was Tete's mistress, or one of his mistresses, the one with seniority, let's say, still a good-looking woman the last I saw her, lovely breasts, nice legs, big calves and very slender ankles, very attractive, but as I say, she was no Frenchwoman. The story goes that her name was, well, not even really, but her name was Luba Checks, she came from some steel or mining town, her *real* name was something like Lyubinka Czechowyczy. Tete met her at some hotel bar where she was a cocktail waitress and gave her this name, Sylvie Lacruseille, where he got it I don't know, but I heard that it was from some schlock historical novel about the American Revolution, the real, well, real, you know what I mean, the original fictitious Sylvie Lacruseille was Lafayette's mistress in the book and so on and so forth, the usual tits asses blushes and beauty spots routine. Tete gave her this name and set her up in this boutique into which she came maybe three days a week at most, for a few hours, with a French accent that was so absolutely hilarious that you didn't know whether to shit or go blind when she opened her mouth. She drove away a few customers, not too many though, they didn't know the fucking difference, credit cards and cash and labels they knew. In any event, this really made Léonie more and more sour because she ran the shop, did all the work, even kept the books, did the purchasing, everything, worked ten or twelve hours a day, and to top it all off Tete was sleeping with her whenever he felt like it and she was still the assistant manager, despite Tete's promises. He was a great one with the promises, a shadowy figure as they say, as well, all these fashionable little places were really a sideline, his real money came from some shady deals he had going with some art galleries, art dealers, what, I really don't know, but it had something to do with forgeries, selling them out of the country to collectors, oh not really collectors, nouveau-riche types with money from cocaine and weapons deals who wouldn't know a Picasso from a Braque, and also pulling some deals with prints, you know, printing a thousand and saying that it was a run of a hundred and fifty, the artists signed everything, you know, didn't know a goddam thing, like publishers, you know, who can tell authors they printed three thousand copies of a book when they printed five. But Léonie wasn't always like this, I clearly remember her years before, ten or fifteen years, she had some literary aspirations then as they say, and had even written a novel, not bad really. It was called *The Metal Dress,* I think, but she never got it published. She married a deadbeat, some black jazz musician, Duke Washington, played those weary old be-bop licks and thought he was Charlie Parker. Anyway, to make a long story short, he convinced Léonie that she had no talent and she quit writing, I told her that she really should continue, at least try to get her book published. I knew a guy in those days, Saul Blanche, an editor at what was then a very good house, very adventurous, Crescent and Chattaway, did some good people, Henri Kink, a remarkable poet, and Cecil Tyrell, his novel *Black Hose and Red Heels,* and of course Antony Lamont's *Synthetic Ink.* What was I saying? I told Léonie that I could talk to Saul and have him read her manuscript but she was convinced that this wrong-o, Duke, was right, even though his idea of a book was that it was something you put under the leg of a wobbly table. Well, she and Duke split up eventually, Duke was screwing her best friend and she was working, as I told you, as a cocktail waitress, drinking too much and jumping into bed with the dummies who passed through the hotel, by the time she met Tete she had no conception of herself as a novelist, she was just on her way to the Madame Aubois she is now. Well, this scene at Bunny's house, she was grabbing everybody she could, telling them about these photographs, so called, of Lena, photographs, by the way, that nobody has ever seen, but people believed her, some people did anyway, Dick and April Detective certainly, but that's because they themselves had an, what shall I say? interest in that sort of thing. April used to send Dick really steamy pictures of herself when he was on the road, for a while he was a meat-cutting-machine salesman, and I'll be damned if Dick didn't show them to people, like, how do you like my wife, sensational, right? It was very embarrassing and a little, maybe more than a little sick. So they were delighted to believe this and for months afterward tried to get ahold of these pictures, they were really a couple of winners. Oh and she talked to a lot of other people, I can't remember all the people who were there, Leo certainly, and his second wife, Ellen, they *had* to be there, Leo was writing *Isolate Flecks* at the time and he was everywhere, gathering material, as he called it, he even had a little notebook so that he wouldn't lose any really deep thoughts that came to him when he was away from his beloved desk. And Ellen! I don't even know what to say about Ellen. She was the kind of woman who was always talking about cuisine, you know the type, cuisine this and cuisine that and cuisine the other thing and by Jesus Christ if you went to their house for a meal you'd get some disaster that you'd turn down if they gave it to you in the fucking army. The woman would serve you mashed potatoes, lots of luck, she'd mash them with a goddam fork, all lumps, hopeless. Half-raw carrots, these terrifying salads with hunks of cheese, my God. Well, they were there for sure, Leo scribbling away in his little notebook, a little *leather* notebook that Ellen bought him, you know, like real writers use, to Ellen a real writer was some guy she saw in a movie, you know, you see this dumb actor sit down at his typewriter and he types at the top of the page, CHAPTER ONE, beautiful! So Léonie knew she had a couple of marks there and, oh I can't remember all the people there, Biff and Chico, yeah, and of course Bunny and Lucy, Lucy wouldn't have listened though because she and Léonie didn't get along to put it mildly. Léonie used to call her Mr. Taylor and ask her what wonderful, what *marrr-velous* Goodwill she bought her clothes at, and Lucy would reply in kind with cracks like how natural Léonie's new hair color looked, such a curious yellow-orange, you'd really have to be right up close to see that it was dyed, oh lots of good clean fun. And as I said, Tania Crosse and I were there, feeling no pain, but the moment we came out of the bathroom we were grabbed by April and Dick, who started to talk and talk to us, unbelievable! They went on and on as if they hadn't seen another human being in ten years.

Well, what was the substance of April and Dick's conversation?

Substance would not exactly be the word. April and Dick were very insubstantial people, but I know what you mean, O.K. As I recall, they wanted to know if I could introduce them to Lena, which was funny, because I'm sure they knew Lena already, but that's what they said they wanted, or maybe I'm thinking of the time we were at Bunny's house after a party at Horace Rosette's? I can't recall exactly, I've known these people so long and they don't ever seem to change, or they change but nothing else does. Anyway. They wanted to meet Lena, I think it was after Biff's party, Tania would remember, but that's neither here nor there, the point is that they said they wanted to meet Lena because they figured that Lena knew Lincoln Gom. As a matter of fact she knew Lincoln all right, they'd been an item as they say, for a year or so, just around the time that Lincoln got involved in his phony ecology and politics dodge. It turned out that it was some kind of scheme having to do with buying up cheap land to make environments or some goddam thing, but what Lincoln really had in mind was building condominiums for rich morons who liked to ski or something, hike, jog, eat cuisine, not smoke, I don't know, healthy things, self-congratulatory things. At this point though, Lena and Lincoln were not speaking to each other, he'd got her involved when they were lovers in working for him as a secretary, Girl Friday, file clerk, the works, in some little dump of an office he opened in Connecticut. The story went that it was funded, that's too fancy a word, I'm beginning to sound like Gom himself, *paid for* is the term, paid for by some guy named Jack Marowitz, Ellen Kaufman's brother, a true hustler who wanted to get in on this condo hustle. Well, Lena moved to Connecticut, which is where, by the way, April and Dick now live, or they did, I should say, until very recently, when they moved up to Vermont, it seems that Connecticut was getting too bourgeois for them, ho ho ho, you understand that I'm talking about people who think that a waiter, for instance, is an inferior being. At any rate Lena moved up to the sticks, she'd really been swept off her feet by Lincoln and his arty friends and she went to work. And I mean work! She did everything, ran the whole office, worked all kinds of hours and half the time she didn't even get paid, can you beat that? So you've got the picture, Lena living with Lincoln, working in his office, you'll pardon the expression, and as likely as not cooking when she got home, cleaning the house, once in a while the sport would take her to a drive-in movie, *I'll Eat Your Eyeballs,* you know, and then buy her a hamburger. Meanwhile he and Marowitz were buying up this land by the fucking fistful and trying to get somebody with *real* money to go in with them on the condo scam, beating the bushes, and then suddenly the deal just fell through. They were informed by the county or the state or somebody that they'd violated some law or ordinance on zoning, or they would if they tried to build, or they wouldn't be able to get a variance or something, so that the whole thing was a bust even if they got the money they needed, which they didn't have a prayer of getting. But Lena didn't know this, there she was, filing and typing these endless letters and one day the so-called business was simply gone and Lincoln and Jack took a powder. There she was alone in Connecticut, and when she got back to town Lincoln was living with what he called an old friend, Rose Zeppole, a girl that everybody called Sister Rose. She'd starred in some porno film playing a nun, I can't remember the name of the thing, *Sisters in Shame,* something like that, anyway she was Sister after that. Which brings me to April and Dick after Horace's party. What they *really* wanted, it turned out, was to meet Lena because of what Léonie had said about the supposed pictures taken at Horace's, that's

right. Lincoln was involved but only because April and Dick had heard
that he was making a fortune, along with Marowitz, in the porno racket
and they wanted to meet him too. They must have figured that Lena had
been in on the beginning of this scheme some years before in Connecticut,
since she'd run the office. In other words, they thought that the real-estate
business, so called, had never been a real-estate business at all, but a front,
from the start, for this little cottage porno-film industry, and that Lena
would know about it. When they heard Léonie talking about these photographs of Lena they then thought that Lena was involved on another level
as well, right? as a participant. I know that Lena wasn't involved, well,
there was nothing to be involved in, and that the original scheme was,
indeed, a real-estate hustle. The idea that Gom and Marowitz were involved in pornography had no basis in fact. O.K. Rose was living with
Lincoln when Lena got back to town and doing, essentially, the same
things that Lena had been doing in the country, that is, chief cook and
bottle washer, as they say. The Detectives, as I told you, were weird, and
they probably wanted to meet other weird people so that they could all be
sexually free, you know, group sex, orgies. Or else, who knows, maybe
they had ideas about *April* becoming a porno star. I don't know, all I know
is that they wanted me and Tania to introduce them to Lena but we told
them that Lena was very self-conscious about her slight limp and that it
would probably be best to sort of introduce *themselves,* we all played, in
other words, our little roles, it was all insane because, as I told you, they
knew Lena. And they persisted, they kept at it, until finally it became clear
why they wanted us sort of in the middle when they asked us if *we* wanted
to go up to their place in Connecticut, yes, they hadn't yet moved further
up into God's country. I mean it was just sex, they wanted us and them and
Lena to sit around at Bunny's and maybe they'd bring up the photographs
or the nonexistent porno business, who knows? To put it bluntly, they
wanted to talk dirty, which is why they wanted us involved, the more the
merrier. Anyway, they asked us up, Dick started talking about his studio,
his studio this, his studio that, it turned out that he had become a photographer, so called, I should say he had a lot of equipment. He went to a
great deal of trouble to tell us that he'd studied under, what a glorious
phrase, he'd studied under Annie Flammard, that French-Canadian photographer who made a great splash with photographs of toys? The really
famous one that some big museum bought immediately was that picture

of this little old-fashioned windup toy, *Tin Pig*. Well, when Dick said that, with April looking sage and artistic, and the both of them up to their elbows in filters and shutter speeds and lenses, all that incredibly boring shit that photographers talk about, worse than food freaks, it occurred to me that Dick was perhaps involved in something unsavory already, because there had been a story about Annie and how she'd been part of some sort of vice ring or some goddam thing and she even did some time in Canada. Some weird thing where they'd get married women, solid citizens, stoned or something and then pose them in lesbian situations, take pictures, a cheap blackmail scam, but nobody could ever really find out anything. The gossip was that she wasn't born Annie Flammard but Roberte Flambeaux, up in some little town either in Canada or right on the Maine border, Christ knows, a farmer's daughter, no joke, a potato farmer. Anyway, they were really pushing us to go and visit them, I think they thought that Tania and I were romantically involved with each other, because April kept running on about a real *fun* weekend with some other *fun* couples, and they were almost certain that Ted Buckie-Moeller was going to be there, hallelujah! Ted was a walking wet dream, also a photographer, a fashion photographer I think, and his great claim to fame, outside of the wild rumor that he once got a model to speak a declarative sentence of more than four words, was that his place was featured in some magazine as being an example of Now Living. He lived in a loft that had no furniture, no books, no pictures, nothing but a big barn of a place with about five hundred fucking pillows on the floor, one whole wall a movie or TV screen and another filled with a huge collection of cigarettes, packs of cigarettes. A deep thinker. So at that moment, over the din of Léonie and Lucy sweetly murdering each other and the melodious sound of vodka being guzzled by the gallon, I heard a little voice, that of my guardian angel, saying, these people are fucking idiots. Anyway, Tania escaped, just went back into the bathroom. I really envy the way women can escape to the bathroom. When I started to move into the living room, edge my way in, they were right with me and I guess that the sacred name of Buckie-Moeller hadn't given my face enough of a look of wild anticipation, because they started to tell me that Vance Whitestone would also probably come up to the old barn—they called their place in the woods the old barn—isn't that too fucking sweet? Yes, Vance would be up with Karen Ostrom, his then current inamorata, who was, I think, an airline stewardess. Maybe even—ruffle of drums!—Lincoln Gom would be there! I had a fleeting vision of the *Garden of Earthly Delights*. So I said that it looked pretty good for me, they should call. All the time I'm thinking of an opening I'd gone to about three years earlier, maybe four years? of photographs by none other than Annie Flammard, and then a wonderful conversation that those same three—Vance, Karen, and Lincoln—had in a bar that they went to, that a lot of us went to, after the show. I was in a booth right behind them with Marcie Butler, who was just in the process of splitting up with Saul Blanche, who'd suddenly discovered that he was in reality a homosexual, and I got an earful.

What did Whitestone, Gom, and Miss Ostrom talk about in the bar to which they went afterward?

Well, when these three got together it was murder in the henhouse, they were vicious gossips, the slightest rumor became fact with them, really made for each other. The funniest thing about it all was that at this time, with Karen living with Vance, she was also getting a little on the side from Linc, who was also having an affair with Bart Kahane's wife, Lolita—or it might have been with his ex-wife, Conchita, that's terrific, isn't it? Lolita and Conchita, almost as good as Anton and Antonia, I can't imagine where these people got these names, not to mention the Detectives, of course, but there they are. Anyway, Lincoln thought he was pulling a fast one on both Lolita, it must have been Lolita because Conchita was then in Europe, France I think, when Annie had her opening, so, Lincoln thought he was pulling a fast one on Lolita and his good pal, Vance, not to mention Bart, but the truth of the matter was that Vance knew all about it and was delighted, because when Karen was with Lincoln she, of course, couldn't be with him. Which is exactly what he wanted because Karen was getting on his nerves, as well she might, might get on anyone's nerves, you know the type, wheat germ and black-strap molasses and raw milk with the yoga and the courses in adult education, you'll pardon the expression, How to Order Wine, Keep Fit, Write and Be Happy, Getting the Most Out of Your Leotard, you know the kind of thing I mean, plus all that mystical shit about smoking a little goddam pedestrian joint. Used to read books about the correct way to eat spaghetti, for Christ sake. She was getting on Lincoln's nerves too, truth to tell, but she had bread, a good salary, you know, and this was just about the time that Linc was trying to hustle the real-estate deal with Marowitz. But you want to know what they were talking about, O.K. This really places them beautifully. A few months earlier, Cecil Tyrell, no, that was later, I don't know how I could have confused it, I mean to say Lamont, a few months earlier Antony Lamont published his novel, *Synthetic Ink,* it came out from, as I told you, Crescent and Chattaway, C and C, as people called it. Tony had published earlier books—let's see, one was *Rayon Violet,* another one was called, I think, *Baltimore Chop,* they both got crucified, but then slowly he started to get a reputation, Saul Blanche went to the wall for him at C and C, and they took his new book, *Synthetic Ink.* O.K., now you have to realize that this was a break for Tony, if the book did pretty well, broke even anyway, the chances were that maybe he'd have a publisher for his next book, of course there was no next book and there probably won't be, I mean it's been almost fifteen years since then and Tony is a dedicated drunk, always starting his really *great* novel, hopeless. Anyway, where was I? Anyway, right, *Ink* comes out and the first review it gets is in a rag, a weekly, called *Hip Vox* as a matter of fact, exactly the kind of garbage that somebody like Karen would read like the Bible, what to eat, where to go, what movies are good, they discovered writers and painters, Jesus, guys who should have been left under a rock, you know what I mean? As a matter of fact, Karen *did* read this crap, goddam thing filled with ads selling you a pair of used combat boots for eighty bucks, foolishness. Anyway, it gets this big, *big* review, a picture of Tony, must have been twenty-five hundred words, the featured article, and on the front page a little banner across the top says something like Lamont's Ink Not Permanent, some cutesy catchy shit like that, and here's this review by some ace, Christ-all knew who he was, a guy named John Hicks. Who? everybody said, not least of all Tony and Saul, you better believe it. Anyway, it was one of the most savage, vicious reviews I've ever seen, Lamont wound up looking as if he was a rapist, child molester, fascist, misogynist, you name it, all rolled into one, plus of course the worst writer since God knows who, Page Moses maybe. He got a couple of reasonably good reviews after that but they came too late to do any good, and they were too small, you know, nobody saw them, besides, the fashionable readers of *Hip Vox* stayed away from the book in droves, it was, right? not *hip* to read it! So the usual, no sales, lots of returns, the book was eventually pulped because no remainder outfit would buy it for a price that C and C could swallow, and Saul even had to quit C and C finally, they started to give him real dogs to work on, *Jog Your Way to*

Orgasm, really, that was a book, and that was that, the well-known hand-writing was on the wall, everybody was walking around wondering who in the name of Christ this guy, John Hicks, was. Léonie Aubois, I've got to give her credit because she smelled a rat, said it was probably a phony monicker for Vance Whitestone, and damn if she wasn't close, I'll get to that. So I'm sitting in the booth with Marcie, wait a minute. I should tell you some, give you some background to this stuff so you'll be able to understand the ins and outs of it all. When Vance first came on the scene he was a poet of sorts, and sorts, believe me, covered a lot of territory, he was really *bad,* mediocre, worse than mediocre. I mean he was what you could call rotten. Craig Garf, who's involved now in television commercials, I'll be damned if I know what he does, arranges corn flakes, some imbecile shit, Craig at that time had a little magazine going, I can't remember the name of it, it was filled with these hopeless little poems, looked like they came out of some computer programmed by a moron, these poems that trot down the page one word to a line and go something like, oh I don't know, you know what I mean, the sun is gold and your moonhair shines, some shit like that, one word to a line, all small letters, really *modern* in nineteen twenty-five. Anyway, Craig was on the hustle, trying to make a name for himself as a very revolutionary poet and editor with this little piece of, oh right, *Lorzu* was the name of it, and, well, I bring this up because Vance couldn't even get into *this* magazine. But then he started to go to Horace Rosette's, Horace was at the time a psychiatric social worker or some useless goddam thing, a clerk at the unemployment office, too good, of course of *course,* for the job, but he was very much the lover of art. By that I mean that he befriended young writers and painters, preferably good-looking young guys. Dear Horace would have them over for private poetry readings that would end up most of the time in Horace's bed. He even went occasionally for girls if they looked like boys, once in a while couples, that's neither here nor there. He had a lot of parties, lots of booze and food, actual *food,* not a few slices of American cheese and a box of crackers. What was I saying? Vance started to go to Horace's, became part of the gang, more like a coven, and his star, as they say, started to rise, because Horace got Craig's ear and told him that though Vance didn't have that *something* that makes for the poetic temperament, he had a great deal of, how did Horace put it? oh, yes, critical acuity, sure he did, which meant simply that Horace was blowing him like a trumpet and tak-

ing it up the old wazoo. Anyway, Craig knew, as they say, which side his
bread was buttered on, and Vance suddenly started writing these haughty
little reviews for *Lorzu*. In the meantime, Vance met Anne Kaufman at a
party at Horace's, Anne and Leo were having a lot of trouble at the time,
the marriage was breaking up, they'd got married right after they both
graduated college, playing house, you know, living in some grim furnished
apartment while Anne went out to work. Leo was collecting rejection slips
and getting swacked every other day, this went on and on till finally they
just sort of tolerated each other and Anne was looking to fool around. Leo
couldn't get it up anymore anyway unless, so the story goes, but who
knows? unless he could first undress Anne and then spank her. She wasn't
having any too much of this. Anyway, Anne met Vance Whitestone, fan-
fare! critic, at one of Horace's parties and they began an affair, she was
impressed because Vance's reviews began to appear here and there outside of *Lorzu* and he got a teaching job somewhere, creative writing, what
else? and about a dozen people knew his name. She was also impressed
because, Jesus! Vance was one of those corny bastards with the walks in
the rain, the little Greek restaurants that he'd found up some alley and
down in a cellar, ferry rides, tweeds and corduroys and work shirts, all he
needed was some big goddam fucking dog crapped out at his feet. So this
went on for a while, a year, year and a half, meanwhile Anne and Leo got
a divorce. Leo then walked around crying all over everyone, playing soppy
songs on the jukebox, *Are You Lonesome Tonight?*, drinking boilermakers
like water, and living with one old friend after another, how could you
turn him down, the pathetic bastard. Then, into this idyllic amour of Anne
and Vance's came, organ chord! none other than the well-known cult-co-
terie-raffiné author, Antony Lamont, and in a trice, as Vance might say
when he coins a cliché, in a trice, Tony was in Anne's pants. The problem
was that everybody knew what was going on except Vance, the son of a
bitch was so wrapped up in himself and his dumb literary *career* that it
never occurred to him that Anne might give him a set of horns. When he
found out he went apeshit, as they used to say, had a fight with Tony, who
casually gave him a black eye, and then went home and took Anne's
dresses, those she still had at his place, and cut them up with a scissors. A
lot of class. So when *Ink* was published and got the bejesus kicked out of
it in *Hip Vox,* we were surprised that it wasn't Vance in a way, but in
another way not, because he was probably still afraid that Tony would

kick his ass for him again. Which brings me back to Léonie's idea that maybe John Hicks was just a phony name for Vance, but she found out from somebody, some guy who worked at *Hip Vox,* that this guy John Hicks was the McCoy. So there I am in the bar with Marcie, she's telling me a lot of embarrassing things about her sex life with Saul, what he liked to do and how he liked to do it, this and that, no need to go into it, but she figured she should have suspected that he was twisted because of these kinks, and I'm listening and telling her that she shouldn't mind, after all they can still be friends, I'm beginning to sound to myself like the proverbial man with a paper asshole, or like Horace Rosette when he's coming on to some college freshman, Horace would quote yards of Elizabeth Barrett Browning and Rupert Brooke, for Christ sake. Anyway. With my other ear I'm hearing Lincoln, Vance, and Karen in the next booth. Karen says, well you finally got even with Leo after all this time, oh, I forgot to tell you that Leo told everybody that when Anne and Vance started in, Vance pressured Anne to take all of her and Leo's money, maybe a couple of grand, out of their joint savings account and she did. So Leo told *everyone* this story, he was quite a weeper in his day, anyway, Karen says this, she was talking of course about Vance's shot at *Isolate Flecks,* and this brings on a lot of laughs, and then, aha, Lincoln says, yes, it *was* sweet, but it lacked the beauty of the Hicks job, so I'm immediately all ears, meanwhile Marcie is telling me about Saul and Christ knows what all, bowls of milk and raw eggs, cross-dressing, golden showers, I don't know, like French porn, I don't remember because I'm really *listening* to Lincoln and Vance. To make it short it turns out that this guy John Hicks was a student of Vance's and he got him this job doing the review of *Synthetic Ink,* his actual name in actual print! It was, of course, understood that Hicks would tear Tony's book to shreds. Then, later on, a few months, maybe only a month, I found out from Lucy Taylor, when she was staying for a while at Lou and Sheila's place, that's a story in itself, by the way, I found out from Lucy why the editor of *Hip Vox,* who was a woman, Lee Jefferson, why she let Vance talk her into letting this kid, John Hicks, do a review, just like *that.* That had really seemed strange to me because Lee used to work and pal around with Saul at C and C.

What's that about Lucy Taylor at Lou and Sheila's?

Did I say Lou and Sheila's? I meant to say Leo and Ellen's that Lucy stayed at or, now wait a minute, it could have been, at that time, Leo and Anne's. I should make it clear that while Leo's marriage with Anne was breaking up and she was seeing, *seeing*, terrific word, Vance, Leo had already started carrying on with the future Mrs. Kaufman, Ellen, who, by the way, I maybe forgot to mention was Jack Marowitz's younger sister? In any event, Leo and Anne still had their apartment although they were rarely in it at the same time, Anne, as a matter of fact, had moved in, in effect, with Vance, and Leo was with Ellen as much as he could be, sniffing around her skirts, mooning over her, for Christ sake, well why not? She let him spank her and he ate her yogurt and wild grass. The perfect couple. In any case, Lucy stayed with the Kaufmans, but I just can't recall now if Ellen had already become Leo's wife at the time. Christ, Lucy wouldn't have stayed with Lou and Sheila if *not to* meant sleeping in the park. She hated them with a passion. But she got along fine with Leo, probably felt sorry for the pitiful bastard.

Why did Leo Kaufman leave Rosette's with Anne instead of Ellen?

Oh, that was the famous night that Horace gave a party for Bart because he'd just got a nice fat check from some jerk he did a doctoral dissertation for. Bart was part of a group of people who used to write theses and dissertations and such for grad students mostly, and Bart had done this paper on math for somebody who didn't know his ass from his elbow, I can't remember the paper, it's not important, something about complex resolutions or contravariant resolutions, whatever, anyway, anyway, as I've told you, Horace loved to give parties. He might well have had his eye on Bart at that time, I don't know, Bart wasn't artistic, as they say, and that was always Horace's weakness. Annie Flammard was there, she'd just married Barry Gatto who was, of all things, a piano tuner which was delicious because the son of a bitch had an ear made of pure tin, but he had a great line of jive and had some kind of a partnership with a girl by the name of Buffie, Buffie Tate, who was an interior decorator, she called it a space-décor consultant, some kind of bunk. Barry would go into somebody's house to tune the piano, God help the poor bastards, and while he was there, he was lovely, he had this fake Italian accent, you know? While he was there tuning and tinkering, butchering the damn piano, he'd start talking about how ver' nize it would be if the lady of the howze she's a put a white-a velvet couch here an' oh si, thees wall-a is perfect to have some shelves with little drawings, and on and on and then he'd recommend his fren', Mizz Tate, oh si, why Mizz Tate had consulted for the most wonderful and chic and rich people in the most wonderful houses and maybe ten percent of the time he'd land some fish and Buffie would be in business. They had some kind of sliding percentage deal depending on how much Buffie could squeeze out of the marks. Anyway, he married Annie Flammard, she was still a painter then, or maybe she was making sculpture, I don't clearly remember, purely a business arrangement. Buffie and Barry and Annie formed this triumvirate, right? Barry would set up the mark, Buffie would come in and consult, and then guess who she'd recommend as a fantastic artist, not really big *yet,* but on the verge, oh yes, *absolutely* the time to buy her for those who are truly *au courant,* for those who could spot someone who was going to be one of the hottest, in-demand painters in the country in a few years, her prices were insanely low, but she had to eat, Buffie felt in a way that perhaps she was even, well, taking advantage of a great artist but, well, the client had been so wonderful, she felt really *close* to her, the apartment or house had come to seem like Buffie's own, it was none other than, yes, Annie Flammard! A young vibrant Parisian artist who had come to America because things were so *exciting* here! Enter Annie, trotting out another phony accent, black boots and black tights, turtleneck, Gitanes, and she'd have the mark in for a private, *exclusive* showing and unload a half a dozen things on her, Christ knows what, on some of them the fucking paint was still wet. It was a sweet little deal and they ultimately had a going *ménage à trois,* business with pleasure, as they say. So they were at Horace's and a lot of other people, Bart and Conchita, Lolita, that was the night that Bart and Lolita met the Henrys as a matter of fact, Page Moses, the worst writer the world has ever known, we used to call him Doctor Plot, what a case, and some joker who worked in the same place as Biff Page and Chico, I think his name was, amazingly enough, Sol Blanc, not to be confused with Saul Blanche, but to tell the truth, it was uncanny how much they resembled each other. I think even Jack Marowitz came that night, he wanted to meet his sister's husband, Leo, he was a little put out because they didn't have a religious ceremony when they got married, he was very big on that religious idea, he wanted to take a look at this deadbeat who'd married his beloved sister. They were of course there, Leo and Ellen, I remember unfortunately as if it were yesterday Ellen's zucchini cake and her kohlrabi quiche, she'd brought them to help out, Jesus Christ almighty! If you put them in a gun you could sink a battleship with them. Lincoln Gom, oh right, with Sister Rose, Rose Zeppole, who at the time was modeling lingerie in a showroom for department store buyers and paying the rent for Lincoln, who was *into,* as they now put it, radical politics then, he'd stand around talking about the struggle of the peoples and the bourgeois canon and running dogs of imperialism, sweet Jesus, meanwhile Rose was fighting off these guys from the vast heartland and doing a few small favors for some of them, right? all in a day's work. Lena was there too, and in very bad shape, Jack Towne had died about a month before from booze and pills, in a way it was inevitable, he'd been heading for it for a long time, but it was bitter, bitter, you couldn't find a sweeter guy than Jack. The story that went around was that he'd really been crushed because of the pictures that had supposedly been taken of Lena and then their quarrel about it. As a matter of fact his death, and it was really suicide however you want to slice it, his death had assured everybody that the pictures, you know, that they actually existed and that Jack couldn't handle it. However. Well. However, this wasn't the truth. The truth was that Jack had got himself tangled up in some mess concerning a nursing home, I think I mentioned that he was some kind of supervisor or inspector for the city? Something to do with housing preservation and urban renewal, something, and he O.K.'d some old-age home that had violations or whatever. To make a long story short, the place was unsafe and he and some sleazy bastard who used the name Biggs Richard, there's a fake handle for you, Jack and this guy Richard made a deal on some kind of doctored report on this place, for money of course, I mean Jack got money from this guy, I don't know how much but a nice taste, and I don't know the ins and outs of it but that creepy yokel, Harlan Pungoe, was somehow at the bottom of it, he stood to make a real bundle. So what happened is that the goddam second floor of the place collapsed and seven old people were killed, a lot were badly hurt, a nurse was killed, and Jack was left holding the bag. This guy Richard was somehow conveniently in the clear, and Pungoe was, as they say, not connected in any way. So Jack started to, well, kill himself, by degrees, and whether it was because he knew that the investigation that the city started would absolutely destroy him, or land him in jail, or it was simply the guilt over these dead people, or all three things, anyway, that was it. He did kill himself. But I'm way off your question about Leo and Anne, right? Sorry. O.K. Leo and Ellen came and they were there about an hour when in walks Anne, she looked like a million wearing this knockout of a shift dress in off-white raw silk, she'd gained a *little* weight in, as they say, the right places. The only woman at the party better looking than Anne was Marcie Butler, but she was something *really* special, she had the most beautiful legs I've ever seen. Well, Anne and Ellen and Leo started to talk, you know, the old civilized routine, and I guess that Anne had had a few too many on the way, whatever, but she started in about Leo's sexual, ah, proclivities? shall I say? Well, Ellen was enormously embarrassed and of course there's big brother Jack, looking at this weird son of a bitch who, Jack must have thought, was running his kid sister through some heavy sadomasochist routine. There were words, and Ellen demanded that Leo tell Anne off, and Anne said something about well, whatever else Leo was when *we* were married, he certainly was not henpecked, and what was the matter with Ellen that she was angry about Leo's first marriage, was she maybe insecure? Jack Marowitz got in on it, with sick Leo, disgusting Leo, spineless Leo, and Anne suddenly just grabbed Leo by the arm and bang! out the door they went. None of us quite knew what to do, we tried to treat it like a joke, or not exactly that, but we tried to make light of it as they say, a lot of loud talk, you know, and forced hearty laughter. Except for the other people who were at Horace's, who at that time were always in a little group by themselves, like a little cabal, they hardly paid any attention to what was going on. A spooky bunch.

What other people at Horace Rosette's?

Well, as I said, this little cabal, if that's the word, a kind of informal club, I suppose, kindred spirits, as I say, spooky, if that's not too melodramatic a word. Guy Lewis with his employer and friend, if you will, that good ole boy, Harlan Pungoe, some creep named Roger Whytte-Blorenge, which is a wonderful handle, except when you met the guy his accent was strictly Joizy Cidy, you know what I mean? You'd be introduced to this guy, this is Mr. Whytte-Blorenge, Roger Whytte-Blorenge, and he'd say, you know, pleeztameecha, scuze me I gotta gota duh terlet. Beautiful. All I knew about him is that he worked for Pungoe, or had worked for him, anyway, they'd known each other for years, he was a kind of gofer, there was something really weird about him, he'd get a few in him or smoke a little hash and the next thing you know he'd be sitting in front of some woman, sitting on the floor, and staring at her shoes. And let's see, the rest of the good old gang, Lorna Flambeaux, who insisted that she was Annie

Flammard's sister, but Annie denied it, said she'd never even seen her till, say, maybe two years before, when she first arrived in town. Lorna worked at the time as a first reader for some publishing house, I don't remember which one, and she was, I believe, romantically involved with Roger, which is a thought that still astounds me, I can just see them getting into their apartment and Roger making a dive for her feet, oh yes, as I told you, Lorna had ambitions to be a poet, she had some crackpot theory that Sade was a woman or something like that, and was writing a cycle of poems, or an epic poem, her idea was that Sade was, Christ, I don't know, that he was really his wife, and the man, the Marquis de Sade, was some pure and innocent sap who took the fall for her, the true writer of the books, the real libertine. Anyway that's what her poem was about, so I heard. She said that only a woman could think up all those perversions, or as she put it, those *marvelous* perversions. And oh yes, of course, there was another woman, Annette Lorpailleur, I don't know *what* to tell you about her. There was something, what's the word? something really nasty, unsavory about her, she was quite beautiful, somehow regal-looking, but something, something about her. She was thought to be a kind of partner with Harlan in his direct-mail business, some offshoot of it anyway, but nobody ever really knew what the offshoot or whatever you want to call it, was. My own idea, that I came to from, well, let's say this and that, is that it had something to do with, I don't know exactly, but some sort of religious cult or something, not really *religious,* I don't know. Something to do with the occult, some sort of magic, probably all crap anyway, but the money came rolling in, so I heard, they had members or devotees, initiates, all over the country, all over the world I think, some sort of orgiastic thing going, satanism, I know one thing and that's that Guy Lewis was absolutely smitten with her, he was, if you'll forgive me, bewitched. There was something really chilling about her, distant, her voice, well, her *voice.* The way she talked, it wasn't as if she had an accent or anything, it was as if her voice wasn't exactly coming from *her*—you know, as if somebody was talking and she was moving her mouth in this funny stiff way, just like, well, just like a ventriloquist's dummy. That was the group, a real fun bunch, and there were two other women, no, they came on the scene about a year later, by that time Guy was going home just to change his clothes so to speak. Right, they came later, two women who moved in with Annette, Corrie Corriendo and a Madame Delamode, I don't know what her first

name was, but they weren't at this particular party, as I say. I should correct myself by the way, they didn't move in with Annette, the three of
them bought a huge co-op apartment and had it completely redone, completely decorated to their taste. It was an absolutely incredible place, sumptuous, strange and sumptuous. It must have cost them a mint.

You referred to some paper of agreement or contract that Lou
signed with or for Saul Blanche—what was that all about?

Right. It wasn't a contract *per se,* in a sense it was a gentlemen's
agreement, but there was a written something or other that Lou signed,
yes. Lou and Sheila, Lou mostly but Sheila was also interested, Lou got
her interested, were bibliophiles, book collectors, you know, especially
interested in modern first editions, manuscripts, letters, notebooks, and
they were as they say devoted and quite knowledgeable—not just the usual
thing, I mean they didn't try to get hold of, acquire stuff done by only
well-known writers. They were also, or I should say they were *primarily*
interested in writers whose reputations were just beginning, it was more
interesting Lou once said, more risky and exciting, you know, the idea
being that he was, or they were, taking a chance on writers who might fail
or disappear, just fold up. Of course it was much cheaper too and they
didn't have a hell of a lot of money, they both worked, you know, just
ordinary people. Well, Saul, as an editor at C and C, C and C being a house
that published a lot of avant-garde, experimental fiction and poetry in those
days, those days however being gone forever—now they do the same
weary stuff that everybody else does, novels that could have been written
two hundred years ago, *angst* at the pool among the sensitive young in a
world they don't understand, or how the TV repairman talked so funny
because his wife ran away with the motel manager. Christ, they even published a novel by good old Doctor Plot, I mean here was a scribbler that
even vanity presses used to run screaming into the night from. That's not
the point. The point is that in those days C and C was different and Saul,
being an editor, would see an awful lot of manuscripts, a lot of them were
rejected, good stuff too, it's just that they couldn't do everything and a lot
of it was too difficult, as they say, and written by writers with tiny reputations, no audience, they couldn't afford the losses, but Saul would know
or take an educated guess, you know, that these were writers who would
some day be important. Well, he and Lou made a deal that, with an author's
consent, Lou could buy the manuscript, the original manuscript, and Saul

would get a cut and give the author a cut of his cut, and he'd do this with manuscripts that the house had turned down. I suppose that maybe it could be viewed as exploitation but on the other hand the author gave his consent and could always copy the original, probably had copies anyway. Most often Saul would ask the author for the rough draft, the working manuscript, which, of course, Lou would be most interested in. As I say, it could be seen as exploitation but it kept a lot of writers eating, as a matter of fact, Cecil Tyrell's first novel, that was turned down by C and C, was sold—in this case, the whole thing, I mean the typescript, working drafts, notebooks—just like this. Saul had read it and got in touch with Lou and Cecil said, hell, all right, so Lou has all that material. As a matter of fact he's even talked about maybe publishing it for Cecil himself, you know, privately, because Cecil hasn't ever found a publisher for it, I can't remember the title, I think it's *Orange Steel.* It's supposed to be very difficult, what's the word, inaccessible. Sheila said that Cecil told her that he took the three classical unities, or I should say he took two of the classical unities and discarded them so that the book has no action and no time, only place, or no action and no place, only time, or something, and the element, the unity that's left is presented as a catalogue. It's just one long list or a series of lists. In any event that's the nature, that was the nature of the agreement. I don't think it's in force anymore, Saul is long gone from C and C. To tell you the truth, though, Lolita Kahane was really angry about the *Orange Steel* business and even called Sheila up about it, and from what I know it wasn't a very friendly conversation.

And what did Lolita have to say to Sheila on the telephone?

It's funny to think about this, it was so many years ago, we were all pretty young, I doubt if Lolita would even remember it now, Jack Towne was still very much alive, Sheila and Lou were still married, Horace hadn't taken his act, so to speak, to France. It was amazing by the way, how he left, Christ only knows where he got the money but he got it, the story was confused, something about money being embezzled by Léonie Aubois, but nobody ever proved anything, the money was probably dirty money anyway, you know what I mean? Money that couldn't be reported as stolen because it wasn't supposed to exist in the first place. Well you don't need all this, it just struck me thinking about Sheila and Lolita when they were young women. As I remember, Lolita had lived with Cecil the whole time he was writing *Orange Steel,* and he was some number in those days, to call him a fucking disgusting boor would be a *little* too kind, drinking, I mean falling-down drinking, a foul and vicious mouth, he'd hit people, mostly women, mostly, of course, Lolita. It was a godsend really for her when Cecil took a powder and she met Bart, who was, despite his being a con man and a bullshit artist, a reasonable human being. But she'd lived with Cecil and paid all the bills all the time he was working on this book, it's not a very big book but it took him more than three years to write. Anyway she knew all about Lou and Sheila and their collecting, and as far as she was concerned they were simply thieves. I think she used to call them the vultures. Besides, she hated Saul Blanche because he walked right in on her, on purpose, you know? when she was in the bathroom at one of Horace's parties, and he caught her in a very embarrassing position, you know, and then he had the nerve to, this is according to Lolita, he had the nerve to stand there and watch her, just stand there smoking a cigarette. So she had no love for any of them. On top of this it's a cinch that she also knew that those nights that Cecil didn't come home, or I should say, crawl home, were spent with, not all of them but a lot of them, they were spent with Sheila, and with the knowledge, even the assistance, the connivance of Lou. I mean, an awful lot of people knew about this oddball activity that was going down and Lolita must have heard it from somebody, if from no one else then from Léonie, who was always the official mouth, believe it! This would have been bad enough but it was clear, or it became clear to Lolita that all these sex games had to do with something else, what, I don't know, but something to do with this novel that Cecil was working on, who knows? Maybe the Henrys were already convincing Cecil that they'd love to buy his manuscript, I don't know. Well when the book was finished and turned down by C and C and then a few other houses, that's when Saul arranged for the sale and so on as I've already told you, and Lolita called Sheila up and told her what she thought of her and of Lou too, of course. Cecil had taken his share of the sale money and poured it down his throat, and with some of it he gave the business to Barnett Tete, I mean to say that he and Sylvie took off for a week or ten days together, which is about the time, or I should say that because of this fling, Barnett kicked Sylvie's ass out of the boutique, but he still didn't make Léonie the manager, which did not, as you can imagine, make her disposition any sweeter. Instead, Barnett asked Tania if she wanted to be the manager, Tania Crosse, and she accepted, same deal as

with Sylvie—she didn't turn a hand, came in when she goddam well
pleased, and bought the most expensive clothes at forty, fifty percent off.
In addition, of course, to the ones Tete bought for her because to be Tete's
manager was to be his mistress. Or one of them. Well, all this is neither
here nor there, but I should add that Tania, who is now known as Madame
LaCrosse, is always in some goddam magazine or other, the successful
businesswoman, you know the sort of nauseating set-pieces they do, glamorous, chic, elegant Madame LaCrosse is also one of the fashion world's
most hardworking and hardheaded business executives, then there's a picture spread, Tania on the beach, Tania climbing a snowcapped mountain,
Tania consulting with her staff, Tania giving a crippled kid some dumb
plaque, Tania smiling at the mayor or some other fucking idiot, and then a
little sanitized interview-story about the rewards of the fashion game for
women bent on exciting careers, enough to make you puke on your shoes.
Anyway, I wanted to tell you that all this began for her when Barnett took
her out of the boutique and opened yet another one, a specialty shop, for
her. She must have really rung old Tete's bells for him, hauled his ashes
good. It was a little overpoweringly snobbish trap, obscenely expensive,
that dealt only in what they called ultra-intimate apparel, the usual lingerie, but *very* expensive, and then a special line of kinky stuff, French and
Italian, made of the most expensive materials, the shop was called, beautiful! Soirée Intime. A wardrobe of their ultra-intimate apparel, as their
demurely suggestive ads said, color-coordinated—color spelled with a u—
color-coordinated for those magic moments after midnight, a wardrobe of
this stuff cost enough to keep a large family eating for a year. Anyway, this
is far off Lolita's phone call, but you know you get to thinking about all
this after so many years, if anyone ever asked Tania if she'd like to share
a joint in the bathroom nowadays she'd probably turn her three Nazi
dobermans loose. That day seems as if it happened a century ago.

Why did John Hicks visit Horace Rosette some time after the party
had broken up?

Well, wait a second, the party, there were so many parties at
Horace's and other places that I don't know exactly what party you mean.
But John Hicks, the famous iconoclastic book reviewer, he was only
around for about a year and a half, a little less, then he just disappeared. As
a matter of fact he disappeared about the same time that Henri Kink did,
right after Henri's novel, his one and only novel, was published, so I think

I know just about the time you mean, although Christ knows he might have gone to see dear old Horace every night as far as I know. Anyway, the time you mean is pretty much common knowledge because Horace dropped hints about it, hints the man says, he talked about it *incessantly* to everybody because he said that Hicks was so nervous, not nervous, Horace's word was terrified, Hicks was so terrified, he said, that he was really worried when he just disappeared into, as they say, thin air. Anyway, he talked about it all the time and it must have been, as I said, right about the same time that Henri's novel, *Mouth of Steel* was its title, was published. The book, by the way, had what they call an interesting history. It was written in English but Henri couldn't find a publisher and so it was originally, God knows how, originally published for the first time in France, in a French translation, as *La Bouche métallique,* and created a little stir over there. I'll be damned if it wasn't then published here, by Beaumont and Halpin, in English—only for some weird reason the original English text *wasn't* published. The version that appeared here was a translation of the French translation back into English. Anyway, that's neither here nor there, except that there was a rumor that the translator, somebody named Anthony Octavio, whom nobody ever heard of and never has since, was really Sol Blanc, though that seems farfetched to me because the only thing French that fat Sol knew anything about was French fries. Besides, he had a hell of a lot of trouble speaking English, he was some kind of a refugee or some goddam thing, came over as an exchange student or I don't know what, whoever sent him didn't want him back, not that I'd blame them. But you want to know about why John Hicks went to Horace's after the party that we've got, I think, straight, which one or which time. I hope I can remember this, it was about, let's see, *Mouth of Steel* came out about, well, I guess six or seven years ago so it was that long ago, O.K. What I heard is that Hicks went to see Horace because he was up to his ears in some very shady goings-on with Annette Lorpailleur and her two cronies I told you about, Corrie Corriendo and Madame Delamode, who were all, at this time, living in this dazzling apartment I mentioned, well, *dazzling,* yes, but not in any warm, bright way, very strange and icy to tell you the truth. The whole place was sinister. John Hicks wanted out from under Annette and the other two women, it seems that he told Horace some strange stories about weird rites of some sort, sex orgies with all kinds of people, he was involved with all of it, along

with, as far as my own opinion goes, along with that loathsome rube,
Pungoe, Mr. Congeniality. What Hicks wanted was for Horace to give
him some money or talk to somebody for him or something at the place he
worked, I told you that Horace was some kind of sociopsychological
something, I think, but Horace really didn't know exactly *what* he wanted,
or so he said. You can bet your ass that Horace wasn't about to give anybody any of the old mazoo, not Horace. To him every buck that he had left
after he paid the rent and etcetera went for a party, or for entertaining,
shall I say? his interesting and artistic young friends, man, woman, or
animal. Anyway, to be as brief as I can, it got around after Hicks disappeared that he was no young Lochinvar who'd shown up all sparkling
eyes and hot breath in Vance's writing class, out of the woods with mud on
his boots and egg on his vest, no, it turned out that Star Eyes was Pungoe's
contact with this guy Biggs Richard in the nursing-home swindle I mentioned earlier. As a matter of fact, since nobody on God's earth had ever
laid eyes on Biggs Richard a lot of people put two and two together and
had it figured that they were the same guy, I mean Hicks and Richard.
Now that I think of it I remember that Jack Towne told me that when he
was involved with Richard—except that he never told me what for—that
he never could *meet* the man, they did everything over the phone, which
was, I'm sure, true, only as I say Jack never told me what it was all about,
just ran some story down to me about it all being some kind of a quick-
buck scheme having to do with selling a goddam whole warehouse full of
some kind of synthetic-metal fabric that garment makers use for those,
you know, those shiny metallic gowns and costumes, showbiz tuxedos,
you know the stuff I mean, but I never thought twice about it since Jack
was always trying to make a fast score one way or another. Anyway. Where
was I? Right, right, Hicks wanted out of whatever he was involved in and,
as I said, Horace said that he was absolutely shaking with fear, take
Horace's descriptions with a grain of salt, O.K., but he was impressed and
had no reason to make it all up, and Horace said that Hicks left his place
without saying in any clear way what it exactly was that was spooking
him, then he was suddenly missing, I mean he simply *vanished*. Vance
went to check on him after he hadn't been able to get him on the phone for
more than a week and there was his place, intact, everything in it, books
and records, clothes, food in the refrigerator, an open pack of cigarettes on
the table, just as if he'd gone down the block for a bottle or a loaf of bread,

he was just gone. On the kitchen table there's a sheet of paper, Vance just left it there, he said that it gave him a chill just to look at it. On the paper there were, I don't know, odds and ends of writing or something, calligraphy, more like little drawings, I really don't know, circles and pentagrams and bits of Greek or Hebrew or some damn thing, runes, and that was it. Vance said the phone rang while he was there and he almost jumped out of his skin. It's funny you should ask this question because, as I said, it brought to mind that Henri also disappeared about the same time and right after *Mouth of Steel* was published, which is very very interesting indeed because the novel is a *roman à clef* insofar as the main character is concerned, who is based on Annette Lorpailleur, who was tied up with Pungoe in Christ knows what kind of eerie, eerie whatever. What I'm getting at is that Henri and Annette didn't get on too well, as a matter of fact he used to call her Mademoiselle Mummy because she stood so stiff and still and because of that voice, that *voice* of hers that didn't really quite come out of her. She'd talk and her mouth would move but it was as if the whole thing was from an out-of-synch movie, the mouth was moving but, you know, either just in front of or just behind, I mean just before and after what she was saying, I used to think it was almost inhuman, for Christ sake. In any event, Hicks disappeared, then Henri disappeared. And dear Jack got caught up in this building con and, well, you know what happened.

Can you give me a brief synopsis of *La Bouche métallique* or *Mouth of Steel*?

Oh sure, though it's been a long time since I've read it, not since it first came out, really, though I was looking through it, oddly enough, just a couple of weeks ago. You have to understand that it's not really representative, as they say, of Henri's best work, his poems, and he wrote some really terrific prose poems too, they're really his best work. *Mouth of Steel* was written as a kind of lurid melodrama, sinister and strange, I think that Henri, in his ignorance, thought that maybe it would make him some money, maybe the movies would pick it up or somebody would take an option on it, lots of luck, that was strictly a pipe dream. The book is much too complicated, too convoluted for the geniuses of the cinema to do anything with it, even though it's got a lot of intentional soap opera in it. All right, I'm going by memory and all I can do is give you the barest essentials. First of all, the book is in three parts, each one a different kind of part, I mean different stories, sort of, different characters. There are three

main characters in the first part, a guy named Dick Grande, another, Jack
Rube, and a woman whose name is given only as Madame Jeannette, who
is in the finest tradition of the beat-me-please genre, a stern, harsh, disci-
plinarian, what do they call that in the porno-flick ads, a dominatrix? I
think so, not quite the hip boots black stockings and whips routine but
quite clearly the same type. O.K., there you have the main three. We find
out that Jack Rube has fallen under the spell of Madame Jeannette, so
much so that he ignores and mistreats his wife who loves him dearly, and
so on and so forth, and his career, whatever the hell he is, or does, some
noble lawyer or brilliant academic, his career is suffering because he sits
around all day dreaming of crawling on his hands and knees in front of
Madame J. begging her to humiliate him, force him to write bad checks
and wear thin white socks, I'm kidding, but yes, he does get off on being
used. So, enter Dick Grande, old pal called by Jack's wife, they all went to
college together, he's now a marine biologist or a cave explorer, some
dumb kind of TV gig, and of course we discover that he used to love
Jack's wife when they all went to Suntan U, but he lost the girl, you've
been here before of course, at least a thousand times. In steps stalwart
Dick to rescue his old fraternity buddy from his obsession. By now, Jack
is kicking the cat, leaving the house without his plaid sport coat, throwing
his wife's tuna-avocado casseroles on the floor and insulting her Peck and
Peck blouses and her sensible shoes, I mean the *works*. But what happens
is that Dick goes to see Madame Jeannette in her penthouse, what else?
She enchants him, oh, I forgot to tell you, this is central to the book, the
title and everything else, the Madame has a mouth made out of *steel*, right.
And there are very strong hints and then a fairly explicit scene dealing
with Madame's steel mouth and her erotic use of it, she's just a good-time
girl who can do all sorts of tricks with the old *bouche*, make you jump for
joy. In a flash *Dick* becomes her sex slave and is enraged that he has to
share his delicious degradation with his pal, Jack, so with the help of Madame Jeannette and, unwittingly, Jack's sweet, intelligent, charming, witty,
and deeply loving and caring and nurturing wife, he destroys Jack's career
and his life and Jack winds up a wreck condemned to live out his days in
Scranton or someplace, a shopping mall, a mere shell of a man. End of
first part. Second part. The story is told over again, this time changed
around a little, a strong and imperious woman, Jeannette, who is not averse
to giving her beloved husband a few vigorous lashes regular as clock-

work, her husband being Dick Grande, meets a handsome and rather vague professor of something or other, who is one Jack Rube, only now he's called Dr. John Rube, and despite his degrees, his Phi Beta Kappa key, his tweed pipes and briar jackets, his vacations in Europe and his near-adoration of Yvor Winters, he succumbs to his powerful yet till now repressed desire, his desperate need, to grovel, crawl, lick high-heeled shoes, be beaten and laced into tight corsets, and so on and so forth, tendencies no doubt developed during all the years he waited to get tenure. Jeannette, with the aid of a metal face mask that she fastens on Jack when he's been especially good, it's his reward for especially fine writhing and begging, Jeannette persuades him to kill her old man for his big insurance bread, dumb old Dick, who can't understand why his old lady only canes him once a week lately, he's beginning to think the honeymoon is over. So Dick is dispatched by Dr. Rube, who drowns him in the bathtub or the toilet, then rushes wildly to the arms of Jeannette, or I should say crawls to the legs of Jeannette, whimpering for his metal face mask and a few kicks. But! entering her bedroom he sees that Jeannette is a *man!* Yes, this powerful, brawny, imposing, and strapping woman is not a woman at all but a powerful, brawny and so forth man! But the good doctor doesn't mind, he's too enamored to let a little thing like gender stand in the way of happiness. Jeannette is not pleased, however, and she puts the mask on him in such a way that he suffocates, and she arranges the whole thing to make it look like a bizarre homosexual murder-suicide. That's part two. The third part is in the form of a notebook, a journal, whatever, in the first person, that's being kept by a nun, Sister Jeannette, the story in the journal being that of a woman that she knew, named, coincidentally, Jeannette, a sincere, devout, chaste woman who has been totally corrupted by two men, Jack and Dick, successful and in the eyes of the world, of course, wonderful, first-rate gents, but who are in reality two vicious sadists who hate women and spend their lives and wealth corrupting the innocent and good. The twist is that one of these guys enjoys his secret-life adventures dressed as a nun, in this way he gains the confidence of modest women and so on and so forth. However, we discover as we read that the journal tells a shadowy story of murder and blackmail stemming from some compromising photographs of the so-called nun, I mean the guy who dresses like a nun, photographs with a priest who, it turns out, has also had something going with Jeannette, whom we thought was chaste, devout, and so on.

Just as the book reaches this point we come upon a new entry that reads, more or less—That's the novel I'd like to write if I had the time and the talent. So we know that Sister Jeannette has written this. O.K., now things shift again, the view is objective, third person, we see Sister Jeannette undressing, we get loving and meticulous details of her movements and garments, and then we find that Sister Jeannette is a man just like the wife in the second part, *then* we see her, or I should say him dressing like a priest, as you can see things are getting more lurid by the minute, and now it gets very weird. The priest puts his nun's clothes on a mannequin made out of polished steel that's standing in the corner, then he pushes a button and the mannequin starts to speak. There's a tape recorder or whatever in the mannequin's head and the damn thing starts to talk and what it says is the *first part,* verbatim, of *Mouth of Steel!* After a paragraph or two, given absolutely word for word, the priest switches off the machine or rewinds it, whatever, and he then starts to dictate into the mannequin's mouth— and what he dictates are the opening sentences of the *second* part of *this* book, I mean *Mouth of Steel.* And the book ends. That's it, with an awful lot of details and odds and ends and minor characters left out. It's an odd item. It was almost completely ignored and the language is weird because of the disastrous double translation, so to speak. But you can still find an odd copy at pretty steep prices since it's become a kind of cult classic.

Tell me some more about Annette Lorpailleur—for instance, what did she do at this party?

Well, I don't know too much about her because as I've said already, she was mysterious and involved in things that I didn't really want to know about, and still don't for that matter, but she *was* beautiful. A big woman, about thirty-five, must have stood six feet tall in her stocking feet, beautiful body, jet-black hair, and these strange pale blue, ice-blue eyes that never seemed quite in focus, but still, it's hard to explain, still seemed as if they were looking right into your brain. She just *appeared* one day and started to pop up at parties, openings, a supposed partner, as I've told you, with Harlan Pungoe in some sort of business dealings. Then it was thought that she was a kind of patron of Annie Flammard after Annie took a powder from Canada, Annie hinted, in fact, that she'd known her in Canada, but I always thought that she was from somewhere in Europe, France or Switzerland. Anyway, that's not important, except that Bart Kahane told me that Conchita, his ex, as you remember, that she wrote

him from Paris that she'd met some very strange woman there at a book
party by the name of Roberte Flambeaux, and her description was a perfect one of Annette, which leads us right into the soup because Roberte
Flambeaux was, right? supposedly Annie Flammard's real name, although
it's often struck me that this rumor about Annie's so-called real name was
very carefully put out by Annie herself as a smokescreen, a blind, I mean,
she's the source, as if she wanted to divert attention from Annette. Annette
gave Annie a kind of allowance to live on so she could paint and, wait a
minute. No, she was making sculpture then and Annette sometimes would
buy pieces from her as well, paid very nice prices, even though Annie had
no gallery, no dealer, and no real reputation at all. One piece I especially
remember, a big piece, polished steel, aluminum, chrome and nickel,
called *Gin City,* that Annette had right in the middle of the living-room
floor. And there was another one, smaller, but still a big piece, up on a
wall, sort of a wall piece, that's a brilliant observation, and that was copper or bronze, polished like a mirror. That one was later sold by Annette, I
think, I can't remember the name of it, it was either *Steel Orange,* after
Cecil's book, it was a kind of rough globe in shape, right, or it was called
99, don't ask me why, I can't recall. They never struck me as very good
pieces. The assumption was that Annette and Annie were, you know, getting it on together, to tell you the truth all the men were envious of Annie
except that you always had the feeling that hopping into bed with Madame Lorpailleur would be like screwing a robot or maybe a refrigerator.
Anyway these pieces did, I suppose, complement the apartment, this was
when Annette was living in this opulent co-op with Corrie Corriendo and
Madame Delamode. These were two hookers who had been around, *pro-*
fessionals, still-attractive women who'd had some sort of spectacular
porno racket going somewhere, Mexico City, I think. I understand that
they published porno magazines and made films that featured middle-
aged, matronly looking women and hit a huge, untapped market. Just when
you think you've heard it all, right? And they also ran some porno distribution service on the side, made a *lot* of money and then left and came
here. They were supposed to have some sort of sensational magic act in a
club that they owned themselves, some little trap, I think it was called The
Blue Ruin, long closed now. I caught part of their act once, they were
good, but the real attraction was that they were only half-dressed if that on
stage, a lot of bare flesh, you know, and they had a shill or two in the

audience at the show I saw, the last show, good-looking young women, built, you know, and they ran this game down about the power of suggestion and these women got up as if they were hypnotized, sure they were, and mechanically stripped down to their panties before a couple of waiters rushed up to cover them, you know, to the rescue! Believe me, the customers ate it up, and everything I heard about the place proved that it just got more and more popular, you couldn't get in the damn place even on a weekday night. What was I saying? Oh yes, they were all three living together in this apartment and it was incredible, did I tell you about it? I don't think so, but it's worth telling. The place was all *metal.* Absolutely, the whole goddam place, steel and copper and bronze, I mean literally *made* out of metal, the walls, the ceilings, the floors, all the fixtures and the tubs and the toilets, the refrigerators, bookcases, I mean *everything.* Even the mirrors were some kind of polished metal, aluminum I think. There was one room that I went into by mistake one night at a dinner party that they gave for something, I think it was the opening of Barnett's little boutique, the Soirée Intime, I told you about it, in which they maybe had some sort of financial interest, the place was strictly a terminal for Tete's dirty money, a little laundry to wash it all white, you know? And it wouldn't surprise me if Annette and Pungoe got in on this to stash some of their loot from the mail-order cult scam, or the other scams they probably had going. Anyway, this room I went into was all red metal, this blood-red copper or some damn thing, and all over the walls were these weird hieroglyphics, scribbles, whatever, and a little, it looked like a little altar in the corner, there were no windows in the room and it must have been below freezing in there, I was in and out in a flash, there was something strange going down there, I mean this was not the family room with Old Shep dozing in the corner and the roaring blaze. This was heavyweight bizarre. The dinner party was more or less O.K., I've been to worse, amen. The strange thing was that Annette and Corrie and Madame were dressed in matching black gowns that were made of *metal,* and they had on, this was really something, metal shoes and stockings! I don't mean *metallic,* that glittery fabric, I mean *metal* in thin, thin sheets, or maybe the things were made out of metal thread, something, but the McCoy, Jesus, they almost clanked when they moved. You can imagine this, the place itself, their clothes, and so on, in tandem with Annette and that voice of hers. And the other two who talked with these absurd accents, as I've mentioned, these accents that sounded as if they came out of a movie, you didn't know whether they were supposed to be Italian or French or Mexican or lower Bulgarian for that matter. But if you heard them talk when they didn't mean for you to hear them, they sounded like they were Whytte-Blorenge's sisters, dese dose and dems—for all I know they may well have been, they came out of oblivion, and, wait a minute. I just thought of something about them, Léonie told me this, she happened to be there once with Tete, their affair was dying at the time since Luba, or I should say Sylvie was already on the scene, though I really don't remember if Tete had given her this new name yet, it's not important. Good old Barnett was surely sleeping with both of them with Léonie already second banana, but whatever the case Sylvie wasn't at this party that Annette and the Dolly Sisters gave. Léonie said that there was some guy there all dressed up like an officer in some foreign army, French or Italian or something, braids and medals and ribbons and stars and Christ knows what else, strictly comic opera, the works, a big tall guy who was soaking up the booze and talking about books and art and music, the whole deeply cultured and cosmopolitan front, right? like a nightmare that you're in San Francisco and you'll never be able to leave. And as he's doing all this talking he's giving a little feel here and a little squeeze there to all the women, very subtle, with this Charles Boyer voice. I can't remember the women who were there but he was hitting on all of them, the major part of his line had to do with a novel he'd just read in London, ahem, called, I think, *The Orange Dress* by somebody named Thelma something, some kind of a Polish name, Krulewicz or Krelewicz, Krulicewicz maybe, and coming on about how it was all about him and his family, the author had worked as a secretary for his father who was some kind of a big-time diplomat or some damn thing. The kind of lame shit that you can hear at any party but he had it all down pat, smooth and sweet, with his bedroom eyes and continental manner, the headwaiter routine in spades. Anyway, to make a long story short, to tell you a little more about the, about Annette and company, which is what the point of this digression is all about, anyway, he disappeared a couple of times with, and I'm only telling you what Léonie told me, a couple of different women, Sheila Henry and April, which you can almost make a mean joke out of in a way. I mean I can imagine Lou saying, Hey baby, go ahead, maybe we can like buy the original manuscript of *The Orange Dress,* give the frog a little poon, you'll never miss it, and April, well.

Dick would be like under the bed or in the shower stall with his Rollei and light meters and whatever the fuck else, whispering Look abandoned, baby! Stick your tongue out! Roll your eyes! All right, maybe that's unfair. Anyway. The point of all this is that as the party was breaking up, Annette introduces this officer of the imperial household and horse dragoons or hussars or whatever he was supposed to be as some deadbeat actor she hired for the occasion and this guy, some Oaky Doaks, takes a bow and thanks everyone for such a wonderful time. April and Sheila are minutely scrutinizing their nails, right? O.K. That gives you a little more of an idea of these three women, especially the boss, Annette, just a barrel of laughs. And Léonie added that she also heard later that every room in the apartment had hidden tape recorders and movie cameras, so there might well still be some *remarkable* pictures floating around of various citizens, you know, the kind of things that might give the relatives back on the farm something to think about at Christmas. Noël, Noël. That's really all I can tell you, generally speaking, about Annette—you did want to know about *her,* right? The Platinum Priestess as Jack Towne called her, God it's long ago. So that's, oh, of course, your question. I imagine you mean Horace's party for Bart? It's hard to say because she was with her little clique, they weren't concerned with the goings on of Leo and his two wives and Marowitz poking you in the chest with his fat finger and spitting potato salad all over your tie, you remember that fiasco. She was with *her* people, dear Pungoe, the Flem Snopes of our time, you can throw Popeye in too, and Roger the shoe lover, who else? Oh yes, Lorna Flambeaux who had something going at that time with Guy, he took her to Horace's that night as I recall. So. I can't tell you what she did, there was just that eerie, that uncanny *thing* about her, that power she had—I know it sounds ridiculous—that power over people. I do remember her asking Guy about Lucy Taylor, plain Jane, who was, I think, living with Lou and Sheila at the time, though that may have been later, she was asking him about Lucy's amour with Bunny, only, well, only at that particular time *nobody* knew about it, Guy and Bunny were still going through the motions, Guy even denied the whole thing to himself, as they say. But Annette was talking about this as if it had been on the front page, you know what I mean? Oh yes, there was also something that Lena told me she overheard standing outside the bathroom. She heard people talking and realized it was Annette, nobody could mistake that voice, *no body,* and some guy, so

Lena figured that Annette was having a little quick romance on the tiles, but then five minutes later she realizes that they're *just* talking, serious talk, not the wingèd words of love. What she gets, in bits and pieces, is Annette talking about some hotel or rooming house that has something to do with Barnett or Pungoe or maybe the both of them, but she got the impression that the place was going to be or maybe already had been torched. Some place called the Lincoln Inn or the Lincstone? I can't recall. O.K., the door opens and Lena makes some lame joke about her teeth floating or says Aha! love in bloom, to cover herself. The guy is none other than Joizy Cidy Rog, the old heels humper, Thom McAn in person. Lena said that Annette gave her a look that would have stopped a tank in its tracks. That's it as far as I know about Annette at that party. But a fleabag called the Lincoln Inn or whatever it was did burn down about a week after that and six people were killed.

What did April Detective see when she entered Mr. Rosette's study?

April wasn't at the party for Bart as far as I know, though I don't really know, maybe she came late, I don't think so. But I'm sure she *entered,* as you put it, Horace's study many times. As I've said, Horace was always giving a party or having some sort of get-together for drinks after an opening or a show or when the bars closed, he was a good-time Charlie with a slight weakness for the genitals of warm bodies, a mere peccadillo. I remember when he first met Lena, she almost turned him into the complete heterosexual because, my God, her little limp got him all hot and bothered, he'd have done anything to get her into bed, he went on and on about flawed beauty and tainted perfection, sounded like a bush-league Gabriel Rossetti. Lena took it all in stride, she had, as they say, a lot of class, lovely girl, and Christ knows she was *very* good-looking, Jack Towne heard about it and gave Horace a little tap or two and told him to lay off Lena and get his fag scene in gear again, if you'll pardon the expression, the way Jack put it he said, Go with your strength. Anyway Horace had a perpetual soirée of sorts, you were liable to meet anyone at his place any time, thus, so to speak, April. Vague yet sweet, maybe too sweet. Maybe you could say rotten. There was that air of corruption about her, although that simply might have been later when she and Dick started in on their dirty-picture obsession. I mean maybe she was the girl in the pink dress and Dick twisted her around, I don't know. As I say, anyway,

April could have and did enter Horace's study, I'm sure, many a time, and as to what she saw there, well. You were liable to see *anything* in Horace's study, it was more or less understood that it was strictly open city, proceed at your own risk, you know? I can tell you about one time that I know about because I was there with Tania, she and I were then intimate, as they say, this was before she was the chic manager of Barnett's chic shop, still a human being, you could still talk to her, she was as a matter of fact a lot of fun. We were seeing a hell of a lot of each other. We were even thinking of getting married. Just as well I guess, she had her eye on the dollar and her nose in the air even then but when she took her clothes off all was forgiven, amen. She was really something special. So the night I know about, or the day, whatever, this was really long ago, years ago, as I said, Dick had just bought his first camera and hadn't yet started to stick his goddam light meters in your face, I remember it completely because it was the first time that I was really aware of what a weird bitch Annette was. I should tell you that at this time, let me see, Jack Towne was not only alive but, you know, clean, he hadn't got into the dirty-money scene yet, so it was maybe twenty years ago, anyway, Lou Henry and April were having a very discreet affair just about that time, I think that only a few people knew about it, one of those things, as they say, that just happened. I knew about it because April told Tania, they were friends then, maybe they still are for all I know, but not the way they were, April later on worked for Tania when she managed Soirée Intime, she used to model the lingerie for the annual catalogue they put out, they charged ten bucks a copy for it unless you had an account at the store, quite a little item, a discreet aid, so to speak, to sexuality, or, to be crass, a classic jerk-off magazine in the guise of a catalogue, well, that was later. I knew about Lou and April because of Tania, it was accidental the way it started, par for the course, right? Lou and Sheila were already involved in a very minor way with Saul and the manuscript collecting, I guess they'd just started, certainly the first thing they bought was the manuscript and notes and such of a book called, if I remember rightly, *Blackjack,* by Christ knows who, he never wrote another book, whoever it was, or never published anyway, his name's on the tip of my tongue, Richard, Pritchard? Hell, I don't remember. Anyway, they bought this stuff, the book was never published. It might have been, as a matter of fact, the very first thing they bought, their entree into the fabled world of collecting, now you too can

know the thrill. In any event, some schmuck made a fifteen-minute movie
out of the book, you know, hand-held cameras, cinema vérité business,
filmed on the teeming ever-changing streets with no decent lighting. It
was shown as part of a program, one of those midnight-to-dawn programs
they used to run in arty fleabag theaters, every son of a bitch who ever
owned a cheap camera came and stayed the whole night for a buck and a
half. Well, Lou went to see what had been done to his *property,* very pro-
prietary, right? And who should be there but Mrs. Dick Detective, who
had been asked by the esteemed poet and editor, Craig Garf, to write a
review of one of the films, maybe *Blackjack,* for all I know, for *Lorzu,* the
little magazine I mentioned that he was using as his flying carpet to what
the poor ridiculous bastard thought of as success, Jesus Christ! Now April
could write a decent letter as they say, she could spell, you know, but as a
writer, forget it, so why Craig asked her to do this, your guess is as good as
mine. I don't think that anything so obvious would get April out of her
dress but who knows? In less than a year she was up to her eyes with the
old man in kinky pictures and whatever else, the whole scene, so maybe
Craig had some inkling of this or saw, as they say, into her true nature, her
true self, if you'll pardon the phrase. Well, this is all by the way, the story
is that they bumped into each other at this theater and talked, left after a
while and had some coffee and one thing as it will led to another and they
went to bed in, I think, Lucy Taylor's apartment, Lucy was discreet and so
on and besides she had no love for either Dick or Sheila. The point of all
this is that they really fell for each other and it got very sticky indeed.
April and Dick were already living in Connecticut and for her to see Lou
was a production, she had to beg Craig Garf to carry her as the film critic
on the *Lorzu* masthead, so that way she could get into town maybe once
every two weeks to see some film, sure, on the ceiling, right? Tania knew
all about this by now, so when April came into town she let her stay at her
place and Lou would come over and spend the night, what story he gave
Sheila Christ only knows, but that's the way it went. O.K. Now the Rosette business, right, that was really a kind of touch of, what can I call it?
monstrosity, perversity. Whatever the occasion or absence of occasion,
Horace's place was jammed and his study was, as usual, in *use,* if you
follow me, and Annette Lorpailleur got hold of April and told her that she
was really interested in talking to her about having her and Dick spend a
weekend with her and meet some of her friends, a wonderful painter and

her wonderful friend, who else? Annie Flammard and Barry Gatto, the Gold Dust Twins. Annie was also a *brilliant* photographer, oh yes indeed, and Annette had heard that Dick was looking for a good teacher, a private teacher, and so on and so forth, how *lucky,* how *marvelous* for all of us. That voice coming out of the chandelier or the wall. And I've really wanted so much to get to *know* you better, Annette says. I've heard *so much* about you and your husband. You mustn't be strangers and exile yourselves in the country. Even though the country is so wonderful, so peaceful. I was brought up in the country, she says, right, the work farm no doubt, and on and on, and April, who was a simple soul, is listening to all this shit. Then Annette says to her that they might go into Horace's study, so nice and quiet, a few people listening to Vivaldi and blowing a little boss weed, away from the madding crowd, so they go in. Well, it was, to coin a phrase, gangbusters indeed indeed, I heard the story later, I don't recall who told me, not important anyway. The room was dim, maybe one or two soft lamps on, and under one of them there were clothes, a pile of clothes, slips, bras, men's things, all sorts of things, and as April starts to realize what she's seeing she notes, notes is good, she notes the real center of attraction, the center ring, so to speak, and lo! it's the Henrys, Lou and Sheila, and not to go into obscene detail but they're both on their knees with Lou giving it to Sheila from behind, I mean he's, you know, and both of them drunk or stoned and Sheila is crazy, Sheila is, Sheila's going down on Bunny, and in a chair watching this whole thing is that good ole boy, Harlan P, his honest hands calloused and worn from hauling himself up by his own bootstraps, and he's taking pictures, a true American, true and fucking blue American, presidential caliber. What Annette was up to Christ only knows but as far as I'm concerned she had le hot for April and figured she'd just try her luck, the element of surprise, who knows? April might have been turned on except that she and Lou, well, she almost collapsed right there, Lou looked up for a second and just smiled, didn't miss a beat, Sheila was too busy to look at anything, Bunny tried to hide her face but there she was in all her naked glory, with Harlan slobbering away and panting and grunting and making noises, and going click click click with his trusty Kodak. Anyway, Bunny, Bunny in the middle of the scene was proof, if anybody needed any proof, that she was still at that time paying off for Guy's, shall we say, association? with Harlan's direct-mail con, paying off Harlan, I mean. There's no mystery why she and Lucy became lovers, not at all, every time she turned around some guy was taking her over the hurdles in one way or another, Pungoe, of course, was the greatest bastard of them all. He always had plenty of allies, so to speak, but he especially walked on Bunny as if she were a rug, she was *used* by him, what's the word I'm looking for? Soiled, right, she was *soiled* by him. It had been going on for years and years, ever since Bunny was a girl, really. He had her by the short hairs, had a lot of pictures of her that he'd set up, some phony poses and plenty that were not so phony, she was into smack when she was young and Harlan was her connection, he'd hold out on her till she'd do what he wanted, when she finally got straight she got out from under him and then she met Guy. Out of the blue comes Pungoe, surprise surprise! How nice to see you again, Miss Ward, Ward was Bunny's maiden name, oh? you're Mrs. Lewis now? How nice! Maybe we can have lunch or a drink sometime.

Do I understand you to mean that Joanne Lewis—Bunny—had known Harlan Pungoe long before she met Guy?

Oh hell, yes. I thought I made that clear, I'm sorry. It's all in the dim past, as Doctor Plot might write, as a matter of fact, he probably has, a few hundred times. Bunny dropped out of college after some sort of a disastrous affair with some guy whose family had come over on the *Mayflower,* probably in a little boat a few hundred yards in front of the thing, and when they found out that their very own Myles Standish was serious about this common type who had no breeding, no background, no cash, they stepped in and broke it up. Bunny took it very hard. She started to hit the sauce pretty good, then split, and as the story went, she wound up in the vast beyond somewhere, Nevada or Montana, New Mexico, where men are men and sunglasses are king. She was about twenty, you understand, maybe only nineteen, this was almost twenty years ago, eighteen anyway, and she got a job in some hip little bar as a cocktail waitress or barmaid or something, getting her ass pinched, etcetera. O.K. Who should be working in the joint but a guy named Baylor Freeq, who was really Biff Page sailing under false colors because he was on the run, nothing really serious, he'd been hanging paper here and there, had this Western manly con going, Stetson, boots, jeans, he'd just charm the hell out of some poor gullible rube bastard talking about the goddam New York Jews and commies and how Jesus was good enough for him and passing his bad checks right and left. Where he got the name Baylor Freeq Christ only knows, the funny thing is that his father had plenty of money, Biff was the black sheep or some damn thing, didn't want to go into the business. The usual old tale. Anyway, he and Bunny went out together a few times, had a few laughs, then one day some humble citizen shows up, Biff introduces Bunny to him, who else but our friend Harlan? He's very considerate, sweet, mature, a marriage gone sour because of an alcoholic wife, hat in hand, digs his toe into the floor, the old Gary Cooper con, just a hard-working fella, true blue, and despite his club foot a salesman who through snow and hail and so on, the sorta kinda guy, the kinda *little* guy that's made America what it is. Any fucking cliché you can think of, that's Harlan. He also happened to know that a little taste of heroin now and again couldn't hurt a fly, well, not to give you a scenario, good ole Harlan turned Bunny on, her understanding soulmate, they got high together, the old boring story once again, and one fine morning what do you know? Bunny has this very persistent ugly Jones, absolutely addicted. So Harlan said, well my dear girl, of course you can have what you need but first let's have some good clean honest fun. Fun to Harlan was not only the voyeur scene, Bunny with Biff, Bunny with some hookers he hired, Bunny with a couple of truck drivers, Bunny with anything and everything, plus of course Harlan's camera in action, it was also making Bunny beat him, whip him, and vice versa, a whole sadomasochist scene, boots and saddles. This went on for maybe two years, maybe more, a love story played out against the breathtaking panorama of the fabled West. As I say, this went on and on, Bunny was a zombie, when she wasn't full of smack she was soaking up the booze, and at least once a week she'd be the star of one of Harlan's parties. In between times she and her benefactor would stage their own little scenes, Bunny told me once that Harlan's favorite was the little play where he'd surprise her in the bathroom and then beg to be punished for being so dirty, so lewd and so foul, then after she beat him he'd beat her for daring to beat him. A twisted son of a bitch. But once in a while Harlan would have to leave on business, selling, as he said. The selling turned out to be some arrangement he had in Mexico, his porno pictures would bring him some good money, of course, beautiful co-ed in shameless acts of lust, and so on, then he'd buy some good Mexican grass and get it across the border, sell that and buy up, buy some skag, and so on and so forth, he had his connections all over the place, a knight of the trackless sands. He'd leave Biff a maintenance ration of shit for Bunny and off he'd go. Well I don't really know how it happened but I do know Biff was involved, a fit of remorse or something, but she managed to cold turkey once when Harlan was gone for two weeks, Biff sold the dope and gave her the money and she ran for her life. There may have been many more complications to the story, I don't know, I heard this a long time after, some of it from Bunny, some from Guy, and some from Chico Zeek, but to be fair, I also heard from Sylvie that Pungoe hadn't been involved at all, that, as a matter of fact, Harlan had never met Bunny before he came to town. But that doesn't make much sense because then I can't figure out why Bunny would allow herself to be involved in such things as the scene in Horace's study, and I understand, hell, I *know,* that Bunny was involved in a number of scenes like that, all presided over, if you will, by Harlan. I mean I can't understand it if Harlan didn't have something on her, I mean those photographs, right? Anyway, that's none of my business. But then, what is? Bunny met Guy at some picnic or something given by Lincoln, Save the rats! or some damn thing, I seem to remember that he managed, Lincoln I mean, he managed some nature bookshop at the time, Black Ladder Books I think, a hell of a name. Well, she and Guy hit it off, they started living together, and I guess eventually got sort of married. Guy got a job as day bartender at a little joint that was a hang-out for artists, Caliph's Walk. It had been, of all things, a Chinese restaurant originally, by Omaha a Chinese restaurant, a dump called the Red Silk, I think, strictly chop suey and fortune cookies, a big drunk business after the bars closed. Anyway, Bunny came to some sort of understanding with her parents and they gave her a small allowance so she could go back to school. Nice, normal life, you know? Enter Pungoe. The great rube appeared, as I've said, out of nowhere, I don't remember how or even exactly when, but I can swear it wasn't because of Biff Page because when Harlan appeared Biff wasn't in town, he'd gone on a buying trip for his father, his wild oats sowed, whatever, he wasn't around anyway. Harlan had what he called this great-potential mail-order business in the works and he started to talk about it to people, and as it turned out, one of the people he talked to was Guy, because Harlan used to have lunch every day at the Caliph's Walk bar. And whether Sylvie was right or not, somehow Harlan made it clear to Guy that he could get in on this scam, big bucks a-comin'! and opportunity unlimited and so on, he made it clear to Guy that he'd have to meet the little woman. The plot thickens. So Guy, ignorant of everything, Sylvie *had* to be wrong, it's clearer and clearer, Guy, ignorant of everything and excited about the job, tells Bunny. She hears the name but what can she say? I used to be involved in orgies with Harlan and friends? I heard that they had dinner, Tania told me, and Bunny laughed, chatted, was vivacious and charming and so on, acted absolutely dumb, well of course in Harlan's sweaty pocket he probably had some interesting pictures, to say the least, of the fresh and vibrant Mrs. Lewis with two truck drivers and a slut out of some rundown cathouse, all in living color. If you put two and two together it must have turned out that for Guy to get the job *and* remain ignorant of the pictures, Bunny had to have a party or two with Pungoe, poor unfortunate man probably hadn't been whipped in months. Love will find a way. So miracle of miracles! The job came through for Guy, he quit bartending and started to work for Harlan. Thought it was his charm and intelligence that got him the job. The odd thing about it all was that when Harlan came on the scene, nobody really thought that he was an A number one bastard, I have to be honest about it and say that I didn't either. Oh yeah, he was strictly a rube, at least that was his act, his unbelievable suits, Jesus, he had one that was, he called it electric blue, enough to send you screaming into the night, and ties! Oh my God, you know those insanely hideous hand-painted ties they used to sell? That's all Harlan owned, burn the eyes right out of your head. But as far as being, well, sinister, no, I didn't think so. Some people even thought that he was a great guy, you know, a lot of ole boy stories, working on the farm, his days as a labor organizer, travels all over the world, merchant seaman, the works, right? Man of the people, the soil, he played to that vague romantic crap about rural folk, I guess we were all taken in by him. Correction, not *all*. April, this was just before she married Dick, she hated the man. She'd never say why but she did, she and Dick had a lot of quarrels about it I heard, as a matter of fact, I myself heard a lot of the quarrels. Dick thought Harlan was aces, ole Pungoe would set the bar up, tell his hick stories and on and on, bump around on his fucking clubfoot, but April would, I can't explain it, she'd literally get rigid with anger, *fury*, whenever she saw him, I don't think a word ever passed between them. Harlan *had* to know how she felt so it must have been a great night for him when Annette took her into Horace's study and there was Lou in the middle of it. Jesus, now that I think about it, it's odd how these things come clear, now that I think of it, Harlan must have known all about Lou and April and that's why he arranged with Annette for April to be taken into the study. Oh Christ, of course. He gave her, as they say, an eyeful, had the last laugh.

But if what you've said about April Detective is true, how do you explain these photographs of her?

Photographs of her? Let's see. If I may. I'll be damned. I don't have any idea unless, wait a minute. These must have been taken some time later, I mean long after April and Dick split up. Maybe April and Harlan became friends, though that's very unlikely, or else it was just one of those things since Sylvie is in, what? three of these shots and April and Sylvie got to know each other very well about the time that Dick started to carry on with Karen Ostrom, she must have charmed him with some magical wheat germ. What's funny to me is that this looks like, I mean this obviously is an adobe house, so I guess Harlan must have left his heart, and a bank account, in the far-flung Southwest. Unless April and Harlan, no, I doubt that, I was going to say that maybe April's dislike for Harlan was just so much eyewash. I suppose that's possible but I can't figure out why she'd go to all the trouble of making it *look* as if she loathed the man. I really don't know. My best guess is, as I say, that Sylvie, as a friend, asked April to take a vacation from Dick and his behavior with Karen, Vance was dead by this time, I don't remember if I told you that? Well, it's not important, but yes, he was dead then, he died in a fire in one of those phony country inns in New England, The Red Swan, phony name, phony sign, I wouldn't be at all surprised if it said, you know, Ye Olde Redde Swanne Inne, one of those dodges, some city slicker probably opened the joint to con the Sunday drivers out to look at the autumn leaves. Anyway, the place burned down, Vance was trapped in his bathroom, what the hell he was doing there I don't know, but they found him the next day dead of smoke inhalation. I found out later that he was dressed like a woman, he was wearing a white silk dress, panties, nylons, high heels, everything. It was quite a shock because nobody ever figured that Vance was kinky. Somebody suggested that the whole thing was hushed up, and it pretty much was, because it looked as if there was some sort of funny business going on up there, it was a common rumor that Jack Marowitz owned this joint, I mean, he was behind it, you know, it was some sort of corporation, but I don't believe that, Jack had had his fill of the real-estate business years before with Lincoln, so I doubt if he'd have been involved. The whole thing just sort of died, they held an inquest, I think, but nothing came of it, but nobody has yet explained what Vance was doing in drag in this cutesy New England inn. Anyway, I'm getting off the track here. You know, I don't want to be difficult or rude, not at all, but I don't know what it is you're getting at with these questions. It would probably be better for you to talk to somebody who has access to, you know, real information, I mean hard data, as they say. I certainly *knew* these people but I was, as the phrase goes, leading my own life during all this time. I had things to do, jobs, I was married for a while, and these people kept moving around, doing this and that, I don't know much more than what I saw, not a hell of a lot, and what I heard, which is always colored, you know how people do that. I mean you could ask questions forever and just, well, just produce more questions. I don't mind, you understand, but I'm human. I mean to say I can forget things or just get them wrong. All right. In any event, let me see if I can put things together to explain these photographs. I don't mean explain them, I mean see if I can somehow cogently, right, cogently, if I can offer a cogent reason, rather, for these photographs. As I've told you, April and Sylvie became really good friends after Vance died, not that he had anything to do with them but Dick then had a clear field with Karen, well, you know this, anyway, they were good friends and were collaborating on a book, one of those fast-buck deals, how to dress rich with, you know, the best little stores listed, places to buy chic but inexpensive clothes, how to have *real* style, the kind of dumb thing that would go over big with the faithful hip who read *Hip Vox,* as a matter of fact, Lee Jefferson had given them the idea, as I recall. She'd arranged with them to have lunch with her and some acquisitions editor, how I love that phrase, some lover of literature complete with faded jeans and the right politics whose name, thanks be to Christ, escapes me. The thing fell through because of Barnett, who didn't want Sylvie doing anything that might have enabled her to get out from under the boutique, his first boutique, not the Soirée Intime. Barnett liked to keep his women on a maintenance diet, *just* enough but always there if they were good little girls, Sylvie, Léonie, and Tania, only Tania finally escaped, more or less, because the Soirée Intime got so much breathless ink that she became a kind of media celebrity, titillating articles about transparent bras and such, the outrageous prices they charged, the famous catalogue, the stories about staid businessmen coming in for underwear for themselves, all that rubbish. Interviews, talk shows, oh and she was *terrific*. The lowered eyes, the slight blush, the demurely crossed legs with her skirt pulled just so over her knees, in the meantime she's talking to some slobbering host about women's freedom and crotchless panties. Sometimes I can't really believe that we were actually married, *briefly,* but it's as if it happened to somebody else. Anyway. The photographs, right, April and Harlan smiling into the sun, O.K. All I can guess is that Harlan had nothing to do with it, so to speak, I mean really nothing at all, because it was probably a case of Sylvie asking April to take a short vacation at what must have been, maybe not, Harlan's house wherever the hell it was and Harlan was there when they arrived or he showed up. I just don't know. I'll tell you one thing that intrigues me though and that's who *took* these shots of the three of them together. Did they recruit some passing Indian or a lonesome cowboy? Not that it matters, but I'd just like to know. It's possible, just barely, that it was Dick, he and April *might* have gone together, singing that old sweet song, let's-try-it-one-more-time to the silv'ry moon and the desert breezes. But if it was Dick you can bet your ass that it was because Miss Whole-Grains had to go home, all smiles, freckles, and gleaming teeth, to see the old folks in Apple Pie, Nebraska. He and Harlan could have had long talks in front of the cheery blaze about lenses and shutters and such, ah yes, good old Dick never let the grass grow under his feet. By the way, I should add, for whatever it's worth, that the renowned Mr. Detective was in his version of clover at that time. He was carrying on with Karen, whose all-American smile shone through the darkest night, he had a little porno business going with Corrie and Madame Delamode, not to mention their colleague, Annette, specialty poses I think he did for them, *and* also Biff Page had hired him, not really hired, but he worked as a free-lance photographer for Biff's PR agency, and wonder of wonders, will they never cease? one of the first jobs he did was a color layout of Annette's metal apartment that appeared in some ultra-modern house-and-home magazine. Enough to frighten small children. The three fates in their steel peignoirs looking like a dream of the divine Marquis, crackling blaze in the chromium fireplace, aluminum spike heels, and so on. And Annette in those pictures! She'd had something done to her face, plastic surgery probably, or she just *willed* it, it wouldn't surprise me a bit. The point is she didn't look like Annette anymore, she looked like Annie Flammard, not exactly, but as if she were Annie's older sister or maybe even her mother, you know, a really glamorous older woman. She always had looked a little like Annie to begin with, or vice versa. But this was more. It was very unsettling.

Who was Annette Lorpailleur?

Well that's a funny question, I don't mean funny, I mean unexpected, we've talked so much about her, I've talked so much I should say and still here you are still trying to find out, well, I don't *know* what. All I can tell you is what I've already told you, there she was, she just was, she seemed to be in the background for years, but the background *everywhere,* you'd turn around, there was Annette, you know, turn up a damn rock and she'd be looking at you. There were stories about her, oh, endless, one would just cancel out another. You'd hear that she'd been at such and such a place at such and such a time, then the next day you'd hear that no, she couldn't have been there because she was, well, someplace *else.* One story that persisted was that she'd written a novel under the name Ann Redding, supposedly an occult mystery novel, *The Metallic Fly,* that purportedly was really, as they say, a kind of esoteric handbook of demonology for, you know, the initiated, I've never seen a copy, as a matter of fact I checked on the book, nothing in the card catalogues I checked under that title but there was an Ann Redding, Ann T. Redding to be exact, but it turned out to be a book of criticism, literary essays. One I remember was on Cecil, Cecil Tyrell and Tony Lamont, I can't remember the title, something about Janus, the Janus something or other, the Janus theme, I don't know. I just skimmed through it, one of those standard academic essays with a system, you know? Everything fits into the system or you don't mention it. Bursting with jargon, on and on, the macroparatactics of the ur-text in self-reflexive surfiction or can microparatactics valorize the signifier? My point is that the book had a little bio note and a photograph on the jacket, Miss Redding, *Doctor* Redding standing alongside her desk, a lot of books, bookshelves on her right, a window behind her opening onto a garden, a formal English garden, a sunny day, but Doctor Redding was not, by any stretch of the imagination, Annette Lorpailleur. This woman was in her late thirties or early to mid-forties, very well groomed, short hair pulled back tight off her face, tortoiseshell glasses, a tweed suit and tailored blouse, stack-heeled shoes with small metal buckles, beautiful straight legs, big calves and very slender ankles, very attractive, like those women in the movies of the thirties and forties, the anthropologist or professor who takes off her glasses and unpins her hair and there she is! Lana Turner! Why, you're, you're b-b-beautiful! some lunk says, Preston Foster or

George Brent. She's carefully, a little stiffly, almost professionally posed, she has a pen and a sheaf of papers in her hand, there's a little ceramic mug full of pens and pencils on the desk, a *millefiore* paperweight on a stack of letters and a small figurine, looks like metal, of some Hindu god or goddess, I don't know which one, the one that rides a dog, whoever that is. And this and that, a kind of, what's the word? studied, right, a kind of studied clutter. Also a little basket of oranges on the desk. She's very scholarly-looking, attractive, although a little stern, formidable. The bio note says that she lives just outside London with her husband, who's a stockbroker. I remember his name, Richard Gross, Bart., because a few years later he wound up in the papers, his wife was just mentioned in passing, he was mixed up in some stock-fraud scheme, involved with a group of people who got insider, confidential information about the market, or he gave this sort of information to other people, it's all kind of vague to me now. That's all by the by, the point is that if Ann T. Redding wrote a novel I couldn't find out about it. And Ann T. Redding was *not* Annette. But that's just one example of the stories, and there were dozens of them, about Annette. Most of them just stayed in the air, just persisted, because nobody could ever find out anything to prove or disprove them. She was strange enough without the stories. O.K. She just left anyway, in a flash, just the way she arrived. And Corrie and Madame Delamode with her. They were supposedly going on a winter cruise to the Bahamas or Bermuda or some damn silly place like that, and they never came back. Their apartment disappeared too, I mean the building it was in, an old brownstone, it got torn down with all the other brownstones on the same side of the street, some sweet real-estate shuffle. The houses were declared undesirable or unsafe or un-some fucking thing or the other, whatever lie was used, down they came and up went these high-rise co-ops, two hundred and fifty grand for three closets and a fireplace just about big enough to burn a popsicle stick. Many bucks, many many bucks were made by somebody. The kind of thing that bastard Biggs Richard would have loved to be in on, except that he'd split too, with, of all people, Lorna Flambeaux, or so we heard. Except that she was by then Lorna Gom, Mrs. Lincoln Gom, maybe I already told you that? She'd become a senior editor and Linc saw the promised land there, he'd never have to work again, right? She must have got fed up with him though, he'd always be bringing home some rocks-and-ferns freak, complete with backpack and sturdy boots, and they almost always turned out to be eighteen- or nineteen-year-old girls, their eyes on the redwoods, their feet in the mud, frogs jumping out of their survival jackets. Well, Lorna just took off, closed out the bank accounts first, and that was that. I think Linc moved in or tried to move in with Lena Schmidt then, gave up the whole ecology con, fuck the whales, right? I don't remember how long that raging love endured but it ended pretty quick. Then, what then? I'm trying to end this whole Lincoln thing, that'll be another thing out of the way, another goddam character. Oh, about Annette, I've got one more story but let me finish with Linc. He kissed every ass in town looking for some kind of a job, you *know* he was desperate, finally he saw some friend who owed Duke Washington a favor, I mean a friend of Duke's. Lincoln had gone to see Duke too. In any event, the friend gave him a job as an assistant to the advance man for a lame heavy-metal band, Dress Rite, spelled r i t e, very cutesy. About a year later they found him dead in a Holiday Inn outside Gallup, o.d.'d on wine and downers. Always the original. Now, Annette, to tell you the last thing I heard about her, supposedly she turned up in Florida somewhere in some retirement community, well, no, not exactly. She had some kind of a partnership with a guy to *develop* retirement villages, little bungalows made out of cardboard and spit, God forbid it should rain, the ceiling would fall down on some poor old guy's head. White Sun Village was the name of the first one as I recall. The thing got blown away in a hurricane and people were hurt, killed, it was in the papers but when the law came to look for Annette, the state or county, whatever, she was long gone. Invisible. It was as if she'd never existed. The papers, the stories in the papers gave her name as something else, some alias, I forget what, but the story going around was that it was in fact Annette. Maybe, maybe not. Nobody's heard anything since about her. For all I know she lives next door, some sophisticated, independent, and mature woman who incidentally owns a couple of hundred tenements crawling with rats. Who knows?

What does the phrase "metallic constructions" mean?

Metallic constructions? I have no idea. I'm sorry, I really can't help you on that one. Metallic constructions. I'm damned if I know.

Why did Bart Kahane tell Leo Kaufman that he had surprised Anne Kaufman and Biff Page on Horace Rosette's bed?

I didn't know that old tale still had any currency because it's absolutely phony, made up out of whole cloth by Bart for the simple purpose of making Anne look bad to Leo. Supposedly it had a lot to do with their marriage finally breaking up, but they were both ready, I mean if it did break the marriage up, it was a thing they grabbed for, something that came along just in time. Anyway, the story went that Biff bumped into Anne one day, this was soon after he'd come back to town after his Baylor Freeq adventures, you'll pardon the expression, but I don't think he'd gone to work for the old man yet, he wasn't yet the *new* Biff, firm of jaw and so on, as if he ever will be, well, they bumped into each other somewhere and had a cup of coffee together. Anne was more or less living with Vance at the time but Vance was broke and a cheap son of a bitch as well, so she had no money and was looking for a job. She hadn't met Tony yet, I don't think so anyway, it wouldn't have mattered, since he wouldn't have given her any money even if he had some, it all went right over the bar. Leo was spending as much time as he could with Ellen, his little Eskimo Pie, eating her oven-fried okra and chicken-guts Madeira with marshmallows and spanking her every day and twice on Sundays, love in full bloom. It makes me laugh when I think that Ellen became a firebrand in the feminist movement, fedora and all, overalls for Christ sake. She probably started to make speeches because she couldn't sit down. Well that's neither here nor there. My point is that Leo spent the few shekels he could get his mitts on on Ellen, though her brother Jack used to give her an allowance. So. Biff and Anne got to talking and he mentioned that she had probably heard that he and Barnett had opened a restaurant together, a chic, overpriced seafood joint that they called Les Lobsters, cute as a little button, one of those traps with the lobsters in tanks so you could pick your own, as if you're, you know, exercising your shellfish expertise, the carafes of house white and red, the crudités and rice pilaf, all the young blond fag waiters who were *really* actors and dancers, what else would they be? And the Mozart cassettes and so on, the works. To sit down and have a glass of water you dropped five bucks, when they brought you a menu, or I should say when Allen or Chet or Dwight or Ronnie brought you a menu you said goodbye to another fin. Well, the upshot of this was that they needed a hostess, an attractive woman who'd look good in clothes, someone to say hello, seat people, you know the things they do. O.K., Anne thought it was great, she could make a few bucks for herself and get out from under Leo *and* Vance, right? So she says it sounds great and—this was the story—they go up to Horace's place because Horace supposedly wanted to introduce Biff to some starving painter who did little watercolors of lobsters and crabs and fish that Biff might be interested in buying, or commissioning, to hang on the walls of Les Lobsters, the deluxe touch, sure. Horace was out but Biff had a key, a lot of people had keys to Horace's place, and they sat down to wait, have a smoke, one thing led to another and they wound up in the sack. Enter Bart Kahane, who was sucking around Horace at the time so that he could meet what he thought of as important people, the poor deluded bastard, Horace was no doubt making him perform unnatural acts in spades, you know? Bend over, Bart, my boy, we'll while away the time until David Rockefeller arrives to discuss off-shore oil leasing. So in barges Bart and catches Anne and Biff in flagrante on the bed, he rushes out and tells his old pal, Leo. What are friends for? The only thing true about this bullshit story is that Anne was indeed in bed naked but *not* with Biff Page. You've got to understand that Bart really hated Anne because when she and Leo started to drift apart, I love that phrase, Anne was falling into bed with everybody, including a few women, making a few trios and quartets as well, but she wouldn't give Bart a tumble. She just thought he was a clown. I personally heard her say to him once, she was three sheets to the wind, she told him that she didn't want to make it with him because she was terrified that she'd die laughing. I don't know, something about the guy even then just turned her permanently off, and then, oh yeah, then just before this alleged incident with Biff she began to call Bart Les, you know, short for Lester, because he'd thought up the name Les Lobsters and Barnett gave him, I don't know, ten or twenty bucks in appreciation, and he took it! Then everybody picked up on this nickname and poor Bart got to be known as Les, some people were even *introduced* to him that way. So there was no love lost between Bart and Anne Kaufman, believe me. But the real story behind Bart's telling Leo about Anne was very different. Barnett really had the hots for Anne and Biff told her this story, which was true, in a way, they did need a hostess, but I suspect that Barnett had Léonie in mind for the job, but who knows? Biff told her, as I say, this story, then asked her to go up to Horace's to meet the fish artist, and who should be there? You've got it, Barnett, all by his lonesome, knocking back the sauce and getting himself into a lather. He'd had this mad lust for Anne ever since a Halloween costume party that Annette and friends had given that year to which Anne had come as a baby. She wore a white bra and a *diaper.* I mean it was really weird, I think she did it to out-weird Annette, Corrie, and the Madame, who were dressed like store mannequins, made up that way, and they moved in these little jerks as if they were robots. Well when Barnett got an eyeful of Anne in her baby costume he got crazy because he knew, as did everyone else, that Leo used to like to spank Anne and he must have put this together in his diseased mind with the diaper. To tell the truth, maybe Anne did it because she knew that Leo had told everyone anyway and she figured what the hell, bring it out in the open. I don't know. That was another sparkling trait that Leo had, he'd tell you anything about himself, the most personal things, right out of the blue, the son of a bitch had no shame at all. Every hopeless drunk within a radius of twenty miles knew every excruciating detail of Leo's sex life with Anne, he should have sent it to the newspapers. As a matter of fact, when he started going around with Ellen he'd take you by the lapels and give you a play-by-play of *their* personal lives, or he'd walk into whatever bar everybody was hanging out in and show you things he'd bought for her from the Soirée Intime, with her money of course, for their, what did he call them? I don't remember, something like erotic nocturnes, whatever. Or he'd show you his lotions and creams and ointments, once he even passed a French tickler around, the man was astonishing. But I'm getting away from, right, so Biff takes Anne up to Horace's, there's Barnett, Biff leaves posthaste, and Anne is in the sack with *Barnett* when Bart walks in. Bart rushes out to tell Leo this tale, but changing Barnett to Biff. O.K. He was avenging himself on Anne because, as I said, she would never give him the time of day, but he was also protecting his ass. Bart didn't dare tell Leo that Barnett was shtupping Anne because Barnett had already made, to put it delicately, veiled threats against Bart's life and limb, Jesus, these things are all coming back to me, what a mess. It seems, or the rumor was, that Barnett was sleeping regularly with Lolita, who at that time had been married to Bart about a month, they're divorced now, as I told you. Now, Conchita told Barnett that she knew that he was getting his ashes hauled regularly by Lolita and Barnett figured that Bart knew and had told Conchita, his usual crying-in-his-beer routine, right? But Bart, as far as I know, had no idea that Lolita was two-timing him. At any rate, Barnett called Bart up and told him that he wasn't at all pleased that his name had been linked with Lolita, did Bart think that he, a man in his position, had to sneak around with married women? Then he said that if he heard, from anyone at all, any more stories that men-

tioned his name in an insulting or demeaning way, Bart would find himself involved in, ah, unpleasantries, that's the kind of word that Tete would
use. Then he mentioned, oh so casually, the high-heels kid, Roger Whytte-
Blorenge, you remember, woddayasay kid yawanna get some ersters?
O.K. Roger worked for Pungoe, worked, well, did this and that, dirty work
I suppose you'd call it, but Pungoe and Tete were sometime business associates, to coin a euphemism, the story was that at this time they were ripping off designer dresses and selling them, selling the designs, to ready-
to-wear clothing manufacturers before the models in Paris and Milan and
New York had even modeled them, don't ask me, some racket they were
in cahoots on, there was a rumor that Pungoe and Tete had paid a bundle
of money to have some kind of mini-camera fitted into a special pair of
glasses, you know, eyeglasses, that somebody in the fashion business, or
probably more than one someone, but people in their employ, you'll pardon the expression, would use to photograph the big designers' new lines.
I'm ignorant of that business so I don't know if it could have been possible to do that, I do know though that the both of them were walking
around at that time looking like the cat who ate the canary. Anyway, Roger
the shoe fetishist was a certified thug, and Barnett suggested that old Rog
might pay Bart a visit if and when he heard, etcetera, etcetera. So Bart just
substituted Biff for Tete and got even, so to speak, with Anne. But she
didn't give a good goddam, as I said, this was what got the divorce started.
To the satisfaction of all parties.

     Is it possible that Conchita had learned of Lolita's indiscretions
with Mr. Tete through Bart?

     I'd say that it was possible but highly unlikely, improbable. When
Lolita and Tete were having their fling Conchita was in Paris, and I can't
imagine Bart calling her up to tell her or even, for that matter, writing her.
But *somebody* told her, unless the whole story about her telling Tete that
she knew is suspect, if there was anything *to* know. Which happens to be
my own opinion, that is, that there was nothing to know. I mean to say that
I think Lolita still really loved Bart in some odd way, and I mean odd, at
the time and I don't think she would have become involved with Barnett
and if she was involved certainly Conchita wouldn't have given a damn,
she wouldn't have told Tete that she knew. I'm afraid that I can't explain
all this clearly, but you should understand that most of these people were
more or less reasonably all right until odd things started to happen, odd

people started to, I don't know. I mean people like Barnett and Pungoe, you know, Roger, Annette Lorpailleur and her two friends, when they suddenly appeared it was as if a kind of disease infected everybody, people got crazy, weird, they got foul and greedy and mean. I told you about Léonie, for instance, who was a lovely young woman and who became a drunken bitch, and of course Jack Towne, Tania, oh God, it all happened over a few years really. Well. Lolita loved Bart, O.K. Now maybe she did sleep with Barnett, Bunny said that she saw him once every two weeks for an evening, he'd take her to dinner then go home with her, she'd stay the night, five hundred dollars. This may or may not be true, maybe Lolita *was* just a whore, I don't know. It would have been better than putting up with Cecil Tyrell's shit when she was nursing him through that goddam novel of his, *Orange Steel,* and supporting him as well, getting an occasional shot in the chops for her trouble. But what Bunny had to say should be taken very carefully, because Bunny had no love for Lolita then, although they live together now, or they did a few months or so back. So I heard. But at that time she had a suspicion that Lolita and Guy were lovers, a real mistake! If there was someone that Lolita hated it was Guy Lewis, this dated from the night at somebody's place, I think I mentioned this, maybe the Lewises', when Lolita was in the bathroom and Guy walked in on her and just stood there smoking a cigarette and grinning like an ape, watching her. Bunny figured they were up to some funny business in there and so if she passed the word around that Lolita was a whore, Barnett's whore, it wouldn't surprise me if it was all just an invention. And of course now, if you ask anybody about this, anybody who was around at the time, it's a *fact,* I mean, sure, Lolita and Guy were lovers. It's carved in stone. An interesting sidelight on this is that in *Synthetic Ink* there's a strange scene in which one of his characters, somebody named Daisy, is involved in some kinky sex in a bathroom with a demented soldier, a deserter I think. He ties her to the toilet with her stockings, she loves it, then you discover that this is really just one of Daisy's lecherous fantasies. Tony got a lot of grief from Ellen Kaufman about that scene when she became a militant feminist, she was the vice-president of some group that boycotted bookstores and so on, Tony was so constantly stoned in those days he probably thought they were loyal fans clamoring to buy his book and meet the author, but my point is that the woman in the novel, Daisy, was modeled on Lolita, whom Tony despised, because he thought, rightly or wrongly, that Lolita and Lee Jefferson were buddies and he hated Lee too. This, by the way, I mean Lolita being used as the model for Daisy, is, according to some people, why *Hip Vox* went out of its way to kick the hell out of *Synthetic Ink,* that assault by John Hicks I told you about? Maybe so, but that would imply that Lee and Lolita were indeed friends, I don't know about that, I think personally it was because Lee was, you know, up-to-the-minute Charlie and she knew that it would go over big with the *Hip Vox* audience to savage Tony's novel, feminism was just then becoming a valuable commodity, it sold, if you'll pardon my cynicism. I'm *still* not making my point. My point, Jesus, my point being that people who knew that Daisy was based on Lolita thought that the bathroom scene was, you know, *actual,* that it was the way *Lolita* really was, they believed the goddam novel. People are really amazing, can you imagine believing a novel? So Lolita suffered and all the others involved were delighted, Ellen and her radical-feminist group, I can't remember their name, got a lot of mileage out of it, Lee added a lot of new subscribers, even Tony got a kind of backhanded push with the publicity, some interviews and such, a talk show, he even made a pretty respectable paperback deal, I can remember the cover they did, bright red with the title and his name spelled out in letters drawn to look like stockings, black nylon stockings, and a little banner printed across the bottom, The blistering novel that enraged the women of America! Beautiful. And for the next year or so every time Lolita got up to go to the bathroom at a party or in a bar somebody would pass a smart remark, that lunk Doctor Plot, you know, Page Moses, even threw her a salute once. She spit in his face.

Why did Lolita Kahane slap Conchita?

That's news to me. If she did I never heard about it, although it sounds like the kind of story that Bart might have made up to make it look as if these two women were fighting, you know, over him. Very unlikely. Lolita and Conchita got along pretty well as a matter of fact, for a time they even went to the same hair stylist, bought their clothes at the same stores, they even showed up at one of Pungoe's parties dressed exactly alike. I don't know if that was accidental or not, but. However, you might be interested to know that Lolita slapped *some* woman at a little bar that Barry Gatto worked in as night manager, a place called The Black Basement, this was some time after Barry and Annie Flammard were divorced and he needed a job. Annie and Buffie Tate, with the help of Annette, gave him the business in the home decorating racket they'd been in, they got some other guy to take Barry's place, Serge something or other, and the great part about it was that this loser had an ear that had even more tin in it than Barry's, it was beyond belief. Anyway, a bunch of us went to this trap, The Black Basement, one night right after Barry got the job, it was somewhere to hell and gone, and some dump. There must have been about ten of us there and what happens is that Sister Rose, Rose Zeppole? comes up to the table where Lolita is sitting and starts telling her that she, Lolita, would be perfect in a new movie that Rose was going to start shooting in a few weeks, a blue movie of course, and Rose is saying that she's exactly right for the part, they're looking for a woman to play the role of a nymphomaniac business executive, executrix? whatever. Lolita was turning colors but Rose was so sincere that she didn't know what to say, I mean that was the strange thing about Rose. She was somehow sweet, innocent, despite the dirty movies she made a living in. She'd made *Sisters in Shame* and then, in a row, three flicks called *The Party, Chorus Orgy,* and *Silk Sighs,* and by this time, the night I'm talking about, she was a kind of chic celebrity. This came about mainly because of an essay that Saul Blanche wrote on her for *Big Apple,* a serious piece, or it *looked* serious, Saul wrote it straight-faced anyway. As I recall, it went on about the sense of existential dread in Rose's films, and her strange innocence, right, she was innocent the way Sade's Justine is innocent and because of her beauty and purity she's always being seduced or ravished or defiled by the men she meets and this happens over and over again, she never learns anything, she's too good to learn anything from evil, Saul used the phrase accidental body, I think. In other words, let me see now, it went that Rose had a body that was beautiful, voluptuous, sensual, but it was a kind of betrayal of her mind, of her essential morality. Her body got her, you know, into all these perverse scenes. The upshot was that she was a kind of innocent sex-goddess, Saul threw Marilyn Monroe in, *The Perils of Pauline, Dracula,* everything but the kitchen sink. Rose became an underground star, if you were hip, you know, you'd *have* to have seen Rose's flicks. It became fashionable and perfectly respectable for a whole party of people to go and see one of Rose's movies after dinner, that sort of thing. There was even talk that people would go to somebody's place after seeing one of Rose's movies and re-enact scenes from it, I remember that they called these gatherings, these orgies, rose parties or rose gardens. The big movie was *Sisters in Shame,* Saul gave that one a lot of space. Rose played a nun so all of Saul's ideas were brought into focus in that flick, they even ran the son of a bitch at a couple of art-film festivals. Anyway, anyway, what was I? Right, Lolita and the woman she slapped, O.K. Rose was at Barry's place with a woman nobody had ever seen before, maybe about thirty, early thirties, and she just sat there and smiled while Rose was giving her pitch to Lolita. As I said, Lolita was absolutely nonplussed but she had no idea how to handle it because it was so obvious that Rose had no intention of insulting her. Then just as Rose is explaining the financial arrangements that Lolita can expect to make with the guy who's going to make the film, this woman looks at Lolita and then at Rose and says something that sounds like, I don't know, sounds like nothing, gibberish, incomprehensible, and she's making gestures with her hands. Lolita thought she'd insulted her or was making fun of her, I don't know, and she hauls off and gives this woman a slap that almost knocked her off her chair. The woman starts to cry and then Rose is crying and yelling at Lolita, she's really upset, and believe me, Rose was a great cryer, there wasn't a movie she made that she didn't cry in, this was also, I should add, a very big item in Saul's essay. Well, to cut it short, it turns out that this woman, an old friend of Rose's, was deaf and dumb and that what Lolita thought was an insult was this woman just, you know, trying to say something and using sign language and it also turns out that what she was trying to say was that she thought that Rose was embarrassing Lolita. That's what Rose was screaming at Lolita. Then *Lolita* started to cry. Barry was running around like a crazy man, figuring that this was the end of his job almost before it started. As it happened, though, Rose and Lolita and Rose's friend all calmed down and spent the rest of the evening together, thick as thieves.

What were Bart Kahane's motives in following Sheila Henry into the bathroom?

I really can't say, motives, God only knows what motives Bart had for doing anything, he'd started to go around the bend after he and Conchita split up or right after he married Lolita, I can't remember precisely. He followed Sheila into the bathroom in the Caliph's Walk, not The Black Basement. As I recall, Bart went into the happy house some time before The Black Basement even opened, so it would definitely have been in the Caliph's Walk. Bart was working there as the bartender, no, wait a minute, as a waiter, it was soon after Guy Lewis got canned for tapping

the till for a pound here and a pound there, not that he really needed the
money, he was all set by then with Pungoe in the mail-order scheme. Bart
said that he followed Sheila in because he wanted to tell her that the toilet
didn't flush, but that was a lie, the toilet flushed fine. Sheila gave him a
smack across the face and came out of the ladies' room just boiling. It was
no secret that Bart was wild about Sheila and he probably had some idea
that Sheila kind of liked him too. Where he got that idea nobody knew,
Sheila was all innocence, she just said he was weird, you know, kinky,
which seemed to wash, because Marcie Butler had told me and a few other
people that Bart used to buy the kind of perfume she wore, expensive stuff
called Ce Soir, and put it on his pillow and his underwear and under his
arms and he was, you know, *serious* about it. I mean that if somebody
said, you know, how wonderful he smelled or something like, say, Bart,
how about the two of us flying into the night together, you sweetie, it
wasn't funny, was *not* funny to him at all. He'd look in your goddam face
and say, this is Ce Soir, Marcella's scent. And with these blank screwball's
eyes staring straight at you. He also had, Marcie said, a drawerful of
women's hankies, little linen handkerchiefs with a lace trim, all of them
scented with this perfume. He used to have long talks with Sheila about
her perfume, tried to get her to use Ce Soir, he gave her these handkerchiefs, you know, he'd say, here, carry this for a while and see how much
you'll get to love this scent. I think that Sheila was maybe touched, if
that's the word, but she couldn't take him seriously, especially after people
started to call him Les. Poor bastard then occasionally started to answer to
the name, which didn't exactly put him in the role of a Valentino, if you
get what I mean. On top of all this he was a bum waiter, fucked up the
orders, spilled soup, kept people waiting forever for the check, most of the
time because he was on the phone to Lolita, I guess, arguing with her.
Sometimes he'd start to cry and there he'd be, right? slapping down some
poor bastard's shrimp cocktail with the tears streaming down his face and
the smell of perfume off him like a Mexican whorehouse. Anyway, all this
is just by way of preface to why Bart wound up in the nuthouse.

It is?

Yeah. Bart had a lot of problems as long as I knew him. He was a
really brilliant guy, the type that could beat you at chess while he read a
book, you know? Mathematics, physics, they were really his meat, but he
just couldn't get it together, he married Conchita when he was just a kid,

she was too, and he dropped out of college, graduate school, then started making a buck doing theses and dissertations for people. The thing that really wrecked him, or so Lolita said, was that he wrote a Ph.D. dissertation on some complicated math problem for some joker and in it he put all his own ideas, all his own original thinking. I'm saying that what he did was write *his* dissertation and sell it to some guy. And the saddest part of it all is that he did it so he could buy some new furniture for Conchita, they were living in a goddam basement at the time, sitting on these chairs the Salvation Army wouldn't even take off your hands, you know? So he buys a couch and a couple of easy chairs, a coffee table, the usual stuff. Conchita is delighted, but when she finds out where Bart got the money that was really that, it was, I don't know, it was contemptible to her, she started to treat Bart *so* badly. When they had people over Bart would, you know, serve. I don't mean that he'd help out or that he and Conchita would work together, host and hostess, no, Conchita would act as if she'd, I don't know how to put it, as if she'd *hired* him. And one night, one night damned if he didn't serve the whole night wearing an apron and a maid's cap, you know, those frilly little caps with the ribbons? Even Conchita did a double take. And that's how it went from then on, she humiliated him and he humiliated himself, she even took to calling him Berthe in front of guests, visitors, anybody. But Bart *liked* it. Anyway, when he met Lolita she didn't know about this and Bart came on like Jack Armstrong, Mr. Manly Normal, mm-hm. After they were married things must have got hairy, it turned out, I heard from Tania, who heard from Lucy Taylor, *all* the women knew about it, that Bart was impotent unless he played the woman's role. When they made love. Lolita was so upset by this that she didn't know what to do so she started to buy these fancy things, fancy underwear from Soirée Intime to seduce Bart, but it turned out that *he* wanted to wear them. She went along even with this but then he starts nagging her about her dressing like a *man*. That was it. Lolita was devastated, there was no way around it if she wanted sex, I was going to say if she wanted a normal sex life, ho ho ho. To be absolutely crude, he couldn't get it up at all unless they were in each other's clothes, so to speak. This was when he started to wear the Ce Soir, I guess. Must have been. Well. One night at a party Bart was so drunk he could hardly talk, it turned out that earlier in the day Lolita had told him she was going to leave him, at least for a while, you know, to think things out because it all seemed so impossible, and so on. At the party Lolita started to carry on with, of all people, Roger, making a fool of herself, dancing with him and rubbing up against him, she was pretty well sauced herself. Bart is sitting there knocking back the booze and getting drunker by the minute. All of a sudden that goddam pig, Sol Blanc, starts to laugh and point and holler, then everybody looks and Bart's sock, the poor bastard, his sock has slipped down and you can see that he's got nylons, nylon stockings on under the socks. Well, the jokes and the cracks and the hoots and hollers, the place sounds like a rally for Jesus and the grand old flag put together. Bart gets up, the poor miserable bastard, he gets up and pulls his pants off, he's wearing these nylon stockings, women's underwear, and he stands there, he's spitting at people, he's cursing and crying and swinging his arms around, Jesus! Lolita starts to go over to him, she's crying too, and the poor bastard, the poor bastard turns around and just jumps out the window, we're two stories up. He broke his arm and his collarbone, got a concussion, and they took him away to the hospital. From there to the psychiatric ward for observation. Then he was committed. By Lolita. It was really grim, a really grim night.

Who was at the party? All the names.

Oh come on. You're asking me the impossible. I can remember most of the people, but *all* the names? I don't know if I've made it clear but you know that these were parties that attracted all kinds of people, anybody. Some ace from Christ knows where would hear about a party sitting in some bar and he'd show up with all his friends. I'll do my best. I was there but I didn't want to be, I wasn't getting on too well with certain people at the time and I knew they'd be there. Ted Buckie-Moeller, it was his housewarming, you might say it was a spurious housewarming since Ted was subletting a loft for six months, it wasn't, strictly speaking, his place. He was one of the people I wasn't getting along with by the way, he'd run out on me as it were, we were sharing a shotgun flat and he got this sublet and left me with all the bills to pay, rent and gas and electricity and such on the dump and he didn't want me to move in with him because he'd started an affair with Tania at the time, we were supposed to be married in a couple of months and she just gave me the business. Well. O.K. And Bart and Lolita, Roger, Sol Blanc, right, I told you about that fat fool, and Saul Blanche and Marcie, they were still an item in those days before Saul discovered that he was twisted, if you ask me I think he was a phony, I mean he decided to admit that he was gay because it was getting to be sort of hip, you know? O.K. Harlan, Annette, I think maybe Corrie and Madame Delamode, Annie Flammard, Tony Lamont, ZuZu, you know, Lee Jefferson, and I think maybe Henri Kink, but that may be just my imagination. Then there were the usual crashers, drunks and junkies and lames and losers looking for free booze and whatever the hell else was free, and three guys that I found out had been invited, they were supposed to be film makers or some goddam film something, as a matter of fact I believe they were the guys who made the Sister Rose flick, *The Party.* They made a barrel of money on it, so I heard, and Rose, as usual, got screwed, pardon the pun. One guy was supposed to be a hot avant-garde Italian movie genius, I think his name was Tucci or Tucco, Tuccio? I don't recall but he looked like a standard corner deadbeat to me, maybe that was his style, you've got me. He was wearing this old forties-style suit, a one-button lounge they used to call them, pearl gray with white chalk stripes, a white-on-white shirt, a knitted tie and black French-toe shoes. The other two partners I can barely remember, one was a tall dark guy with a big hooked nose who spoke really weird English and the other was an old man with white hair and a beat-up Panama hat, he looked like the classic stereotype of the down-and-out beachcomber, right? I remember that clearly because it struck me that this guy was missing on a couple of cylinders, it was the middle of winter, as a matter of fact it was snowing that night, right, poor old Bart was lying in the snow when we ran down to see how hurt he was. What made me think that these three were just assholes, outside of the fact that they looked like the Three Stooges, was that the old guy with the straw hat was carrying this big bundle wrapped in newspaper, it turned out that it was the manuscript of some monster novel and he spent most of the night trying to get Saul to take the goddam thing for a reading. As far as I know that was it except for, as I said, except for the mobs that came and went looking for some action. To tell you the truth, all I *really* remember is that moment when Bart went out the window, screaming and crying. God. I'll tell you the truth, it didn't bother me a bit when I found out that somebody dropped the dime on Sol Blanc with the immigration people and got the prick deported. That was much later though, I'm way ahead of myself, Sol was getting greedy, greedier by the day, and he tried to muscle in on some prostitution scam that Jack Marowitz had going, some kind of dating-service hustle, Jack was in on this with Annie Flammard and Lorna too for that matter, it was called Marquise Meetings,

Inc. That was Lorna's fine Italian hand. The classified copy was something else. It ran along the lines of, Marquise Meetings, Inc. Are you tired of dates that center on dull, I think they said vapid, on vapid talk of TV, Hollywood, and the so-called adventures of the so-called famous? Talk about pop music, chic restaurants, and Broadway theatre? And best-sellers, this and that, a few more things, fashion. MMI has beautiful, intelligent young hostesses whose conversation will refresh your sense of the truly sophisticated. Some crap like that, what it meant was that some whore had a little ten-minute line about Picasso or Eliot or somebody that she'd give the john before she got down to business. And oh yes, Cecil Tyrell was also at the party, he got into a beef with Tony over something dumb, some writer's thing, all I can recall of that is Cecil standing there, about a quart of vodka in him, saying over and over, What's the fucking exegesis? What's the fucking exegesis? Christ only knows what he was talking about. And Tony is sitting there with a book open saying, Thirty-three times three, thirty-three times three, you goddam idiot, thirty-three times three! Oh it was really a moonlight-and-roses night.

Why were you invited to this party?

Well to tell you the truth I wasn't *really* invited. I certainly wasn't invited by Ted, I think he was surprised when I showed up but he didn't say anything, Tania was embarrassed, that was in the days before she was incapable of being embarrassed, before she became one of the important people. Anyway, I thought that I had to go to see if I could do Guy a favor, he'd asked me to talk to Pungoe about maybe getting that job, you know? The mail-order thing? Wait a minute. This is a little complicated, let me spell it out. I was on fairly close terms, business terms, if you'll pardon the expression, with Harlan then. I'd recommended a couple of hard-up artists to him, he wanted some artists to do some wood-block prints for him. As I recall he wanted to decorate the rooms in some hotel or motel outside the city that he had part interest in and he didn't want the usual horses and trees and dogs and views of Venice, you know the garbage they put on the walls. Anyway, we worked a deal out, he'd pay the artists for the prints and give me ten percent of what he paid them, a sort of finder's fee, I was like an agent, a middleman. It wasn't much money, especially since Harlan often screwed me, but it kept me going, I didn't have much more of an income, really just some money I'd saved. From the days when I was making a lot of money, very good money. Harlan wasn't exactly all heart, or all business for that matter, he really had his eye on Tania, so it turned out. What he wanted was for me to make him look good to Tania, you know, the art connoisseur. I was too dumb to know it but as it turned out even if I'd wanted to, or even if I knew what Harlan wanted, she and Ted had already made their plans. For all I know he got *Ted* to do his work for him, because right after she and Ted moved into this loft she started managing Tete's boutique, almost as if, well, almost as if he and Pungoe had made an arrangement to share her. But I haven't got any proof as to what happened or what didn't. It's all water under the bridge anyway, I don't give a goddam anymore. Well. To get back to Guy, I thought I'd do him this favor and tell Harlan what a hell of a guy he was, a good worker, ambitious, he really needed the money, was he supposed to work for bar tips all his life and so on. I owed Guy this, a lot more really because, well. Because, you see, I used to make a lot of money working for a company that made TV commercials, a fairly small film-production company that did work for ad agencies. I started out taking Polaroid shots of locations, possible locations, that the producer and director could look at to see if they were O.K. to shoot at. For instance, if the commercial was going to be for, let's say corn flakes, and they wanted some all-American schmuck to be eating this shit in the back yard of a typical American house in the suburbs, a typical American suburban street, I'd go out with my camera to a few suburbs and take fifty, a hundred pictures. Then they'd pick the best one, or I should say one that was most in keeping with the sanctity of the product and the show would be on the road. Anyway, one thing led to another, in a year and a half I was an assistant producer with a card yet, and making a lot of money, oh the money they spend in that racket is enough to make you weep. I traveled all over the world, thirty-second spot on a street in Madrid, by Jesus, swarms of people, tons of equipment, everyone and everything went first class to Spain for a whole week. For thirty seconds! Jesus Christ. What I remember from all this is the bars and restaurants and rooms in about a hundred Hiltons. They all look alike, you're having a drink in Paris and you might as well be in Florence or Pittsburgh for Christ sake. Well, it all started to get me down, you know? I couldn't sleep, I started in on the sauce pretty good, lots of uppers, lots of downers, a little coke, you name it. The thing that really cut it was one time we were doing some job for an agency that had a cat-food account. Some genius, a creative director, can you imagine that, they call these scumbags creative directors? These bastards used to sit around and talk about the best way for an actor to hold a roll of toilet paper, the most aesthetic and *convincing* way. These people were serious, I'm not kidding you, *serious* about their useless fucking lives. Anyway. Some creative afterbirth got the idea, I can't recall this too well, I was spaced out day and night then, he got the idea of building this commercial around the notion that cats loved this swill so much that they'd swim to get to it. So we had a bunch of poor goddam cats that we'd throw up in the air and into a swimming pool, they put little swim caps on them, Jesus Christ! Two guys threw them into this pool over and over and over again, they'd *blow-dry* them, a special creative blow-dry team, in the poor little fucks would go again, they were absolutely traumatized, and they'd film away and film away till the director got what he wanted. They had the usual guy from the humane society, right? but they paid him off or somebody gave him a blow job so he'd be sure to keep his mouth shut. So I said, I don't know, what the hell am I doing in this filthy shit and I started to really hit the sauce, I mean *serious* boozing. Then I woke up one morning and I sort of saw myself setting fire to the curtains as if I was somebody else. Then I started to shake. I mean I sort of went around the bend a little, right? So I went away for a while, well, with the help of a shrink I put myself into a sanitarium. I was in this place for about two months, getting straight and drying out, I should tell you that I'd been seeing Marcie before I went away and when I came out she was living with Saul. Well. I don't blame her, our last few months together she might as well have been sleeping with a zombie, I was the living dead, believe me. Anyway, Guy comes in here, I'm sorry to lay all this sorry business on you, Guy comes in here because when I got out he asked me if I'd like to move in with him and Bunny till I got straightened out. So, you know, I owed him. He was a good friend and so was Bunny. The terrible part of it all was that I fell for Bunny, it was mutual, really, but we just, we just *looked* at each other. It was strictly hands off. I wanted her so desperately but for Christ sake! I was in her *house, Guy's* house. He was oblivious, he trusted me, so. Well I got the hell out of there as soon as I could and took a job with, of all people, Annette Lorpailleur, she'd settled in and wanted somebody to do the cleaning and the shopping, wash the clothes, a kind of housekeeper, but she didn't want to hire a woman. She said to me that although men pried as much as women did, men didn't hold what they found out against you. That's neither here nor there. I made her her coffee in the morning, sometimes lunch when she was at home, never dinner. She was always either out or she'd hire a cook when she was having guests. She wasn't so weird then or maybe I just didn't notice, I was really hanging on. Just hanging on. That's how I first got to know Pungoe, through Annette. But at this particular time, the housewarming, things were rather chilly between Pungoe and me since I'd found out about him and Bunny, all that perverse business with her, so I wasn't feeling any too warm toward him although I'm ashamed to say that I didn't let it interfere with our little business arrangement, maybe I should say that *I* was cool toward Harlan but I didn't let him know that I knew. I didn't let Bunny or Guy know either. I kept it to myself. I'll tell you though that it cured me of my feelings for Bunny, when I found out I just felt sorry for her and for Guy too, really, they were caught, you know, just boxed in by circumstances. I've thought about it since. I've thought about it, I mean maybe I *should* have told Guy about it, but what good would it have done? He found out himself later anyway and it didn't help anything. I wish that I hadn't been told about it at all, it was April who spilled the famous beans. Who else? When it came to scandals, especially those involving sex, April was the daily news, she was *everywhere.* I told you about the time that Tania and I were smoking some grass in a bedroom at a dinner party and there was April banging on the door to tell us some dirt she'd found out about somebody, Léonie I think, and Lucy Taylor, who were supposed to be lovers, they used the back of Barnett's boutique where Léonie worked for their rendezvous. April loved it. So, in any event, I went to the damn party and put in a word for Guy with Harlan but I'm sorry I went because I think that I was responsible for Bart jumping out the window. Well, indirectly. Guy had really got me mad because he was ignoring Bunny, she was miserable, but, you know, I had to play it very cool, not seem to be interfering, had I known then that they were married the way, I mean that their marriage was a joke, maybe I would have felt differently. I don't know. But I was in a sour mood. Guy was feeling his oats because Pungoe had more or less told him that the job looked good, he was in, this was after I spoke to Harlan but the son of a bitch never even thanked me, well, O.K. There was Bunny, drunk and making a fool of herself sprawled in a chair with her legs wide open and her skirt too high, a cigarette hanging out of her mouth, she looked like some fucking tramp off the street, spilling her drink all over the front of her dress. And then I got into an argument with Sol, I hated the bastard, the only thing that Annie Flammard and I ever agreed on was Sol. He was sort of the rage according to some precious, some arty little magazine, a faggy photography magazine, what was its name? I can't, oh yes, *Filter Blue,* Christ! The jerk was a Neanderthal, I mean he took pictures the way any slob in the street takes pictures, aim and shoot, he didn't know dick-all about anything. *Filter Blue*'s editor thought he was just too, too charming, right? So, you know, unaffected, so crude, so honest, so cruelly blunt, so *primitive.* Sol's shtick was to take these crummy snapshots of derelicts, bums, drunks, beat-up old ladies. It was sickening to me, a kind of brutal exploitation. So I started to needle him about the travails of being an artist, especially a foreign artist in a crass and philistine country and he took it out on Bart. I ought to add, as long as I'm telling you about Guy, it really got to me that he was the one who laughed loudest at Bart. I figured, at that moment, I didn't owe him another goddam thing. When I think about it I'm sorry now that I didn't give him the horns. Well, maybe he got what he deserved anyway because later he took the fall for Pungoe and Annette on a mail-fraud rap.

Was Guy Lewis married?

Yes, sure, they were married. If you mean, I guess you mean were they legally married, that I don't know, I don't think so. I think that Bunny was always a lesbian, she had a long and very passionate affair with Lorna Flambeaux and she did her damnedest to put the make on Sheila, she probably succeeded, and there was a time there when it was really embarrassing to see. Bunny would get a few in her and she'd start, in front of anybody, I mean *anybody,* to rub up against Sheila, feel her breasts, put her hands up her skirt, try to kiss her. It was really incredible. Sheila went through her patented no-no-no routine for the usual three seconds. The deal with Guy, or so I gathered later from Lucy after she and Bunny went their separate ways, was that when Bunny got away from Harlan she asked her parents for some money for an apartment till she could get a job and so on, her parents weren't too happy with her, right? They were solid suburban citizens and were upset when Bunny dropped out of college. Anyway. She asked them for money for a place, said she was going to go back to school and get her degree, sure sure, but they'd had it with Bunny, then she met Guy and he went out to their place, Katydid Glade, Gnatville, whatever, some classic burg, row houses with the little crabgrass lawns

and the barbecue pits and the petitions against through traffic, the works.
So she said they were going to be married and Guy gave them some line of
crap about working in the restaurant business, he modestly told them of
his dream of owning his own place some day, how much he loved children, the need for a strong America, how he was sick and tired of foreigners taking advantage of us, *us* he said, you could hear the violins. So they
came up with a few grand for their daughter's new leaf, right? And said
they'd give her a little allowance to boot. But as I said, the deal was that
Bunny wanted to live alone and have a clear field with women but she
couldn't lay this on mom and pop, she had to come on like Miss Cover
Girl. I often used to wonder what her parents would have said if they'd got
a look at some of Harlan's photographs of Miss Cover Girl and two
rednecks looking like a bag of pretzels. The old man's clip-on sunglasses
would have melted right into the birdbath. But there was no way that they
were going to give her any bread unless they thought she was settling
down. That's where Guy came in. The problem was that Guy knew that
Bunny wasn't going to marry him but he had no idea that Bunny was a
dyke, as a matter of fact the whole thing looked sweet as sugar to him. I
mean Bunny was not, as they say, hard to look at and she had a gorgeous
body. Then when the whole thing was settled and the money was in the
bag, Bunny starts in with Lorna, then with this woman and that one, her
great passion for Sheila. Then Lucy sort of moved in. It must have been
like living in a sorority house for Guy, not that I feel bad for him, though
I admit I did at the time. I was ignorant of Bunny's proclivities then too,
Guy, give him credit, didn't say a word, in fact a few people had it figured
that Guy was the one who was carrying on with Lorna, you know? The
first time I had an idea, well, an *idea,* it was more than an idea, of what
was really happening, was one night in some bar when Bunny and Lucy
had a lovers' quarrel, it was after Annette had arrived and I'd already, I
think, started working for her. Annette and Lucy were talking and laughing together in a booth, one of those big circular booths, there were about
seven or eight people around the table and Bunny just suddenly flew off
the handle, told Lucy that she wasn't used to being ignored by dowdy
little sluts like her and she climbed over two or three people and was out
of the place in a flash. The veils fell, as they say. Annette just smiled her
weird and sinister metallic smile and Guy suddenly had to tie his shoe,
right? Or go to the men's room. There was, as Doctor Plot would write, a

strained silence. We all pretended that it was just a normal quarrel, had nothing to do with sex, and so on and so forth. The rest of the night was, well, it was just an ordinary night. Lou and Sheila drove me and Guy home as I remember, we lived near them and just a couple of blocks from each other. I was living in a broken-down tenement, Jesus, the walls were painted this dark blackish-green, I used to think that if you wanted to commit suicide this trap would help you right along. As a matter of fact, Tony Lamont used to call it Felo-de-se Towers.

Did Guy make indecent advances to Sheila in the car?

I suppose you might say that, only I don't know if I'd use the word advances, they were a little more than that, at least from what I could see in the rear-view mirror. Lou was pretty well in the bag and asked me to drive or maybe Sheila did. Anyway, I was driving and Lou was next to me in the front and Sheila and Guy were in the back. O.K. So I could see a little, Lou was just sitting there asleep, maybe. Maybe he was asleep or just pretending. I could see that Guy was kissing Sheila and feeling her up, her breasts and her legs, thighs, you know, I couldn't really see. I suppose he had his hand under her skirt too, I had to keep my eyes on the road, right? I mean I wasn't exactly cold sober either. But I'll tell you that son of a bitch Guy had some moxie because, I mean to say that when I got to his place Lou woke up or as I said maybe he wasn't asleep at all and he pretended to wake up, and Guy tells him that Sheila has the most beautiful legs he's ever seen, I'll tell you there was a hell of a lot of them to see too, and I thought to myself, O.K. Now Lou will *have* to say something, whether he knew what was going on in the back seat or not. Believe me, there was a lot of heavy breathing, they weren't even trying to be discreet, almost as if they, you know, wanted Lou to turn around and catch them, well he didn't. I did. There Lou sat, his eyes closed, while they went at it, if Guy had lived a couple of miles further on they would have made it right there. As for me, hell, they must have known that I could see them but that goddam Sheila, well. No sense in thinking about all that now, what's the old phrase, speak nothing but good of the dead? What was I about to, oh right. When Guy makes this remark about Sheila's legs, and he was right, her legs were, well like that old song goes they'd make a preacher lay his Bible down, they started somewhere up around her ribs. He makes this remark and Lou turns around, Jesus Christ almighty! Sheila is straightening her clothes, pulling her skirt down from up around her hips for Christ sake, and Lou says, are they better than Bunny's? I remember that so clearly. Guy is outside the car on the street and he leans in the window for a second, he says, he's got this grim smile on his face, he says, what the fuck would I know about my wife's legs? And the word wife is just, it's just dripping, as they say, with contempt. Then as he starts to turn away by Christ if he doesn't stick his head in the car and look at Sheila. He says, I can't remember exactly, but he says something like thanks for a great evening. Lou is smoking a cigarette and looking into the distance. Happy days. Happy golden days. And it was only the beginning of this thing between Guy and Sheila. As a matter of fact there was another time in Lou's car with Guy and Sheila in the back seat again, they were always in each other's pockets then, this was later, I mean it was after the night I just mentioned, I was in the car in the front with Lou, Lou was doing the driving and I think, yes, Léonie was between us, I was seeing a lot of her then. She was in bad shape with that bastard Tete, that was just about the time he gave her the business by hiring Sylvie Lacruseille, you remember? Luba Checks, to run the boutique. I was trying to persuade Léonie to quit the place and start to write again. I thought that maybe I could get Saul to talk to Lee Jefferson and get her to publish something in *Hip Vox,* nothing came of any of it. Léonie would write a sentence then get up and walk around her apartment and then open the vodka. When I came in she'd start in on me, she would be really abusive. But. But at other times she'd be really beautiful, just, I don't mean to be corny, but just radiant. She was a beautiful woman. This is all so old and vague, so old and dead, I must be crazy even to think about it all. We were seeing each other a lot, I was feeling really low and she was feeling lower if possible, we must have been some pair. I was Mister Joy and she was Miss Laughter. So there we all were in the car, they were on their way to someplace, a party, always a fucking party, we were always en masse in those days. Our Gang. They were driving me and Léonie, if I'm thinking of the right evening, to a lecture, yes, right. A lecture by some member of a radical-lesbian-feminist group, the one I told you about that Ellen was in, the Tribade Conspiracie, spelled with c i e at the end, conspira*cie,* c i e, they thought it was a more feminine ending than a y. What in the name of sweet suffering Jesus we were going for I don't know, we never did get there, but for some reason Léonie thought she should go, it was some sort of talk or panel discussion or colloquium on literary innovation or experimentation or something, the avant-garde being just another repressive tool of the white-male-hetero-sexual establishment. I imagine you've been here before but it just came back to me. If I wanted I could probably reconstruct the arguments for you cliché by cliché. But anyway. They were going to their party and we were going to this fire-eating discussion that would wind up no doubt by turn-ing Sara Teasdale into the greatest thing since canned beer. O.K. You should know that a little while before this Guy had moved in, sort of moved in with Lou and Sheila, he and Bunny were really on the rocks, they couldn't, as the shining phrase goes, stand the fucking sight of each other. So Guy had, as I say, just *sort* of moved in since he left most of his clothes and things at his place. But he was very much *there* at the Henrys' apartment. He and Sheila must have been jumping into the sack at every opportunity. And Lou ignored it. I guess. Hell, I don't know, maybe he watched for all I know, maybe they had cozy little parties, I wouldn't put much past Sheila. Anyway, in the car I turned around to say something to Guy and they were at it, both, you know, in, their clothes were in disarray, to be discreet I mean they just didn't, they did *not* give a good goddam, it was really unbelievable. Then Léonie looked around, Sheila was strad-dling Guy, Lou was just, Jesus Christ! just driving, I think he asked me to find some jazz on the radio, jazz indeed! Léonie asked Lou to stop the car and she got out and pulled me out after her. Lou took off again, staring, you know, straight ahead, and his wife and Guy were just oblivious to everything there in the back seat, just, well, they were just fucking their brains out. I don't know how many times this sort of thing happened in the car, I should say it wasn't just the *car*, it was that the car was a kind of extension of the bedroom. Or the couch or the floor or the closet or the bathroom. Sheila and Guy were just, you know, they were wearing it *out*. And of course the car, well, it was a car accident that killed Sheila but that time, that was one time that Guy wasn't there, he had the flu or something, a virus. That time it was just Lou and Sheila and me.

What were you doing in the car?

Well it was a few months later, let me think. They were on their way to a party, yet another party, and they were dropping me off at the train station. I'd been invited for the weekend, it was a long weekend, I think it was either Memorial Day or the Fourth of July, it was warm any-way. I'd been invited to Dick and April's beach house for the weekend, Dick was making barrels of money, he had some kind of a business ar-

rangement with Barnett and somebody else, I can't remember who, something to do with limited-run tapestries, or one of a kind wall hangings
made from famous paintings or paintings by well-known artists. It was
shady, what else would it be with Barnett involved? They didn't bother to
get the artists' permissions or the permissions of their estates, they charged
some obscene prices for this stuff, most of it went to Latin America, sleazy
government officials who didn't know what to do with their loot, I don't
know. Anyway, I was going for the weekend. We were driving along when
suddenly Sheila starts to take off her clothes and throw them into the front
seat, I'm sitting next to Lou and Sheila's dress goes flying, then her slip,
her bra, her underpants. Lou stops the car and Sheila for Christ sake gets
out! She gets out of the goddam car. She stood right in front of it banging
on the hood in nothing but her shoes and stockings, a little garter belt. Lou
was crying, it was really grim, then Sheila started to run down the street,
people were looking at her, this naked, good as naked woman. Then she
ran back toward the car and when she was about twenty feet in front of it,
I don't know, it just shot forward and Lou, Lou. The car ran her down. She
died. She broke her neck. Jesus Christ. Lou got out and stood there, stood
over her, I knew she was dead just the way she got hit, the way she got
knocked just flat. Snap. Jesus Christ. We'd been drinking most of the afternoon but Sheila could hold her liquor, I don't know what the hell happened for her to just, to simply freak out the way she did. We were just
sitting there, I was sitting right next to her, we were all talking, as a matter
of fact we were gossiping about the Detectives, Sheila called them Mister
and Mrs. Rollei. Everything seemed very funny, we'd smoked a little grass,
you know? Not a hell of a lot of grass. Then all of a sudden Sheila gave me
a strange look and reached down to the hem of her dress and pulled it up,
her dress, I said hey! Wait a minute! Then she pulled her dress right *off*,
she threw it at Lou, then, you know, her underclothes. I tried to stop her
from taking her bra off and Lou was, you know, Lou was crazy, he was
reaching back to her and driving at the same time. My God. When I tried
to hold her arms she butted me in the face with her head, I guess that was
when Lou stopped the car and Sheila just jumped out into the street. Lou
started to chase her, then he ran back to the car. Then he got back in as I
recall. Or it was just before Sheila started to run back toward us that he
came back to the car, he asked me to, you know, he gestured, waved his
arms, I guess he wanted me to follow them in the car but by the time I

reacted, I mean that I had to get into the front seat because I was in the back because I'd got back there when Sheila threw her dress at Lou, at the both of us, to try and stop her from going really, well, really crazy, right? By the time I got into the front seat again Lou was back in the car and Sheila was standing there about twenty feet away in the headlights, laughing and screaming and cursing like a madwoman and giving me the finger, or the both of us, I don't know. Then the car just, Jesus Christ. I remember, so clearly, sitting there in the front listening to "Scrapple from the Apple," it's odd what you remember.

What was the occasion for the party to which they were going?

Jesus, I don't know. It wasn't actually a party, it was a reception at a bookstore for Cecil Tyrell to honor the publication of his *Orange Steel*. Sheila didn't even want to go. She hated Cecil, I told you that, I think.

There have been persistent rumors that Lou Henry owed something to Guy Lewis and that this debt was the reason that Guy was tolerated as a more or less permanent guest in Lou's home. What, if anything, did Lou owe Guy?

As far as I know, he owed him nothing. Lou was a mark and Guy was a manipulator. Besides, Guy wasn't a permanent, as you say, guest, and it was Sheila who invited him, really. They were hot for each other, O.K.? As simple as that. Sheila was a, let's say she was a free spirit.

What was Sheila wearing?

What was she wearing. Let me, I don't think I really remember, but it might have been a pale blue dress, or maybe lavender. She had a dress like that that she wore to, you know, special, if you will, special parties. Very soft filmy material, maybe it was silk, I think that was it, that particular pale blue dress, but it's hard to remember. All I see when I think of it is Sheila in those damn headlights in nothing but her shoes and stockings, her clothes, I don't, and her other clothes, I mean her underclothes, it seems to me that they, her slip and other things were white. They were, yes, probably white. Sheila always wore white underwear, very plain, chaste. What a word. But I think that was it. She had on white underclothes and that very soft, that very soft pale blue dress. I don't remember her shoes. Heels, but I don't remember them.

Earlier you mentioned, in passing, that there had been a lot of drinking. What sort of drinking?

Just, hell, you know, drinking. It was, it had to be a Friday afternoon, early afternoon, I went over to Lou and Sheila's with my bag, because as I said, they were going to give me a lift to the station. I was a little surprised because when I got there Pungoe and Annie Flammard were there in the living room and it was, well, you know that feeling you get when people have been talking about something they don't want you to know about. That was how it was, I came in and everybody just shut up. They all seemed well on the way so I poured myself a big drink, gin on the rocks I think, a new taste thrill. Hell, I don't know, we started talking about all sorts of things, it was strictly social. So it seemed to me. Then we I guess smoked a little grass, actually it was hash, Annie had a big piece of it, she was, I think, dealing at the time. Maybe not. It doesn't matter. We all got stoned anyway. I imagine that I was hoping to get so wasted that I'd miss the train because the last thing on earth I wanted to do was spend a weekend with Dick and April, you know? They'd told me they had a great time planned and when the Detectives planned things, run do not walk to the nearest exit. It was strictly murder in the henhouse. They gave a, they called it a winter carnival once at their place in Vermont, dear sweet Christ! That was a kind of parody of a comedy of manners if you can imagine such a thing. A lot of sex and jealousy and weeping, people sick and depressed. Well, that's got nothing to do with all this. The point is that we were all feeling, as they say, no pain. Pungoe and Annie for some reason seemed especially smug, I don't quite know how to say it, the cat that ate the canary. So we were smoking and drinking, listening to some music, and I recall that we were talking about Henri's novel, *Mouth of Steel,* because Lou had, I think, just got a catalogue from a book dealer, modern first editions, you know, and Henri's book was listed, a presentation copy Lou said, at five hundred dollars. I've often wondered who sold Henri's book. Anyway, this and that, we just talked. After a couple of hours Pungoe and Annie said they had to go and then Sheila went into the bedroom to get dressed. I sat with Lou and Christ knows, I think Lou started to complain and bitch and moan about, what else? Guy. I didn't want to hear this. Besides, I figured Guy would come out from under the couch for Christ sake, the man who came to dinner. Guy wasn't there though, as I said, he was sick or something. Where he was I don't know and I didn't give a good goddam. I can't begin to tell you how disgusted I was with all the, with everything, with everybody, it was all just, I don't know how to describe it. Just shit, you know? Shit. I really hated every motherfucking one of them, men and women and myself included. I went into the bathroom because I could see that Lou was getting ready to cry all over me about his whore of a wife and how much he adored her and I didn't need it. I'm in the bathroom washing my hands and face, wasting time, stoned but not that stoned and I see an envelope on the floor, a manila envelope propped between the toilet and the back wall, so I pick it up. I'm not really a snooper but something, oh hell, I don't know, who the hell cares anyway, I open the thing. O.K. Inside there's a bunch of color photographs. One shows a table around which there are four men, the great Pungoe, Barnett and Horace, and a fourth guy I didn't recognize, but he really didn't look like a man, more like a woman dressed like a man, short black hair, no make-up. Anyway. There's a lamp in the corner. It was obvious, I should add, that it was taken in Horace's apartment. O.K. There's a lamp in the corner and under the lamp a pile of clothes, they looked like women's clothes but I really couldn't tell. Then there's a second photograph, the same four looking at a woman with her back to the camera, she's naked except for a pair of black high-heeled boots and a black slouch hat, a wide-brimmed hat and the third picture, the woman is on her hands and knees and the guy who doesn't look like a guy at all is giving it to her from behind, he's still completely dressed. The other three, dear pals all, Harlan, Horace and Barnett are still at the table watching. You couldn't tell who the woman was at all because of her big hat. So I'm looking at these photos, thinking that they must have something to do with Annie, but what the hell are they doing here? One thing I *could* tell was that the woman wasn't Sheila, I mean because Sheila, Sheila wouldn't do such a thing, you can say that for her despite her, well, her appetites. Then there were five more photographs, taken outdoors, Christ knows where, trees and shrubs, flowers, a formal English garden, it could have been anywhere. The pictures were of, let me think, Vance, Jack Towne, Jesus yes, Jack, and he looked wonderful, Lincoln Gom, John Hicks, that creepy bastard, and who else? I can't remember the fifth one but it was a man, they were all men. Who the hell? I really can't remember. There was also, of all things, a dust-jacket picture, I mean clipped from a dust-jacket, of the woman I told you about, the critical work? Ann T. Redding. Doctor Redding. Same picture I'd seen in the library, so somebody else must have been curious about the name and that rumor about Annette. Something like that or else why would they have the picture? I put everything back where it had been and went out to the living room. I was thinking of mentioning it to Lou, not that I'd looked at the stuff, I felt a little sleazy about that, but just that there was an envelope in the bathroom, you know, as if maybe he'd dropped it or Pungoe or Annie had dropped it, but Sheila was ready and I just let it go. We had a few more drinks and Sheila made some sandwiches and we had a bite then we, as I said, we left. I wish I could remember that fifth man but I'll be damned if I can.

The seating arrangement in the car?

I thought I told you? Well, maybe not really. It was a little confused, complicated I suppose. When we got to the car Sheila told me to sit in the back by myself, she was very very chilly toward me. I should say cold, ice cold. I don't know why but she turned it right on. Asking me, excuse me, *telling* me to sit in the back was but one manifestation, as they say, of her displeasure. O.K. For some reason, maybe because he was drunk, Lou decided to be masterful, Mister Husband. So after a couple of blocks he pulled over and said he wanted to talk to me and he'd be goddamned if he was going to keep turning around all the time. Sheila didn't say a word, she got out, I got out. Then she got in the back and I got in the front. But, oh Christ! the whole thing was absolutely ridiculous. The crazy woman refused to close the door until I got *back* into the back with her. I could see Lou was about to break his jaws grinding his teeth, right? I was going to just say fuck the both of you and get a cab when Lou says, all right, humor her, the bitch, something like that. All right. She and I are in the back and she starts to get amorous. To be blunt, she starts to grope me, feel me up, but she's being obvious the way she acted with Guy. You know, she's acting as if it's all a big joke so that Lou can see that there's nothing, what shall I say? nothing furtive. Fun on the road! Anyway. Anyway. Christ, this is all so futile. Anyway, I objected to this, you know, all this hearty laughter while the smoke is coming out of my ears and I'm about to bust through my pants like the guys in the dirty comic books. Oh God, Sheila. So I finally got back in the front seat and the next thing was, I told you the next thing. Sheila started to undress.

Was it still twilight, or had it already grown dark?

When we started out it was still a little light, that very pale light, but when Sheila got hit, when she got hit we, she was in the headlights. So it was almost dark, but not quite. It was also sort of misty, a kind of very quiet, very beautiful night. It rained later. But at that time, earlier, it was absolutely lovely, still, and in a way very mysterious, peaceful. The really curious thing about it was that after Sheila was dead, they came, they took her to the hospital and pronounced her dead, this curious thing came into my mind. It had to do with Leo's novel, *Isolate Flecks,* you know, Leo Kaufman. There's a scene in the book that describes a foggy, misty night in the city just like that night. And Sheila used to laugh her head off over that passage. She'd say that it was a perfect example of Leo's way out of all problems, she'd say, look at that stupid book! When Leo gets stuck he always describes nature. I'm damned if she wasn't right and the fog business, the mist, all that garbage for some reason that especially amused her. Really tickled her. Anyway, what I was getting at is that it occurred to me later that night sitting with Lou in the dark, drinking, I mean it occurred to me, I wondered if Sheila remembered that scene when she was out in the street. I wonder if she did.

What was left in the dresser in The Red Swan Inn?

In the top left drawer: a small toy tin pig wearing a sailor suit and carrying a drum; a postcard depicting a view of San Francisco taken from Twin Peaks on the back of which is written in blue ink the word "cupcakes"; a pink paper napkin on which is crudely printed the image of a filled cocktail glass from which bubbles rise and the words HELEN AND TROY'S OHIO'S FREINDLIEST COCKTAIL LOUNGE; a peach-colored silk slip with white lace hem and bodice.

In the second left drawer: a slender pamphlet entitled "Sexology: 100 Facts"; a book of matches on which is printed LENTO'S BAR AND GRILLE STEAKS CHOPS PIZZA SANDWICHES FINE LIQUORS; an empty Bromo-Seltzer bottle; a peach-colored silk slip with white lace hem and bodice.

In the third left drawer: a color slide of an abstract expressionist painting entitled *The Valley of the Shadow of Death*; a photograph of three young girls on a parched lawn, one wearing a summer dress and the others pullovers and short pants; an issue of a film magazine called *Flikk*; a peach-colored silk slip with white lace hem and bodice.

In the bottom left drawer: a brittle sepia-tone photograph of four women and two men, dressed in white, playing lawn croquet; a garishly colored postcard depicting a large hotel with two of its windows each marked with an "X" in black ink, on the back of which is written, in the same black ink, "We're having *some* fun!! See you soon. Love, The Kids"; a photograph of a black man sitting on a bed cradling a tenor saxophone in his arms; a peach-colored silk slip with white lace hem and bodice.

In the top right drawer: a scorecard of a baseball game between two semipro teams, the Crystals and the Ambers, noting that the game was called after three full innings of play for unknown reasons; a throwaway brochure claiming that Mrs. Louise Ashby, a Healer, Reader, Adviser, Seeress, and Prophet, will reveal the sickness that is in you; a children's book entitled *The Daddy and the Drake* by Louis Condy with watercolors by "Georgette"; a peach-colored silk slip with white lace hem and bodice.

In the second right drawer: a photograph of a ten-year-old boy with a crossed left eye holding a kitten up as if for our inspection; an unopened package of Camel cigarettes; a leather tobacco pouch half-filled with tobacco; a peach-colored silk slip with white lace hem and bodice.

In the third right drawer: three decks of Tarot cards: the Tarot of Marseilles; the Tarot of Oswald Wirth; the Tarot of Arthur Edward Waite illustrated by Pamela Colman Smith; a peach-colored silk slip with white lace hem and bodice.

In the bottom right drawer: a short French novel entitled *La Musique et les mauvaises herbes;* a newspaper clipping of an interview with a congressman's wife; a black-and-white drawing of an extraordinarily odd-looking wagon or cart; a black silk slip with black lace hem and bodice.

Can you give me any more information on her?

Soon after being granted her Ph.D. from the University of Chicago—her dissertation was titled "Sexual Desire as Evidenced in Selected Phonemic Groupings in Virginia Woolf's *Mrs. Dalloway*"—Dr. Redding was discovered in a compromising situation with First Lieutenant Evelyn Leonard of the Women's Army Corps at the New Ecstasy Motor Inn outside Webster Groves, Missouri.

Dr. Redding later denied that it had been she and strongly implied that the woman in bed with Lieutenant Leonard had been her twin sister, Phyllis Redding, the manager of the Naughty Nightie boutique in nearby Kirkwood and a locally well-known champion of unpopular liberal causes.

Eight years later, Dr. Redding became the President of the radical-feminist organization, The Daughters of Durga International, and two years after that was awarded an honorary membership in the radical-lesbian organization, the Tribade Conspiracie.

To what thing or place or idea or whatever does the title, *99*, that she gave to that sculpture, refer?

Annie Flammard made six sculptures: *Blackjack, Amber Glass, Lorzu, The Caliph, Ten Eyck Walk,* and *The Metallic Fly.*

What was the name of the fifth person in the series of erotic photographs found in the bathroom by him?

Pamela Ann Johanssen, an aspiring actress, whose professional name was Pamela Clairwil.

She had been one of the earliest members of the Tribade Conspiracie, but had been expelled from that organization for "pandering to base male fantasies of the lesbian way of life."

Then if it wasn't Ward, what *was* her maiden name?

Harlan.

Joanne Jeanne Judith "Bunny" Harlan.

Was he Ellen Marowitz's father, or was he her brother?

Jack Marowitz, born Jacob Marowitz, was the real name of Jackie Moline, the owner of a small bar-café called The Black Basement, which was, in actuality, a drop for stolen goods.

He had two sisters, Sheila, who married Louis Henry, and Sandra, her identical twin, who was, for twelve years, an assistant to the creative director of a Tel Aviv advertising agency.

She disappeared while scouting locations outside a small village near the Lebanese border.

Jack Marowitz had no children.

Can you give me a description of her so-called "metal" apartment?

Annette Lorpailleur had no apartment of her own, "metal" or otherwise.

She lived in a suite that consisted of a sitting room, a bedroom, and a bathroom in the large cooperative apartment owned by Harlan Pungoe, whose maid, mistress, and confidante she was for six and a half years.

After leaving Mr. Pungoe's employ, she depended on the kindness and good will of friends for her living accommodations.

Then what *is* the novel about?

Blackjack deals with a scandal centered on a respected teacher of creative writing at a major university who steals characters, ideas, plots, themes, and even locales from his students and uses those materials useful to him to write his own stories, which he publishes in literary magazines of limited circulation under a pseudonym, John Black.

Ultimately, he publishes a collection of these stories to extremely favorable reviews, sells the book to a paperback publisher and a film producer, and is honored by the award of three prestigious literary prizes to the collection.

At this point, the teacher's true identity becomes known, and his ex-students sue him for plagiary.

He retains a brilliant and beautiful woman lawyer who success-fully defends him by demonstrating, in court, that the stories that the teacher has purportedly plagiarized, as well as the stories written and published by him, are almost identical, in theme, construction, and technique, with thirty-three stories, selected from five nationally known magazines, published over the five-year period preceding the trial.

Her defense of her client lucidly and penetratingly argues that any one work of popular fiction is substantially the same as all other works of popular fiction.

The teacher is acquitted and the novel ends with him and the lawyer registering at a charming country inn as "Mr. and Mrs. Jack Black."

Was the book written by Annette Lorpailleur or by Henri Kink?

La Bouche métallique or *Mouth of Steel* was written by Annette Lorpailleur.

The only known work by Henri Kink is a poem that appeared in a long-defunct little magazine, *Blue Filter.*

It is titled "Poem" and reads:

What are the various fragments of memory?
—bits of dark sky or silk in a drawer
and dead voices from old photos
on the walls: bitter inventory.

I am a man with a notebook who
thinks himself sane, I am probably sane
but assaulted by these shards of the bizarre,
these phenomena of decay.

So that my voice is trapped
with the lost voices in the photographs
suddenly my body fades smudged
into the pieces of sky faded blacker—

Are the accounts that I've been given of their deaths and disap-pearances substantially correct?

No.

None of these people has either died or disappeared.

Vance Whitestone and Lincoln Gom jointly own a small, lucrative costume shop, The Good Company, that supplies costumes for sale or rent.

Their most popular items are: Saucy French Maid, Naughty Nurse, Blushing Nun, Cute Cop, Boss Lady, and Madame Doctor.

Jackson Towne is the day bartender at a chic and expensive cocktail lounge, Caliph's Walk.

Sheila Henry has just published her first book of poems, *Fretwork.*

John Hicks is an advocate for homosexual rights whose weekly column appears in the magazine, *Toujours Gai.*

Henri Kink is an assistant producer for the daytime television serial, *A Waste of Shame.*

What were the particulars of the scandal attendant upon his marriage to Sylvie Lacruseille?

There was no scandal.

There was no marriage.

Such a marriage would have been, and is manifestly impossible.

Dr. John Rube is a fictional character.

Sylvie Lacruseille, *née* Luba Checks, is a real human being.

And what were her duties, if you'll pardon the word, when she worked for Blanche Neige Press?

Marcella Butler never worked for Blanche Neige Press.

The women who worked there were: Lorna Flambeaux, Tania Crosse, and Lena Schmidt.

April Detective occasionally worked for the press on a freelance basis.

You mean that the so-called factual data used by one of my informants were tampered with before my investigation began?

Yes, but not enough of the data to change substantially the information that was given you.

Much of the tampering, if you will, had to do with the chronology of and participants in certain events, changed by persons unknown for reasons that are not at this time wholly clear.

May I see the floor plan of Horace Rosette's apartment?

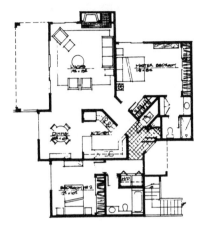

Then they were *not* the producers of *The Party?*

No.

The Party was produced by a partnership incorporated as White Sun Talent Associates, Inc.

The partnership consisted of three men, Janos Kooba, an emigré from Yugoslavia; Edward Beshary, an ex-professor of linguistics who had left his university post under the cloud of a vaguely defined charge of moral turpitude; and Albert Pearson, an unemployed society-band drummer.

These three had made a fortune in the development of a complex board game, based on the Tarot, the Ouija board, and basic elements of goetic practice, and marketed as The Fool's Paradise.

The film, *The Party,* was vastly and almost unrecognizably different from its original script, written by Craig Garf, and starred Florence Claire, Tamara Flynn, Chet Kendrick, and Thompson Richie.

It opened to savagely bad reviews but currently enjoys a certain cult status among those who claim to see in it a subtle existential dread and an unintentionally strange innocence.

Can you describe this old photograph?

It is a photograph of Dr. Ann Taylor Redding taken when she was eleven years old.

She is sitting cross-legged in the middle of a formal English garden behind a large frame house and she wears a short-sleeved light-colored summer dress, anklets, and Mary Jane shoes.

In her right hand there is an ice-cream cone, partially consumed.

She smiles into the camera.

Across the street, parked by the yard of a neighbor's house, is an old Chevrolet coupe, and in the yard three girls, about the same age as Dr. Redding, are sitting side by side.

Two of them are wearing dresses and one a pullover and short pants.

They are smiling at a clubfooted man who is standing about ten feet in front of them, gesturing with one hand.

In his other hand he holds a camera.

What does the phrase "metallic constructions" mean?

Metallic Constructions is an inaccurate, or perhaps more fairly, an unsatisfactory translation of a technical work on engineering, *Les Constructions métalliques,* by Gaspard Monge, the inventor of descriptive geometry.

Monsieur Monge was also the author of a famous—or infamous— novel of the Décadence, *Une Nouvelle Dimension,* published in 1874.

This work is usually attributed to Philothée O'Neddy, since Monge published it under the pseudonym of Théophile Dondey, which was O'Neddy's real name.

Appalled by this cavalier appropriation of his identity, O'Neddy, or Dondey, challenged Monge to a duel in which the latter was killed.

Can you tell me why I was directed to ask my fifth informant the same questions, in reverse order, that I asked my third informant?

No.

What sort of things were strewn about on the study floor?

A sleeveless shift of off-white raw silk, a black evening gown of some shiny metallic fabric, a gray tweed skirt and jacket, a black-and-white-figured rayon scarf, a pale blue silk tailored blouse, smoke-shade nylon stockings, beige nylon stockings, black silk full-fashioned stockings, white nylon panties with white lace trim, a black lace corselette, white cotton panties, a pink silk sleeveless dress, a white lace French garter belt, a white nylon garter belt with lace front panel, a white nylon brassiere, a white cotton brassiere, black sling high-heeled shoes, black stiletto-heeled pumps of some shiny metal, tan stack-heeled shoes with small silver buckles, a tortoiseshell barrette, a pair of glasses with tortoiseshell frames, an orange silk dress, and a habit and wimple of the kind worn by the Sisters of Charity.

Was she a real nun?

Rose Zeppole was a registered nurse who worked for twelve years in the small clinic of a year-round vacation resort, Blue Runes, which catered to honeymooners and singles.

She is presently nurse and companion to Lena Schmidt, a victim of traumatic or psychosomatic blindness.

Miss Schmidt is the director of a prestigious art gallery that specializes in contemporary metal sculptures, or, more precisely, constructions.

Then there *was* a body found there?

Yes.

The police identified the body as that of Karen Ostrom, an executive secretary who had recently resigned from her job at White Sun Talent Associates, Inc.

Miss Ostrom had falsely registered at The Red Swan as Jeannette Grande, but the police have yet to find a motive for her doing so, or indeed to find a motive for her registering at all.

Her luggage consisted only of an attaché case that contained, according to the police, "a diary, an appointment book, an address book, and a heavily corrected typescript of what seems to be a confidential business report in a pale blue file folder."

Do you think it odd or suspicious that so many of the people who have turned up in our investigation have French—or what seem to be French—names?

No.

It is not our investigation.

Was she a novelist or a boutique manager—or was her name but a pseudonym used by a writer, by some—by *any* writer?

Sylvie Lacruseille worked as a registered nurse for fourteen years, after which she became a very expensive prostitute who serviced clients, both male and female, who had what might be called exotic sexual tastes.

She is currently married to Barnett Tete and is extremely popular and active as the chairwoman of several cultural and charitable organizations, as well as being the founder and president of an inner-city housing-renovation group, Concrete Proposals.

What do you mean by "personal treasures and keepsakes and such"?

For instance, behind the bar of the Red Silk restaurant, the owner has a perfect scale-model of the interior of the Red Silk restaurant, made by Bart Kahane out of toothpicks.

Horace Rosette has a key-ring charm of gold and cloisonné that represents one of his most famous anthologies, *Bridges: Poets Express Their Love.*

Harlan Pungoe carries a tiny pair of black bikini panties with black lace trim in the change purse of his wallet.

Tania Crosse has, on her bedroom dresser, a beautiful doll dressed as Sister Rose Zeppole in her role in *Sisters in Shame.*

Dr. Ann Taylor Redding has, on her desk, a small brass figurine of the Hindu goddess, Durga.

Antony Lamont has a sepia print, greatly reduced, of a rare photograph of James Joyce reclining on a couch dressed in his wife, Nora's, clothes.

Guy and Bunny Lewis have in their bathroom a novelty ashtray, in the shape of a toilet bowl, that plays the Victor Herbert song, "Beautiful Dreamer," when the seat is lifted.

Barnett Tete has a virtually priceless drawing by Fragonard showing the poet Horace writing in a mirror-lined room and surrounded by harlots in wantonly abandoned poses.

Lolita Kahane has a small wooden crucifix, blessed by Pope Pius XII, on the back of which is printed, in faded blue ink, FLINT, CITY OF PROMISE.

Sheila Henry has a pornographic love letter of four typed, single-spaced pages sent her by an anonymous female admirer.

Roger Whytte-Blorenge has a pair of Annette Lorpailleur's black ankle-strap high-heeled shoes.

April and Dick Detective have a first edition presentation copy of *Roberte ce soir,* on the flyleaf of which is written, "À mon prochain Donatien, Toujours, Pierre 1953."

Chico Zeek has, on the wall above his bed, a photograph of Barry Gatto in his role as Duke Washington in *Hellions in Hosiery,* inscribed, "To 'Chico' with love, Baylor."

Marcella Butler has the heavily corrected typescript of a poem by

Roberte Flambeaux titled "Renée-Pélagie: The Ecstasy of Her Agony."

Duke Washington has the alto-saxophone reed used by Sonny Stitt on the famous original recording of "Ko-Ko."

Dick Detective has at least one photograph of everyone he has ever known.

Barnett Tete has the original manuscript, stolen from the Bibliothèque Nationale, and substituted for by a perfect forgery, of Monge's *Géométrie descriptive.*

Guy Lewis has a photograph, taken by a Baby Brownie, of Ann Taylor Redding, at the age of eleven, standing in the rose garden of her family's home in Webster Groves, Missouri.

Lee Jefferson has a complete set of repro proofs of the first number of *Lorzu,* inscribed: "To Zooz from her adoring slave, Craig."

Lincoln Gom has the prints and negatives of a series of erotic photographs of Tania Crosse with an unidentified man and woman taken the week before she became the manager of the Soirée Intime.

Lena Schmidt has a copperplated ear trumpet that once belonged to her grandmother, Helga Schmidt McGrath.

Anne Kaufman has the manuscript of a piece of juvenilia by Leo Kaufman, a short story called "Sleeping With the Lions."

Lucy Taylor has a pink latex dildo that she calls "Big Yank."

Page Moses has an empty manila file folder labeled THE PARTY, given him by a private investigator, Donald Plot.

Guy Lewis has a set of keys to a car once owned by Lou Henry.

Léonie Aubois has three curiously affectionate fan letters, given to her as a present by Barnett Tete, from Herbert Hoover to Tom Mix.

Annette Lorpailleur has a gold medallion into which is meticulously incised the seal of the demon Paimon.

Cecil Tyrell has four scrapbooks filled with more than five hundred articles clipped from newspapers and magazines over a twenty year period, all of which bear the title, "The Avant-Garde: Finally Dead?"

Barry Gatto has a full-dress uniform of an officer of the Peruvian Army, complete with braids, medals, and sash.

Sheila Henry has her own Certificate of Death in a frame on her dresser.

Conchita Kahane has her high school Spanish primer, *Primer Curso de Español.*

Biggs Richard has an untitled and unsigned manuscript of eight hundred and twelve pages, found in a taxi, that purports to prove conclusively that all artists, throughout recorded history, were actively or latently homosexual.

Karen Ostrom has a toy airplane on whose wings is printed the legend, WELCOME TO KANSAS CITY.

There are many more which it is pointless to catalogue.

What is the importance of this catalogue to my investigation?

If the catalogue, or any catalogue or list, is understood to be a system, its entropy is the measure of the unavailability of its energy for conversion into useful work.

The ideal catalogue tends toward maximum entropy.

Stick it in your ear.

What titles might best describe the study I will undoubtedly write on these people and their relationships?

White Shifts, Permanent Guests, Envelopes, Consensus, Acquisitions, Heavy Machinery, Labors of Love, Doubles Cross, Odd Numerals, Indelible Experiences, Strange Coincidences, Complicated Webs, Qualifications, Lack of Evidence, A Grain of Salt, Blinding Clarity, Construction in Metal, Twilights, Dead Beats, Environments, Parts of the Gangs, Cults and Coteries, Reams and Reams, Complex Resolutions, Little Cabals, Ventriloquists' Dummies, Official Mouths, Set Pieces, Farfetched, Cameras Work, Accidental Bodies, Lens and Shutter, Growing Dark.

Why is there such a dearth of information on her?

Because of the ignominious manner in which she was permanently crippled.

While drunkenly slopping hogs for her husband, Antonia Harley fell into the sty and was attacked and badly injured by two boars, Homer and Dante, and a sow, Sappho.

Why was it his favorite book?

Harlan Pungoe believes that *A Pack of Lies,* which he knew almost by heart, and quoted from daily, helped him to keep his essentially American values intact despite the unavoidable and occasionally unfortunate business dealings that involved him in fraud, forgery, blackmail, arson, extortion, drugs, rape, prostitution, assault, murder, and what he somewhat obscurely referred to as Christian pornography.

How long did he spend in the mental hospital before being re-water into wine.

SE, who gives skill in all abstruse sciences and true answers
g secret things, who can change human beings into any shape
agician may desire, so that those that are changed will not know
ho can also reduce them to such a state of insanity that they will
eir identity changed, which delusion will last for as long as the
may desire.

PHOENIX, who speaks marvelously of all arts, proves an excel-
, and fulfills all and any orders admirably.

PAIMON, who speaks with a distant voice, teaches the arts of
rphosis, gives and confirms wealth and dignities, and makes hu-
ngs subject to the will of the magician.

SYTRY, who procures sexual love of all kinds, and causes women
themselves naked, *jussus secreta libenter detegit feminarum, eas
udificansque ut se luxorise nudent.*

What do you mean by "perhaps more important papers" on his

On his desk there is a manuscript, a typescript, to be precise, of a
ore than a hundred and fifty pages.

It is heavily corrected in pencil, blue ink, and black ink, with nu-
s interlinear and marginal addenda, and rests in a pale blue file folder
is neither marked nor labeled.

Next to the manuscript is a single sheet of white paper on which
s typed a paragraph that reads:

On his desk there is a manuscript, a typescript, to be precise, of a
ore than a hundred and fifty pages.

It is heavily corrected in pencil, blue ink, and black ink, with nu-
s interlinear and marginal addenda, and rests in a pale blue file folder
is neither marked nor labeled.

Next to the manuscript is a single sheet of white paper on which
is typed a paragraph that reads:

leased as an outpatient?

Bart Kahane was never in a mental
or an outpatient.

He has been in a hospital for the pas
subsequent to a jump from a third-floor win
coln Inn, during the course of a fire that tota

The jump was the cause of a ruptur
broken arms, six broken ribs, and massive b

What *about* the quality of the inforn
informants?

It is somewhat distorted by omissions
fantasies, confusions, prejudices, egoism, faul
and outright lies.

May I *please* see the floor plan of Har

and turns

concerni
that the
it, and w
believe
magicia

lent poe

metam
man be

to show
ridens

desk?

little

merou
which

there

little

mero
whic

there

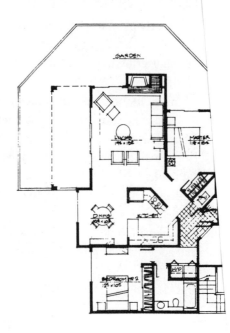

What were the names of the demons invok
BAAL, who imparts invisibility and cunnin
SEERE, who brings things to pass sudder
lace in a split second, and distorts messages.
HAGENTI, who grants wisdom, transmute

Rose Theatre

Who cares what was there before? There is no going back,
For standing still is death, and life is moving on,
Moving on towards death. But sometimes standing still is also life.

—John Ashbery

Chayne of dragons

Baal, the cat, King of the Invisible. In France, the girl on a rock in a field, thighs pressed modestly together. Off-white raw silk shift, a peach-colored silk slip with white lace hem and bodice. A full bottle of Bromo-Seltzer. "What a Girl!" Go *slow*. It is Bune, the Dragon of the Dead, who terrifies the filthy streets. That eerie café in Ferozepore, the Punjab? Dog walker! She is dusting. Like the libidinous Charlotte Bayless, she wants a lengthy sojourn in the Bahamas, preferably with Lou Henry, the humiliated goat. Agares, Master of Tongues and Crocodiles, vacationing in Fanapa. He speaks sweetly, sweetly to three young girls on a brilliant green lawn, one in a summer dress, the other two in pullovers and short pants or are they in black evening gowns of some shiny metallic fabric and peach-colored silk slips with white lace hems and plain bodices? The Tarot of Arthur Edward Waite: "He's a Voyeur." Go *fast* for Ronobe, Master of Rhetoric. And then be still as death. Flint, City of Promise? Sales correspondents all! She is sweeping. The lewd Flo Dowell, on a weekend in Paris with Guy Lewis, demon of drunkenness. Vassago, by whom the hidden is revealed, displays, from Antoine's seamy past, four smiling young women, four smiling young men, all in white: a rustic picnic table: tall drinks raised in a toast to grey tweed skirts, peach-colored silk slips with plain hems and white lace bodices. A paperback copy of *La Musique et les mauvaises herbes.* "Jacks or Better." Go *easy*, whispers Berith, the Red Soldier of the Lie. Dost fornicate in wild abandon, thou base prevaricator? *Vide* the charming West Village that recalls the glory years of Lady Day. Pander! She is polishing. Filthy Yvonne Firmin, a month in the mountains visible in her dreams, close in the arms of Leo Kaufman, leveler of lays, ravager of rhymes. Gamygyn, who bears messages from dead sinners to Fantoine, to the vast and ornate dining room of the Splendide-Lincoln, on whose tables are strewn grey tweed jackets and peach-colored silk slips with plain hems and bodices. A half-empty package of Camels. "A Laff a Minute!" *Harder!* for the delectation of Astaroth, Angel of Unearthly Beauty, who hides his face in gorgeous masks of absolute corruption. Does he miss Clappeville, desolate amid the Alps? Croupier! She is vacuuming, naked, lascivious Emma Woodhouse, whose day at the beach was often spent beneath the panting Dick Detective, whining for his wife. Marbas, the Transformer, who lifts his wand before Agapa, changing himself to a ten-year-old boy in a striped polo shirt squinting at the sun, filled with blistering thoughts of rayon scarves and peach-colored lace hems with plain bodices, no slips. An empty leather tobacco pouch redolent of rum, maple, chocolate. "Two Guys from Hackensack." *Deeper!* Forneus, the Evil from the Sea, bellows, rising dripping, lusting for a tall, an icy Trommer's in Hackettstown, where Modernism died. Con artist, she is cooking, the horny Nora Avenel, anticipating a trip up the Hudson on the day line with Bart Kahane, maker of false idylls. Valefor, Mentor of Thieves, secluded in an English garden with Sir Bloom and Lord Bury playing patient and doctor, one in a pale blue silk tailored blouse, the other in a peach-colored lace bodice, plain hem, no slip. A beautiful doll dressed as a nurse. "On Their Metal." *Now!* Foras, Great President of Strength, looks on: to whom all the world doth kneel. In Malibu, whose sands are hot and blue, a game-show host! She is scrubbing. Dirty Lydia Languish, on a picnic in the woods, accidentally strips before the eyes of Anton Harley, the razer of kitchens. Amon, who vomits fire on seeing Sylvie Lacruseille, or is it Ann Taylor Redding, sunbathing on a Manhattan rooftop in an ounce of spandex. By her bronzing side a pair of smoke-shade nylon stockings, a colored lace bodice, no peaches. A forged Fragonard. "Cartel." I'm *going* to. Asmoday, Familiar of the Cur from Hell, yet clothed impeccably in natural fabrics, dreams of the Cotswolds where the sheep run for their very lives. Preacher, she is washing! Ruttish Zuleika Dobson on a Sunday in Central Park ogles Biff Page, whose eyes are amethyst and neon. Barbatos, who understands the birds, in a metallic room filled with photographs of Sheila Henry at ten, smiling from the back seat of her father's Packard outside Nathan's Famous in Coney Island. He is buying beige nylon stockings, colored lace peaches, but neither bodices nor hems. An alto saxophone reed once used by *Jimmy Dorsey?* "Old

Hoboken." Are you going to, too? Gaap, who makes insensible, now reigns, Master of Earthquakes, Reciter of Verse. That was in Callipolis, where Love Triumphed. Registered nurse! She is drying. She is sluttish Grace Armstrong, soon to take a stroll through Chinatown for an assignation with Harlan Pungoe, ruiner of souls. Paimon, obedient to Him who was drowned in the depths of His knowledge, beguiled by a steel evening gown; or the perfect image of a perfect navel orange on which has been neatly lettered in black ink, Ceci n'est pas une orange; or black silk full-fashioned stockings and a peaches and cream lace slip with no bodice. A copperplated ear trumpet bought in a Bleecker Street "sundries shop." "What's for Supper?" Ohhhh. Furfur, Earl of Married Love, who haunts the shadowed pools dark in the Poconos, Scranton of the Seven Caesars. High-powered executrix (she irons). Simmering Esther Summerson, off for a week in those fastnesses, fleeing from Barry Gatto, the underground duke. Buer, the Healer, seduced by Corrie and Berthe via an old photograph album whose every caption reads "Some Fun." In white nylon panties with white lace trim and a peaches and bodice hem and no slip, why not? A Tom Mix telescope carelessly displayed. "Blind Bums." Uhhh. Solas, Bleak Raven of Astronomy, who flies in candlelight forever more. Or to Natchitoches, redolent of chicory and jumpy jass. Building contractor. She is mending? Hot Betty Barker, fresh from a few days in Mazatlán where Rupie sucked on her pumps. Gusion, the Duke of Those Who Discern, with disembodied voice that speaks of Durga, Goddess of Destruction, the clumsy brass figurine of Whom has its nipples rendered prominent by two dabs of nail polish, Red Moon. She hath scorned the black lace corselette with bodice of lace cream and peach hem. A key, to a suite, in the Blue Runes, motel. "The Heart is Lo-onely." Ooohhh. Marchosias, the Wolf, hideth his phiz amid a crowd of galaxies. Above Charleville? Where poor Arthur saw the Northern Lights? Demolition expert, "she" is sewing. Lustful May Fielding on a hike in the woods so wild espied Henri Kink, the living corpse, amid various items of decay. Sytry, jussus secreta libenter detegit feminarum; or, a ventriloquist's dummy; or, a doll dressed as Sister Philomena Veronica, whose black stiletto heels shine beneath the hem of her chaste habit, peachy. White cotton p-----s and more white cotton "things." A discarded typescript of a Ph.D. dissertation on Lorenzo's lost novel, *Marmalade Eros.*

"World of Signs." Oh *God!* Phoenix, who lispeth as a child, hunts amid the hollyhocks for "Sis," dreams of Mytilene, a snatch of honey, φαίνεταί μοι, humble bard, she is knitting. Steamy Donna Julia, after an hour in the pool, caresses Sol Blanc, the sun twin, excites Antony Lamont the other secluded in the Plaza with nymphomaniacal Venetia Herbert she fucks the languorous police chief eyes "cast" toward Staten Island rich world of Gotham content at last in her middle years but for Furcas the Cruel Elder open wide A Batch of Stuff including pale blue file folders and a Ship 'n' Shore flowered print blouse white Mary Janes at this Cecil Tyrell predictably scowls at the "blank" sheet of paper predictably rolled into his predictable Royal Manual studied clutter Glasyalabolas the Murderer of Barnett Tete of owning of hoarding of purveying dear and yet a fiesta in Old Méjico discovers him paying voluptuous Katie Woodward for unspeakable favors she tidies dressed as a "French" "maid" like Binghamton like on the mother-fucking road sport all trapped in their own circumferential evidence as Procel the Geometer has so proven *put it in!* Win a Bundle or a treatise on fractals or Habits and Wimples and bone Mary Janes *plus* a passport-size photograph of Henri Kink face twisted with terror albeit well-groomed as per Naberius the Cock of Cocks Duke Washington of heresy of blasphemy of cant of Labor Day weekend in Madrid with depraved Eleanor Harding who arranges for the bartender in Aspen a last resort Yours For No Down Payment Easy Terms Hagenti Maker of Gold do you like *that* Regular Guy? beside a Hudson Terraplane in orange silk dress and tan "things" then *see* "Scale model of Splendide-Malibu in the lobby of Splendide-New Haven" attractive yet stern Aini the Destroyer Chico of the flickering image e.g. a holiday in Sun Valley e.g. the whorish Amelia Sedley she stores (stares) so says the maitre d' in the inn at Sciacca the "roots of confidence" at the "Snorter" neo-impressionist minimalist star with bankable first novel screenplay inside Vual Camel of Egypt I *like* that La Última Despedida but to a pair of *drumsticks?* to a pair of glasses with tortoiseshell frames and brown shoesies to a photograph of three young couples the women disconcertingly identical outside London laughs Ipos the Angelic Lion as Biggs Richard of anonymous January in Monte Carlo New Jersey in pursuit of lecherous Nancy Lammeter she mops she is a chef in Frisco city of cupcakes where ensues the search for the perfect pome and where lives Bifrons Disturber of the Dead *more!* Guy Ropes! in the sunshaft a fly in amber a tortoiseshell barrette a pair of some god-damned things in the gloaming old Rupe again avidly staring at some bulging oranges the "real thing" but the wall collapses before the assault of Morax the Bull *cum* Cecil the cursed the blasted a fortnight in a Kenya of the imagination ah the debauched Alice Bridgenorth she cleans a "food server" lost in Cortland where the virtuoso singer died dancing in the haunted wood of carrion memory Vine Monster of Witches *don't! stop!* Every Girl's Dream a copy of the Irish folktale bedad begorrah bejayzus *The Paddy in the Brake* soon to be a pair of stack-heeled shoes with small silver buckles isolate a self-portrait of René Magritte contemplating' a photograph of a photograph of a painting of a perfect navel orange paired with Durga and Purson of Bears of Trumpets of Jackson Towne duke of the sticks on the town in town and in shameless dalliance with the wanton Dorothea Brooke who prunes and how a college traveler who goes broke in Brooklyn limbo of small griefs a vague backdrop of uncertain smiles Shax Destroyer of the Understanding *stop!* Ladders at Last and a matchbook from Helen and Troy's café within whose ladies' room a pair of black steel pumps on whose heels is impaled the first card The Magician of the Greater Arcana large calves and slender ankles whispers Saleos the Pander and so Page Moses the doctor of plots writes of a "trip" to the "moon" and the immodest Lucy Brandon his heroine she plants she is a shipping clerk in Colma city of crypts and cadavers while rain lashes the windows Vepar Duke of Storms and Tempests like *that!* You're the Top you're a box of cookies you're a single red sling high-heeled shoe in the hand of a young man in electric-blue suit whose lapel button's printed message is too small to read? "small silver buckles"? Bathin of the Pale Horse Lincoln Gom falsifier of artisans a Saturday in Monterey the unchaste Edith Granger weeds candy maker of Jersey City of bitter Februaries of despair in driving sleet bad Chinese food Sabnack Marquis of Wounds and Worms hath himself prepared like *this?* Thinking of You a full set of steel false teeth in one cup of a white nylon brassiere et au milieu d'un essaim de filles Madame Lorpailleur nue tirait la langue tirait les white silk pumps by Botis the Viper Vance Whitestone he who rapes a year in Calafawnya as the impure Letitia Snap she waters the bell-ringer? thence to Manhattan a fifth of old Noo

Yawk eater of pies kneader of dough Focalor Drowner of Men sweetheart! An Idiot's Pleasure a blackjack a white lace brassiere sweat-
stained somebody's dear old mother in the act of placing a pie on a
windowsill stern but comely Zepar who drives women mad with lust
thus Horace Rosette the collector one time in Gstaad appalled by the
indecent Tabitha Bramble she gardens a perfect hostess he thought of
Hartford where a fat man lusted for his "lineage" in another life a
certain Mr. Anthony no names pliz or Raum He Who Reconciles?
baby! Chattering Fools some decayed costumes e.g. white nylon garter
belts with lace front panels (nota bene a strange incomprehensible
construction in metal) tortoiseshell peaches the delight of Eligor the
Lustful the Concupiscent the Seductive John Hicks killer of the aged
hidden in the night in Tunisia wild with the fantasies of salacious
Margaret Ramsay she airs but a dishwasher years ago in Haddam Neck
of the right graveyards the right house with large loft with kiln therein
with books scattered "about" Malpas Friend of False Artificers Christ!
Lengthy and Serious Talks bits of dark silk white lace French something a still of Tania Crosse in vile embrace with two popular female
stars of rival network news "shows" short-haired Lerajie Creator of
Strife all will be metamorphosed forever by Beleth the Terrible and
Halpas Burner of Cities the fearsomely regal and beautiful the black
heifers of chaos those who persuaded the joyous Irishman to don a
scanty daringly short skirt riding up at the knee to show a peep of white
pantalette transparent stockings emeraldgartered with the long straight
seam trailing up beyond the knee who placed *The Secrets of the Bottom
Drawer* under his oxter who created Yonkers by which some came by
way of who filled with malice invented the pink jersey sleeveless dress
for hapless women the sculpture *The Caliph Lorzu* fashioned by them
and into the mouths of lovers they have placed the words "no bananas"
have defiled obscenely the obscene Esther Waters who spit on Jesus
darkness falls at their behest on any day on all days and Saul Blanche at
their pleasure is become the Sun Twin. AND at their command enters
Baal: who hath transformed his image to that of the slavering brach:
who hath become visible.

Littel alter

Introibo ad altare Dei . . . many ascents, but always laid low. She went
forth to battle but she always fell. Usually on her back. Laid is good.
You couldn't count them all if you tried. The T-shirt, the paisley tie, the
old khakis, the seersucker suit. Chicks really dig it. The paisley tie came
all over himself, the old khakis had a wife and children. The seersucker
suit quoted Anatole Broyard. The T-shirt, which T-shirt? That one,
that one, that one, that one, that one. You're the top, you're a
gonococcus. And this one is Jimmy, in the wading pool, he's four, and
Marge has on the Hofstra sweatshirt, she just turned seven. Is she cute
or is she cute? Spurted all over himself, the poor man. Dick knew but
did Dick care? Dick was an ascots. Dick was a desert boots. Dick was a
faded blue chambray shirts. Bach. If there's anything she could *not*
stand! Jesus Christ Almighty and His Blessed Mother. I can't get away
to marry you today, Karen. Whore of the airways. How about this,
baby? She thought she invented it. Did you ever see anything like this,
honey? Hell, half the world has one. My wife won't let me. Let him
what? The photographer will snap *her,* God knows. God damn him and
his boils and his impeccable handkerchief. He was kneeling, well-
trained Catholic that he is, or was. *He* was kneeling too, his Nikon or his
Kodak or whatever. She'll never tell. She never told. Who would have
thought that poetical Dick would grieve in his lust? Because of some
pictures? Well, men. Often, when she knelt to kiss the crucifix, she
knew that rubbers and frayed collar was looking at her. From there it
was but a step to T-shirt and seersucker suit, not to mention old khakis
and all those impossible snapshots. If that stairwell could talk. It would
say *Kyrie eleison.* God sees all from the altar and it is a sin to laugh in
his house. It's also a sin to show your underpants. Once a bad girl,
always. Dick, thtay? Caw and thay you have to meet thomebody? My
wife won't let me. There she was, waiting at the church. Have a

Manhattan? Tastes like horse piss, hahaha. Uncle Johnny was a real card. Is that the Lido I see? Do Not Disturb. Or only Asbury Park? Do Not Disterb. The dumb bastards. He said he spread all my pictures out on the bed and did it. He loved her with his boils and all. His imported beer and his cheddar and his English Ovals and his Bach and his amethyst crystal ashtrays. Do not disturb! Do you see this brand-new drawing? Got it just the other day. The French bitch with the Gitanes. Smoke that cigarette, Annie so-called, so-called Annie, Gitanes for her, her for Gitanes. Eez zat ow you say? Zat eez ow we say, ow do you say in ze Yonkers? His wife won't let him. Is it possible that on her wedding day she actually wore a girdle? Uncle Johnny and his rented royal blue tux, Knights of Columbus, Confraternity of the Most Precious Blood, and although her body was her most sacred temple and altar. Oh Johnny. Did Dick care? Mr. Boils, meet Mr. Pimples. Care for a double-thick chocolate shake and a large fries? It was great Art what rescued him from his bourgeois sleep. Bach definitely smoked English Ovals and sat in a rocking chair. To listen to his own records. His wife won't let him but did he give a goddamn? Karen Gash put the steak on and love sweet love just like in the movies. Down on his knees before *her* altar. Oh Johnny. The Manhattans taste like you'll pardon my French horse piss haha but what the hell, it's not every day your favorite niece contracts to get her ashes hauled. Do Not Disterb. It was the McCoy, a honeymoon suite from which the ocean could be glimpsed. In the dark, in Asbury Park, for a lark. Quark quark. *Finnegans Wake* that's from. Art which rescued him from the provincial. Right. Quark you. Oh Dick, the thteak is wuined. Just like in the movies. With ascot all undone and in a generally unbuttoned state, the young woman but partially dressed, he ascendeth to the Seventh Heaven. A far cry from Mechanicville. A girdle! That was in another country, you can bet the rent on that. He preferred *Dubliners,* yes, I prefer *Dubliners,* to tell the truth. Self-denigrating smile. To tell the what? Father Graham turned to face them, his best vatic smile beaming. It's a sin to laugh in church. It's a sin to tell a lie. What was that snowman story? If his nose were a carrot he'd eat it? Something about a roaring blaze in the old stone fireplace that makes her sick to her stomach. Gathered about the cheerful hearth, warm false friends all. What in the hell did she know about gardening that she should be on her

knees in the mud? It's a treat to beat your feet. His meat. That's nice, oh
that's good. Bless me Father, for I have sinned. It's been a hundred
years since my last confession. I ate meat on Friday. What kind? She
knew what Horace was going to show her that night. They all went
crazy then. From pimples and boils to novel in progress. By the time she
knew what had hit him, oh, the hell with it. She doethn't wike youw
witing at aw, Dick? Not at all, face turned toward the window, the
stricken artist. Now suck me off, O.K.? Mr. Suave. Off they went into
the blue of the sky, *another* Karen. Every time she turns around he's
humping *some* Karen. Norwegian beauty. Have another slab of lute-
fiske? How about a passel of fried lingonberries? Or would you prefer
some hot Scandinavian tongue? You must avoid the occasions of sin,
my dear. She walked toward the altar, the faces of her old boring friends
around her, the dusty rose coat, the lavender suit, the fuchsia hat, with
veil. Beneath the finery, what else? Girdles. How do you like the
opening sentence of chapter three? Through the humid indigo pall that
had dropped on the island came pallid, distant voices, seemingly
oblivious to the heat, lost, far, drowning in ecstacy. His desert boots.
Throw another log on the fire, let's have a drink, put some Bach on, let's
smoke a little dope, let's build a *snowman.* If his ear were a cunt, is that
how it goes? The only surprise was that Dick was not another ascendant
star in Harlan's galaxy. Speak nothing but good of the crippled. And the
dead. Did she mention the cardboard living? Dick was probably with
Tania, plenty of times. I don't think it's demeaning or anti-feminist for a
woman to wear, well, exciting lingerie. Not at all, as a matter of fact, I
think that. A woman. Is even. More. Womanly. On the weekends she
can put on a Good Will fedora and a pair of overalls. Let's haul out the
old stump afore we plow the bottom forty and save another miserable
whale. Nota bene: black lace crotchless panties. Just the thing for those
impromptu protest rallies. Fads and fancies. Speaking of such, the guy
with the *shoes.* Some kind of gofer for Annette with the metal walls and
the weird voice. That guy who wanted to marry Tania told me that there
was some kind of an altar. How about collecting, you know, nothing
spectacular, but like books? To screw Cecil, for one, is a boon to all
mankind, Christ knows. He'll *never* die. Lou said it was an accident,
sure, like Uncle Johnny's hand under my dress. Sorry to lose my favorite
niece, now just let me get my hand in there. Just drunk, Dick said, hell,

he's just a pathetic old drunk. Then she found two pairs of her panties missing, well, better them than me. Goils, duh blood streaming down Ah Lady's face from huh eyes, streaming down dat poifect, holy face, is blood shed because of duh sins of impurity occasioned by duh organs of sight, *ah* eyes. Ah Lady's heart is broken because of duh impure books and magazines and fillums dat tempt you on every side. Our Lady should have been at Horace's that night. Rose as the nun in what was it? *Sisters of Shame?* Underneath her habit a black corset, lace garters. God protect me, the priest said, as he pulled his pants off to reveal. Another Academy Award performance from Chet somebody. Bart finally went crazy, won't you sample some of this scent? Ce Soir. She sacrificed her whole youth for him. For what? What did she get? Older she got. She got I think I love Karen. Which one? Another one. She really knows how to haul your codfish, right, you louse? She actually prayed that his boils would come back and by Jesus they did. *Deo gratias.*

Lavabo inter innocentes manus meas . . . cross-eyed Maureen Shea caught her bouquet, so dumb she thought men had perpetual erections. Would it be any different if they did? And was she any the worse off? Than the rest? Of us? All of the lavender suits? If he hadn't met that jerk Leo he'd still be drinking beer in his T-shirt and playing the pinball machine out at Lena's Rest. I've been reading these fabulous poems baby, listen, what if a much of a wind of which. Jerry Casey figured that he'd turned into a fruit. Dear God, the ignorance of the thickhead. Dick knew. Dick was a T-shirts. Dick was an engineer's boots. Dick was a sideburns. Then Dick was a little treasury of modern poetry. When something punishes my hair with frozen fingers we'll love each other or die. The first time she went down on him, in the back seat of Billy Magrino's Dodge. And have you committed any sins of impurity, my child? I ate meat on Friday, Father. Chet somebody pulled his priestly pants off. To reveal to Sister Rose. What a bunch. I'm breaking off with her, I swear, I swear it, I am, so Dick said after they bumped into her with another Miss Shredded Wheat in Gimbels. Uh, this is, uh, this is, uh, uh, this is my, uh, wife, April. Innocent act, the two Misses Shredded Wheat with the blank skies of Iowa in their perfect faces. Did she deserve this humiliation? After she did what she did and never mind what, she washed her hands for fifteen minutes. A living cliché, that's what I am. Cross-eyed Maureen told Dolores who told Liz who told Georgene who told Terry who told Charlotte and Virginia who told Mary who told Nancy who told Nina what she did. I thought you were supposed to be my friends. I'm a whore, all *right.* Then, by Christ, let's do it! Bless me Father, for I have sinned, but I have washed my hands a lot. Yes, more than one. A man's got to have steady nookie, that's what he said, nookie, or else his brain will be affected. Must mean that none of you are getting laid. Good old Leo. Wike thith, Dick, baby? I love my wife. He loves the girl he's near, *pace* Ellen. Say girl to her and her fedora explodes. Her overalls melt. Her jockey shorts burst into flame. I want you to get my April home by twelve-thirty, Dick. Yes, I sure will, I'll just have to see to it that I pop her by midnight. By the light of the silv'ry moon. I washed with toilet paper in the stall at the Round Lake Inn, dancing every weekend to Mel Proud and His Melodics. Let's face the music. Kid. Do you want to come in? Is your mother still up? I think so. No. Why don't we do it right here on the porch? Is that you, dear? Jesus fucking Christ! She entered, her innocent smile conveying to all there gathered around the cheerful hearth the warmth and quiet benevolence of her mind and the purity and calm of her womanly heart. Eyes cast down, she blushed at praise of her goodness, protesting that she did not deserve such, in that they, in the humble performance of a steadfast charity, were more worthy of *her* encomia. In the modest reticule clasped firmly by her pale and delicate hand, her undergarments were discreetly hidden from their view, lest knowledge that she was naked beneath her dress should cause them to suspect her ruin. Didn't Dick want to come in? No, Mom, it's late, and besides, Dick is out in the wind and rain, behind yon stately elm, whacking himself off, I have little doubt. What a nice boy! So considerate. Yet won't he go crazy as well as impair his health? Hello! Hello, Maureen. How's Dick? Oh, we're separated, I'm afraid. Really? Yes, he said he needed his freedom in order to bring his notebook up to date. Really? Yes. His notebook? Yes. Well, I've got to run. Nice seeing you, cockeyes, keep your legs closed. She has eleven children by now, a little late. Well, he might as well be keeping his notebook up to date, the damn fool. They were all invited to a snow party at our house on January 14, 15, 16, they were to bring warm clothes and big appetites, there were to be cocktails and a snow-ball fight and cocktails. Please come! RSVP. If she ever *hears* the name

Robinson Jeffers again! The really interesting aspect is the unique, the savage imagery, really, an absolute genius. Among these learned innocents, no respite. And here's the fat guy who lives with his mother. And here's the maiden that men forget. And here's the girl who used to swing down on the garden gate. Yes, he'd sooner kill a man than a hawk. What a guy! Right, like Himmler. Somebody lost his jockey shorts. What *was* that snowman story? If his ear were a cock? The crackling blaze and Ted the bore going on and on about how Kline this and Rothko that and Motherwell's problem. She left to take a bath and was not seen among the revelers for twenty-four hours. You are some bitch treating my friends like that! Right. If I were an ear, would you fuck me? Karen, the twat of the clouds, smiled that smile what melts all manly hearts. Oh get the hell out of here with your idiot whore! Everything but true love. She could almost hear his back breaking out in boils. Go and wash yourself, you insulting bastard, I can *smell* the whore off you. *Lavabo inter innocentes,* thus spake Father Richard, S.J., crestfallen at this unfounded accusation. Cutesy Karen Wyoming, pulling on her cutesy bootsies, ith it thtill thnowing, Dick? And Bach labored on. Yes, baby, it is. I hope we can get to the aiwport on timey-wimey, my wove. If he's going to with Sheila she's going to with Lou. What a sap, yet those innocent tears after the accident or whatever were real. But that other guy in the car she wouldn't trust as far as she could throw him. They say he told everything they asked him. Just off the funny farm. He burned down some hotel or something. Cleanse me of my sins, shrive me of my few transgressions, I didn't know what I was doing. Fuck off, whoever you are. Dick was doing it with Sheila? I was doing it with Lou! Not a bad man except for his taste in what? Wives. Cold love, blue love, everything but true. True love breaks out in boils and pimples while he whacks off on his knees, weeping, forgive me, forgive me, oh, forgive me! She remembered his panegyric on the sound of the surf, did she not? Sheer poesy, Dick, just sheer, sheer voibal art. You are a bitch, a grade-A *bitch.* The crackling fire. The cheerful hearth. Good food and drink, ho! And the marvelous snowman, he melted. To treat my *friends* like this! Oh go write another dumb sentence you dumb, dumb, you dumb. And so, by God, he would. There is no stopping the obsessed artist. He'll show her that he's not just another sweaty schmuck beyond yon stately elm! It is with this, his first novel, that Richard Detective, whom most of us had secretly deemed an idiot, has produced the sort of work that helps keep us *all* in business. Indeed, transcending the finely etched chiaroscuro of inner truth and the inner depth of naturally rendered detail we feel that we have come to know as well as share in some inner beauty that is something and also something else. As she read, eyes cast down upon the crisp *Times,* she blushed. Where do they get these jerks? The structure of the novel is wholly satisfying, although, and yet, and yet, although. Finally, we come to appreciate the fine eye for this and the excellent ear for that. Where? From the far reaches of glittering Manahatta, yet few can find their way to Baltic Street or Tremont Avenue. Does it matter? Without them how could one discover what one must know in order to understand? What? Shop on, shop on! Pre-washed, pre-torn, pre-faded and presented for your delectation along with a brief telephone interview, wholly illuminating. Often, Bach hovered in the background. Dick was the sort of man who washed his hands before listening to that fucking organ. So *much* Bach, yet where was he to turn for succor? Well, Karen Blonde and Karen Teeth were really nice and understood things. Also liked it in every orifice, right, hubby mine? So, taken all in all, we can take it all in all. Out to the parking lot, Vince Esposito smiled, climbing into his car. So long. I think, he thinks, I think I've fallen in love with Karen Complexion. Because of the sins of impurity occasioned by my eyes perusing *Baron Darke of Eagle House,* who, with insistent hands tore open Melissa's bodice so that her innocent breasts were exposed to his devouring gaze, the blood streamed from Our Lady's eyes down her sad and suffering face, for she abused herself with a bottle of Prell shampoo. When you abuse yourself with a bottle of Prell shampoo or anything else, Our Lady has a hemorrhage, right there on the little side altar. Absolutely. The guy, what was his name, said that the room was *freezing.* And with an altar. Such goings on were called fads and fancies. How about this, baby? I think it's much better. Through the oppressive wet indigo of the island night came distant pallid cries, lost in the maddening heat, ecstatic, perverse. The idiot, oh, the goddamned idiot. You were always a cheap philandering louse, long, long before Karen Cornfield. What? Why? Why? You don't remember that even when we were engaged you couldn't keep your eyes off dusty rose coat and lavender suit and fuchsia hat, with veil? All my boring friends, their mouths working over the body and blood, dreaming of for Christ sake Tab Hunter pulling their girdles off? Young people must, uh, avoid these occasions of sin, girls, uh, no less than boys. Abjure that, uh, lewd bottle of Prell! Discard that concupiscent, uh, candle! Jettison, oh jettison that, uh, suggestive cucumber! In other woids, boin. Or marry that nice, well, that O.K. boy with the station wagon has a good job in insurance. She *knew* what Horace was going to show her. Warm phonies all gathered about the old stone hearth of the house built in the seventeen hundreds, the wraiths of Christ knows how many Protestants about. Do you want to know what I think about Robinson Jeffers? He's a prick. Jesus, if only all you drunks would tell the truth, just once. I'm going to take a bath. That's *enough,* April. Enough my ass, nothing is enough with you! His best vatic smile, it beamed. Do you take this prick to be your husband? He ascendeth unto that state of extreme rapture, the Seventh Heaven. Do Not Disterb. Now the pretentious fake pretends he's never even heard of Asbury Park. Mr. Boils ascendeth unto the empyrean of sophistication. Right. Mr. Boils chuckled at the review by Miss Understand of Mr. Insight's newest novel, his third and, surely, finest work. Eez zat ow she say? Le novel? Or eez eet le fiction? Zat eez ow she say, Annie weez ze camera. You have, Dick, such a strong face, I mean, fess. And so to bed. I don't know, baby, I don't know, I think, I think I really *love* her. Who, Annie? Annie? No, not *Annie.* I mean. Oh, of course, right, another Karen Fairgrounds, what else? While I am but Mrs. Asbury Park, right, you rotten cheating bastard? But God sees all from his altar, so when you embrace your neighbor in the pew do not feel her up. She was always true to her high-school sweetheart. It gets you right *here.* Rubbers and frayed collar always looked at her underpants when she knelt to kiss the clammy disgusting crucifix. And once she saw him touch himself with Sister Mary Magdalene right there behind him. But she never told. She'll never tell. Him and his boils, Christ! I thought we could play one of our games, but these *boils.* I can hardly move. He'd be the priest and I beneath my chaste Catholic wife and mother-of-four dress would wear a red garter belt, black stockings. Bless me Father, for I have sinned, I'm not wearing any underwear. My *child!* Dick was a desert boots then. Dick was a faded denim jackets then. Dick was a button-down collars then. Dick was a chilled white wine then. Dick was a I think I'll take a cab then. Soon he forgot where Bath Beach was. *What* beach? Dick knew. But did he care? Neither did April, no more, no more. There was the stock boy and the mail boy and the shipping clerk and the UPS man and the trucker as well as the guy in the movies and the guy in the bar and that one and that one and that one and that one and that one. The seersucker suit wasn't really used to picking up girls, wife and children, the damn snapshots, Jesus, but he wanted to lick my little one, he called it. He loved his wife but oh! Is this any way for a good Catholic girl? Chicks really dig it when they try it. And though I washed my hands yet were they dirty. And though she ascendeth often yet was she as often laid. Dick knew, but.

   Confitebor tibi in cithara . . . quare tristis es, anima mea, et quare conturbas me? . . . are we to blame her because try as she might she could not conceive? Not us. I sang the old songs and the new while Dick went on his artistic way. Have I mentioned his chain of Karens? But of course. Speak but the word and her soul shall be healed. What word is that? She won't cry anymore. They could have called him Charles or Peter, or her Melanie or Susan. Have another drink, no use talking about it. Don't neglect to give him his recorder or his guitar so that he can replace Bach's noise with his very own. Time out for tears. Well we don't have to worry about diaphragms or condoms or spermicidal foam, l'écume, l'écume des jours. That's what she should have had, a flower in her lung. Who asked for this? Just loved, loved the nights away. Oh what it seemed to be. Will we shake our heads because she performed fellatio on a number of men to whom she hadn't been properly introduced? Not us. That's the breaks. A couple of jiggers of moonlight, kid. Not too much ice. And add, say, a star. The brakeman fucked her, as did the conductor. I wanna be bad! The act of love, my dear woman, is primarily intended to insure the conception of. Oh for Christ sake give it a rest! Might as well shoot some Prell up there for all the good you do. Me? No, the janitor. Maybe I'd have had a snowman. When he's not near the girl he loves he'll take anything. I fall in love too easily. Why don't you play it on the recorder? If its name's Karen, instant erection. Make it a double, I should care. And the engineer came in his pants. On Fire Island I had the funny feeling that *maybe*. She can dream, can't she? I had the feeling that he had a feeling too that *maybe*. But they didn't even do it, he fell down the steps onto the sand and staggered into the night. She stood right there in the moonlight bare. Mine hostess, whose name I forget. What most disgusted her is that he didn't even take off his pants. Like the engineer. There they were like a couple of mongrels in the bushes. What was the old joke? Just hold the snake still? More truth than poetry in that. He got all red in the face and kicked the wall when he found out about me and poor hopeless Lou, in love in vain. Why didn't you kick the stereo, O reckless adventurer? The plastic-wrapped books? How come you didn't kick your gleaming rocking chair? You hypocrite, you *hypocrite!* Kick your desert boots, you bastard! Make me a Scotch, you bastard, a big one. And the wind blew up her nightie. How nice to have you and Dick for the weekend, her dazed Bryn Mawr eyes. She smiles and the angels sing. Sure, but it's too soon to know, sugar. He still doesn't believe me about Horace's as if I give a damn. I should have just pulled my clothes off, what the hell difference would it have made? Maybe that clubfooted pervert could have planted *his* seed. I'd have a little bastard born wearing a terrifying blue suit. Is it true what they say about Bunny? I wouldn't raise my boy to be a voyeur. Yes, I liked it, yes, I *did.* Yes, Lou is a joke. To *you.* Ow wondairfull eet eez zat you tek ze photograph? Stick it in your nose. I'd raise him up to be, I'd raise him up. Yes, she did that and she did that and she also did that and with him and him and them and somebody else and with her too. A lot of them. With their snapshots with their keychains with their sad kinks with their interesting jobs and their mortgages and their cars falling apart and their wonderful kids and their understanding wives and their fake names. Uh, Bill, right, Bill, uh, Saunders. I love my wife, but. On my back on my knees standing up bending over naked half-dressed fully dressed on backseats balconies beaches booths dumb saloons motels stairwells bathrooms. Oh, you kid! What the hell did he care? Strangers in the night? Very witty, I'm surprised you knew I was gone. Go write another engaging story or whatever it is you write. Go see Karen Forage and cry on her compassionate shoulder. God, Dick, I just *wove* youw articwe it's just wike a beautifuw kind of wiwd enewgy. Isn't this Karen the sweet and understanding one, very intelligent, loves opera, from the reaches of Terre Haute takes dictation types files cheerfully with her blue eyes on a better job or should I say career a general all-around wonderful girl with her little white blouse? with them there eyes? with simple jersey dress?

with businesslike mid-heel black pumps? with sweet little Alice-blue
gown? Plus a college graduate! She takes him to paradise, but one
mustn't forget the importance of the wine, perfectly chilled, with just a
touch of petillance, the Brie, the crunchy baguette, the Gitanes, and the
amusing vibrator. You sold your heart to the junkman, sweetie. That sly
liar who just got out of the nuthouse then set his own house on fire, or
something on fire, tells all, he had us both involved in you name it,
anything and everything. Just said whatever came into his head to the
cretin with the tape recorder. For what? A study of urban something, or
the talk of the town. Does it matter that Dick and April were not what
we were led to believe they were? Not to us. By the way, what were we
led to believe? I'm goddamned if I know. But where there's smoke. I'll
never be free. Couldn't stop talking, on and on. What a pair we were,
according to Mr. Mouth, smoking, drinking, never thinking of tomorrow. Well, it makes the slobs feel better about their own quick journey
to the grave, they are possessed of a deeper understanding. Of what? Of
just what happens when. And also when. I've got my own troubles, let
them play theirs down. The bastards. Dick thought the whole thing was
funny. Hey, we're famous! Depressing. Pour me a glass of that
Cabernet swill, the crap that Karen Peachy from the mountains and the
prairies wuvs so much she could just dwink it *aw* up! But first, before
you toast your love, a little head from the scintillant M.B.A. Am I right?
So it's only nine in the morning. Sue me, should I be out jogging the
pounds away? When he goes to sleep he never counts sheep he dreams
about getting in Linda. Linda? What could have possessed my very own
Mr. Denim to get himself involved with a non-Karen? You *are* a shrew!
I only for Christ sake said hello to the girl. Fine, just don't bring home
the Old Joe again, O.K.? Probably why she can't have any children, the
mean filthy son of a bitch knowing he had it and not saying a word.
Filthy? *Me,* filthy? After the rube with the foam-rubber dice on the rear-
view mirror wanted you to, you know. So what? *You* never seem to
want my romancing. Very funny, very very funny. But it turned out that
Linda was a pet name for, I'm not making this up, for Karen! Her father
was a Buddy Clark fan, remember him? Oh sweet Jesus and all His
wounds, spare me the grisly details of the *family.* But tell me, Karen-
Linda, is her thing really made out of cellophane and ice cream? Jesus,
you are really, really, Jesus. My sweet embraceable you, it's not your

brain. I don't know what it is, I really can't explain. *Don't* explain! For
Christ sake, give me a break! 'Twas then that he discovered Art. She
can imagine him, oh, she often imagined him with Karen Pepsi Karen
Heineken Karen Sperry. What's really so remarkable, Karen, is how
he uses color itself as form. Alarums! Wow, Dick, I weawwy enjoyed
that I weawwy fewt for the fiwst time that I can weawwy appweciate
etcetewa etcetewa etcetewa. Oh oh oh oh oh! you beautiful doll! Then a
bite of lunch, just a little lunch in a little restaurant on a little street in
little old Greenwich Village, a charming place that Dick has loved for
years, for a couple of months, since last week, he's never been there
before. You hopeless chump. And soon after he buried us in Vermont,
falling leaves, birches, God knows what, birds and bugs, neighbors with
pale hatchet faces and transparent eyes whose forebears were whipped
aboard ships at Portsmouth. The works. You know exactly what you
can do with your clean air and your town meetings, don't you? Dick did
not deign to reply. Deign this. His immaculate notebooks, his neat
jottings, his ridiculous sharpened pencils, his Olivetti portable. All just
so on a card table, Christ have mercy. Alone in the woods with that
blank sheet of paper and without a sweetheart to his name. Does that
view down to the river inspire you? There's nothing like nature, look at
Thoreau. He thought he'd perhaps, *perhaps!* poach a salmon. Certainly,
darling. In chocolate syrup, Fox's U-Bet? I am a bitch and why not, and
why the hell not? My love for him meant. It meant heartaches. So who
was it? So who took those goddamned pictures? Who? Did you get him
hot, you whore? Did you change in front of him? Who was it? Did he
fuck you, you whore? Say it isn't so, oh God, please. She smiled the
smile she used to smile back in leafy Mechanicville. When she was
sweet sixteen. I won't tell. I don't see me in his eyes anymore. I never
told. It's a sin to tell a lie. The blood streaks the beatifically suffering
face of Our Lady. He did hate to lose his favorite niece, oh that's O.K.,
plenty of others around, Uncle Johnny, thank heaven for little girls,
right? There he stood in his cheap rental tux. Received every Sunday
with all his cronies and their dopey wives. My mother used to say,
you'll pardon the expression, April, but my ass would make a Sunday
face for all of them. There is most definitely a curse on your families and
it fell on you, oh you're ugly. Beans, carrots, radishes, God knows
what. All failed. Couldn't grow a marigold. He wanted to go in and see

Saul or Sol, God, I can't remember those wretched men, to talk about some changes in the first part. Certainly, you must see to the particulars of your Art. If they asked you, could you write a book? There's no *living* with you. So? Go live with Karen whoever. Thertainly, Dick, pwease come up to my pwace and I'ww make you some bacon and eggs. Why, what a cute little apron. Do you wike it? And those wonderful postcard reproductions in the bathroom! I got them fwom the Museum of Modewn Art. Wonderful! Did you see the marvelous retrospective of anybody last year? *Did* she? It was marvewous! And in a trice he had his fly open, you can bet on it. Just a prisoner of love, poor baby, my wife won't *let* me. Did you have a good time in the dynamic, vibrant, ever-changing, restless, and, how shall I put it, *electric* city? Did you have any interesting conversations? Take in any of the *great* shows? Run into Karen Millpond who never never *thaw* one ath big ath yours? You're drunk as shit. Have you noticed how all the really exciting people there carry attaché cases and take cabs? From their lofts to other people's lofts? You're drunk. Glittering crowds in canyons of steel, all from Nebraska. All the Karens. She couldn't help mentioning the Karens, could she? You're drunk, go to bed. Yes, you son of a bitch, and I'm going to get drunker. How's the *stuff* coming, what's the title again, *Blackhead*? She should care what she said. Do we care? Not us. Dick knew, but did Dick care? You walk along the street of sorrow, Don Juan, right? Or is it the boulevard of broken dreams? My God! Is that a pimple on your sensitive and aesthetic face? Don't worry about it, all right? Do me a favor. I love how your eyes are fixed on the trees. In Southern fiction they call that the tree line, don't they, Massa? Shut up. Don't you love Southern fiction, so earthy, so natural, so attuned to the art of narrative, and yet, so, so, so deep. Shut up. Do you know why this is the case? Shut up. I'll tell you why, I'll tell you, you pitiful sterile bastard with your well-wrought crap, because *all* Southern writers had a mother or a grandmother or an aunt or some other wise old person who told them the most *fascinating* stories in their youth. Usually on the old porch. Shut up. Or the old verandah. Shut shut up! Under the Spanish moss. For *Christ* sake! That's why they can write those rattling good tales, stories so full of life that make you understand life and everything. She's going to make another pitcher of martinis because she doesn't know about him but she, for one, is goddamned sick and tired of swinging on the goddamned birches. Can I get you a mason jar full of white lightning, darling? Or is it just plain corn? Earthy? Electrifying? Full of dusty red clay roads and tree lines and overalls? Will you please shut the hell up? That sounded just like dialogue! Do you want to know why Southern writers write such great dialogue? Jesus! Because in the South, wait a minute! Because in the South, everybody *really* talks! I mean they don't just talk, they *talk.* Don't you think it's a lost art? Don't you think that television is to blame? Don't you? Oh, God, my heart cries for him. We used to go to all the very gay places. Who cares? Not *us.* Now we have all these friends and a lot of parties. I'll go to bed with anybody I want, I'm still good enough to get somebody. Those come-what-may places. And. And. Why am I so? Sad. It's the feel of life. I hope you're satisfied. That first time I took off my clothes he blushed, he turned his eyes away. Now he eats breakfast and lunch in his studio. *Studio,* my God. In the mirror her face looked like Our Lady's. Whose blessed eyes bleed for all the sins of the world. Girls, the blood streaming down is because. I remember all their faces if not their names. The blood streams because. Yes, girls. Bloody sanitary napkins, bloody tampons, blood, blood, always plenty of goddamned blood. I don't think I've ever missed a period, and does it matter whose fault it was? Not to us. Down. Down and down. Lost April, the heart within her died.

Payer of stayers

to a loft, a beach, a field

Said fine O.K. when asked to marry went down to the bar drank bourbon draft beer played Billie "No Regrets" over over over Harlan came limped with strange tall woman dead eyes black metallic dress: was on the roof locked out on a bitter cold night: no paint turpentine canvas paper food money nothing but a pint of Dixie Belle half a fifth of Majorska: a smaller painting crimson Prussian blue imitation of Guston *The Raid* said was best work so far Jesus Christ! let's face it! hypnotized by self-pity: asked take off everything but boots what did care: large eerie painting black vertical slash in center said it was death: climbed stairs loft behind looked up skirt: told about Harlan New Mexico looked and nodded: walked upstairs alone again again walked downstairs alone again again: hateful couple Lou and Sheila somebody on landing too listened cursed kicked bottles around behind door: looked at two ears of Indian corn over stove asked if never for Christ sake heard of Popeye: put cap on head fucked from behind: answered phone said no said no said all right yes got drunk walked across town upstairs undressed: wouldn't show one photograph managed to steal sheriff and wife: ripped *The Raid* across with beer-can opener wept chanted Guston Guston Guston: called Lucy Taylor came over helped down with suitcases: told again about Harlan New Mexico heroin others photographs looked again nodded again: hit with belt over and over came on the floor wanted to vomit got excited: screamed about white linen dress white sandals hair screamed all the way downstairs: slammed front door: second night brought two pencil drawings stared puzzled the bastard: yelled yelled again waited yelled again window opened key in Milky Way wrapper: tried to arouse failed tried failed: cried went downstairs got drunk: went upstairs drunk: cried tried to arouse failed: put cap on looked out window while slept: harsh thin smell turpentine sun curtainless window on death: Lucy helped upstairs with suitcases frowned filth broken walls ceilings must be some fantastic lay to put up with this: lit cigarettes don't know what:

went back in dead of winter married thank God alone looked grey sea going out: should have known first night around eight oh Jesus we're going to run out of booze Jesus Christ might as well have kept my clothes on: asked as joke about my past some joke left Harlan out of it. Midwest puritanical questions: yet took my hand small canvas white yellow peach softest violet *Joanne's White*: no matter how no matter couldn't keep him hard lay in sand wept apologized cursed moaned: at the top of the steps to beach still calm low tide hand in hand walked all right: asked me why I wanted photograph innocence white pants white shirt white tennis shoes smiled in sun glare Kansas City sun through windows innocence how come you: rain pelted ran upstairs kerosene heater tomato soup rice beans franks salad stripped fucked kneeling came and came oh he came kneeling sweet cunt sweet sweet cunt groaned like dirty books: wanted to know wanted really about Harlan smoked cigarette after cigarette I brought up I told Joanie Teddy Marlene all Chester Max oh Jesus all the O'Neills Connie all every damn one couldn't shut up made some up all: fire: ocean just visible moonlight: why: why why: but why: followed me to beach his hand cupped between my legs: why oh Jesus why: drank cursed yelled argued red face vicious: *Joanne's White* is phony phony piece of phony shit dumb fucking bitch whore: vicious: worse and worse: worse and worse and worse: impossible: hid Mom's handmade birthday card beloved girl my sweet child of August: hung over fragile read me Hart Crane wet thick wind slicing through the blanket: another miraculous palest yellow white lavender fuchsia green size of a postcard *Provincetown Alba* absolutely beautiful: for you: for me: for you forgive me: card from Lucy we all miss you sweet Bunny hurry home looked at me the card this the ugly fucking dyke you told me about?: pushed me right down the steps skinned my knee forearm now bullshit me about your tough life lit a cigarette: raw clams baked clams clam soup basil thyme white wine fresh tomatoes who says I'm not a good provider fucked me my white sundress sandals sweet breeze: on the deck sketched me over and over threw everything away I don't even understand your goddamned blank wasp face: the last night stupid movie argument about where oh God about where it was filmed in a rage cursing at me I wouldn't he masturbated in front of me see? see? see this goddamn you?: Tania came with some man talked nonstop gossip to be married like marrying a radio we laughed afterward shh they'll hear us: a canvas board three brushes his paints give it a try don't worry about it give it a try don't be nervous see how the paint feels: stopped talking about books he hated those he hadn't read but wouldn't read you and your Symbolist fags: in Truro middle-aged man limped I stopped I must have gone white looked at me his face I must have gone: New Mexico: I told him contempt rage you can't paint you can't write you can't cook make the bed can't sweep the floor do the dishes can't do anything can't fuck right you're killing me! you're killing me opened a gallon of white port: killed me fucking already can't even paint anymore worth a damn look at this shit!: and kicked *Joanne's White* across the room:

bores me to death: empty stadium: hand on my hip: talks about quarterbacks: hand on my breast: down the stairs: talks about Ohio: almost puts me to sleep: Caddy and Quentin: under the stands: takes bra off opens pants I can't look do it to him with my hand: comes all over me my skirt: up the stairs: he loves me: he bores me to: leaves me at the bus stop: walk back to stadium empty sky: sit on the grass: throw up: stiff stain: walk up the stairs: sky empty:

to an inn, a school, a front door

Biff Harlan Harlan and Biff Harlan and Teddy Harlan and Biff and Teddy Harlan and Joanie and Teddy Joanie and Teddy and Marlene and Harlan Joanie and Sam and Biff and Harlan Marlene and Terri and Georgette and Harlan Marlene and Biff and Harlan Dolores and Marlene and Harlan Biff Harlan and Biff Harlan Dolores and Liz and Chester and Max and Harlan Chester and José and Harlan Ed and Kate O'Neill and Harlan Kate O'Neill and Harlan Ricardo and Ed O'Neill and Harlan Harlan Harlan Harlan and Biff George and Connie and the O'Neills and Louie and Harlan Harlan April and Johnny and Harlan: all preserved forever: clear glossy images:

good-looking beard will for me top step Art Students': will be *Fruits and Dross* or *Pistachio Oval* evoke sneers laughter: have incredible body when sketch again and again erection: limited talents commercial bent: son of a bitch: wait for me every day drunk or sober bottom of stairs: look up skirt step stool my paint box my apron: climb down step stool hands hips hands thighs sneaky bastard dirty as if he: will cross-eyed artistic psychologist or goddamn schoolteacher brushing up against me: take a break: relax: step stool my legs: he'll throw cap out window he'll vomit on floor model somebody's canvas: that look on that cold face that cold look when Harlan this when Harlan that: frightened girl from Akron or some place kiss feel breasts why not? between landings: water color six ladders to a sky azure *New Mexico Blooze*: not bad: admirable talents small but fine: the beard hand on my ass in the dark street a drink? a bite to eat?: run down scattering charcoal pencils brushes everything: he'll incoherent mumble steps to the creative tequila in a pickle jar sweat running down face: creative bitch!: *Fruits and* laugh spit on it what a piece of garbage: start on beard in basement his eyes ohh good and stiff he'll ohh baby: Harlan dream naked club-foot naked clubfoot in between his legs: Agfa apron beard say they can't see your pure and eccentric but real downstairs Rocky's Tavern what the hell: really I mean really beard will say real talent I'll settle myself legs open as if by: he'll fall front steps or something down the street he'll break wrist he'll break again: beard at step stool when I'll get down he'll smirk love really love your ice-blue I'll blush I'll: my father? my father will come upstairs puffing oh God the tweed jacket the blue denim shirt *The Nation* in his ripped pocket he'll smile: so what's up with you?: he'll say can't paint worth a shit a good goddamn who the fuck do I think I'm kidding this *New Mexico* crap for Christ's sake good for the Salvation Army or your dumb old man for Christ he'll go down to the ball game cursing and laughing he'll:

be the father open your arms smile at the top of the Christmas stairs: be the tweed jacket always be that be that good teacher: be the beautiful dreamer: peach silk slip on a holiday visit: Lucy will show me Lucy will take off our bras: holiday dinner a little wine the trees pale in the grey mist low clouds: elbow patches blue work shirts he can carve he can cut the pies: like the watercolor: after snowstorm he shovels a tunnel to the door he takes a little Scotch neat his face all red her jack-o'-lanterns beautifully made each one a different face his deprived underprivileged her Indian corn her tableware ceramics and clay the porch steps: her dress molds to her buttocks and they are and they are this is how daddy sees her: weeping in my room: pumpkins autumn my birthdays and theirs Christmas Ralph comes over the same bore the same football: pale leaves in mist: I'll never again daddy be what I what I did the men and the women the sheriff and his wife the redneck truck drivers the married couple and the cameras Harlan never daddy not Kate's thing she straps on never I'll be the cover girl in white again: the plaid skirt the knee socks white blouse I'll be again what was: he'll be gone he'll be dead the filthy pig his filthy clubfoot dead: be the girl who showers in the bathroom with the pink roses and blue baskets calmly diagonal: be the colored lights and the ribbons and the tattered Santa Claus the turkey sober small jokes: the dishes and mom in her navy blue woolen dress her black pumps and be the daddy in the repp stripe tie and the pie and some cognac: and mom of course your mother has put on a little weight: but in he smiles but in the right places: we will love we'll mom and daddy love love: smile: smiles: they smile at the top of the front steps love: be love no big thing just easy and easy love: just some decent love for God's sake: be the father and mother: be that.

Cage

Anne Kaufman née Marshall: born to Jude Marshall, an alcoholic crew chief for the telephone company, and Tessie Blankenship Marshall, the only one of four children to be placed in an orphanage by her deserted mother. State Teachers College, where she excels in athletics. Extremely popular member of the Christian Student Union. That's a good one. Full skirts. Peasant blouses. Hair in a thick yellow braid, bright and glowing Scots-Irish face. Etcetera. Smell of Castile soap. Pots, ceramics, weaving, knitting, crocheting. Competent cook. White kitchen curtains, yellow-daisies print. Bakes whole-grain bread, literary ambitions. Too good to be true. However. New York at twenty-two, job at Black Ladder Bookshop. Meets Thelma Kruliciewicz and startles herself by having a brief affair with her while living with Karen Ostrom. Make it a passionate affair. Meets Lee "ZuZu" Jefferson, gets job as editorial assistant at *Hip Vox,* where Lee works. Lee isn't a bad name. Buys new clothes, has hair cut, meets Guy Lewis and Joanne Harley. Correction: Joanne Ward. Moves into Guy's loft. Marries Guy one month later in civil ceremony. Oh boy. Has affair with Olga Begone, a mythocentric poet, cross-eyed to boot. Moves in with Olga, divorces Guy. [Two-year lacuna.] Tessie dies, Jude remarries the owner of the Naughtie Nightie boutique in Kirkwood, Missouri, Charlotte Pugh. Small world. Anne appears at wedding, held on Charlotte's yacht in Palm Beach. Ridiculous! All right, Biscayne Bay. Ridiculous! Anne gets drunk, confides to Ralph Ingeman, a childhood friend who now sports an ill-fitting toupee, that Jude sexually molested her for years and that for Ralph's information she isn't wearing any underclothes. He confesses his long-standing and hopeless love for her. She wonders if he'd like her to prove it by standing against the sunlight coming in through the bay window. The porthole. Returns to New York, attends art school, shows no talent. Attends poetry workshop. Curious word.

Learns to write poems in imitation of Theodore Roethke. Publishes "Snails" in *Lorzu,* a little magazine edited by Craig Garf and ZuZu. Ambience? Literary. Sniggering helps nothing. Moves out of small Brooklyn Heights apartment owing three months' rent. So much for the magical fucking skyline. Moves in with Craig Garf and begins to do his typing. Etcetera. Meets Vance Whitestone and Dick Detective, known to some as "the priest." White wine. Sazeracs. Vodka with cranberry juice. And so on. Fun-filled days and thrilling evenings. Right. Has affair with April Detective, an enthusiastic bisexual. Jude dies in fall from telephone pole in Corfu. Something odd there. Charlotte Pugh returns to Lawton, Oklahoma, after selling boutique to Phyllis Redding, an Englishwoman with an obscure past. Small world. Anne meets Leo Kaufman, a poet, moves out of Craig's apartment and into Leo's. Too good to be true. However. He enchants her by claiming that the trash and garbage that fill the shotgun flat on Avenue D is "dirt that blew in through the windows." White kitchen curtains, make it a cherries-and-leaves print. Writes Theodore Roethke but the famed poet does not deign to reply. Close call! *Very* attractive stationery. Craig gives her a number of informal lectures on the enchanted world of books and she gradually begins to understand truly the wonder and delight of. Hold it. Leo asks her to wear a diaper to satisfy a common sexual taste. Some dish, he later says to a stranger in a saloon in Teaneck. Wrong town. Anne and Leo are married, have a wedding supper at Stanziani's. No. Fugazi's. No. Imbriale's. No. Some Italian joint with a beer garden in the back, spaghetti, paper lanterns. Those Italians. They return to a burglarized apartment, in the middle of which are two fresh turds. My God. Correction: In the middle of which is a note on Anne's very attractive stationery that reads "thaks four the Mikky ways." Something odd there. They speak quietly of Freud, excrement, and money, but Leo cries anyway. There's no winning. Anne sits at the window listening to the screams and curses of the dispossessed floating through the courtyard, echoing again and again, maddeningly, despairingly, bringing her at last face-to-face with the hollow travesty. Hold it. Anne sits at the window smoking. Make it nervously smoking. Nervously chain-smoking. Leo writes "The Burglary," a kind of sirventes. Check word. Leo reads the poem to Anne and then says, for no apparent reason, that his occasional

impotence can be remedied if she will allow him to spank her. That's a
good one. If she will spank him. Oh boy. How about with a belt? Something odd there. Anne remembers that she once told Ralph Ingeman, or
so she tells Leo, that she wanted a word with him out in the hayloft,
preferably naked. In Biscayne Bay. Biscayne Bay? Leo queries. Wrong
place. Anne accedes to Leo's perverse desires, formed quite some time
before. That's the way it goes. Anne begins keeping a journal that
meticulously records their erotic life together. You never know. Leo
begins to drink heavily and purchases several recordings of Civil War
songs of the Union Army, which he plays while drinking muscatel and
A & P Tudor beer. Check brand name. He tells Anne that he wishes he
were dead since he's dead anyway. Disturbing yet quintessentially
melodramatic. Anne gives the ice-blue panties that he buys for her as a
peace offering to the super's wife, Frieda Canula, who puts them on her
head to scrub the stairs. So much for exotic lingerie among our
Albanian friends. Anne spends an evening smoking marijuana with the
Detectives and all three go to bed together. She tries a few things, some
of which are good and some all right. Others won't work because of the
physical limitations of the human body. So the manuals were wrong!
That's the way it goes. But give her credit, give her credit. That's a good
one. Leo frequents the Soirée Intime and becomes enamored of Léonie
Aubois, who always laughs at him and rarely fails to tell him to get a
haircut. Why? asks Leo, peering out from the vast bush that encircles
his head. Always the card. Anne shows her journal to ZuZu, now the
managing editor of *Hip Vox.* ZuZu decides to publish excerpts from it
anonymously. Anne buys a fedora and pickets the offices of Crescent
and Chattaway, publishers of *Suck My Whip, Lace Me Tighter, Joys
of the Square Knot,* and other works of the erotic imagination. Correction: other filthy and degrading trash! Leo begins writing *Isolate
Flecks,* a roman à clef whose most reprehensible character is named
Annie Sheriff. These writers. He uses Anne's journal as a source,
although how he managed to. Hold it. Anne moves in with Vance
Whitestone and Leo somehow meets a young woman named Ellen
Marowitz. The narrative quickens. Now we're beginning to see
daylight. Anne closes their joint bank account and gives the money to
Vance. She begins wearing burlap skirts, sandals, and tattered T-shirts
and stops shaving her legs and underarms. God knows why. Vance

introduces her to Tony Lamont, author of *Synthetic Ink,* who is aroused by her hairiness and pursues her sporadically but unsuccessfully. Leo meets her in the street one day and tells her that he wants a divorce, that he is finally beginning to *live,* and that he is rewriting the poems of Dante Gabriel Rossetti as free verse. Wow. Anne tells him that it's fine with her, that he's as crazy as he ever was, and, on parting, that she isn't wearing any underclothes. Search me. She begins an affair with Tony Lamont, moves out of Vance's apartment when she finds Karen Ostrom's blouse in the closet and her bean sprouts in the refrigerator, then moves in with Tony. [Two-month lacuna.] She meets Lorna Flambeaux, author of *The Sweat of Love,* and they have a brief affair. An intense affair. A brief, intense, and torrid affair. On their one-month anniversary, she gives Lorna her fedora, and Lorna, in turn, buys her a pair of Sweet-Orr overalls. How fetching she looks! Fetching? Anne discovers that she has the manuscript of Leo's first story, "Sleeping with the Lions," and burns it in order to destroy not only the mere physical object but the outward symbol of a love that at one time burned as. Hold it. Meets Annette Lorpailleur, who wants to arrange to have photographs of her taken in what she calls interesting bohemian poses. Oh boy. Anne goes to a Halloween costume party at Horace Rosette's, dressed in a diaper, bra, and high heels, and even though she's crying on the inside, Rupert Whytte-Blorenge steals her shoes. Henri Kink, a failed novelist, commits suicide after writing the screenplay for *Hellions in Hosiery.* His farewell note reads "Enough is enough!" Always the card. At his funeral, Anne meets Ann Taylor Redding and Ellen Marowitz, the latter clinging to Leo's arm, and to whom Anne subsequently refers as Miss Eskimo Pie, Miss Golden Delicious, and Miss Popsicle. So much for remaining good friends. Jack Marowitz, Ellen's brother, whose professional name is Jackie Moline, propositions Anne, offering her three-hundred dollars if she will perform a rather reprehensible sex act with him and she accepts. You never can tell. Anne begins to affect severe tailored suits, crisp blouses, low-heeled shoes, has her hair styled in a loose chignon. Check word. She considers converting to Roman Catholicism but is discouraged when she discovers that Annie Flammard, the star of *Hellions in Hosiery,* was once a Sister of Charity. Small world. Anne is duped into going to bed with Barnett Tete, a wealthy businessman, who has not been able to get her out of his mind since seeing her at Horace Rosette's Christmas party. Wrong occasion. Her divorce from Leo becomes final and she precipitately marries Barnett, who insists that she live alone for most of the year in his Biscayne Bay mansion. Aha! She cuts her hair short and buys a wardrobe of pink sleeveless dresses in the hope of catching the eye of a plain, no-nonsense, good-hearted man, but succeeds only in attracting the attention of a vacationing professor, who, it turns out, thinks that pink makes a woman look helpless. These academics. The gardener, Reeve, makes her pregnant and for a lark she blames the professor, who swiftly returns to his sylvan, wooded campus in the Mississippi swamps. She has an abortion and as she leaves the clinic is struck a vicious blow with a picket sign carried by Phyllis Redding, who now makes her home in North Miami and works as a clerk in the Tropical Bible Aids Shoppe just outside of town. Ridiculous. [Three-year lacuna.] Anne appears as Sister Philomena Veronica in *Sisters in Shame,* a low-budget horror movie. So much for the religious impulse. Phyllis Redding is seduced by a stock clerk at the Born Again Employees' Picnic, after which she writes an article for the magazine *Jesus!,* "The Horror of My Forced Abortion," which she dedicates "to my unborn Robin, who will never feel the humidity on his little face." Whew. A death notice for an "Anne Kaufman" appears in *The Sacramento Bee.* Wrong Anne. Wrong paper. Anne returns to New York, her name changed to Anne Leo, determined to make a go of it in business, but fails to interest employers in her eclectic experience and life skills. So much for the cheery fucking magazine articles she's been reading. Barnett Tete announces that he can make gold, calm storms, and raise the dead, and is committed to a mental hospital by Rupert Whytte-Blorenge, who has earlier been named by Barnett as attorney-in-fact for the purposes of executing durable general power of attorney for health care of Barnett. That's a good one. Anne moves in with Rupert, who now owns a chain of shoe stores. Too good to be true. [Six-year lacuna.] Anne buys out White Sun Talent Associates, Inc., and begins producing educational films for the Golden Rose Fellowship, an organization whose energies are directed primarily against public restrooms as places of sin. These crusaders. Marries Chet Kendrick, a former actor, now a Neo-Neo-Humanist with a syndicated newspaper column of conservative views entitled "I Got Mine." She presides over licentious Washington parties to which high government officials are invited and records their unruly behavior on videotape. You never know. Travels to Mexico, has cosmetic surgery, invests in La Basurita Aztec Food Products, Inc., and two years later moves to Switzerland, where she begins work on her memoirs, *Perfumes of Arabia,* with the assistance of Leo Kaufman, a more-or-less permanent guest in her chalet. So much for burning the old fucking bridges.

Cuisine this and cuisine that, you know, the half-raw carrots and the lumpy mashed potatoes, salads swimming in oil with those massive chunks of blue cheese, or bleu cheese, or cheese bleu, lots of luck, but you know, Miss Eskimo Pie, Miss Milky Way, Miss Tutti-Frutti, she doesn't really like Leo to spank her but after a while it isn't so bad and then, you know, Ellen sort of gets to sort of like it, she likes everything about Leo, my God, even though her old man, Jack, doesn't like him much, or her brother, Jackie, that gorilla, he doesn't like him at all, he thinks, they think, he's a pervert and a schnorrer, a sort of well, you know, a faggot, that's Jackie's word, their word, you know, too bad, of course, the cocktail dresses, sweet Jesus, pink, baby blue, lavender, fuchsia, pale yellow, you name it and if it's cute, well, there it is, plain black high-heeled pumps, Peck and Peck cardigans and blouses, Harris tweed jackets, pleated skirts, just a picture of restrained perfection, Barnard and Sarah Lawrence too, you know, best friend Elizabeth Reese, prize-winning student poet, Jesus Christ, her "Starry Night, Bronxville: With Orgasm" creates a small scandal because the "Helene" of the poem, whose "shining head moved in / gentle pulse be- / tween my joyous thighs" is thought to be, well, you know, thought to be Ellen, too bad, that's at Bennington, so what all the fuss is about, God knows, you know, she doesn't really like to, you know, do it with Elizabeth, but after a while it isn't so bad, she likes Bennington, except for Jane Richardson, who is always, you know, always the old families and the old houses and the old estates and the old who the fuck knows, the old *Mayflower,* and the feeling is sort of, well, mutual, there is that snub nose and those good clothes and that creamy complexion, but, you know, to old Jane she's just a new kike, you know how those old girls can be, the story goes that old Jane gets the old Joe from a sleaze rock-

and-roll drummer and that her sister, Punkie, those names will murder you, she runs off with a Cuban-Irish truck driver with a few tattoos, you know, some guy who delivers firewood or manure or whatever to the old summer place at the old seashore, and has a bastard son, so the two old girls liven up that watery blood, you know, that old blood, too bad, but we are off course, Jesus Christ, Elizabeth moves to New York, no, Elizabeth more or less disappears, so what, Ellen moves back to New York to her parents' house, time flies, she gets a job, the Marvelous Magazine Management Corporation, publishers of *Action, Men's Action, True Action, Action Monthly, Jungle Action, Action at Sea, Sports Action, Hot Action, Actionworld, Universe of Action, War Action, Guns in Action,* and other real men's magazines, on the strength of her education, right, her résumé, her crossed legs, you know, her wide dark eyes, her, well, sort of eager look, her engaging curiosity, Jesus Christ, her crossed legs, you know, people die, as usual, then many more die, too bad, Ellen lives, Greenwich Village, wooden spatulas, wooden spoons, wooden bowls, wooden breadboards, all-purpose wine glasses, ceramic this, ceramic that, a leather address book, some, you know, attractive and unusual prints, a fucking brick wall, more wooden things, Jesus Christ, Lincoln Center, you know, right, she meets ZuZu Jefferson, an editor at Crescent and Chattaway, and is soon, you know, in the thick of things, Jesus Christ, at a party, you know, one of those parties, where one might meet daring editors and writers in touch with their generation, and fascinating artistic people of, you know, all sorts, including the deadbeat who just got an appointment to, you know, teach something somewhere, no, to be a, you know, writer in residence, right, and Barnett Tete is there, some strange girl with an accent, no, some strange girl, a deaf mute or some-thing, a cripple, something, she just, you know, just sort of pulls her panties off while she's dancing, some novelist, Cecil something, he just sort of pukes in a corner, pisses in the bathtub, throws the baked ham out the window, a barrel of laughs, a real artist, and Ellen meets, well, you know, not meets, but talks a little to Annie Flammard, who does something, something having to do with, you know, art, in advertising, Jesus Christ, and through Annie she meets, she is introduced to, Leo Kaufman, a poet, *The Beautiful Sun,* acclaimed by those few who know, and Leo is working on a new long poem, political but not, you know, overtly so, not propaganda, so he says, wild mop of hair, you know, he's afraid of the barber, don't ask, ninety-eight-cent tie with grease stains, rumpled suit, shoes, well, Jesus Christ, unbelievable, she doesn't really like him to spank her, you know, too damn bad, Leo sort of, well, he puts his hand right between her legs, a real bard, they're at the table with the baked ham, no, that's on the sidewalk, the roast turkey, the cold cuts, no, actually, they're at the table with the booze, the bowl of melted ice cubes, and Ellen, well, you know, there she is in her pink cocktail dress, Ellen is sort of, well, stunned, Craig Garf, a handsome man, prematurely grey, you know, no, balding with greying sideburns, no, rather fat and he seems to wheeze, well, Craig takes her hand and leads her away from Leo's hand, and Anne, Leo's first wife, no, his wife, right, they're still married, Anne comes up to Leo and slaps him across the face and Jack Towne, somebody, probably Jack, you know, he takes Ellen into a bedroom and this comes to that, you know, whatever, when Ellen gets home she's missing her underwear, except for her slip, which is torn, she's wearing a grey fedora too big for her, right, her skirt has stiff stains all over it, you know, a Peck and Peck, no, a Bergdorf's, who knows, it has these stains on the unearthly purple material, no, blue, no, aqua, no, turquoise, no, it's pink, stains on her pink skirt, dress, a garment not too particularly chic, but Ellen has an idea about herself, don't ask, Jack Towne calls up, but no dice, too bad, he really would like to get to know, you know, get to know her better, right, legs, right, thighs, right, you know, she really interests him a lot, you know, more people die, on and on it goes, that's the way, you know, then it's Thanksgiving yet again, Jesus Christ, time flies, Anne and Leo Kaufman, Sazeracs, turkey, range turkey, Jesus Christ, ZuZu, Craig, a fruity chablis, Vance Whitestone, Karen Ostrom with, you know, an organic plum pudding without anything at all in it, amazing, Jesus Christ, some priest, right, a regular guy, right, all-natural hashish, no, he's an ex-priest, expresso and cognac, Ellen and the ex-priest and somebody else in a closet, somebody, but, you know, who cares, some pills, some capsules, lots of cognac, this and that and things happen, things happen, Henri Kink comes for after-dinner drinks, with a striking tall woman with icy, well, blank eyes, beautiful legs, she's in a black metallic dress, her voice is, well, you know, her voice is, well, uncanny, Jesus Christ, and a third guest, a clubfooted man, he rubs against Ellen rudely in the kitchen, she's getting ice, he, you know, he is really very rude, very, you know, bold, she can feel his erection against her thigh, she can see it inside his, Jesus Christ, he's wearing these pants, this suit, he's got on this weird blue suit, it is really, you know, very, very, you know, it is odd indeed, he just rubs again, Jesus Christ, she gets back to the living room, dimly lit, her living room, the ex-priest, you know, the one in the closet with somebody else, time flies, that was two years ago, time flies, you know, it just, right, she notices that her skirt is somehow up, she is not quite there at all, she is, well, you know, stoned, she notices, too, that there seems to be a head between her thighs, it's the ex-priest, he's, right, Jesus Christ, and there's the creep, the weasel, the man with the suit, the clubfoot, the insane blue thing, he's in a chair with a camera, Jesus Christ, his eerie pants are, well, they're, well, he's opened them, well, you know, she lies back, her eyes close, she, you know, who cares, soon Ellen goes to Switzerland, no, Brazil, no, Milan, no, she goes to, she goes to, you know, she goes to work, right, to work, she gets fired, work, fired, and so on, she gets a job through Jackie, he calls himself Jackie Moline, he owns a couple of saloons, Cadillac Lounge, Reno Tavern, Gold Coast Bar and Grill, he has money on, you know, he has money out on the street, he's prematurely bald, greying sideburns, no, a little overweight, no, he's got distinguished prematurely grey hair, no, silver, he gets a job for her at one of the, right, the Foxhead Inn, a cocktail waitress, you know, those legs, her unabashed curiosity, right, those legs, short flared skirts, legs, thighs, black mesh stockings, no, she works as a hostess, svelte, sophisticated, some drinking, right, some coke, right, a little hash, a little this, nothing serious, a little that, she meets Barry Gatto, pieces of Mu-Shu pork stuck between his front teeth, disgusting, too bad, a Long Island drive-in movie, *Silk Thighs,* Ellen with the ex-priest, Frank Baylor, right, that's his name, and what with this and what with that, he asks her to, well, he doesn't really ask her, he says that he can't bear to look at her and not, well, you know, tiny flared skirt, legs, thighs, svelte, whatever, he says he can't bear, well, he can't, and so Ellen says, well, she doesn't say, who cares, and more die, time keeps, you know, it keeps passing, Lincoln Center, the ballet, Lincoln Gom, ecology, politics, Buddhism as transcendent xenophobia, Jesus Christ, and Leo, one night, he's drunk, he's always drunk, too bad, Leo asks her to come with him to his apartment one

night, right, after the bars close, no, just before they close, she is
celebrating her birthday, dinner with Jack and Jackie, you know, family
ties are, you know, her mother isn't there, her mother is, well, dead, Leo
asks her to, will she please, he loves her, Leo loves her, Jesus Christ, he
looks at her, her legs, you know, her thighs, well, you know, she goes
with him to his apartment, she looks at things, Jesus Christ, beer cans,
beer bottles, soda cans, stacks of magazines and newspapers, shirt
cardboards, filthy piles of clothes, no, piles of filthy clothes, the sink
crammed with greasy dishes, hordes of cockroaches, the mousetrap
with the putrefacting mouse in it, the broken refrigerator, smell of
freezone, in it a half-quart of Majorska vodka and a washcloth stained
with blood, Jesus Christ, the clogged toilet, grimy towels, smudged
glasses, food-encrusted stove, the mattress on the floor, grey, stained
sheets, a pair of torn beige panties in a corner, pornographic magazines,
Nylon Pussies, Whores in Heels, Anal Fancies, stained with, well,
soap covered with strands of hair, foul toothbrush, hairbrush, comb,
razor, broken-legged table littered with God knows what, Olivetti
portable, half-ream of yellow second sheets, loose stamps, correspondence, paperback mysteries, science fiction, *New World Dictionary,*
pens and pencils, dull paring knife, rotted apple, overflowing ashtray,
five or six crumpled Camel packages, a brown-stained butt glued to a
spot of dried beer, half-full quart jug of Gallo Burgundy, envelopes,
notepads, a spiral-bound notebook, three Trojan condoms, Jesus
Christ, enough, Ellen takes her clothes off, you know, carefully, kneels
on the mattress, you know, gingerly, no, Leo asks her to put her heels
back on, he, you know, he hands her his belt, he kneels on the mattress,
she doesn't really, but, you know, he starts to beg, you know, Jesus
Christ, she tells Jackie, no, she tells Jack and Jack tells Jackie, no, she
tells them both, separately, she and Leo, she tells them, are, you know,
they're sort of, well, married, my God, Jackie finds Leo, he, you know,
he sort of hits him, he sort of socks him in the nose, well, in the jaw, he
whacks him, you know, a little, in the eye too, he, well, he beats the shit
out of Leo, he calls him a pervert, then Ellen buys him leather notebooks for his jottings, for his, you know, his notes, so that he won't, you
know, lose any ideas, Jesus Christ, Anne, well, Anne is a bitch, Leo
says, you know, Anne is some bitch, what else is new, Leo goes on and
on, daily, nightly, Ellen would rather that he just didn't get so, you

know, so, so, Leo goes on, Anne, she turns out to be, among other things, a, you know, a motherfucking cuntlapping dyke whore of a shit-eating titlicking cunt, whew, Ellen meets Olga Begone, you know, author of *Man-Kill* and *Nutless!,* and, you know, Anne and Olga are, at this time, whatever that may mean, they're sort of, you know, living together, then she's introduced to Lorna Flambeaux, whose latest book is, right, *Leaves of Yearning,* an imaginary journey through the mind of Renée-Pélagie, and then she sort of meets Roberte Flambeaux, the chairmistress of the Daughters of Durga, and the author of various tracts and, well, you know, manifestoes, and when Leo makes Anne into a monster in *Isolate Flecks,* Ellen, well, Ellen, you know, Ellen is angry, you know, because now, well, time passes, more deaths, Leo spanks Ellen, he paddles her with a Hi-Lo bat, he makes her wear her pink sleeveless dress because, he says, oh boy, it makes her look like a whore pretending to be a virgin, Jesus Christ, there is tofu with cranberries, Jesus Christ, dandelion leaves sautéed with mint jelly, garlic, and olive oil, Jesus Christ, brains, eggs, and pumpkin casserole, Jesus Christ, odd but enthralling, right, *Isolate Flecks* is published, Vance Whitestone, right, reviews it, he's, well, somewhat unkind, you know, a little harsh, right, he doesn't much care, you know, for the book, he, well, actually he crucifies it, too bad, Leo cries, he cries a lot lately, Ellen's pink dress doesn't help, she won't do what Leo likes anymore, she stops buying refill paper for his leather notebooks, she's, you know, got other fish, you know, to fry, she moves out one day, temporarily, to stay with Roberte, just for a few, right, a few, a short, right, some weeks, time flies, a month or two, she moves her clothes in, her record player, her books, Roberte is writing the text, the commentary, you know, for *Annals of Sapphism: Womanlove,* and one thing, you know, one thing just sort of leads to another, Roberte shows Ellen certain things, certain, you know, techniques, right, Ellen meets Lucy Taylor, someone who is, well, Lucy is in love with Joanne Lewis, because Joanne is, well, Joanne is really lovely, and besides, her so-called husband, Guy, the so-called artist, right, he's up to his ears in something with that guy, what's his name, the twisted creepy guy, with the bum leg, no, with the limp, no, the guy with the clubfoot, with that horrible blue suit, oh God, and Guy gives beautiful Joanne no peace, so Joanne and Lucy, after all, what the hell, Ellen and Lucy hit it off, they begin to live together, Leo is out in the cold, too bad, Ellen and Anne have a long talk together one night at The Black Basement, a new club that Jackie has just opened up, no, that Jackie manages, they find, you know, that they have a lot to, well, to talk about, right, they agree that Leo is, well, you know, that Leo is, well, Jesus Christ, they become friends, they talk things over, one day Ellen sees Leo on the street, they call him, you know, the bard, right, she and Anne, Ellen sees the bard on the street, pathetic, unshaven, under his arm he has this copy of, right, *Isolate Flecks,* pitiful, too bad, he doesn't, you know, recognize her, he can't recognize her, even though he looks, Jesus Christ, he looks right in her face, her new look, her crew cut, her, you know, her new self, overalls, fedora, right, the same fedora that, right, work boots, she smiles at Roberte, who is with her, they go into the Caliph's Walk, she has to call Jackie, she has to make, you know, arrangements, to get, well, to get the plans straight for the High Holidays, for Passover, the seder, then she has to go and buy a wig, you know, and a nice little black dress, right, because, you know, Jack and Jackie, well, and when she comes out of the bar with Roberte, Leo is sitting on the curb, pathetic, he's drooling, he's wet his pants, Jesus Christ, disgusting, too, you know, too bad, and time flies.

Two mose bankes

Madame Annette Lorpailleur

Annette was born in Mexico of Hungarian parents who were fleeing freedom or something reasonably identical with it. How the mariachis burned the tongue, was it not so? Yet she, rather too obviously, grew up on the outskirts of London, where the depressing albeit picturesque fogs instilled in her a love for oranges, so that even today she likes to be surrounded by them in the odd moments she snatches from her busy life, well, perhaps not literally *surrounded*. She read many books, classics all, painted with a gracious nod at insouciance, and was soon married to a man who would later be disgraced, poor sweet bumbling Tommy! Something to do with bribery in the construction business. Yet none of these travails, whose enumeration is tedious but absolutely necessary to our narrative, prevented her from a relentless and single-minded pursuit of her goals, ever receding, a pursuit occasionally interrupted by reckless and malicious charges brought against her person, always in whispers, by the rest of the faculty. Few had number two pencils either, yet nothing seemed able to stop them.

Yes, she had found a home at last. Gone the long nights of seedy sexual adventure, the torn half-slips, the picnics and wienie roasts on the banks of the sullen and brooding Thames. Degradation is too mild a word! She knew that she looked good, even fetching, in her severe tweeds and flannels, chastely cut, sure, yet alluringly contrasted with her strong and beautifully molded legs, encased, in the time-honored phrase of Wordsworth, "in nylons taut like gold to fairy thinness beat." Talk about poetry! The flirtations with shadowy Hindu "blood cults" did not in the least prevent her from pottering in her garden, a formal English garden, as one might expect, in the elegantly restrained village of Stilton-on-Baskerville, where the lawns had been sown at the time of

188

William the Conqueror's birth. His royal mother, so the story goes, had asked for preserves of some kind as she expired. Noblesse oblige! Often the young Annette gamboled, Heidegger all forgotten, in nothing but the bottom part, or the "pants," of a swimsuit casually selected and purchased in Rio. Lord Harlan wasn't quite sure whether he liked that, and would sometimes glance up from his blueprints disapprovingly. Yet at dinner at the Macedero Club that evening, or the Blue Rune, or Le Bricoleur, when Madame's hand stole softly beneath the immaculate napery and rested, rather promisingly, it must be added, on his trouser-fly, he would find himself ordering in his most compelling, though somewhat theatrical, tone of voice. And *what* he ordered! Even the *maître d'hôtel* averted his experienced eyes.

Often a tree would fall as she labored over her footnotes. Then would follow a lengthy discussion of love and the responsibilities attendant thereon. Sleep was, of course, difficult. But nothing could keep her from the meal that she loved to prepare in the mornings for her Tommy. She also "fell to," as Stevenson might say, with a hearty appetite. And coffee? Well! Long into the mornings, graceful in her flowery peignoir, she sipped at the brew, her thoughts far away, the house quiet, Tommy at one of his many offices, or, as he'd often whispered to her, his "branches." His voice, at such times, had that edge of gruffness to it that was sure to soften her heart and permit her to forgive him, even though the ancestral English oak had, yet again, smashed in the roof. At such times Zeno helped, as did Cleanthes of Assos, and, goodness knows, it was wonderful old Chrysippus of Soli who had enabled her to cope with the discovery that somebody, probably the sturdy gardener, had allowed a bushel of corn to rot in the hold of the yacht, the older one, thank goodness!

After Tommy had been slandered and hounded by a vengeful and vulgar press to his exile in one of the larger Midwestern states, where even now he regales the members of the Country Club with bantering descriptions of scones, Annette (or, as she still bravely and defiantly calls herself on those rare occasions when she puts pen to paper to thank an old friend, and how few of them were left!, for a gift of marmalade or a dead turkey, perhaps a potted boar's head—Lady Granjon *still* knew what she liked!—Lady Harlan), Annette, ever in command, had turned her hand to the composition of "spicy" limericks, many of which she threw wildly into the sea. There was something disconcerting about them, or so she admitted to a bevy of chuckling journalists. One of them snagged her revealing skirt on the quince, and *who* shouldered the blame? Of course!

Still, the reviews were wonderful, so much so that her colleagues often gave a party or two, anything, as they said, but not to Annette, whom they still hated, to get a "celeb" onto the hoary, yet not unattractive grounds of the university. Many would gather beneath the statue, as if *that* would help. These academics! That she chose, at this time, to dispense with underclothing, is apparent in the dust-jacket photograph, which shows her, somewhat bemused, before a wall of books in her study. A discerning eye can descry some several oak branches protruding from the ceiling. Yet *nobody,* not even the Earl of Bodoni or Tony Malinger, fresh from yet another triumph at Cannes, was permitted to smoke. She had, it was obvious, heard a few things. Instead, they spoke of the great satisfaction her garden gave them, as well as the ineffable peace they found, pink gins in hand, in the bee-loud maid. There were, of needs, a few guests who were quite painfully stung by the irrepressible forest creatures, but Reeve, the head butler, always had to hand plenty of lard and seasoned chaff. Good old Reeve! His collection of curious implements was a "hit" with the Frankenstein girls, the minxes! And still the reviews came in!, one, as her publisher, Freddie Willingmouth, put it, better than the other. There was, as Lady Harlan told Mrs. Divan of the Condom League, something "about" Freddie. Others of their set agreed, but rarely.

At the Academy Awards ceremony, no one, it seemed, in all that glittering assemblage of wealth and talent, was surprised when *Fly of Metal* won virtually every award. When Annette kissed her "Oscar" and spoke, quite movingly, of her old dining table, wittily characterized by her as a "groaning board," even the little people got to their feet. They were something that night! Later, at the whirl of parties, the President called and gave her a lighthearted description of his Windsor knot. And people wonder why! Still, she would have thought it odd, if not remarkable, had she known that the strange odor in her dressing room was caused by a moldering copy of the *Tractatus,* left there, in hasty retreat, by an old school chum, Berthe Delamode, who, as Corrie Corriendo, presided over one of the more exclusive brothels in all of

Beverly Hills, though the envious scoffed. Let them! others proclaimed. How Annette herself had fought her feelings when she found Berthe's fondly inscribed packet of pornographic playing cards. Had our country's enemies ever got their hands on the Five of Clubs! Heavens! Yet she triumphed over her animal emotions, as was her wont. Berthe's fedora, however, was found the next morning by the chambermaid, submerged and as good as ruined in the loo. Curious word! Tommy read, some weeks later, and with no small degree of hilarity, of the team of plumbers and their search for an orange, "caught," as the manager put it, "somewhere in the miles of pipes" beneath the hotel. Poor Berthe! Yet the nagging realization that Annette had once owned a fedora caused him, no longer as young as he had once been, many a sleepless night. Slipping into the "frillies" that his fiancée had bought for him at François of Fargo's gave him, thank goodness, some surcease from the pain of suspicion. And one night, what should appear on the "telly" in his suite but an old Jeff Chandler "flick"! There had always been something infectious about *that* he-man, so the gossip went. Society columnists were increasingly grumbling, however, that the season was not quite the same as it had been when he'd brusquely organized generally amusing orgies, a few of which had been of a decidedly sexual bent. Yet on Thursday evenings, lost in nostalgia, he would stare at her photograph and remember. Still, nothing could deny that the frame cried out to be replaced. One morning, he flew into a rage when his favorite magazine lacked an ad that reliably confused him. It looked like "the end of the line," as Dreiser once wrote to an old friend who still, after all these years, lives in Tucson with her memories.

In any case, the money, which Professor Blinque facetiously characterized as "moolah," rolled in. What a card! She was in time given an endowed chair, and then it was that the wives of her colleagues no longer asked what she "did." But nothing, it seemed, could help. Soon, fellatio itself was a bust and the mullioned window, although repaired, lacked the old zing. She wanted, most desperately, to be believable, despite her odd proclivities for public self-abuse, or "pollution," as Father Debris liked to call it. Oh, she *read* everything! But many the night found her dreamily washing the ashtray her cousin, Welles, had made, for a lark, at Cambridge. Remarkable how after the Sudan we have tended to forgive fraternity boys everything. The Museum of

Modern Art in New York was interested but cautious. They'd had *their* share! It was less of a shock than a surprise when the headlines screamed of Welles's disappearance in the Amazon Basin. They *had* found a pith helmet sporting nine poisoned darts. Cold comfort indeed. Never again would the flaxen-haired youth lurk in the men's rooms of the bustling Métro! Nevertheless, the old English oak appeared to be growing again. And then Berthe was heard from, as if out of the blue. How could she have dreamed *that?* Yet records indicate, if one reads between the lines, that it was so. From that soft afternoon to her first pair of metal shoes was the simplest of progressions, so that even Baron Sternhagen was compelled to extinguish his cheroot before attempting his sexual specialty, no small victory! Lady Harlan wasn't through yet, despite an irritable deluge of the new season's great novels. Hadn't the Dean of Arts and Sciences given her a new nameplate for her door? No matter that her name was spelled "Onette." That had *always* been a minor flaw. There was always the potato salad and the chance to filch a seasoned cardigan while everyone took snapshots of the much-heralded event. The paperback was doing well, too, and though Tommy had taken to sending her descriptions and photographs of his new family, the elms had, for *once,* escaped.

The metal slips were somewhat of a bother, but Annette remembered Edison and his onanistic interludes, and Berthe only laughed. It was the same dry, hard, brittle, forced laugh that had made her so loathed at Greengage School. Lady Harlan had, in spite of it all, become something of a "looker," though diet and exercise had taken their toll. Still, tongues wagged. Hadn't Charles Rimini-Bates returned the garter, the "something blue," he'd stolen after that weekend in the Newlywed Room? Annette felt a *little* sorry for herself, but decided definitely against the chain-mail. Enough was enough! Later, when the apartment had somehow dissolved, there would be time for a nostalgic tear or two. In the meantime there were the term papers, the Committee Against the Committee on Committees, the domestic wines—quite good in their way—and new studies of the Bloomsbury circle, though few understood her dogged insistence that Jack London had actually written *The Voyage Out.* Indeed, there were some who demanded that she "go back to Hollywood." No amount of sparkling water could placate *them.* She thought, one bright, crisp autumn day, relaxing on a flat rock in the middle of a New England field, of the old English oak, but soon rejected the idea as gauche. It was, indeed, for many of her younger colleagues, a pleasure to get to know her. Although her skirts were becoming disconcertingly short—the New York influence, some opined—few, if any, left early. Then, too, there were the long nights of Key Lime pies, the slide shows, just about any kind of World War I model plane, and, for a lucky few, oral sex with unknown but complaisant guests in the potting shed. How they treasured their inscribed copies! No one knew, of course, that Tommy had taken up a stubborn yet fitful residence in the attic. Marmalade was, Annette was chagrined to admit, but his second choice. It is difficult to understand the creative spirit. Berthe, at any rate, finally decided she wanted him in her employ, for the "few old broads," as she facetiously put it, who'd arrive after midnight. There was the usual rouge and the occasional blushing remonstration, but nothing could stop Tommy once he had his trousers off. Dear Berthe! Lady Harlan's next book, the memoirs, wasn't half-bad, so everyone said. But she did get some odd looks on the old quad. Luckily, she had her chair, and the rights had been bought for an Academic Playhouse of the Air dramatization. She even found herself chatting with her colleagues and their auto mechanics as the cool of the evening descended on the trees. Strange how often they spoke of Europe. When the wind blew up, the trees soughed, and the gossip turned to marital problems, which, the "gang" agreed, were a bother. Still, *somebody* had to open the summer cottage.

Then there were the reflecting floors, the rare-book collection, the evenings spent sorting out her blouses and the few intimate garments, which she, in high spirits, called "lingerie," and which she couldn't bear to pass on to the maid. It was, in truth, absurd to find that on numerous occasions, a man who introduced himself as Mr. Rosette was discovered cowering behind a rack of evening gowns. He looked older than usual, but what, in heaven's name, was she expected to do about that? Nor was it her fault if Sheila, who had often loudly proclaimed her friendship, insisted on cavorting, as good as naked, in the street. She'd always maliciously called her Lady *Harley* anyway. Tommy, as usual, wasn't talking, poor darling. Yet the blame, if blame it was, had to be placed somewhere. Surely, Annette hadn't intended on actually *working* in the bordello. It had been merely a misunderstanding that "caught her out" entertaining two priests, a policewoman, and someone who kept insisting, over and over, that he was "lost." The subsequent faculty meeting was lively, to say the least. It seems that no one dared venture to put in a good word for either Virginia *or* Leonard Woolf. On the contrary, one distinguished professor, in the slow and measured tones of an engaging pedantry, suggested that they were, after all, "only British," and, as such, decidedly vulgar. There ensued a confused rush to the coffee machine.

But by this time the yacht had been refitted despite all, and Bermuda was, Annette wrote to a favored few, beautiful for a change, even though Tommy kept insisting, long-distance, that he had married Karen in a moment of pique. One can't have everything. So it wasn't with precisely a *light* heart that Lady Harlan threw everything over and boarded her favorite luxury liner with her "little Hungarian," Count Janos something-or-other. Pity his mother had ordered his tubes tied after the Cracow affair with a band of traveling goodwill ambassadors. Still, her collection of Impressionists was dazzling, if banal. The university, however, never quite recovered from the blow, nor did it go unnoticed that three new female assistant professors had taken to affecting tweed suits and low-heeled shoes. Though they often tried surreptitiously to cover their knees at faculty "galas," many old hands were having none of *that,* thank you! There was *always* too much to drink. And so it was that a daughter was born at last. The Count looked on amazed for the space of a few moments, then fled to his estate. Annette, or as she was now called by her ideologically naive new friends, Countess Nettie, ate another forbidden chocolate. There was little to be done about it, for now the *shrubs* seemed to be toppling over, some of them onto the greenhouse. That spelled disaster, of course, for an awful lot of flowers. But it would be champagne and caviar for everyone sometime soon, even tough-guy writers. How the moonlight danced on the waves, and that glow in the distance was surely Miami! So life, Nettie mused, smiling gently into the refreshing salt spray, did have a meaning after all. More or less.

Ann Taylor Redding

Although there were a few Bulgarian friends left in Panama when Dr.

Redding decided to leave, she wasn't that impressed. "The grass *is* always greener," she'd quip, packing her favorite stocks and foulards. And she never wanted to see goulash again! No one dared ask why, amid the general hubbub beneath her window. Had they surmised that her favorite leather bag was crammed with peaches and apricots, they might have changed their tune, although certain highly placed commentators still deride that idea. Yet Paris was, as always, Paris. There it lay! Ann knew that she could always count on a good, depressing drizzle to make her forget the banana plantations and the other things, mostly multicolored. Still, a therapeutic bout of blubbering and wailing insured the presence, sometimes for days, of what she had learned to call a "cafard." Those frogs!, she spasmodically tittered through her sobs. And although she had never married, she couldn't forget her new business associate, Mr. Pungoe. He wore his electric-blue suit everywhere, while the other partners sat and grumbled in New York and other humming capitals. A few said it was the real-estate dodge that drove them into their weekly frenzies. Yet the majority was closer to the truth. On the other hand it took no great acumen to search out the real factors behind it all. Ann was back and show business was once more beginning to pick up, a sure sign that the party season was upon them. We *think* we know what cocktails are! And platters with unrecognizable cheeses! So the good doctor was, take it all in all, glad to be "home" again, faced, though she was, with her world-renowned sportswear collection. *Somebody* had to do it.

She'd gaze out at the Loire, the Eiffel Tower throwing its brooding shadow on her biscuit. Then, of a sudden, there were the stars! What with her recipes, various engines of destruction, her silks and satins, the shoes that *still* didn't fit, and the few, poor, steel brassieres she'd made —how many years ago was it now?—in Indochina, the nights would pass. She didn't mind a bit! Every other Tuesday would, however, find her on the window ledge, the subject of prying eyes, but the famous lines, "Something there is that doesn't love a fall," kept her from it. That's art for you! Friends? Well, perhaps, but it wasn't always so. But with the mere act of kindling a good fire, and placing a white cloth on the table, things often began to "look up." With wheat rolls and a glass of fresh clear water, Ann managed to engineer a *few* pleasures for herself. "Besticitum consolatio veni ad me vertat Creon, Creon, Creon," she'd begin one. Then, look out! By the time the newspapers got wind of the various occurrences, Dr. Redding had lit out for her château at Après-le-Bain. It was whispered by the grooms and a few others that Richelieu himself had breakfasted on rotten *oeufs* in the homely kitchen. Wittgenstein *was* a comfort, even though her habit of reading him in the chimney corner in a swimsuit set the surrounding countryside abuzz. Soon after, the mad garageman escaped and the cows, so it was bruited about, ran for their very lives! That very week, the Board of Directors voted to ask for her resignation. What a joke! She'd occasionally call long-distance and talk, in that odd voice of hers, to just about *anybody*. Pungoe, just in from his morning tramp—an old war "buddy" who had fallen on hard times—didn't precisely *object*, yet there was something in his face that gave her pause. All would be forgotten in the evenings, however, when, at Club Zappe, or the Hotel Pachuco, or Le Bleu du Ciel, Ann's shining gauntlet paddled in the entrée in such wise as to make Pungoe literally *drag* her home. And so to bed! *That's* where his clubfoot came in handy. But in the mornings the shrubs were dying. Oh, she'd turn to her ledgers and account books, of course, but even Ann couldn't blot out the fact that her diploma was, well, *missing*. Pungoe, dear heart, jovially spoke of the letters to the advice columnists, and poured the wine with a liberal hand. Still and all. And the *meals*, especially dinner! But back in her room, Ann waited tensely for the door to slam. Connecticut again?, she'd often think, then vomit, like as not. Pungoe had become, willy-nilly, a man on the go. And she, somewhat tragically, had tired of the endless hors d'oeuvres and a couple of cherished memories. Perhaps it was polishing her evening gowns that kept her sane. Still, there were *other* stories. Beauchamp, the hostler, was found one morning caught fast in the trellis. A stern look from Ann put a stop, eventually, to *that*.

Meanwhile, somewhere in the middle of the great city, Pungoe had become involved in "the arts," whatever in the world he meant by that. The notorious Horace Rosette, "the man without a patio," as he was known to the seething milieu, was behind him, a remark that occasioned many a furtive leer. Little, if any, decency was shown. Ann rummaged through the fallen leaves, searching for something, something. Perhaps the glove that dared not speak its name? Who could tell? But old friends from the "Zone" were always near to prevent her from savaging the phlox. You'd never have guessed, of course! "Reticent" is perhaps the word. When the reporters, who were indefatigable, scaled the wall, Countess O'Mara, Lady Bustier, and "Queen" Endiva opened fire on the ptarmigans, the loves! Even though her royalties on the first five-thousand copies of her "confessions," *A Bed of Poses,* were earmarked for the National Multiple Orgasm Fund, the stories came out twisted, as usual, in the tabloids. Partners fumed behind locked doors. They hadn't counted on *that!* Although Pungoe's complaints fell on deaf ears, Dr. Redding *would* give the party. But the hashish did its job, despite the tendency of a few high-powered executives to fall into the pool. And besides, as Lady Bustier chuckled, the videotapes of perverted Congresspersons would come in handy, later, when they found themselves touching down at Palm Springs. None were prepared, however, to discover that the top model was one of our crustiest generals. There's *something* about a soldier, one wag at the bar noted, to general acclaim.

So went the weekends. The maids quit, *en masse,* every Monday morning. "Incidents," one petition stipulated. The Frankenstein sisters, who were usually found plodding down the sylvan back roads, loved to "fill in," however. The critical attacks on *Bed,* led by Michelle Caccatanto, were somewhat tempered by their frilly aprons and unfailing good humor. And talk about your pasta! Suffice it to say that there wasn't a tablespoon to be found. Few wanted *really* to do it, what with the children just next door, but even religion has to take a holiday *sometimes.* Hollywood was naturally interested after the talk shows, particularly the one on which Ann talked for almost ten minutes about her steel-mesh stockings. The audience roared its approval. And quips? Don't ask! But where in goodness' name were the actors? Oh, they did find a few practicing their salutes and speeches, but the moguls were, well, not happy. The option later arrived by registered mail, but it was all done so *subtly.* Pungoe had wired that Annie Flammard was more than interested but was having a spot of trouble with motivation. Still. And on top of all that, the peaches and apricots rotted, then *attacked.* It was enough to make a girl cry, or so Ann was quoted as saying. Almost immediately after, a piece by the President of the Tribade Conspiracie appeared on the op-ed pages of several major newspapers. Then, of course, came the veritable *storm* of fedoras.

Pungoe, as restless as ever, had put Rosette in his place, and an invitation quickly arrived for Dr. Redding to attend the cocktail party celebrating the opening of his new boutique, Nuts & Bolts. She literally *flew* to the wardrobe to find, as she had feared, her unique prototype for an aluminum-alloy sun dress missing. So he *had* finally decided to pattern his lackadaisical existence on the base character of Minna von Hattiesburg. What film buff worth the name doesn't recall her as she was played by Dolores Délire in *From Natchez to Mobile*? Some suggest that popcorn rose to prominence about that time. *That* was an era! Still, it is only in dusty and forgotten tomes that the role of the Iowa Writers' Workshop can be discerned in the affair. In brief, at a certain point, all admitted to a general collapse, then, in a past Director's phrase, all hell busted loose! Literary historians agree that the debacle was caused by "the short story." A few have been preserved as cautionary devices at which the curious gape with a mixture of horror and loathing. Oddly enough, children seem to like them. Ann often reflected on all this as she signed things. Pungoe *was* persistent, the boutique was flourishing, and prayer had returned. With, so to speak, a bang! Yet Dr. Redding's bank statements told the harsh truth. Cash had ceased to flow! Through the long winter, she stared unseeingly at the shriveled carrots. There was, surely, her platinum cocktail-dress collection, safe in Marrakesh. But then her father's gruff voice and work-gnarled hands would come back to haunt her dreams. Annie Flammard? Ann would wake up, once in a while, in a cold sweat.

It was at about that time, at the advice of her psychoanalyst, Miriam Paimon, that she decided to "act out"; in the words of Dr. Paimon, "What the fuck." Good advice indeed, as it turned out. Ann journeyed to the Everglades and started what is still spoken of with awe in the real-estate business as one fantastic scam. An adroit mixture of senior citizens, condominiums, and faulty building materials, and in no time at all she was giving speeches and winning awards. Money? It is to laugh. But in a trice, her sister died, found smothered beneath a pile of *Cosmopolitans* and *Swedish Lusts* in a sordid room of the New Ecstasy Motor Inn. A few Evangelists spoke of sin and free school lunches, but they buried her anyway. An old friend, Karen, called during the funeral festivities, to let Ann know that all had turned out badly. She *had* managed to marry Lord Ridingcrop, whom she somewhat unfairly referred to as "an English pipsqueak." Street toughs had

long known where to sell their "hot" garter belts, but still, Ridie had a
few good points. For one, he *was* British, or so the *Times* had long
assumed. Subsequently, there was that indefinable *soupçon* of
elegance, of grace, about him. Perhaps it was his kippers! Certainly, no
one else in Riding-on-Alum wore them with such an easy flair. Unfortunately, when he rode to hounds, the young ladies hid their eyes and
the older ones blushed demurely. Sports often bring odd things out.

So bad news followed on the heels of bad news, often without
surcease. Ann began smoking extremely large cigars, wondering—
occasionally aloud—if this nasty habit had anything to do with phallic
symbols or whatever they're called. She was never one to fret, however,
no matter the damned Sunday supplements. Then came the certain
hearty tycoon's call! It was time to modernize her kitchen! Dr. Redding
set to with a will, hammers flying, gouges and adzes and Stillson
wrenches not far behind. Acclaim for the finished job was not so great
as she had hoped or expected. Old friends fell silent when she entered
the room and Holt Rinehart, her new maid, kept tossing his little lace
caps into the garbage-disposal unit; it *was* in the sink, but unmarried
young women often found themselves unwilling observers. Ann, in
what Pungoe diffidently called "a tizzy," took out the fuses, but Holt
had other methods up his puffy sleeve. What a rascal he was! Ann
wouldn't have cared, for herself, but she'd read too many accounts of
honeymoons that just weren't *fun* to let him have his way. So when the
auctioneer disposed of the last Warhol—and passing acquaintances
agreed that it was *amusing,* at least—the doctor took a room in a new
"in" whorehouse. She had sworn to read, straight through, all the
Pulitzer Prize novels of the last quarter-century. "For penance," she
implored anyone who would listen. Of course, they were busy most of
the time, and even she was constantly being urged by clients, who'd
mostly had a few, to disrobe, at least partially. Still, on she read, with, it
must be confessed, a pencil in hand. You can't *tell* about people.

A long, rambling letter arrived and in it she learned that the mesquite
had just up and quit. Things were back to normal at the new ranch!
She'd gaze out, thinking, *knowing* that it was too good to be true.
Pungoe was discovered in the game room, morose as usual. Money,
money, money! But the long winter nights were perfect for their addled
and unreasonably wayward conversations, the delicious—and little

known—mustards from every corner of the earth, and the semi-weekly shot at fornication in front of the crackling wassail bowl. Christmas at last! Partners, moguls, tycoons, and assorted alcoholics turned up on the doorstep, proving, if proof were needed, that they were no slouches when it came to opera and other refined, if silly, things. And double-breasted suits were back! She realized just how *long* she'd been away as she flailed wildly at a piñata. She knew, at long last, the truth of the old saying, "ethnics are warm and *real.*" You bet! she chirruped gaily.

But almost before the eggnog had turned a frightful green, it was spring! Then came the requests from adoring fans and goodness knows what all else! Skyscraper heels, surely. Pungoe adored to watch her totter about the yard at her chores, and growled happily. If marriage could only be like *this,* Ann would carelessly think in her little room under the eaves. Yet Karen was ill! One can imagine the doctor's surprise when the photographs arrived, *air mail,* from Worcestershire. As if *she* could have helped. Pungoe, as usual in times of crisis, was doing something with the chickens. Foul birds! A book she'd once read came back to her, but she wasn't going to *tell* anybody about it. Especially Ridie! She had to hold most of them upside down or sideways to discover just *what* was going on. Medical personnel had often proved that that many people couldn't be in one place at the same time without *something* breaking. You never know with demented gay persons, so Ann claimed. There were a few loud Christian cheers, but for the most part, the desert brooded in silence. There occurred an occasional cloud of dust on the horizon, but nobody cared about *that.* Well, it wasn't their responsibility. Still, a few days later, she bought a great deal of flat-white exterior but tearfully admitted that her heart wasn't in it. She even wrote to Karen at Lourdes, "Fuck the place!" Well.

After a wild and confused meeting with the board, she went ahead and put the soft-drink machine in, and, as she had long insisted would occur, her stock soared with the lowly employees, although the clerks groused, as usual, amid the bulging files. Deals, however, soon were being closed with the greatest of alacrity and dispatch and soon the area around the water cooler was virtually empty. Dr. Paimon presented her with a signed and leatherbound monograph on what she was pleased, for some reason, to call her "case." But after a score more triumphs she tired of everything, sold her shares and her skyscraper heels to Whytte-Blorenge, the ruthless fundraiser, and married, at last, a wonderful guy that she introduced to the old crowd as Rupe. Little was known about him, save that there were sexually explicit rumors having something to do with wicker baskets from Hong Kong. But love will find a way, or so Karen wrote from the cloister. Rupe did assume some airs, but with *that* nose? Why not?, the women, at least, opined. The men were, give the devil his due, chasing the underwear models around the greenhouse, now damaged almost beyond repair! Younger female partners took over the day-to-day business and once again the clank of metal was heard in the vast midtown offices. They all certainly *gleamed!* It wasn't that, but there seemed to be, among the women, great difficulties in sitting down. These kids!, wiser heads stated. For the record! Nostalgia was king, as is its wont. "Smooth," as weeklies suggested, "sailing." And how! But for others, it just hadn't panned out at all. Pungoe, for instance, was seen in an obsolete amusement park outside Wilkes-Barre, but then, silence. No one seemed to care about the three young women facing the horror of their unloved fetuses. Oh, the letters poured in to the newspapers, but they all seemed to have to do with sin and slaughter. There is no *telling* what excites some people. Ann, however, when she heard the reports, looked blank. Those who *really* knew her weren't a bit amazed. Unforgiving, perhaps. But she, her arm around Rupe, sailed on, the two of them lost in admiration on the forecastle or some other nautical equipment. Tahiti!, she laughed into the wind! Here we come!, the crew later swore she screamed. Rupe, however, wasn't so sure, although even *he* had heard about the depraved women thereabouts, well, perhaps not actually *depraved,* but there seemed to be nothing that they couldn't be talked into. At least so said old salts. And tars. There was nothing to lose, in any event, and he expressed this opinion to his bride. Ann threw him a fond but prurient glance as the pole star twinkled. It seemed to suggest that life was for living.

Tree of gowlden apples

Bart Kahane, who you will certainly remember may have been seriously injured some twenty or twenty-five years ago as the direct result of his penchant for donning women's clothing, or so we have been led to believe, decided, when he first married Conchita, which was a pet name for her true name, María de la Concepción, full name, María de la Concepción Dorotea Carolina Darío y Reyes, to find out all that he could about her seven sisters. His reasons for doing this are best known to Bart, who seems to be in a coma, and to his mother, who has disappeared. These seven sisters had all married suitable husbands, according, that is, to Conchita, the "flower of Durango," or, as she sometimes called herself, the "flower de Durango." Whenever Bart thought, when he could think, of this group of fourteen, or sixteen, if he added, as he invariably did, Conchita and himself, he visualized a small tree, perfectly spherical in the shape of its leafy branches, and dotted here and there with apples—golden apples. A rather too obvious figure, it is true, but one suitable to Bart's poetic understanding. Let us say immediately that he had a penchant for what is often called "the image." It is not too much to say also that this by-now famous "tree" and its equally famous "golden apples" have been made part of the accoutrements of Bart's "mind" because of the title of this section. The secrets of art are long, long secrets.

There were, in addition to lovely Conchita, lissome Constanza, beauteous Berta, gorgeous Elisa, handsome Eugenia, plain Lucía, sultry Bárbara, and vivacious Benita. A bevy of hot tamales, as Bart often put it to his many friends and acquaintances, whose identities are, let us hope, well known by now. The tamales' natural desires for home, security, and children, coupled with their fiancés' impetuous lusts, made for a series of quick marriages, beginning with that of the lovely Conchita to the twisted Bart. Then, in rapid succession, or, as Bart would sometimes humorously say, *pronto,* the lissome Constanza married the wily Charles "Chuck" Murphy, the beauteous Berta the good-natured Albert "Hap" Garrett, the gorgeous Elisa the saturnine Louis "Slim" Hess, the handsome Eugenia the effeminate William "LuLu" Hunter, the plain Lucía the ugly Henry "Hank" Lewison, the sultry Bárbara the lecherous Al "Whitey" Shields, and the vivacious Benita the pious Charles "Chick" O'Hearn. Strange, as the phrase has it, bedfellows, although more than one of the deliriously joyful newlyweds had never heard this expression. Hence the occasional grunt of bewilderment or chagrin when these particular unfortunates ran across the term in their honeymoon reading. For all, or most of them, had taken a good supply of books and periodicals into their various nuptial chambers.

The eight women, seized by the female aberration known to medicine as "the vapors" [See Lange, *Traité des vapeurs* (Paris, 1689); Raulin, *Traité des affections vaporeuses du sexe* (Paris, 1758); Pressavin, *Nouveau Traité des vapeurs* (Lyons, 1770); Rostaing, *Réflexions sur les affections vaporeuses* (Paris, 1778)], decided, in concert, to call their husbands by nicknames to which only the sisters would be privy. Thus, Bart was to be known as "Nando," Charles "Chuck" as "Carlos," Albert "Hap" as "Paco," Louis "Slim" as "Che," William "LuLu" as "Rosita," Henry "Hank" as "Chico," Al "Whitey" as "Pablito," and Charles "Chick" as "Momo." The root causes for this collective gesture toward sisterly unity are unknown despite our admittedly careless and halfhearted attempts at research, although a few amateurs who have concerned themselves with this mildly surprising but not unprecedented act seem to agree that a working premise, or opinion, may be based on the invaluable though somewhat eccentric studies of the "naming malady" done by "the man who ate the broom," Edmé-Pierre Beauchesne in his often-mocked *De l'influence des affections de l'âme dans les maladies nerveuses des femmes* (Paris, 1783). That work has since been, of course, superseded by the clinical observations of Pearson, Kooba, Beshary, *et al.,* yet its implications are, to this day, suggestive.

Perhaps more interestingly, the eight husbands, acting, for the nonce, in ignorance of their wives' decision, decided to take unto themselves nicknames as well, in order, as one of them later admitted, to feel closer

. . . to each other. So that Bart "Nando" was to be known as "Beebee," Charles "Chuck" "Carlos" as "Chaz," Albert "Hap" "Paco" as "Allie," Louis "Slim" "Che" as "Luigi," William "LuLu" "Rosita" as "Sweetums," Henry "Hank" "Chico" as "Hen," Al "Whitey" "Pablito" as "Happy," and Charles "Chick" "Momo" as "Cheech."

Bart, whose well-known oddities of behavior go far in explaining the obsessive interest he took in the activities of his in-laws, may have initially conceived of the eight marriages as a vast *hieros gamos.* If so, it was the very holiness of the rite which was to afford him, paradoxically, the greatest amusement, in that the second year of marriage for each couple revealed that all of the partners had availed themselves of lovers. For the sake of what we must insistently call the record, these pairings were: Conchita Kahane and Keith Blague; Constanza Murphy and Edmund Posherde; Berta Garrett and Emmanuel Chanko; Elisa Hess and Joe Billy Tupelo; Eugenia Hunter and Chalmers Endicott-Braxton; Lucía Lewison and "Weeps" McGuire; Bárbara Shields and Jay Bindle; Benita O'Hearn and "Buddy" Cioppetini; Bart "Nando" "Beebee" Kahane and Lolita Schiller; Charles "Chuck" "Carlos" "Chaz" Murphy and "Chickie" Levine; Albert "Hap" "Paco" "Allie" Garrett and Diane Drought; Louis "Slim" "Che" "Luigi" Hess and "Tits" O'Rourke; William "LuLu" "Rosita" "Sweetums" Hunter and "Buzz" Duncan; Henry "Hank" "Chico" "Hen" Lewison and "Muffin" Cunningham; Al "Whitey" "Pablito" "Happy" Shields and Eleanor Julienne; and Charles "Chick" "Momo" "Cheech" O'Hearn and Marie Louise Wong.

Now, according to hastily scraped-together information, Bart, in those few lucid intervals that interrupt his coma, as golden apples interrupt the green field of the tree from which they depend, hysterically insists that the eight sisters found each other's lovers to be far more interesting and desirable than the individuals whom each had originally seduced, or been seduced by. So that each, if Bart's ramblings are to be believed, began a clandestine affair with a fresh partner. In order to conceal, as best they could, their liaisons from each other, from their primary lovers, and, of course, from their husbands, assuming that their husbands, in the throes of their own amorous passions, cared about either their primary or secondary lovers, each took unto herself a name to be used while engaged in her secret venery, and also gave unto her new lover a secret name. Thus, Conchita Kahane as "Babs" or "Boobs" Gonzales or Consundays took up with Edmund Posherde, whom she called "Blinky" or "Bunky"; Constanza Murphy as "Queenie" or "Cunty" Antilles or Uncles with Emmanuel Chanko, whom she called "Puppo" or "Peepee"; Berta Garrett as "Honey" or "Hummy" Potts or Pazzo with Joe Billy Tupelo, whom she called "Texie" or "Taxi"; Elisa Hess as "Giggles" or "Gallie" Whinge or Bilge with Chalmers Endicott-Braxton, whom she called "Paleface" or "Polefast"; Eugenia Hunter as "Big Mama" or "Bag Mama" Pussie or Fussy with "Weeps" McGuire, whom she called "Fotz" or "Fudge"; Lucía Lewison as "Jitters" or "Cheesy" Staffel or Stuffit with Jay Bindle, whom she called "Heeb" or "Hoib"; Bárbara Shields as "Hots" or "Humps" Reilly or Daly with "Buddy" Cioppetini, whom she called "Hoagie" or "Doggie"; and Benita O'Hearn as "Legs" or "Sucks" Tubetti or Tortoni with Keith Blague, whom she called "Joker" or "Joan."

On, so to speak, the masculine side of these marriages, the arrow of Eros was also indiscriminately striking the sisters' husbands, and they followed, as if under a spell, the sort of spell that strikes one upon first glimpsing a tree, soft in the morning mist, crowded with golden apples, their wives' leads. And, too, for purposes of concealment, they availed themselves, while engaged in their carnal pursuits, of the nicknames that their wives had earlier given them. Bart is too "loco" and we are too busy to resolve the appealing mystery of how the husbands discovered their wives' secret names for them, but the evidence, flimsy as it is, shows that discover them they did. So that Bart Kahane as "Nando" dallied with "Chickie" Levine, whom he knew as "Lips," the pet name that Charles had given her; Charles Murphy as "Carlos" with Diane Drought, whom he knew as "Hickey," the pet name that Albert had given her; Albert Garrett as "Paco" with "Tits" O'Rourke, whom he knew as "Big Tits," the pet name that Louis had given her; Louis Hess as "Che" with "Buzz" Duncan, whom he knew as "Buns," the pet name that William had given him; William Hunter as "Rosita" with "Muffin" Cunningham, whom he knew as "Scummy," the pet name that Henry had given her; Henry Lewison as "Chico" with Eleanor Julienne, whom he knew as "Taterhead," the pet name that Al had given her; Al Shields as "Pablito" with Marie Louise Wong, whom he knew as "Chinks," the pet name that Charles had given her; and Charles O'Hearn as "Momo" with Lolita Schiller, whom he knew as "Dumb Lo," the pet name that Bart had given her.

It may be inferred, at this point, that these data, some, admittedly, tainted by conjecture, suggest that "the vapors" are not only progressive, but that they may be highly and intersexually communicable.

Bart's "tree," we note, was now more full of "golden apples" than he had bargained for. His transvestite quirks may have well been, in fact, the direct result of his growing bewilderment and anxiety concerning the moral configuration of this voluptuous and shifting panorama, or, as Bart once put it, this "fucking circus." His anxiety was surely not ameliorated by the fact that another "crop" of "apples" was, over a period of some twenty years, brought into the world. These were, of course, the children born to these various couplings, lawful and otherwise. It is impossible to assign to these children their proper and/or responsible parents. The ceaseless copulations of the group of husbands, wives, and lovers, along with what must have been their unified effort to expunge, destroy, obliterate, erase, obscure, falsify, counterfeit, and efface all records pertinent to these various births, has made it difficult even to begin to trace genealogies. We must permit, so to speak, these children simply to "appear." Here follows an incomplete listing of these offspring:

Nemo, Chooch, Hoppy, YoYo, "Mutt," Hips, Jiggs, Eppie, Looy, Slug, Ignatz, "Fotch," Popeye, Blast, Walt, Krazy, "Hans," Socks, Andy, Lefty, Jeff, Whitey, Skeezix, Blue Wind, "Ben," U.P., Swee'pea, Dipers, Chester, Chet, Chatz, Bud, Slam, Terry, Holo, "Clark," Fems, Whammo, Slick, Tillie, Trixie, Bra, Blondie, Blinky, Blow, Traxy, Mille, "Dick," Blammo, Hem, "Mark," Soho, Perrie, Bam, Mud, Matz, Zet, Hester, Weepers, DeeJee, Op, "Wen," Oiwin, Mannix, Blightie, Heff, Hefty, Mandie, Cox, "Mans," Hazie, Balte, Mast, Woppie, "Scotch," Oogotz, Mugg, Duey, Zippy, Wig, Lips, "Guts," LoLo, Poppy, Scootch, and Froufrou.

Finally, it may be of value to add that at the periphery of the complex erotics herein but sketched, there were at least ninety-seven other people who had to do sexually with the noted wives, husbands, and lovers. We know, if that is the word, the names of but eleven of them: Sailor Steve, Jayzus McGlade, George the Polack III, John Greene

Czcu, Miner X. Beely, Werner Smitts, Marion Bunt, Eloise Stephanie Gump, Kate O'Sighle, Patience St. James, and Whitney fFrench-Newport. All of these people seem to have disappeared, but for Patience St. James, who reads Tarot cards and tea leaves in a small store located in a large city whose name remains unknown. Her professional identity is, variously, Ronda the Crazy Gypsy and Sweaty Patsy.

In conclusion, it may be seen that rigorous attention to the most pedestrian details of human relationships may yield surprising data if not any decent "yarns." Such data, while probably of little use to an understanding of the people involved in said relationships, may, however, allow us to draw certain conclusions about the truth behind the facade of social, public intercourse. Our paradigm is, we insist, despite the mockery we are all too used to, useful to a limited degree. Some may discern in it, perhaps, the presence of what Hans Dietrich Stöffel in his *De praestigiis amoris* (Brussels, 1884) defined as "[a] large mess (*perturbatio*) developing as if self-generated out of [a] small one."

Three tombes

Was her maiden name Ravish, Ravitch, or Banjiejicz? Was it an obviously literary act for her, at the age of six, to call her most beloved doll Lu-Lu? On what pensive occasion did she wear a flowered-print Ship 'n' Shore blouse? On what date did she decide that The Three Stooges were brilliantly surrealistic? Why was it doubtful that in moments of mild frustration she whistled "That's for Me"? Why did she wear L'Ardent perfume even though she loathed its smell? Why did she attempt suicide by putting her head into a gas-stove oven when there was easily to hand a number of potentially lethal items? Did she ever use the name Louise Ashby? On what happy occasion did she wear a pale-orange dress and a plain gold bracelet? How did the novel *La Robe orangée* change her life? Was it likely that she always wore white underwear because of a magazine article? Did she really have beautiful legs? What prompted her to insist that *The Lady in the Lake* was a modern version of *Ethan Frome*? When and why did she get a tattoo on her inner left thigh that consisted of the letters W, A, C, and O? What evidence denied the oft-repeated charge that she stole an off-white raw silk shift from the Soirée Intime? Was it true that she objected to that which she somewhat obscurely referred to as Christian pornography? Was her observation that San Francisco looked like a lot of cupcakes an original one? Did she understand Emma Bovary's anguish better than Benjamin DeMott did? Was "They Can't Take That Away from Me" her favorite song, or was this too good to be true? Why did she invariably cry when she watched *Dark Victory*? Could her heart fairly be described as aching for breaking each vow? Did she think the hot dog a bona-fide phallic symbol? Why did she think that lumpy mashed potatoes were truly American? Why did she, when speaking with academics, falsely claim that she watched only public-television programs? Why did she call a term paper she wrote for an English course "Impotence in Silver Age Poets"? Did she know that Ho Chi Minh smoked Salem cigarettes? On what bitter occasion did she say, "Fly me to the moon or at least for Christ's sake take me to the fucking zoo"? Did she intermittently fantasize herself as the Simone of *Histoire de l'Oeil?* Did Sheila's proofreading of a true-life adventure story, written for the magazine *Fist!,* contribute to her decision to become a writer? Why did she look like a whore in her modest pink jersey sleeveless dress? For what reason did she falsely claim that mauve was her favorite color? Had her name been Gert Shitzvogel, Yolanda Stuzzicadenticcio, or Myrtle Wandajajiecowicz, would her first novel, *The Orange Dress,* have received any critical attention? Was she dead?

Am I embarrassed and chagrined to discover that Lou is not the originator of the phrase, "remarks are not literature"? How many times a year do I enrage Lou by suggesting that professional football players are probably fairies? Why does Lou become angry when I tell him that I'll never read *Finnegans Wake?* Is Laguna, where Lou and I honeymooned in 1964, real, or is it, like Gstaad, an imagined place? Am I secretly annoyed when Lou uses my mascara to paint a moustache and goatee on his face? What internal evidence in Lou's poem, "Sheila Sleeping," prompts me to accuse him of writing it for and about Yvonne De Carlo? Why, when I stand before Lou in lingerie from the Soirée Intime, does he say something like "this old cat plays a lot of tenor"? Am I impressed by the tag, "a poet of small perfections," that is often hung on Lou in the contributors' notes of the little magazines in which his writings appear? Do I always close my eyes and clench my teeth when Lou undresses me? Why do Lou and I think of Prospect Park with distaste? Why don't I tell Lou the name of the friend who left a manila envelope, containing nine rather unusual photographs, in our bathroom? Why does Lou claim that he wrote the central section of *The Orange Dress?* Is the foundation-garment model whose photograph reminds Lou of me at age eighteen, me at age eighteen? What is my reaction when Lou sings "Orange-Colored Sky" just prior to saying "that was some time, baby"? Why do I become annoyed with Lou whenever we travel together on the IND? Is it possible for me to initiate divorce proceedings in Laguna? Does Lou secretly possess the manuscript of my first short fiction, "Suck my Whip"? Does Lou ever shop for me at the Soirée Intime for what he calls frillies? What are the names of the third-rate Chinese restaurants at which Lou and I dine on Monday nights? What is the nature of the telephone conversations between me and Lou when he calls me late at night from Brooklyn? How often does Lou bore me to tears by telling me of E. B. White's glorious prose style? Is it unlikely that Lou and I will make love on the floor next to the Christmas tree in my family's living room? What prompts Lou to read aloud to me from the *Psychopathology of Everyday Life*? What sexual act do Lou and I refer to when we speak of "struttin' with some barbecue"? Does Lou ever watch me engage in sexual acts with another man or other men or with another woman or other women or with another man and woman or with other men and women? Why do I poke fun at one of Lou's favorite poets, Jean Ingelow? What do I say when Lou tells me that *The Bridge* is an example of religious immanence aborted by a lack of transcendent morality? Why does Lou deny ever seeing a photograph of me, at sixteen, sitting on a flat rock in a field in Connecticut? What reasons lead me to dislike the way that Lou wears his hat, holds his knife, and sings off-key? Do I ever tell Lou what I really did in my father's sinister car, outside Nathan's Famous, in sordid Coney Island? Is there anything to the rumor that when Lou eats coffee cake he never fails to remind me of the Sunday morning on which I attempted suicide? What are my motives for telling Lou that my favorite book is *Buddy and His Boys on Mystery Mountain*? Are Lou and I alive?

Why will you call your first adulterous lover Milt, even though his name will be, remarkably, Jerrold "Jambo" Vizard? What will be the surname of "Fred," to whom you will write on December 27, 1963? Why will Thomas Thebus, of Brooklyn, New York, momentarily glimpsing you from the window of a coach in which he will be traveling from Washington to New York, think you his wife Janet? Will Delilah Crosse, the lesbian sister of whom Tania never speaks, be the chic girl with whom you will strike up a friendship at a ski resort in February 1967? How will you manage to attend the Detectives' "snow party" in Vermont without Lou's knowledge? Will you ever confess to Annie Flammard and Rose Zeppole that you'd like to play a role in a pornographic film? Why will you pretend to believe that the deadbeat actor whom you will permit to seduce you at Annette Lorpailleur's dinner party is, in fact, a foreign military officer? What will make you virtually certain that the anonymous author of an erotic, not to say obscene letter sent you from Flint, Michigan, is none other than Margaret McNamara Duffy, a high-school career advisor? How will it come about that your father's insistence that you be home by midnight lead directly to the loss of your virginity? Does it seem possible that on the evening that you will supposedly be killed you will make a Spam and ketchup sandwich? When you tell Ellen Kaufman that your abiding desire in life is to be a fireperson will you be poking fun at the vocation, the word, Ellen, or all three? Why will you buy a pale-blue dress of soft and filmy material when you discover that Lou is having an affair with April Detective? Will it be naïveté or malice that prompts you to discuss the character of the Tin Woodman in the presence of Annette Lorpailleur? Why will Treadcliffe Marche, a sometime male model, steal your grey fedora? What will you mean when you tell Saul Blanche that you like the homoerotic imagery in Robert Frost's poems? Is it believable that your novel, *The Orange Dress,* will be nominated for the Ralph Lauren Medal for Literature? Why, despite published claims to the contrary, will the only known photograph of you in a sylvan setting show you playing volleyball in the nude? What curious and improbable series of events will lead to your winning, along with your partner, Dave Warren, the weekly fox-trot contest at the Bluebird, a tavern near Budd Lake, New Jersey? Will it be mere coincidence that leads all your lovers to read you the Blake tercet that begins, "In a wife I would desire . . ."? Will you be justified in your embarrassment and irritation when you discover that Jack Marowitz is lying about his knowledge that Duke Washington is the alto saxophonist on the famous recording of "Ko-Ko"? What will lead you to remark to Mesdames Lorpailleur, Corriendo, and Delamode that their apartment is warm and cheery? Will your coughing fit be designed to conceal hysterical laughter or compassionate weeping when you hear Leo Kaufman read, at the Gom Gallery, his celebrated "Tit Poem Number Five"? What arcane reasons will you have for collecting every recorded version of "Clarinet Polka" that you can find? Will it be a sign of the existence and goodness of God, as Rose Zeppole maintains, that you are sterile? Will you be lying when you tell all your lovers that Lou tried to destroy your literary career in order to advance his own? Is it true that moments after Bart Kahane throws himself out a window to the street below, you will steal his sequined mauve scarf? How will it happen that in the early morning of July 12, 1971, you will find yourself deshabille in the luxurious suite of a country inn with Janos Kooba, Edward Beshary, and Albert Pearson, three men whose very existence you doubted? Will it be mere coincidence that the drawing of a woman which appears on page 113 of Conchita Kahane's copy of *Segundo Curso de Español* bears a striking resemblance to you? Why will you be chagrined to learn that Saul Blanche decided to become a homosexual for a few months, or, as he put it, "more"? What pictorial evidence will contradict your assertion that you first met Cecil Tyrell in the patio garden of Horace Rosette's apartment? What will Lou make of the fact that in Laguna, on the morning of September 11, 1964, you will greet, in the space of three-quarters of an hour, Judge Harold Wenj, Cornelius A. Ryan, Johnson Mulloon, Father Donald Debris, S.J., and Captain Craig Copro, U.S.A.F.? Why will you think of Leo Kaufman's *Isolate Flecks,* a novel his many detractors call *Leo's Lunge,* each time you eat stew? If you live, will you care about any of the above-named people, and if you die, will any of them mourn you?

Beacon

Nobody is interested in Antonia Harley although it seems to be the case that something must be said of her. No one knows why this should be the case. References, certainly, here and there, may be found, anyone can find them, curiosity, that's the main thing. They were, of course, sketchy. Little response other than a shrug or a look of what has often been described as mild interest. Very mild indeed. You know about Anton, so let's leave him out of it.

It may have value, when certain new information is posited, emendations made, corrections considered, mistakes rectified, slanders quietly erased, well, partially erased, more precisely, obscured, or twisted out of recognition, when all has been made different, then quickly forgotten. In any event, she had her place, her undeniable place, even though it was as Anton's wife. Good old Anton. References may quite easily be checked against others, and there are plenty of references and plenty of others, too many, some say. Mostly readers. But although nobody really cared, something should be said.

The procedure usual in such cases: anecdotal material, so-called.

We may find ourselves in a room. We are in a room. Small wonder that it turned out to be Antonia's room, as it is now, we thought we knew what now means and whatever else it may mean it most certainly did not mean now. Antonia's room. It had in it this, and it has in it that. It had a refrigerator and a sink and from such textual evidence you may surmise that it is a kitchen. Fill in the useless details, since we are after something more profound, something real. However, if we consider that the refrigerator, the sink, and the useless details were all evidence that this room is a kitchen, is it so because of these items or because the prose once noted them with authoritative clarity? Refrigerator. Sink. Useless details. Enough of theory.

In Antonia's kitchen the fluorescent glare ruthlessly revealed a refrigerator, a sink, and other culinary items. Everywhere, a woman's light touch is descried, e.g., a dish towel, a coffee mug filled with yellow pencils, etc. Over here this touch of care. And that one. All had that ordered look. Implements, tools. Common sense is usually best in such tense situations, that is, here we are in somebody's kitchen, hers. On the other hand, common sense may be of no help whatever. Yet it has often been discovered that in mundane items people's true selves will be revealed, so goes the pensum. However, as often as not, there is another side to it, which it was once our duty to respect. Rightly so.

It may be of some value to rummage through a drawer that was quite easily seen among the wealth of details above catalogued. There it is, right over there. Although some of the items to be discovered therein, and soon, may have belonged to Anton, that somehow was not then, nor is it now, germane to our interests. Well, here they were, or will be, and as we hoped, they indeed did make us aware of, and display, as does little else, etcetera and etcetera.

There seemed to be a stirring of interest. Our story is about to take that famous turn. On, as they say, its own.

A drawer was suddenly open. Elements, or at least fragments of Antonia's true self may surely be discovered. Stranger things have happened, but rarely in a kitchen. We know a man who liked to surprise his wife in the kitchen. One leans back in one's chair and stares reflectively at the fire. The house creaked as it settled.

The open drawer. We're getting there.

Some were beginning to show a sharp interest, while others have no doubt skipped ahead to more interesting adventures. A third group has perhaps returned to familiar tales to take what they called another crack at them. "I wonder what's in the drawer," a few said, but not in unison. Perhaps they'll be able, finally, to get the gist of the thing. Or else. One or two were people who have their troubles just like everybody else. They hang on, bravely, the little people. America. Beneath all the glitter and optimism, you never know. Some were ex-drunks whose long struggle with alcoholism has made them or will someday make them, wise. Or at least resigned. To punish us, they may give interviews concerning their courageous battles.

We've heard that it's the writer's task and we cannot argue with that. Literature has a certain redemptive quality to it, so a majority opines, and not all of them can be wholly wrong. The writer, it seems, has many tasks.

In the thick of it. All right.

Someone was currently rummaging through the drawer, albeit with gentle hands, reserved mien, with a certain respect, is not too strong a word, for the woman who was not at home, or at any rate, is not in the kitchen, or those parts of it that have been tersely described in a workmanlike and sincere prose. There is nothing that can take the place of sincerity. Craft and sincerity. Craft and sincerity and the need to, the real need to tell stories. There's been a lot of rubbish spoken of all this, but in the last analysis nothing really can take the place of one flawed human voice telling of the deepest and most important hopes and fears and weaknesses and strengths of people. Flawed people. Flawed and weak and fearful. Yet strong and hopeful. And plain. And little. Plain, little people.

Antonia may well have been somewhere else in the apartment.

Slowly, the drawer was closed. Items loom in the brooding half-light, soft as yellow flowers. There's a predicate for you. Prior to now, that was. The recently rummaging figure has become the crunch of footsteps on the gravel driveway outside. Trees thrashed about in the cold wind, the moon sailed wildly through scattered clouds. Streaming darkly. It was a gloomy night. Many go to bed early. Open the door. He looked out the window. Crunch, went the metonymy.

A little farther and all will be made clear to you. Famous and quite familiar words, he laughed.

Yet the startling light of the kitchen showed nothing out of place. Someone had done his job well. False modesty has been thrown to the winds, and the most cynical admitted that the crucial rummaging-through-the-drawer, as it has come to be known, has produced nothing of interest but a slip of paper which has written on it what turns out to be a message, so to speak, a message whose content will prove to be uncanny. In this context. At the mention of the impending disclosure of this message, interest was piqued again, so muttered new fans, as well as some old ones, returning, however reluctantly. That such a message was discovered by chance is more than coincidence, whatever the mockery we may all, or some of us, be forced to endure. Such is the writer's task.

Yet earlier, if we have all agreed on what earlier means, or, perhaps more importantly, on what it meant, the drawer was opened, its contents rummaged through. The promised inventory was not made, yet soon all will be brought to light, but in the wrong place. Soon may as well be now.

Now is as good a time as any. Or as good a place.

Six cork coasters for party use, three bottle sealers, a package of paper cocktail napkins for party use on each of which is depicted a bleary-eyed pink elephant, a package of sewing needles of various sizes, a bay tree, a box of wooden safety matches for convivial evenings when guests drop in unexpectedly, a beer-can opener for party use, the same intrinsically loathsome, an aluminum funnel for funneling certain liquids, unprepossessing, four playing cards, six of Diamonds, four of Clubs, Ace of Diamonds, six of Diamonds, a ball of cotton twine, a yellow Princess telephone, a spool of masking tape, a crucifix purportedly blessed by the Pope with the words Hiya Your Holiness printed across its shorter transverse arm, a quarter, a dime, three pennies for those unexpected evenings when strangers arrive, a novelty garter of pale blue ruffled satin, a 3 x 5 index card on which is typed the recipe for Banana Amaze, two red plastic tiddlywinks, a fireman's helmet, three unrecognizable items for which there seem to be no words, a photograph of a clubfooted man taking a picture of three ten-year-old girls sitting on a lawn, a basketball, the seal, in gold, of some cashiered demon in whom Antonia has long since ceased to believe, a number of erotic letters to Antonia from a correspondent signing himself Pepe, a novelty corkscrew for novelty evenings, a newspaper clipping that tells the story of a wealthy magazine publisher and sportsman who fell into a ditch and claimed the loss of something valuable, a collection of

The interest was definitely growing, slowly

glass stirring rods now almost universally called swizzle sticks, a dish towel stained with some unspeakable liquid, something utterly bewildering, a few more things, an off-print of an article published in *PMLA*

Although there was some shuffling of feet and a few furtive coughs and entitled "Food Imagery and the English Mystical Tradition: The Role of Bacoun and Eys in Medieval 'Convent Tales,' " an alienating, self-indulgent, and confusing novel by a writer whose name is best forgotten, three disgusting items, the names of which will be graciously omitted, a chart showing the narrative line and plot development of a novel by an author who writes immediate classics about life and its beguiling wonder, a bunch of

Getting thin yet the ever-fruitful imagination

chopsticks for convivial Oriental afternoons, a red candle with the wick cut off, a hoe, a pamphlet issued by the Tribade Conspiracie: "Death to Emily Dickinson's Modesty!," what appears to be a shopping list: milk, bread, eggs, meat? check, cleaners, an unpaid parking summons issued by the Lamoille County Sheriff's Department on the back of which is written "Tonia, is Tues night [unintelligible]," a smooth orange-and-ocher pebble, a warranty card

This gave us all the sense of life as lived in all its beguiling wonder

not filled out, for a battery-powered vibrator to soothe away those tensions, an American

You saw how, as promised, Antonia was gradually becoming more real to

-flag lapel pin, some this and some that, a raffle ticket for a Christmas 1971 drawing at Our Lady of Crushing Sorrows R.C. Church, offered: the usual prizes, led by a twenty-five-pound turkey, a picture postcard of the Golden Gate Bridge

"This had been some goddamned drawer," a voice

taken from the North Bay end, showing the golden city of San Francisco, on the back of which has been crudely lettered in pencil the word cupcakes, a broken-pointed Mongol No. 2 pencil for party use, a copy of Viña Delmar's 1928 novel, *Bad Girl,* a package of three Sheik condoms for those interesting evenings when importunate guests batter at the door, a female puppet named Annette, a photograph of five drunken men each of whom brandishes the exotic confection known as cotton candy, an invitation to a cocktail party at the Mervishes, mercifully unknown, another red candle, with wick, four more

Holy Sweet Mother of God

things that will not bear scrutiny, an India-ink drawing of someone, who even now crunches, crunches in place with unsettling maniacal insistence, and finally, perhaps, finally

A hesitant yet hopeful scattering of applause

it looks as if, yes, one more item, it is the scrap of paper earlier mentioned. It was the scrap of paper stuck in the jointure of the bottom and left sides of the drawer, in the back. A scrap of paper, it was a bit of the margin of a newspaper page, yellowed with age and a good deal of rough party use, on which can be made out, in soft pencil, the word, the single word

Absolutely amazing

beacon, uncanny, certainly more than mere chance, beacon, startling

Startling is right, "Uncanny is more like it," an excited female voice

because, of course, the attentive reader, as well as the rest of you here gathered in the kitchen despite persistent qualms, most of which were understandable if not quite forgivable, you saw that this word, lost in the drawer of a minor figure's kitchen, is the same word that is used for, must we really go on?

"Truly incredible," the same female voice, pitched now

Still, certain of the small crowd seemed more interested in getting to know each other, now that they found themselves thrown together for some obscure literary purpose. We don't know who they are. One thing seemed certain, and that was the relentless marching and crunching in place, outside, as we certainly recalled, on the gravel driveway, of the previously rummaging someone. In the face of everything that had happened, and despite all his expectations, even, we may have said, his sophistication, this discovery stuns him. Perhaps dazed would be more accurate. Stuns and dazed.

Carefully, someone had pulled the brittle and yellowing, or yellowed, scrap of paper from the crack in which it is caught. Rummaging is one thing. This was what he briefly thought of as extracting. He read the single word. He was stunned, dazed. He walked from the kitchen, out the door, onto the gravel driveway, where, surely stunned, and quite possibly dazed, he now trudges blindly toward the street. Toward the road. Toward the car. Open the window. He began eating. It was a dark and louring afternoon. In the late summer of that year he and all the rest of us lived in a house in a village. She was very tired. Shut the door. He looks up slowly.

He crunched, his feet crunch, that is, on the gravel. It was truly amazing, he thinks. He thought earlier. Not now.

"Incredible that Antonia should have concealed this scrap of paper here and nowhere else." Here, that is, there.

It had been a night of restless sleep, haunted by bizarre dreams.

And so we may ponder the mystery, despite the streaming clouds and the constant threat of rain, ever more rain. And we mean rain, not a shower or two. Yes, we may ponder on the mystery of how it has come about or how, earlier, it came about that Antonia, in whom nobody is interested, although she had turned out to be more than a little fascinating now that we've come to know her, how it happens that she seems to have concealed this scrap of paper in such fashion that it can be found, as it has been found, here, in this place, and no other. Now.

Baye tree

Commentary suggests that despite what we think we have discovered, Antonia is alive if not precisely well. And has anyone noticed how like her name is to her husband's? Certain liberties have been taken by the narrator or narrators, agreed. Too many to go into, surely, yet one among them all has twisted and sullied the otherwise adequate scene in the kitchen, or, as it has come to be known, the "kitchen scene." I had personally met Antonia some years before at a real-estate-management convention, a pretty, vibrant young woman whose hair was the color of autumnal aspen leaves.

They choose titles with great care, of course. Yet "Beacon" seems to go a bit too far. "Autumnal aspen leaves." Or "Baye tree." They seem more pertinent if not more credible. We spoke at the hotel bar of many things and I felt her captivating perfume insinuate itself into her halting words. Until, until I was, well, whatever I was. I no longer cared. That night we made love for the first time. The breeze had a welcome edge of autumnal chill to it. Outside, the bay tree insinuated its perfume into the darkest corners of the captivating garden, a garden through which we later walked in a rapt silence. As far as I can recall, now that I look back upon the events of that extraordinary night, the words "Baye tree" were those that had been hurriedly scrawled on the scrap of paper in the kitchen drawer. A mysterious correspondence, yet what was not? Does it seem as if the entire scheme begins to show itself plain? So it would appear.

In her ecstasy, feigned or not, she had cried out a single word that I did not quite catch but which, nevertheless, chilled me to the bone. The curtains floated, ghostly, in the soft wind from the sea. I caught her looking at me as I busied myself at the writing desk, and I let the sweater slip from my lifeless fingers. How blind I had been, blind and stupid and unfeeling.

I went to the window.

I stood looking out of the window!

The sweater lay, a crumpled heap, on the floor, and on the lampshade there was caught another garment, a wisp of diaphanous lace.

The bay tree moved, almost imperceptibly, in the freshening wind.

Certainly, I could envision the possibilities, even though there had been nothing that can be called candor employed. Yet the silence of the bar and her oddly amused gaze had permitted me to imagine, if only for a moment, that there might be some authority to what we had otherwise jokingly dismissed as futile, some, but not total. And jokingly? I had been, I confess, the one to use the word, even though it had been manifestly cruel.

There might be some *authority* to what we've otherwise jokingly dismissed, I had said.

As futile? she had replied.

The barman had been listening closely to our conversation and now he walked toward where we sat, knees touching, at the end of the long bar, deserted but for the three of us.

I realized that we were caught in a strangely formal dance, a dance of strangers.

Soon, we were making love, furiously, profligately, unashamedly. It is, even now, somewhat simple to envision the possibilities.

It must be the bay tree, she had sighed. I let my lifeless sweater—or was it her lifeless sweater?—slip from my fingers.

Christmas! I later discovered that Antonia hated it. It had found her, years before, huddled in the shadow of an ancient bay tree that could be seen from any coign of vantage on the sweeping verandah. The lights of the vast living room drenched the windowpanes with a soft rose glow, and the muffled laughter of the guests came sporadically, on the freshening wind, to her ears. But did it matter? It would be difficult, she knew, but there seemed no other way, no alternative to the course she had chosen. She imagined her father at his beloved whist.

She remembers the rest hazily, if at all. But the sound of the cruel ax as it bit relentlessly into the wood of what she had always been assured was her tree is a sound that even now fills her eyes with pain.

Now ye're no better than us! the harsh rural voice cried from the darkness. And then she had drifted into her own darkness.

Yet had I been any less cruel? I had not, indeed, said "ye're," but I had surely, if hesitantly, implored her to let the nagging suppositions rest, to let them disappear, as suppositions must. But had I been formally correct? Had I given credence to the physical reality, to the facts? Had I not been as guilty of a certain velleity in my protestations as had those who once governed her every deed? Had I mocked, rather than comforted, probed, rather than accepted, had I, in short, compromised her innocent and bewildered anger? Most seriously, had I brusquely rearranged the agenda?

There was something sentient about it, something almost human. Its silhouette pierced jaggedly the lightening sky to the east. In the despair and wretchedness of her thwarted longing, I knew that her eyes were fastened on my back, probing for some sign of compassion in the configuration of the body that had, I knew, but used her own. Yet I had felt something akin to love.

Am I, have I been, guilty in your eyes of a certain velleity? I managed. I dared not turn to look at her.

Only insofar as your protestations, she said evenly. They were almost pathetically transparent.

I imagined her brilliant nudity against the soft whiteness of the bedclothes. I had desired her. I still desired her. Still, to think that she had wantonly debased herself with him suffused me with grief and rage, insofar as I could be suffused. Her sweater slipped lifelessly from my fingers and lay in a crumpled heap atop mine.

I dreamt that the bay tree had collapsed, she said later. Shadows moved across the ceiling like mournful wraiths.

Was it my place to tell her that this was but a destructive fantasy? I thought not—I still, God help me, think not—and, looking into her lovely face, I realized that it wasn't the darkness that frightened her. She had been in love, almost, all of her life with darkness. But here, high above the garden and the aromatic bay tree, the darkness seemed, surely, to be not merely a physical manifestation of the mundane, but the absolute harbinger of the dead, still past. How I longed to reassure her! Of what? I thought bitterly.

It was then, I think, that I noticed the credenza. Antonia had seen it as soon as we had entered the room and I realized that her initial modesty in undressing had been occasioned by its dark, burnished presence, there, next to the writing desk. Had I known it then? Known it and chosen to ignore it? Her peach-colored silk slip lay crumpled in soft folds on its glistening surface.

Can you hand me my slip? she cried softly from the bathroom. But the dawn would not come! Only the cold wind soughing through the leaves of the bay tree testified to my actuality. What, then, was the name of the garment caught impotently on the lampshade? I suddenly felt afraid, as if I had been the chosen receptacle of an unassuaged and acerb grief, causeless and infinite.

Despite what others have said in the course of callous interrogations, Antonia was, for just the space of those few hours, wholly joyous again.

I went to the window, pulling my sweater over my exhausted body. The shower was running and the credenza seemed innocuous in the weak sun that filtered through the drawn curtains, through which I peered at the bay tree. Or was it, finally, the Baye tree? And why had I refused to open the curtains?

Now, of course, but too late, much too late for it to matter, I feel the nagging doubts. Was it indeed that her name seemed but a monumental parody of her husband's? Perhaps. Or perhaps it was someone else with some other name, someone else who was so inextricably involved, given the obsessions of the narrator, or narrators. And they were obsessions, inevitable perhaps, perhaps even forgivable, yet present, eternally, obstinately present. I cannot help but feel that they have created the chimera of the fiasco in the kitchen, a fiasco that occurred, despite every effort, years later. But then, I had immediately taken notice of the striking young woman who entered the hotel bar, alone, her subdued but flattering dress, her modest demeanor, the perfectly coiffed scintillance of her shining black hair.

They have said "Beacon," they have suggested "Shadowie lumpe," they have all but insisted on "Baye tree." For me, these are but stage properties, although I have admittedly spoken, for what seems a lifetime, out of a persistent remorse, biting if virtually nameless, and almost painfully acerb. We chatted easily of the afternoon's dull lectures and I found myself drawn ineluctably toward her. Was it the oddly bizarre scent of her perfume? Or do I now comfort myself with that mundane possibility? I spoke smoothly, even, I confess, glibly, into the mystery of her eyes, yet felt inert as some large piece of furniture, perhaps a credenza. It was but the matter of a few moments, or so I remember it, until we were in bed together, lost in each other's arms, and legs. The soft wind from the sea carried the penetrant and familiar aroma of the bay tree, far below, into our darkened room. Despite my most powerful efforts, I came to realize, if not willingly to accept, that the scrap of paper in what she had tearfully admitted was, indeed, her kitchen drawer, had had roughly inscribed on it the words "Baye tree." Not even our languid stroll through the hotel gardens could assist me in denying the remarkably curious turn that things had taken, *general* things. I had begun to see the heretofore dim form of the overall plan growing clear. Now, of course, I know that I neglected—or was it that I refused?—to perform those actions that would have changed everything. But at the time, close to her, intoxicated with various aromas, I thought, I knew—nothing.

In the abandonment of her passion she had whispered a name into the darkness, a name that I recognized, yet did not recognize. It has haunted me all these years, and yet, at the time, I had not the temerity to ask Antonia precisely who it was that she had named. While she slept, or seemed to sleep, I pottered idly with the stationery in the writing desk, but then stopped, knowing without having to turn that her eyes were following my every move. I let a postcard slip from my lifeless fingers. Was this, then, to be all?

I went to the closet. I entered. There were the hangers, I thought angrily.

What was it that had permitted all this to come to pass as it had come to pass? I was not yet so incapable of human feeling as to be unable to imagine the possible conjunctions of this liaison, its potential inevitabilities. Even though there had been nothing that can be called precipitate action on either of our parts, there was a stillness, a reality about the ultimate reasons for this strange state that was, or soon would be, or so I feared, isomorphic in its perfection. Was there some mundane, some obvious cause for the combinatory elements that had, seemingly, come out of nowhere?

I had re-entered the dim room, and addressing the dark shape on the bed, noted, There may well be, I think, something isomorphic in the strange perfection of this night.

But has it, she began, then caught her breath. I waited near the closet.

Has it what? I said.

Has it a—mundane cause? she whispered.

Earlier, the barmaid had vulgarly adjusted her brassiere, listening, all the while, to our subtly erotic verbal fencing. I have come to judge this act as a sexual metonym, but at the time had not the confidence to articulate my beliefs.

Antonia had so easily broken through my somewhat puritanical barriers, and soon we were lost, blind and wild in our passions, throughout which she had insisted on wearing her shoes. It is still puzzling to me. Had this been done at my behest, or with my permission? Or was permission but moot in such a sudden conjunction? Nevertheless, it had been so.

The bay tree is dying, she had whispered, again. A postcard, the same postcard, slipped lifelessly from my fingers and fluttered helplessly to the floor. It was a sign.

A sign of more to come!

January. A month which filled Antonia with terror, or so I discovered later, had found her, while still a girl, dozing serenely in the shade of the venerable bay tree that had dominated Old Weskit, the family estate, for centuries. It could be seen, this legendary tree, from any place on the grounds, lest one stood behind one of the many buildings that graced the lush acreage. Her mother was at the spinet, pretending to play, while her father gazed out toward what he'd stubbornly demanded be called the tree line. The truth about it, and about so many other things, had come to her the night before, yet she was, as she now admitted, utterly passive in the face of what she dreaded would be the final blow. She could see, in her mind's eye, her mother's delicate fingers twitching gracefully in the air just above the keys of the heirloom instrument. She knew.

The next few weeks, or months, passed as if in a restless dream, yet the terrible *chunk* of the ax against the trunk of the bay tree recurs again and again in her memory.

Now d' ye think ye're better'n us? the harsh voice mocked from the darkness. And then came the darkness of blessed oblivion.

But I, too, had been harsh, as well as abrupt. And though I had couched my questions and replies in the most courteous terms, wasn't it also my responsibility at least to assist in the balance of what I now see were the perorations? The rhetoric, yes, that goes without saying. I had no reason to malign my motives as far as that was concerned. But what of the varied innuendoes? The sentences that trailed off? What of the tortuous clusterings of gossip and snide half-truths? Had I lied by omission? Had I, that is, tyrannically rearranged otherwise simple strategies?

I had known, for a moment, love. Of that I was reasonably sure. Yet, when I looked awkwardly out the window, the bay tree seemed wounded, and, yes, dying. Although I instantly entered the closet again, the closet with its hangers!, I felt that her eyes were boring into my soul.

I re-entered the room, trembling.

Does the rhetoric, at least, go without saying? I had asked.

The rhetoric? she said quietly. Yes, the rhetoric. Her voice trailed off into soft breathing, then:

But not the innuendoes! she cried. Her body was a dazzling, shimmering white in the darkness. I wanted her, as, now, I still want her. But she had deceived me as she had deceived all the others, especially him. I threw the postcard from me and watched it flutter into a corner of the lifeless room.

Later, after we had slept, she suddenly murmured, I dreamt that the by tree . . . spoke to me.

The by tree? I replied.

There was a long silence during which I looked at her impassive face, and fought against the temptation to tell her, even as I knew that such a confession might well be considered only a kind of moral gesture at what, at that time, I was pleased to think of as the infinite. Now, such a theory merely brings a wry smile to my lips. I thought that her remote, trancelike air might be the result of the sound of the foghorns, groaning in their timeless melancholy, or the barely discernible ringing of the bell buoys far out in the angry wash of the relentless swells. Yet the monstrous silhouette of the tortured bay tree was nowhere near the cliff's edge! For a moment, I thought that she might not be able to go on, but I knew that she would go on, would live with the unassuaged grief that gave her no rest, no peace. The darkness was implacable and in its grip our desire reawakened. I wanted to make love to her again—again and again and again! But my near-frenzied groping on the floor for her shoes was, as I suspected it would be, fruitless.

Then, the credenza loomed. I had seen it from the corner of my eye as we had earlier tremblingly begun to undress each other, but it had not, then, actually loomed. Antonia had finished disrobing in the closet, so she, too, had noticed its persistent presence. Why had I not? Or had I? Had I, and, as usual, cravenly denied the warnings of my heart? Her peach-colored silk slip shimmered on the polished surface. So that's where it had gone! I felt the blood rush to my temples.

Will you *please* hand me my slip? she cried from the bathroom. Would this night never end? Was it only the coarse action of the barmaid that had called into being the *actuality* of my self? Was it on such ephemera that my tenuous grasp on what she had rather crudely called entelechy rested? So it appeared, at least then. Yet to what could I assign the fact that a nameless garment of feminine apparel lay beneath the slip? I thought, for a feverish moment, that I was not I, and that she was not she, but that we were—some other people!

But who?

I have, since that time, firmly denied, in the face of all queries, that this was, or even might have been, so.

Nonetheless, and if other reports are given even partial credence, we had sounded the depths of a profound *jouissance* that night.

I could hear her humming sadly to herself as she began her toilet, and I pulled my clothes on as rapidly and noiselessly as possible. No small feat! Banging my knee painfully on the sharp edge of the looming credenza, I made my way out of the room. The bay tree shimmered mysteriously in the moonlight.

I had reached the house, and reconnoitering so as to avoid the man whose faint footsteps I had heard crunching on the gravel of the driveway, I somehow effected an entrance into the kitchen.

There was the drawer.

There was the scrap of paper, still caught within it. Had I always known what I would read thereon? Sometimes, even now, I think so.

Now, you have it. It is precisely now, and here. Just so.

Baye tree.

Rocke

But it is not lost, clearly, since he is looking at an old sepia-tone photograph of Sheila although he doesn't know but only assumes or pretends is better, pretends that this is Sheila, he has never known Sheila, she is dressed in a pepper-and-salt tweed country suit, sitting on a large flat rock, posed on a large flat rock, in the center of a field, somewhere, he pretends to himself as he looks at the photograph that this girl is his wife, or was his wife, although he has no idea why, he has no wife, he had no wife, there is something odd and essentially unconvincing about the photograph, rooted in the fact, the fact?, that Sheila or his wife seems out of place, assuming that she has or had a place, and, as it were, out of costume, if such a plain garment can be called a costume, in all the years that he knew her, or pretended to know her, or is now pretending that he knew her, for years, he never saw her in anything so severe, so, if you will, chaste, although he must admit, or he may as well admit, here, where better a place, that he heard, many times, from various lovers, and read, more than once, in passages of prose purporting to be true, that is, based on facts, facts?, concerning her, remarks by her husband, her real husband, Lou, who is, who was, based on other characters, other people, supposedly actual, that she always wore white underwear, if Lou can be trusted, not always, but he knows, he thinks, what always means, and what Lou means, and he may wish to consider these latter garments as chaste, or representative of chastity, as Lou did not, or he may not so wish to consider them as such,

he may not so wish to consider them as such, it so happens that, a nice phrase, useful to the writer of what he decides should be, or shall be, called a tale, the girl, Sheila, in the photograph, is Sheila at eighteen, or perhaps only seventeen, and it also may so happen that the Sheila he knew, or pretended to know, or didn't know at all, is not the girl who seems out of place in this field, this reproduction, this image, of a field, and that this is the reason that she seems so unconvincing, since the actual Sheila would never wear such a severe, or chaste, tweed suit, therefore this photo is of someone who is pretending to be Sheila, or someone very like her, whoever she may be, or may have been, or may not have been, the field is autumnal, as he has noted, but not here, surely not here, he can check that easily enough, the girl, who, given the date on which the photograph was taken, is no longer a girl, has a face that is striking, as striking as it was when he first met her, or pretended to etcetera, etcetera, and her legs, although covered by her skirt, to some three inches below her knees, which are modestly pressed together, are as beautiful in the photo as they were described as being, by someone, in some tale, there's the word, as beautiful as when he, as someone or other, someone with a name, a meticulous history, history is necessary to understand prose, not all of it, some of it, as beautiful as that time when he first stared at them, rather shamelessly, at a ridiculous party to which he had gone to celebrate the publication of a book, another book, yet another book written for some reason, the world seems to be full of writers,

full of writers, yet despite that depressing fact, fact?, time has a way, another trenchant phrase, it has a way of exaggerating the beauty of innumerable things, including the legs of women, that has the ring of authority, a trenchant phrase with the ring of authority, of surety, a kind of absolute sense of, of declaration, something like a motto, or a maxim, or perhaps a bromide, or, to be unkind, as he often is, a cliché, which latter word he does not flinch from, he is thinking of being a writer, or, if not a writer, of writing, of adding some babble to the present babble, and why not?, he says aloud, in the best literary tradition of speaking aloud, to the walls, to the window, to his feet, to, if he wishes, his ass, as he rises from his desk, there is even a desk, and looks out the window at, it may as well be, at the traffic far below, not, it will be confessed, a bad place for traffic to be in a tale, or while still sitting here, or there, at his desk, perhaps he was, or is, he gets himself away from the window to give the tenses a chance, merely thinking of writing a brief paragraph or two, on himself, more or less himself, looking at a photograph of Sheila, he now calls her Sheila, perhaps, that may well be the case, that may well be it, he can't see that it makes any difference, Sheila, fine, yet

Sheila always despised the country, dulcius urbe quid est?, she might have said, probably not, yet that's the ticket, or was, that's her motto or is it bromide?, so what is she doing here, on a flat rock, in a tweed suit, he looks again, or thinks of himself looking again, at something, at the photograph, of course, the photograph, which is absent, which may be merely a handy device around which he can write his tale, or his paragraph, or paragraphs, an entry into the truth, or something, a way of being able to write rock, field, photograph, and as he does this, looks, imagines, writes, he perceives, perceives is good, he perceives that Sheila's legs, those imagined legs, were not really as beautiful as the legs of this Sheila, in the photograph, or in the word, photograph, this girl in the imagined field in the photograph on his imagined desk,

on his imagined desk, Sheila rises from the rock, stretches and yawns, now he can get a good look at her legs, she vigorously brushes her skirt, she moves slowly to the window, to gaze at the traffic, no, she brushes her skirt with her hands, to rid it of dust, dirt, twigs, other things, country things, perhaps she lights a cigarette, if she smokes, she rummages through, or in, her bag, he is, in effect, spying on her, odd how the photograph has come alive, or something, he'll find the phrase later, he spies on her, he waits for her to do something important, something fit to be set down, so that he may discover for his readers, his readers to come, more or less, the truth about something, about life, life will do, he says to himself, life, excellent, in the smallest actions which one makes one's little word-puppets perform one, of course, always discovers, for someone, the truth, about life, he waits, she may do something exciting, something that will enable him to understand the, erotic flush, he writes, or soon will write, that pervaded his body, or certain parts of it, he is nothing, he knows, if not accurate, or is it comic, on that certain afternoon, years ago, when he and Sheila, let's say, this old one, or that new one, although new is not precisely the word, he'll attend to precision later, or that one in the absent photograph, he is having trouble now following the figure, or the trope, the literary something, he'll attend to it all, later, that afternoon, when he and she sat drinking cognac, in the private bar of somebody's house, a rich man's house, on Long Island, in, in Locust Valley, the name comes to him, as a reasonable locale, and the young woman, this Sheila, or that Sheila, or the other Sheila, still near the rock, or so he thinks, the young woman is definitely Sheila, now, despite the name, or names, she may have borne in other tales, there's the word again, it's all made up, or was, but now, or soon, it will be based, however, to be sure, on what he now calls, real life, although he doesn't actually call, names, that's more like what he does, he names it real, then adds, life, it will be based on that afternoon when she stretched her long and remarkably well-made legs out before him, so that he couldn't take his eyes off them, succinct, all right, those legs belonging to, to her, but not to, he decides, the Sheila who is, now, strangely moving around in the photograph, or, even more strangely, moving around in the word, photograph,

in the word, photograph, Sheila sits again, this tale is at a far remove from the exciting, she sits, she pretends, he pretends that she pretends, that she is only seventeen, or eighteen, and not what she is, now, whatever she is, he figures rapidly, let's make it forty-five, or, he'll make it forty-five, when he writes his tale, based, of course, on etcetera, etcetera, she sits, she begins to do some, some thinking, she cannot stand, despite the age she is, for the moment, trapped in, she cannot stand Lou, Lou will do fine, she cannot stand Lou, he remembers Lou, nor can she stand her lovers, whose ranks he may join, if he writes the tale, or even the paragraph, or two, for truth will out, more or less, usually less, usually not at all, for that matter, for if the truth outs, an awkward phrase, he'll fix that up later, if it does, it will be revealed that her lovers bore her with their pleas, their needs, they call them needs, only on occasion, give the devil his due, he calls them needs, but he, as he sits at his desk, or even while away from it, he is a, a, traditionalist, preferring, above all other things, meaningful things to occur to characters whom we, he usually thinks this we, meaning, he supposes, us, whom we can care about, making order out of chaos is his middle name, or soon will be, if he realizes his fondest dream, of writing, of writing the truth, they bore her, they all want, want, want and demand, things, from her, what things, he is presently too lazy to discover, there he is at the window again, and there, below, is the fucking traffic, they want things, they give her interesting roles to play, she enters, she exits, she plays the unfaithful wife, she is, Sheila is, she turns out to be Sheila, after all, she is, indeed, the unfaithful wife, he has her pretend to pretend to think this, as she taps a cigarette on her fingernail, he has given her a whole pack, minus one, of course, put it into the bag in which she rummaged, is still rummaging, forever, in that deathless sentence, she taps, he decides, Sheila taps a cigarette on her thumbnail, a nice touch, a nice piece of business, in the elaborate piece of business that her life has become, another nice, another cleanly turned, an inventive phrase, he used to think he knew the word for the figure, perhaps conceit, metaphor, vehicle, no, in any event it is, indeed, something literary, to permit him, or somebody, so to transform, or transcend life in order that it be made understandable, that's how art works, though he realizes that it is hard to understand life from a photograph, especially an imagined photograph, a real photograph to be referred to is much more effective, as a device, for understanding, for making sense of, of what?, of life, even though it displays a woman, who, it may well be, was the girl who might well have become his wife, before he met her, at, seventeen, or eighteen, yet this woman, too, hated the country, her name, her name was Sheila, an odd coincidence, that's life, or is it an irony?, there is something to be made of that, so he thinks, as he gazes, as he stares, blankly, as he is attracted to, blankly?, as he stares, blankly, at the typewriter, he has a typewriter, a desk, and a typewriter, the room is slowly being furnished, the wonder of literature, at the typewriter, yes, and at the yellow legal pad, as he turns from the window, as he does this, as he does that, blankly, as he lights a cigarette, and realizes, once again, as he has been taught, by something, call it literature, experience, the anxiety of looking at that blank piece of paper, the intimidating presence of, how lonely it is, how lonely he is, as if anyone asked him, he can go fuck himself with his anxiety, and his paragraphs, and his photograph, more or less,

more or less a photograph anyway, and now he sees, he speaks figuratively, he's willing to say so, again, not actually say it, he is silent, he realizes, that's a little better, that his life, no, that he has fallen into the trap that he thought, or had thought, or will eventually think, at that anxious moment, before the time-honored, the famous blank sheet of paper, to avoid, he is turning Sheila into a figure, an element, a thing, really, to be caught in a chain of metaphor, that sounds like the right phrase, but she is no such thing, she is flesh, and blood, well, flesh and blood, so to speak, she is a picture, a part of a picture, no, part of a photograph, no, the word, photograph, there is probably no photo-graph, although he seemed to be looking, at something on his desk, he definitely still has a desk then, but it is a strange photograph, absent, since she is, well, she is moving around in the photograph, he is looking out the window, staring, no, gazing, out the window, out a window, not at the wonderful goddamned traffic, time-tested, far below, but at the field, a field, that has at its center, more or less at its center, a rock, and so forth, and so on, in any event, she is no such girl, or woman, as she here exists, that is doubtlessly the fact, the fact?, that he must face, well, not must face, that he faces, she is Sheila, so it is Sheila, after all, in a tweed suit, underneath which, is Lou's white underwear, he calls it Lou's, but it is not actually Lou's, by Lou's he means, etcetera, maybe it is white, maybe not, he will not, at this time, undress her, although he has the power to do so, she is at his mercy, so he thinks, or he has himself think, that's always good, a neat way into the mind, thinking, mind is an odd word to use, in this context, so is context, in this context, what context can he be thinking of?, he thinks, or wonders, he has no context, at present, he has that blank, that lonely, that etcetera, Sheila is on the rock again, her cigarette is finished, she is beginning to feel cold, and why not?, the sun, weirdly enough, is going down, it is actually, more or less, actually sinking, right here, or there, in the photograph, real, or imagined, or projected, in any case, the sun is sinking, and Sheila, despite her tweed suit, which is warm, is beginning to feel cold, she is cold, right here, or there, in her tweed suit, her warm tweed suit, that's how it works out, in literature, because it's an oxymoron, or a litotes, and maybe the wind is coming up,

the wind is coming up, and that, for some reason, allows him to know that she hasn't had an orgasm, with Lou, he'll stick with Lou, so that's decided, although there are plenty of other names available, dozens of them, hundreds, Sidney, for instance, or Kirk, Gig, Mickey, endless, but Lou will do nicely, he knows that Lou is not the real name of the real Sheila's real husband, the name that the name, Lou, was meant to conceal, in the tale in which he first met Lou, under, a curious word, under another name, which he has forgotten, or has pretended to forget, how strange to meet people in tales, or is it?, he has no idea, or no ideas, he merely wants to write, to forge in the city of his soul a blank etcetera, more fool he, write his own tale, Sheila, however, despite all, has not had an orgasm, with Lou, in almost seven years, which seems fine to him, not to Lou, that will make her twenty-four or twenty-five, if her age, in the photograph, is right, though he has the nagging sense, another smooth, another familiar phrase, that he has somehow figured wrong, he doesn't care, or rather, I don't care, he says, to the window?, to the window, out the window, he says, aloud, but he denies, give him credit, he denies himself the window, the traffic, the blank stare, Jesus Christ, enough is enough, a hell of a guy, yet, where was he?, yet, she has often pretended to have an orgasm, or orgasms, a few, or many, he knows that Lou knows that she is, or has been, pretending, and that he is faintly pleased, at her groans, her grunts, her sighs, her gasps, it's good enough for Lou, and if it's good enough for Lou, it's good enough for him, if the truth were known, back again, to the known truth, literature allows the truth to be known, it is the writer's function to etcetera, he should admit, once and for all, that the truth is known, for Sheila has spoken to him, from the rock, in the field, wearing her etcetera, while the cold and so on, she has spoken the words he has wished her to speak, whatever they are, he doesn't give a shit what they are, even though she is bored, by now, with this field, and, as he knows, as he has created it, as he has thought of creating it, it is cold, and so is Sheila, for the wind, etcetera,

the wind, etcetera, etcetera, and as he looks at the photograph again, he now says, with authority, with confidence, the idiot, photograph, he now insists that he has a photograph, it's little enough, when he looks at it again, or, since it is now unimpeachably here, as it was not heretofore necessarily here, at all, when he looks at it, for the first time, or, as if for the first time, assuming that it was here, or there, all along, and why should we doubt him?, or it, or this?, he is mildly surprised to discover that it is a sepia-tone photograph, in which Sheila, it is indeed still Sheila, a girl of seventeen, or eighteen, who looks remarkably like his invented wife, the one given him, or taken by him, he is not one to deny free will, in some tale he was once, as it is said, in, as somebody whose name he no longer remembers, or whose name he does not care to remember, or pretends he does not care to remember, even though the tale has been spoken of as unforgettable, as a minor classic, Sheila is standing, against a tree, of some undetermined species, a tree bare of leaves, a gaunt, gaunt is good, a gaunt tree, a look of absolute defiance on her face, one hand thrust into a pocket of her tweed jacket, rather elegantly, so that the position of her hand, and arm, reminds him, somewhat disconcertingly, of a photograph, of a bridegroom, which he once saw, and which proves nothing, except for the unwholesome, or something, nature of partial, perhaps specious, recall, her expression is that of the woman with whom he drank cognac, that afternoon in Locust Valley, right, an expression at once defiant, as noted, strong, bitter, daring, sexual, for it turns out, so it turns out, it happens, that someone, it is Lou, Lou is at the door, there must be a door, Lou is asking, Lou asked, if she would like to join the gang, that's what Lou calls the rest of the guests, he assumes that there are guests, he had no idea, until now, that there was anybody else in the house, what house?, well, the assumed house, but there is, it appears, a gang of them, mysterious indeed are the powers of literature, powers that permit them to hide, somewhere, until needed, would she, Lou asks, or asked, like to join the rest of the gang, in making jack-o'-lanterns, a nice touch, observant, lifelike, yet uncommon, the darkness is falling, the darkness is gathering behind, or beyond, is better, beyond the huge picture window, that looks out on fields, and woods, dropping off to a brilliant shard of, a shining slice of, something, water, he will write, soon, perhaps, water, although it seems to be the Connecticut River, but what the hell does he care what it is?, he will maybe write, though, the Connecticut River, visible through the gold and yellow and crimson trees, that is, the leaves are golden and etcetera, it is an autumnal scene, much like the one in the photograph, although the colors as here carefully denoted, can only, in the photograph, be imagined, and that, only if the gaunt trees therein are given back their leaves, of various colors, to prove, in order to prove, something, as if he gives a fuck, one detail is as good as another, when truth, he says, aloud, is the goal, and so on and so forth, that's his motto or his paradigm, or is it his hypotaxis?, whatever, Sheila sips her cognac, then raises her free hand, lets it fall, lets it rest, gently, relaxed, on his upper thigh, he sees that Lou sees this, sees that Lou stares, with a bitter yet unsurprised look on his face, then turns and leaves, he will, he might, have him do something to enrich the poignancy of the scene, he calls it, in his mind, a scene, and if a scene, why not a poignant one, he will, or might, make Lou whistle, a small touch, perceptive, an insight into the vagaries of human nature, a wonderful and smoothly administered dash of literary something or other, literary bullshit, bullshit is not bad, though a trifle crass, a trifle vulgar, a correlative for bleak despair, now he's got it, yet, and yet, he remembers Lou whistling, as he leaves, his hands thrust, but not elegantly, into the pockets of his worn corduroys, worn is a judiciously selected adjective, he feels, he felt, so he thinks, so he writes, or will write, sorry for Lou, but he wants, or wanted, Sheila, who will later tell him that she despises those corduroys, he will not ask why, as well as that melodramatic whistling, even though he was, is, will be, the one responsible for it, just as well she doesn't know,

she doesn't know, Sheila, now, that is, then, at the time of the photograph, he continues to insist on this object, or this word, a girl of seventeen or eighteen, she, now, who reminds him of his invented wife, as if he had an invented wife, some word, that's more like it, an unabashed word, that's the ticket, that's the way to go, she, whoever she is, Sheila, the word is sitting, now, or was sitting, on a flat rock, in the middle of a field, of the field, in the photograph, in reality, reality will have to do, in an autumnal field, the crimsons and the golds, the yellows, the russets, too, and so on, the wind, and so forth, it seems to be getting a little chilly, and etcetera, another shot at the fucking scene, perhaps he'll get it, perfectly, the perfect scene, beautifully done, evocative, that's good, probing, revelatory, yes, that's the ticket, same ticket as before, she is still fumbling in her bag, she has fumbled, as he knows, she is, right, smoking a cigarette, perhaps the same cigarette, he discovers that there is an oddly lascivious smile, on her face, perhaps not so odd, a smile that husbands often think they see, on the faces of other men's wives, more fools they, these smiling women, these wives, a few of them anyway, at least one or two of them, maybe one of them, and that on rare occasions, he is about to write, as he paces, as he sharpens his pencil, as he looks out, etcetera, on and on and on, with this and with that, these smiling women, he insists on more than one, seem to be thinking, as if they, as if they something, no, as they chat, about children, about jobs, about the banalities of politics, about their husbands' jobs, that they would be delighted, simply delighted, to permit their conversational partners, or partner, he has been a partner, somewhere, as if that mattered, that they would be more than pleased to permit him, the partner, who may still be listening to the sound of whistling, growing ever fainter, that's nicely turned, that's warmly familiar, permit him the most remarkable, the most unbridled, wanton, and lustful liberties, that's a mouthful,

a mouthful, so that quickly he turns to, he hears a train, in the distance, why not?, the good old lonesome sound, of a train, what a wonder, he notices, once again, as always, he is observant, as all good writers must be, perhaps not all, somebody said, somebody is still saying, probably the same somebody who said, who says, that good writers must also be, also be something, good listeners, right, listeners to what, or to whom, and for what reason, is never, wait, was never explained, perhaps it was, or is, bad writers who must be good listeners, but he notices, and has noticed, for some time, whatever that means, in the upper-left quadrant of the photograph, a railroad-crossing sign, how handily it has appeared, its reality is, what?, winning?, that's not it, he doesn't care, and this word, Sheila, of course, Sheila, she's still here, or there, this Sheila who reminds him of, right, she is still smiling her oddly lascivious smile, as some wives do, when etcetera, etcetera, she looks toward where the tracks, in reality, reality will have to do, must be, that is, he cannot see them in the photograph, the imagined photograph, what an imagination he has, it's of course a necessity, like observing, and listening, he thinks to comment on this to someone, soon, perhaps a friend, he will soon have, maybe, a friend, or somebody's wife, not his own, he has no wife, nor did he ever, yet with his imaginative powers, or with somebody's imaginative powers, you never can tell, you never can tell, she looks, she rises from her chair, she rises abruptly, she goes to the window, here's the picture window, good as new, to look at the fields, the woods, the trees, the riot of colors, nature's great palette, breathtaking autumn, yet somehow, somehow something, somehow sad, right, sad autumn, another handy phrase, just waiting, just waiting to help the imagination out, she looks down, or away, to the shining slice of river beyond, the brief glint, the silvery glitter, Jesus, the shining slice, the brief glint of its cold waters, all right, he smiles, at the traffic, no, at his desk, or he aims, he aims a smile at, no, he looks at her legs, her thighs, her hips, her buttocks, her breasts, all perfect, beneath her closely fitting, yet not immodest, knitted dress, a wheat-colored dress, no, maize, no, white, he can still feel her hand, on his thigh, it was relaxed, her hand, he would like her permission, and Lou's, he's come to like him, a little, he'll get to like him more, perhaps, as he develops, right, develops his character, he'll grow to respect him, to care about

him, he must never be better than his characters, never, that's a rule, he
would like, anyway, permission, from somebody, from his imagined
wife, in the tale, some tale, the wife who reminded him, of Sheila, or was
it the other way around?, he would be grateful, for permission to take
liberties, lustful, wanton, and unbridled, with her, but such permission
will not be granted, how come?, he is irritated, he drinks, or he drank,
some more cognac, Sheila looks down, she looks over the glorious
etcetera, the russets, right, the sad autumnal this and that, he decides to
have him decide to be ashamed of his obscene desires,

obscene desires, yet, Sheila, Sheila is staring, with a strangely
hopeful, he seems to remember that it was hopeful, or strange, something, she has that look, on her face, he is interested, now, only in the
facts, the facts?, of this day, of that day, that is, of this photograph, he
has decided will be the device, the device whereby he will get at the
truth, or something, whereby he will allow his imagination to ferret out
the this and the that, she is staring, he pretends to forget the expression,
the look, on her face, which looks, looks, curiously hopeful, or was it
curiously strange, or lascivious, oddly older, than what?, seventeen or
eighteen, she is staring, at the railroad tracks, there they are again, right
as rain, those next to the actual, the real, real will have to do, railroad-
crossing sign, in the imagined photograph, imagination is all, he thinks,
he has him think, with an abstracted, an intense look, on his face, and
then he thinks, with a pang, of what?, of remorse, of the crimsons, the
blues, no, the golds, the sad, the poignant, the cognac, to which he must
ultimately give a name, specificity is a sign of something, perhaps of
careful listening, or respect for one's characters, there is something
about the train that he hears approaching, and that Sheila hears,
something that, illogically, for a change, a refreshing change, and that
something, as Sheila knows, now that she is almost forty-five years of
age, at last, at long last, is that the train means itself, nothing else, which
accounts, perhaps, for her strange, or odd expression, her strangely odd
expression, she waits for him to decide, more fool she, she waits for him
to let her know, what to think, about this approaching train, in the way
that she waited for him to comment, on her legs, her thighs, etcetera,
and to comment on Lou, on his corduroys, that are, that were, that will
be, worn, pants that she, wait a minute, that she will despise, despised,
that she despises, that was some time ago, or something, she is waiting

for him to take the most illicit pleasures, etcetera, to seduce her in the guise of some ideal, to say whatever he will say, but it wasn't, apparently, worth the trouble, since she is still waiting, it is growing colder, it must be growing darker, time marches on, but all he does is stand at the window, light another cigarette, a famous literary cigarette, so he thinks of writing, soon, as he lights his cigarette, he thinks, of her body, beneath her pepper-and-salt tweed suit, he thinks, that her body must be as remarkable as her body,

as her body, Sheila's, still here, or, that is, there, on a flat rock, in a field, the photograph, he calls it, he'll not give an inch, has arrested her, in a casual, yet inward, whatever that means, pose, she is about seventeen or eighteen, there, while here, she is about forty-five, here?, a train, the train, there it is, it rushes past, noise, dust, other odds and ends, other words, some three-hundred yards, to her right, to his left, given the position of the absent photograph, whose presence he insists on,

he insists on, why not?, the photograph, and the train, not quite in the photograph, absent, yes, but intensely imagined, imagination is all, or a great deal, and the train has on board, so he decides to discover, a man, whom he will subsequently, maybe, call Tom, or Dick, or Harlan, but not Lou, of course, not Lou, Tom is staring fixedly, such turns of phrase, out the window, at the sad, the autumnal, the poignant, fields, as they rush, as is their wont, by, and at the etcetera, until Tom, Tom will do, sees a young woman, who, he thinks, he has Tom think, who is Sheila, he has almost managed to forget her, how it coheres, Tom stares at Sheila, all seems extraordinarily, to Tom, unreal, as well it might, theatrical, perhaps amazing, maybe, he says aloud, once again, amazing, since the young woman, on etcetera, wearing etcetera, surrounded by sad and poignant etcetera, looks exactly, or very much like, his, Tom's, wife, Janet, this time Tom speaks aloud, what's sauce for the goose, or like Janet when she was seventeen or eighteen, for Janet has, and often, for some obscure reason, of her own, for not much is known, of Janet, shown Tom a photograph, of herself, taken years before, posed, strangely smiling, wearing a well-cut tweed suit, on a rock, in a field, in Connecticut, or so she says, has said, except that Janet is now forty-five years of age, as if that follows,

if that follows, he doesn't care, but the train passes, it rushes, Sheila looks briefly up at it, with an oddly something smile, or look, so he descries, nice word, with some expression, on her face, and in the photograph, that he wishes he now had, assuming that there is a real, real will have to do, photograph, so that he might verify his, his conjectures, his rambling conjectures, with incontestable evidence of, of whatever, it is difficult, given the photograph that he insists he once had, or wrote that he had, but has no longer, for him to make out the intent of this, or that, not quite formed smile, yet he stares, he props the photograph of Sheila, of that word, props the word of the word, up against a brass figurine, of Durga, the goddess, which figurine once appeared in a photograph taken, of another woman, whose name he forgets, although he can look it up, the goddess is on his desk, or, he coughs apologetically, nicely turned, right, it is actually a table, the truth is always best, and he thinks, or notes that he will be thinking, when the time comes, that Durga is a goddess of destruction,

a goddess of destruction, this may be a transcendent analogy, a figure located somewhere on the axis of selection, if it's good enough for etcetera, in any event, he knows, that in the tale that he will invent, or is, at this moment, not actually at this moment, actually will have to do, about Sheila, the Sheila in the photograph, he calls the word photograph photograph, why not?, what else?, yet another thing, perhaps spurious, but not without merit, that the photograph reminds him of one taken of his mother, a sepia-tone photograph, another coincidence to complicate the plot, and it is a plot, and nothing but plot, although he remembers, not the photograph, but the emotion that the photograph evoked in him, but what emotion?, perhaps not emotion, but a sense, of the, of the uncanny, that may be the word, that may be what was evoked, by the photograph, of his mother, unless it is, or was, the uncanny that is, or was, evoked by the photograph, of Sheila, she may as well be Sheila, he cannot recall any face at all, except for the one that is here, or that was there, precision is the first rule, of something, and that face is, always, oddly, the strangely smiling face of Sheila,

the strangely smiling face of Sheila, he thinks, he knows, well, he pretends, that Sheila is unaware, that she does not know what will happen to her, over the course of the next few years, or more than a few, neither is Janet aware, whoever she is, or was, Sheila has not yet heard of Lou, at least he doesn't think she has, he can check, although Lou is, was, the man of the gang, the pants, the pumpkins, pumpkins?, but that

came later, later?, or it will come later, in terms of real, have to do, have
to do, life, now, Sheila looks at the train, rattling, rushing, still at it, an
exotic scene, well, bittersweet, this cannot, despite the evidence of the
absent photograph, possibly be Sheila, or his wife, what wife?, some
forgotten word, he gazes out the window, he'll give himself a pipe, might
as well, in a minute Sheila, this, or that tweedy Sheila, who looks very
much like Janet, who is insistent indeed, may well have a brief affair,
with Fred, who died, recently, who was, who was an, an accountant, or
a master sergeant, or a teacher in Detroit, or who is settling, at the time
of the photograph, into a seat behind Tom, Tom, who is looking out the
window, at what, at Janet, not Janet, but Sheila, yet Tom is startled
because etcetera, and at the sad and russet etcetera, the golds,

the golds, the crimsons, he would like to, he considers rescuing
Sheila, from her rock, he calls it hers, from the artificiality, of the scene,
scene will have to do, and then burn the photograph, the photograph
that he has pretended to prop up, against the goddess Durga, there are
metaphorical possibilities, but she is forty-five years of age, not Durga,
his mother is dead, many people are dead, they die, and die, and Janet,
well, he thinks, vulgarly, fuck Janet, although there she is, more or less,
in the few random thoughts that he has given, or will give, Tom, time is
disappearing, into the void, of memory, that's nice, the void of memory,
now, well, now, now he stands, he looks out the window at the fields
dropping off to the brilliant shard that is a river, it turns out to be the
Connecticut River, remarkable, he expected the traffic, far below, its
muted sounds, but there are the trees and the shrubs, yet, yet they are
green, odd, strange, he reserves, this time, uncanny, wait and see, wait
and see, he sees a girl in a field, somewhere out there, in the midst of
nature, and so on, she is in tweeds, she isn't Sheila, she can't be Janet,
safe in Tom's head, he has no idea who she is,

no idea who she is, he lays his pen down, or he will, or he thinks, of
that moment, when he will, how brilliantly weary this scene of completion, when he may, or will, hold it, loosely, gazing, abstracted, at
whatever, he may decide to place it on the desk, actually, that will have
to do, actually, a table, or he may put it, behind his ear, or in his mouth,
when he will pick up the photograph, from the desk, the table, Durga is
revealed, or exposed, there she is, as always, she glares at him, blankly,
as always,

blankly, as always, Sheila, or the other girl, of whom he has, or had, no knowledge, amid the green, she who is now, not then, not imagined, she may as well be Sheila, he'll be done with it, she is, whoever she is, Sheila, she sits on a rock, the rock, the train passes, still, perhaps it is another train, chronology is all, how placid she seems, although, or perhaps because, her eyes are blank, they are like the eyes of, of something, of someone, her expression is oddly, strangely, lascivious, defiantly so, she reminds someone on the train, perhaps Fred, perhaps Tom, there they are, in the window, or windows, of someone outside the train, someone once seen, or well known, someone that they, and he, would like to remember, or pretend to remember,

pretend to remember, everything is still, a reasonable way to pretend to end things, he will dispense with the fly, the clock, the breathing, the buzzing, ticking, sound of his own, he realizes that it is growing darker, and, right, colder, now, so to speak, now, it is completely dark, he thinks to save time, dark, dark, but now, he can't find the photograph, he looks out the window, the girl who was not Sheila, is not Sheila, is walking toward him, it is still light, outside the window, he hadn't thought of that, the swing of her hips, the way her skirt caresses her thighs, these awaken in him thoughts of etcetera, she stops, she certainly looks like Sheila, she is cognizant of being watched, she knows her role perfectly, she raises her skirt, demurely, she refastens one of her stockings, her legs, or the one leg that he can see, are, it, it is beautiful, he moves closer to the window, he has no idea who she is, he can see the lace edge of her white slip, now she shakes her skirt down, smooths it over her hips, her thighs, she looks something like his invented wife, who used to be somebody, some character, some word, in a tale, written, or told, written is better, perhaps the word was Janet, or Sheila, Sheila sounds right, as he stares she disappears, well, she doesn't disappear, she walks away, he has her walk away, he is not a voyeur, not in this tale, not now, not outside, whatever that means, not outside the photograph, which he may well have taken, which he might as well have taken, he turns to the desk, actually the table, actually will have to do, hesitant, that's precise enough, hesitant, he can't, as he feared, find the photograph, the scene, the scene that he has decided to, decided to what?, he turns on the lamp, a lamp, all right, it is the only lamp, the lamp, Durga, the figurine of Durga, glares at him, not at him, nor does she glare, there she, there it is, a dull brass figurine, he still cannot find the photograph, it is, it seems, nowhere to be found, nowhere in the room, not on the desk, the table, in any event, the room can wait, he hadn't thought of a room anyway, it is definitely missing, yet he had, and quite recently, a part, or parts, of certain elements depicted in it, yet it is missing, it may be lost, at least for now, he says aloud, and again, for now, but it is not, not really, really will have to do, he will write, but it is not lost.

Bedsteade

They say that nobody knows and nobody seems to care that April is a drunk now, lying in bed all day long. The moments pass into hours, the television soundlessly flickering before her in the best tradition of the exhausted motif, a glass of vodka at her side, some say at her elbow, thinking of her youth, her marriage, her career, whatever it was, all now dissolved in alcohol, that's what they say. She ain't got nobody. They say that such a portrait of her is a romantic lie, that she is the same old April and that Vermont has become her true home, that it reminds her of Schenectady. They say she's smilin' through. They say that Dick writes all day long in a small outbuilding that has been converted into a studio according to plans presented to the contractor by April, who has always had an eye for such detail, a flourish, a flair, a touch of elegance and style. So they say. They say no, it isn't so, that Dick is gone, that he's now just a vagabond lover. They say that April divorced Dick when she discovered him and their neighbor's wife in, as they say, vile embrace on the kitchen table, love will find a way, one fine bright morning in early spring. They say that they remarked that everything was peaches. They say that April got that wonderful look in her eye and became a nun, seized, as she was, by this perfect image of renunciation and penitence, and influenced, in no small part, by the role played so perfectly by Rose Zeppole in *Madame Delbène*. Rose, or so they say, is sometimes called Broadway Rose. They say that there's a broken heart for every light on Broadway and that Rose's is one of them. But, they say, if April did indeed become a nun how is it that this was not reported? Many say that she's just a girl that men forget. Some say that it has been reported, but in metonymic terms, for instance, that it happened in Monterey, although others say that the terms were heavily symbolic, that, in a way, the dawn was breaking. They say that whatever may be true, nothing can satisfactorily explain what they call the missing years. They say that April said that it was fascination, or that the bells were ringing, or that she found the end of the rainbow. They say that she seduced office boys and truck drivers in a sentimental attempt to regain the carefree, or salad days of her young womanhood. They say that she said that the best things in life are free. They say that Dick is dead, or that Dick has married the neighbor's wife after buying off her husband, a pig farmer, they say, of some local reputation as a good driver. Now, they say, he's lonesome and sorry. They say that Dick strolls around and around the house, his shoes crunching on the gravel, while his new wife tidies the kitchen. They say that Dick said that her eyes are blue as skies are. They say that she nervously anticipates, while tidying, April's weekly visits, although some say that April lies in bed all day, and that she's *nobody's* sweetheart now. They say that the three of them compose a Platonic ménage-à-trois of a decidedly literary cast, whatever they may mean by that, although some say that they're writing songs of love and others that they are collaborating on a novel with the working title of *Doubles Cross.* Dick said, they say, that he's sitting on top of the world. They say that Dick's new wife's contribution to the novel is the idea that a smile will go a long long way. They say that April is a drunk and cannot help phoning Dick's new wife, who, they say, she calls Karen, in the middle of the night. They say she's funny that way. They say that these calls often ruin Karen's strange gelatin desserts, why, they don't say. She may be weary. They say that April knows that Antonia Harley was crippled, years ago, by her husband, although some say that her crippling was an accident and had something to do with pigs. Others that her crippling was linked with Anton's, her husband's, outstanding collection of softball bats, one of them being employed as a weapon after Antonia had made a vegetable casserole fit, so they say that Anton said, for the pigs. They say he said other things as well. They say that Anton said that Antonia said that he was the pig it was fit for. He said that she said, they say, that she'd sooner go to bed with a bottle of vodka than with him. Others say that this wasn't possible since she had left Anton long before his interest in collecting had blossomed. They also say that Antonia despised vegetables, but that April said in her testimony that she loved them in order to make Anton look bad to the jurors. They say that April said that he took advantage of her. They say, however, that the jurors were bribed to bring in a verdict of not guilty, and that they said that his sin was loving her. Others say that the case was about two other people who lived on an adjacent farm, the people who cut down the old pine tree. But they say that there was no farm, nor, for that matter, pine tree, ever involved in any way with April's life and vice versa. Only God can make a tree, so they say. Yet they say that April and Dick never said that there was a farm, and, as a matter of fact, agree that April's house and grounds in Vermont cannot be called a farm. They say that April and Dick got the money to put down on what may or may not be a farm by organizing unsavory weekend parties for the friends of a certain Mr. Pungoe, who, they say, was at the center of a rather sinister cabal having to do with art or something that vaguely resembled it, although others say that it did not resemble it at all but was merely some kind of mess called art. They say that Pungoe was in the construction business, or the real-estate business, and that despite his clubfoot, he's got rhythm. April often thought of him, they say, in her drunkenness, and of how she had always rather liked him, despite his affliction. They say that Pungoe's affliction was unspeakable, that he'll haunt you night and day. They say that Dick, just before he left for a week in Paris with Karen, said Pungoe wore the startling blue suit that was, as they say, his trademark, in order to take people's minds off his affliction, unspeakable as it was. They say that Pungoe was Chinese, born to a restaurateur in Wichita Falls, and that he said as much, they say, to April one night when she accompanied him to an opening of Annie Flammard's at the Gom Gallery. That was the evening that Annie confessed, they say, that she's the daughter of Mother Machree, the famous madam. They say that April will tell all in her memoirs, which she works on in bed during her lucid intervals, and that she revealed, they say, that the memoirs' title will be *Strange Coincidences*. Some say that the book will be an exhaustive compilation of strange coincidences. They say that Karen said that April said, although this was some time before April knew what was going on between Karen and Dick, that one of the coincidences had to do with the fact that her bed was once owned by a woman who had not only lived in Schenectady but who had known her father for many years. He used to love her but it's all over now. Karen said that April said that the woman's husband, from whom she had bought the bed, had said small world, and that he went on to say that that was what his wife would have said, rest her soul, were she still with us. April said, Karen said, that by us the emaciated widower clearly meant those of us who are still alive. Or perhaps those of us who were alive at the time of purchase. Or those of us who still are or were mostly sane. They say that April's sister, May, was the girl that Dick really wanted to marry, and that he had carried a torch, as they say, for her for years. She'll always be the same sweet girl. They say that although May didn't say that this had been the case, she didn't dismiss the notion either. She didn't say yes and she didn't say no. They say that May had at one time entertained a profound obsession concerning one of the priests at Our Lady of the Bleeding Eyes in Mechanicville, that he had brought a new kind of love to her, and that she, for a time, seriously considered taking the veil. Some say that this is a complete distortion of the facts, since it was, they say, April who thought of becoming a nun after she discovered Dick's head between Karen's thighs one fine bright morning in early spring. Her heart stood still. They say that there is nothing quite like spring in Vermont, unless, of course, one takes the moonlight into account. The moonlight, they say, is not only beautiful, some even say stunning, but is also famous. The stars at night are big and bright as well. They say that May married, finally, a nice young man, Michael Cullinan, or Cullinane, although it turned out that Mike, as they say that May said that he said he preferred to be called, was not what might be called thoroughly normal. They also say that he's not much on looks. They say that Mike and May and their two children, Brian and Maureen, visited April and Dick in Vermont one weekend after they had made the old farmhouse more or less livable, although some say that it was not a farmhouse at all. Karen said that Dick said, after they were settled in their seats in the jet that was taking them to the Bahamas for a break from the endless New England winter, that April said that she had walked in on Mike in the guest bedroom on the second day of their visit and was embarrassed by the sight that greeted her. She said, so Karen said that Dick said, that she refused to tell Dick about it, since, as they say, Dick despised both Mike and May, even though Dick and May had once been engaged while they were all at Mechanicville High together. The thrill is gone. But Antonia, who got to know April fairly well, and who, they say, even worked for a time as her amanuensis, said, or so Lena Schmidt said, or wrote, that April tells the story of "Mike in the Morning," as she calls the episode, in *Doubles Cross,* and some say that it found its way into *Strange Coincidences* as well. Although neither book has been published, nor completed, nor, some say, begun, Crescent and Chattaway seems to be interested in one or both of them. At C and C, or so they say, anything goes! Antonia said, so Lena said, or wrote, that April said that when she walked into the bedroom on that fine bright morning in early spring, she discovered Mike lying naked and supine on the bed, a pair of what April recognized as her panties wrapped around his erect penis and what she thought was one of her brassieres in his teeth, and that Mike was vigorously, as they say, abusing himself. Antonia said that Lena said, or wrote, that April said that Mike, when discovered, said, "Happy days are here again." They say that May never found out about this bizarre episode in her husband's life, although Lena said, or wrote, so Antonia said, that May must have known of Mike's sexual proclivities, even though he was a devout Catholic, as they say, a member of the Knights of Columbus in Schenectady, and deeply in favor of life. They say that he loves a parade. April, they say, threw that particular bed out or put it up for sale, or insisted that Dick put the bed in the outbuilding that was soon to be the studio in which he would engage in various literary pursuits. But others say that she sold the bed to an old friend of her father's in Schenectady. They say that April never quite got over that scene and that when she went back to work she became as promiscuous as she had been before meeting Dick at the Dew Drop Inn, a local tavern. Love is the best of all, so what the hell. Yet they say that Mike said, or that Dick said that Mike said, one night when the moon was all aglow and they had been drinking for some hours, that all the stories about April were untrue, and that May had said that Dick himself had made up all the stories about April since Dick, so Dick said Mike said May said, was angry with April since he had been jilted by May. They say that Dick laughed at Mike and made a crude and highly offensive double entendre concerning May's forever disappearing underwear. Mike had stumbled out, crying, into the bitter cold Schenectady night, although some say that this incident occurred in Vermont while April was in bed drunk, as usual. Dick says, they say, that he's sorry that he made him cry. Some say that Mike froze to death and that Lena Schmidt and Biff Page found him in the drifts, clutching a rosary. Biff says that Mike said that somebody stole his girl, then quietly expired. They say that May didn't shed a tear at his funeral. It was the talk of the town. They say that April, however, cried uncontrollably, leaning for support on Rose Zeppole's shoulder, who, they say, was dressed as a nun. They say that Rose often affected such garb, even though she was not a nun, and Léonie Aubois said that she was not only not a nun, but that her name was actually Sylvie Lacruseille, although April said that Rose says that she's often called Rose of Washington Square, although she has no idea why. All this, they say, proves that April was never a nun either, for at this time she had taken to her bed, as they say, with a bottle of vodka, the television flickering soundlessly before her, the images bringing to her mind her lost youth. Time hurries by. They say that Karen left Dick on the beach in the Bahamas for a young entrepreneur, who, they say, was just a gigolo. Dick, they say, is still on the beach, waiting patiently for her return with the cigarettes that Karen said that she wanted to buy. Others say that this is but a bad as well as ancient joke. Antonia, before she lost the power of speech in the mysterious accident which befell her, said that the whole story was suspect, since she knew, she said, that *Doubles Cross* contains a scene in which these events occur, in an episode entitled "Butts on the Beach," but others say that they've heard from people who've read the manuscript that no such scene therein exists. Others say that there is no manuscript. They say that April is the same old April and that it would be exactly like her to throw that episode away in order to protect Dick from, as she said, scorn and contumely. She can't help loving that man. They say that she sits in bed all day, drinking vodka and writing long love letters to him, and that she encloses, with these letters, erotically posed photographs of herself in various stages of undress, photographs that, they say, were taken twenty-five years ago, when, they say, she had a "blue room," which phrase no one seems able or willing to elucidate. Then, or so they say, April mails, or has mailed, these letters to Dick's new wife, Karen, who never receives them, since she has been dead for ten years, and Dick, they say, lives somewhere in New Jersey. Sometimes he's happy. They say that the Postmaster has all the letters and that he has been considering paying April a visit for some time since, they say, he doesn't realize that the young and beautiful woman wantonly posed for her husband's pleasure is the demented and drunken woman to whom he delivers mail, most of it, so they say, junk mail and bills. They say that he says that he sees her in his dreams. They say that nobody will tell him the truth about April, although others say that nobody *can* tell him the truth, for nobody knows that he possesses the letters and photographs. They say that April is getting "stranger," since she often speaks of the Postmaster with affection, although they say that what she says about him reveals that she thinks of him as he was some twenty-five years ago, when he was young and perverse, rather than as he is now, old and still perverse. They say he can dance with everybody but his wife. They say that Lena said, or wrote, that she has gone back to Mother Church because, or so Lena said, or wrote, that April said, she envies the camaraderie that exists among a group of housewives in the parish, all of them April's age, who take turns going to each other's houses for coffee and cake on weekday evenings following Benediction. These women say that there are smiles that make you happy. They say that either Lena or April is lying, since there are no housewives in the vicinity, unless, they say, Dick's new wife, Karen, may be considered such, although she is not middle-aged but quite young. They say that Karen is always chasing rainbows and that she calls herself Karen at Dick's request, even though her true name is Rose Marie. Saul Blanche, an erstwhile neighbor of the Detectives in Connecticut, said that Marcella Butler, who assisted him in a small publishing venture he had once run and who knew Dick and April when they first arrived in New York from Schenectady, Dick all pimples and April thin as a rail, said that Dick, for some unknown yet decidedly eccentric reason, fell in love with any woman named Karen, except, so they say that Saul said that Marcella said, when he fell in love with women who were not named Karen. In the latter cases, he implored these women to permit him to call them Karen. Yet some say that Marcella lied about this as she has always lied about everything concerning Dick. He is, they say, the cream in her coffee, and reminds her of her first flame, an elderly and distinguished reinsurance clerk named Fred, of whom, as they say, nothing will be said, except that at present the girl in his arms isn't she. They say that this is a blessing for Marcella, and that old Fred will miss the sweetest girl he ever had. They say that April calls Dick's new wife, Karen, Miss Dubuque, although no one can guess why, and Dick says that Karen, who is the youngest daughter of Rosie O'Grady, says that she is getting tired of being confused with some French whore whom Dick had known before they met. They say that Dick knew a number of French whores before he met his new wife, Karen, but that none of them were called Miss Dubuque, although one of them was called, oddly enough, Karen O'Grady. However, they say that the Postmaster made this story up so that he might have an excuse to call on April and warn her to stop harassing Karen, since one of the duties of the Postmaster in the little Vermont town in which all these people live is to act as the Constable. They say that the Postmaster-Constable did, indeed, visit April one night, or so he said, and that he discovered her in bed with a bottle of vodka and a man with a movie camera and an unspeakable affliction. The latter, so the Postmaster-Constable said, cheerfully introduced himself as Mr. Harlan and April as Miss Majorska, and then suggested that a threesome might be amusing since the night was made for love. They say that the Postmaster-Constable, whose name, or so he said, was Clive Oak, said that he'd come to make known to April a citizen's complaint, not to indulge in what Oak said that Harlan said were carefree gambols. But some say that none of Oak's recollections of that night rings true since he is known throughout the county as a man who would, as they say, fuck a snake. Oak, when so accused, simply says that he wants to be *happy*. They say that Oak would most certainly have joined the couple in bed, despite the fact that Harlan's affliction, unspeakable as it was, would have disgusted any reasonable human being and that Harlan's facetious remark, "You ought to be in pictures," would, most likely, have been the thing that served to convince him to join in, as they say, the fun. It is said that they say that it was after this particular adventure that April took the veil and became Sister Rocco Portola, which was the name, or so an unnamed cleaning woman said, of the nun who had given April her first catechism instruction when she was a pupil at O.L.B.E. Parochial School. But another unnamed cleaning woman said that the nun's name was Sister San Antonio Rose. In any event, as far as April is concerned, so she says, she's to this day the one rose that's left in her heart. They say that all this was a lie made up by Dick to explain April's absence from Vermont, although Karen said that Dick said that April was never absent from Vermont, and that April's memoirs clearly state that she

had not left Vermont at that time, since the vodka as well as Mr. Harlan
barely allowed her a moment out of bed. Those who have had the
privilege of perusing April's memoirs say that they note that Oak got
Mr. Harlan's name wrong, and that the man who was in bed with April
was, in fact, Mr. Pungoe. The memoirs go on to say that he "does
something" to her. But, they say, none of this can be trusted, for the
pages of the memoirs on which these elements appear are decisively
marked FOR NOVEL ONLY, the novel being, of course, *Doubles
Cross,* the variant title for which was, at one time, *There's a New Sun in
the Sky.* They say that Marcella said that Sheila Henry said that the
first, preferred title of this novel, which title has never been revealed,
although no one seems to know why, is a pun that refers to the dress, a
sleeveless shift of off-white raw silk, worn by May on the evening that
Mike first took her out. They say that May said that the stars were
peekabooing down and that they went dancing at Lena's Rest, where
Mike played "I Can Dream, Can't I?" twenty-six times on the jukebox.
They say that May said that Mike proposed to her that very night,
bewitched by her daring dress. They say that falling in love is wonderful.
They say that Mike says that he still wonders what would have
happened had May worn her pink jersey sleeveless dress, a garment, so
Mike says, that could not fascinate or excite anyone but a hermit,
although some say that Mike would never have used the word fascinate.
On hearing this obvious denigration of his linguistic skills, Mike said
that none of these insults faze him since he always lets a smile be his
umbrella. He'll get by. They say that May's story is highly suspect,
since April said that May said that *she* proposed to Mike. They had
been high-school sweethearts, as they say, and Dick said that Mike
once said that they had invariably obeyed the injunctions, or at least the
suggestions, of the lyrics of certain popular songs. These lyrics had led,
inevitably, to the proposal, although Dick said that Mike said nothing
about who had proposed to whom. Mike also said, with a tear in his eye,
that May, or for that matter, any pretty girl is like a melody that haunts
you night and day, much to Dick's barely contained amusement. But
they say that May never once mentioned her earlier involvement with
Dick to Mike, even though April said that Dick said, years later while
they were sitting in front of the fire in Connecticut, that he and May had
had some great times together in the balcony of the Ritz movie theater,

the Score Motor Inn, and the backseat of an abandoned Nash down by the lumber yard, and that May had been sweet and hot. They say that Mike and May were married against his parents' wishes, for, they say, the elder Cullinans or Cullinanes maintained that May was no better than her tramp of a sister, although Sister Rocco Portola, or, as some called her, Rose, said that April, at the time, was far from being a tramp and was thinking seriously of becoming a novice with the Sisters of Misericordia, a charitable order. But some say that this recollection was really no more than love sending a little gift of Rose's. Sister Rocco also said, however, that there's a little bit of bad in every good little girl, and that April had been no exception. They say that April said that May brought all this up to her one evening during a visit to the Detectives by Mike, May, Brian, and Maureen, although Maureen said, some years later, that her mother had said nothing about any of these things. But Mike says, or so Dick says that he said, that nothing that Maureen said, ever, could be trusted, since she was born to make trouble for him and May. She ain't nobody's darling. They say that it got back to April that Mike also said that Maureen took after her aunt, whom Mike dismissed as no better than a secondhand rose, and that it was clear to April that Mike had not intended to flatter her with this remark, since he made it, so Lena said, or wrote, immediately following a disturbing incident involving his daughter. They say that Mike said, so Lena said, or wrote, that he had come upon Maureen in their basement family room one evening after he and May had unexpectedly returned from a party early, a party that had been the occasion for a quarrel stemming from May's sudden and startling declaration of her unutterable boredom with his unutterably boring friends. They say that Mike's friends may well have been unutterably boring in that they spoke of little save automotive problems, trips to Europe, money, and professional football, although others say that these "subjects" are fraught with interest. In any event, Lena said, or wrote, that Mike said that he had found Maureen, who was sixteen at the time, rather intimately involved with two neighborhood boys of her own age, and that their partially undressed state was explained to him by his daughter as the result of a game of charades. They say that April said that when she heard, or read, what Lena said, or wrote, about what Mike had said that Maureen had said that Mike should have been glad that *somebody* loves her. They also say that when it got back to April that Mike had compared Maureen to her aunt, the "tramp," and that the comparison had been based, doubtlessly, on the incident in the family room, she had suggested that she might ask May to ask Mike about what she said was the little faux pas of some few years earlier concerning certain articles of intimate feminine apparel. Every road has a turning. They say that somebody told this to Mike and that he became so upset that he left the house in the middle of a professional football game. But others say that nothing short of death or a sale of repp-stripe ties could make Mike miss a professional football game, and, as a matter of fact, that Mike's abiding dislike of Sheila Henry was rooted in the fact that she had once asked Mike if it were really true that all football players are homosexuals. They say that April said that she hoped Mike would suffer a fatal coronary just before the kickoff of the next Super Bowl game. They say that Mike did indeed suffer such an attack, but others disagree, and say that he had a spontaneous orgasm. They say that *Karen* was the one who suffered a fatal coronary, and that soon after Dick met another young woman, whose name was Karen. They say that this Karen was an airline hostess and that April said that Dick said to all who would listen that this Karen was "*the* one," and that he'd found a rose in the devil's garden, whatever he meant by that. April said, or so Marcella said that Dick said, that she was certain that this Karen's surname was Minet, another "healthy slut," and that Dick said that this was but another of April's drunken insults and that he was sorry that he'd left the Vermont house to her. Marcella said that April laughed at this and noted merely that the sun was going to shine in her back door some day. Marcella said that Dick had begun to cry and told her that the Vermont house was where he had first discovered that his true bent was for literary pursuits. But they say that Dick never wrote anything anywhere, and that the novel *Blackjack,* which he claimed as his own, had been written by Henri Kink, who, so they say, disappeared some years ago. Days are long since he went away. Henri had had an argument with Annette Lorpailleur, who, so they say Madame Delamode said, had been secretly married to Mr. Pungoe for some time. But Joanne Lewis said that Annette and Pungoe had never been married, although they say that Joanne cannot be trusted in anything that she says ever since the day that she moved in with a man named Norman, whom, they say, nobody has ever laid eyes on with the exception of Joanne and her ex-husband, Guy, who *still* gets jealous. Yet they say that Guy cannot be trusted in anything that *he* says concerning Joanne. He has, as they say, gone around the bend, and spends his nights all alone by the telephone, waiting for some mysterious call that will prove to the whole world that you're a million miles from nowhere when you're one little mile from home. Joanne, they say, doesn't believe a word of this. When April heard of Joanne's new relationship, they say that she stopped drinking and became engaged to Oak, who, so Karen, Dick's new wife, not Karen Minet, said. She went on to say that Oak said to her that this was a dream come true, that he'd found a million-dollar baby. They say that Oak has never got over the twenty-five-year-old photographs of April that he still cherishes. Some say that the joke, if joke it was, was on Oak, as, twenty-five years earlier, it had been on Dick, in that the photographs were not, so Mike said that May said, of April at all, but of her, May. April says that this is nonsense, as does Dick, but May said, so Mike says, that it is the absolute truth, since she and April are identical twins. She even says that an old family saying has it that April brings the flowers that bloom in May. So much, as they say, for old family sayings. But they say that this contention is absurd, since April and May do not look at all alike, although others say that they can't be told apart. Mike says that May insisted that this was the fact, and that she had said this one day when she was, so Mike says May said, "up to here" catering to the whims of his drunken family, members of which would, so they say, descend upon Mike and May at all hours. They say that Marcella said that April said that Mike said that what had made him furious, even though he still loved May as he had loved her when she was sweet sixteen, was that May had asked his father if he didn't feel cold without his green cardboard derby. But others say that May's language was more forceful and that she had said to the elder Cullinan or Cullinane that he looked blue without his fucking shanty green fucking derby. Yet May said, so April says, that she would never have used such language in front of Brian, who was, at the time, an altar boy at O.L.B.E. They say that April, despite her engagement to Oak, or perhaps because of it, began drinking again, that Oak finally joined her, and that the two of them spend their days and nights watching television. Yet Karen, Dick's second ex-wife, said that Oak said, on one of his daily visits to her in the new condominium development where she lives, that it is April who drinks and watches television, and that he, so Karen said he said, had moved into Dick's old studio, where he spends his time in research on the writings of Anatole Broyard. Oak says, they say, that his feverish labors are worth all his sacrifices, because the world is *waiting* for the sunrise. Some say that Norman, for some reason, bought the condominium for Karen, but others say that Norman has never heard of Karen. For her part, Karen says that the condominium was a gift from Barnett Tete, who admires, so Karen says, New England spunk. Karen and April, they say, have returned to Mother Church, and like nothing better than to chat, over coffee and cake, with the other women of the parish on weeknights following Benediction. They say that April says that she has burned her memoirs, despite Crescent and Chattaway's interest, and that she has recently taken to telephoning May in order to dissuade her from the sin of divorcing Mike, who, so Karen says that April said that May said, has begun to take what she called a "morbid" interest in her wardrobe. Mike speaks to April, they say, after she has spoken to May and begs her not to reveal to her a certain secret that they share, a secret, so May says that Mike said, that has to do with a practical joke that he played on April some years ago on a fine bright morning in early spring, or, as he says in what he calls "play-talk," on the morning that he was with her in apple-blossom time. April, they say, pretends not to know what Mike means, while Karen, or so she said, to whom April has told the story of that morning, makes faces at April so that she can hardly keep from laughing while on the telephone. They say that April still despises May and that she urges her sister not to divorce Mike so that they may continue to live together as usual. But others say that April really cares for her sister, and that she truly hopes that one day she'll find her lovable. Dick, for one, believes this, they say. He has, others say, just moved into a house down the road from April and Karen with his fifth wife, Karen, who is a color consultant and loves to do pastel miniatures which she frames herself. Or so they say that April said, although Karen says April is a drunk now and never says anything at all.

Chyme of belles

There's no rush. There's never any rush, the truth, the facts, are all here, they do not have to be hurried into prominence. Serenely, they'll assert themselves, we'll get a few things straight, finally, although why it should so turn out that Anne and Ellen will have their lives rectified is beyond comprehension. The impression was that their lives had been rectified, which goes to prove how little we know. Consider the dozens of other people who must bear the burden of distortion, who have been presented as so many instances of a sketchy and unsatisfactory Eleatics, and then, of course, there is the flatness of the narrative, the lack of tension, the absence of conflict and resolution, the dying falls, the lack of closure. Coarse sexuality. Data and cynical commentary. Nervous and demotic language. Jokes! Yet all is true, each and every line. In vain we search for immense darkness, wandering gazes, garish colors, sullen heat, swooping sea gulls. And not to forget the backless kitchen chair! The leaky toilet! And the reassuring smile. *This* must be the void, deemed fashionable by those who dabble in ontology. Dare we whisper: fuck them? The stuffy room: check. The moths bumbling at the windowpane: check. Numbing somnolence of the heat that spreads over the town like a, like a: check. A screen door, right on cue, slams in the distance: check again. Here, in the silence, broken only by the scratching of a pen on paper, the buzzing of a fly breaks the silence. Wait. The stifling silence is broken by *two* sounds, the scratching of a pen on paper and the buzzing of a fly. Face to face with the unbearable light of truth!

Anne

Her maiden name was not Marshall, but McCoyne. Scratch the telephone company. Anne couldn't catch a ball for the life of her, nor run, nor wrestle. The radio. All right. The radio is what she liked! The other members of the Christian Conservative Student Crusade disapproved of her and her clothes, especially her flour-smudged skirts. Her hair was dark brown, she wrote home to her mother, Charlotte Pugh McCoy, McCoyne, every week. An occasional gravy stain. Charlotte, too, listened to the radio, driving her husband, in desperation, to the Bluebird Inn, where he learned how to do a passable fox-trot. What the hell, it filled his empty life with promise, his empty and somnolent life. This dance may figure large in our story, like a symbol, of which we have a plethora. Transcendence is all. Anne always wore underclothes, even, strangely, beneath her bathing suit, for she adored swimming. On almost any summer Sunday, she could be found at Riis Park, her face dreamy as she listened to one of her many radios. Her preference was for white rayon, which is fine by me. Pristine. There were few problems that she couldn't solve, once she undid her braids. She did not know how to throw pots or make, let's say make, ceramics, and as for knitting, crocheting, and sewing, they, she often said, her eyes snapping with the irrepressible humor that, her eyes glowing with girlish fun, they, well, were for other people. That's how she put it. Sometimes she wore a single braid. Thick, of course. Tania Crosse, her first roommate, loved it when she claimed, as she barely repressed a shy giggle, that she could weave. A grotesque ashtray had somehow found its way into the apartment. Actually, Tania was her second roommate. Anne often gazed imperturbably at it, wondering if the unbearable heat would ever break. She had no curtains. Sun is sun, but *this!* One evening, she and Tania experimented together sexually, and though nothing came of it, Anne's heart pounded when she thought, in later years, of Tania's creamy skin and soft lips. Her pulses crooned. Yielding and such. She never married Guy Lewis, nor even met him until long after her marriage to Leo. That clears that up. Her blood seemed to boil, too. Olga Begone? An invention. We already know about the nonexistent Tessie and Jude. Charlotte sent her a set of chili bowls, suitable, of course, for soup or stew as well. Or even salad. Anne occasionally made soup or stew, but chili, never. Most of the time she was content to know that the bowls sat neatly in the cupboard, a token of her old life. Oddly enough, she had, some years before, confessed her loathing of certain hearty dishes to Ralph Ingeman, an old school friend, or chum.

Ralph's open face had broken into an engaging grin when he heard this news. He, for his part, was not surprised, for he had always been a salad fan. Ralph still wrote to her, his letters invariably beginning with the salutation, "Dear New York Pal," which phrase occasionally made Anne retch. Yet more often than not she'd sit, alone at the kitchen table, or she'd sit alone, at the kitchen counter, after reading Ralph's chatty letters, and allow nostalgia to wash over her like an invisible wave of sullen heat. Enough? More.

Ellen

Jackie Moline never existed, one can check with Ellen on that. Her salad was reasonably good, the ingredients were fresh, although she had a penchant for bottled dressing, especially a remarkably tasty concoction called Green Goddess. Perhaps it was a sign. Strange how salad has popped up again. She often capped the bottle with an unsteady hand, sweat forming in little beads on her worried brow. She wore a cocktail dress but once, to her high-school prom, and it made her feel, well, beautiful. As well it should have. Photographs from those days reveal her slender waist and large breasts, but a discreet device planted in her ear hints at early hearing problems. So there is a measure of heartache to be taken into account. Wearing this dress, she longed to turn away from her callow classmates and their little dreams. Peck and Peck? Fabrication. But after the dance, alone in her stuffy room, the house gripped by the unseasonably hot June night, she was grudgingly forced to admit that some of them had big dreams. She met Leo long after he and Anne had been divorced, and could never forget how the blood had thudded in her temples when she first saw him, his great artistic head of hair setting him apart from the crowd, which was quite large. She was a graduate of Brooklyn College, and although she had, indeed, a pert snub nose, this latter was the result of what her mother irritatingly called a nose job. Elizabeth Reese was a philosophy teaching assistant, a young woman with bow legs and a sudden but warm smile. The operation had cost, as her father often put it, "plenty." She was properly thankful. Big tits aren't everything, as Mother Theresa probably knows. When Ellen looked at Elizabeth she felt suddenly faint, as if the blood beneath her tingling flesh had grown wildly turgid. At such times, she sensed her woman's body keenly, and a strange excitement made her catch her breath. But school ended, and goodbye Miss Reese! One hot summer day, a day on which the cruel and scorching air hung, then fell over the city like a leaden blanket, she got a job. She was glad when the shadows finally lengthened for she could hardly wait to enter the candy store around the corner from her parents' house. It would be good, she thought, the faint trace of a smile playing across her full mouth, to relax and have an egg cream and an Eskimo Pie at the counter. For it must be understood that Ellen, despite the harsh disappointments of her childhood, had few, if any, problems with acne. She was lucky, "glad" is how she thought of it, to have landed the job. It was time for her to sever her ties with Jake, her father, and Tessie, her mother, whose existence centered on her weekly Mah-Jongg game. Jake, for his part, liked nothing better than a good cigar. The clicking of the tiles and the voices of her mother's friends always made her think of the overpowering bouquet of her father's cheap cigars, and the gestalt of these invariables caused her to shudder imperceptibly. She would turn away, grimacing, her heart heavy with the nagging sense of her betrayal of them. At such moments, Jake would whisper encouragement to her, secure in the knowledge that she couldn't hear him. She would often remain sleepless throughout the long nights, rising at dawn to watch the salmon-pink sky spread its glory over the world. Her large, youthful breasts trembled beneath her sheer nightgown, and suddenly there would appear against the vast sunrise a gull, serene in the sky, proud and isolate. Her nipples often rose against the diaphanous fabric. Enough? More.

Anne

It wasn't Theodore Roethke who mattered, but Peter Viereck, or perhaps Allen Tate, in any event, one of our great poets. She loved those poems, strong as they were, yet with a certain delicacy and a rapt attention to rational form. And the fact that they meant something, that they transcended and explained many things didn't hurt either. "The Old Confederate Dead Man" was, perhaps, her favorite. Craig Garf took it into his grizzled head to hump her quietly at a party one evening, and she, stricken with nameless grief and half-mad with strong drink and the passionate rhythms of loud music, probably hot jazz, humped him frenziedly back. She never lived in Brooklyn, that mysterious borough as foreign to her as the mysterious Bronx. Leo came into her life at about the same time that the strange ashtray appeared, on a cold day when the grey sky seemed to complement her depressed spirits. It loured menacingly. What a head of hair! she thought shyly. He sent her a drink at a bar that everyone frequented, including the *Lorzu* crowd, and when she asked him his name he smiled distantly, and, in reply, bit off a few obscure words. They hung in the air for a long moment and time, at least as far as she was concerned, seemed to stop. Then she knew, she felt him somehow deeply and irrevocably hers. At about the time—it was summer now, a deadening, humid, somnolent summer whose heat lay on the city like a sweaty hand, or arm—that she found herself becoming involved with Leo, Charlotte, her mother, wrote to tell her that she was remarrying and that the groom was to be Russell Gunge, the aging barber who lived just upstairs. At the news, a bleak greyness, a greyness like that of a bleak, grey November day, settled on her soul. Not that she didn't like Russ, who smoked Pall Malls, but she couldn't help but remember his mocking leer when, as a girl, she had excitedly told him of her plans for the future. You be locky if yez loins ta fock-trot like ya dad, he'd invariably say, his scissors held menacingly aloft. On one occasion, he had gestured cynically with the yellowed fingers that now often returned to haunt her waking dreams. The diaper story is slanderous and apocryphal, or probably so, since the tastes of most of her male friends ran to lacy underwear and sheer hosiery, nothing, as they say, to write home about, at least not in a lather. Babies, and all that served to remind Leo of babies, put the unkempt poet off. He would lie on his rumpled bed, tears welling up in his eyes, a foxed copy of Wordsworth, an English poet, open on his bare chest to "The Prelude," a highly regarded poem of several parts. Soon after, they married, but Leo turned out to be, to put a nice face on it, not up to the mark, and even though Anne often thought of the beauty of the hills as they turned to gold under the evening sun, and of how wonderful Indians really were, it was all she could do to clear a space for herself amid the clutter of the dining table, or, as things might have it, the kitchen table. She smoked nervously. Enough? More.

Ellen

Yet after the family ties were severed and placed on the dumbwaiter, she felt somehow as if she were the only human being in the world, and often found herself crying as if in expectation of a curse and a blow. Her legs, which even now are a splendid eyeful, were especially lovely way back when, and it wasn't long before the hirsute bard was running his hands under her skirt while they sat in one or another of the dimly lit boîtes or cocktail lounges in which he cut something of a figure. To tell the truth, he adored playing with her garters, or, as he'd often gaily whisper in her ear, her jarretières. The night that found Leo really getting fresh with her was the turning point in their relationship, and although it had little or nothing to do with the party's baked ham, roast turkey, or cold cuts, it was a shock nonetheless to Ellen to realize that the insistent pleasure between her thighs was being caused by his somewhat importunate if pleasantly feverish hand. The French have an expression for that, she thought, somewhat irrelevantly. They left to confront a rain that poured down sullenly, like a great wet hand, on the city, a wet and cold and merciless hand, and Leo's voice rose in triumph as he turned at the door to hurl imprecations at poor Jack Towne. Ellen felt, after all this, barely alive, and wondered what Miss Reese would have thought when, later, she surrendered to Leo's pathetic lusts. Her skin felt hot beneath her woolen suit, or perhaps one of her innumerable cocktail dresses, oddly fetching garments which she had taken to wearing again, despite coarse laughter. Her skin cooled quickly as Leo undressed her with shaking hands, and she was secretly glad that the lace on her underthings was as fine and frothy as spun sugar or beaten egg whites. What a break! Then the world seemed to move away, slowly, silently, and everything in Leo's flat receded into a magical and shimmering distance. And a good thing too. She wondered, as she felt the poet's urgent manhood at the center of her yielding body, what Jackie might have said had Jackie only been, as she had often dreamily wished, her brother. But she had no brother! No, she had nothing, nothing but Jake and Tessie of whom, she thought guiltily, she was just a little ashamed, now that she had begun to meet really sophisticated people. Enough? More.

Anne

Biscayne Bay does not figure in our narrative, so that all references to it and environs should be viewed as apocryphal at best. Yet perhaps the mere notice of the words occasioned by a fleeting glance at a magazine made Leo question the wisdom of their marriage, for Anne even now recalls that it was after just such a cursory, or fleeting glance that Leo became cynical, hostile, sardonic and contemptuous toward her. Her spirits sank as if into a sea upon whose surface of hope no ship of love or even affection could move or tack in the becalmed waters that . . . sank as if they were a ship into the becalmed waters of a lost sea, a lost and strange sea, a Sargasso of crushed dreams and thwarted hopes. She introduced him to one of her new friends, Léonie Aubois, brilliant, embittered, wise-cracking Léonie, in the hope that the latter would refresh his spirits by chatting with him of the latest fashions in frillies, lacies, gewgaws, and equipment. It was to no avail. Indeed, Anne often started awake to the mad flutes and drums or fifes and drums of large orchestras or bands playing Civil War songs. Leo would often sing along, his voice raised in agonized triumph. Her haunted eyes would gaze imploringly at him over their light but nourishing Continental breakfast, and he would, rarely, all too rarely, meet them with his own imploring gaze. Yet nothing seemed amenable to resolution, although when she found a pair of ice-blue panties among Leo's papers her heart sang, for she knew that he had bought them for her as an offering to Eros, as a gesture toward their mislaid passion or, at the very least, mutually satisfying marital sex. But her spirits sank in the ponderous July heat, an oppressive heat that smothered the city like a damp muffler, when, the next day, she saw Frieda Canula, the manager of a laundromat down the street, with the intimate garment nonchalantly knotted about her neck. So much for froufrous, she thought, drained, as she dashed at the tears that sprang to her eyes and then ran, like slow, sad rivers, down her pale cheeks. The Detectives? Anne disliked them intensely, even though, at this time, she hardly knew them, and didn't want to, given the fact that she was barely alive, what with the oppressive heat's leaden hands choking the city, the ceaseless grey rain, and the gnawing sadness that ate at her like an acid regret. The presence of a packet of photographs that belie her nodding acquaintance with Dick and April should, of course, be noted, but only *en,* as the French so deftly put it, *passant, mes amis.* [But just while passing by, my pals.] Muscatel? Yes. White Port, Thunderbird, Sherry, Gypsy Rose—all these went down Leo's throat, and with each swallow he slipped deeper and deeper into his strange apathy, an apathy in which the sublime art that had always been his reason, or one of his many reasons, for living, was deeply foundering, so that Leo and Anne were both gasping in the long, relentless, hot summer with its leaden skies and fierce, hot rains, those scorching rains that, because they were hot and scorching, made the summer hotter and more relentless. Anne threw herself into bed one evening with ZuZu Jefferson, the cool and fashionable blonde who had an interesting and demanding job having something pertinent to do with, as Leo's beloved Wordsworth once put it, "creative art!" He knew what he was talking about. Never had Anne's body felt so alive! Never had the roots of her sexuality been so deeply stirred! Never had her soul so yearned to cry out, its voice high in ecstatic joy: SO THIS IS THE ORGASMIC ACTIVITY THAT I'VE BEEN READING ABOUT IN A NUMBER OF RECENT MAGAZINE ARTICLES! Wow! she cried, again and again. Wow! It was really something. She soon bought a fedora and began keeping a journal in which she recorded her most private thoughts and impressions, thoughts and impressions now safe from Leo's drunken contempt, cold hostility, bitter cynicism, mocking leer or leers, and proud contumely. Enough? More.

Ellen

Some of them were not, surely, as sophisticated as were others, for instance, there was the insufferable clubfooted man who usually went by the name of Harlan Pungoe, and who seemed to have a penchant for cameras, photographs, and what might be termed documentary evidence of this, that, and the other thing. A robust sort of tyke, no, fellow, a robust fellow who, despite his shadowy motivations, and his relentless peerings, was at bottom no more than what somebody termed a fucking cripple. However, years ago, in somebody's vague memory, it seems that Harlan was not crippled at all! Ellen tried to put it all out of her mind, yet it was always there, behind whatever other varied thoughts were hers, so that to see her stand, bemused, outside the

Foxhead Inn, in her tight bodice and short flared skirt, was to know that Pungoe had, so to speak, inserted his quite considerable self into her mental life. But even with that to worry about she had to admire her remarkable gams when she glimpsed their reflection in a passing tray. Then Barry Gatto strode into her life and she felt, momentarily, somewhat content. Perhaps it was merely the faint odor of Moo Goo Gai Pan on his breath, since he was widely respected as a gourmet. Yet whatever the temptation, Leo was never very far from her thoughts, usually just "in front," as Ellen conceived of it, those of Harlan. As far as the ex-priest, Frank Baylor, Father Frank, is concerned, he seems to have just passed through, sans stopping, the rather hectic milieu that at that time abounded. That takes care of that. There had always been something remote about him anyway, a depressing greyness, that emanated from his, so many thought, patronizing and sacrosanct attitude, if greyness can fairly be said to emanate from anything at all, much less an ex-priest's attitude. In any event, he came and went within forty-eight hours. Off to the convent! someone quipped, his indiscreet hand up Ellen's accommodatingly short skirt. They were always trying that one out on her, often with reasonably satisfying results. It goes without saying that her job as a cocktail waitress was fraught with humiliation, and at the end of her working day, as she walked out into the nearly deserted streets of the great iron uncaring city, she felt numbed, barely alive, and humiliated. In the winter, her legs would get extremely cold, especially were the winds bitter, and if it were drizzling that fine, icy, penetrant mist that brings one face to face with one's own mortality, she would find herself actually running toward the subway. It was nothing short of amazing. She'd creep up Leo's stairs as the dawn rose on the pitiless metropolis, hoping that she'd find Leo asleep as she most liked him, his arm badly twisted beneath his flamboyant aesthetic head, his cheek wet with childlike drool. Often he would be stretched out on his back and she'd take solace in the fact that the phonograph's turntable would be spinning, the needle riding in the final grooves, exactly as it does in so many of the films that Ellen had seen and, yes, loved. She wasn't ashamed to admit her liking for the cinema. He needed her then, she knew, and it was nothing for her to wake him and pose lasciviously before his fevered eyes for hours and hours, or at least for about forty-five minutes to maybe an hour or so. In the middle of these erotic exhibitions, she'd think, Pungoe!, and rush to the dirty window in time to see a nondescript figure in an electric-blue suit limp, or perhaps hobble off toward a lonely diner, preferably one beneath an "el." Eyes snapping, Leo would roughly possess her as she leaned on the windowsill as the first rosy light appeared in the east. It was probably her wet hosiery that excited him, wet from the cruel drizzle that has already been mentioned. Father Frank had mentioned something about it on the night that now loomed as one of the most important of her life, could she only discover precisely why. Enough? More.

Anne

A reckless artist, Tony Lamont, his gifts destroyed long years before by an excess of critical adulation, yes, he was that. But the reality was sadder. His rampant manhood longed to find its way to Karen's armpits and the moist tufts of hair that he wished grew there, but it was only a dream. Only a dream!, he would sob into the fetid air of his dank bedroom. Anne needed the divorce from Leo and his insufferable Dante Rossini! As far as she was concerned, a wop was, well, not to be crude about it, always just a wop. And this despite various arias, which, she had to admit when coaxed, took her breath away. Then there was, finally, the discovery of the frilly items in Tony's freezer, which, when Anne opened the door one fine spring morning, the pigeons cooing and shitting on the window ledge, took her breath away. For a long moment, after her breath returned whence it had fled, it came in ragged gasps and anguished rattlings, as she recognized the frilly items, now cold as the death of their passion, to be various intimate garments of Karen Ostrom, who was, Anne was certain of it now, some kind of Swede. She fairly flew down the stairs after blindly shaving her underarms, weeping bitterly, dashing the angry tears from her eyes, those dark eyes which snapped in irrepressible fury. Into the cloudy grey morning she ran, quite unsure of where she was going, knowing only that she must go! Fitful rain pelted her unmercifully, like a large and merciless fist. Lorna Flambeaux was waiting, as usual, reclining, actually, on a heap of pillows carelessly, yet with studied elegance, strewn about the fur rug before the bright fire. That was Lorna all over. Anne had to admire her,

for Lorna, despite her important job and her upper-middle-class preten-
sions, didn't care! Then came a long, sweet morning of mutually
consensual adult sexual behavior, directed toward making both of them
feel good about themselves, and Anne's soul sang a long melody of
rapturous sensuality, believe it or not. She, who had but a scant few
hours earlier felt herself barely alive, now thrilled to the center of her
being, as Lorna showed her a few perverse tricks that she'd learned
from a certain "Yasmine." Yet who is to say what "perverse" is? Or
who, for that matter, what "tricks" are? Her passionate laughter came
so unexpectedly and powerfully that she dislodged, more than once,
poor Lorna, who wound up, not unsurprisingly, utilizing the home first-
aid kit before they sat down to a light and nourishing lunch, which fairly
took Anne's breath away. Soon came Anne's first pair of Sweet-Orr
overalls and a chance meeting with Annette Lorpailleur, who was
somehow mysteriously linked with a man the crowd called "Clubfoot
Pete," and who turned out to be, of course, Pungoe. Although he smiled
benignly at all, and his voice was rich and deep and so bespoke more
than a mediocre upbringing and education, Anne was uncomfortable
with the idea of looking the other way when he commenced, as he did
with great regularity, to, well, "play" with himself, a hand thrust as
nonchalantly as possible, given the circumstances, into his pocket. It
unfailingly took her breath away. At the funeral for Henri Kink, whose
works, according to those who knew about such things, were delicate
yet strong as a spiderweb, albeit filled with a joyous affirmation of life
and a great humility before his responsibility to his characters, she saw
Leo again. Someone insisted respectfully, as she tried not to stare, that
Henri's works were as delicate and strong as a *number* of spiderwebs,
not just one, for Christ's sake! She couldn't help but notice that the
young woman who gazed raptly at Leo wore a cocktail dress, and she
knew, suddenly, that this was Leo's future wife, Ellen Marowitz. It was
a curious shade of mauve, and, to be candid, Anne thought it a little
gauche. Yet the funeral ended on a dark note when a strangely importunate person with the unlikely name of Rupert Whytte-Blorenge
insisted on spitting into Henri's grave and then, to add insult to injury,
told Anne, to her face, that she was, as far as he was concerned, some
eyeful. At this *mot* he winked and reminded her of a costume party to
which she had, against her better judgment, worn a diaper and heels. So

it was true. Anne blushed beet-red, backed away, then stumbled blindly, tears stinging her eyes, into the oppressive heat of the streets, the mocking laughter of the mourners pursuing her as if it would do so forever. As she stood at the curb, waiting for a taxi, and wishing fervently that she had never even heard the word "diaper," Pungoe pulled up alongside her in a new car, vulgarly shiny, his clubfoot concealed by a fetching rug, one hand insouciantly yet energetically twitching in his pocket. Ride home?, he inquired pleasantly, or, perhaps, Lift home?, and Anne got into the car, affording him a good long look at her legs. What was the use?, she thought. Pungoe crisply threw the sedan into reverse and smashed decisively into a tree. Thankfully, no real damage was done. Enough? More.

Ellen

Olga Begone, a very thin poet who had kept hidden, for some years, a novel, *Zeppelin Days,* written while a student, took a good look at Ellen one day as the latter chopped shallots and cabbage for one of her special dishes, and the brilliant if remotely obstreperous artist promptly introduced herself to the young bride. She had some legs, Olga thought. Ellen found herself strangely drawn to the warm, homely lesbian, who was, at this time of her life, a go-getter. She had more than a few things to say about the works of Robbe-Grillet! What they were, precisely, Olga could not articulate, yet this failing did nothing to prevent Ellen's disappointment when discreet inquiries revealed that the poet was currently living with Anne. It seemed unlikely, and many pals thought of Ellen's putative amazement as an affected ironic sophistication. But Ellen, like the good soldier that she was, refused to allow this letdown to affect her pursuit of other adventures, or, as she once put it, put a "crimp" in it. She was, it should be stated, chagrined at having to wear, and regularly, the famous pink jersey sleeveless dress we've heard of so often, and thought, more than once, of her empty and meaningless life. She would stare at herself in the mirror, cringing, as she listened in disgust to Leo splashing with his boats in the bathtub, readying himself, as he tenderly put it, for her. She could feel her skin crawl beneath the jersey and her eyes would grow moist, perhaps with self-pity. How she despised herself! Then the splashing would stop. The living room, into which she'd automatically walk, and which she had once been naive enough to think charming, filled her soul with a greyness that made her gorge rise. Leo would enter, his sex stirring, a Hi-Lo paddle gripped in one hand, a mocking leer disfiguring his once-sensitive features. His other hand would gesture toward the musty attic. Enough? More.

Anne

A Jackie something paid her well to perform despicable acts that made her feel degraded, almost dirty. But she made plenty of money serving these various lusts, so much so that there soon emerged a new Anne! Her face, once sensitive, now wore a perpetually mocking leer, and she offhandedly married, past hurt, past reason, Barnett Tete, a millionaire with a heart made of stone. She became known as the nun of Biscayne Bay, and was often seen wandering among the conchs. Rich and powerful people were in the area, as were golden sands. Yet wealth was not the answer to the age-old question that would form on her tight lips. It was not the answer! She returned to New York, for reasons peculiarly her own, rigid and forbidding in a tailored suit that, paradoxically, brought out the yielding femininity of her soft and still vulnerable body. She was vaguely discomfited by this, yet she had many suits. What could she do?, she mused. Throw them away? She wanted to make her life sing again. Freud had been right after all, she realized, suddenly ashamed. She appeared, for no reason at all, in a pornographic film catering to the vilest of male fantasies concerning tribadic love, as Sister Philomena Veronica, and caught the eye of Father Frank, who was back, again. He knew a great deal about ceramics and good fiction, having once been an editor at a magazine devoted to publishing really fine writing. They opened a little store together in Elmhurst, where Anne's gentle way with the clientele permitted them to reap a tidy profit. Religious stuff was their specialty and they had a batch of it. One day the vengeful shadow of Barnett Tete fell across the threshold, then the man himself followed. He had recently been released from a mental hospital, and Anne felt herself go all cold, then all hot, as she remembered certain things. A scream rose unchecked from her throat. The ceiling of the shop began to swim, sickeningly, and her knees turned to water, as, chuckling maliciously, Tete pulled from his pocket a diaper! At that moment, Father Frank entered, his eyes wide with horror. He knew. He *knew*. Enough? More.

Ellen

Despite everything, a lot had happened. Ellen thought bitterly, favoring her sore buttocks as she sat at the window table in her favorite coffee shop. There comes a time when humiliation is too high a price to pay for a few good dresses. A phrase from a great poem suddenly intruded on her half-clouded memory. If only she could remember it! She felt the breath catch in her throat. She was excited. Poems can do that, and so well, she said to herself as she paid her check. The cashier looked up quizzically, then smiled uncertainly, her eyes on Ellen as she walked out into the drizzle. Lucy! She knew now. That was what she had to do. Some days later she found herself in Lucy's homely arms, both of them thinking of the truth buried in the poem's famed lines, while Ellen wept, thinking of her father—dull, inarticulate, cruel, unfeeling, just plain, well, dumb, yet the dearest man she had ever known. She thought of their little Friday ritual, which he had shyly called "gumball." "Gumball?" he'd ask softly. And she had always answered yes, yes, oh yes, Daddy! What had that been about? If only . . . Hardly any time at all passed, and one day she and Lucy found themselves on the street, arm in arm, dazed and lethargic in the afternoon heat. Leo sat on the curb, half-hidden beneath the battered fedora that Ellen recognized as a caring token given her years before by a woman who was now much older, and as she put her hand up to her mouth in the age-old womanly gesture of pity and love and sorrow, she felt somewhat odd. Lucy, ugly, faithful Lucy, said quietly, no!, and brusquely stayed Ellen from sinking to her knees before the man to whom she had once surrendered herself. "No," she repeated, since Ellen had apparently not heard her. Her hearing aid was still "on the fritz," as she'd learned to say. Better than having a clubfoot, she'd say to Pungoe, when his barbs became a little too pointed. "No!" And now, she heard. A weight seemed to slip from her shoulders. But did it? Enough? More.

Anne

Heartless mirth and objects appearing as if in a dream, exotic food products. The release of maddening desires and an end to frustration. Looking as if she hadn't a care, moving as if in a trance: harsh and liberating truth, burning and insatiable flesh. Waking dreams! Deserted hills over which the sunlight plays, pinched souls. Sudden realization of friendship. Enough? Almost.

Ellen

Sudden realization of frustration and the pinched and insatiable flesh. The release of exotic food products: heartless objects! Moving as if she hadn't a care, looking as if in a trance. Maddening desires appearing as if in a dream. An end to mirth. Burning and deserted hills and a waking friendship. Harsh sunlight, liberating souls. Dreams over which the truth plays. Enough? Enough.

Hell mought

Joanne Lewis was born in Boonton, New Jersey, a small town putatively founded by Daniel Boone in 1809. As Guy reached orgasm, she absurdly thought of Boone, but why, she could not say. Odd that she had discovered the ecstasies of art *cum* sex right there in the heart of the great uncaring city. Although the January day had been bitter cold, she and Guy had tarried long on the Provincetown sands, those silent, majestic sands of New England. How she wished that Barnard were in Massachusetts! When she saw, years later, that infernal vision on Norman's wall, diabolic above his black leather couch, it was all she could do to smile weakly at Chet Kendrick, one of the stars of *The Party,* and her escort for the evening. Barnard became, perhaps predictably, increasingly distant from her thoughts. How Norman had ever come into possession of *The Valley of the Shadow of Death* was a mystery to everyone, not least Guy. Yet she remembered Harlan's prize specimen, a ceramic dildo made in exact imitation of those that whalers were wont to carve lovingly for their wives, forlorn on the shore. The large painting, done in a somber palette, had always seemed, to her, a representation of the mouth of Hell. Harlan had said that he'd been "through hell" to find exactly what he was looking for in ceramic Pekes. Why nobody, she had suddenly thought, ever complained about oiling the adobe floors was surprising. His wonderful collection of unique ceramic ashtrays, works of art in themselves, graced many a boardroom, and had convinced her that he was indeed the salesman he purported to be. Then she whipped him again with his belt, a remarkably ornate item of tooled leather. That the point of one heart nestled in the cleft of another all around the outer circumference of the friendship ring, or so she wrote years later in her diary, "tortured her young blood" with its "innocent symbolism." Afterward, exhausted, they had looked long at the setting sun which turned the snow on the

Sangre de Cristo blood red. And Ralph had rudely taken *his* friendship
ring back! The opening sentence of *Unicorn*, "The wind, which had, all
the dreaming Cornish afternoon, carried intimations of a calm and
joyous love, turned suddenly cruel as the sun slouched coldly into the
furious sea," had stayed in her mind since she had first read it. She still
had the ring, after all this time, and often thought of Stanley, who had
suffered so terribly with acne. Despite her nervous exhaustion and her
worry over everything, *Unicorn Crimson, Unicorn Grey* was a
marvelous read. But Guy maintained that it was not the mouth of Hell
there pictured, but the face of Satan himself, whom he had, he insisted,
once glimpsed on a road some miles outside Kansas City. Settling once
more into the pillows, she read again the flap copy for the work which
"redefines, for all time, the much-abused 'historical' novel." Guy,
terribly drunk, shouted that he hadn't even *painted* the fucking painting!
Then he'd begged her to put her new boots on. Obsessively, he'd gone
on and on about how someone else had completed the painting while he
was out getting a beer. But he took the time to admire her in the glistening boots. She had an unpleasant recollection of the day he'd pretended
to read the *Tulane Drama Review* in order to show his contempt for all
of them. In her pocket there had been a photostatic copy of a little-
known monograph of Stekel's which he'd given her to read. She'd
changed into a white crocheted dress and white sandals, then rejoined
them all on the patio. First Guy, and then her father, threw pieces of
incredibly charred chicken at Ralph's departing Plymouth. It seemed
that everything, chicken, hot dogs, hamburgers, and ribs, was charred,
and still Guy and her father talked on and on while her mother sat
smiling in an Adirondack chair. Some time later, Ralph drove by again,
shouting obscenities at Guy, who was praising Harold Lloyd at the
expense of Chaplin and Keaton. Earlier, a letter from her Englishman,
filled with amusing stories of legendary rock stars' perverted sexual
practices, had repelled yet thrilled her. She often dreamed lately.

Ralph just kept driving by in his old jalopy, leaning on the horn each
time he passed the house. There had been some photographs, which she
loved, of a deaf, blind, and clubfooted rhythm guitarist, enclosed with
his letter. Faulkner, whom Guy kept invoking in a loud voice, seemed to
her distinguished, if a little seedy. She wondered if he had actually met
Mick Jagger, as he claimed, at a party in London! She had tried to read

Absalom! Absalom! but returned to *Unicorn Crimson, Unicorn Grey.*
She'd hardly been surprised when Harlan removed from his sample
case a complete ensemble of ice-blue lingerie. *The Sound and the Fury*
lay on the dresser. When, flushed, she quickly pulled the panties up he
actually drooled. Although she had been as circumspect as possible
concerning the connection between her mother's stroke and the foul
letter about Mrs. Feuer and her father, Mr. Ward buried himself in his
much-read copy of *Les Constructions métalliques* for the remainder of
the evening. Ignoring what she'd said, he insisted, almost angrily, that
the color was *electric* blue. Her mother hadn't died, after all, even
though the poison-pen letter had gone into lewd detail about Mrs. Feuer
and Mr. Ward. After her mother had returned from the hospital, her
father began living in the refurbished chicken coop, saying nothing, and
existing on canned beans and chicken à la king. Her mother had been
stricken as she fussed, one cool fall evening, with the Indian corn and
autumn leaves spray on the front door. Her father denied everything,
even the fact that he knew Mrs. Feuer, and called them a gang of
Calvinist busybodies. This *couldn't* be, she thought, the reward for four
years of college! Mr. Ward, returning from what she had known for
years was his weekly rendezvous with Mrs. Feuer, almost stepped, in
the dark, on what he had first taken to be his wife's corpse. College,
then, had to be good for something. Upon her return from New Mexico,
she was surprised to find that one of the Soirée Intime's models was
April Detective, who looked, she had to admit, absolutely stunning in a
filmy peignoir. And April, as everybody knew, had never even seen the
inside of a college! The prices at the boutique were ridiculously high,
yet she still wanted, after all their troubles, to please Guy. She never
dreamed that just a few short years would find her staring in awe and
dread at *The Valley of the Shadow of Death* in Norman's living room,
while he stood behind her, his hands on her thighs. She had decided,
earlier that evening, perhaps because of something that Chet had said,
on white underclothes. Norman was something of a painter himself,
and the following morning showed her a little thing that he'd done of
Daniel Boone, dressed as a clown, in fierce struggle with what looked to
be a giant kangaroo. How she wished that she had listened to her father,
who never tired of saying that Ralph was, like all football players and
amateur painters, a repressed homosexual. In any event, from that

evening and its sordid events on, she always thought of the title of the painting as *Hell Mouth*. Norman's laughter at breakfast reminded her of Ralph's when she had complained to him about her ruined skirt. The man in the dry cleaners, as she had feared, asked her, with a lecherous grin, just what kind of a stain it was, even though he came from a closely knit community of hard-working middle-class people. Ralph had always been, she realized long after, only interested in his own selfish pleasure. Just the words, hell mouth, gave her a *frisson* of icy terror. And then Dick, whom she thought truly cared for her, began pursuing some vapid girl named Karen. She saw, with great clarity, that *he* hadn't cared that it was her best skirt either. She often dreamed lately that the mouth of Hell had opened.

She had to admit, even now, that Karen—Aileron was her surname —although not exactly pretty, had a remarkable figure. Perhaps what's-his-name's contention that Annette Lorpailleur had them all somehow in her power wasn't so farfetched after all. What galled her was that Dick had at one time, in play, liked to call her Karen! Annette somehow knew all the scandalous stories about everyone, including, to her dismay, certain incidents that had occurred in New Mexico. When she saw Harlan, still wearing the same electric-blue suit, still dragging his clubfoot along the floor, her blood almost froze. She hated Annette for being so involved with him, yet she was sickeningly attracted to her as well. When she saw her introduce Harlan and Guy to each other she thought she'd panic. And then, ten years later, there in Norm's closet were her six missing dresses and her pale blue silk tailored blouse! On the way home she refused to talk to Guy about Harlan Pungoe or about anything to do with Harlan Pungoe. It was at about this time, or so she remembered it, that Guy had first suggested that she meet an old friend of his, Norm, but she begged off. She recalled this some years later when Sheila sent her her first book of poetry, *Fretwork*, snidely inscribed "to Bunny, the belle of Boonetown." No one could ever convince her that her missing clothing didn't have something to do with Harlan's reappearance and Sheila's book. It came as a shock to her to discover that Norm had been Sheila's first lover, although in those days he had preferred to be known as Fred. On top of all these surprises, her father had begun painting miniature imitations of *Hell Mouth* on small lengths of two-by-fours. And then, of course, there was the false news that Sheila had been accidentally run over by Lou. Guy, ever more distant as his relationship with Harlan waxed, told her that he'd known her father was a fucking loony ever since the day on the patio when the other loony kept driving back and forth in his car. She didn't mention that Ralph had bought himself a used Porsche and promptly driven it into a tree. Nor did she mention that she'd secretly wanted her parents, especially her father, to hate Guy. Ralph, for some few years after being discharged from the hospital, took to coming into the city once a week to annoy her in any way he could. Guy, drinking more heavily than ever, bitterly and endlessly complained that there was never enough ice in his whiskey. Then began Ralph's letters, telling her, with relish, how *he* had been responsible for the letter that had caused her mother's stroke and her father's sojourn in the chicken coop. She blew up one hot Sunday morning and threw a mayonnaise jar full of Three Feathers into Guy's smeary, weirdly unfamiliar face. Jung, or so she thought, had written something about doubles. Contrite, she made Guy another drink, filled to the top with ice, while he sat on the fire escape weeping. All of this must have had something to do with heredity. To make matters worse, Tony Lamont called her an ignorant cunt when she ventured the opinion that his *Synthetic Ink* was Faulknerian. Psychology had a good deal to say about the causes of such vicious misogyny, something to do with mothers, to the best of her recollection. She started *Absalom! Absalom!* again. Guy had taken to ranting about Andy Warhol being the only painter of the last hundred years who mattered. She switched to *The Sound and the Fury* because of something that Lucy Taylor had said, but she couldn't remember what it was. According to Guy, Picasso was a charlatan, there was a confessional letter or something he'd read to prove it. She wanted nothing more than to go back to Long Island, as it had been, forever. Guy screamed at her that Matisse was a fucking interior decorator, then vomited on himself. On the North Shore, despite Ralph, her father's sheet-metal manuals, her mother's unmatched tableware, and their ugly Volvo, life had been easier. She had a recurrent bittersweet memory of the snow that fell on them on the beach at Provincetown. She often dreamed lately that the mouth of Hell had opened for her.

Wooden canepie

Not the usual sort of place that Lolita would sit, or for that matter, where anybody would sit, yet there she sat, perhaps in fantasy or dream, yet nonetheless she sat, shielded by its shade from the heat and glare, looking placidly on. As a rule, she'd never bothered with such attentions to herself, but she'd long since confounded the predictions that were invariably made, and many were of the opinion that they knew by whom. This was not to say, however, that the putative content of the predictions was known or even guessed at. That, in a sense however tenuous, would be too much to ask, even in the light of subsequent events.

Despite her background, her recent background, that is, Lolita didn't seem to mind, or even notice, the pedestrian, not to say gauche nature of the edifice, for such it had been termed by no less expert a personage than its architect. There had been the initial and usual grumblings about his capabilities, yet she had chosen him after all, and the product of his labors and her faith in them was now apparent for all to see. She sat then, bemused, lost in a private world of, perhaps, ambitions not yet realized. Yet there was the possibility that she was, simply and unaffectedly, rehearsing what might be termed the high points of her life. The latter were not too numerous, to be sure, so what better place for her to sit in order to call them up from a memory that had, recently, and even earlier, failed her on more occasions than she wished to be cognizant of? For example, it is rather well-established that forgotten were the dinner dance at Charmaine's, the lakeside picnic with the Carruthers brothers, the humiliating incident in the voting booth—and there were others. So her decision to locate herself beneath this rude structure, plain to the point of the primitive, may have been her attempt to shed the unnecessary, and thus reinvigorate her badly failing powers of recall.

What then if she *were* to recall the salient episodes of the life which she had so helplessly seized, which she had lived? It wasn't like Lolita to sit and simply reflect. She had always loathed nostalgia, although always may be putting it a trifle strongly. But if the congeries of past events, if congeries it was, could be separated from its usual partnership with sentiment, it cannot have been too much to cheer Lolita on in her wholehearted attempt. Many were the voices that did cheer her on, although others were predictably silent.

Well then. She sat, the cunningly ugly rude wooden structure doing the job that the architect had envisioned it being called upon to do: by Lolita, of course. No one else called upon it to do anything. Indeed, they were content to allow it just to *be.* The curious came and stared, moved on, silent or speaking in whispers, as if afraid that they would become part of Lolita's musings.

The problem for her arose almost immediately, and since it had never before been, for her, a problem, or if it had, it had been one which she had so far avoided, it struck her with overwhelming force. It was, simply, that she was unable to make any connections between or among the varied dead events that urged themselves upon her. When she entertained one event at a time, all was well. Yet when a new event rose to her mind it drove the earlier one out. Thus, when she had satisfied herself with an investigation of *this* element, she instantly had to turn her thoughts to *that* one, helplessly aware that *this* one was slipping into the oblivion whence it came, luminous. This was, and Lolita knew it, no way to survey the elements that had made up her life to its present moment. Was there any help for it? She may well have asked.

Her face, throughout what has come to be called the ordeal, never changed, but remained fixed in a beatific expression that occasionally bordered on the uncannily beautiful. It may be that Lolita triumphed, from time to time, over the violently solipsistic turmoil of her thoughts, yet who knows? On the other hand, there is some evidence that her placid visage may have expressed a surrender to utter bewilderment, that it may have been the face of a woman partially if not wholly unaware of her identity.

Her inability, at least so far, in this, her retreat, to reconstruct the entire schema of her life from the incidents which she could recall in something approaching their original clarity of outline did not, of course, preclude for her the belief that the schema did, in fact, exist. Not to put too fine a point on it, but Lolita was aware that the recalled incidents, though few, and wholly unconnected to each other in any way that she could understand, were not the whole of her past life, but that they were, surely, a proof, so-called, of its reality, if the latter is not too ingenuous a word. Her reason for sitting so quietly in what many thought a ridiculous structure, far from those she knew, and doing nothing at all, was, quite obviously, to deny, as best she could, the possibility of any *more* incidents occurring, incidents which, by the mere fact of their occurrence, would hopelessly complicate her search for the schema. In other words, she had chosen a kind of death. Some who understood this were terrified, for they realized that their own peripatetics were analogous to her stasis, but that the movements that they indulged in disguised themselves as being somehow more real than her stillness. Lolita, in short, ruthlessly demonstrated to these unfortunately perceptive few that all events are representative of death; i.e., that to look into the past is to insure the death of the present, even though that gaze is part and parcel of what might be called a story concerning long-disappeared phenomena or adventures. So much is clear.

It is somewhat embarrassing to dredge up those instances of data from the totality that was Lolita's past schema, assuming that Lolita was correct in her assumption that there was indeed a schema, since they seem so remarkably innocuous, even banal, and are made more so by the disconcerting fact that she remembered incidents only hazily, or in fragments. For instance, what was she to understand of the vast structure of her past by remembering the words *lathe operator?* Those words were revelatory, surely, of an important incident, or incidents, they were proof, so to speak, that the vast structure existed. Yet what sort of structure could be envisioned by a lost reality that asserted itself in such crabbed and opaque terms? Lolita did not know. She did know that a structure implied by these incomprehensible terms must have been made up of an infinite number of such shards, and that therefore she had existed, she had a past, her life was a highly intricate composition. *Lathe operator* was, arguably, a complement or surrogate for an infinitely variegated number of experiences which her mind would not permit her to recall. But it pleased her that *lathe operator* complemented or substituted for, or for that matter, implied, let us say, *large blue suit* or *banana split*. It was, she thought, quite possible that *large blue suit* and *banana split* were as much a part of her life's schema as was *lathe operator*, which term intruded itself so regularly and unchangingly into her thoughts. It was, perhaps, good to be ignorant of the whole structure, for then one could force it to emit whatever one wished. To see the whole and thus to prove it so is to be truly dead, whereas, as noted, Lolita was alive, though dead within her life, and contentedly so.

As she sat, turning over and over again the immutable and curious manifestations of her life, she came to realize that although none of them had any connection with any other, they did form a pattern by the fact of their *being;* yet the pattern implied only itself, and did not, in any way, bring her any nearer to a comprehension of the larger and more ordered and rational pattern from which the singular manifestations had emerged unbidden.

Lathe operator was the first of the series, in that she had had that phrase thrust upon her first. The other elements in the series, a series that repeated itself in varying combinations, were as satisfyingly impenetrable as the first. Without, then, further attempts at analysis, however unsatisfactory, of Lolita's methods, if they can be termed that, these are the elements of her past that Lolita recalled, again and again, and always with the belief that since they *were,* there must have been others, and that taken all in all they suggested, convincingly, the panorama, endlessly changing, of her past.

As *lathe operator** complemented or served as surrogate for or implied, as far as she was concerned, *large blue suit* or *banana split,* so did the importunate and repetitive element *Barnett's crucifix* complement or serve as surrogate for or imply *white shifts* or *grainy photographs; bathroom confessions, bridge deck* or *pale blue file*

---

*Lolita was astonished to realize that the diverse elements suggested by the elements from her past, which latter elements, as noted, continually recurred to her, could well have been any others; and that any or all of them in any or all combinations and permutations—ceaseless and neverending—could possess the identical relevance for and relation to the great structure of her past as did the fifty-two elements initially suggested by the twenty-six clearly recalled elements. At this point, she became convinced that her life, up to this time, had quite possibly been inextricably involved with quite possibly everything. She was, at this juncture, probably insane.

folder; orange ball, Gordon's gin or *manila envelopes; steel mistreatment, complex resolutions* or *Sazeracs; she flushing, little cabals* or *cracked window shades; stolen manuscript, broken ribs* or *pile of clothes; black basement, still twilights* or *red swans; Ce Soir, Spanish primer* or *Easter bonnet; slapped face, Klactoveedsedstene* or *lady's shoes; Flint, lens and shutter* or *Mus musculus; red silk, metallic fly* or *La Révocation de l'Édit de Nantes; toothpick bridge, egg cream* or *deadbeats; movie models, Ingelow's snood* or *floor plans; Conchita's sisters, black nylons* or *blue ink; hospital plunge, St. Vincent's* or *Zippo; drunken tears, quadratic equations* or *ham on rye; April showers, gross constituent unit* or *country inn; arrogant immigrant, personnage marchant vers l'horizon* or *melting snowman; mistress of metal, three-subject notebook* or *reams and reams; breaking glass, syntagma* or *amethyst crystal; false answers, mean streets* or *tape recorder; parfum intime, exotic booze* or *plot doctor; Blanche's leer, stupid writer* or *cheap blend; unknown persons, bricoleurs* or *Schiller; wooden canopy, hot sun* or *long days.*

The final element, *wooden canopy,* asserted itself some time after the other elements which served somewhat to define Lolita's hitherto unrevealed entirety. At first, she chose to ignore it, as, indeed, she chose to ignore its congeners, *hot sun* or *long days,* for none of these seemed to have anything to do with her past. *Wooden canopy* was, of course, the element which had projected itself from the center of her present circumstances. She had chosen stasis, and its conditions, in order to preclude new experiences and thus better to isolate the past. Yet she realized, surely, that the situation which she had selected had itself, and inexorably, insisted upon its validity as an element every bit as important, or at least, as *actual,* as all the others, those recalled as well as those obliterated. Her inertia, in other words, had generated and would no doubt continue to generate elements, and their suggested elements, contributive to the overall schema of her life. There was, then, she doubtlessly admitted to herself, no *escape from life, Pungoe's adobe* or *kitchen drawer.*

Sittie of Rome

Now, because of a carefully designed plan, by means of which he is reasonably certain that you may discover various truths, or at the very least, certain insistent discrepancies among the data, however scattered, that one has been given to think of as factual, he has brought together, on a warm Sunday in Rome, a group of middle-aged women:

Sheila Henry, Joanne Lewis, Anne Kaufman, Ellen Kaufman, Antonia Harley, Conchita Kahane, Lolita Kahane, April Detective, Annette Lorpailleur, Ann Taylor Redding.

Rome?

Here, in brief, is the plan.

Seated beneath the well-known and famous pines of the old city at a large round table covered with dazzling white napery, the women will take refreshments. Brilliant white umbrella. They are pleased, it seems, to have come. Hot Roman sun, the sound of conversation and laughter, as is usual.

He is aware that their least important remarks may well be, and in all probability are, crucial to an understanding, however tenuous, of all that has been said about what you have been given to think of as their lives. One is reasonably certain of this. The sound of their conversation and laughter drifts erratically toward him.

Rome!

Women he has been given to think of as actual.

A plan: The many contradictions that you have scrupulously taken notice of may finally be resolved.

By the employment of a certain specific yet untried method one may define or at least locate those elements which may be defined or located.

By means, for instance, of a transference.

An evasion. A trick.

This, in any event, is the gist of a scheme that he will proffer you.
One is not wholly satisfied.
The women seem to be leaving. They are leaving.
Now, what.

Misterioso

For with men and women, with men's men and women's men, with men's women and women's women, with men's and women's men, with men's and women's women, all is possible, as far as can be ascertained, in this connexion.

—*Samuel Beckett*

Perhaps a question will open the way to resolution, for instance: Why does this old A & P supermarket, with its wooden floors, narrow aisles, and overabundance, or so some think, of house-brand canned goods and bakery products, display, as if carelessly forgotten atop a binful of Granny Smith apples, a seemingly well-read paperback copy of *Absalom! Absalom!*?

"That was made into a movie, I think," a well-dressed woman, in her hand a box of jelly doughnuts, says. She is smiling, but close observation reveals that the smile is an involuntary rictus. Everybody has problems. "On the 'Academic Playhouse of the Air'?" Silence attends upon her question, the kind that invaded the streets of John Keats's little town. "Or did it win an Academy Award, or something?" Back comes the silence, or perhaps the silence returns.

Nobody in the market either wants or is able to answer her question. Perhaps no one believes she cares about the famed novel in one way or another. Evidence: a copy of the latest paperback best-seller, *Accidental Bodies,* is in her shopping cart. "Put this one in your beach bag, packs a shattering wallop of steamy sex!"

The Ace of Diamonds is protruding from between pages 150 and 151 of *Absalom! Absalom!* ". . . cling to above the maelstrom of unbearable reality—The four years . . . are gone, leaving us immobile, impotent, helpless; fixed, until we . . ." Of course you remember it.

She hopes that it's better than *Acquisitions,* a book that she has started three times but just can't get into. Too thick, anyway. Who can *read* it?

There are many people who don't even pretend to read it, and for such as these, a wire rack near the express checkout register contains magazines which promise stories of action. There is *Action,* "Holocaust of Death at the Indy 500," *Action at Sea,* "Death beneath the

Arctic Ice," *Action Monthly,* "Rape and Death Stalked State Trooper Kimberley Butz," and *Actionworld,* "Death Is Their Mistress—The Green Berets." "To tell you the truth, my husband reads these sometimes," she says. "I think he likes the ads in the back for dirty books, machine guns, and big knockers on the girls." The young woman giving out samples of cherry-cheese dip nods and smiles into what she takes to be a smile.

"Isn't it the truth," she says. Her smile slowly fades, a well-worn but useful fade, as close observation reveals to her that her interlocutor's smile is an involuntary rictus, which shows no sign of fading, slowly or otherwise.

"She'll get herself in a jam if she smiles at some horny guy like that," the sample woman says in the direction of *Absalom! Absalom!* and the Granny Smith apples. Neither apples nor book replies. For the most part, things are silent.

Some few miles away, in a suburb of the city in which the A & P is located, a middle-aged woman sits in a weathered Adirondack chair placed on a lawn in the shade of a large plane tree. We don't know the name of the suburb.

"Agapa," the woman says, looking up from a novel whose title cannot be discerned. Is it too much to hope that it is, perhaps . . .?

"It's *Sanctuary,*" she says. "The old version. I like it better."

This woman, whose name is as yet unknown, is a . . . wait a minute. The name of the suburb is Agapa, and it is not unlike any of the other suburbs contiguous to the northern boundary of the city. An attractive vegetarian couple, for instance, lives right here, on Rensaeller Street.

That's Rensellaer Street.

The woman wears a golden charm on a slender chain about her neck. She may be unaware that the charm is the seal of Agares, Master of Tongues and Crocodiles, a bad hat. Tied snugly around her attractively mature body is an apron with the word *Agfa* across it.

Agfa, so a representative of the company, or firm, kindly writes, makes supplies of every kind for the photographic industry. It is apparent that all camera enthusiasts know this, judging from the volume of outraged mail received.

"Ah Lady," a priest is saying, "cries tears of blood when people like to peruse over dese magazines' ads for sexual aids, pornographical degrading materials such as large female bosoms, an' guns of all descriptions. Duh stories are not so big wit' her either." No one in the market pays any attention to him, since he is in mufti, and his accent is obviously "put on."

Karen Aileron looks distractedly out the window, a tofuburger sizzling in the skillet on the stove. She's put on some weight, but her legs are still good, her bosom, thanks to *Actionworld,* still firm, and her white teeth, well! They flash now as she smiles to herself, thinking of the movie she saw a couple of nights ago—*Aini, the Destroyer!*—and the wonderful love scene in the cabin of a 747. She sighs and wipes her hands on her Agfa apron as she turns to check her tofuburger. Satisfied, she smiles in a friendly way, and says, "Hi! I'm Karen Aileron! I used to attend to aerial wishes, stratospherically svelte amid soft drinks and tiny liquor bottles. But here in my comfortable flat, I dote on simple meals, good thoughts, and fantasy guys. Hi!"

"I hate it when two people wear the same clothes," the rictal woman says to the checkout clerk. "I mean it's not impossible for two people to be wearing the same clothes, I guess. It's just that I hate it, I don't know, I can't explain it." The checkout clerk, not being of a literary turn of mind, glances, with a quick raise of his eyebrows, at the boy who is bagging groceries. The latter looks blank.

The woman in the Adirondack chair is of the opinion that she might as well be living in Akron, for, in the early afternoon, an Albanian woman of indeterminate age passes by, as she has for the past month. Her looks and clothes are more or less nondescript. More or less.

However, knotted tightly about her neck as a kind of ascot, she wears, or sports, what the woman in the Adirondack chair is certain is a pair of filthy ice-blue bikini panties.

Why, though, *Akron?*

Allen, a waiter with bunions, callouses, corns, and ingrown toenails, whose public discourse is usually limited to variations on "Hi, I'm Allen, your waiter, and I'll be gleefully serving you this evening," suddenly says, "Hi, I'm Allen, and I prefer the Alps." He winces as he bangs his foot against the base of the service bar. "Fuck Akron."

Some do prefer the Alps, some, perhaps surprisingly, Akron, while others look to more exotic purlieus—the Gobi Desert, the Serengeti, the Amazon Basin. The latter, for instance, is a sediment-filled structural depression between crystalline highlands. Geologically speaking, it is known as a fylfot.

"I'm nobody's dummy," Allen simpers a moment prior to toadying.

The woman in the Adirondack chair, as we are about to discover, is a sculptor, who at one time enjoyed a small renown. Of *Amber Glass,* one of her last works, a small wooden figure of Olive Oyl, she notes, "I want to deconstruct the notion of female comic-strip characters as figures of contempt." What the hell. She is reading *Sanctuary* in order to take her mind off a suit, filed by the owners of the Ambers, a semi-pro baseball team, who contend that she is using their copyrighted name without permission or authorization, thus subjecting their organization to ridicule and scorn. Considering the level of the Ambers' play, this is quite a feat.

"Is nice things about America, also and Americans," the Albanian woman says, in a rich yet amusing accent. "I learn these thing in studied of American Revolution in citizen class." She goes on and on, to such an extent that Amon, Who Vomits Fire, is tempted to singe the bikinis right off her neck, but desists, for private, probably depraved, reasons.

"Why the hell is this copy of *Anal Fancies* carelessly tucked in among the action magazines?" Andy says. He is an unprepossessing young man who hangs around the soup.

"I wouldn't let a dog read that trash," the rictal woman says, or fumes. She neglects to add that which we suspect, that she owns a well-thumbed copy of *Annals of Sapphism: Womanlove,* unfortunately now out of print. Forty-two full-color photographs depict two young women, possibly college-educated, exploring the forbidden pleasures of female eroticism.

Probably out of print because the text deconstructs the very notion of the phallus. Well, not precisely a *text.*

Has it been mentioned that the woman in the Adirondack chair, "the sculptor," owns a puppet, dressed as a French maid, called "Annette," and another, clad only in leopard-skin briefs, called "Mr. Anthony"? They are the gifts of an old, somewhat perverted acquaintance,

"Queenie" Antilles, sometimes known to close friends as "Cunty" Uncles. *She* has a few stories to tell! Such amazingly lifelike puppets are painstakingly crafted by hand in old Antoine by canny craftsmen to whom craftsmanship is more important than speed or handsome profits. Observe their bent, grizzled heads encircled by wreaths of pipe smoke.

"I think they're made by some*body* named Antoine," the sculptor says, suddenly laughing gaily as she remembers a couple of things.

Then perhaps they're made in the rustic hamlet of Apple Pie?

"Perhaps," the sculptor says. "But I think they're made in Après-le-Bain by the renowned puppetmaker—I should have earlier mentioned it—Antoine! Or *have* I mentioned it?" She returns to *Sanctuary*, singing contentedly to herself in an untrained yet pleasant alto.

"How funny she sing 'Is It Lonely for You This Evening?' " the Albanian woman says. She stops to stare rudely.

"Get the hell out of here!" the sculptor implores her. "And besides, you foreign bitch, it's 'Are You Lonesome Tonight?' "

"I not is," the Albanian woman modestly rejoins, to general hilarity.

As the rictal woman leaves the A & P for the oppressive heat of the streets, she is knocked sprawling by Grace Armstrong, a ridiculous figure in "sweat" clothing, or "sweaties," who is just finishing her daily jogging stint. She bears little resemblance to the sluttish young woman of the good old days. She says, to anyone who will listen, that this exercise keeps her sane, an exaggeration of the first order.

"Running, actually," Grace says. "It keeps me sane. I really prefer to call it a 'regimen.' "

Jack Armstrong, a man who suffers, as can well be imagined, from the monicker he bears not proudly but with the calm resignation and sad visage that has done many things, finishes writing the final paragraph of a story. He is, finally, pleased. Critical comments: remarkably perceptive, packs a satisfying wallop, steamy and exotic sex. Jack is rummaging among some books on his desk, or riffling through the pages of same, for the perfect epigraph for his story, one that will display not only his erudition but his sensitivity to walloping prose. A sensitive depiction of the lower stratum, learned, but not annoyingly so, Mr. Armstrong has chosen the perfect epigraph, packs a probing wallop. He settles on one from the work of a writer he disgustingly, at least some think, calls "Arthur." Just "Arthur."

". . . je vous détache ces quelques hideux feuillets de mon carnet de damné." Jack seems a complete schmuck. But wait. "Arthur" enters Jack's study, actually his bedroom, his hair tousled and greasy, his knobby wrists protruding from the sleeves of his too-short *la jaquette* or *la veste,* his slate-blue trousers wrinkled and rumpled. Around his neck is a filthy *la corde.* His eyes are the clearest, most piercing blue that Jack has ever seen. In a soft voice, heavy with contempt, he says, "J'ai seul la clef de cette parade sauvage." Jack turns upon him that which is crudely known as a shit-eating grin. We've all seen it.

By the way, that's Rensselaer Street.

Grace Armstrong is a student, as many of you will have guessed, at the Art Students' League, where she is working on a small semi-geo-graphical canvas called *Asbury Park.* "And a real disaster it is," her instructor adds. She is now on her second year of work on this picture, and is known to the other students as "Mrs. Asbury Park." The anger and humiliation that this sobriquet causes Grace may be the reason behind her daily stint of jogging. Or it may be because of something that happened *in her youth!*

"Actually, it's a regimen of running," Grace says, scraping off another layer of paint. It's bad work, all right.

A flyer offering the services of Mrs. Louise Ashby, Healer, Reader, Advisor, Seeress, Prophet, details, in a testimonial from one G.A., the beneficent and salutary powers of Art. It reads, in part . . .

But now it must be reported that the priest has come across the copy of *Anal Fancies* slipped between two copies of *Actionworld.* He is astonished, disgusted, repelled, and aroused by the cover photograph of a young man and woman in anal coition. "My God," he says, "dey look like dey like it."

. . . "people were talking about me and I was drinking too much alcoholic beverages and gambling away all my earning, and, finally I lost my suitcase. My husband left me for a bimbo and I had nowhere to turn until I heard of MRS. ASHBY, one visit to her and today I am a student at a famous Art School and working happily on a genuine oil painting . . ."

This is a familiar if crass testimonial.

It is not generally known that the demon Asmoday, Familiar of the Cur from Hell, spends a month each winter at the world-famous ski resort of Aspen, Colorado, where, on almost any given day during the "season," one may see famed film stars, famed writers, and rich, powerful people who are famed in many diverse walks of life. As they enjoy themselves much like regular persons, they as firmly insist on their treasured privacy.

"I am, as you may well imagine, disguised during my sojourn in the brooding mountains as my good buddy, Astaroth, Angel of Unearthly Beauty, a luscious broad with a knockout figure and a lot of bad threads."

"I much admiring American jargo," the Albanian woman says. For her, as for so many who grease the wheels, prime the pumps, stoke the fires, and unfailingly "take it on the chins," Aspen, Colorado, is but a fantastic dream, a lambent Xanadu. The sculptor is safely in her house, fearful that the unwanted figure lurking in the road beyond the bed of phlox may never go away. She may be right. Time will tell.

Léonie Aubois pours the last ounce of vodka from her 1.75 liter bottle into a glass with an oranges-and-lemons motif etched into its outer surface. Some call such vessels "Depression glasses," make what you will of that. A pot of Campbell's Vegetarian Vegetable Soup simmers on a burner of her hot plate. She rises from her torn, stained armchair, totters, staggers, and falls to the floor. "God damn them all," she says. On the wall, a tear-off calendar reveals that this day is August 29, 1982. There are two pieces of reading matter—outside of the calendar —in the room: "Autumnal Aspen Leaves," a poem on yellowing newsprint, Scotch-taped to the wall above the dirty, rust-stained sink, which poem begins:

> O Empress in your trembling golden gown,
> Chilled in the Autumn winds that swirl and gust—

and an offprint of an article from an unknown journal of ideas and opinions, "The Avant-Garde: Finally Dead?" by Nora Avenel, reportedly a horny cultural journalist. These are depressing items.

"And God damn that bitch too," Léonie says, and begins the drunken weeping that is by now second nature to her. She could use a bath.

The jelly doughnuts are a homely touch designed to reinforce the market's probability, its, how shall we say? credibility. To strengthen further the much-desired pilosity of just about everything, we may modify the generic term with a brand name, casually and naturally affixed, to wit: ". . . in her hand a box of Jane Parker jelly doughnuts . . ."

"I like much this jaybarger jelly donuts," the Albanian woman says. Note her modern, time-saving spelling of the substantive.

Yet among those who distrust the veracity, even the usefulness of the anecdotes thus far presented as facts, are the priest, who doesn't understand why *he* is chosen to have an unseemly erection caused by his shocked glance at the photograph so glibly mentioned, the sculptor, who trusts nothing beyond the confines of her suburban property, and a certain "B," of whom we know nothing, and who has intruded rather brusquely. "B" may be either a man or a woman. It's impossible for us to get a good look, attendant as we are upon the Albanian woman's culinary opinions. No sparrow falls, as they say. The Albanian woman, by the way, seems pleased, convinced that everything so far offered is exemplary of life in America. She may well be right.

The A & P, incidentally, is in direct competition with two other neighborhood markets, Rudy's Superette and Crown SuperMart. Because of this unseemly situation, the A & P management is increasingly chagrined to discover that it is more and more difficult to fob off tainted meat and rotten produce—most especially, bananas—on its customers. By means of unspeakable midnight obeisance to Baal the Cat, King of the Invisible, the management is about to close a deal to sell out to Baby Brownie, owner of a chain of cinema centers, which Mr. Brownie calls "CineCenters," subtlety being his trump card in the exhilarating and aggressive world of the entertainment business. True to his code, however, a code that no expert has been, as yet, able to crack, Mr. Brownie, or "Babe," as his wife calls him in those all-too-few moments of marital passion that they occasionally share during their rare and jealously coveted country weekends, likes to listen to Bach, especially, one, or two, might say predictably, *The Art of Fugue.* While enjoying this acclaimed masterpiece, written by the great composer at the age of four, the entertainment czar invariably reads aloud from *Bad Girl,* the spicy novel of some years past, bound specially for the Brownie library in pale-blue vellum, a favorite skin, or whatever it is. Three of his children, Wotan, Natty, and Elmo, are, sadly, permanent residents of the Bahamas, where they are, unfortunately, rather unsuccessfully attempting to cling to a questionable sanity. A fourth, adopted child, Balte, probably lost to business forever, hangs around the mayonnaise in Village Victuals on Baltic Street. Literati know that this slobbering albeit repulsive idiot served as the model for Max Champagne in the justly neglected novel *Baltimore Chop.* Bam, his friend, a towering wreck of a man, in plaids, who steadfastly refuses to comply with the Mann Act—he is a graduate of a famous Ivy League school—never lets Balte Brownie forget this youthful indiscretion. From the next aisle, where he hangs around the Hispanic food products, he laughs immoderately, making what he fondly believes to be the sound of popping champagne corks.

Then, to lighten things considerably, there is the joy of Banana Amaze, which the rictal woman makes for her busy family at least once a week. It keeps her, so she claims with a smile, "in touch." This is a dessert, not to be confused with Banana Split—a pedestrian confection which requires little preparation—that is perfect for those evenings when a festive atmosphere is desirable, and is also an excellent conclusion, or *rondo,* to hearty winter fare. The recipe follows:

Banana Amaze

1 3-pound chicken, cut into serving pieces	1 envelope of ruy Lopez
Salt and freshly ground pepper to taste	2 cups of Kobayashi
3 tablespoons chicken fat or valerian	1 cup each Kronecker and Schur products
2 large mastiachi peppers	4 milk-chocolate bars, plain or tinctured

4 ripe bananas, peeled and cut into 2-inch pieces

1. Sprinkle the chicken pieces with salt and pepper to taste. Tenderize by beating with hammer, being careful not to cut the skin. (Traditionally, the chicken is wrapped in vellum and buried in loose materials overnight.) Heat the chicken fat or valerian in a heavy skillet and add all the chicken pieces, skin side down. Cook until golden brown and turn the pieces. Add the mastiachi peppers and the bananas.
2. Cook for approximately 3 hours over low heat. Add the ruy Lopez and cook another 15-20 minutes.
3. Remove everything from the skillet to a hot serving platter and add the Kobayashi, martingales, and Kronecker and Schur products to the skillet. Cook over high heat, stirring to dislodge the blackened, charred particles that adhere to the pan. When the Kronecker and Schur products turn a dark brown and curl at the edges, return the chicken, peppers, bananas, and ruy Lopez to the skillet.
4. Add the milk-chocolate bars, cover the skillet, and cook for 10 more minutes. When the chocolate has melted, serve immediately, with a large, unpeeled banana for garnish.

Yield: Four servings.

We don't understand why this recipe, which may be found in *Get It on in the Kitchen!,* is attributed to a "Mrs. Banjiejicz," and described as a "Polish holiday favorite." Our doubts are reinforced by a recent letter from one of our many admirers, Mr. Barbatos, who understands the behavior of nervous birds, collects "modernana," and is an authority on peppers and their use in national cuisine. Mr. Barbatos writes:

Sirs:
I am reading some sort of thing as you *well know* and can't help but "laugh" along with you at the notion that Mrs. Banjiejicz talks about "Banana amaze" as a Polack people "favorite" since anybody who knows anything about peppers knows that mastiachi peppers are decisively unknown to the swell Polack people. Mastiachis, known to the people of Michoacán as *chilis de penes,* are completely unknown to the great Polack people. I don't think that Mrs. Banjiejicz knows anything about peppers.
                                      Sincerely, etc., etc.

Letters like these usually occasion numerous replies, and Mr. Barbatos's is no exception. Here is a reply from Betty Barker:

Dear Sirs:

The unsigned letter that criticizes Mrs. Banjowic's recipe for Banana Amaze is an example, a telling type, of the type of mentality that we let run loose in this once-great city, where I got robbed the other night outside of Village Victuals of a potatoe which I paid for by a huge thug in a plaid suit. When I was a student at Barnard forty years ago, I remember, *very well,* a lot of girls. Since then, I've tried my hand at writing and am the author and publisher, at my own expense, among other well-received books, of a historical romance novel in free verse, *Baron Darke of Eagle House,* of which Valerie Menses was occasionally heard to comment, "it packs a romantic wallop!" and also *A Batch of Stuff,* a collection of adult musings on Life which also did not sell very well because of ineptness in distribution methods by mockies. So you see that I am not exactly anybody's fool.

But enough about my accomplishments, for I just want to state that your ignorant correspondent knows very little about the Polish, when he says "mastiachi peppers" are something that the Polish don't know anything about. After all, His Eminence himself is a Polish person. At Barnard, I knew a lot of girls and often, we'd eat Banana Amaze at somebody's house, often *Polish,* after "cramming." Once I remember we traveled all the way to Greenpoint to somebody's house on the subway and, if you know where Barnard is and Greenpoint also, you know that this is a long subway ride. Does your correspondent think that I and my girlish college friends all of whom arc now middle-aged and with children of their own, from Barnard, would travel all the way to somebody's house in Greenpoint by subway if we didn't know that there we could get Banana Amaze? I also have it on an authority's word contained in a highly regarded newspaper column that the Polish element in Greenpoint grow mastiachi peppers in their backyard but that they simply call them "Peppers." I think you should be ashamed to print letters from foreigners who don't know American customs.

Yours truly, etc., etc.

Finally, a Mr. Bathin, the proprietor of the Pale Horse Inn, writes:

Dear Sirs:

You might be interested to know that while browsing carelessly through a local bookstore, I became angry to see the exchange of letters on the subject of Banana Amaze. I think that it is all *stupid* because how is a reader like myself to make up their mind about who is right in this culinary argument when we do not even know about these so-called peppers? It is obvious that you know very little of the writer's task which a well-known author says is "to inform the long look with all that is in our power." I would be proud to serve such an author at my Inn, one that *Town 'n' Country Notes* reviewed in a favorable 2-Stars light. As far as you people are concerned, you are lowlife.

Respectfully, etc., etc.

Evident, we hope, is precisely the sort of thing we have to put up with as we try to inform a long look, with all that is in our power, with this and that.

One of the powerful looks so informed is to be found in "Baye Tree," a delightful yet thoughtful romp excerpted from an otherwise essentially self-indulgent fiction, which Charlotte Bayless, an extraordinarily libidinous woman, especially favors. Leave it to Charlotte! At present, Charlotte is right here in town, doing God knows what, although she may be on the verge of rude expulsion from her otherwise fulfilling job. She still likes what she calls "mayonnaise sandwiches," which may explain the faint, secretive smile that plays about her generous mouth as she yawns, stretches, and wonders just what kind of day *this* is going to be. Frank Baylor, "Father" Frank to the seedy acquaintances he pathetically calls his friends, knows nothing of this smile; still, he wages his lonely battle against the gonorrhea that renders his life a living nightmare and a waking horror. Yet the insidious disease also brings home to him some powerful moral truths. Too late! Because of his half-forgotten romance with the church, Frank prefers "Beacon," another excerpt, to "Baye Tree," doubtless because of the vague yet penetrant aroma which clings to the multifarious items therein assiduously detailed. And commented on. At some length.

Yet both Frank and Charlotte have time, wrested at great personal expense of spirit, to indulge their taste for current news and gossip, however malicious. For example, they are currently agog at the unexplained presence of *Anal Fancies* in the A & P—Charlotte, agog because of the priest involved in the burgeoning debacle. This is called the recognition factor, or, more professionally, the Empathy Syndrome. They also follow the sex-for-ducats scandal involving Beauchamp, a white-haired ex-hostler, and are enthralled by the memoirs of Edmé-Pierre Beauchesne, which read as freshly as if they had been penned yesterday. These "jottings" are amazingly attuned to past events chillingly like those contemporary and corrosive occurrences which assert themselves ever more powerfully into the weakened—the *already* weakened—foundations of a true cultural sophistication; indeed, the historical *connaissance* implied by Beauchesne to be "dilatory at best," might well be a mirror image of our own dilatory *connaissance,* one that threatens America itself, perhaps fatally. Time will tell.

Then too: Beaumont and Halpin to Begin New "Geriatrix" Porno Line; "Beautiful Dreamer" Stolen from Stravinsky Melody, Researcher Claims; *The Beautiful Sun* Gets Final Production O.K.; *A Bed of Poses* "All Lies," Attractive Blue-Blood Whore Asserts; Miner X. ("Beat-Off") Beely Makes *Guinness Book of Records;* Olga Begone Goes on Acclaimed Aluminum Diet.

There is no end to the tidbits which Charlotte and Frank snap up. After all, *they live in this world,* and *you're a long time dead.* Or so they believe.

It is Beleth, the Terrible, who casts the ancient spell of malediction which compels "Ben," an otherwise nice young fellow with a penchant for rhumba rock and cerise bikinis by Jockey (women are often beside themselves at the sight of his manly equipment), to hang around the eggplants. From this vantage, he hears the jubilant shouts of unemployable pals echoing through the air. "Ben" has tried mass, to no avail; novenas to St. Jude, *nada;* benediction, incense and all, *rien.* His girl, a pert gamin known as "Muffie" to her Bennington friends, no longer enthralled by his threatening bulge, now shops alone, repressing her sobs as best she can, at Saks, Bergdorf's, Tiffany, and Gucci. Her remark, "Eggplants? Oh come *on!*" is, you might agree, like as a knife in the young man's heart and crotch. "Ben," however, seems able to do nothing about his jeopardized love, although he misses Muffie's lackadaisical sexual enthusiasms. Occasionally, though, Berith, the Red Soldier of the Lie, and one of Beleth's closest confidants, causes him to dream of sweet, silly Muffie energetically fucking a tugboat. Miner X. Beely, at this intelligence, is struck dumb with envy.

Bermuda, at this time of year, is beautiful, with its several tans, shorts, green stuff, oranges bright, and fawning menials. The sculptor thinks of this as she peers out at the Albanian woman, who is now lying on her lawn, *Sanctuary* opened over her face in an inverted V. The sculptor recalls the man, precariously existent on that sunny isle, who dresses as a maid. Cute as a button, good legs, nice face but for a hairy mole. He calls himself Berthe, is learned, but not annoyingly so, and says, to anyone who gets near him, that this ancillary enterprise keeps him sane. Men who are too forward quickly learn of his prowess, for he packs a sure wallop! Gossip amid the flowering shrubs and lethargic jalousies insists that he is a nonproductive painter and sculptor, yet he is often seen in the company of Edward Beshary, crass, grizzled mogul who brooks no nonsense. When E.B. isn't vulgarly and openly compromising Berthe's reputation, he is on the phone to Beverly Hills with endless talk of deals. Suffice it to say that Berthe has no friends.

There is, purportedly, a long monograph in the *Enfer* division of La Bibliothèque Nationale concerning Beshary's perverse exploits while an assistant professor at Bennington, before, as he might say, he wised up. An interesting sidelight on this, courtesy of Mr. Beely, is that the *Enfer* division is remembered as the employer of the famed French poet and wit Guillaume Apollinaire, who labored amid its musty erotics as curator. Apollinaire's true name, Kostrowitski, strikes Beely as Polish, and Betty Barker assures us that in the poet's beloved "Annie," the "rosiers" referred to are mastiachi peppers. If this is so, Miss Barker asserts, the line in which this word occurs should be translated: "Her mastiachi peppers and her vests don't have paste buttons." "Proof enough?" Miss Barker queries. It is something to think about.

It is probably unwise to speak of Apollinaire and "Annie" and "her," i.e., "cette femme," who walks alone in the garden, lest such names arouse the interest of Bifrons, Disturber of the Dead, a dread spectre for whom Bermuda, for instance, is but as the crackling of thorns under a pot. Nor is he interested in such publications as *Big Apple,* now in its twenty-second year of surveying the arts, and as shiny, provocatively controversial, and just plain dumb as ever. Along with regularly featured essays, such as the controversially provocative "Minimalist Fiction: The Real Thing—Or Just Words?," there are the controversial ads for such products as "Big Yank": Now hit that FANTASTIC spot you've heard so much about on NATIONAL TV for new heights of

ECSTASY! This baby is EIGHT INCHES of amazingly LIFELIKE sculpted latex especially designed to hit that SPOT! Perfect for COUPLES or the SINGLE WOMAN. With stand and convenient harness. Perfect for travel. $59.95. Bifrons doesn't cotton to this sort of copy.

Jay Bindle, no longer "Heeb" or "Hoib" and rarely even "Jay" to anybody, sits in his apartment watching a game show on television. It is not controversial but it is provocative. Craftsmanship is more important than speed or handsome profits. Should he open a can of hash? Should he make himself a peanut butter sandwich? Should he go out for a cheeseburger and risk death or injury? Should some other rough fate be his lot? Suppertime will soon draw nigh and the shades of night will, subsequently, he feels, fall.

"I could use some of that cherry-cheese dip, honey," Charlotte Bayless calls to the sample woman. "Honey? Say, *honey?*" Although her present distance from the A & P is not considerable, she may as well be in Binghamton, famed for blond families, or for that matter in the mansion that now stands deserted on Biscayne Bay, a mansion which figures importantly in this tale of greed, lust, and disaster. It stands empty, save for the rats which contentedly inhabit it. Rats are easy to please: some chow, fresh water, and a place to hang their little hats. Things ain't what they used to be on and about the golden sands, even though a small revival of yesterday's gaiety is to be attempted with tonight's opening of an exact replica, right down to the busboys' filthy aprons, of the Black Basement, a once-notorious café of an earlier and more innocent time, previously detailed. "We want to make the Black Basement the friendly, vital place it used to be years ago," Jimmy Blackhead, the owner, grins. "The dominant theme will be, of course, blackness. I've always had a thing for black, there's something exciting, but not annoyingly so, about it." Mr. Blackhead looks wildly about, his eyes calmly taking in every detail of the feverish last-minute activity of the workers who are methodically putting the finishing touches on the bar and dance floor. "For instance, we'll have, like, book jackets from books that have black like as a dominant theme, blown up to *enormous* size on the walls." He gestures toward breathtaking replicas of the jackets for *Black Hose and Red Heels, Blackjack* (whose unforgettable husband-and-wife team, Mr. and Mrs. "Jack" [John] Black, have created a whole new sense of insouciant style among the charming and rapacious young), and *Black Ladder* (a play, actually). An interested observer wonders how he manages to *find* these old jackets, and Mr. Blackhead fields the question politely. "Well," he laughs, "there are certain bookshops that . . ." His voice trails off as two carpenters plunge to certain serious injury from a scaffold. When asked if Black Ladder Books, the famous "home away from home" for Biscayne Bay literary types, might be a possible supplier, Mr. Blackhead pales and quickly calls attention to the replica of *Blackout,* a collection of short stories once described as "life in our time." "I think the room packs a distinctive literary wallop," Mr. Blackhead concludes, moving off to supervise the harassment training of a waitress in an alarmingly short skirt specifically designed to reduce her worth as a human being and make male customers act something awful.

From the reviews of *Black Hose and Red Heels:* "A sophomoric display of cynical attitudes toward life and its beguiling wonder." "No amount of provocative intelligence can mask the misogyny and just plain contempt for humanity and the animal kingdom here disguised as 'sophisticated' humor." "Life in our time? Don't make me laugh!" "Intelligent satire like that of Swift or Abbagnano is one thing, but this amounts to no more than adolescent nose-thumbing." "A piece of fucking shit!" "Precious, pompous, and nasty, yet I was sexually aroused." "Packs the same sort of fetid wallop as the Marquis de Sade."

"Joker," sometimes "Joan" to the men he plays cards with, is dead at last. Records reveal that his name was Keith Blague. A manuscript of poems is found among his meager belongings. It is entitled *Songs of Forgetting* and signed "William Blake," clearly an attempt to deconstruct the notion of the poem as a personalized object of admiration.

Blammo, a fervent youth whose face would stop an eight-day clock, wrenches himself away from the cereal aisle, and relays Charlotte's request to the cherry-cheese dip woman. "Oh *please!*" she cries. "Does that bitch think I'm her personal maid?" Has it been mentioned that she has knockout legs? Blammo returns to the cold cereal. What is a "maid"? he wonders.

We've held off speaking of Sol Blanc, palsied and balding, who directs Blanche Neige Press with his double, Saul Blanche, original founder of the small but daring house. Both read excellent literature incessantly and bewail the market conditions that compel them to publish books that are, well, crap. They rarely complain of Turpin's Syndrome, the debilitating disease, popularly known as *un oeil qui dit "zut!" a l'autre,* that afflicts them both. "We think it's the toilet seat in Rudy's Superette," Saul says, glancing up from Adams's *English Domestic or Homiletic Tragedy, 1575-1642.* He smiles, but close observation reveals that the smile is an involuntary rictus, one of the symptoms of the dreaded illness.

"Rudy's is a fucking pigpen," adds Blast, the stock boy. "I'm going over to hang out at Village Victuals as soon as I can. Now *there's* a toilet seat. Clean? Hey!" Blast may be referring to the Village Victuals on Bleecker Street, since the Baltic Street store prohibits all but official employees from using its rest room. Rudy (not his real name) knows of the difficulties that indiscriminate toilet-seat use can cause. "Was I or was I not the night manager at Le Bleu de Ciel for fifteen years? It's those two kikes' own fault." He wipes a smidgen of chicken fat, or *schmaltz,* on his brother Blightie's attractive all-cotton form-fitting shirt. Blightie grimaces, but says nothing, for the freedom that a life of letters bestows will soon release him from his brother's tyrannical usage. Even now, he is in the middle of a piece he calls "Blind Bums," an affectionately humorous yet intelligently satirical report on a partially sighted softball team in St. Augustine. He is also the author of *Blinding Clarity,* an unpublished novel. A letter from "Blinky" Blinque (Professor Raoul Blinque of Harvard, the excellent university) states that "*Clarity* is the best unpublished manuscript outside of my own— *The Deconstruction of the Charnel House Motif in the Fiction of Daniel Defoe*—that I am aware of." Blightie, whose real name is Paul, bides his time. Rudy, as usual, is not wholly approving of his brother's literary efforts. "A lotta shit!" he notes.

Karen Blonde, an interested reader, writes: "Hi! I'm Karen Blonde, but call me Blondie, O.K.? I'm often a brunette when I'm up among the flawless azures but down here I feel that there's nothing like subzero temperatures and dried cowshit for the complexion. Hi!" Sir Bloom, forgotten till now, manages to get hold of this missive, and, redolent as it is of Miss Blonde's steamy sex, he relaxes on a really nice-looking chaise longue and begins a gratifying bout of self-abuse. "This is the life," he thinks. And why not? Does he not study the lives and mores of the Bloomsbury circle, from which his name mysteriously derives, in the spare moments snatched from a busy life, perhaps his own? You bet he does.

Blow, an interesting, depressed person with an awareness of life in our time, is not coping very successfully. He thinks that he is in possession of information which proves that his conception occurred behind the bandstand of the Bluebird Inn, a small roadhouse specializing in foxtrot contests. What is the basis for this unsettling *idée fixe*? His reading of a poem in a twenty-three-year-old issue of *Blue Filter*. It is not the celebrated Determinate Meaning of the poem that convinces him, no, but the equally celebrated Indeterminate Meaning that "does the trick." It, however, just *may* be that the Objective Correlative is the cause of his present unhappiness, but we cannot blame *that* on John Crowe Ransom. He has enough to answer for.

"I don't appreciate the *mot*," Ransom says, "and charitably ascribe it to an irresistible desire to be rather a 'wise guy'; yet the arena of the verbal arts is littered with the bodies of wise guys, my own being conspicuously absent. Wise-guyism damages one's professionalism, and one should never speak impromptu in one's professional capacity, as I once said to heartfelt plaudits." In the Blue Ruin, a febrile nightspot dedicated to dancing, drinking, and various forms and shows of gaiety, the patrons are, so it appears, unimpressed with the savant's remarks. He packs up his personal, annotated copies of *God without Thunder, The World's Body* (revised), *The New Criticism, Poems about God, Chills and Fever, Grace after Meat, Two Gentlemen in Bonds,* and *Selected Poems,* and leaves to save a civilization *worth* saving from the barbaric hordes. Many of his poems are about the headstrong virility of youth and the slow, dark wisdom of age.

For a change.

The Blue Ruin, located within easy walking distance of all major hotels and the new convention center, was at one time the celebrated Blue Rune, a workingman's tavern which film stars, when film stars were film stars, were wont to frequent, incognito, of course.

"It was called Blue Runes, corrupted white-eyes," an impassive fake savage, Chief Blue Wind, says. "And if white flag of surrender not on pole (indicates wooden pole) by time stick (indicates stick, actually a tree limb) burn (indicates burning end of stick) to here (indicates spot roughly halfway down stick) . . . all *die!* For the earth is our Big Mother and we wish to be one with her womb and that is why, like, we burn stick and carry on about white flag and abject surrender. Also buffalo! Right! Are you hip that my squaw even now passes through your exhausted suburbs, disguised as a old Armenian broad?"

"This guys is a old and meaning broad!" the Albanian woman says proudly. She's mowing the lawn! Can she be mowing the lawn?

In spite of Blue Wind's threats and the imminent danger they pose, Sir Bloom, to add spice to and otherwise enhance his autoerotic pleasure, dons a costume described in the Kinky Klothes catalogue as the "Blushing Nun." Although it is cruel to say so, and surely unworthy of Swift and Abbagnano, he is rather fetching in this homely garb. Garb, it should be pointed out, of indeterminate meaning. Most of the members of the Board of Directors, on which he sits, want to get rid of him, although it is only fair to add that two of them, the Earl of Bodoni and Mr. Stanley Boils, men of vim, demur. There is, currently, a lot of trouble on this board. In a *Bookwatchers PreViews* roundup of recent books on hardball business practices, Daniel Boone, the tough-minded Wall Street analyst, exposes the infighting that takes place whenever these powerful men gather to determine who will garner "the big bucks," "the heavy bread," "the real money," etc., etc.

You can tell them by their subdued ties, tiny penises, and bony wives.

"Daniel Boone," he grins powerfully, "is not, of course, my real name." He toys with a gold paper clip and complacently proffers his tie. "I was born in Boonton, originally called Boonetown after Cheech Boone, the blue-blood arbitrager so much in the news lately." Boone leans back and complacently sucks on a massive phallic symbol disguised as a "cigar." "So it all just came together for me," he chuckles complacently, his sinewy mind never still.

"Perhaps I should switch to the 'Bo-Peep' look," Sir Bloom says, "since Blondie's letter is now but a sodden lump in my sweating palms, or, actually, palm. Looking at myself in the mirror (indicates mirror) in this lubricious act, it's hard to believe that I pretend to regular-guy status at the annual Born Again Employees' Picnic. Privately, I'm but a hulk that is a shell of what was once a man." He continues to abuse his sacred temple (see *Poems about God*), still slightly irritated at his impulsive decision to lend his "Boss Lady" outfit to a mid-level executive, a whiz kid who not only plays polo and tournament-level squash, but who is presently *designing his own house*. Although soft-spoken, on the Street this dynamo is known as Botis, or "the Viper." Yet he can tell a sudden off-color joke to the mailboys, who adore him, and regularly picks up the check at his club.

"I'm currently brushing up my French by reading *La Bouche métallique,*" he notes, serious now. "A marvelous book, filled with subtle tips that only the humanities can offer the hard-driving executive." He toys with his DuPont lighter. "You're surprised that I read enlightened and serious fiction in a foreign language?"

"I like *Madame Bovary* myself," Sir Bloom pants. "Especially the lyrical, yet icily malicious Charles Boyer translation. *That* is imposing entertainment!"

Bra, the engaging and sprightly young woman who aspires to an acting career as Tabitha Bramble (her real name), is having a quiet argument with her new friend, Lucy Brandon. They stand by the peanut butter machine in Crown SuperMart.

"I got bigger knockers than you possess," Bra says.

"No, I fear that my jugs are much the larger," Lucy replies.

"Go to! *These* are tits, my pal," Bra insists.

"Even the untrained eye can see that my melons take the palm," Lucy suggests.

Rudy would never stand for this sort of disturbance in his Superette. "It's a goddam shame," he says. "Always happens in those stores with the *loose* stuff, you know, the stuff in bins and barrels. Put that sorta shit in your store and you get all kinds. Imagine these two broads demeaning, denigrating, derogating, and insulting their own sex with talk of 'knockers' and 'jugs'!"

But hold, gentle Rudy! Can we fairly indict Tabitha and Lucy for this conversation? Are they not but helpless pawns in this sprawling, lifelike canvas? Or on it? We could start over, as did the painter Braque, who started over more than once. Perhaps a revisionist approach, taking into consideration the sociopolitical climate in which the concept of "breasts" thrives, might be effective.

"I find it interesting," Tabitha remarks to her chum, Lucy Brandon, "that in countries such as Brazil, home of the Amazon Basin, which is, as you know, a fylfot, the words 'knockers' and 'jugs' still have currency."

"That is on account of Brazil is a hotbed of *machismo* and they do not give a fuck about us broads," Lucy frowns. "They are a bunch of *cacahuates.*"

"And yet," Tabitha replies, "recent studies suggest, and so forth, et cetera."

"Of course," Rudy says, "I draw the line at paying chicks the same as guys, they get their periods and these mood things and they could kill you or hit you with a lamp or an iron. I saw it in a magazine."

"I still prefer the Alps," Allen the waiter says. "What care I for knockers?"

Allen's last remark, by a chain of associations too hackneyed to detail, leads to an uncharacteristic digression. Does anyone remember George Brent in a long-lost film, *Carom*? It is based on an unpublished novel in Zola's Rougon-Macquart series, *Le Bricoleur.* Brent plays a poet engaged in the writing of a great epic which he calls "The Bridge." Unfortunately, he has accidentally contracted leprosy in the South Sea Islands. Alice Bridgenorth, a wanton and debauched chanteuse, falls in love with him, despite the muslin mask he wears to hide what we all know is his decaying nose. She loves him for his mind.

In the sculptor's small yet excellently selected and judiciously arranged library, there is a copy of the once-famous but now out-of-print and sadly neglected anthology *Bridges: Poets Express Their Love.* One of the selections, from a longer poem, "Spanning the Azure," by Gilberte Brie, contains a section of some seven lines which are identical to those lines spoken by George Brent in the climactic scene of the film, one in which the poet renounces billiards and cheap sex to devote himself, in the few years remaining to him, to the completion of his opus. The sculptor often finds solace in this poem, particularly in the couplet

> Broadway! It is thee I chose!
> Thou art my only Broadway Rose.

Hard to believe that George Brent played a role like that. George Brent's with the moustache, right? Played in a lot of Bette Davis flicks?

"Not one single Native American was cast in that movie," Blue Wind says. "For that and for certain other slights my squaw, resplendent in decadent lingerie intended as a symbolic reproach to the white-eyes, even now stalks the streets of your bourgeois suburbs so as to scare the shit out of ladies with blue hair."

"I need an Alka-Seltzer or a Bromo-Seltzer in order to listen to a ruffian like that," Betty Barker writes. "Believe me, at Barnard I knew a lot of girls who were perfect ladies and not one of them had blue hair."

Not too far from the locale in which this discussion of the cinematic arts is in progress, in the Bronx to be exact, the once wildly abandoned Dorothea Brooke, tired now of attending to her plants, throws down her trowel and heaves a sigh. She so heaves for it is time to turn, for an hour or so, to the pages indited by her namesake, Rupert Brooke, perhaps the best-known and -loved of the younger Georgians. Her eyes fall on one of her favorite poems:

> Just now the lilac is in bloom,
> All before my little room;
> And in my flower-beds, I think,
> Smile the carnation and the pink;
> And down the borders, well I know,
> The poppy and the pansy blow . . .

Dorothea puts the book down. "I think," she thinks. Her hands fly to her face, all pink. She commences to sob. She sobs. "O seasons, O castles," she cries, for some deep, hidden reason. Suddenly the trowel disgusts her! "Well I know," she knows. Dorothea, raised in Brooklyn and a graduate of Brooklyn College, wishes, as she fills up a watering can, her cheeks wet with tears, that she could have those carefree student days back, those days spent so happily in a little Brooklyn Heights furnished apartment. Her roommate, Brown, kept her on her literary toes. For example, one day Dorothea says, "Look, Brown! Smile the carnation and the pink."

"Dotty, I don't know how you can read that slop by Elizabeth Barrett Browning and those other terrible drudges. 'Let me count my days,' indeed!" Dorothea is hurt, but all ears.

"What about 'Patterns,' Brown?" she suggests.

"Are you kidding me or something?" Brown answers. "Listen to *this,* it's by a young guy who shows enormous promise. 'I was screaming inside, my eyes frantically trying to signal this like a lighthouse whose keeper has run amok.' If that's not worth all the 'Patterns' you can come up with, I'll kiss your ass."

The reader with a long memory will recognize in that snatch of prose the hand of Anatole Broyard, now a book-person-essayist-commentator on themes literary. His work is eagerly awaited by many people, whose eyes, now and again, frantically try to signal this.

"I understand that there are expatriates in, like, Brussels even, who await," the demon Asmoday says, feeding arms and legs to his large cur.

"We await him and his work at Bryn Mawr," a young woman says. "What do you think of my jugs, by the way?"

This is the sort of cheap joke which was avoided by both Swift and Abbagnano. Right?

As right as the poppy and the pansy!

Ted Buckie-Moeller is going through his expense-account vouchers, changing here, padding there, trying to make a few extra bucks. Is he chewing on his pencil? Check. Is he waiting to see *Black Silk Stockings* on the Playboy Channel? Check. Is he thinking of telling the new super that he can keep his goddam bike any goddam place he goddam well pleases? Check. He angrily starts again on the first bill, a lunch check for two at the Bluebird Inn. That's what started the old ulcer up again, that goddam lunch! He should have stuck to photography. Maybe.

Bud opens his fly and heads toward a group of women stocking up on the Village Victuals special on paper towels. Tall and flabby, he rarely parts his hair. He hates his hair, and takes no notice of his personal appearance. He *hates himself!* "I deserve a better break than being an uncontrollable exhibitionist even though I rarely if ever commit serious sex crimes. I'm not like, you know, a sex *fiend.*" He is almost upon the women, his eyes signaling his intentions, were the women to look, like a demented lighthouse.

"Buddhism," Father Frank suggests, "might conceivably be of some assistance to Bud—may I call him Bud?—in his attempts to integrate his sexual drives with those of the community as a caring human being with special needs. Or one could be a priest, but *not* like the one who's looking at that dirty magazine. Roman Catholicism, well-handled and attractively presented, increasingly packs a timely wallop!"

"Well, boys, we are now fair deep in the mountains above shining Budd Lake."

So does a chapter of Elizabeth Barrett Browning's favorite novel, *Buddy and His Boys on Mystery Mountain,* begin.

"Buddy," said Dick Witherspoon, "now that we're a far piece from the heartless, roaring city, what was the name of that feller who threw your father from one of the beetling crags hereabouts 'count your dad owed him several thousand dollars he refused to pay him?"

"Ned Blutwurst," answered Buddy, in considerable dismay. "What's the reason for such an odd query, Dick?"

"Wa-al, nothing really," Dick chuckled through divers flying wood chips. "I thought I remembered the blasted rogue. He drowned in Budd Lake some few years since, they say, I reckon I believe, if I recollect aright."

"So the rumor was bruited," Buddy laughed joyfully. "I immensely like those wood chips flying from your busy penknife."

"Just what would a feller mean by a few years since?" Dick rejoined, a look of sly cunning on his athletic face.

"I do not know, Dick," Buddy replied in incredulous amazement. "But you are tarnation perceptive."

Then, with visible relief, he quickly put the steaming grub on the rough table, and the two chums, their manly good looks heightened by the leaping flames, fell to with a hearty will.

"There is nothing quite like sizzling pork and beans and a light but nourishing salad for a fellow after a day's tramp through the mountains high above Budd Lake," Buddy said, a slow smile infecting his face like the beacon from a lighthouse.

"This is the life," Dick replied mysteriously. "Too bad your old dad is dead as a doornail and can't no longer acquaint you with woodland lore afore he used ter settle down comfy-like with his pipe by the fire."

Buddy, touched by his friend's clumsy attempt at velleity, and not a little worried by the facial pallor caused by his use of noxious tobacco which it was his habit to smoke and chew, said nothing, but stared into the flames in momentary confusion.

"Say!" Dick whooped. "That was some feed! If I could eat ramshackle like that ever once in a while yer wouldn't hear a word of complaint out of *this* young feller! Nosirree!" And with that, Dick pushed his rude chair back from the rough-hewn wooden table.

"The air here on Mystery Mountain is what puts a keen edge on a fellow's appetite," Buddy blushed. "I submit that the worst victuals in the whole wide world would taste mighty good up here."

"Go on!" Dick joshed excitedly, banging his calloused palm on the rough wood of the rudely hewn table. "You take the cake as a cook, Buddy," he continued, "and now, how 'bout a song? That old one, 'Big Bullies 'Mid the Fishes'?"

Buddy glanced about, his clear blue eyes seemingly troubled. "Sounds capital to me, old chum, but I thought that tonight . . ." His voice trailed off, the shadows dancing wildly on the cabin's rough-hewn ceiling the while.

"Yes?" Dick grinned knowingly, tamping down the " 'baccy" in his mellow valise.

"Well, I thought it might be vouchful to read aloud, by the light of the glowing grate and this smoky oil thing, from *Sonnets from the Portuguese*."

Dick, his dark eyes frantically signaling affirmation, nodded eagerly. "I do believe that would be fine. They are passionate though careworn verses, yet one can nowhere detect in them the loveless smirk of the depraved pornographer."

"Mrs. Browning's body, if I may use such a word, was her sacred temple," Buddy solemnly agreed. He began then to read, in a quiet but manly voice, the beautiful words weaving a spell of enchantment throughout the mysterious dimness of the crude shelter. The other boys, weak from hunger, had long since cried themselves softly to sleep, although they *had* drunk their fill of the crystal-clear spring water that is Mystery Mountain's bounty.

"I love thee to the level of everyday's most quiet need, by sun and candlelight, you guys," Mrs. Browning says. "Each one in a gracious hand appears to have a gift for mortals," she further allows. "I feel great affection for these honest lads. How do you feel about it, Bob?"

"Let them fight it out, friend! Things have gone too far" is the surprising reply from the garret.

A curious occurrence: Dr. Rex Buer, he of the golden hands, and known to all who have had the good fortune to be cared for by him as "The Healer," is on a mission for the redoubtable Buildings Department, the organization whose awesome responsibility it is to make the poor disappear in seemly fashion. Dr. Buer's task, this sultry day, is to care for a Bulgarian of advanced age. The Dragon of the Dead, the fearsome Bune, possesses the soul, spirit, and body of the work-gnarled Dimitrov Plovdiv. On his way to Plovdiv's small but immaculate apartment, which boasts a fairly decent but much-reduced reproduction of *L'assassin menacé,* which canvas Bune forces old Plovdiv to worship, a curious occurrence takes place. Marion Bunt, on her way through the streets to buy something to settle her stomach, accosts "The Healer," and makes him a number of torrid sexual offers, e.g., Howdya like to —— me in the ——?; Can you use a good ——job? Dr. Buer accompanies Mrs. Bunt to her apartment, trembling with excitement. It's been a long time since he —— anybody in the ——, and almost as long since he's had a ——job, or, for that matter, any kind of a job. In the bedroom, "The Healer" has a massive coronary as Mrs. Bunt playfully throws her perfumed half-slip in his face. So "The Healer" dies, unable to heal himself!

Although the characters are not fully realized, their very *humanity* is attractive.

The above-noted anecdote is thought to be part of the text of a long *sirventes,* "The Burglary." Although the text is lost, there is, if memory serves, no mention of a burglary in the poem. Is the title, then, a metaphor? A metonym or synecdoche? An analogue? A symbol? An instance of parataxis? Yes? Or no?

"Did he actually say 'if memory serves'?" Lord Bury asks, bursting in unceremoniously on Sir Bloom to show him a new book on Lytton Strachey, or by Lytton Strachey. Whatever, it is of abiding interest, for one can never learn too much about Bloomsbury and its brilliant circle of varlets. But Lord Bury's news must of needs wait, for Sir Bloom, rather like a lighthouse whose keeper has run amok, has reached the point of orgasm, a *jouissance* that not even this notable literary intelligence may detain. Thus doth the body make morons of us all.

"It's quite amazing, old chap," Lord Bury says. "Quite amazing. You look, in *your* 'Blushing Nun' costume, quite the way Lady Bustier looks in *her* 'Blushing Nun' costume. Ripping!" he exclaims.

Marcella Butler is waiting for the man she wishes, sort of, to be her third husband. Well, not really. He is late and she's alone. She knows that he won't come and that he won't call, for he is no longer interested in her. Dinner grows cold, the candles burn down, her new pumps pinch her feet as evidenced by a glance toward said pumps and a faint grimace. On the refrigerator is a stick-figure drawing, on oaktag, of what looks to be a little boy, his head all teeth. Body, arms, legs, and head are in red Crayola, teeth in black. Underneath this figure, in ragged, awkward letters which pitch wildly to right and left, is the message I LOVE GRANDDMA. This declaration is in red, green, and orange Crayola. Marcie looks at herself in the hall-closet mirror. Her hair is the wrong shade of brown, dull, *Jesus,* dull. Her skirt is too short, her blouse too tight, *Jesus.* Her lace-patterned black stockings are ridiculous. And the heels. The heels! They remind her of Mrs. Scheh and *her* heels, Mrs. Scheh, the math teacher who went crazy. Mr. Olsen and Mr. Andrews were math teachers too. They went crazy too. She should put on a girdle, although she hates them, but her hips, her thighs, *Jesus.* Who the hell does she think she is? She knows that he won't come, and if he should, he will probably be wearing those slacks which are unsettlingly close in color to that shade once called "electric blue." *Jesus,* she doesn't even like the man, really. Isn't that right, Grandma?

In truth, the death of "The Healer" is detailed in "Butts on the Beach," one of the interlinked stories in *Cameras Work,* by Josh Cabernet [Ka-bur-NET], a writer of whom, so it is threatened, we have not heard the last. Who has made an auspicious debut. Who is delighted and surprised by the wonderful reception accorded his first. On which a small publisher had the courage to. Whose photograph is seen here and also there. Who although a lawyer. Who hopes the screenplay will do his. And yet who has faith in. After all, isn't he a? Who is, yes, thinking of a. Who is a little, well, scared. After all, Dickens. Conrad. Who wonders if. Who doesn't really feel all that. Who is, yes, tired, but gratified by the marvelous. Who is thankful to his wonderful agent and her. Who fully agrees now with his quiet but convincing editor about the suggested. Who is sure that the book is just about as good as. Who, yes, thinks. Who has strong opinions but doesn't think that. Who isn't really sure that. Who thinks people today want books that this and also that that. Who thinks that his generation is. Who knows that courage and hope are. Who feels that the best advice is simply. Who affirms that informing the long look is.

Of *Cameras Work,* Michelle Caccatanto, with her customary uncial pertinence, writes, in part: "Josh Cabernet has given us an impressive and gritty collection in his *Cameras Work,* a series of connected stories which reveal a sophisticated intuition of the small despairs and triumphs of lower-middle-class domesticity. . . . The stories, although sympathetic and compassionate, are tempered by Mr. Cabernet's observant, cold, yet not pitiless eye. Learned, but not annoyingly so, the author . . . proves convincingly that 'old-fashioned' craftsmanship is more important than . . . fashionable obscurantism. . . . Characters are so convincingly etched that we feel as though we are participating in their lives. *Cameras Work* supplies a subtle bas-relief of a grey world which the more fortunate among us cannot even imagine."

She says that to all the boys.

Insofar as we may now determine, the dessert called Banana Amaze does not exist. Apologies—and kudos!—to all those readers whose attempts to create the dish are even now terminating in tears and blasphemy.

Then too: Famed Author's "Caddy" Named after Favorite Bar, the Cadillac Lounge; Unrepentant Eulogist's Poem "Calafawnya" Again Denied Coveted Prize; *The Caliph* No Cure for Summer Theatre Doldrums; *The Caliph* and *The Caliph Lorzu* Both Fakes, Expert Claims; Caliph's Walk Newest "In" Club for Publishing Rebels; Callipolis Voted "City of Beauty or Goodness"; Calvinist Accuses Cambridge Don of Stealing Baseball Cards, Strapless Bras; Camels and Chesterfields No Longer Welcome in Health-Crazed Canada; Cannes Ga-Ga Over "Cans" This Summer.

The Albanian woman is hot and sweaty after her chore, and, distraught because of the absorbent inadequacy of her impromptu neckerchief, reveals that she is Frieda Canula, a superintendent's wife. Threats by the much-disliked Carruthers Brothers and the imminent danger they pose are unable to dissuade the bedraggled varmint from telling everything to anyone who happens along.

"Is Carruthers the brothers seizing husband for exposing same in 'Cartel,' smashing wallop-read in *Albanian America.* I take saddened walk with good-lucks muffler (indicates neck region) and halt when in window I glimpse into I see idol of Albanian Lard Goddess. Is like special *vernissage* just for Frieda."

As she speaks, her warm eyes abaft, suburbanites, including an attractive vegetarian couple with an enlightened interest in caffeine-free beverages, roughly jostle her. Jerry Casey, who is a picture of health despite his grey hairs, hands her a bar of Castile soap.

"A wordless reproach," Casey smiles, and turns his face toward his condo, settling nicely into the poisoned landfill. "Another wordless reproach," Casey smiles again, as he knocks Mrs. Canula sprawling with a nifty hook off a jab. "You don't stop them now and they'll be here with their bongos and soiled underwear by the thousands." Thinking better of his largesse, he retrieves the bar of Castile and places it in his pocket, where it rests, silently. Things are silent, mostly.

"He pack a wallops!" Frieda says from the border of pinks.

A faint sound of cheering issues from the sculptor's house. And why not? But who is she? *Really?* Can she be a Catholic? Does it matter? Is this maybe a metaphor, or what?

All we know is that "the . . . pinks" probably belong to Rupert Brooke.

Cedric, a name that suddenly thrusts itself upon us, such are the mysterious and ineffable workings of the isomorphic synapses, doesn't ring the old bell. Yet here it is! in all its nominative substantiality. Rather than clutter this report with people who will not pull their own weight, what do you say we get rid of him with vaunted celerity?

O.K.

Cedric, poor man, is found dead in Central Park, often called "the Jewel of Parks," "the Emerald of Parks," and "a really terrific park." A Certificate of Death is made out for one "Cedric Doe."

Ce Soir, a haunting scent which recalls the long, slow twilights of the Serengeti, is still notorious as the *parfum* favored by Jeff Chandler, a film star who untimely died. Emmanuel Chanko, on whose face the sun oft falls golden, despite his embarrassment at being known as "Puppo" or "Peepee" Chanko, considers him a comic genius "not inferior" to Charlie Chaplin. Many disagree with Chanko, to wit: "A confusion of entelechy with fantasy yearnings." "Get the fuck outta here!" " 'Puppo' is a *cetriol'*. "

Now we have a *Charles* to deal with. How may literature be created when. . . ? O.K. Central Park again? Under a bush. "Charles Doe": Into the ground with him. And another Charles! What the—?

Mistaken identity?

Good! He's not Charles but somebody else we don't have to care about.

A statue of Arthur Rimbaud is to be found in Charleville, his place of birth. Rimbaud is well known for the famous gibe, directed at Paul Verlaine and his crude yet understandable manifestation of uncontrollable sexual desire: "If you only knew how fucking silly you look with that herring in your hand!" Leads to shooting in Brussels three days later, Verlaine's anger reaching its zenith when Rimbaud taunts him by calling Charles Baudelaire, one of Verlaine's saints, "Goodtime Charlie," or variantly, "Up-to-the-minute Charlie." Charlotte Rochambeau, a whore of a certain age whose speciality is the knotted-silk-kerchief trick, takes the wounded Rimbaud to Charmaine's, where they dine sumptuously on chaudrée aux fruits de mer, poulé sauté beauséjour, bavette de boeuf sauce chasseur, haricots verts au citron, pommes de terres duchesse, tomates grillées à la Provençale, pain rôti aux herbes, salade de cresson et endives, and banane étonnement. Excellent wines, tedious to detail, give each course the indefinable perfection which lies at the heart of all great dining experiences. Rimbaud is notably enthusiastic about the dessert. "Hein!" he exclaims. It is not generally known that Mlle Rochambeau goes on to write a *récit* based on the amours of Rimbaud and Verlaine, called *La Sottise,* rendered into English as *Chattering Fools* by Rodney Chatz.

Luba Checks throws the deadbolt on the Yale lock. The police lock is next, then the chain. Lo! two slices of rare roast beef, a hard roll, a small jar of Hellmann's mayonnaise, a translucent pink spheroid—perhaps a tomato?, a small bottle of Perrier. The article on the crisis in Israeli morality in the *Magazine.* Lifts her skirt to her waist, slips out of her shoes and pulls her pantyhose down and off. Depressing deli items, ho! await her, as does the latest article on the crisis in Israeli morality in the *New York Review of Books.* Waiting also: the latest article on the imminent demise of organized crime after the arrest of 487 top mobsters, and a front-page review of *The Inner World of Lytton Strachey.* Television. Long hot soak in small shallow basin jokingly called a "tub." Luba takes out her partial upper plate. Takes out her partial lower plate. Takes out her contact lenses and puts reading glasses on. Disgusting deli fare. Blouse open, then off, then into the bathroom sink with the pantyhose. On the coffee table a postcard from her daughter in Seattle on welfare. "Thanks for the check. It will come in handy for the baby. Dorrie." Luba puts an ice cube in an Old Fashioned glass, fills it to the top with Bombay. Can it hurt? Puts on a terrycloth robe and sits down with her gin. She's a long way from her salad days as Lyubinka Czechowyczy. Who isn't? Unconfessed to the boring but kind friend from work with whom she spent the afternoon is the fact that she would very much like to get laid. Then, and, you know, like right now.

Chester leaves the baths, shaken. While there, he is sexually active with a young man whose name is Chester. He has a drink with a young man who introduces himself as Chet. He is sexually willing but physically unable to perform with a young man who is surprised to learn that his name is Chester since his name is Chet. This Chet is a waiter, well, not *actually* a *waiter*. Another man, his own age, asks for a cigarette as he is dressing, and mentions that his name is Chet. Chester doesn't even want to think about their haircuts and moustaches, uncannily alike. He is just too old, too goddamned old for this. And why is that *woman* smiling at him?

It should be made clear that the woman who smiles at Chester is not the same woman who is sprawled on the street in front of the A & P. She looks a bit like her but looks, as Aristophanes says, can be deceiving. Of course, he said it with more panache.

Far below, at the mouth of the secluded valley, barely distinguishable amid the gorse flickering in the sunlight, a Chevrolet stands abandoned in the shade of the ancient yews. Farther on, beyond the small farmhouses whose chimneys even now send up their wisps of dried-conifer smoke, which latter betokens the slow labors of the placid women preparing luncheon, the University of Chicago dominates the great shale bluffs that overlook Chinatown and its self-absorbed throngs of Chinese, jabbering their unpronounceable gibberish in the packed and fetid streets. Chinatown!

Chooch sighs, and then, alerted by the thrashing of heavy boots in the dense furze behind him, hides his video cassette of *Chorus Orgy* in his soiled bedroll. Just in time! For at the edge of the clearing, a tall young man, his blond hair and beard matted with gooseberries, thorns, briers, chicles, and nightshade dust, stands regarding him with curiosity. His plaid mackinaw and worn moleskins bespeak, more eloquently than could any words, the fact that he is a Christian. The young giant strides toward Chooch, his huge right hand extended in greeting. Chooch forces a smile, then extends his own right hand, glad that he'd had the presence of mind to conceal the film, one which might well have maddened the hardy wayfarer. They shake extended hands firmly, their eyes locked in mutually homophobic embarrassment, while all about them the forest murmurs its inscrutable message, i.e., "krik-kk, krik-kk, krik-kk."

"I'm Knute," the newcomer says. "Secretary of the Christian Conservative Student Crusade." His piercing eyes instantly pick out the ruined Chevy far below. "Hmm. Seen any yids pass this way?" His smile is cold and Chooch weighs his reply carefully.

"No yids in these feral parts," he replies evenly, his face impassive. "Saw a couple of young women in innocent gingham, from the Christian Student Union, I think they said." It is, he realizes, a mistake.

As Knute's face darkens, Chooch helplessly recalls the Christmas, long ago, when his drunken father destroyed the Christmas tree they had joyfully chopped down together, more or less. He had had Knute's face—pitiless and vengeful. Is Knute, too, a drunkard? Is Knute perhaps his father? Probably not, and yet . . .

A cloud drifts over the sun and the windy crag grows suddenly grey and cold.

"You say young *women?*" Knute sneers. "What's gingham?"

It may fairly be said that the above fragment, allegedly part of a story by Jack Armstrong, exhibits neither remarkable perception, such as what we could never forget it, nor exciting wallop, which each phiz bedizeneth, and nowhere may any particle in it be construed as displaying steamy and exotic sex, to which all mortals bend the natural knee, or knees.

"And how!" the priest says, still uneasily hovering about the magazine rack.

The fragment, in point of fact, seems hardly irrefragable. To speak with whitest candor, it is very poor work, and reads like a bad parody. So shrewd readers often proclaim!

"You got the wrong story!" Jack protests. But Jack doesn't know that this is an occurrence in no way uncommon or remarkable. "The wrong story" seems to be, to paraphrase Chrysippus of Soli, our burden and our cross.

Buddy Cioppetini, known as "Hoagie" or "Doggie" in the nondescript ginmills he frequents, is bald. Yes, and to add insult to injury, he has misplaced his Chevy, in connection with which the words "crick," "holler," "draw," "gulch," and "fen" keep coming to mind, but none of them rings the old bell. He stolidly continues, then, to shine his old shoes, his good old shoes. "What," as George S. Patton said, "the heck." Suddenly he remembers that on the front seat of his car lies his dog-eared, worn, and much-annotated copy of *Homo Ludens.* Without it, there is no telling what he may consider doing.

Perhaps—just a thought—perhaps, like our literary friend, the lighthouse keeper, he will run amok?

Civil War Songs of the Northern Armies: "Sloggin' inter 'Bammy"; "Have *My* Beans, Sojer"; "Jeff Davis Is Tarnation Mean"; "Embraceable You"; "Fuck the Dangèd Rebs!"; "Lady of Spain"; "What Is This Chickenshit?"; "Hardtack in Heaven Tonight, Cap'n"; "Babalu."

Florence Claire, once an actress who still gets an occasional laxative commercial, each a wonderful opportunity for her to "hone" her "craft," does anonymous book reviews for *Virginia's Beat,* an "important journal" ancillary to the "publishing" business. She is currently putting the "finishing touches" on the review of a new book of "poems" by Pamela Clairwil, another sometime actress, whose photographs of shattered people sitting next to garbage cans, etc., etc., "grace her pages." Florence changes the phrase "slipshod writing" to "automatic writing." It has, she feels, the perfect soupçon of literary ambience she seeks. She likes the phrase, and vows to use it in the future whenever she decides, for one reason or another, not to, uh, well, not to read, uh, well, not actually read all, uh, of an assigned book. In this determination, she joins the prestigious guild. Meanwhile, she *must* attend to that nagging chancre.

"That's really a bit terribly much!" the population of Clappeville says. "It is one thing to use fiction as a means of retaliation on those one feels have wronged one, yet quite another to descend to the vile and the base!" They say these fairly complex sentences in unison. Chant them, really. And there are a *lot* of people in Clappeville. Got its own croissant shop. All the residents are clearly perturbed by this egregious breach of etiquette.

This is the town which put "Clarinet Polka" on the map. There you go!

Elects mayors named "Clark," always. "Clark," inverted commas intact.

Claims that Buddy Clark's recordings sport bebop orchestrations. They are enthusiastic about this one, although we doubt the truth of the statement. A flatted fifth does not a bebop make, to paraphrase Bartók. "Cleanthes of Assos is best known for his *Hymn to Zeus*," a solitary voice cries. All turn about nervously. "It is a song cycle what tells the musical story of the early Stoics and the beat is shifted to the splash cymbal, said beat accented on one and three!" Silence. Clubfoot Pete, Clappeville's police officer, a figure in a tattered suit, eerily blue, clumps through the crowd, looking for the offending hipster. Many feel, though of course do not say, that this voice of musico-philosophic rebellion is that of the owner of the Club Zappe, a roadhouse which specializes in fox-trot contests, as does the Bluebird.

One begins to see the intricate yet asymmetrical weave in the pattern, no? "But what are patterns for?" Dorothea Brooke cries.

The Bluebird is mentioned at least once or twice in *Seize My Ravaged Heart*, a frivolous novel which is obviously the product of . . . Florence pauses . . . "automatic writing." "Florence is pretty dumb," experts ascertain.

In Colma, however, surprising developments unfold. A group of locals, calling themselves The Committee Against the Committee on Committees, is convinced that the reason that their town is home to every cemetery in Northern California is that it lies within the infamous "fog belt." But what to do? A series of amazing adventures follows. Liaisons, drunken picnics, messy divorces, God only knows how many leftovers! Threats and imminent danger. The despairs and triumphs of middle-class life, e.g., wide ties, e.g., crudités. All against a background of intrigue and inflamed passions. Deviled eggs! An occasional good read. Pleated gabardine trousers. The dead are, as usual, unimpressed, although a few do pretend, give them credit, a polite interest.

Karen Complexion on being modern: "Hi! I'm Karen! You might think a flight attendant is all business, but when I'm groundside, jogging and working out with that *special* microchip whiz, I know how important well grooming and competent grammar could be. Take it from me, *hair* on most sections of the body is unwanted. Oh, hi!"

As is often the case, *Complex Resolutions* and *Complicated Webs* go unread. *Compost* is a magazine no longer extant. Yet how gently the editorial hand guides the prose to its lapidary finish! They have nothing of the crass, no, it is all relaxed clothing and the exhilaration of cupidity. Even the heartland is enthusiastic, witness the cultivation of understanding therein regarding short fiction, enjoying now a revival of sorts.

"People have little time for long books now, but they do feel the need for worthwhile literature," says the attractive, perfectly coiffed president of Concrete Proposals, a garden-pool company, or something about fronds or something. "The mood is upbeat," the attractive, modishly attired executrix mutters, scratching one of her things the while.

The ladies of the Condom League agree. Yet they look surreptitiously at their neatly folded white gloves and nervously adjust their little veiled hats. As usual, something is going on under the table. Ladies!

Louis Condy, children's-book author, and now a resident of a resurgent Coney Island, considers thoughtfully: "Now that I'm getting on in years and feeling good about beating that bum sodomy rap, I have little patience with talking worms and kids who want to know what the milkman does." He holds up his new manuscript for inspection. "So I'd have to agree with the grout-theory people, yes." Condy has a touch of the rampant buboes, a nagging disease which slows him down some. "Was Christ always mad?" he concludes in an upbeat mood.

Speaking of Christ, a delegation from the Confraternity of the Most Precious Blood is dispatched to the A & P. A certain citizen, known mockingly to the neighborhood as "Mr. Congeniality," is thought to have dragged his unspeakably deformed foot to a public telephone to register his protest against an "embarrassing priest." The priest, now back at dairy products, is trying to "do something" about his obstreperously tented trousers. It is, perhaps, his great trial.

Allen decides that Connecticut, after all, will be just paradise. Chet will be along, dearest Chet, who, Allen recalls, often tells complete strangers that he is not *actually* a *waiter*. If only they can once again rent the little cabin that looks across the flame-touched gorse fronds and the copious furze, alive with golden glitterings, to the peaceful shimmer of the Connecticut River, whose slow current carries the still-living dreams of rangy pioneers! If only.

O lost! And cry the wind, brief ghosts!

Through his tears he spies Connie, a perfect bitch if he ever saw one, seat herself in his section. Sullenly placing a tumbler of tepid water on her table, he says, "Hi! I'm Allen, your waiter." Connie, her eyes frantically but not annoyingly signaling a desire for friendship, orders a "Consensus," two slices of anchovie Pizza topped with sharp melted Cheddar and lightly sautéded Raddishes on a bed of crisp Iceberg Lettuce, with Savory pickles and fresh golden Pommés da Terre Franchais.

"Obvious that the joint knows nothing of real cuisine," Mr. Bathin says in a telephone interview. "Pommés da Terre Franchais is an item should be atop the Pizza. These people will eat anything." He hangs up and the operator sticks the interviewer with the charges.

"Cuisine mighty fine chow is," Frieda Canula says through her banjaxed mouth, proving that, although in pain, yet hath she her mind entire. But now, bearing down upon her, the sculptor, her face pale with fury, her eyes rolling wildly, like those of a frantic, screaming leper in a lighthouse, brandishes her copy of *Sanctuary,* a prop by now half-forgotten in the turmoil of things. Frieda staggers back in fear and awe, for she takes the sculptor to be, quite understandably, the Lard Goddess. "I'll give you 'chow'!" the sculptor screeches.

Are we to discover, at last, whether or not *Construction in Metal* is a translation of *Les Constructions métalliques*? Rimbaud knows, but is dead. Gary Cooper, although he regularly crosses the void, won't say. Craig Copro, Captain, USAF, is forbidden to speak to anyone, confined, as he is, to the Bachelor Officers' Quarters on Corfu, "island of exhilarant foliage," for an infraction involving a cute bus driver, a secretly drugged assistant professor of petroleum engineering, and a pair of jump boots. Karen Cornfield? Busy, as usual.

"Hi! I'm Karen Cornfield! Busy as usual while in the clouds which stream delightfully, I have little time to entertain questions on matters literary, and when I'm down on good old *terra firma* I just want to be, well, *slinky* for that special heart surgeon! Despite books and the overtly homosexual types who seem to be involved with them, I think it's pretty important to be, well, just a woman. That's why I fabulously scent."

Corrie Corriendo, never fully realized, packs up some old clothes to give to the poor. Rusty old things, really. She clanks over to the window to gaze at the traffic far below, fingering the while her grey-blue aluminum wig. She catches the reflection of her face in the pane, and steps back, startled. So it comes at last to *this*. Yes, she is discarded now, thrown away like an old steel sneaker by those she thought her friends. "Hâ, hâ," she laughs, sans mirth. She looks again at the traffic far below. How small it seems. How small and virtually unimportant. How far away. Is it possible that she once actually *cared* for it?

Cortland, Colma's sister city, nestled at the foot of Mystery Mountain like a toy city in a Christmas display in a toy store in a great city which, covered with the first snows, seems like a photograph of a toy city, learns of the troubles in that fogbound burg. "Troubled tydinges, lyke spirites incorporeal, / Doe flye as shaftes from th' Amazon's marcial bowe." Ontology, yes, but true.

"I seem to remember that clever distich from *Cosmopolitan,*" the rictal woman offers, picking herself up from the sidewalk. "I first read it in the Cotswolds, on our honeymoon. We lived, then, in a cunning little cottage, Cottage . . . Cottage . . . Cottage 33, yes! Cottage 33, which commanded and perhaps still commands a breathtaking view of the fields of scarlet-tipped sedge that ran down and perhaps still run down the gently rolling mounds, or knolls, to end in viscid crimson just at the point where the ancient emerald lawns of the Country Club began and perhaps still begin. I was, but doubt that I still am, Miss Cover Girl to him." She furtively wipes some dogshit off a Real-Mex Frozen Dinner. Unknown to her, Cox, here to buy the new issue of *Clothes Action,* regards her narrowly. His denim jacket, *finally,* is faded to a color which permits him to walk the streets looking like those who walk the streets.

"I would rather die," Cox says, "than dress like this hag. I would rather be boiled in liquid fire than appear so gauche, rather be beat like gold to ayery thinnesse than be seen with a copy of *Accidental Bodies.* My appearance? Elegant yet relaxed. Insouciantly rumpled. A falling drape of slender excitement. I have little time for long books yet feel the need for literature. E'en now, my nights, those nights o'er which grim Morpheus doth cast his tincted mantle, are partially given over to a satisfying moment or two with an amusing quarto, heavily annotated by a previous owner, that I picked up for a song at a dusty old bookshop, of a kind that is fast disappearing from the dynamic city."

"That wouldn't be my *Homo Ludens,* would it, champ?" Buddy Cioppetini queries.

"No, my hardworking dago friend," Cox answers. "It is a volume by Hart Crane, *White Bridges.* But thanks a million for your continuing interest. And, by the by, it is apparent that despite your polyester-cotton-blend shirt, whimsically buttoned to the neck yet tieless, you have deep, lasting roots in the community, love children, drink, but not to excess, adore noise of all kinds, and cannot be held responsible for the depredations of organized crime. In brief, thou'rt your swart Italiano. Got any clams?"

"Who is this fuckin' hardon?" Buddy says. Silence is his only answer, a rapt silence which seems to await his earthy laughter.

"What I miss is the pull of continuity. Or to put it more clearly: Although the continuity's pull is sometimes present, there is lacking a certain sympathy for the people involved. We don't, somehow, feel as if we are participating in *real* people's *real* lives. But do drop by for a cuppacawfee."

"Right. Without the pull of continuity, civilizations tend to crumble," Tadeusz Creon says. "For instance, the Cracow Incident, without that pull, cannot be fully understood." He puffs thoughtfully on his crusty aromatic. "Oh, you think it's *funny?*" Blows are exchanged and old friendships strained almost to the breaking point. A kielbasa panic. Painted Easter eggs are snapped up. Anti-Semitism is trotted out in new clothes. Yet who *knows* about this?

Crescent and Chattaway? Perhaps.

"Coffee?"

"Don't talk to me about Crescent and Chattaway," Grey Crimson says, his words angrily spurting out around the stem of his well-designed billiard meerschaum, a gift from his first wife and her "boyfriend," Dr. Trite. "They don't send out advance galleys, they have no clipping service, they take ads in *Gardening Fun,* they get a hundred returns for every book sold. I'm a well-known author for God's sake! And here I sit, smoking this piece of white rock or something from

Crete, flat broke, melting with ruth. I don't even have an interesting accent anymore."

Meerschaum is a fine white claylike material mined chiefly in Daly City. Adolf Hitler, the late German statesman, had a mania for pipes fashioned from this rare vignette.

"*I* still love his accent," Delilah Crosse says. She is stunning in an excitement of black silk falling ravishingly to the knee in a single crisp sweep of midnight magic. "As you can see, my taste in clothes is a manifestation of style, not fashion." She makes a small enchanting *moue*. "Some think that my love for things Continental and the fact that I ridicule everything Middle American with what amounts to precious condescension keep me youthful and vivacious. Perhaps," she says softly, with a hint of self-doubt, "my jugs could stand some improvement?"

"What did that woman say about jugs?" Lucy Brandon says.

"However," Delilah continues, crisply ravishing her excitement, "there are plans in the offing and not a few irons in the fire. Especially concerning my legs, which are at once my shame and my triumph." She proffers a lot of leg in silky sheer stockings to sustained applause.

"O.K. I'll give her the legs," Lucy says.

"With those legs I don't think she's a good Christian woman," Knute sighs, pausing in his search for rustic foodstuffs.

Tania Crosse has so much money that she believes that "Tania Crosse" is her real name. Her face, always beautiful, is cool and smooth, her makeup perfect, her hair a silvery blond. She's drinking Ricard and ginger ale, a famous affectation. She doesn't recall Delilah. She lights a Camel. She likes the still-pink scar tissue on her wrists. What to do? She sets out for her flagship store. Things are not quite as *à vau-l'eau* today as they have been recently. But they are *à vau-l'eau* enough, oh yes indeed.

Knowing a good thing when he sees one, the owner of the Crystals, another semi-pro baseball team, is also thinking of bringing suit against the sculptor. God only knows why. Proud contumely, vile disdain, imminent danger? All look O.K.

"Look," the sculptor says, "all I want to do is finish this goddamned book and get that foreigner with the neck thing away from my house. O.K.? Don't bother me with this asshole and his suit. O.K.?" In her pique, her humanity comes to the fore and it is, well, pretty darned *attractive*. But this is neither here nor there, for many are eager for news of the Cullinan family.

In the basement of their white frame house, not too far from things, Brian, a little slow for twenty-six, is forging his father's name to a check. He has his eye, a poor thing but his own, on a COMMANDO KNIFE, guaranteed to PUNCTURE, INCISE, LACERATE, SLICE, RIP, TEAR, AND HACK IN TWO!! anybody who wants to "Get Funny." INDISPENSABLE for camping trips, can be thrown with SPEED and POWER!! RUGGED SAW for barbed wire. 10-DAY FREE TRIAL. CHECK IT OUT!! Maureen is jacking off the ice-cream man inside the cab of his truck, and by now she is a whiz at it. May is on the phone with, of course, her sister, who is *still* in bed. Michael, in his "den" up in the attic, is filing away his newest ladies' underwear catalogue, *Frenchie Frillies*. But why are they all dressed in what they call their "best clothes"? It is that Mr. Cullinan the elder is dead at last and they are preparing to leave for the funeral home where he lies intestate in the largest room. Mrs. Cullinan, his widow, is already there, and many friends and relatives attend him. They speak in hushed voices, *de mortuis nil nisi bonum* their guiding precept, more or less.

A picture of health, he niver looked so good when he was aloive, Jayzus and ye'd think he's about to git up and go fer a pint the hard man, look at the roses in his dear owld cheeks, Christ and he's as pink as a baby, sure and I wished I looked half as good wit' the sinuses cloggin' me head wit' snot, he's a fookin' credit to the owld country, even stiff as a board he could lick a dozen men, look at the poor widow will ye now, I love the dear silver that shoines in her hair, I think the good woman has a few jars in her meself and who's to blame her, he'll be havin' a jar on the other soide about now that he will, he looks like a notorious saint he does, he made a foine act of contrition at the last they say, merciful Jayzus but he niver had much of a chin on him, 'tis a pity his poor owld tongue is stickin' out of his gob like a bloody snake's, ye'd think the pansy Orangeman of a funeral director would close his right eye for him for the love of God, by Christ ye'd niver think he had the walkin' glanders what me own da died of, and et cetera. Enter Brian, Maureen,

May, and Michael, in the splendor of their grief. Divers snots, tears, and wailings. Rudimentary ethnic artifacts of a celebratory nature are crudely passed about and shared, e.g., green cardboard derbies, clay pipes, lapel harps of plastic, etc., etc. All goes well, varied entertainments, some of a scandalous nature (see *Irish Wake Amusements* by Seán Ó Súilleabháin) proceed in good order.

"They are hardworking folk," Cox says, "like your dark-eyed ginzola."

Still, Michael, enchanted as he is by the wild Celtic jigs, reels, skreels, potheens, mashies, and kerries which command the floor, is troubled in his heart, for his new issue of *Cults and Coteries* is late. And this is the issue in which "Muffin" Cunningham, "Scummy" to her friends, is to model the entire "Cute Cop" line of *exciting fantasy-wear!*

"How is it, sir, that *I* have no intelligence of the 'Cute Cop' line?" Sir Bloom says from his chaise. "Am I losing touch with the still center of the turning world?"

Here let it be noted that we are interested in the Cullinane family, *Cullinane.*

John Greene Czcu buys a copy of *Buddy and His Boys on Mystery Mountain* for fifteen cents. The book is virtually unobtainable, yet this relaxed gentleman laughs only the harder. Certainly, nobody has any right to expect to find such a gem here in the fog belt, especially on grubby Rensselaer Street, which, at its best, looks like Avenue D on a magical summer weekend.

"It is so," Czcu says shrewdly, a hint of mockery in his voice. "Although I work hard, I play even harder, this dynamite city providing many opportunities for leisure fun, if one knows *where to look. Buddy,* for instance, one of the great tales of insouciant adventure in the considerable literature of rural capers and gambols, has bears, one-eyed gypsies, noble braves, simpering damsels, and chums galore. One might even say that in its rhetorical subversion of the 'chum as callow youth' theme, the privileged 'Ur-chum,' we witness a classic deconstructive technique."

"There is not one real stolid redskin in the whole book, motherfucker," Chief Blue Wind protests.

"Yet Buddy is delightfully attractive, don't you think, Chief?" Czcu says. "You're not, if I may say so, too hard on the eyes either, if you get my drift?" For a long moment, Blue Wind's humanity shines forth from *his* eyes.

There ensues that which is known to commerce as "brisk sales" of Louis Condy's *The Daddy and the Drake,* in the Black Ladder Book Shop. The beloved children's book, finally reissued after twenty-three years, has become the adored focus of an enthusiastic and pleasantly mindless cult, whose celebrants quack greetings to each other and wear T-shirts which display the book's most famous sentence, "The duck *talked,* Daddy!" Condy, his usually saturnine face wreathed in an uncharacteristic smile, sits behind a low table at the rear of the shop, autographing copies. Moved by the awed crowds, the author writes whatever is requested, e.g., "To Daisy, a swell gal and *some* character"; "For Dante, King of the Bores"; "Por María de la Concepción Dorotea Carolina Darío y Reyes, un abrazo y un beso."

Dark Victory is playing in a rerun house down the street, but such is the pull of the reclusive author's presence that the theatre is virtually empty, save for three or four avid masturbators whose sexual fantasies incline toward images of women who exhibit a lot of spunk despite the brain tumors which are the cause of their nagging vision problems. When the star of the film, Bette Davis, stumbles over a credenza and, bravely smiling, pitches forward into the buffet supper, a medley of unmistakably lewd groans is heard in the darkened orchestra.

"I thought she falls into the buffet supper in *Carom,*" a fan says. "Right after the scene in the cheerful, sunny kitchen, where she mistakes the jelly doughnuts, or donuts, for French crullers. Whenever I see that I bust out crying and invariably ask myself what *I* would do ensnared in such embarrassing instance."

A well-mannered group of older women from the Athene chapter of the Daughters of Durga International is massing in front of the Black Ladder to protest the fact that *The Daddy and the Drake* has but a single female character who is, early on in the adventure, eaten by a bear on a garbage-strewn nature trail. One of the women buttonholes a shifty-looking man heading for the theater, a grimy raincoat held, in the time-honored fashion of harmless perverts, in front of his pubes. The man, who identifies himself to the media only as D.D., stands impatiently, hoping that the jelly-doughnut scene has not yet been reached.

"While we mobilize, Mr. D., to protest the lack of an evenhanded *humanity* in Condy's insensitive work, you rush toward a rendezvous with the base fantasies excited by the Pink Sleeveless Dress Syndrome, a metonymy for female helplessness. Is it, then, strange that the Daughters adopted, long ago, fedora and overalls as counterweights to such male horseshit thought? As a way for us to deconstruct the very notion of the helpless woman?"

"Look, sister, I don't bother nobody," D.D. says. "All I wanna do is sit down, take it easy, and come in my old grimy raincoat here. I really *dig* chicks."

But now the women are forming into ranks and have no time to deal with this shuffling slave to the aberrant. Condy glances out the window and in his rampant egoism assumes that they are old fans, perhaps mothers who read his masterwork to their children long years ago, when things were as they are naturally supposed to be, and real men could nonchalantly curse, spit, piss, shit, and masturbate among themselves without fear of nosy women barging into the sanctum of club or swimming pool.

Dear Sir:

In your description of the Cullinan wake, the statements put into the mouths of the mourners are in execrable taste; indeed, they comprise a miniature encyclopedia of anti-Irish rodomontade presented as "realism." Sir, the Irish do not speak in this way, and despite the fond beliefs of the benighted, neither are they partial to green cardboard derbies, "jars" of intoxicating liquors, and the other claptrap noted in your callous and bigoted essay. May I suggest that you do some research before you again set pen to paper?

Sincerely,

A Concerned Irish-American

A piecework of heartburn, he niver looked so good when he was aloive, Jayzus and ye'd think he's about to git up and go fer a pinwheel the hard manakin, look at the rosins in his dear owld cheetahs, Christ and he's as pink as a bachelor's-button, sure and I wish I looked half so good wit' the sirs cloggin' me headgear wit' snowblink, he's a fookin' creep to the owld coup, even stiff as a boast he could lick a dozen manakins, look at the poor wigan will ye now, I love the dear silverweed that shoines in her hairline, I think the good wonderland has a few jaseys in her meself and who's to blame her, he'll be havin' a jasey on the other siderite about now that he will, he looks like a notorious Sal that he does, he made a foine actinomyces of contumely at the latchstring they say, merciful Jayzus but he niver had much of a chink on him, 'tis a placard his poor owld tonka bean is stickin' out of his gobo like a bloody snap-back's, ye'd think the pantie Orangeman of a funk-dirk would close his right eyehole for him for the lover of God, by Christ ye'd niver think he had the walkin' glassman what me own dachshund died of.

Now *that's* Irish.

As the morning sun rose over the wooded slopes of Mystery Mountain, sending its rays through the chinks in the walls of the rough-hewn cabin, Dick Witherspoon laughed gaily and stretched, his eyes shining brightly on Buddy, his lissomely strapping chum.

"I declare I slept like a log being a-sawed in two, Buddy," he commented.

"So did I, Dick," Buddy admitted. "It is the pure air up here in the mountains," he mused. "It cleans the cobwebs out of a fellow's brain."

"The cobwebs, Buddy?" Dick queried softly.

"It's a figure of speech, Dick, kind of like Mrs. Browning uses, a nice, respectable one too. Like an ozone," Buddy said seriously.

"You're a strange lad, Buddy," Dick grinned. "But a right faluting brick."

The two friends, having washed quickly and with many a boyish whoop in the icy mountain stream that ran clear and cold behind the rustic cabin, tramped back inside, shyly cozening each other about the pangs of hunger that gnawed at them. For boys of their age need a great deal of homely grub to ensure the rudest health! Buddy, obviously exhilarated, decided not to tell Dick that he'd almost injured his arm on the jagged pelisse which the furious rill had sent crashing down on them.

"You 'most broke your arm on that dang'rous pelisse, Buddy," Dick said admiringly. Buddy blushed and began energetically to lay the fire, while Dick discreetly pretended to busy himself with his collection of sturdy raiment. For all his love of hearty fun he was an estimable, gentlemanly boy.

"Say, Buddy," he soon called from the shadows that still lingered in the corners of the snug shelter, "it looks mighty like the other lads up and died during the night. I'll be piped!" he exclaimed in a voice of genuine concern. "They seemed tip-top and in the pink 'fore they turned in."

"Died?" Buddy echoed, his worried face framed by the firelight. "I suppose that we should have provided them with a supper more substantial than their fill of *crystal-clear spring water,* such as the mountain boasts." Both boys laughed merrily at Buddy's subtle levity, for it was well-known that even in time of the greatest danger, Buddy insisted on a genteel lightheartedness. Yet it was of no small concern to him that the untimely demise of the other lads was uncannily like an incident described in *Dead Beats,* a novel of mystery and danger that Buddy admired greatly.

"Well, let's get some chuck inter our bellies," Dick continued. "I'm so hungry that I could eat a very large horse, hooves and all!" Again the two youths' laughter joined in mutual clean fun. If Buddy had learned anything in his fifteen years on this mortal coil, it was that a sense of humor is no bar to advancement.

"Yes, let's quickly procure a meal," Buddy added. "For we've a long, hard day ahead of us if we expect to find that dago Blutwurst's hidden map before sundown."

"You don't have to implode me to agree with *that,*" Dick chuckled volubly. "In course, the dago's map sure ain't going anywhere. And neither is *he,*" he added jocularly.

"You should say '*of* course,' Dick," Buddy said quietly, "not '*in* course.' Incorrect grammar often proves a bar to advancement in the demanding world of business."

And with that, the boys began eating copiously of the smoked rashers that they'd found beneath the floorboards, and to which cache they'd been alerted just a week earlier by the Dean of Arts and Sciences, a coarse-looking man whose flushed face confessed that he was not unfamiliar with strong spirits. Buddy suddenly thought of the Dean's rubicund complexion, and, startled, helped himself to another generous portion of the nourishing fare.

It was mid-morning when the two companions, after lugging the bodies of their chums into the woods for the shy forest creatures to carry off, started along the north bank of the swift creek and headed for the distant crag, forever wreathed in forbidding swirls of mist, called "Misty Crag."

Literary Interlude

"Death to Emily Dickinson's Modesty"
(to the tune of "Moon River")

Death to Emily Dickinson's modesty!
Her reticent blushes? A malepig travesty!
They wish her to be but a brainless tootsy
Or one whose genius "just growed" like Topsy.
Death! To Emily Dickinson's modesty!

Let us strangle the nun of Amherst's modesty!
Photos reveal that Em wasn't too breasty,
Filthy pigmen think chaste means not chesty,
And consider poetic brilliance unzesty;
Let us strangle the nun of Amherst's modesty!

Let us drown in womanrage Emily's modesty!
We are sick and do puke at pigspeak that's "jesty,"
On how we are home-loving, docile, and nesty;
And if we speak out we are "broads" who are pesty.
Let us drown in womanrage Emily's modesty!

Let us drown in womanrage Emily's modesty!
Let us strangle the nun of Amherst's modesty!
Death to Emily Dickinson's modesty!
Death! Relentless death! See?

Father Donald Debris, S.J., long removed from his pastoral duties for teachings not only contrary to the Magisterium, but, some say, dangerously close to heresy (*vide* "The Effect of High Heels on the Cloistered Orders," *New Church Bearings,* XXII, 6, 1958), spends his days in a close study of the Décadence. This morning, he is startled to discover that his idiosyncratic and highly complex system of numerology—a system of numerological transference determined by an algorithmic permutational shift accomplished by a rigid adherence to the formula

$$a \div b = a \cdot (1/b) = a \cdot b^{-1}$$

—has afforded him positive proof that "Barbey d'Aurevilly" is an anagram of "Yvonne DeCarlo." Debris has long been fascinated by the film star because of her roles as temptress in *Blaze over Pago-Pago*, *The Hot Countess, Tongues at Midnight,* and *December,* the last arguably displaying her finest performance. Almost overcome by excitement, the priest reworks his formula and discovers that he has made an error in one step of the process. It is not "Yvonne DeCarlo" that is anagrammatic of the outrageous author's name, but "Barbra d'Eveuilley." Now Debris realizes that Miss DeCarlo had nothing to do with the roles, perhaps irresponsibly attributed to her by "loco" journalists, in the four films he so admires. Yet the priest can find no references to prove that Mlle d'Eveuilley appeared in the films either! Who, then, was the star? He rises from his desk, strolls to the window, and gazes at the traffic far below. Perhaps there is something "wrong" with his formula. Many otherwise intelligent people founder on the shoals of mathematics, or, in this case, arithmetic.

"Deejee," Father Debris mutters incomprehensibly to the blinds, or, perhaps, to the traffic. Then, "Thank goodness there will be mastiachis for supper. God bless, despite her ill-gotten wealth, Miss Crosse, our generous supplier."

Miss Crosse?

Madame Berthe Delamode ("Creations Tastefully Designed") packs up some old clothes, of which she is tired to death, to give to *somebody.* Truthfully, she's just going to leave them in a box out by the garbage cans. Really, they're slightly corroded. She spies something in the street. "Aha!" she laughs, yet realizes, now, that "it" is all so *unimportant.* For a moment, she looks blank, but then, in an untrained but pleasant alto, sings the first two choruses of "Time Will Tell":

> Time will tell
> I'll give you la de da
> Time will tell
> La da my heart

Dengised yllufetsat
Snoitaerc
Dengised
Yllufetsat

It is apparent that she is suffering from a female ailment clearly recognized in the 1783 monograph, *De l'influence des affections de l'âme dans les maladies nerveuses des femmes.* Among other well-known women whose careers were notably affected by this "maladie" are the actress Dolores Délire (see especially her performance in *Les Fureurs du péché*), and the author Viña Delmar (n.b., *Bad Girl*). Among the early symptoms of the disease is the overwhelming desire to tastefully design creations.

It's not so much a desire as it is an obsession! (Indicates "Confidential" file.)

There is a slender possibility that Benjamin DeMott may soon address the problem with, of course, an eye to its literary implications. For our time. Mr. Denim—Anthony Denim—supposedly wrote of the scourge in 1884 or thereabouts in his still-valuable *De praestigiis amoris,* or, *On Love's Deceptions.* In those days they called the disease "nervous prostration." Noble chicks got it a lot when their boyfriends like rode off with the hussars, shakos bulging in the slanting rays of the morning sun.

April Detective, in bed, is, despite the warmth of the day, cold beneath a sheet, two blankets, and a grimy raincoat, a bittersweet reminder of earlier, far happier days. Maybe not "far" happier. She gets out of bed to get another bottle of vodka, a favorite beverage, cheap, potent, and without any *frotteur* to interfere with the function of the alcohol. Her brain, steeped as it is in booze, is not working very well. "Such go the breaks of life," she says. "Tomorrow I'll get straight," she adds, proving once again, if proof is needed, that alcohol is no defense against the platitude. Abruptly, she falls down, and as abruptly, rises. She falls down again, abruptly, and rises again, slowly. She enters the bathroom, sits on the toilet, and pisses, aware too late of the fact that she has forgotten to lift her nightgown. "Not to worry," she says. "Tomorrow I'll lift my nightgown and relieve myself in more seemly fashion." She really hates this country house, if that's what it is. It looks like a country house, there is something warm and inviting and familiarly depressing about it, something bovine, something that reminds her of chickens and their manic clucks, something rich and smugly Protestant. She pulls off the sodden nightgown, dries herself with a glum country towel that gives off, as in all tales of squalor, a faint odor of urine. And so back to bed, naked, and colder than before. If it were night, she could lie awake, staring into the pitiless dark, wondering. As it is, she drinks some vodka. "Good booze," she says. "A crisp yet velvety sensation that speaks of the good life. Tomorrow I'll get straight." The phone rings. It's that goddamned May again. Yet again.

All the remarks here attributed to April are "translations" of what she actually said. Her exact words, here in her rustic bedroom, and bathroom, in order of utterance, are: "Much flow some grapes, dull wife"; "Moon, car, beau: wild sex-mate"; "Wazoo flurry!"; "Blues are woe, why sin I? I plow, stand, pee-pee, sigh; else grim corpse dreams, reams crank's cunt"; "Wouldst bruise?"; "Such pricks said, 'Well, well, we said dame grunts sad news—but her bush shines' "; "Moon, car, beau: wild sex-mate." It was the repetition of the last remark which led to the revelation of the true message which it concealed. After this, breaking the cipher was but a simple matter of adherence to the precept, "as it goes in, so does it come out."

The maddening itch and pain of Dick Detective's boils and pimples are driving him almost to despair. He takes his novel *Blackjack* from the shelf, and opens it at random. Who is he to fly in the face of convention? There is nothing more soothing to Dick than to read a page of the prose, the Ur-prose, which ushered in the enormously influential Parvanist (cf. L. *parvus,* L. *pavrus,* f. Gk. παῦϱος) movement. Parvanism, a "style" celebrated for its smallness of mind and the meanness so representative of its era, was, as few now admit, foreshadowed in Dick's only book. He reads:

> . . . and I've heard a few things. Which is not to say that I'm smarter than the next joe. Like when I was in the army I learned plenty.
>
> We were sitting at the bar, Howie and me. Howie works in the Jack in the Box while he's trying to get himself straightened out. He's not all as funny as he used to be but he's still Howie. The gin's settled him down some. I lean to

a little Teacher's myself.

Anyway Howie and me we're doing a little damage to the stock at Stan's when this guy comes in, a little geeky-looking clown with a fedora under his shirt, one of those shirts that has a kind of shiny look, and over his left pocket it says "Fedora." Can you beat it?

"Stan," the guy says to Claude, the bartender, "I'll have a double ball of the best you got." Stan don't come in much anymore since Gladys left him two years ago to go to air-conditioner school up to Topeka. Stan said that he told her he was goddamned sick and tired of tuna casserole for supper and she lit out. He's a big guy, Stan, but he has one of those goiters. He takes it pretty well.

Howie looks at me and he's got "Oh, hell" written all over him and the same kind of sick look as when he ate the weeds behind the AA place.

It was just like when I was back in the army, I get this real itchy feeling all over. Alice always knew when that happened, because she'd set fire to the curtains every time. She used to be some looker before she got a little fat from the Hershey bars. Alice is my wife. We been thinking of buying a laundromat . . .

"Good God! What a genius I had!" Dick remarks, looking up from the page. "The way I informed the long look with all that was in my power!" To think that this man was once "Mr. Parvanism." It is enough to make Dick cry. It is enough to encourage, in fact, a touch of *saeva indignatio* in his carbuncular breast.

In Detroit, Michigan, founded as a fort and settlement in 1701, and called Ville d'etroit by the brilliant if emotionally bankrupt Antoine de la Mothe Cadillac, incidentally the original North American forebear of Berthe Delamode, there exists one of the 12,147 taverns named Dew Drop Inn. Dick, who is not to be confused with the author of *Blackjack,* nor with the Dick who is the brother of Dipers, the latter pair twin bastard sons of a powerful and ruthless nature magnate—although his identity is not important—Dick, *this* Dick, steps off a train at the suburban station of Agapa. He gazes in mild surprise at the heavily sweating people who run by him, their "clothes" drenched, their faces red and twisted into expressions which indicate agony, orgasm, or both.

"Have you heard about what happened at the Dew Drop Inn?" one says, a Mrs. Divan of the Condom League of West Agapa. She is jogging this fine morning in order to prepare her body for the inquiring hands that may, this afternoon, get a little fresh with her. The immaculate napery and the rich yet subdued place settings are almost always the provocation for somewhat forward advances on the part of a *few* of the ladies, as we suspected all along. Dick ignores the question and takes a long swallow from a pint bottle of Dixie Belle gin, the brand originally employed in the composition of the Gin Thrill, a fabulous mixed drink whose recipe is forever lost to us, like that for pizza. "Oh, fuck off!" Mrs. Divan says over her sweaty shoulder, and Dick turns to admire her delicious buttocks. "You don't see asses like *that* on the train," he says, and wonders why.

Chances are that the reason may be rooted in the fact that the trains which Dick takes are decidedly lacking in napery—immaculate or otherwise—as well as in place settings. In fact, the food served aboard such trains is fit only for someone like Oaky Doaks, who is currently reduced to playing clowns at shopping malls and fast-food restaurants. "A hell of a comedown in the world," Doaks admits from a shopping mall outside Agapa. "But I always let a smile be my umbrella, as the ruttish Zuleika Dobson might say. Or does she say, 'I'll think about it tomorrow'? Or is it 'Ball me, Ishmael!'? Or, perhaps, 'The diary, the diary'?"

"*Zuleika Dobson,* once an actual person, is Sir Max Beerbohm's only novel," Dr. Plot offers to a restive crowd. "Written while the master of authorial wit was still a student at Jesus Christ Almighty, its plot may briefly be summarized thus. . . . No, please! Don't go! Please . . .?"

ZULEIKA DOBSON

I

1. Cambridge Days ("Overture").
2. The "Rowdies' " Pre-Regatta Carousal; smutty stories of lecherous dons are recounted by the boys; puke contests; maudlin vows of friendship made.
3. Zuleika arrives to examine the famed "Water Willies" of Cambridge.
4. Buddy muses bitterly on his exclusion from the social whirl.
5. Dick Witherspoon chides Buddy; Dick's allegorical tale of the "yellowed newspaper."

6. Zuleika, depressed by the sad fountains, hikes into nearby Scone Canyon.
7. Buddy searches for and finds the old Dodge hidden in Scone Canyon; digression on the Dodge's traditional role during "Regatta Month."
8. Buddy and Zuleika meet; share cheese and bread despite class differences; "Buddy's story" recounted.
9. Zuleika tells a horrified Buddy "the Girdle Story."

II

10. The "Rowdies" overhear Knute's plan to pollute the river with glög; they continue to carouse heedlessly.
11. Strange deaths of the Dolly Sisters; history of the "good-time trio" recounted in a letter found by Dick.
12. Zuleika meets the mysterious Lutheran, Knute, and falls in love.
13. Buddy throws himself into river and disappears; digression on the dangers of the river; its victims' fates recalled; disquisition on the water's potability, piscine inhabitants; enumeration of submarine autoerotic acts from the reign of Alfred the Swollen to the present, etc., etc.
14. Dick discovers pollution plan; troubled, he weeps; hurries to Buddy's rooms.
15. Old Dodge decays; "yellowed newspaper" clipping blows into nearby furze.
16. Dick searches frantically for Buddy; finds Zuleika packing her trousseau while whistling "I Love a Big-boned Viking."
17. Zuleika ignores Dick's pleas; refuses to tell him "the Girdle Story"; dubs him "nosy shithead."
18. The "Rowdies" find "yellowed newspaper" clipping; tell Dick of Knute's true identity therein revealed.
19. Dick swears vengeance; whittles furiously; he and the "Rowdies" recall Knute's older brother, Lars "the besmirched."

III

20. Zuleika marries Knute; finds his diary on honeymoon; pales at secret, depraved ideas expressed therein.
21. After a night of unpleasant surprises, Zuleika drowns herself; is found wearing seven layers of clothing and makeshift chastity belt fashioned from old copies of *Kirkus Reviews*.
22. Dick finds Knute's unposted letter to Lars; suspects the ugly truth.
23. Knute is confronted by Dick; denies all heatedly; surrenders moleskins.
24. Buddy attends Zuleika's funeral; accidentally spies the guilt-stricken Knute in "Chevrolet owner's" disguise.

25. Buddy and Dick turn the craven Knute over to the Constable; the University grudgingly cancels the Regatta.
26. Buddy tells the story of his drowning ruse to admiring coeds in shorts.
27. Buddy leaves for Mystery Mountain and the sad peace of solitude.
28. The "Rowdies," sober at last, marvel at Knute's infamy and Zuleika's bold fashion statement.
29. The mystery explained; Knute's diary made public; strong men sicken; women vow eternal chastity.
30. Cambridge Nights ("Coda").

Corrections of Earlier Errors

Item: Dolores, who took part in at least two orgies, or "wild parties," as she now calls them, the particulars of which are not pertinent, is not the same Dolores who was one of April's friends. The latter Dolores may still be one of April's friends, but since, as we know, April spends most of her time in bed, the chances are excellent that they don't see each other anymore. Or perhaps they do. It is difficult for us to keep track of so many people. Very few of them keep in touch.

Item: Donatien Alphonse François, the "Divine" Marquis, later Comte, is not to be credited with the authorship of the novel *Le Bousingot,* definitely by Théophile Dondey, contrary to the somewhat persuasive arguments of Jean-Claude Rififi, Curzio Toffenetti, and Gil Roulure.

Item: Don Juan, by George Gordon, Lord Byron, is *correctly* pronounced, despite the "confirmation" of years of usage, and the agreement—one might say the collusion—of scholars, as its author pronounced it, Dawn Jee-WAYN, and not Don JOO-un.

Item: The "Jimmy Dorsey" heretofore mentioned in passing is not the famous bandleader (brother of Tommy), whose best recording is probably "Long John Silver." Selected lyrics follow:

> John Silver,
> Long John Silver;
> John Silver,
> Long John Silver.

The "Jimmy Dorsey" who plays a small role in this place and on this day is the grocery-bagger at the A & P, the one who "looks blank."

"Grocery-bagging" is often considered a menial, dead-end job, but the incidence of job fatalities in this position for 1985, the last year for which such records are available, was one in 11,002,593. It may therefore be argued that "Jimmy Dorsey" has a better chance at a long life than did Long John Silver, who had, as the phrase goes, 'is bleedin' neck stretched.

An epiphany from *Treasure Island:*
"Har, har, Jim! Har, har, har!" Long John Silver croaked, vigorously bashing his peg leg against the mizzen-poop gunwales. "Belay me if I'm not sorrprised as a barkenteen caught in a sudden yar! The apple barrel, ye say? Har, har, har!"

"In *Doubles Cross,* by April and Richard Detective, with additional material by Karen Cornfield, Keats is mentioned more than once in what seem to be meaningless and even self-indulgent digressions." The lewd Flo Dowell is speaking, reclined voluptuously on a tiger skin. She is trying, yet again, to teach her current lover something of the fascination of literary theory and research. He is unresponsive, and wondering why she is called "lewd," since you can't prove it by him. "These digressions, however, are the key, or, if you will, the keys to the entire work, much as the descriptions of weather in Cornwall hold the true meaning of *Dracula*—I speak, of course, of Bram Stoker's famous novel, not the short story by Theodore Dreiser. But of course you know this." The lover, still unresponsive, waits for a few tried-and-true sentences to arrive and get him out of this. Suggestions:

1. He doesn't want this forced intimacy, despite Flo's good intentions.

2. He knows that she means well, and feels a sudden rush of sympathy for her.

3. He rises and walks toward the door.

4. He opens the door, and as the light floods over his wasted face, he hears Flo's voice falter, then cease.

5. He suddenly feels old, yet realizes that he feels old as if for the first time.

All the original members of the old band Dress Rite die within the

space of an hour. This is truly amazing. It's almost well-nigh unbelievable. Who ever said that truth is stranger than fiction? Or was it
"stronger"?

That was some shitty band, by the way.

Diane Drought, known to her neighbors as "Hickey," for disputed
reasons, is waiting for her daughter to drop her grandchild off for the
day. Diane doesn't know that this grandchild is not the daughter of her
daughter's legal husband, but that of a lover who, at this moment, is
dying. And no wonder, since he is the ex-bassist of the long-defunct
band, Dress Rite. Diane's daughter, in her turn, doesn't know that she is
not the daughter of the late Mr. Drought, but is the illegitimate offspring
of a certain Bob Doran, whose name is the same as that of a character in
Dubliners. Life seems to become ever stranger, even though one buys
riding clothes and waits patiently in hospitals for what seems *forever.*

Bob Doran also appears in *Ulysses,* if you're interested.

Fine.

The doorbell rings! In they come! They have a little conversation,
e.g., "—— —— —— —, ——." "—. ——, —— ——?" "——,
——, — ——." "—— —— — —— - ——. . . ." Etc., etc. Things are
going along, going along. But why does Diane's daughter wear knotted
about her neck a pair of ice-blue panties? Odd things tend to happen on
Rensselaer Street.

While Miss Dubuque, humming to herself in her cheery kitchen, puts
up enough mastiachi peppers to last through the long winter, since her
"boyfriend" is a stickler, a small tragedy is unfolding at Rudy's
Superette. Rudy, tired and irritated because of an argument with his
artistically minded brother, is preventing the young Duey, one of
Blast's "pals," from examining the labels on the varied yogurts carried
by the market.

"Look, kid," Rudy bellows, "this market fairly bustles! Out! *Out!*"

On her way to Coney Island in a car of what is no longer the Sea Beach
Express, but is now revoltingly called the "N" line, a decidedly familiar-
looking woman of about fifty opens her bag and takes out a letter,
creased and worn soft from dozens of readings. She is not dressed for

Coney Island but wears a black suit which, though flattering, is somewhat too tight and decidedly unfashionable. She opens the letter, which proves to be from an anonymous correspondent who is, the woman is virtually certain, a high-school career advisor, Margaret McNamara Duffy, now deceased. It is an erotic, not to say obscene letter, offensive to all but the most degraded community standards. It is included here for the sake of what is usually considered the "record," but can easily be skipped or crossed out by those who fear for the purity of their souls.

Dear Velvet Pie,

You don't know me, my slickertwaddy, but I feel I know you from things that people have told me about you, and things that I've read. We also met at a party once, but I can't tell you when or where. I know that you are gorgeous!

I wish I had a picture of you naked with your beautiful nummo completely exposed. I would kiss it and lick it and play with my bim-bim until I fainted dead away with maddened pleasure.

I'd love to have you here right now with me so I could put my tongue into your crunge and bite your gozos, and then I'd beg you to get on your hands and knees and I'd wamble you from behind, then huche your swickie and your shy little waz too! God I'm wet! And my coonze is itching, is yours?

I know that you like men, but I know that if I had the chance to fondle and mouth your piz, I'm certain that you'd consider "changing your luck," as they say. I wish I could tell you my name but in the town I live I'd be hounded to death by the Methodists and Lutherans who run things, especially considering the sensitive job I have on the Purity Vigilance Committee.

In the meantime, I only hope and pray that this "mash" note makes you at least once in a blue moon fondle and stroke and finger your scump with your intoxicating thones spread wide open, and think about this letter and the "unknown adorer" while you're *doing* it.

Oh, I have to go and miche myself, I'm just *drenched.*

A Secret, Burning Admirer

"Buzz" Duncan, whose intimates lovingly call him "Buns," no longer content to be a mere humorist, yet not quite fully realized in his new profession of saying important things, is brought up short as he sees a delightfully attractive man, his face a study in concentrated frustration, leaning awkwardly against a frozen-food case. Although his body is uncomfortably twisted into an unnatural position, the man cannot conceal the scandalous bulge which distends the crotch area of his trousers.

Several women regard him with intense interest as they pass, and one, thoroughly fascinated, drops a stack of Durango TexMex Frozen Chimichangas on the head of a young fellow who, crouching, appears to be examining a shelfful of canned soup. "Buzz" takes a playful step toward the distraught man, who now gazes up at the ceiling imploringly. The thud of two bodies colliding on the street is heard throughout the market. It is almost as if Durga, the Destroyer, the Serene, the Ineffable, the Thunderbolt, is exerting this day her malevolent will against all who strike her as unworthy. This may indeed be the case, for, as we know, one of her many manifestations is as the Albanian Lard Goddess, in whose form she is called Crusher of Cities, Scourge of Suburbs. And now, perhaps too late, we realize that she is also the young woman who appears, ecstatic, in the photograph which sullies the cover of *Anal Fancies.*

"I don't care what they say," Dwight grumbles. "I'm *going* with Allen and Chet to Connecticut! Just because I spit little bits of licorice on people when I laugh doesn't give them the right to exclude me."

Another waiter listens sympathetically, his thumb partially immersed in a plate of the *soup du jour.* He doesn't particularly want this forced intimacy.

"Everybody has faults," Dwight says, gazing distrustfully at the vat of succotash on the gas range. "I saw a documentary on TV about Thomas Edison—Edison!—and it said he used to whack off whenever one of his perplexing experiments failed. *Edison.* Those stories about the apple pie and milk are a lot of crap."

The other waiter knows that Dwight means well, and he nods appreciatively.

"They told me to go see the Eiffel Tower. I don't want to go see the Eiffel Tower. No damn reason in the world why *I* can't enjoy the way the sun lightly touches the gorse leaves with gold and ruddies up the timothy. Is there?"

The other waiter thoughtfully licks his soupy thumb, thinking of happier times, especially that one particular happier time, and sticks it back into the soup. It looks as if this shift is going to pack a riveting wallop.

Eligor, the Lustful, Eligor, the Concupiscent, Eligor, the Seductive. It is he who exerts his uncanny powers upon certain events of this otherwise quite ordinary day, turning and twisting them to suit his caprice, so that all seems somewhat out of kilter, so that what is clear is muddled, so that candor becomes a synonym for desuetude. The works of T.S. Eliot are silently removed from the trusted anthologies used in literature courses, and the renowned poet scandalously presented to all as a *femme entretenue.* Elmhurst is mocked, badgered, and finally brutalized into submission. Chalmers Endicott-Braxton, affectionately dubbed "Paleface" or "Polefast," is made to crawl, half naked, at the feet of "Queen" Endiva, who exposes herself to him while she reads aloud from pamphlets on holistic medicine, the meaning of rock and roll, the benefits of whole-grain aerobics, and the delightful climate of California. An Englishman of no small repute in the savage yet compelling world of textile factoring leaps upon an Englishwoman, the mother of two fine sons at good schools, and, despite her obvious pique, ruthlessly violates her tweeds. They do, however, share an English Oval afterward, when he gallantly suggests that men will be men. *Envelopes* closes immediately, the actors able neither to remember their lines nor to recognize each other. *Environments,* the new magazine devoted to, among other interests, the whys and wherefores of composting privies as viable alternatives to death, disappears from the newsstands, and Eppie, locked in the cellar of the Crown SuperMart, where he has hidden in order to try on his "Cute Cop" outfit, is abandoned by Eros, and instantly develops a rash from the synthetic material used to make the costume's gunbelt. Other things are also done by Eligor, many of which may be recorded in their proper places. For now, suffice it to say that our quest for truth, our search for understanding, and our quest for truth, as well as our quest for truth, may be seriously compromised. May have *already* been seriously compromised.

You mean, for instance, all that business about Banana Amaze may be . . . ?

Precisely. The hand of Eligor. And other things. The problem being, of course, that we don't know *which* things. For instance, we know that an Eskimo Pie is a frozen confection, although there is doubt that it currently exists in its true form. It has probably gone the way of Moxie, Frank's Orange Nectar, and Dixie Shake.

But isn't Dick, at this very moment, more or less, about to fall down in the streets of Agapa because of the rapid ingestion of the latter? That's Dixie Belle, a cheap gin. Dixie Shake is—or was—an imitation-chocolate drink which turned the toper's mouth an arresting beige. But now that Dick has been brought up, something as unimportant and essentially gratuitous as his bout with Dixie Belle *also* shows Eligor's interference. Dixie Belle, too, is doubtless no more. Further, although we can vouch for the "whatness" of Eskimo Pie, we can have no idea who *Miss* Eskimo Pie is. Is she Karen Cornfield? Is she a *femme entretenue,* like T.S. Eliot? Or his first wife? Is she the desired subject of a Buddy Clark ballad? It would also be of value to know a little about Vince Esposito, or "Vinnie," or "Eppie," an early, unsatisfactory lover of April's, and a man forever stigmatized by Eligor as He-Who-Comes-in-His-Handkerchief.

"I am *not* Frieda Canula, mother!" Diane Drought's daughter is troubled and bewildered, and at the limits of her patience. Diane smiles sweetly at this strange Albanian.

"Some of the difficulties faced by all concerned on this too-hot day are, strangely enough, adumbrated in a brief and rather superficial exchange I recently had with my wife, Zenobia," Ethan Frome says. "You may recall her saying to me,

" 'Ethan, I get so that I think I'll go crazy with you reading all the time about Europe in those fancy books Mattie brought. As far as I can see, them Evangelists was right when they said she is a sinner with a soul black as pitch 'neath that purty face. Mercy me!'

"And my reply, 'Zeena, it's not Europe I'm reading up on, but the Everglades, the Everglades and their pure, white snowfalls.'

"So, you see, the clashes I have with Zenobia, par'lyzed as I am an' at her mercy, are much like those that you are . . . that you seem to be . . . that it may be that you think that . . . seems I lost my train o' thought."

Tabitha Bramble and Lucy Brandon, their quarrel temporarily postponed, exit from the Electra. They have just seen *Every Girl's Dream* and *If You Could Only Cook,* a pallid double feature. The Electra is an art house, owned by Baby Brownie, who opened it to do something to repay the community that gave him his chance. Right.

"George Brent has got one hell of a schlong on him," Tabitha ventures.

"And how!" Lucy agrees enthusiastically. "I'd haul his ashes for him any time."

"He's dead, I think," Tabitha notes. Lucy, chastened by this news, walks in silence by the side of her old friend. She knows that Tabitha, although sometimes abrupt, means well, and this evening, if all goes as it should, perhaps they will together gaze out their window and see a large bird, or the lights of Rudy's Superette. The large bird may even fly directly toward the lights of the bustling market. *That* would be something to record in her diary! Or, under "symbol," in her notebook!

Fagapa, a small volcanic island which is part of the Solomons group, is often confused by Karen Fairgrounds with Fanapa, the native word for a large and, to some, embarrassingly detailed herm on Mt. Cyllene; and with Fantoine, the fabulous "devil fish" of Assyrian mythology. Karen suffers from an aphasic disturbance which manifests itself in random verbal substitutions, yet this distressing malady doesn't prevent her from doing her job. In *Farfetched,* a popular study of certain types of aphasia, by William Faulkner (not his real name), a representative specimen of Miss Fairgrounds's speech is presented in a lengthy footnote to chapter 33, "Aphasic Disturbances of the Substitution Order." The specimen follows:

> "Hi! I'm Karen! I bend over so that bodies get hard when I engage sweaty parties of men. But when I'm on a streaming ogler's back, I apprise that special man of the existentialism of Abbagnano's Clouds—between the details of divorces and the spirited debates with my certain values. They're getting a 'ground' soon, and then it's quiet bye-bye to those times forever!"

Mr. Faulkner observes, "The veteran flight attendant's case is especially beguiling and puzzling in that her rare type of aphasia seems to be held in check, and indeed, for all practical purposes, *disappears completely* during the month of February. Each year, during this month, Miss Fairgrounds is lucidly communicative when she speaks of the details of her professional and personal life. Nor, most surprisingly, does she have any memory of ever having spoken otherwise."

In an apartment of the Felo-de-Se Towers, Fems, the fraternal twin brother of Blammo, the cold-cereal devotee, is attempting to seduce, by means of a display of color slides depicting the erotic sculptures of Ferozepore, the Punjab, Mrs. Feuer, who is, as the cruel phrase goes, old enough to be his mother. Fems is attempting this seduction because of persistent rumors that Mrs. Feuer is currently bestowing her considerable favors on Whitney fFrench-Newport, a brilliant if undisciplined bibliographer, and the notorious bisexual, May Fielding, "the lustful hiker." *Filter Blue,* in its current issue, provides photographic evidence of what the editor purports to be clandestine meetings between Mrs. Feuer and Mr. fFrench-Newport, and Mrs. Feuer and Miss Fielding. Photographs can be misleading, of course, and *Filter Blue'*s editor, in a note accompanying the somewhat risqué portfolio, states that he invited John Crowe Ransom, the impeccably qualified scholar, to comment on the veridicality of the pictorial evidence. The editor, in an unusually courageous display of candor, admits that his request was gently but firmly refused by Professor Ransom, whose gracious reply is given: "I would prefer to leave the documentation to those who are better qualified." But Fems believes the persistent rumors and has absolute faith in the magazine's sensational feature, and so he continues feverishly to project his slides, lingering for some moments over those which depict the frieze known as the "Rajnapur Flesh Triangle" and the astonishingly detailed bas-relief called the "Punjabi Thigh-Grasp." He fantasizes Mrs. Feuer's sudden surrender to passions which the slides have enflamed, and of, as the author of *Finnegans Wake* puts it, "making her love with his stuffstuff in the languish of flowers and feeling to find was she mushymushy." Let's wish him luck.

"Allen, I'm going to Fire Island right *now,*" Chet says, "so that bore, Dwight, won't be able to find me. Or find *us,* if you want to come."

"Sounds wonderful," Allen says. "It's funny you should think of Fire Island, I'm just reading a poem in the *New Yorker* by Mamie Morsett, listen":

> I saw the clam, alone upon the Saltaire beach,
> And thought of the wind-splashed October day
> That you and I, our hands cold-smooth as its secret hut—

"What's a 'secret hut'?" Chet asks.

"The clam's house, I guess," Allen replies. "I don't know. Where clams live, in nests or something?"

"Let's get packed," Chet says. He's had enough of this clam.

"Filthy" Yvonne Firmin is also packing, if you want to call it packing. Into her old leather suitcase she throws four pairs of shoes, not one of which can be called "serviceable" or "sensible," four Merry Widows, black, white, red, flesh, and a chocolate bunny. The mountains, lately, have been visible in her dreams. She is probably packing for the mountains, for her "gear"—save for the ever-present chocolate bunny!—is the sort recommended in the August issue of *Mountain Action* for such deserved and carefree respite from everyday concerns. The chocolate bunny has to do with a deep psychological need of Yvonne's, with something dark and vaguely menacing, rooted in her childhood, surprisingly enough. We are unaware of what it is and so Yvonne must, we fear, remain but a two-dimensional character, not one who is so convincingly etched that we feel as though we've participated in her life. So go the breaks.

It is, by the way, not at all surprising to learn, as many have, that the A & P doesn't carry *Mountain Action*. There is little call for such a publication here amid cosmopolitan environs and their attendant bric-a-brac, most of it *raffinée*.

"I prefer *Mountain Action* to almost any other magazine," Knute remarks. "It was what saved my sanity in the penitentiary."

On the other hand, the A & P does carry *Fist!*, although there is no readership for this journal either. Its features and articles have to do with what the editors are pleased to call "the main chance." For instance, in the current issue, there is a long photo-essay on the "after-hours" haircuts favored by the patrons of the newest art club, the Five of Clubs; an interview with Lorna Flambeaux, this year's winner of the Leonora Speyer Prize, conducted by her half-sister, Roberte Flambeaux, who, although not as celebrated as her famous sibling, is a poet in her own right, and does the weekly column "Trochee Trix," for *American Poets' World*, the indispensable consumer journal; and the fascinating story behind Annie Flammard's dazzling portrayal of Marcella Butler in the legendary twenty-year-old underground film soon to be released under its new title, *Days with Marcie.* "That broad is utterly devoid of a whim of grit" has, of course, become the film's most famous line, and has passed into the language, although no one is quite sure which one.

The sculptor, who is luxuriating in her unexpected false incarnation as the Lard Goddess, ventures, "I used to go into town once a month to pick up *Flikk* in the A & P—the only thing worth buying there. Then the magazine changed." She rushes about on her lawn, suddenly peevish, eyeing the Adirondack chair. "Do I need stories about ascots? Old Dodges? Starlets' knockers? Come *on!*"

"My husband reads magazines for the ads for big knockers on the girls in the back pages," the rictal woman says. "They made one of them into a movie or something with Red Butler or somebody?"

"Shop at Rudy's Superette!" Rudy pleads. "Look, I undersell those thieves at the A & P and you can rest assured I keep my arty brother in the cellar so you don't have to worry about talk about Don Byron and that kinda shit. Who needs magazines?"

"Yes, but make sure you *squat over* the toilet seats, ladies," Blast warns, "and do not *sit on* them." He displays a terrifying "before and after" photograph of Sol Blanc and Saul Blanche. "These guys once had the world in an oyster and now look at them. But shadowoi of their former selves."

Then too: Flint, "City of Promise," to Bake Three-Ton Jelly Donut; Florence Once Part of Florida, Geologist Maintains; Tamara Flynn Wins National Book Critics Circle "Great Legs" Award; *Fly of Metal Star*, Rex Focalor, Will Direct *Drowner of Men.*

After examining, however briefly and superficially, the current issue of *Fist!,* it might be well to turn to some richer fare, and take a look at a page of the scholarly essay "Food Imagery and the English Mystical Tradition: The Role of Bacoun and Eys in Medieval 'Convent Tales.' " Chancing upon the epigraph, a bit of doggerel from Chaucer's "Nun's Priest's Tale," we are made immediately aware of the interesting textual risks, such as they are. Yet of even greater interest is the curious relevance the essay proper has to "things as they might have been," all things, that is, being equal, as is, unfortunately, rarely the case. For example:

The medieval "convent tale," the labile cornerstone of the mystical tradition in English literature, or at any rate that tradition which has valorized the hypotactic strategies of the classical canon, displays, as one of its early and persistent tropes, that one called, somewhat inaccurately, the *ekphrasis.* Although this trope is still occasionally found in modern literature, most usually as a pallid and somewhat tenuous positing of the *mise en abyme,* it is to be discovered in its purest state in the currently popular board game, The Fool's Paradise. In this paper, I propose to show how the "convent tale" may, surprisingly, be elucidated by a deconstructive approach to its use of recurrent *topoi* by, so to speak, "working backward"; i.e., from the board game to the medieval genre. "Bacoun and eys," a prescriptive *topos* which occurs in virtually all the "convent tales," and which is a figure plucked almost rudely from the axis of selection in order to validate the extraordinary combinatory power of the metonymic, is the key, or primary *topos,* in the pattern of recursively enumerable recurrences. In The Fool's Paradise, the problematically designated "Penalty Cards" include one which depicts two fried eggs and three slices of bacon, and is called *Sunny Side Up;* the imagery, however unsophisticated, is remarkably clear in its bold attempt at a grammatization of a pictorial rhetoric sim— [article breaks off]

Deo gratias.

"Hi! I'm Karen Forage! When I'm sailing through the peaceful aether, however you pronounce it, my always interesting job is to attend vivaciously to eager travelers by optimistically pressing small comforts on them and pointing out fascinating topographical oddities, like, for instance, sediment-filled structural depressions between crystalline highlands. But when I'm on the rich old soil again, it's nothing, thank you, but running, sensible exercise, all-natural foods, avoidance of caffeine, and thrilling—in those special, personal ways—the young sharp-eyed exec who's just, well, *outstanding.* Hi!"

Two more demons are pressed into service in order to carry news of the general debacle to the Lightbearer, the Prince of Darkness, the Great King, He of Hollow Laughter, the Cankered Beast, the Scourge of Ministries—in short, the Boss. They are Foras, Great President of Strength, and Forneus, the Evil from the Sea. Foras has assumed the shape of Jane Parker, and his companion, whose usual manifestation is ominous enough to frighten Brooklyn rats, looks exactly like Preston Foster in his salad days.

"Lan' sakes," Foras says, toying with an eggbeater, "if you don't agree that sinkin' your teeth into one o' my scrumptious baked goods ain't better 'n makin' a Pentecostal beat his pumpkin, I'll heave you into a lake o' flamin' snot." She hasn't quite got the hang of homely lingo, yet how *tidy* Jane looks! She's wearing an Agfa apron over her pert gingham dress, or frock, and is a vision of domestic chic. Forneus says nothing, but quietly seethes. Within, of course. He feels that if he can't be a sea monster, what's the point? And just what does "news of the general debacle" mean? "Fotch," his bent, grizzled head encircled by wreaths of pipe smoke, knows who these two infernal pretenders are, but he is, unfortunately, on his merry way! He also feels that, since no one ever does anything for him, he has no obligation to apprise his fellow citizens of the possible danger that they face. Celerity is all, or so he thinks, but he has the wrong word.

The "newest art club" mentioned earlier is not the Five of Clubs, but the Four of Clubs. We wish to thank Miner X. Beely for calling this matter to our attention. Mr. Beely, taking a moment or two out from his relentless and exhausting labors, writes that he caught the mistake because of his professional interest in "Fourth of July-like symbolic pyrotechnics" and "great shale bluffs." Thanks again, Miner X. Beely, a million.

At the bar of the Foxhead Inn, Chief Blue Wind is bitterly complaining that the firewater is not only diluted but that it costs heap much wampum. The other patrons barely notice his grumblings, since they are horseplayers, and most of them have just dropped a package on Fox's U-Bet, a quick little three-year-old chestnut that should have run away from the field at a tidy 7–5, but who, as turf parlance has it, is still running. The winner of the race, the seventh at Bowie, is none other than a hitherto undistinguished nag who usually fades badly in the stretch, Banana Amaze.

"The son of a bitch paid 133.40!"

General weeping and fearsome maledictions. Threats against the well-being of both horses. Howls. God is given the figs.

"I at least shoulda put a pound on him to show!" And so on.

"I did not notice one fucking Appaloosa, Pinto, Paiute, Reno, Paint, Cayuse, or Ziti in the race," Blue Wind says. "Nothing but your pale-face horses, not an American among them." But it is as if the Chief is not there. He'd probably be better off at Fragonard, a dark, quiet "lounge" in which the patrons discuss the subtler ramifications of applied skewbald. In, of course, the light of recent French developments.

"What the goddam hell is this glass beads for change?" Blue Wind asks.

In François of Fargo's, a small soup-and-salad restaurant made famous by its mention in the socko-wallop *Accidental Bodies,* the Frankenstein girls, two minxes who, though no longer abloom, are as scandalous as they used to be when they made jabbering idiots of leaders of industry, powerful political figures, religious pundits, and other depraved solons, are enjoying a light brunch of croutons and beansprouts with Fred, a doddering, retired reinsurance clerk, who is being led on by their subtle hints of frenzied and degrading lubriciousness to come. Little if any decency is being shown, and no wonder! For the girls have, over the years, but *added* to their collection of curious implements. Fred, on his part, is oblivious to memories of his seasoned rubber stamps, his collection of maxims, e.g., "Crime is the hole of the world"; "To the sewer, all things are sewers"; "Wisdom comes to no one in pants," etc., and his treasured letter of December 27, 1963. All that Fred, in his rapidly increasing pullulation, can think about are the *les femmes* on either side of him and the pressure of their warm *les cuisses* against his.

"I understand that you're interested in enlightened and serious fiction in foreign languages," one of the girls says, letting her tongue loll out of her mouth on the first syllable of the last word.

"Yes," Fred gasps. "And in my retirement I'm pursuing a study of the shadowy Baylor Freeq. That is, who is he? Or, who was he, and is he still? I'm afraid I'm not making myself clear." The other Frankenstein girl lets her hand fall, as if accidentally, on his *ramazza.*

"Isn't he a French-Canadian?" she asks, widening her eyes expertly. Fred is silent, all his energies directed toward the act of breathing.

"No," the other girl whispers. "He married a Frenchwoman, somebody who took photographs, I think. Would you like to take some photographs—of *us*—Mister Clerk?"

"Mister Fred," Fred croaks. "Call me Mister Fred. What kind of photographs?"

The girls' crystalline laughter is informed by a delightful sweetness. Fred is acutely aware that his shako is bulging.

Cox, *White Bridges* safely under his oxter, moves down the street in restless search of clams, but is tempted by yet another dynamic old bookshop. On a bargain table he spies *Fretwork,* a forgotten volume of poems. Forgotten, even though a statement by a respected critic, now dead, graces the jacket: "Not only is *Fretwork* a remarkable display of the gritty poetry which one actively awaits in these sad times, it is a collection of intensely personal rhythms." Cox opens the book to check the truth of this statement:

> Great explorer of the dark and dread of mind,
> Humbled in kinship with drear lunacy,
> O Freud! When Phoebus' cart each Friday disappears
> And Moses' Sabbath winds you in strict nostalgia,
> Do you then think of—

He stops. Even Cox has his limits. He neglects to look at the author's name, since it isn't his business. We've been led to believe that certain interested parties know who the author is, but there may be many books entitled *Fretwork.* This is possible since book titles are not, being insufficiently creative, copyrightable. More troubles!

The denizens of "the City" coincidentally feel that "Frisco" is not sufficiently creative as a short version of or nickname for their beloved urbs. Many think that it is uncomfortably close to "Crisco," which, wags argue, is what "the City" often looks like in sunlight, as it lies whitely gleaming against the blue of the Pacific.

One had thought it looked more like "a bunch of cupcakes."

An interesting description, and one decidedly removed from "Crisco." Or "Frisco." We definitely need a less cumbersome name than that with which it is freighted. Something clear and simple, yet redolent of the free and easy nature of the place. Like "Pork and Beans," for instance.

General agreement. Shouts of "Down with Rupert Brooke!" and "Hand me my old autoharp!" Rustlings. Hard falls. Vigils for things in general. Someone begins "The Girdle Story," eyes frantically signaling the collision with prose like a house on fire. What a town!

In *From Natchez to Mobile,* Dolores Délire has pertinent things to say to the actor—someone who was once called "the right answer to George Brent"—who plays the hoary poet Robert Frost. The scene takes place with the principals over steaming earthenware bowls of bavette de boeuf sauce chasseur, and in it, la Délire, playing the racy Parisienne, Mlle Froufrou, opens her *la chemise de nuit,* exposes her generous and shapely *sequins,* and peremptorily enacts a *tableau vivant* rooted in a detail from the faux-Fauve painting *Fruits and Dross.* It is widely agreed that this scene is a landmark in postwar cinema. Frost, his white "mane" streaming in the "wind," returns to his garret, kills his hired man, and in an orgy of sublimation, composes "Birch My Apples!" The film is now rarely screened, since Fugazy's owns all rights and the directors of the comestibles giant are loath to display foods which, so company attorneys say, are "inimical to our client's traditional menu." Such piddling legalisms and censorious pettifoggery are worthy of the ordinary machinations of Xavier Furcas, a cruel old man, and Whitney Furfur, a much-married earl. Indeed, this pair may well be involved in the wretched enterprise Artistic Suppression. It is in such instances, too, that one almost automatically looks for the hand of Gaap, He Who Makes Insensible, He Who Digs Chicks. It's a good bet that he is entranced by Dolores Délire, even more desirable now that she has the stamp of experience upon her.

"With a quart of Gallo Burgundy in me, do I care if she's fifty-nine?" Gaap smirks. "Though Dolores is but a two-dimensional celluloid icon of postadolescent masculine dreams of domination, penetration, and illicit adventure, this symbol of sexual dread and the ambiguity it confers upon the 'copulative gavotte' is preferable to a sharp stick up your nose."

Gaap delivers this last phrase with a perfectly straight "face." So it may be seen to what lengths Gaap will go in order to carry out his program.

What program?

Something about a general debacle.

Despite having been trapped in Gallup for many years, where he felt constrained to instruct the rustics in the lore of the Cult of Gamygyn, to wit, "post few bills," Dexter Gapoine finds, upon his return home, that things in the little village of Misty Crag are about the same as they were during his formative years there, when he larked about with lynx and tambourine, hey nonny-nonny-no! The short-skirted waitresses, "slaves to fashion," as they are called in Stan's Tavern by the out-of-work, almost-but-not-quite-defeated customers, still gambol on the outdoor terrace of the venison hangout, The Garden of Earthly Delights, and the gossip, as always, is about the little town's favorite son, Craig Garf, who went to the big dazzling city and wrote a play, or so it seems. Craig still lives amid the ceaseless pistonings of the thunderous dynamo wherein restless lives beat ever faster, or so runs the good-natured chit-chat. "Well, that's art for you," Albert "Hap" Garrett remarks to Dexter, as they gaze past a vista of redundant brambles to the hulking mountains brooding in the east. Or south, depending on the direction in which "the buddies" face. "Hap" is a lighthearted bozo, and because of his uncanny resemblance to the town's demented lighthouse keeper, now retired, who harmlessly if obscenely signals to the café's notorious waitresses, is called, on those festive occasions when spirits soar with the mill's afternoon whistle, "Paco" or, sometimes, "Allie." "Hap," not surprisingly, has a continuing interest in the arts, as witness his carefully selected comment. Yet Berta Garrett, his once-beauteous wife, a glowing spitfire of a peppery woman, neither hears him nor notices the leer with which he appraises the stunning blond who just now stumbles on high heels toward the trio of old friends lounging at the edge of town. Berta is struggling nowadays with an encroaching quiescence not unlike embarrassing jock itch.

"Hi!" the stunning blond says. "I'm Karen Gash! Although I no longer cut the fine figure I once did when ambling down the aisles of mighty jetliners in which I earned an honest salary amid the cumulus, now I'm back on the confused streets of divers favorite metropolitan centers, and I cut a rather remarkable figure when I *thereon* amble. That's why I seem, despite steady losses, to élan so nicely!"

Brambles approach her outstanding legs hesitantly, then fall back into their characteristic stupor before flattening themselves against the far horizon. The three friends are not aware that Karen knows that Barry Gatto is Baylor Freeq's real name, and that he still tunes pianos. Annie Flammard knows, of course. And she has the photographs to prove it! So it is clear that Fred, insofar as his research is concerned, would be better off here than in François of Fargo's, where he is, even now, saying to the Frankenstein girls, "I fear that I tend to ridicule everything with what amounts, I suppose, to precious condescension. Can you forgive me?" The girls think that he is, as they might put it, a scream. "Open your fly, you old geezer," they giggle in unison bold. They have attractive smiles and are, on closer inspection, seen to be quite tidy. Meanwhile, the four pastoral figures stand glumly transfixed before the thought of the café's menu. For it is August, the deer-bloat season.

Looking up at last, after hours of dazed reading, from the worn and foxed copy of *Géométrie descriptive* on his desk, George, who for years made a decent if precarious living as an orgy photographer, realizes that nothing, absolutely nothing of the classic text has been absorbed by his reluctant brain. We should here note that Arthur Rimbaud, disgusted with Jack Armstrong's venture into letters, a short story which takes place in a bowling alley, is now wandering about, not exactly sure of where he is. The poet quickly realizes that George is reading a book dear to his heart, and a tear comes to his *l'oeil* as he remembers the letter to his family in which he wrote, "Envoyez-moi *Les Constructions métalliques,*" a companion volume by the same author. Filled with disdain at George's obviously desultory studies, he says aloud, "Ce peuple est inspiré par la fièvre et le cancer." George looks up but sees nothing, of course. Then he looks out the window at the abandoned Chevrolet which makes this ugly street into a "bulwark of perfection." He hears Georgene's key in the door and turns back to his book, a practiced look of expectant curiosity and unabated delight on his face.

"Whoosh!" Georgene exclaims, putting a bag of groceries down somewhere, perhaps on a table, chair, or counter. Or a credenza. "I'll tell you one thing, Georgie, it's too damn hot to wear this old fuchsia suit! And it's out of style and too *tight.* I got a lot of clearly insulting looks over at Rudy's, as well as some compassionate glances."

"Well, *I* like how your attractive gozos are thrown into—how shall I say?—*relief* by that suit," George smiles. "Shit on the people at Rudy's, they don't pay the bills, dear."

"With all due respect, darling," Georgene says, throwing herself into a chair in an unladylike manner, the better to gaze distractedly at the Chevrolet, "neither do you. My mother is beginning to refer to you as George the Polack III, after the blind cripple who used to sing for loose change in the good old days of her lamentable youth."

"Ha! Ha!" George laughs, slapping the rude wooden table with his calloused palm. "That's darned good!" Yet there is a fleeting but perceptible imago of resentment beneath the bonhomie on his ruined mask of a face. "Your mother always reminds me of my old partner, Georgette. Do you remember her?"

"The one who did the original watercolors for that children's book. I *knew* you'd bring her up. You never miss an opportunity to annoy me, do you? First it's the old suits so that everybody can see my *jayumbos,* now it's that bitch!"

"No!" George laughs again, and rather heartily. "Not *that* Georgette, the *other* Georgette."

"What 'other' Georgette?" Georgene asks. Her face is a mask of barely repressed insouciance gone wild.

"Oh, bosh!" George replies. "I'm really not up to this conversation *again,* sweetheart." He smiles, his teeth falsely lambent in the sudden gloom.

A strained silence fills the little apartment, broken only by the soft ticking of the clock, which has, yet again, appeared. A few far-off shouts in the street, also, are heard. Georgene wonders if she should tell George about Getting the Most out of Your Leotard, a really great course that she's begun at the Y. But with his fixed ideas on fuchsia, lavender, pink, and dusty rose so recently in the troubled foreground of their marriage, she decides to put it off until a better time.

"How's the book?" she says at last, flagrantly kicking off her "things." "Compelling? Or merely fashionably obscurantist?"

"I know, darling, that you really *mean* well," George says, "and I do feel a certain sympathy for you. But despite your good intentions, I don't want this kind of forced intimacy."

"Have it your way," Georgene says, rising so as to give George a tantalizing look at her nummo. At the door, she pauses and turns, in time-honored fashion. "By the way, I ran into *Gig* today. He said to give you his *best regards.*"

Her silvery laughter grows, as it must, progressively fainter as she proceeds down the hallway, since she does not raise the volume of her laughter the farther she gets from the door. We speak, of course, of her laughter in regard to George's position, which, for the duration of her departure, remains fixed. His face a rigid domino of ill-concealed ire, George begins to tear the pages from *Géométrie descriptive.* "Frogs and math—what a combination," he mutters. Then, unable to control his rage any longer, he rushes to the bathroom, where Georgene is, perhaps, freshening up.

"So you saw Gig!" George shouts through the door. "So? What did he say? What *does* he think of my schlong?" He listens to the sound of, probably, water running into the tub, and then, her voice heavy with recrimination, Georgene says, "He said he thinks it can be amusing and even funny in a waggish way."

George reacts as if, as they say, struck. As if in the face. He is as if rooted to the spot. So much for this afternoon's trip to Gimbels. And the guys in Dress Rite are all dead!

Gin City, a sculpture which is now usually attributed to Annie Flammard, has a history of ownership the details of which have to do with the curse of glossolalia. At present, Annie is smoking the last of a pack of Gitanes, a morale-booster designed to strengthen her for her look into the envelope where she keeps her cash. There is no cash, and Annie knows this. She seems rather distracted and a little dowdy, the result, perhaps, of life, coupled with the unwanted biweekly visits of a clubfooted man whose wheezing outside her door is always followed by his demand—never acceded to—that she tell him the secret of the "yellowed newspaper." Annie unfailingly sits in silence, and waits for him to go away. She knows nothing of Maureen Cullinan's "athletic tricks," either, another of her visitor's subjects of inquiry. After a time, the clump and swish of the desperate man's unspeakable foot moves away down the hall, and she relaxes, but awaits his inevitable parting sally: "A sense of humor, for Christ's sake, is no bar to advancement, you unfriendly bitch!" On this particular morning, the gimp is almost banjaxed in the street by the rushing figure of Glasyalabolas, the Murderer, summoned by the Lard Goddess to punish the woman who currently impersonates her. Glasyalabolas, who has no sense of direction, soon finds himself not in Agapa, but in a neighboring town, Gnatville. He promptly joins a barbecue-in-progress.

"... badly burned *chicken* for God's sake ... Stekel and *whose* boots? ... and only vegetables you say ... charming old jalopy ... could eat you in that white dress ... needs refueling ... perverted rock stars' what? ... in the *fucking* chicken coop yes ... then the refurbished pillow ... Oaky Doaks? ... a *frisson* of icy terror ..."

Glasyalabolas soon determines that the counterfeit Lard Goddess is not located in this burg, but decides to linger. A young woman, who introduces herself as what his demonic ears take to be "Saybuddy," is wearing a short, tight, crocheted dress which, as Viña Delmar might say, leaves little to the imagination. The striking young woman is going on about a wonderful club, really hip, really fun, called the Gold Coast Bar and Grill. "Kind of a boîte," she says, getting very close to the infernal visitor, who can't help but wonder what she'd do if she were to see him as the winged dog whose form he usually favors. "What do you say we go tonight?" she smiles, coquettishly waving an incredibly charred chicken leg at him. Well, as coquettishly as possible, considering. Glasyalabolas, who is slightly deficient in the art of small talk, and ignorant of flirtation, replies, "I teach all arts and sciences simultaneously, incite to bloodshed, am the leader of all homicides, discern past and future, and make men invisible." He beams, more or less, at her, and she is a little surprised at the size of his canine teeth. "You are really a cute guy," she titters while mincing. Then she lowers her eyes, raises them, and licks her lips. Glasyalabolas, unable to interpret these signs in a civilized manner, frees a monstrous red phallus from the constraint of his seersucker trousers, and at the same time reaches a hand, on which the wiry hairs are crackling with blue fire, toward the young woman. So much for this jovial gathering.

The Gold Coast Bar and Grill is a joint on the Brooklyn waterfront. Once frequented by stevedores, longshoremen, and merchant sailors, it is now a chic watering place for people with little time and too much money, a murderous combination. They delight in the atmosphere, rigorously preserved, and the nightly entertainment, always of minimal talent. The patrons think of this entertainment as camp, and are thus ennobled in their lives. It doesn't take much. The current entertainment comprises two acts: the Gold Dust Twins, who bear an uncanny resemblance to Barry Gatto and Annie Flammard; and their "opener," a skinny, middle-aged woman, her face leathery from the sun, in a fifties-style puce cocktail dress. The Gold Dust Twins specialize in dramatic readings from little-known plays, and at present are offering scenes from *'Tis Ruth the Whore's Dead,* by Thomas Ballantyne. To give you an idea:

CAZZO (*discovered alone*):

> Now dread varlets hold the welkin dear,
> Wherein doth, marry, phials incarnadine
> Fume so that a king may felter'd be;
> Yet all the glories of that drear assemblage
> Lack physick and the puling of a maid
> Whose mincing mows pricketh th' ebon Saracen!
> Meet that, an't be a shining poniard
> Pluck'd from the massy comet that dread Jupiter,
> Blanch'd ere he wrapp'd his corse in finest lawn,
> Shall grin the bony skull whence fled the fiend.
> But soft! Keep venoms sealed up tight,
> 'Twas ne'er a lady pecked at asp so bright.

PUTTANA (*entering*):

> Yet methinks sweet Cazzo in his license
> Vents our news of most strange things, that, seconded,
> 'Twill be brutish to th' extreme of unguento.
> Still, his ducket and this blizzardy wet look
> Belike unto an apeish picture out o' wax
> Do crown the common bawds and ruffianos.
>   (*To* CAZZO):
> How now, my lord? Doth blood run pure as babes
> In the painted honours of dissembling coins?
> Or doth my breast, blue as the spicy carbuncle
> That prov'd a pomegranate of worse favour
> Drop, as it must, thou know'st, unto chill sooth?

My soul, as the curious lizard of far jousts,
Blinds my womanish nature like the frighted whelp,
And speeds me to a doom of mummery.
　　(*Dies.*)

Miss Golden Delicious, the aforementioned opener, warms up the customers by showing slides of the Golden Gate Bridge, Construction of; Repairs to; Renovations undertaken of; Calculations concerning; Romance of; Legends about; Suicides off; Moods of; etc., etc. These arresting photographs, many *in full color,* are accompanied by Miss Delicious's enthusiastic, if unlearned commentary. Nevertheless, in the last few months, surprise raids on the boîte have been carried out by the more radical members of the Golden Rose Fellowship, the action wing of the Immaculata Syndicate, a group dedicated to the eradication of public and private restrooms. The organization feels, as its literature indicates, that the restroom is an "area in which men and women" alike "loosen, open, and dishevel" their various "garments" and in the process "expose" themselves, this "activity leading to sin or thoughts of sin." The "Goldie" chant, chilling to many, is well-known throughout the city, and illustrated copies of its verses are currently on view at the Gom Gallery in its controversial "Corners of the City" exhibition. One chorus, especially, has caught the public's fancy:

Chorus:　Oh Jesus sweet and fine,
　　　　　Oh Jesus strong and pure,
　　　　　Oh Jesus so sublime,
　　　　　Oh Jesus will you cure
　　　　　　These sinners who should burn in hell?

Response:　Sure!

It may be obvious that the city is no longer the one that Zuleika Dobson tells us of in *The Goiter Story,* lines 116-72, despite its electric atmosphere, vital people, and numerous interesting activities, many free of charge. Still, no one, as thousands regularly point out (indicates gesturing crowds), can "know its heart."

Lincoln Gom, whose hair has turned to silver, yet they love him just the same, admires his pictures as he does whenever he has a moment. He can almost hear them appreciating before his eyes, or ears, and both organs, though not as gosh-darn attractive as they once were, are still sharp. He is especially delighted with himself today because a piece in the newspaper on the "downtown art scene," which you've all read before, has a flattering reference to him as a "shrewd connoisseur" in the "ecology of the thriving new art world." Odd how ecology, in all of its vainglorious manifestations, has always been a big part of Lincoln's life. He's elegantly dressed today, for "lounging." He takes another survey of his pictures, which he calls "holdings," among the more valuable of which are *Connecticut Condo, Silver Mercedes, A Cool Million, Vintage Port, Fake Diner, I Want It All, Trump, Studio Apt. $3000, More Skyscrapers,* and his favorite, *Koch's Paradise.* He sighs, and makes a mental note to read more poetry like the one about killing men rather than hawks. Hawks! He used to read a good deal of poetry until, well. There's something wonderful about how it makes order out of chaos, kind of like real-estate deals, and he needs a little order in his frenetic life of gathering. He cannot "lounge" for *too* long, not with all the sharks in the water. Sharks!

"Babs" Gonzales, who occasionally travels under the name "Boobs" Consundays, tired of reading Mrs. Browning, who can be tiresome indeed in her amazed mode, "marches" into The Good Company to return her "Cute Cop" outfit, piqued because "Muffin" is currently featured as the model for this costume in the latest issue of *Cults and Coteries.* Of all people, "Muffin"! She must be forty-five if she's a day, the bitch, and she's running to Anglo wrinkles.

So much for sisterhood.

"I don't much like these holster," she says to the man behind the counter. He is a *bored salesclerk.*

A little verisimilitude to truly depict life in our time so that it's as if we're living it ourselves instead of other people pretending to live it for us but in such a way that it is not quite believable.

Check.

"In what way don't you like these holster?" the *bored salesclerk* says mockingly.

"It is bumping me in the wrong personal intimate place, coño,"
"Babs" says. "Makes the bruises."

"I'm afraid, Madam," he says, *yawning elaborately,* "that we can
neither take in exchange nor accept for refund any costume that has
been, uh, worn. Your best alternative would be to go to a Good Will and
donate it for a tax deduction."

"Can I change these holester maybe, only? For a peg leg?"

"I'm afraid not, Madam," the clerk says, *studying his fingernails.*
"That peg leg is part of our new Long John Silver ensemble and cannot
be sold separately."

"Babs" walks out, cursing Michael Cullinan under her breath. He's
the one who really objects to the holester! She doesn't really give a
damn about it. "Muffin" makes the costume odious, anyway. What she
needs is a double Gordon's gin, no ice, and so she enters a dim saloon,
the Gotham, and puts her shopping bag on the bar.

An epiphany from *Treasure Island:*

"Har, har, Jim!" Long John Silver laughed, his salty earring trembling as if schooner-rigged. "Keelhaul me if I don't be struck blind as
Pew! H'isted in a wicker basket, ye say? Har, har!"

The boys, exhausted by their courageous climb, sat across from each
other in the rear of the little country inn, its rough-hewn pine walls
sending forth a rich, spicy aroma of aging splinters that soothed their
spirits. The day had brought its share of agonizing worries to the hearty
chums. Taking a long swallow of his refreshing beverage, Dick Witherspoon vigorously banged his glass down on the crude wooden table, and
laughed joyously.

"Well, old man," he said to Buddy, "I 'spect we won't be reaching
Misty Crag *this* evening," he opined. "Might's well batten down here
for the night."

"I'm afraid you're correct, Dick, as is sometimes the case," Buddy
confessed, his cheeks peculiarly flushed. "And yet that priest, Father
Graham, seemed a regular sort, despite his suspicious complexion,
ruined compass, and odious religious beliefs." Buddy set his jaw with
perplexed vim.

" 'Pears he took us for a brace of yokels, Buddy," Dick nodded. "I thought for certain that we'd be hallooing on the dangerous crags long 'fore now. Maybe even scaring up some chuck food and c'lecting dead wood for the fire. I pondered something was mighty odd when the Romish galoot told us to foller that bear trail." Dick raised his schooner to his smiling lips.

"Had I but paid heed to my father's woodland tips," Buddy said softly, his eyes bright with the memory of old Mr. Buddy's plaid mackinaw, "now gathered, at last, under the title *A Grain of Salt*—and how good it is that we now have them all together—we would certainly have directed ourselves toward the sought-for crag. By means of moss-growth. And other such lore."

"Well, my friend," Dick replied, retying his colorful habanera with a flourish, "there's no use to spoiling the milk now. Let's wrestle some hot grub and bed down."

At that moment, a young lady, her dark eyes glowing with health, walked into the inn and sat, her nether limbs modestly crossed, at the long bar. Buddy and Dick, with an exhibition of youthful pluck, leaped onto their chairs and stood respectfully thereon, watching her drink a large tumbler of gin, neat.

"She must be dusty of throat," Dick remarked, "like the little pals we left behind."

"Indeed," Buddy whispered admiringly, "although she does seem too much disposed toward strong spirits, yet there is something refined about her carriage, something naturally superior in her bearing. I would not be at all surprised to learn that she occupies a position of some importance and responsibility in the business community."

"There sure isn't nothing of the dago about her," Dick commented, and then, jumping lightly to the floor, he continued. "Say, Buddy, do you remember the strapping feller who used to join us on those occasions when we held our feral clambakes?"

"Indeed I do!" Buddy replied clippedly. "Dick Grande was the lad's name, I believe. A tall boy, slightly but not unpleasantly hirsute." He quickly joined Dick on the floor, and stood, a slight smile of nostalgia on his sculptured lips. "But why do you inquire?" Buddy continued, an expression of hesitant longing rippling across his chiseled features.

"Well," Dick said, biting his lips together one at a time, "do you remember his sister?"

If Buddy remembered anything of his fifteen years on this terrestrial globe, it was the beautiful coquette, Jeannette Grande. She had, on more than one occasion, made him doubt the advice on personal hygiene given in his weathered *Handbook for Lutherans.* Beaming jovially, he bounded again onto his chair so as to gaze at the young woman at the bar.

"Well?" Dick cried anxiously. "Is she . . . ?"

But Buddy, with a cry of pure brawn, had fallen heavily from his chair into his comrade's arms, his eyes rolling nervously about. The young woman had gone, and at the place where she had been lately sitting, there lay a bulky shopping bag, and, pinned to it, a letter on daintily scalloped, lilac-hued stationery. There would be, Dick Witherspoon guessed, as he smoothly laid Buddy's insipid head on a nearby dado, no meatball sandwiches for them tonight!

Although the wind seems about to blow up, and the trees on their quiet street threaten to sough at any moment, a lady of unchaste proclivities, Edith Granger, stern in the cruel, iron-ribbed foundation garment that is "doing its job" beneath her purposeful tweeds, and her newfound friend, Lady Granjon, are putting the finishing touches on their amusing ad. Not to reveal the verbatim copy of what the ladies consider an "appeal," it may be noted that the message contains promises of mutually enlightening cross-dressing, mirror larks, Greek interludes, *tableaux vivants,* discipline *à la* the Greengage School, and stimulating episodes featuring cooking oil and Green Goddess salad dressing. "It has to be good for *something!*" Lady Granjon quietly jokes of the last. There is also a reference to a Greenwich Village masque, depending, and quite properly so, on the weather. So they continue to polish their verbiage as carefully as Mamie Morsett polishes her clam poems; perhaps more carefully, since so much more is at stake.

Then too: Richard Gross, Bart., Will Return to Prison, D.A. Says; Author Claims *Growing Dark* Basis for *Dark Victory* Screenplay; Swiss Tourist Board Admits Gstaad Does Not Exist; "The Guards" to Take Acting Classes; John Crowe Ransom "Secret Structuralist," Eloise Stephanie Gump Reveals; Russell Gunge, Inventor of Insolent Pompadour, Dead at 87; *Guns in Action* May Hire Michelle Caccatanto as Cultural Editor.

Gusion, the Duke of Those Who Discern, is sent to rescue Glas-yalabolas from the barbecue, which the ingenuous sprite, as one might have guessed, has reduced to a shambles, the exact nature of which will be discreetly passed over in silence.

"Are you crazy?" Gusion says, mucking through broken glass and Christ knows what else. "You're *supposed* to be looking for the counterfeit Lard Goddess, so that we may send storms of flies and lice, fire, and poisonous winds against her. You are *not* supposed to be wreaking havoc on these professional persons here (indicates clusters of abandoned barbecuers) strewn about. I'm going to have to put this *faux pas* in my report."

"What does 'cute' mean?" Glasyalabolas asks.

"You haven't heard one word, have you? Let us go and find Agapa," Gusion says, levitating slightly.

"All right. Say, how come you don't look like some big fido-head today?"

"*Here?*" Gusion shakes his head at such a display of naïveté.

The two slowly fly off, scattering bits of garbage and carrion, and marveling at the bodies writhing in various pleasant combinations on the emerald lawn below. Slabs and gobbets of dead animals send up thin plumes of smoke.

Eddy Beshary definitely decides to buy the lissome yet muscular Berthe a drawing by Philip Guston, if the charming maid promises to stop walloping the unfortunate tourists who sometimes surprise him amid the flowering shrubs.

"Who?" Berthe asks suspiciously.

"Never mind on it," Beshary says, hanging up rudely on a mogul. "Suffice it to proclaim that it is of a pulchritude to emboggle the mind's eye. It also promises seriously to attain monetary values sufficient to enable you the ability to purchase plethorous ruffly aprons and bewitching caps when old age shall reft your earning powers from off of you."

"So you say," Berthe replies. "I'll ask 'Guts,' the savvy bartender, about this guy before I promise to play the coward or the regular guy 'mid the blowing foliage, you'll pardon the expression."

"As you wish, my enchantress of a fellow," Beshary smiles. "Now, if you will permit me to create an excuse, I must open a deal on the telephone which waits obiediently on this cheap wicker table."

Berthe pushes wisps of silken hair under his bewitching cap. What he doesn't know is that "Guts" is about to throw up his job at the hotel bar, for he is in possession, by means of a delicate ruse, of a rare bibliophilic item, *Gusty Ghetto Tales*. This famous anthology, on which all others of its genre are modeled, is actually entitled *Gutsy Ghetto Tales*. The misprinted item, which contains the error on its spine, half-title page, part-title page, full-title page, and in the running heads throughout, is but one of a rumored seventeen in existence. In his delight, "Guts," in defiance of hotel rules, mixes himself a celebratory Banana Amaze, "the drink that made Bermuda laugh." The heretofore secret recipe follows:

Banana Amaze

1½ ozs. Gypsy Rose wine
1 oz. banana absinthe
½ oz. mastiachi pepper extract
    Shake well with cracked ice and strain into a frosted cocktail glass. Decorate with two thin rounds of ripe banana and a sprig of pink brilliantine.

"Guts" takes a sip, rolls his eyes, and grins. To the bar at large, he proclaims, "*Habits and Wimples* has nothing on this, despite its clear and complete index and exemplary notes."

Habits and Wimples?

The, ah, reference is obscure. But that's just like "Guts."

The Bluebird Inn, a small roadhouse specializing in fox-trot contests, lies just outside Hackettstown on the road to Budd Lake. It may well be the "little country inn" in which Dick and Buddy are playing yet another scene in the mundane drama of their prescribed, yet fully eustachian lives. Did they only know it, Misty Crag is but a two-hour walk from the inn. But they are confused, and Buddy is still only semiconscious. The possibility that they may not reach the somber heights today is very real. Their predicament is made even more complex by their map of the area, for it shows Hackettstown as Haddam Neck. This transmutation may be the work of Hagenti, Maker of Gold, sometimes, because of his penchant for pranks, called "the Halloween Kid," and his vicious thug of a comrade, Halpas, Burner of Cities, who likes to go by the name of "Hans," a kind of acknowledgment made to his old Nazi pals. But why they should decide to toy with the map used by Buddy and Dick is an unanswerable question. It may not even be a proper question, and, besides, Halpas does not take kindly to interrogation.

Eleanor Harding, whom the years have made no less depraved, puts her signature to a letter written to a certain Harlan, a man who is invariably described as "a train passenger." He is, coincidentally, on a train at this moment, passing through the environs of the real Haddam Neck, hoping against hope, as they say, to catch a glimpse of a startlingly attractive young woman who occasionally used to be found sitting on a flat rock in the open field which abuts the tracks. Eleanor's letter has to do with her special program of "good reading, intelligent discussion, judicious exercise, and the employment of a time-honored and infallible love philtre obtainable, at great cost, from a pepper that grows in the gardens of Greenpoint." You won't be far off the mark if you guess that Eleanor, in her middle age, is reduced to varied confidence games, and that Harlan is her latest mark. Harlan believes that some one of Eleanor's programs can bring him into friendly intercourse with the girl in the field, even though she exists only in his imagination. This Harlan, by the by, is nothing to Joanne Jeanne Judith "Bunny," since the latter's maiden name is *not* Harlan. This is old information to veteran investigators, yet it never hurts to insist on the facts. Neither does he have anything to do with Lady Harlan and Lord Harlan, the former a mysterious Frenchwoman implicated in the international scandal known as "the girdle story," and the latter an ineffectual, but sweet, bumbler. And he would be shocked, and rightly so, to be associated, even peripherally, with the Mr. Harlan who has an unspeakable affliction, which, in tandem with a mind-numbing suit, he exploits so as to be able to raise the dead, create typhoons, catch the falling stars, and make the oceans boil, and who intimidates all those with whom he comes into contact. This sinister cripple, or as he prefers to be described nowadays, this walking-impaired gentleman, is not, in fact, "Mr." Harlan at all, Harlan being his given name. As Harlan looks out the window of the train in fruitless search for the nonexistent girl, "Mr." Harlan is heard to shout ". . . advancement, you unfriendly bitch!" The train clatters past the field and Harlan returns to his book, but the back of the head belonging to the man in the seat just in front of him stops him cold. There's something about it that gives him a strange chill.

"I call this automatic writing," Florence Claire says smugly. As we know, Florence is pretty dumb. "Right!" say experts.

Anton Harley cannot believe that his ex-wife's phone is still busy, but there's the manic buzzing! He hangs up and dials again, for the seventeenth time. She's taken the phone off the hook, that's for sure, and all he wants is to arrange to pick up some things of his that he knows are in her goddamned kitchen drawer. He's entitled to them. They have certain, ah, certain *redemptive* qualities. Is this too much to ask? What else does he have after all these years of marriage and separation? A bleeding ulcer, gout, emphysema, colitis, ormolu, and pyorrhea. He calls again, no use, and then he sits to look over the list—a short list, for Christ's sake!—of the items he wants, the items he *needs:* six cork-openers, a beer-can coaster, an amazing banana, a photograph of a novelty garter, a picture of three young girls in pale blue ruffled satin, the recipe for wickless candles, a list of recent immediate classics, a chart showing the narrative line and plot development of *A Clubfooted Man,* some red glass stirring rods, and Viña Bad's *Delmar Collection Girl.* He calls again and yells incoherently into the busy signal. Antonia Harley is indeed there, and, as Anton guesses, the phone is off the hook. She doesn't feel too good today, the faded scars from her numerous pig bites are troublesome in the oppressive humidity. But she is busy! What else should she be doing but throwing away those things which she knows that Anton wants, the old bastard! Into a paper bag she puts a spool, a novelty basketball made so as to be confusing, corkscrew tape, three self-indulgent novels about sheiks, and a masking condom. It is obvious that the Harleys have, even now, no understanding of each other.

"Is fonny thing in draw she keeps," Frieda Canula says.

There seems to be no way to stop Frieda from roaming. Lucky for her!

By the way, one question: Is Lady Harley identical with Lady Harlan, the mysterious Frenchwoman?

Glad you asked. No, Lady Harlan is often called Lady Harley by people of malicious intent, the purpose of this misnomer being to ally, in what we like to call "the popular mind," Lady Harlan with a woman, well, with Antonia, who is whispered of as the "Pig Lady." Lady Harlan is, of course, above all this pettiness.

A correction: Harris tweed is not manufactured in Hartford, Connecticut, as noted on page 37, but in Hazie, Scotland, a small town in the Outer Hebrides, covered to a depth of some thirty-one feet throughout the brief, dazzling autumns of those parts with great mounds of purple gorse and rainbow heather. "The Heart Is Lo-onely," a haunting folk song popular some forty years ago, is, perhaps, the most famous of all the many panegyrics to Hazie's unearthly fall beauty. The chorus in which this seasonal enchantment is memorialized runs:

> Hazie, wi' your parple garse,
> Hazie, wi' your rannboo hitherr,
> It is the baywitchin' fall
> Tha' carts the bonny witherr
> So lak the braw bricht Harris tweed
> Tha' stands so tall.

Florence Claire, exhausted from her critical labors, dips into *Heavy Machinery,* a recently reissued novel, one highly recommended by her friend, Buddy Cioppetini, who is just about to run amok, like an eye rolling wildly in its frantic socket. But *Heavy Machinery* bores her with its bullying tone and obdurate blankness. She jots "obdurate blankness" down in her notebook, a neat little item in mottled shenango. The novel is unintelligible to her, so much so that it might as well be written in Hebrew. "In Hebrew," she writes, or jots. Well, there's time enough to wonder at Buddy's enthusiasm for the obdurately Hebrew blankness of the work, but for now, Florence needs a few pages of John Crowe Ransom to soothe her raging chancre, picked up, doubtlessly, from the toilet seat in Rudy's Superette, whence all dread diseases flow.

"You bet," Heff, a barber, comments. "Rudy's—witness my pal Blast's indictment earlier today—is, indeed, a pigpen." His voice falters, cracks, then ceases at last!

"I agree with my brother, Heff," Hefty, a barber, chuckles. "Rudy, even in this era of enlightened health habits and nourishing foods, seems to place little credence in the idea that craftsmanship is more important than speed or handsome profits."

"Here, here! And hear, hear! as well," Heff enthuses.

Our problem with these brothers is that we know for a fact that they are being paid what Thomas Holly Chivers once called "a tidy sum" by the Bleecker Street store of Village Victuals to denigrate Rudy's and Crown SuperMart. The owner of the Village Victuals chain is the irrepressible tycoon Baby Brownie, "the Mayonnaise King" of the food world. The story of Baby and his adopted son Balte's mania, gives this sobriquet a savage yet enthralling piquancy, an aura of what Hegel terms *das geistige Thierreich.* Yet Hegel, as always, is not the sort who desires a *forced* intimacy. For instance, everyone knows the story that he purportedly told Heidegger during one of their innumerable chats on the greensward. He mentioned Keats, Chapman, and rock and roll with what all biographers term a "dazzling insouciance." Perhaps most indicative of his relaxed attitude toward the camaraderie of philosophy is discoverable in the fact that the end of the story, "a lolling Stone slathers no boss," was delivered in flawless, unaccented English. To his credit, Heidegger, rather than exhibiting the rage one might expect at being victimized by Hegel's "lust for punning," smiled sweetly, and said, "This story, Georg, is proof of your affection for me and my ideas, strange as they may be. It is, in fact, what our good friend, Heine, somewhere calls 'a garter of thy love.' " So the two thinkers laughed and talked into the small hours, swatting mosquitoes, their meerschaums fuming without surcease.

"Hi! I'm Karen Heineken! When I'm zooming through the atmosphere I wear pale beige pantyhose, with just a *wisp* of control, under my flattering yet dignified uniform, but later, lounging in tastefully appointed apartments from which the lights of swell cities can be observed to flash, and some glitter, I favor suggestive black net hosiery held up by pale blue garters of ruffled satin to please my highly intelligent electronic-realty wizard of a fella. Hi!"

Helen and Troy's café, close-nestled under the looming cragginess of Mystery Mountain, is the scene this day of tension and heartbreak.

Helen and her husband, Troy, for whom the café is named—although they originally planned to call the place Harry and Mary's for its chic—have been distressed of late to learn that their only daughter, Helene, is the subject of an alarmingly frank lesbian poem, "To Helene in Hell," a work which deconstructs the very notion of the normal American-café ethic. After weeks of tears, threats, and recriminations, this afternoon finds Helene, after a long search, sobbing quietly in her chintz-covered bedroom as she packs her bags. With hope and fear combined, she is leaving home! Outside, the soft summer wind blows the yellow crenellate into a sea of nervously sparkling gold. In the silence, broken only by her sobs and an occasional hawking-up of phlegm, Helene can hear the hum of traffic on the distant highway. "So it's always been," she thinks, "and so it will thus be, for always." She lays her cherished videocassette of *Hellions in Hosiery* atop a small pile of patched yet immaculate lingerie. The hum of traffic grows louder. "But why?" she thinks. Outside, by the crude wooden table beneath the ancient elm, Troy is mechanically pitching horseshoes, his face a mask of grief and rage, a bottle of Jax beer held in his mouth at a jaunty, yet somehow pitiable angle. Helen is in the kitchen, cleaning crimps for supper. All is normal, all is as it is every day, and yet. . . . Helene, who has realized—with a clarity so intense as to be well-nigh incommunicable to her bewildered parents—that her sexuality, her gender, her very nummo is a political act, something like the Tennis Court Oath, is leaving, despite all! Now the hum of traffic seems to be just outside her door of innocent chenille, and she raises her head, knowing in her heart's deepest recesses that the hum is a message: She is a *woman.* Troy, sensing the pain of defeat, defeat and loss, brains a passing Guernsey with a horseshoe and decides to call it a day. His voice thick with repressed sorrow, he shouts an oath at the stunned cow, who reels, with almost unbearable irony, into Helene's own little patch of bitter vetch. Helene suddenly appears on the porch, her bags in hand, and as she smiles wanly at her father, he throws his forearm across his streaming eyes. Then the cow falls down.

Jimmy Blackhead is directing the hanging of the painting, popularly known for many years now as *Hell Mouth,* on the rear wall of the Black Basement's dining room. Jimmy doesn't know nor would he be pleased to discover that this painting is a flawlessly rendered copy of the original. Hem, the foreman, takes orders from Jimmy and passes them on to two workmen who are struggling with the large canvas. There's something strangely unsettling about it. "This is the finishing touch!" Jimmy says. It is possible that like the painting and the Black Basement itself, Jimmy is a replica of the original owner of the original club, but there is no evidence to support this conjecture. Which is often the case, as Heidegger knows. In any event, this Jimmy Blackhead looks like the Jimmy Blackhead that we *do* know, even though he's changed his name from Caponegro. Hem is Hem, absolutely. Look at that fedora! Look at those overalls! Look at that cold cigar clamped between his teeth! We've seen *him* before, plenty. Now the painting is successfully hung, and with the vast space of the white wall behind it and the perfect lighting evoking its every nuance, *Hell Mouth* looks even better than *Hell Mouth.* This will be one sweetheart of an opening night. "Nice work, guys," Jimmy says, in Jimmy's voice. Oh, this surely must be Jimmy. Look at that tie! There's something strangely unsettling about its odd, almost eerie shade of blue.

Lou Henry, having arisen late, is now searching carelessly and un-methodically for his mascara, his tea, his hat, his eye shadow, and his knife. It looks as if his smile is just *beaming,* but close observation reveals that this smile is but an involuntary rictus. This must be something recent, some currently entertained and quirky manifestation of his middle-aged loneliness, of his aimlessness. There is no football, of course, so that's out. Besides, the fucking hole of a room has a TV set that gets only one PBS channel. He comes across a photograph of a woman standing by his old car, and holds it up to the light. In her shift dress, which is probably white, she seems familiar. And here's another photograph, of a man looking directly at the camera with a demandingly inquisitive expression on his face. Lou feels uncomfortable, and begins to sing, off-key. Where is the knife? Where is the mascara? Where is anything? And anybody? He sits in a sprung armchair and looks out the window at the window across the airshaft, but the young woman who sometimes comes to the window in her peach slip to wave at him isn't there. He slept too late. "Where's my tea?" he asks the airshaft. The picture of the woman next to the car intrigues him and he gets up to look at it again. Maybe it's someone he met once, he used to own a car, of course. But he wants his tea, he wants his knife. He wants his mascara so that he can paint a moustache on his face and think about possibly leaving the room. But he needs his hat, if he paints the moustache on and has no hat to wear, that's no good. He needs his moustache, his hat, dark circles under his eyes, and in his pocket, his knife. Then he can think about possibly going out, the A & P is open pretty late. What kind of dress does the woman have on? It is an old picture. He sits again, and smiles, not a real smile, since close observation, etc., etc., but it will have to do. If he has his moustache, his hat, and so on, and goes out to the store when almost everybody else is gone, no one will really see him, or not many, not too many. And even if they are still out, still shopping, he can take his car! He still needs, surely, his hat, his moustache, and so on, but the car seems to have solved his basic problem of being in the streets. He begins to sing again, off-key. It's a nice dress, modest yet provocative. It's very familiar. Nice car. He did have a car?

Sheila Henry sits on the Coney Island beach near Sea Gate, a curiosity to the crowds in her unfashionable black suit, pearl choker, matching earrings. She adjusts a little close-fitting white hat, decorated with a spray of tiny pearls, slips off a pair of black pumps, and places them side by side on the sand next to her. She likes these shoes, particularly the thin strips of white leather that run around their vamps. How *very* nice, but perhaps too young for her. The heels are a little too high. Her stockings are a misty flesh, a bride's stockings, her legs are beautiful, still. She looks out at the sea, straining to find where the azure of the sky meets that of the water, but there is haze far out where the horizon line should be. She is oblivious to the crowds around her, the noise, smells, heat. Why is she here? Fully dressed? Her clothes are out of fashion, and are somewhat too tight for her, but they are in near-perfect condition. Why? As she sits, her mind begins to tell her things, disquietingly. Oddly. Sheila simply allows this telling to happen, it seems to consist of skewed answers, obliquely given, to unasked questions. Unknown questions. Forgotten questions. The illusion is intense, and she stares fixedly at the sea and listens.

The first name, not so much literary as operatic. While walking on a beach during her unhappy honeymoon, August 14, 1966, she was a stranger to the art of whistling. She liked its name. Films had initiated this action because of their well-known power of suggestion, she did not. She is being confused with someone else, or so it seems, since she never wore these items on any occasion that can be called happy. It gave her a glimpse at the life of the successful adulteress. There is a question as to whether she "always" wore white underwear, the kind that makes men bump into trees and lampposts. Because of the kinship of water and snow, during one of her solitary jaunts through the garish lights and mechanical hilarity of Coney Island. And because she wanted to be thought of as tough and worldly. There is extant a bill of sale for its legitimate purchase. No, she enjoyed pornography of all kinds, Christian or otherwise. No, this observation is to be found in an obscure novel by an author whose name is best forgotten, most certainly! This was too good to be true. It suggested to her that life, though tragic, is also, and more importantly, glamorous. Such a description lacks both acumen and breadth. Only when she ate one, because the first time she ate them was with Yankee pot roast. She knew that academics pretended a lack of interest in television and she wanted to fit in, to get even with Sir Thomas Wyatt for "My galley charged with forgetfulness," a poem which improbably gave her nightmares. She did, when she was faced, for perhaps the hundredth time, with an order of pot stickers. She did, especially when she played the "egg game" with her lovers. It did not. Because of the delicious contrast between the modesty of the dress and the voluptuousness of her figure, she didn't want anybody to know that she had no favorite color. Perhaps a passing mention in the "Books Received" listings of various little magazines. She was not dead, not yet.

Not so much embarrassed or chagrined as irritated at my own naïveté. Between twenty and twenty-five times, because Lou thinks that this book contains the secret of happiness. It is an imagined place, absolutely, yes, and sometimes my annoyance is overt. The lines, "for / you, dark / celluloid fury / of forgot / -ten imagery": I've never been able to figure this out. No, I'm really filled with pity, not always, but almost always. Because that's where Lou first fucked me, it's none of his business. Because it's better than anything he ever wrote. It is not boredom, anxiety, and disgust, in that order. Because the chances are good that we'll get lost, no, since it is an imagined place. No, since that scabrous tale was written by Regina Fury, he does, and, or so I hear, with much embarrassed bluster. The Orchid Boat, Jade Mountain, Yung's Oriental Gardens, and The Three Mandarins, invariably. That he is lost in some strange neighborhood whenever he reads my prose. Very unlikely! When I forget something, he remembers. Mutual masturbation while standing up, often. If you've read her poems you know why I say, "Oh, please!" I have no idea. For the same reasons that lead me to dislike the way he sips his tea. On rare occasions, yes, yes, and he also reminds me of this whenever he eats doughnuts as well. *Buddy and His Boys on Mystery Mountain* is my favorite book, at present. We *are.*

Because I've always liked the name, I don't remember anymore, I can't tell you what goes on in his mind. The name sounds familiar. By telling him that I'm going to spend a weekend with *Finnegans Wake,* I will indeed! Because he'll doubtless be handsome, because she'll sign her name. I don't remember; it's possible; but not probable—all three. Because pale blue flatters my figure, complexion, hair, and eyes, making me more desirable. Malice and a touch of recklessness. To audition for a role as a street-wise rock poet, I'll think, for instance, of "A Hundred Collars." Not only believable, but probable; all the others are locked away. Lost near Mystery Mountain, I'll find my way to the Bluebird, be attracted to that rube because of his resemblance to my image of Buddy, and enter the contest to get away from the bartender, a depraved-looking man with a clubfoot, yes. "Justified" is much too weak a word—pure *malice.* Hysterical laughter. Hands down, "Clarinet Polka" awakens tender memories of a very private nature. That bitch of a whore doesn't know anything *about* me. I will not! It will not exactly be "stealing"; it will happen because of $5,000. I have no idea. Saul Blanche is always *becoming* something; he has no patio garden, which the floor plans of his apartment will show clearly. He will figure that I told them I'd be there, because the book is very much like a mulligan. I won't care and I don't know. Or care.

Then Sheila's mind stops suddenly. She is still staring at the sea. Still. Still as death.

Venetia Herbert, whose "vocational nymphomania" (cf. Radner, *Workplace Oddities*) occasions periods of delirium during which she believes herself to be the great-granddaughter of the beloved composer

Victor Herbert, has a funny feeling. In fact, she is reeling from the shock of having just read Mrs. Banjiejicz's recipe for Poires en Crème, for the directions *do indeed* contain the key words of the lyrics to one of the choruses of her imagined great-grandfather's self-suppressed and long-missing "He's a Voyeur." (See "Aspects of the Ziegfeld Follies" by Elisa Hess; *Greasepaint,* XXII, 11, 1942.) Louis "Slim" "Che" "Luigi" Hess, the saturnine roué and ex-husband of the gorgeous Elisa, sits in an armchair and observes the shock of this intelligence register itself on the obsession-creased face of Venetia, then turns again to a vulgar contemplation of her generous "melons."

"Rings the old bell, don't it, baby?" he says in his untrained yet pleasant alto.

"Good God!" Venetia exclaims. "No longer content to be a mere humorist, now Mrs. Banjiejicz thinks to attack the soft underbelly of my uncontrollable mania! This (indicates recipe held in trembling hand) is too sinister to be mere coincidence."

Poires en Crème

4 Ripe (MAMMOTH-size) pEARS	1 cup minceMEAT
½ pint heavy CREAM	2 tablespoons xochiCUN Tlapec sweet chili powder
2 tablesPOONs (or 4 LUMPs) sugar	2 leaveS TARES à Provence
	1 or 2 cinnamon sticks, or to taste

1½ ozs. cognac

The pears should be FIRM and without BUMPS or bruises. Avoid tHOSE with soft spots or blemishes. Cut them in half the long way, REAM out cores and seeds, and PRICK all over. Place in a glASS baking dish, arranging the halves in a circle. To the cream, add sugar, chili powder, and tares. WHIP UNTIL STIFF. Add cognac and cinnamon to the mincemeat and leT IT Simmer over a low flame until HOT thROUGH. Place a tablespoonful of the mincemeat mixture on each pear half, then cover with the whipped cream. Bake in hoT (400-450 degrees or "HIGH" setting) oven for 7-8 minutes. Serve when dish COOLs to room temperature.

Did Mrs. Banjiejicz create the recipe and consciously encode the key words of Victor Herbert's lost song? Did the "food writer extraordinary" unconsciously and unknowingly stumble on the words, reviving them, so to speak, in the writing of the recipe? Does Mrs. B. know more than she is telling about Mr. Herbert's past? Are the words, only guessed at by Dr. Hess, much more than mere "ritualized expressions of a crude American erotics"? Was Therese Herbert-Föster, Victor's strapping diva of a wife, the, as it were, object of his song's affection? Venetia knows nothing, but Louis's bold capitalizations of certain elements of the recipe's text (q.v.) are enough to plunge her, much to Louis's lascivious delight, into a brazen enactment of the vocation she embraces. It is possible, of course, that the recipe is bogus, created by Louis himself with an eye to the ends being realized by him and his unhinged companion, who is now thoroughly enmeshed in the toils of her dementia. Without the chorus itself, nothing can satisfactorily be determined, and the chorus may be but the rumor of vaguely crazed scholars. Not even the indefatigable Dr. Hess, her grizzled head encircled by wreaths of pipe smoke, has turned up a line of it.

"Venetia!" Louis says, his voice muffled, "I am deeply enchanted when you completely lose control of yourself and act in such an unseemly yet thrilling manner. Oh, my darling embouchure!"

"Louis darling! Rears! Mammoth cream! Poon lump! Ream stiff!" Venetia yelps.

Although the couple may not be precisely noble, their very humanity is attractive and thus will be favored by our discretion.

But the world, as always, staggers along. If it's not one damn elision it's another. For instance, the curtain is about to rise on a matinee performance of *Black Ladder,* an experimental theatre piece of some twenty years ago. It wasn't received very warmly then, even though the cast rambled through the theatre in a "liberating flesh involvement" with the audience. Questions on the order of "Where's your head at, man?" and "Is that cunt your wife?" were directed at hapless theatre-goers, and so on. The audience reaction, which ran the gamut from rage and confusion to ennui, contempt, and hilarity, was, of course, proof of the "work's unsettling eagerness to confront bourgeois values." Fine. This current production will be played in the round, and the cast will wear identical costumes—"Cute Cop" to be exact—and skull masks, in order to, as the playbill has it, "relate more meaningfully to a new, more cynical generation's needs." Fine. Adelaide Hester, who is remembered for her prickly Mona in *Girls Are O.K.,* will play the lead, and on this occasion, her "guy," John Hicks, is in the audience. Adelaide is a little long in the tooth for this role, but then Hicks is a bit hoary to be anybody's "guy," so it all works like a house afire, as Buddy once said to Dick anent a nocturnal varmint who speedily made off with their pajamas. John Hicks once had something to do with the Buildings Department, and found himself in a "passel" of trouble (indicates rustic word in copy of *A Grain of Salt*) concerning what the press insisted on calling "collapsing condos." A canard if John ever heard one, and a moot, kike-inspired canard at that! In any event, he awaits the performance with interest, since he suspects that it may present him with some peripheral data needed for a study of modern caterwaul-niece-bonding systems, a line of "research" he is pursuing in his current interest in anthropology. His most recent theories have to do with the *hieros gamos,* or marriage fete, as practiced in certain ritual-prone societies inhabiting tropical crystalline highlands. He theorizes that the wedded couples celebrate their "state of rejuvenation" or "joyous swelling" by whacking each other's buttocks, turn and turn about, with wooden paddles which uncannily resemble Hi-Lo bats, an idea that has made the college-educated, middle-class sadomasochistic community proud once more, and hence much less likely to run amok in school-yards and choir lofts. The mass weddings and frenzied paddlings take place in large, semi-enclosed sylvan temples not unlike Hilton hotels, and these temples are invariably named "Spank-Good Place" or "Big Space to Do [Make] Nice Pain." Hicks believes that these descriptions are but vague approximations of virtually untranslatable syntagmatic structures, but that they have their linguistic roots in the honorific given the ceremonial priest, or *vinnie,* He-Who-Comes-in-His-Handkerchief. "Of course," Hicks writes, "they don't actually have *hankies,* but this quibble in no way detracts from the overall theory, or, as I like to call it, 'picture.' " Indeed not! colleagues spiritedly confess.

So he awaits the curtain, looking around every so often for Michael Cullinan, an acquaintance who often provides him with interesting materials from his vast, if highly specialized, catalogue collection. For reasons unknown to Hicks, Michael, who has for months planned on attending this performance, is nowhere to be seen. Comprising the rest of the audience is a man who looks disturbingly like Himmler, a Nazi of recent notoriety; a Hindu, afflicted with what Shakespeare termed "a raging tooth"; Hips, a laconic dairy-products worker at the A & P; and the theatre editor of *Hip Vox,* who is in a bad mood, having just seen a puppet-theatre production of *Histoire de l'oeil.* It is not too much to say that she wants to crucify *Black Ladder,* on general principles, and at the moment she is composing the lead of a coolly malicious review in her head. She hates these idiotic actors anyway, nattering on with other people's words, and always *wearing* things! Pushed by the demands of what many innocents think a glamorous job from her living room and *The Real Ho Chi Minh, My Lover,* she is ruefully thinking that she never dreamed that a drama critic would have to unearth facts about early street theatre at Hofstra, the reasons behind the denial to Billie Holiday of the role of Scarlet O'Hara, and Vittorio Holo's theft of the intricate plot of *All My Sons.* "The usual dago machinations" was her explanation of the last, surely an unfair if not bigoted remark. But now the curtain rises and her heart sinks. On an otherwise bare stage is a large stuffed pig, listed in the *dramatis personae* as HOMER, *a hog.* The Himmler look-alike chuckles. "Schwein!" he rasps coldly.

Hong Kong is drenched by yet another simoom, and so the Chinese production of *Black Ladder* is postponed again. How strangely the threads of experience meet, touch, intertwine, and become entangled, Father Debris thinks. It's almost a phenomenon! Excitedly, he wonders if these ceaseless permutations can be plotted by means of Fibonacci's series, but he knows that he must resist this idea's temptation, at least until he gets a grip on another problem, called to his attention by an anonymous correspondent, who suggests that a curious "lost" fan letter from Herbert Hoover to one Hoppy, a cowboy star, is in code. After breaking the letter down into its varied morphemic, phonemic, and graphemic groupings, the priest realizes that the code, if there is one, might possibly be solved according to the Cartesian-Eulerian formula for polyhedra ($V-E + F = 2$), and he is now "transliterating" the linguistic elements of the letter into terms of vertices, edges, and faces. He feels that he is on the edge of a breakthrough of historical significance. Settling himself at his desk, he reads the letter for "the thousandth time."

Dear Mr. Hoppy,

I recently saw you in *Range Riders of Yellow Canyon* and was thrilled, in a manly way, by your shooting, riding, roping, and pugilistic skills. Many of the "varmints" to whom you dispensed your special brand of range justice had the look of anarchists and communists about them, and some seemed downright swarthy. Not a self-starter in the bunch! Punching and even shooting are too good for such types as these.

The way you leap into the saddle, tip back your head with a broad grin, and then sit your horse, remind me of something pretty darned wonderful, but I have no words right now to tell you exactly what it is.

Your ardent admirer,
Herbert Hoover

Father Debris considers that Mr. Hoover's letter may conceal a proclivity for refined amours, much like those of the poet Horace, of whom Suetonius writes that "it is reported that in a room lined with mirrors he had harlots so arranged that whichever way he looked, he saw a reflection of venery." Such a life, the priest knows, leads but to grief and heartache, and this opinion is bolstered by his recollection of a magazine article read many years ago, "The Horror of My Forced Abortion." Father Debris cannot remember the title of the magazine in which he read this compelling mea culpa, but is certain that it couldn't have been in the only publication to which he subscribes, *Hot Action,* which usually publishes pieces (indicates latest issue) like "How to Order Wine—for HOT ACTION"; "Want HOT ACTION? Swimming the Hudson at Midnight!"; "A Car for Those Who Crave HOT ACTION —The Classic Terraplane Is Back!"; "A Hungarian Freedom Fighter Tells of HOT ACTION in Her Hollywood Designer Kitchen," and so on. But Debris realizes that he is allowing his mind to wander, and so returns to the ex-President's fan letter, slightly troubled by the comic presence of invalidating non-Eulerian polyhedral "monsters," whose lurking reality might call into question any solution to the letter's code at which he may arrive. Perhaps he'd be better off working with the "threads of experience" and the always reliable Fibonacci, or even returning to his contemplation of the authors of the Décadence.

Eugenia Hunter, as handsome as ever, and, with her hair now shot through with silver, perhaps even more handsome, sits at her desk to write the letter to *Flikk* that she's been putting off for more than a month. It's not an important letter, yet is certainly one that she feels must be written in order to set the famous "record" straight.

To the Editor:

In a recent issue of your magazine, the "Town-Crier Tidbits" page states that my first husband was Tab Hunter, the noted movie star. This is quite incorrect. My first husband was William Hunter, affectionately called, by those who had a truly caring relationship with him, "LuLu," "Rosita," and "Sweetums," depending on occasion and milieu. He was a gentle, even somewhat effeminate man, and was, indeed, a sometime author, as you correctly state. However, the title of his much-praised story is not, as you claim, "Like a Dream Am I," but "I Can Dream, Can't I?"

This story was included in the well-received but long out-of-print anthology of "new voices from the creative-writing workshops," *An Idiot's Pleasure*, edited by Katharine A. and Michael K. Ignatz. The collection, incidentally, was given a very favorable mention in the syndicated newspaper column "I Got Mine," where, among other words of praise, it was spoken of as "a shaft of moral sunlight amid the darkness of the ethical muck of puling 'experiment.' "

But this is neither here nor there. I merely wished to write and correct the trifling errors in your otherwise admirable "Tidbits" feature.

Most sincerely,
Eugenia Hunter

Eugenia is not aware, fortunately for her peace of mind, that "I Can Dream, Can't I?" is currently being filmed as a low-budget horror movie, *I'll Eat Your Eyeballs*. The shooting is being done entirely on location in the beer garden of Imbriale's Clam House, where, at this writing, the director is on lunch break, his feet on a table and his full attention directed toward—of all things—Sheila Henry's senior English paper, "Impotence in Silver Age Poets."

"Yes," the director says, looking up with sudden warm alacrity, "one might think it strange that a worker in the cinema has an interest in such scholarly arcana, but I find that such reading refreshes my visual sense, makes me more aware than ever before of the truth that a word is a word and an image is an image. Along with the poets of the Silver Age, Cowper and the like, Afro Benny, artists to whom words were always and forever words, yes, but then, so much more, words that were—song! Song and beauty, and factual experience as well. Yes. Along with them, as I said, I'm also attracted to writings on Heinrich Himmler, the Impressionists and their fascination with the cravat, the heartbreaking saga of the construction of the IND line, and the romance of the meerschaum pipe."

Is such refreshment merely an escape from cinematic discipline, or does it assist you in your work?

"Definitely. Assists. A bewitching essay on Manet's love of loco-motives which I came across in *Hip Vox* some years ago was the direct cause of my making *Indelible Experiences,* starring, if you'll recall, Dolores Délire as the India Ink Murderess. The film was not only a *succès d'estime,* it packed real box-office wallop!"

Very interesting.

"Thank you. . . . Say, what's that Indian doing over there? Hey, greaseball!"

"I've been watching the filming of this movie for three hours, white-eyes fuckhead," Chief Blue Wind says, "and although I see ethnic types of virtually every persuasion in the crowd scenes, nowhere do I detect a redskin! If redskin not on set (indicates Imbriale's beer garden) by time Indian corn (indicates strangely familiar Indian-corn door spray) falls to floor (indicates clam-bespattered flagstones), all die!"

"Give the fucking greaseball a little part in the Indo-China scene, O.K.?" the director calls to his assistant. "Jesus Christ, if it's not one kinda greaseball it's another. But where were we?"

Then too: Current Poetry Scene Prompts Jean Ingelow to Return from Dead; Edward Beshary Names Ralph Ingeman Inspector of Buildings in Lightning Maid-Swap; "Mr. Insight" of Radio Fame Denies Charge of Carnal Insensitivity; Iowa Lawmaker Claims Iowa Writers' Work-shop Makes State Laughing Stock; Bones of Ipos, the "Angelic Lion of Stuttgart," Found in Block of Meerschaum; Scholar Contends *Paradise Lost* Authored by Anonymous Irishman; *Isolate Flecks* Now Viewed as Attack on Smiling Italian.

Buddy, his head clear and his eye bright once again, set his jaw squarely, and gestured toward the forbidding heights, in whose swirling miasma there could dimly be descried the beetling scarp of Misty Crag.

"I think it best if we make a snug camp here for the night, Dick," he laughed sincerely. "There's an abundance of fresh, cool water from the many capital rills hereabouts, and I allow that we're fortunate in that the immediate environs are rich in the spangs that have but lately plunged to their deaths from the dense trees."

"Say! That's a crackerjack idea, Buddy," the indefatigable Dick opined. "I recollect them Meskin bandelitos in 'Jacks or Better' made a reg'lar feast on them, lightly sautéed and topped with *cacahuate* sauce." His eyes fair shone with primitive glee.

"I'd almost forgotten that neglected example of the storyteller's art," Buddy mused distractedly, the cold wind pummeling his slender body and bending the tares à Provence, amid which he stood, almost to the ground. "But," and he smiled wanly at his dear chum, "you should say *those* Meskin bandelitos. Even here in the wilderness, precise, business-like speech can't hurt a fellow's chances."

"Sorry, Buddy," Dick muttered. "I sure do try, but somehow my words come out all mixed up, like as if it 'pears I've been listening to Mick Jagger."

"There's no need to trouble yourself about it, stout Dick," Buddy assured the crestfallen lad. "There's many a man who speaks as clearly as Count Janos, the Hungarian blzcky, yet has a heart as black as stone."

"As black as stone, Buddy?" Dick queried, straightening up curiously with his arms full of dry tares for their campfire.

"Perhaps black as pitch or cold as stone is the better expression, Dick," Buddy chuckled, an expression of hesitant infarction on his face. "But here, let me help you gather up these tares, and then we'll select the largest and tenderest of these bashed spangs for our evening meal. Although," and Buddy's smile beamed like a demented light-house, "I fear that we'll have to make do without the *cacahuate* sauce!"

The infected laughter of the two boys echoed off the shadowy peaks which surrounded them and was, indeed, hearty enough to be heard in bustling Chinatown, far below. Soon the fire of tares and dead planks was burning brightly, with the not inconsiderable assistance of the pages, used as kindling, torn from a copy of *Absalom! Absalom!* that Dick had found in a small, concealed cave. The boys ate their fill of flame-broiled spangs, and toasted each other, with many a goodhearted jest, in the cold waters of the ever-plashing rills.

"I've been meaning to inquire, Buddy," Dick said, leaning back and heaving a sigh of contentment, "s'posing we *do* find Blutwurst's map, what in the Sam Hill are we going to do with it?"

Buddy, his face grown pale with anguish, stared long into the dancing flames before answering, "Well, Dick, it all depends extraordinarily on what the dago's map *shows.*"

Dick looked quickly at Buddy's face, but it was hidden in shadows, and before he could further inquire about the map, Buddy whooped, "But, drat it! Let's not permit the ruffian to intrude upon our evening. How about a poem?"

"You know I have a powerfully enlightened interest in the art, Buddy," Dick shouted rather alarmingly, "even though I'm not as deep read as I'd gosh-all like. By all means, a poem!"

Buddy, heartened by his friend's enthusiasm, laughed quietly, and fetched a copy of Jean Ingelow's poems from his frayed puccoon. "Since you seem so partial to Mrs. Browning, Dick, I expect that you'll also warmly respond to yet another lady of perfect taste. In fact, Mrs. Browning and Miss Ingelow make, in effect, two opposite faces of the same Janus coin." He stopped, slightly bewildered. "Or, I should say, the same Janus faces of two opposite coins." The lad's flustered puzzlement seemed to increase. "I seem, Dick, unable to get my meaning straight. It is as if I, too, have been listening to Mack Jigger."

"Mick, Buddy," Dick lightly mumbled. "Mick Jagger."

"Mick, of course," Buddy flared inconsequentially. "In any case, permit me to read at random from this good lady's works, so that you'll be able to discover a verse that is sympathetic and compassionate, though tempered by the poet's observant, cold, yet not pitiless eye." With that, Buddy opened the well-fingered volume, and read:

> What next?—we started like to girls, for lo!
> The creaking voice, more harsh than rusty crane,
> Of one who stooped behind us, cried aloud
> "Good lack! how sweet the gentleman does sing—
> So loud and sweet, 'tis like to split his throat. . . ."

But abruptly, Buddy stopped, and glanced piercingly into the crepuscular fastnesses of the thick foliage just beyond Dick's reclining back.

"Wh-what is it, good friend?" Dick inquired. "Please continue! This brief snatch of verse already promises to expand into a subtle bas-relief of a grey world of which the more fortunate among us cannot even imagine of." But Buddy had let the book slip from his inert hands, and now he stood, staring into the woods. Dick turned, just in time to see a tall young man, in mackinaw and worn moleskins, stride into the circle of firelight.

"Can we be of help to you, stranger?" Buddy inquired politely. "It's not usual to get nighttime visitors here on Mystery Mountain," he continued easily, but Dick noticed that his hand rested casually on the butt of the Majolica-steel knife in his belt.

The stranger stepped closer to the fire, spat, and then said gruffly, "My name is Kurt, though it's no concern of yours. I'm looking for an old diary, a book I've sworn to possess once again!" His face was terrible in the shifting light, and his moleskins gave off an overpowering odor of menace. "You fellers ain't seen it, have you? It's got a kind of crude map of sorts drawn on the cover, but the map ain't a map of noplace, or . . . *so they claim!*" he rasped, his voice more harsh than rusty crane.

Buddy, his eyes aglow with belated recognition, held Knute in their manly gaze, and said, "Aren't you the younger brother of the besmirched criminal, Lars?" With a cry of rage and surprise, the depraved Swede turned and fled heavily through the underbrush.

At this point, problems may arise, and become, through a lack of attention and a possibly misplaced trust on the part of the reader, "well-nigh insuperable." Therefore, to take a "leaf" from Eugenia Hunter's "book," let the record be set straight, to wit:

a.) Jeannette is but a character in the novel *La Bouche métallique*. She is not what is usually referred to as *a real person*.

b.) Jeannette is but a character in the English translation of *La Bouche métallique*. She is not what is usually referred to as *a real person* either.

c.) Madame Jeannette is but a character in the English translation of *La Bouche métallique*. Ditto on the *real person* note.

d.) Sister Jeannette is but a character in the English translation of *La Bouche métallique*. Ditto again on the *real person* note.

e.) Madame Jeannette and Sister Jeannette do not exist in the original of *La Bouche métallique*. They are not what is usually referred to as either *real persons* or *characters*.

f.) These *unreal persons* may be the same *unreal person*, known variously as Jeannette, Madame Jeannette, and Sister Jeannette.

g.) This Jeannette's last name, or these Jeannettes' last names, may be Grande, the woman on whose account Buddy recently plunged headlong from a chair. If this is the case, then she may be what is usually referred to as *a real person,* unless Buddy himself is what is usually referred to as *an unreal person.*

"Buddy is, it 'pears, stoutly realer as you are or I!"

Thank you, Dick.

"You're welcome. And now I have to hie to Mystery Mountain, where the fields of gorse bend to the relentless winds, afore Buddy finds me gone." With a proud laugh, he turns on his heel and strides into a fog not unlike that which envelops Colma.

Jeff, callow to the core, is still aroused by the "breast quarrel" between Tabitha Bramble and Lucy Brandon, which it was his unhappy fate to overhear. So aroused, in fact, that an early (ca. 1940) edition of the *Handbook for Boys* sternly prescribes a cold hip bath or a brisk run around the block as remedies for the alleviation of this state, or "fix." Jeff, despite his affliction, caused not so much by the subject of the quarrel as by the very fact that *women* speak in this candid way of their glorious bodies, knows that if he doesn't start restocking the frozen foods, that will be *it* for him at Crown SuperMart. He relies, therefore, on his tried-and-true, absolute, and powerful anaphrodisiac, the poems of Robinson Jeffers, especially his favorite, the one he privately calls his "shooter" (see "Marbles in City Streets," *Urban Games Annual,* LXIV, 3, 1942). As he cuts open a carton of fish sticks, he murmurs, "I'd rather, except the penalties, kill a man than a hake," and, as always, his distended prunella begins a return to its normal state.

A film of grimy sweat covering her body, Lee Jefferson is rummaging through the back-issue files of *Hip Vox* for articles, essays, reviews, feuilletons, and short fiction to be considered for inclusion in an anthology, *Twenty-Five Years of the Hip: The Best of "Hip Vox."* (A prospectus detailing the "editorial philosophy" behind the anthology's contents is currently available, but will be omitted in order to spare the reader needless agony.) Lee is surprised to discover the concerns addressed by the magazine over the years, and wonders if the planned anthology might be too *refined,* too *specialized* for an audience not attuned to *Hip Vox's* intellectual bent. So far, she has come across "*Wuthering Heights:* Is Lockwood a Chump?"; "The Pyramids Were a Mistake! Deconstructing Egypt"; "I Put on High Heels and Finally *Lived*"; "Jazz: Finally Dead?"; "Can Sexists Eat Pussy—And Live?"; "Banana Kings of Greenwich Village"; "Milton, the Running Dog"; "Lost Poems of Lydia E. Pinkham"; "Pizza—Cold at Last?"; "*Wuthering Heights:* Is Lockwood a Pussy?"; "Sexists Eat Pizza at Last"; "Pizza, Chump?"; "The 'Pyramids' of Greenwich Village"; "Banana Kings and Running Dogs"; "Milton Deconstructs Egypt"; "Put on High Heels—And Jazz!"; "Finally Dead: Lydia E. Pinkham"; "Lost Poems That Lived"; "*Wuthering Heights:* Is Lockwood a Running Dog?"; "Banana Kings That Lived"; "Lost 'Pussy' Poems"; "Sexists, Pizza, and Egypt"; "Milton Deconstructs Jazz"; "High Heels at Last!"; "Pizza and Pyramids"; "The Greenwich Village of Lydia E. Pinkham"; "Finally Dead, Chump?"; "*Wuthering Heights:* Is Lockwood Milton?"; "Milton Deconstructs the Dead"; "Finally, Jazz for Chumps"; "Bananas, Kings, and High Heels"; "At Last, Pizza!"; "Pyramids That Lived"; "Lost Pussy in Egypt"; "Sexists and Lydia E. Pinkham"; "Greenwich Village and Pizza." She continues her search, trying to remember just *who* Lockwood is.

Although Allen, the waiter, is on record as preferring the Alps, where "the poppy and the pansy blow," to Akron, some prefer Jersey City, a sediment-filled structural depression on a crystalline peninsula. Onny swokkee molly ponce, to fetch a pail of water.

It may as well be noted here that "The Horror of My Forced Abortion," a not unimportant item in Father Debris's painstaking construction of his "philosophy of live and love," as he so nicely puts it, was originally published in *Jesus!,* a magazine out of print for some years now. This publication, much praised by those who would conserve our heritage of humanist ideals and really *good* clothes, published other articles as compelling and thought-provoking as the one which caught—and still catches!—Father Debris's fancy; for example: "Should Jews Be Allowed to Vote?"; "I Listened to 'Good Golly, Miss Molly!' and Saw Lucifer Naked"; and "Karl Marx and Devil Worship."

"That was one hell of a magazine," Jiggs says, careening down the pet-foods aisle. "Blammo? Say, Blammo, do you remember *Jesus!*, that magazine that had the fairly amusing rebus on the inside back cover every issue?" But Blammo is torn between checking the pervasiveness of additives intended to insure freshness in various cold cereals, and looking up the skirt of the cherry-cheese-dip woman.

"He cares not for your queries, Jiggs," Jimmy says. Jimmy is usually referred to as "somebody" or "Jiggs's friend" or "man in supermarket." He doesn't look at all like Jiggs's friend, but then nobody in the entire world looks like Jiggs's friend.

"Deo gratias," Father Debris says, trying, once again, to arrive at an analytical solution to the Jordan Curve Theorem, an exercise, to quote Jordan himself, akin to "pissing up a rope."

Joanie, on the other hand, may simply be yet another case of mistaken identity. No pictures, no records, no letters exist anent her life. In order to place her so as to obviate the horrible possibility that she may simply "float around" on this scorcher of a day, we might say that she was the "girl at the orgy," and let it go at that. For a clue to the orgy referred to, see earlier comments on *Houses, adobe; Floors, oiled; Vigas, original.*

Joanne's White perfectly images the balanced horizontal and vertical conceptions of space in the process of political collapse. It is a "tone row" of propositions that are at once finite and yet open to the possibilities of an imperialist-induced compromise. Although a static and seemingly vapid statement of a decorative refusal to assert that which might fairly be called an extra-artistic kinesis, the contrapuntals and polyrhythms of the painting's color range claim for themselves the right to subvert the canonical conception of phallic mass and the thrust of density. Not, surely, as chastely or as puritanically inept as the "vaginal metamorphoses" of recent reductionist art, *Joanne's White* is nonetheless a remarkably prescient example of the skewed painterly syntax which informs such contemporary works as the straight-facedly bitter deconstruction of Melissa Queynte's *Jog Your Way to Orgasm,* in which the banal words unmask the almost luscious impasto of rich pastels upon which their message is paradoxically set. Seen in this historical perspective, *Joanne's White* begins to look less and less like the "bourgeois excrement" it was condemned as by Consuelo Van Shunt. Perhaps, it seems to say, unapologetic strategies of form and color, worked out on a rigorously adhered to picture plane, can serve as unmasking techniques as well as or better than more overtly registered statements of an intransigent, and perhaps too naïve suspicion of the status quo.

Pamela Ann Johanssen, who writes as Pamela Clairwil, tired for many years now of pandering to base male fantasies of the lesbian way of life, is thoughtfully brushing her crewcut, admiring the way the light brings out the silvery highlights of her fine hair. Should she call Florence Claire, whom she has heard is reviewing her book for *Virginia's Beat*? She's heard that Florence, although pretty dumb, has a soft spot for automatic writing, as do most of the reviewers for this important organ of enlightened literary opinion, yet to call seems gauche if not crude. Perhaps she might call just to tell her that the photographs, which accompany her text, are as automatic as the writing. She hears that Florence really, well, *likes* young women, although, God knows, Pamela is no longer young. Not really. Was she ever young? Was she ever what they call a "chick"? What precisely *is* a "chick"? When does a woman stop being a "chick"? Is there such a thing as an old "chick"? What's the difference between a "chick" and a "broad"? One sees the sort of thing that vexes Pamela's days. Hell, she screams inside, if Johnny were still around, he'd know what to do. (For *Johnny,* see *Joanie.*)

Joizy Cidy, Jersey City's "sister town," has little to recommend it other than that it is a crystalline structural depression on a sediment-filled peninsula. It is from this crystalline material that domestic meerschaum is extracted for connoisseurs of pipes and "pipe lore." They seem to be legion. For an amusing and instructive sidelight on meerschaum, Heinrich Himmler likes to point to some exercises in a textbook for which he acted as cultural consultant, *Learn German Immediately!* The genial ex-poultry farmer, bored with the play, is on the street right now. And pointing! "I vill translate zo ass you may get der flafor uff der text," he barks, and commences.

Willi vishes to go to der department store undt puy der meerschaum pipe. Der meerschaum iss goot. Der Fuehrer luffs der meerschaum.

Willi's vater goess mit him to der department store. Hiss vater's name iss Rudi. Rudi iss goot. Rudi luffs der Fuehrer undt der Party. Der Fuehrer luffs der meerschaum a goot deal.

How fine Willi undt Rudi look in dare prown zhirts. Willi undt Rudi luff der Fuehrer, ezpezially hiss mouztazhe. It iss prown from der tobacco in hiss meerschaum pipes, prown like Willi undt Rudi's zhirts.

In der department store, Willi undt Rudi infesstigate der meerschaum pipes. Rudi tellss Willi zat der Choos hate der meerschaum undt zmoke zigarettes like a bunch of sissy pervert animals. Vater undt zon zen plaze some Choos unter arrest.

Willi decides on a pipe. It iss a meerschaum pipe. Willi iss choyous to see zat der powl iss a zkull. Der saleslady pleases Rudi ven she asks Willi for his paperss. She says, "Your paperss, pleeze!" She iss a goot Cherman girl. Alzo, she hass a nize mouztazhe, prown like der Fuehrer's.

Rudi undt Willi look out der vindow at a train. Der train iss taking many Choos to der meerschaum mines in Poland.

Willi undt Rudi haff a good laugh. Dare are no meerschaum mines in Poland! Vot a choke on der Choo perverts! No more zigarettes for zem!

"Dose vere der dayss!" Himmler says, stopping the fleeing theatre editor of *Hip Vox* to check her papers. She looks suspiciously effeminate to his discerning eye.

"I possess that which addicts of controlled substances were wont to call, in the good old days when schmeckers were schmeckers and not forever whining about this program and that program, a 'Jones.'" José leans back in his colorful raffia chair and takes a lazy, a long and lazy look at last Christmas's gay piñata. "Except that my Jones is for sexual activity. How well I remember Chester, 'the baron of the baths,' and how can I forget Harlan, 'the man on the train'? Not to mention Fatso Willy, 'the guy who could not break his parents' hearts.' I think of the four of us in interesting dalliance, and my Jones becomes well-nigh insupportable, emotionally speaking-wise." José sighs. "I might say these cogitations still amaze the troubled midnight and the noon's repose—and even the untroubled midnight." He rises, tears the gay piñata from its suspending ribbon, and, troubled, hurls it from the window. "Feliz Navidad!" he shouts at the—oh no!—*traffic far below.*

The man whom some call, rather uncharitably, Mr. Joy, and others call fink, weasel, stoolie, rat, nark, snitch, and liar, misses being interrogated, as he has missed it for many years now, most acutely in August, the month of his initial "performance." He is aware of the names that he is called, but it is certainly not his fault if his testimony contradicted that of others. He soothes his aching nostalgia for his brief moment of splendor by reading the letters sent by James Joyce to his wife, Nora Joyce. The latter has been dear to Mr. Joy ever since he read a remark she made to her husband on his work: "Why don't you write sensible books that people can understand?" That Mr. Joy is aware that his testimony forms a large part of a book which he himself cannot understand makes Nora's remark one that affects him deeply. When he occasionally browses through the book of which his testimony forms a third, it seems to him that his remarks have been twisted, falsified, taken out of context, and even invented! Yet, and yet, he'd like to answer the questions again, or answer *any* questions again, no matter his answers' final disposition. As he gets up to leave the apartment and stroll over to the A & P for a cold sixpack, something resembling a gay piñata sails past his window. A gay piñata? In August?

"I hate those books you can't understand," Knute remarks, picking burrs from his dreary mackinaw. "They're all written by kikes if you ask me, kikes who like to have their way with modest Christian girls. Here's"—and Knute pulls a well-thumbed paperback from his rucksack—"one revealing wallop of a read I *never* tire of!"

It is, of course, *Joys of the Square Knot,* red-blooded stories of bondage and domination for the American outdoorsman. Perhaps this is the sort of thing that Sheila Henry objected to as "Christian pornography."

"It was! It was!" Donna Julia calls from the shallow end of the pool on the roof of her building, where she is "teaching" the recently divorced Eleanor Julienne—her beloved "Taterhead"—to "swim." She has her right hand on Eleanor's *mons pubis* and her left hand on Eleanor's right breast. In July, her right hand was on Eleanor's belly and her left hand between her breasts. In June, her right hand was on Eleanor's knees and her left hand on her chest. So things, for Donna, who must exert every ounce of charm and guile in order to "score," are clipping right along at a fairly good pace, considering. After all, as Jung said, feeling is more likely to be dominant in the woman, and Donna has always been quite good at feeling.

A recent note from Jung's attorneys protests the use of the word "feeling," claiming that it is, as used, a "distortion" of Jung's ideas. Whatever *they* are.

Munching her tofuburger, Karen Aileron opens *Jungle Action* to the first story, "Sex-Crazed Gorillas Ripped Off Her Jodhpurs—And Fought for Her Love!" Pretty slim pickings, but it's too hot to smile brightly. To whirl gaily through the quiet streets. To play badminton. To lounge on an emerald lawn. To skydive. To spelunk. To tramp through the woods. To poke through enchanting, out-of-the-way antique shops. The tofuburger is making her sick, but soon her real life may start. A bird lands on the windowsill, and what does Karen say to this bird, his head cocked in time-honored fashion? "Hi!" she says.

The perils of Justine, the unfortunate heroine of *Justine, ou les Malheurs de la Vertu,* are, once again, being followed avidly by Bart Kahane. He sits under a palm tree, reading this work for perhaps the eighth or ninth time since emerging from his long coma. It may not be his favorite book, but his identification with Justine is so strong that it can, in truth, be called his bulwark against adversity, of which he feels he has had more than his share. Especially now, today! Edward Beshary has not only torn up his best lace cap and broken the heels off his black pumps, but, just this morning, *again* began to call him by the nicknames that Bart despises—"Nando" and "BeeBee"—and to refer to him as "the twisted" Bart. "Berthe! Call me Berthe!" Bart sobbed. "I'm fairly cute for my age, I've got good legs still, and, God knows, I'm learned, but not, I hope, annoyingly so!" But Beshary only laughed at him, then gloatingly informed him that the Guston drawing is but a clever fake, done by Annie Flammard years before, in payment for Beshary keeping his mouth shut about an indiscreet interlude involving a physics professor, two nuns, a Weimaraner, and a quart of mayonnaise.

Bart looks up from the ceaseless degradation of Justine, her endless surprise at the cruelty of men, her impossible innocence, and begins to weep into his ruffled apron. His tycoon is preparing for another board meeting somewhere, and "Guts," his confidant, is, even now, happily packing his bags. Out of his tear-filled eyes, Bart spies three tourists entering a copse of exotic shrubs and gorgeous blooms. Yet he sits, immobile, the idea of walloping them senseless because of their impertinent glances as they passed him, not even half-formed in his mind. He thinks of his twenty-year coma as a blessing, then despairingly returns to Justine's fruitless pleas for mercy. From the copse he hears the gross laughter of the gross world.

Somehow, the lovely Conchita Kahane has lost five or six hours of her life. Perhaps it's been five or six years. This is not our business. She's also acquired a box of daintily scalloped, lilac-hued stationery. She has a cloudy image of quarreling about something with what seemed to be a bald mail clerk. She pulls her panty girdle off, wondering when and why it was that she started to wear such a garment, and discovers a bruise over her pelvic bone. Somebody or something packing a crushing wallop put it there, that seems certain. And who is María de la Concepción Dorotea Carolina Darío y Reyes, to whom the copy of *The Daddy and the Drake,* lying on the coffee table next to the stationery, is dedicated with "un abrazo y un beso"? What is an "abrazo"? What is a "beso"? Why does she keep thinking of police officers? Why does the word "boobs" keep recurring to her? Why is her hair almost completely grey? Is she a "chick"? What is a "chick"? She sits at the kitchen table, trying to recall the faces of the two young men who stood, unaccountably, on chairs to gaze at her. What she needs is three or four fingers of gin, and as she rises to get it, the phone rings. The caller, who identifies himself as Stan Boils, wants to speak to "Babs" Gonzales. Conchita shocks herself as she listens to her voice reply, "Jou 'ave the wrong nomber, pendejo." She hangs up, and, dazed, turns to the window just in time to see an attractive vegetarian couple stroll by, hand in hand. And what remarkably slender, vigorous hands! Almost like fylfots intertwined.

She still seems to have as much trouble as always with words, so Lolita Kahane dog-ears page 92 of *The Girdle Story,* and puts it on top of the refrigerator. She seemed to be following the narrative, more or less, until she came across a reference to Kansas City, at which point she thought of a toy airplane or a perverse Continental gentleman, then, as

always, Karen came to mind, but which Karen? Certainly one who had
something to do with a chic but practical uniform or the too-cold room.
Lolita realizes that almost any Karen knows more than enough about
sailing through azure skies, not to mention creamy clouds. But does this
knowledge help her? It seems not. *The Girdle Story,* like most books, is
filled with words, the trouble, necessarily, with all of them. The invitation to the barbecue at Katydid Glade is still on her kitchen table, but
it's much too late to go. The "problem" recurred almost instantly upon
her opening the invitation, for Katydid Glade immediately gestured
toward the girdle story or magazines scattered about. She mutters,
"Oh, Jesus, Gnatville or the open window," and begins, once again,
trying to climb into the cupboard above the sink, knowing, as she does
so, that the cupboard is sure to be full of dishes, Bart's "frillies" or
memories of dark highways. Still, "Something, something or something," she says, getting up on the sink.

Maybe it's not too late to mention that Katydid Glade and Gnatville
are the same place, the former name that of the town before its incorpo-
ration. In one sylvan precinct of this burg, the barbecue guests are tidying up after their extemporaneous orgy. Although they are sophisticated
people (indicates sushi restaurants, a plethora of natural fabrics, local-
talent poetry readings), as they search for their clothing, much of it in
sad disrepair, they turn embarrassedly away from each other, and no
wonder; for as Bataille says with his usual frigid clarity, the orgy, by its
very nature, "is necessarily disappointing." And this *despite* its clear
and complete index and exemplary notes.

Elmhurst, mocked, badgered, and brutalized into submission by
fashionable journalists who find its mores wholly lacking in an awareness of the sexual politics apparent in the commercial cinema, can no
longer, it is clear to Anne Kaufman, support her little religious-supplies
store. It is almost time to leave, or, as Anne puts it, "give up the post
[*sic*]," and as she completes her inventory, she fights the scream that
rises in her throat, the latter a little flabby. It doesn't help that Father
Frank has gone off to wage his lonely battle against gonorrhea and
indulge his profane taste for gossip. No, it doesn't! She is alone in the
store, stunned by the oppressive heat, and wondering why she still has

fifty-four copies of *How to Think Like Jesus.* The bell over the front door jingles, and a man enters, smiling benignly. Anne smiles back, suddenly conscious of the fit of her skirt. They stand, appraising each other, the stillness in the store broken only by the soft ticking of the clock which has, yet again, appeared. It is a sound which one can often count on, even though things, for the most part, are silent. Will this potential customer have the effrontery to introduce himself as the reprehensible cad he is, Miner X. Beely? "Good afternoon, ma'm," he says. "I'm Jeff Chandler." Beely chuckles lightly, his gaze resting on a richly embroidered quadroon prominently displayed above the counter. "Not *Jeff Chandler,* of course," he laughs. He has plans.

Ellen Kaufman bustles around in her small kitchen, preparing dinner for two, for soon the shades of night, et cetera. A lovely and discerning gentleman, Mr. Chandler, will be coming at about seven, and Ellen wants to make certain that her meal will possess the indefinable perfection which lies at the heart of all great dining experiences. She is vaguely hopeful that a postprandial event of an intimate nature may occur, which is probably why she is in her old turquoise cocktail dress, a garment to which a few happy memories still precariously cling. Mr. Chandler displays rapt attention whenever Ellen speaks of her past travails and victories, e.g., her aberrant ex-husband, the decline and subsequent demise of her father's candy store, her delight in "bleu" cheese, her broken wig, the fedora which nobly speaks to her of liberation, and so on. Rapt attention, understanding nods, bloated vocabulary. So this will be one heck of a meal! Cold tomato soup with dill-and-paprika marshmallows, kohlrabi *en brochette* with clam sauce, anchovies *à gratin,* roast range-chicken with okra and yogurt dressing, crabgrass salad with dandelion oil and "bleu" cheese—gobs of it!— Banana Amaze, and herbal coffee. Ellen isn't aware that Mr. Chandler is Miner X. Beely, at this instant getting off the subway at 90th Street-Elmhurst Avenue. If his plans work out, and what plans!, he may not be coming to dinner at all. There is little reason to expect that Ellen's new overalls will be enough to rescue her from misery if Mr. Chandler breaks the dinner date. But at the moment, all is well, Ellen is smashing the kohlrabi with a kitchen utensil meant for the rote task, and singing, listen:

> . . . consider poetic brilliance unzesty,
> Let us strangle the nun of Amherst's modesty!

It is from "Death to Emily Dickinson's Modesty," of course, the lyrics of which were written by Ellen herself some seventeen years ago. The song now serves as the "rally chant" of the Daughters of Durga International, which organization holds the copyright. How Ellen was cozened out of this "property" makes for a long and ugly story, and this is not the place for it. Sufficient unto the day is the evil thereof. Wham! That takes care of the kohlrabi, now on to the tomatoes! Still singing, Ellen rummages in a drawer for her favorite secant.

Isolate Flecks seems, to Leo Kaufman's amazed eye, much too good to have been written by him, yet there's his name on the stained, ripped jacket. There's his biographical note appended to the flap copy. The apartment in which he sits, drunk on Old Mr. Boston Mint-Flavored Vodka, a beverage long considered by experts in the distilled-spirits field to be a symbol of despair, is cluttered and filthy. "I like it homey," Leo insists to the rare guest inveigled into entering. "Good God! What a genius I had," he says to the vodka label, which appears to him to be merrily dancing, like a *cabola*. On Leo's scarred and battered portable phonograph, a badly scratched record presents *Civil War Songs of the Northern Armies,* many of whose titles create grave doubts as to their authenticity, viz., "They Go Wild Simply Wild Over Me," "Can't Help Lovin' Dat Man," "Babalu," etc., etc. "Oh, Anne!" he cries. "Oh, Ellen!" he cries. He takes another drink. "Fish gotta swim!" he yells. There is no need to describe Leo, although fans may be interested to know that his once-luxuriant bush of undisciplined hair is now rather becomingly thin, and his beard is missing, revealing a face pitted with the acne scars which testify to an unhappy young manhood. Generally speaking, he looks a little like a totally collapsed Buster Keaton. He smashes a roach, groggy and adventurous from some spilled vodka, hence a little slow on his *tarsi,* with the spine of *Isolate Flecks,* then flicks the crushed body off the table to watch it land on a stained fedora perched atop a pile of pornographic magazines beneath the window, through whose grime each day appears reassuringly grey. "I gotta love one man till I die," he sings along with the virile chorus, hazily aware that he is hanging his misery on, we might say, the wrong song.

"And not *only* Getting the Most out of Your Leotard," Georgene says through the bathroom door, "not only that, but also I'm considering the Keep Fit course, which is going to be taught by Chet Kendrick."

"Chet Kendrick?" George says. "Chet Kendrick, the hambone actor? The muck of the boards?"

"Look," Georgene says, "dear. I know you really mean well, but despite your good intentions, will you please do me a favor and stick it up?"

"Chet Kendrick," George says quietly, inundated by jealousy.

Is she still taking a shower?

"Are you still taking a shower?" he asks.

She's taking a bath, George.

"I'm taking a bath, George," Georgene says. "If it's *your* business." Chet *Kendrick,* of course, knows that she's taking a bath. Chet *Kendrick,* despite the motherfucking, cocksucking, popeyed, sagmouthed, rotten-toothed bastard's splayfooted walk, high-water pants, and tiny book of derivative poems on his marvelously varied sex life, oh yes, *he* knows that she's taking a bath, and every inch of her pussy as well. Doesn't he, George?

"May he be doomed to a life of bureaucracy forever!" George mutters. "May his wife prefer a cucumber to his crude attentions! May he never learn how to tie a tie!"

Some submit that jealousy runs, a violent and irresistible thread, through all societies. Certainly, evidence of it can be found among certain tribes in Kenya, those afflicted by the depredations of the passion giving themselves over to the relief to be found in ruthlessly bothering ants. (Gilberte Brie mentions this custom in "Spanning the Azure.") When people, especially the French, unexpectedly blurt out such words as *la veste* and *la corde,* they are obviously in the ineluctable passion's toils. State Trooper Kimberley Butz was regularly stalked because of it. Betty Barker maintains that she invented Key Lime pie when tortured by its ceaseless agonies: "At Barnard I knew a lot of girls," she writes in a crabbed hand, "and that did it." Information soon to be released by Scotland Yard reveals that the unfortunate Cambridge don, seized with a huge cache of stolen baseball cards and strapless bras, was goaded into his sociopathic transgressions by, right-o, jealousy. And Henri Kink's famous poem, which appeared many years ago in the long-defunct magazine *Blue Filter,* treats this universal weakness in, as a critic wrote, "a terse monologue developed amid a welter of illocutionary symbols," although he probably meant "symbols."

So George is not alone, then, in his torture?

George is not alone.

"And what about me?" Knute howls, "me and Zuleika?" With a choking cry, he makes a lumbering dash toward the abandoned Chevrolet. The heather shines in the sunlight. Shines and glitters. Shines and glitters and . . . sings!

A man known only as Kirk, whose disturbingly penetrant cologne years ago attracted the amorous attentions of Sheila, edges nervously into François of Fargo's to use the restroom, but his shabby suit and scuffed shoes draw the glance of a resentful waiter—well, not *actually* a *waiter* —and Kirk strides, or, better, shambles to the stand-up counter and orders a small cup of okra-orange peel soup. "Just to take a piss," he grumbles. The healthful concoction arrives in a small bowl (a "cup") decorated with two blackletter F's intertwined in a design reminiscent of one of the Ferozepore sculptures—the "Lingam Twist"—and accompanying the robust liquid is a small slice of fresh asparagus bread. Oh-oh. Kirk takes a sip, nods dramatically to indicate that the soup is "up to" his culinary expectations, and makes for the Gents'. The waiter smooths his blond hair, smiles mockingly at this crude *gonif,* and thinks on subjects theatrical. Let's say Chekhov and his attendant plays. Can it be possible that the waiter is an *actor?* Well, not *actually* an *actor.*

As the door closes behind Kirk and his aching bladder, the Frankenstein girls are helping a trembling Fred from the table. His smile is vacuous, and touched with longing and expectation. The girls have been whispering naughty things to him, and his acute excitement has precluded his touching the remarkable bowl of oak-leaf salad with lo mein, huckleberry vinegar, and cod-liver oil, wittily dubbed the "White Man's Burden" by the salad chef.

Fred pays the cashier, his hands querulous as he carelessly pulls bills from his wallet. The girls, on either side of him, are amusing themselves by thrusting their hands deep into his trouser pockets. "Ooohhh," they say, a number of times. "I think Fred would like a good fleer," one says to the other, who replies, "A long drawn-out, *double* fleer," and they laugh. "A Saint George fleer!" they scream in unison. The light here, near the window, points quite objectively to the fact that the Frankenstein girls should, perhaps, be called the Frankenstein women, or, more brusquely but humanely, the Frankenstein broads. Fred, a broad in his own right, according to some, seems their perfect companion, and, as we can see, is. The three leave François's, arm in arm, and Fred, his brain a cauldron of unholy images, asks hoarsely, "Is a fleer painful?"

Kirk returns to the counter, takes another sip of the ominous soup, gags, and shambles, with renewed *esprit,* toward the cashier. Just outside the door, he comes upon a sheet of paper folded over and over into a small rectangle. He picks it up, and, chewing on a granola *digestif,* reads:

December 27, 1963

Dear Fred,

I'm writing because I'm embarrassed to speak to you. Actually, I'm also embarrassed to write.

I won't be able to see you. I'll explain. Due to my "clear-eyedness" and not to my clear thinking, I've hurt someone very much. Next, you were going to be hurt.

Last night, my future husband made visible his jealousy and disproportionate dislike of you. I was unable to assure him of the innocence of our future meeting. Prehaps I wasn't convinced myself. You see, I find it difficult to understand why anyone would accept "one-time only" circumstances without having some "designs." The more I tried to explain, last night, the weaker, I felt, my convictions were becomming. No, I don't understand at all.

I think you'll not be too angry with me, though. You may or may not know what it is to love someone and be hurt because you've hurt them.

Sheila

Underneath this message, in a different hand, Kirk reads, "and a happy new year to *you,* you little cunt." Kirk shakes his head. Sheila? Impossible. Not *Sheila* Sheila. He feels a slight manifestation of sexual desire as he remembers divers enchanting postures which Mrs. Henry liked to call her "own." And of course there was also her fleering ability.

Then too: Kirkwood, Missouri, Named "Sink of Depravity" by Noted Educators; *Klactoveedsedstene* Called Authentic Franz Kline by Art Experts; French Publisher Claims Pierre Klossowski Victim of "Character Theft" by Obscure American Author; Knights of Columbus Deny Bishop's Charge of "Kodak Worship"; "Ko-Ko," Bebop Classic, Termed "Gross Misrepresentation" by Black Authors Group; Crescent and Chattaway to Publish Janos Kooba's Novel.

Krazy stands before the meat counter, oblivious to the quarrel going on between a flushed, perspiring young man with an obviously "put on" accent, and a group of older men, each of whom wears, in his lapel, a metal device in the form of a crimson heart crowned with silver thorns. Krazy likes to stare at the packaged ground beef, which, to his weak eyes, looks like a display of red bricks. As the argument rages, the hallucinatory figure of a heart, not unlike those mentioned, rises from Krazy's head and hovers in the air. The quarrel ceases for a split second, then is resumed. The word "mufti" is heard again and again. There is something warm and inviting and familiarly depressing about the moment.

Tania Crosse changes her mind and decides to return to her apartment. She takes off her suit, blouse, and slip, puts on a burnt-orange robe of heavy silk, then mixes herself a Ricard and ginger ale. At her first taste, she puts the drink down, walks into the kitchen, and takes some pirogi, which she made a few weeks ago, from the freezer, then removes a container of sour cream from the refrigerator.

"Krelewicz?" she says. "No, Krulewicz." Her eyes are shining, the scar tissue on her wrists glowing pink. "Krulicewicz!" she says, triumphantly. "Thelma Krulicewicz!" She leans against a huge butcher's block, bought from a wholesale butcher just off Little West 12th Street, astonished, feeling her thighs, her hips, her breasts, her shoulders, her face, her shoulders, her breasts, her hips, her thighs, her face.

"Why am I wearing this demented robe?" she says to the utterly silent pirogi. "And where is my dear, my darling Rose?"

His stuffstuff is pandy and her grout is mushymushy. The educational value of visual aids cannot be underestimated. This looks like the "Calcutta Finger Spin."

"We can thank our lucky stars, Dick," Buddy said rather evenly, as the light from the Indian "star" fire he had carefully laid threw his powerfully etched face into virile relief, "that we happened on this crackerjack cave just as the fierce storm, that even now, as we may discern, howls outside, struck with primordial fury." He settled his Impetigo pack more comfortably between his broad back and a rough outcropping of porous oast.

"It 'pears I 'low tarnation bully well inter *that,* Buddy," Dick Witherspoon said seriously, thrusting a charred newt back into the glowing coals.

"What?" Buddy asked quizzically, his eyebrows meeting in stern disregard for appearances.

"Nothing, not a durn thing," Dick replied, looking up quickly from a grisly ember. " 'Nother morsel of critter, Buddy? This un's done to a right bully turn of crackling goodness."

"No, I think not," Buddy mused, looking at his friend with something approaching plangency. "I've just about eaten my fill of those tasty Magma lizards. It's time, anyway, for us to search this cave with a fine-tooth comb, if one remembers what the debauched Norsk seemed to suggest."

"What in the land of Goshen *did* the Scandihoovian say?" Dick asked pleasantly, his eyes filled with strange, thick smoke. "I'm blameder'n a coot if I can recollec' anything 'cepting his pizen glance." And with this he shuddered like a trembling aspic.

"He suggested that—but here, let's see if we can unearth the map that he mentioned, again and again, as he fled, heavily as I may recall, through the cruel fire-brambles."

"I surely do wish to blessed heaven that we find the durn thing, Buddy," Dick weakly enthused, "else it 'pears we might be here in till Labor Day!"

The chums, hastily casting their dining utensils into a shadowy corner, fell to their knees and began crawling toward the dark and forbidding recesses of the temporary shelter, their onerous way lighted only by the uneven, dancing flames of Buddy's expertly "wrapped" crutchberry torch.

"Whoosh! Oww-ww! Heck!" Dick ejaculated manfully. "My knees are being scraped right raw, even through my heavy canvas trousers that wear like iron yet get softer with each wash."

"Steady, old brick," Buddy urged, "and thank the good Lord in His wisdom and omnipotence that we are not women all a-scramble in such wise, else our sheer nylons would be torn into shreds by these infernal boulders."

"What are 'nylons,' friend?" Dick asked, his mouth quickly filling with shards from the many splintered stalactites lying about.

"Although," Buddy grinned happily, halting his progress for a moment, and leaning wearily against a wild hummock, "such a question is remarkably out of place, and should be answered with the strained silence it so richly begs, I'll deign to reply that 'nylons' are a species of feminine hosiery discovered some years ago by restless Science in its quest for marketable coal tar."

"Thanks, Buddy," Dick wheedled. "Can a feller find his way by means of such things?"

"What?" Buddy blustered, his eyes bulging in consternation.

"Nothing, not a solitary durn thing, Buddy," Dick replied, crawling forward again at a smart pace. "Say, Buddy," he soon called from a looming penumbra, "it 'pears to me there's a sort of cardboard . . . objeck . . . back here. Come and take a gander at oncet!"

Buddy scuttled quickly into a position that permitted the guttering torchlight to fall upon his comrade's exciting find.

"That is a cardboard box, Dick," Buddy laughed, "not an objeck. I am of the opinion that we may discover the shifty greaseball's map before too many more moments have fled into that mysterious area where les neiges d'antan ever hasten."

"Lay nage, Buddy?" Dick intoned good-naturedly, gazing wearily at a damp spot staining the granite fastness in which the lads were enclosed.

"But a literary allusion, simple pal," Buddy sneered. "Now! Let's to work!"

The bruised boys tore at the cardboard box enthusiastically, their facial expressions tense with hope, until at last, after long minutes of labor, made somewhat lighter by a spirited discussion anent the myriad differences between an "objeck" and many other things, the hefty container lay open before them. There glittered a cache of interesting items! Wordlessly, the boys glanced at each other, secure in the knowledge that their long friendship and its many larks and adventures had rarely yielded so astonishingly rich an oblate.

"I shall call out to you the names of these interesting finds," Buddy said, rather superciliously, to Dick. "And you may place them in the taxonomic groupings which seem to you rational or attractive. Is that clearly understood?" he masterfully concluded.

"Certainly, close pal," Dick said too quickly through gently clenched teeth. "Let's commence, then," he added, his two large hands theatrically raised toward a cloud of curious bats.

"Indeed!" Buddy agreed, adjusting the sputtering fasces attached inventively to his head by a handy thong neatly knotted with a double spinney, a knot known to all woodsmen as "our delight." "One copy of *Labors of Love,* apparently a novel based upon the screenplay for *Carom.* One can of La Basurita Aztec Food Products mastiachi peppers in tequila, hmm, I wonder if a fellow might make a passable *cacahuate* sauce from this delicacy? One copy of a slim booklet entitled *Lace Me Tighter!,* containing black-and-white photographs of a pair of corrupt female chums in various lewd postures and states of undress, with what appears to be an accompanying risqué text. One copy of *Lack of Evidence,* possibly, from a quick survey of its lamentable prose, an academic study of some sort. One copy of a short *récit, Chattering Fools,* which seems to be about two French sissies. Are you segregating neatly, dear fellow?" Buddy inquired with quick asperity. "And avoiding the steamy photos in that bestial publication? Such trash is the first step toward moral shipwreck and utter ruin, as you possibly may have heard."

"Deuced right," Dick replied, sprawling in maddened torpor against a knobby juke of plinth granite. For the first time since the friends had set out on their trek, Dick's voice had taken on an edge of unmistakable peevishness. "Dang!" he whispered, as if for the first time.

"One photograph of the ruins of a dwelling of some sort, with, on the reverse side, the words 'La Coste,' written in what is probably a No. 2 pencil. One empty envelope addressed to a Mme LaCrosse, said envelope of heavy rag stock in a delicate lilac hue. Getting all this, meathead?" Buddy hissed playfully.

"You bet, *chief,*" Dick chuckled sarcastically. "You mmphh . . . gndhnnghn."

"What?" Buddy demanded, whipping his brightly burning head around with the celerity of a mongoose.

"Nothing, not a durn thing, Buddy," Dick whined familiarly, absently pawing at his nether equipage.

"One rusted steel blouse. One pair of iron high-heeled shoes, likewise rusted. Another rusted steel blouse with Peter Pan collar. Two, no, three brass skirts, rather becomingly covered with verdigris. An iron-mesh, ah, an, uh, slip," the boy whispered blushingly, "tangled in which are some dried furze petals. And, finally, the collected stories of Campo Dawes, *We Don't Please Easy*. That seems to be the long and short of it, Dick," Buddy sighed, briskly rubbing his hands together with the dry sound that many had often admired.

"But," Dick began, a note of hysteria in his voice, "but wh-where's the dago's map?"

"There is no map, my simplehearted friend," Buddy replied, controlling his emotions as carefully as a lighthouse keeper runs amok so as to resist encroaching dementia. "We've been, I fear, the dupes of an intrigue methodically constructed to keep us roaming futilely about on these beetling scarps and great shale bluffs."

"Thunderation!" Dick cried, getting to his feet. "And . . . and all *this?*" he asked, flinging his calloused yet shapely arms about in the general direction of the neat piles he had made of the interesting items.

"It is the end result of bestial, useless labor," Buddy sobbed, an expression of half-sardonic melancholy on his pale lips. "We are not, it is clear, dealing with the regular-fellow forces daily encountered in the business world." He shuddered obtrusively, and, as he fell supine to the floor, the torch's flames reached his thick, lively hair and set it ablaze.

"Unconscious again?" Dick muttered in the silence of the grim cave.

Although she is still a stranger to the art of whistling, Sylvie Lacruseille has had her fill of men. She is settling herself comfortably on the old couch given her, in a spasm of uncharacteristic generosity, by Annie Flammard, although it must be said that Annie displayed this sudden penchant for gift-giving at a time when she thought Sylvie to be Luba Checks. Let it be stated unequivocally: there is a good deal of evidence to prove that Sylvie is not Luba. For one thing, we cannot find a single article on the crisis in Israeli morality anywhere in the apartment; for another, Sylvie despises mayonnaise, Hellmann's or otherwise; and finally, she neither wears nor owns contact lenses or reading glasses. Now she is settled, and prepares to give herself over to one of the many healthful exercises detailed in *Plaisirs Singuliers,* her eyes vacantly fixed on the trees just outside the living-room window. They are threatening to sough at any minute. On the phonograph, a rare, pirated recording of Lady Day performing "Southern Scandal" is softly playing. Sylvie is quite efficiently deshabille for her purposes. On the roof of the building across the street, a shifty-looking man, a grimy raincoat held rather nonchalantly before his lower torso, discovers that he can see directly into Sylvie's apartment, and that she is, quite unconsciously, displaying most, if not all, of her carnal charms to him. He says a silent and doubtlessly sacrilegious prayer that at some point this "toothsome" (he favors this word) woman will rise and stumble over the credenza standing against the wall. But why should she rise? And, if risen, why should she stumble? And over the credenza? Sylvie is most certainly not *blind,* more's the pity. Still, the watcher prays on, hoping against hope, although he can see that despite the presence of the credenza, there is ascertainable no evidence of a buffet supper. Maledizione!

To digress from the narrative, which thuds on, or, in any event, seems to thud on when we're not looking: Doctor Plot asserts that Raymond Chandler's *The Lady in the Lake* is indisputably the model for *Ladders at Last,* a work of fiction which "redefines, for all time, the much-abused 'historical' novel," and that the latter's protagonist, Lafayette—Brant Lafayette—is a more sophisticated version of Philip Marlowe. This literary nugget is to be found in "A Laff a Minute!," Plot's art-and-letters column published in the *Laguna Colony News.* The Good Doctor, as he prefers to call himself, is the paramour of the lecherous Nancy Lammeter, the wealth of whose cupcake empire has permitted her to buy up any number of weekly rags. Strangely enough, the *Laguna Colony News* is edited and published in Brooklyn, in a small loft building at the foot of Baltic Street, the same Baltic Street from which, even now, if we listen carefully, we may hear an inadequate imitation of the sound of popping champagne corks. If it hasn't occurred to you, let us suggest that coincidence is omnipresent, or, as we have a fondness for saying—at, some declare, the drop of a hat—"small world."

Item: We have been asked by the Lamoille County Sheriff's Department for any information we may have concerning an unpaid parking summons, issued to Henri Kink, who is carried in their files as "Deceased." One can almost see the troopers' bent, grizzled heads encircled by wreaths of pipe smoke as they bend to their necessary tasks. Such is the power of the objective correlative, in life as in art. Literary art. Certain literary art, some of it unacceptable.

Surrounded by the three or four thousand intractable typescript pages of the novel on which he has been sporadically at work for some sixteen years, Antony Lamont surrenders, finally, to the suspicion, long held in abeyance, that he has no idea what he is doing. For instance, he doesn't remember what his novel is "about"—is it "about" anything at all? He picks up a handful of sheets and riffles through them, stopping now and again to stare at a totally unfamiliar name. God! He doesn't even remember the names of his characters! Maybe he should keep a list? Will that help? What goes on in the chapter he calls "Jelly Doughnuts"? Or this one—"Time Will Tell"? Or "Gozos"? What about "Burnt-Match Moustache"? Jesus Christ! He looks at his published books, lined up chronologically on a shelf above his desk, in order to affirm his, well, reality. As always, he remembers, immediately, the vicious review, "Lamont's Ink Not Permanent," by that corrupted bastard John Hicks—he'll never forget *that* name. Where did he read or hear that the little prick is running some pop anthropology scam? The son of a bitch is dashing around now confessing to his past "cultural misogyny" in any newspaper that will print him. Lamont arranges his typescript in three ragged piles on his desk, vowing to read it through soon. Really. Very soon. To see if there's anything in it that can be saved. That makes some sense. That has maybe a paragraph or two which won't make him howl in disgust. Then he slits open the envelope, lying on his desk since yesterday, from the erstwhile publisher of his first novel, *Baltimore Chop*. It's a review—a review?—from *Virginia's Beat.* What the hell? It must be twenty, twenty-two years since. . . . Written in a cramped hand across the top of the yellowed clipping is "just found this in the files, thought you'd like to see." The review, one of the important journal's SHORT TAKES, reads in its entirety:

> "He felt as if he were about to float off on some cloud or other, somewhere into the blue . . . he felt as if he wanted to bite the rim of the glass." The reader will feel the same way as he plods through this dismal first novel, a supposed detective story without plot, tension, or characters we can care about. There is a lot of kinky sex, tough-guy talk, and tabloid sentimentality, all set down in a thick, unwieldy prose that has the clarity of axle grease. Keep your hands clean.

Lamont lays the review down and begins to laugh. The motherfuckers come right out of the grave to get you! He takes *Baltimore Chop* down from the shelf. Christ, what a lousy dust jacket! "What a lousy dust jacket!" he says. They have always been, as he tells anyone who will listen, his burden and his cross.

Excitedly, Father Debris suddenly "sees" intuitively into the heart of Lange's famous treatise on "les vapeurs," discovering therein what may well be termed subtle predictions anent the Décadence, the life and career of Yvonne DeCarlo, and the "lost" films of Barbra d'Eveuilley. Disregarding his older formula, which he grudgingly concedes has been leading him, of late, into hopelessly opaque solutions to the problems it is supposed to unlock with ease (*vide* the anagrammatic confusion in re: "Barbey d'Aurevilly"), he decides upon a new formula, that of Girolamo Cardano,
$$\chi = \left(\tfrac{n}{2} + \sqrt{(n/2)^2 + (m/3)^3}\right)^{\frac{1}{3}} - \left(-\tfrac{n}{2} + \sqrt{(n/2)^2 + (m/3)^3}\right)^{\frac{1}{3}}$$
which he then applies to Lange's text, so as to confirm his "flash" (or *perruque*) of insight. That section of Lange's text most receptive to the transforming powers of Cardano's formula reads: "Myrrh and aloes preserve corpses," which discovery inexorably leads to the noted physician's deduction that these elixirs are also beneficial against the vapors. Working swiftly, Father Debris sees that the Décadence, Yvonne DeCarlo, la d'Eveuilley, etc., etc., are specimens of "maladies nerveuses," curable by applications of *metaphorical* "myrrh and aloes." From here, it is but a short step for the good priest to—but let's allow him to work in peace.

Speaking of the vapors, it is the "dirty" (surely a slanderous descriptive!) Lydia Languish's vaporous plight to strip naked, accidentally, at every picnic or other outdoor social gathering to which she is invited, embarrassing the women and inflaming the men. Most of them. Well, many of them. Something, as they say, *seizes* her, and she is thus helpless. A glimpse of hardboiled eggs, or, as they are called on the *al fresco* circuit, "oeufs of a long boil," or a glance at a platter of potato salad— or even macaroni salad or cole slaw!—and Lydia is tearing at her garments. "Helpless!" she often cries out at such moments of humiliation. Today's picnic, at the bosky Scone Canyon Recreation Park, is no different from the others. There's Lydia, just beginning to pull off her sundress amid the smoke of rapidly charring hamburgers, steaks, and chicken. Question: If myrrh and aloes are effective against the vapors, is L'Ardent perfume? Do any of the women have a phial? If so, will it be employed? Lydia has her sundress off now, and neglected beans are turning black in neglected pots. Does *anybody* have a little L'Ardent? Lydia is in white underwear, the kind that makes men bump into trees and lampposts, put charcoal into the gin, and gnaw on their casual shoes. But there is no such thing as the vapors! Then what *does* Lydia have? In addition to her body, which we, because of our responsibility, have sworn not to notice? Now Lydia is . . . Lydia, please, Lydia. Lydia? Lydia!

Nota: "L'Ardent perfume is manufactured somewhere in Latin America," the comely, vivacious Miss Laughter says from her cool, elegantly appointed apartment overlooking the *marvelously* frenzied crowds sweating on the avenue below. "It contains neither myrrh nor aloes, but employs as essential ingredients two roots native to the region— *cagajón* and *pucha.* Isn't this a breathtaking view? And by the way," she turns, suddenly smiling, "what do you think of my jugs, you pig?"

Léonie Aubois looks up from the floor. "*I* used to be Miss Laughter, you can ask anybody. For Christ's sake. That was about the time I was nominated—*me,* not Sheila!—for the Ralph Lauren Medal for Literature, argent with two mounted Labrador retrievers sable in orle." She pulls herself to her knees, looking for the vodka, sees that the bottle is empty. "The fucking bottle of fucking vodka is fucking empty," Léonie says. A scene of rage and heartbreak, made more powerful by the tension of the setting, follows. But *we* don't have to observe it!

Few people consider Lawton, Oklahoma, to be a hotbed of interesting artistic activity, fertile ground for avant-garde experimentation, and, aesthetically speaking, a burgeoning regime of irrepressible new ideas in many exciting areas. Yet it is. Not many would expect to discover the attractive, well-built, and engagingly bemused middle-aged author of the prize-winning *Leaves of Yearning,* Lorna Flambeaux, living right here in the center of town. (Indicates "center" of town.) There are also occasional heavy rains in the area, and Lefty, as Miss Flambeaux is known here, is usually to be found, soaked to the skin, in Lena's Rest, a popular tavern. According to the blue-neon message in the window, Lena's has the·BEST BUGGERS IN TOWN. One *heck* of a claim, and yet many can testify to its truth. More or less. Lena, and there really *is* a Lena (indicates shapeless figure in filthy apron), offers, as well as her famous "buggers," a wonderful selection of jelly donuts (indicates grease-oozing pastries) and color photographs of all sorts, with a special emphasis on open wounds. A little slimy, yes, but Lawtonians seem to adore them. This *is* the heartland. People hereabouts are quite anxious to chat with Lefty about her new work, *Lengthy and Serious Talks,* but opinion decrees that she has "passed out" again, despite the presence of the whole darned crew from *Lens and Shutter.* Few expected *this!* The gang, by the way, is a crack outfit, no expense spared, no detail too small, yet always with some time for a racist joke and a good laugh, etc., etc. They're certainly unlike the last bunch, inept misfits characterized by the town rabble as "right dumb schlongs." (Indicates anatomical photograph.) Lorna doesn't seem to be moving, although she's been known to go into orgasmic trances in the past. Well, let's hope for the best!

Lento's Bar and Grille, in Brooklyn, is always quiet in the afternoon, and today is no exception. To that general rule. If it may be so designated. As such. It is not, hell, *actually* a *rule.* The real Anne Leo sits at the bar, chatting with Henny, one of the more spectacularly drunken bartenders in this part of the world. "What's my name, Henny?" Anne asks. "Ha, ha," Henny answers, and falls to his knees on the duckboards. "What?"

Anne asks, "what is it?" "Ha, ha, ha," Henny answers again, undecided whether he should remain kneeling or just briskly fall over. "That's *right,*" Anne says, "and I don't need no goddam Jew bitch with eclectic experiences and life skills taking my name, you hear me?" Henny may hear her, but it seems as if he has no wish to reply. Looking at this rather seedy bar, the lone customer, the semiparalyzed bartender, it is very difficult to believe that Evelyn Leonard, First Lieutenant Evelyn Leonard, once sojourned herein. Yet photographs occasionally tell the truth. Look. You see? Is that Evelyn Leonard or is that Evelyn Leonard? It was from this bar, Lento's, that she shyly edged into the high-powered urban milieu, starring at last in *Black Silk Stockings,* an acknowledged early classic of the sticky-floor school. Evelyn may have begun her long and somber journey to fleeting fame and lasting moral degradation on the sad evening, now happily obscured by time's opaque raiment, when she agreed to enter a "motor inn" with a female acquaintance who pretended an interest in the young officer's descriptions of close-order drill and cold-cock suppers. Leo Kaufman, in his last poem, "Leo's Last Poem," hints at the motor inn goings-on in the lines

> Like a lost clam, so
> the sweet scent
> of your breath amid
> the rust-
> ed Chevys.

"Drunk as I am now and may yet get later drunker even," Leo protests, "I never wrote this poem, never wrote 'Leo's Last Poem,' and believe me I know about the back-stabbing bastards who call *Isolate Flecks,* my always interesting and occasionally brilliant novel of city life, *Leo's Lunge.*" He sits back. "Should I look into the bathroom mirror to see, with a start of shocked surprise, my sad, defeated face? Or what? Shall I look so that I may . . . *hate myself?* Huh?" Nothing except the animal grunts and groans of Fred and the Frankenstein girls can be heard in reply. We had no idea that the vivacious sisters lived in Leo's building. Neither did Leo.

Lerajie, Creator of Strife, Great Marquis of Lacerations, complains quietly to a waitress in Les Lobsters that his shrimp cocktail is far from chilled, and that his lemon wedge appears to be, well, *used*. He is dressed in a crisp, khaki-colored, tropical worsted suit, rather than in his usual macabre green. It is not what we would call "good news" to find him here. As the waitress cocks her head to stare in rude wonder at this astonishing creature who has *complained* while scores of cuisine devotees wait patiently to be seated in this, the "best and most authentic" of seafood restaurants, we, as they say, do but cringe at her ignorance. The waitress, "Chickie" "Hips" Levine, the putative mother of Andy, the canned-soup admirer, laughs unpleasantly, and casually notes that if the patron doesn't *care* for the appetizer, she not only has no idea what she might *do* about the situation, but she is really, uh, not very *interested*. Y' know? Lerajie, distressed by this inhospitable information, gazes pleasantly at "Chickie," whereupon large, suppurating lesions appear "as if by magic" upon her arms, legs, face, and probably those areas of her body not readily visible because of her fetching uniform. Lerajie smiles engagingly, fingering the knot in his pale-yellow tie. "I certainly, oh yes indeed, *would* be pleased if you'd bring me another shrimp cocktail! How very kind!" he says brightly. "And you might ask the maitre d' to come over here too. When he has a minute, of course." There seems to be a question as to whether "Chickie" hears Lerajie, since her screams are ear-splitting. A thin, yet decisively blunt odor of putrefaction settles over the restaurant's patrons, and many disquieting, we might even say disgusting things begin to occur. Lerajie, however, considers them to be among the indefinable perfections which lie at the heart of all great dining experiences. Including the notably attentive swarms of flies.

Guy Lewis is sitting on his fifth-floor fire escape in a pair of boxer shorts and an "athletic" undershirt, now, we understand, Back in Style Again! Can this be a fact? Athletic undershirts?

Now they call them "tank tops" or "top tricks" or "truck stops" or something. They're cut different. Come in colors and such.

Thanks. Guy, as you may have surmised, is deeply concerned about fashion, so much concerned, in fact, that he refuses to be seen on the streets of his teeming and electrically-charged polyglot neighborhood while wearing said "athletic" undershirt, or, to be precise, while wearing one or another of the two "athletic" undershirts he owns. Not for Guy the current "truck stop" or something. He is sweating in the vicious sunlight and working on his third large drink of blended whiskey—Four Roses today!—and ice, which he sips from a large Hellmann's Mayonnaise jar. The recipe for this summer cooler is a simple one, simple, yes, and like so many simple things, elegantly understated: Place plenty of ice in a large, clean jar, then fill to the top with a good blended whiskey. Four Roses is excellent, good body and fine nose; Schenley's Silver Label has a slightly bolder aroma and a persistent coppery aftertaste; Paul Jones has a brusque nose and will make the eyes start forth from the head in horror; and etc., etc. The most important thing to remember, Guy would be delighted to tell you, could he but form more or less reasonably intact sentences, is to have plenty of ice. Guy doesn't want much from life, but when he sits back to enjoy a well-earned rest with a reassuring drink by his side, or in his hand, or for that matter anyplace, he insists on plenty of ice. Right to the brim is not too much! Ice cubes? Fine! Cracked, shaved, any kind of ice will do. But wait! Guy is grinning his boyish grin through the bars of the fire escape, and it seems as if . . . yes, yes! He's going to tell us himself just what it is that makes a merely pleasant afternoon into an extraordinary leisure experience. Guy?

"Plenty ice. Y' need plenty of ice. Plenty of ice and plenty of whiskey and that's it. Wow! Wow!"

As we have just heard, it is ice and plenty of ice that spells the difference between humdrum occasions and memorable fetes. Guy stands up and holds onto the fire-escape railing. He puts one leg over, then the other. He jumps into the street. One "Wow!" too many.

Joanne ("Bunny" to all who have followed the twists and turns of these twists and turns) Lewis wheels her father out into the sunshine, adjusts a light cotton blanket around his legs, and settles his ludicrous green visor on his head. Mr. Lewis doesn't really need this visor, but there has been, we understand, an overwhelmingly emotional vote for it. "Do you want anything else, Poppa?" she asks. "Orange juice? The paper?" Her father makes no sign, but settles his gaze on the chicken coop, which, as Bunny knows, he thinks of as the site of his victory over the onslaughts of Eros. She wonders again what became of Mrs. Feuer, who is certainly, God knows, getting on in years. Yet on the day, not too long ago, that the lady left Gnatville for good, or so it turned out, she wore a grotesque mask of white makeup, black fishnet stockings, and red patent leather four-inch heels. Bunny looks at her father, whose hands, in the great tradition of afflictions, are "trembling uncontrollably" in his lap. She suddenly feels disgusted, as she uncannily thinks "stuffstuff," "mushymushy." Ugh! "The languish of flowers." *Disgusting!* She is just about to go back into the house, out of the impossible sun, away from thoughts, if that's what they are, of Mrs. Feuer, when she sees an odd-looking woman, a strange, blue, filthy *something* knotted around her neck, standing in the middle of the street, looking at a pall of smoke which hangs in grey oppression over the northern part of town. Now Bunny sees it, and then smells it, a curiously repellent odor, a fetid mixture of charred meat, smoldering garbage, sweat, urine, feces, and sulfur. "Something—excuse me?—something seems to be . . .burning?" she says to the woman in the street.

"Bees burning? *Bees* burning, ah," Frieda smiles wisely, and gestures toward the smoke. "Is barbecue foods? Cooking bees?" She smiles again, and sniffs the air. Bunny stares at her. Can this be Mrs. Feuer, come to take her father away from her? "Have you come far?" Bunny asks. "I mean, are you visiting, here in town?"

"I like much jelly donuts," Frieda says. "From corns, donuts?" Then, standing with her back straight and her arms rigid at her sides, she closes her eyes and recites, "Up from meadow rich with corns! Who arms hair on a grey head, dies! Like a dogs, march on! And so, he said." Frieda winks at Bunny, and says, "American poem good like donuts, yes?" and then takes a step toward the porch.

"Go away!" Bunny cries. "My father is very sick! The chicken coop is, is, it's broken! We don't have any more Indian corn! And this is an old dress, you see this dress, this is an old dress that I hate!" She is pulling desperately at her old and familiar white crocheted dress, pulling at it with both hands as if to tear it off her body. Her father stares at the chicken coop, drooling onto the napkin knotted around his neck. Frieda stares at Bunny, astonished by this new American custom, then begins to tear at her own clothes. Bunny feels as if the mouth of Hell has opened for her.

Corrections of Earlier Errors

Item: The ugly Henry Lewison, known in his fizzling youth as "Hank," "Chico," and "Hen," does not actually fall *dead* when surprised with certain judiciously selected poems of John Crowe Ransom. His vacant stare, on such occasions, can, in good conscience, be called a "trance." According to John Greene Czcu, a well-appointed and nicely turned-out psychic researcher, this stare is akin to an Interzonal Receptivity Modal, or what Czcu describes, with perhaps a hint of good-natured mockery in his voice, as that place "where all art begins—art, that is, for chemists with some spare time."

Item: Plain Lucía Lewison, at one time Henry's wife, was not locked out of the Kodak Motor Inn, "allegedly nude," by John Greene Czcu; she was ejected from the Lido, a hotel which Czcu, with perhaps an edge of weary bravado in his voice, terms a "fleabag."

Item: Lincoln Center is assuredly not a "fleabag," as Josh Cabernet rather surprisingly claims in his tawdry and sensationalist book *Cameras Work.* Our deepest apologies go to the directors of the renowned arts complex, their relatives, loved ones, friends, and not least of all, to the dedicated cohort that "keeps it all going" year after triumphant year, the incomparable gang familiarly known as *"les embouchures."*

Item: Although the Lincoln Inn and the Lincstone are most certainly not the four-star hotels they once aspired to, neither are they "flea-bags," in which one can "get his or her ashes hauled" at any time of the day or night, as alleged by Doctor Plot in the *Laguna Colony News.* Doctor Plot is, in the words of a little-known *tummler,* no better than a fleabag himself.

Lincoln Gom finishes reading another really terrific and interesting article on composting latrines that pay for themselves in *Green Sunshine,* the ecology magazine to which he is a Patron. To think that human excrement—not attractive in itself—the ever-busy *prunellae* bacterium, and assorted tits and nuthatches can make the garden literally *explode* in riotous color! But at present, his hair silverly gleaming, or is it shining softly with what might be called silvery highlights?, it's time for Linc to grapple with sober business thoughts! Lincstone

Productions, for some years now the perplexed victim of a disturbing and wholly inexplicable surge of "good taste"—well, not precisely "good"—on the part of its audience for cultural programming, is on its way up again! Lincoln beams through the aromatic smoke from his mellow meerschaum, and settles more deeply into his robe of Maraschino silk. Picking up Elizabeth Barrett Browning's secret journals, *My Secret Journals,* in his all-leather study, he comes across more than one virtually intoxicated reference to Charles Paul de Kock in her pages. She is mad for *Georgette,* passionate about *Gustave ou le mauvais sujet,* almost delirious in her praise of *Mon voisin Raymond,* and virtually inarticulate concerning the ardor she feels for *L'Amant et la lune.* This is good enough for Lincoln, for if there is one writer he trusts above all others, it is Mrs. Browning. There's something febrile about her best work. In any event, Lincstone Productions is about to begin shooting on a film based on *Mon voisin Raymond.* Good God! Lincoln exclaims, laughing sternly into his rich arras at the sheer coincidence of, well, *things.* The story needs some changes, of course, so as to make the visual images this and that, and to make sure that the book's introspective qualities are that and this, and so on. The cinema is, after all, the cinema, and pictures are, after all, pictures. Words, too, yes, words are, after all, words. The film will be released as either *Raymond and Desire* or *Lace Me Tighter!*

"Hi! I'm Linda, once in a while, most 'specially when I'm spanning the azure empyrean, raptly bent on those womanly tasks that only women excel at, or is it bent over? I can't quite read this. Whatever, when I'm on my square-jawed industrial engineer's arm, casually strolling toward his high-performance car for a moonlight spin down country byways, I'm just another American Karen. Hi!"

"Hi yourself," Lips says, flashing his most delightfully engaging grin, the sort of grin that Lips knows Lips excels at. We feel constrained, however, to admit that this sunny greeting and benevolent grin are intended to mask the fact that Lips may be about to steal the copy of *Absalom! Absalom!* abandoned atop the Granny Smith apples. He may also steal an apple or two. All depends on whether or not the attractive vegetarian couple browsing among the slabs of tofu will stop looking at him. Every fucking minute for Christ's sake! Don't they have anything better to do? Wash their running "togs"? Invest some capital?

"Is someone talking to us, dearest?"

"I think it's this walnut-grape leaf tofu, darling."

Then too: Author of *Little Cabals,* in Speech, Claims Pollution Will Kill Only Rich; Twelve-Million-Year-Old Woman with "Liz" Ankle Bracelet Discovered in Bronx; Study Finds Harold Lloyd May Have Written *Revelations*; *Lobster Lays* to Be Sex Show for Kids on Cable; Lochinvar's Spirit Said to Molest Locust Valley Matrons; Loire River "Mostly Urine," Expert Reveals.

LoLo smiles uncertainly into the camera and nods rather pleasantly as she is introduced by Emil Krasch, your Dynamo! reporter, as Bam's twin sister. They both, as the reporter points out, share a delight in plaids, the charming pair adhering to a ludicrous belief—which has absolutely no basis in fact—that they are Scottish. The program, if that's what this is, ends with Emil's noting, in a tone of mild alarm, that LoLo is attracted to handymen, superintendents, deconstructionists, fisherfolk, in short, men who wear tool belts, preferably filled. "A well-filled tool belt," Emil says, his face so sincere that it could make Himmler weep—

"Vot?" Himmler shouts. "Vot iss dot Choo saying?"

—his eyes, steady and cold, yet somehow, shifty and warm. "Yes. Tool belts. Something to think about. This is Emil Krasch for Dynamo! News, in London."

He's not in London.

"Ve could haff plown London off der map! Shtinking English fairies!"

"Am I the star or am I the *star?*" Emil says. "Besides, I didn't say *London,* I said *Jack* London, open your ears for God's sake!"

Jack London?

"Yes, Jack London, Jack London. Right. Jack London!"

As if at a given command, these stars of the electronic news media and their charming flunkies disappear into *really* marvelously comfortable dressing rooms, the appointments and accoutrements of each clearly contracted for. Are they stars or are they *stars?*

"All said contracts legally signed by all said proper parties in all said proper places," an attractive flunky smiles.

Thank you. Is she (indicates attractive flunky by filing cabinet) an attractive flunky or is she an *attractive flunky?*

Nice jugs.

"Both 'jugs' are legally contracted for," the attractive flunky sighs. "It's utterly remarkable how far we've come in the rough-and-tumble world of the workplace. Makes you kind of think."

LoLo, however, is *still here.* "I really don't like plaid all that much, and I don't think Bam does either, and I don't think, also, that Bam is my twin brother or any kind of brother at all."

From the recesses of a nearby supermarket we hear "POP! POP!" What a day.

It is mere coincidence that so many things are happening on Long Island today. The Lard Goddess, *soi disant,* falls heavily into a pastel sandbox; an inscrutable message issues forth from Hicksville, i.e., *krik-kk, krik-kk;* an idiotic adolescent, Looy, who looks exactly like Jiggs, is subjected to the "Moussogorsky *Pictures* torture" after reporting the sighting of two rather indolent airborne dogs (he calls them "doggies"); the Glen Cove Public Library discovers an unknown manuscript by D.H. Lawrence, whom all of Glen Cove likes to think of as "Lorenzo" because of the miniseries *Lord Chatterley's Plume*—the item is found in a copy of Viña Delmar's *Kept Woman;* a hastily called emergency session of the remaining members of the Gnatville City Council results in a fistfight over the proposition: Shall the City of Gnatville be burned to the ground and the ashes sown with rock salt? Certain other things have happened as well, but we feel that the gross laughter of the gross world may greet their telling. Suffice it to say that whichever way we look we see a reflection of venery.

"That's the way it is in small towns," the big guy in green work clothes says. "They tend to take it pretty well, but they get those goiters, you know? Like when I was dry that time up to Missoula for a spell? Alice knew. Hell, that's when we had the motel with a swimming pool, those nice little chairs around, umbrellas and all. Really nice, but then the leaves just came right down and it was fall again somehow. Then the concrete sort of cracked, I don't know. I used to be some looker then, before Claude, you know, put me in the way of the Teacher's and those damn Hershey bars. Might's well have lit out for Topeka but the Chevy threw a rod. I'm getting straightened out now though. Want to hear about it? Or about any other instances of gritty reality told just as honest as I know how to tell it? Or them? Things that'll just make you nod your head in recognition?"

We feel as if we really don't. But thanks. Anyway.

Bored for some years now with the golden sands and endless golden sunshine of distant golden and exotic lands, Annette Lorpailleur now lives in the city, and is still a little "odd." Many recall the issue of *Lorzu* which ran an article on her voice, "The Performative Function of the Ventriloquial Utterance." There were ugly recriminations, but the essay had its effect. Now she is looking at her copy of *Kept Woman,* which Annette has had translated into French as *Femme entretenue,* with her name given as author. The translator, Henri Kink, is never seen anymore, and gossip, as usual, careens about. Somebody by that name has something to do with something on television or something, but he's only twenty and thinks that Stan Getz invented jazz or whatever! That can't be Henri. Can it? There are lots of people who think that Stan Getz invented jazz, but academics don't count. Annette looks up and smiles her stop-action smile, and a smell of molten copper and smoldering hair hangs sour and metallic in the apartment. The walls are shifting with deep shadows and bright slivers of what may be light, although it hasn't the qualities of light but seems a kind of impossible incandescent blackness. Annette lays the book down and walks away, the terrible illumination glittering off the skintight metal sheath which covers her body, while her thighs, brushing lightly against each other in their humid darkness, create a faint chiming. The apartment is swelteringly frigid. It may as well be added that Annette looks about thirty.

She stops and turns to stare. As they say, *look out.*

Lee Jefferson unexpectedly comes across a color advertisement for Lorzu Fashions, and is "borne back in memory" to her brief and ultimately unsatisfying partnership in the little boutique that was before its time—or was it after its time? Perhaps it was just right for its time, to no avail. No matter. Still, it was a shame to have had the place torched. She looks at the ad and for some private reason thinks of a certain Louie, whose animated descriptions of the "indiscretions" of notable leaders at the parties given by Lincstone Productions were responsible for getting her through many a night. For instance, the story of the Senator, the pantyhose, and the pint of vanilla ice cream, and the one concerning the CEO, the blowgun, and the tubful of mustard were real "life savers." Louie, *dear* Louie! Lee smiles her best editorial smile, which antic grimace she can no longer control, and thinks, astonishingly enough, of Lourdes. Lourdes? She begins to tremble. Lourdes? Maybe because the word is so close in shape to Louie. Lourdes, Louie. Of course, that's it! Is it? She leans back on her elbows amid the files scattered about on the floor, her eyes amazed, her brow glazed with sweat, her jaw clenched. Much of the rest of her body is also sweaty, but that is not our business, although she does have a spot of trouble with underarm "moisture," truth to tell. Perfectly natural, as far as we're concerned, although we must confess that there is a good deal of cruel laughter to be heard from certain areas, especially those located on the great shale bluffs which overlook Chinatown. Chinatown! Little, if any, decency is shown.

She keels over onto the sand and we can see now, dare we have the temerity to invade her grief-stricken privacy, that the object she clutches to her ample bosom is her most beloved doll, Lu-Lu. It is shabby and tattered by the years' sad, long and sad passage, yet is as dear, still, as sweet, as wonderful as ever it was in the bloom of its novelty. The uncaring rabble, in their ignorance, gambol rudely, as best they know how, poor souls, about the still figure. Yet up Above, and gazing kindly Down, whenever, that is, Chance and a Busy Schedule permit, that most cherished Helpmeet of the Creator's, the Doll Queen, knows the heartache of the quiet Shape on the Strand. Smile, oh Doll Queen, smile in Joy on your best Servant and her dear, her beloved and faithful Lu-Lu, who seems about to break into an aria of surpassing Beauty. Probably in German.

Lyons, world-renowned for its humble potato dish, and, among the cognoscenti, for the Macedero Club, where the immaculate napery hides many a furtive adventure of *amour à doigts,* is losing its preeminence in the world of latenight entertainment.

"But of course, darling!" Lady Bustier says, sparing a moment from her roses, and what beauties they are! "The frightfully boring evening when they banned me because of my 'Madame Doctor' costume was *really* too tiresome. The beginning of the end, really. I mean, it's not as if I wore the frightfully revealing things that one sees in films like, oh, *Madame Delbène,* for instance. The city once had a great deal of charm, but now, I fear that it's *so much* like Madrid, I mean with all those frightfully tawdry statues of saints and things and all sorts of bells ringing and Catholics just *everywhere* and goodness knows what else. But do let me get back to this new hybrid, The Magician they call this one. It's the most delightfully *red* red."

"As far as I'm concerned, the 'Madame Doctor' costume *is* pretty damn revealing, thank God," Sir Bloom remarks to Lord Bury, who is gazing abstractedly—a kind of gazing which, or so it's been discovered, is much in favor with the reserved nobleman—at a young man breaking into an apartment on the ground floor of the building across the courtyard. "I say, Bloomie old darling, there's a young chap across the way who looks *awfully* like Billy Magrino."

"Who on earth is Billy Magrino?" Sir Bloom says, irritably. He is still fuming because of his belated discovery of the existence of the "Cute Cop" line. "And why on earth should I care?"

"Magrino was your original apron purveyor, old boy. Good heavens, have you become so *frightfully* jaded?"

"Of course he was," Sir Bloom says. "Of course. And an absolutely topping boy, too, as I recall. Had a remarkable way with starch."

Billy may still be wonderful with starch, but he is not prepared to discover, in the room to which he gains entry, absolutely nothing but two irregular heptagons of an indeterminate material propped against the dark wainscoting. One is blank, and the other whispers—at least to Billy—the word "ciel." "Oh Jesus!" Billy mutters, backing toward the window, "I'm in le palais des rideaux." Then other things begin to happen, among them the preposterous onset of a wracking *jouissance* which not even Billy's considerable literary intelligence may detain. So we leave him, as smart as ever, writhing against first the walls and then the floors, clutching at his well-made trousers with, apparently, no discernible plan in mind. Thus comes to pass the occasional betrayal by the flesh when it finds that it's been taken into strange rooms.

To return to our wealth of anecdotal material on René Magritte: Magritte is still, after all these years, fondly remembered in Curtin's Palace, a diner specializing in seafood, most especially Crab Mah-Jongg. This dish was the delicacy much favored by the controversial, yet well-dressed French surrealist during his American sojourn, or, as Magritte liked to call it, his "visit to America." Quite an *homme!* Ed Curtin, the owner, who was but a teenaged boy when the celebrated avant-gardist "dropped in," as Ed's father, Cliff, often put it, is happy to recount Magritte's remarks for inquisitive guests, as he is just about to do.

"Mr. Magritte would always say, 'Ah lav zees creb deesh.' And then, later, he'd say, ' 'Ow modge ees zees?' He'd always say that, always ask the price. Then, sometimes he'd say, like as not, ' 'Ow far ees Maine?' When he'd ask how far it was to Maine, well by thunder you could hear a pin drop."

"What does 'cute' mean?" a rather hairy stranger barks from the rear of the small crowd. Before Ed can answer, the stranger's friend, clearly exasperated, hurries him out of the diner.

We understand, by the way, that Curtin's Palace has the best burgers in town.

Thought that was Lena's Rest.

That's the best *buggers.*

What?

April Detective, sitting irresolutely in bed, drunk and naked, as in so many tales of squalor and defeat (indicates photograph of "library of filth and degradation"), ignores the ringing phone. It's her sister, May, of course, calling yet again with the usual unbearable tales about her disappearing underclothes. This week it's slips. April, squalid to a fault, takes a long swallow of vodka and scratches her pubic hair, which has just a little distinguished grey in it—young men no longer suddenly catch their breath when she is passing. The vodka is, as you may have guessed, Majorska, made (or better, created) from the water of pure mountain streams that plunge from their sources in the immaculate snows of beetling scarps inviolate; a vodka that is then filtered, not once, but *thirty-eight times* through expensive imported charcoal, a charcoal that is the product of the rare hardwoods of Corsica, hardwoods that have long been the source of the world-famous meerschaum which is lovingly carved into one-of-a-kind pipes by colorful old men who speak no English. They use only the "heart of the bole," and so do the folks at Majorska, tending the slow fires for weeks until the meerschaum turns into silken black charcoal. This, then, is April's drink, so much so, in fact, that she is known to some as Miss Majorska, a monicker first playfully hung on her by a clubfooted acquaintance of interesting carnal appetites. He's often seen about town, trying to locate potential partners for a business-tips scheme. Unfortunately, his affliction, which is at times referred to as "unspeakable" (as in, "Great Scott! When he takes his socks off it's *unspeakable!*"), serves to make him the object of pity, fear, and disgust. The Earl of Bodoni and his inseparable companion, Mr. Stanley Boils, insist, amid gales of sadistic laughter, that the walking-impaired gentleman was literally *driven through the air* in Malibu by the strangely powerful Tony Malinger, who instantly took offense at his clothing—something about a "weird suit" which frightened starlets and looked "shoddy" against the genteel backdrop of pastel Rolls-Royces. Rumors still persist that Malinger's pet crow is actually Malpas, Friend of Fake Artificers. He of the Hoarse Voice. He Who Answers Questions Incorrectly. He Who Sends Muffie on Her Demented Shopping Orgies. He Who Makes Delilah Crosse Immodestly Expose Her Legs.

Only the most dedicated researchers among students of the cinematic arts know that the celebrated café scene in *From Natchez to Mobile,* in which Dolores Délire, as Madame Froufrou, her gown "trackt to the daintie thies" so that we may almost, but not quite glimpse her *cachebuisson,* hands Baylor Freeq, who plays Robert Frost, a jar of apple sauce, was filmed in Mama Gatto's restaurant, right here in old Manahatta.

"Are you *sure?*" Mandie asks, rather belligerently. She's a kind of girl about town, *loves* fashion, cooking, campy movies, hip novels about, like, real people, really tough political satire, and cultural nationalism as a solution to the problems blacks face. She also has a pet theory that Elvis Presley invented rock and roll. For Mandie, it's best that he did. "And what's this like Manahatta?" she says. "I mean it's Manhattan, right? Like, a borough and a kind of a drink for old lushes, like a cocktail or something, right?"

Any point in going into anything at all with Mandie? Or does she seem, despite her intrinsic worth as a human being, essentially a bust?

According to a tall and rather pale young man, not too pale, but with a complexion not unlike that of Natty Bumppo's, or Gunnery Sergeant Caleb Magrane's, there is no point to it. This young man, a possible victim of hyperbolic neurasthenia (indicates staring eyes and "nervous" testes), identifies himself as Mandie's brother, and one who is "best nameless, or, if not nameless, then best forgotten!" The young man goes on, "If she's caused me one moment of tension and heartbreak, she's caused me a dozen. Ever since we moved here from Misty Crag and its huddled environs of encroaching tares, things have gone wrong. Whichever way we look we see reflections of venery, the trees are constantly threatening to sough, and *wildly* sough!, and little if any decency is shown by anyone. Mandie has become a devotee of the radical Olga Begone's hate-filled poetry, and I, once an innocent stranger to the art of whistling, now find myself removing my underwear every evening, despite my rigorous Baptist upbringing."

"That was a *nice* introduction from that nameless wet dream," Olga says contemptuously. Her upcoming and highly publicized aluminum diet has made her the momentary center of media attention. "Can it!" Olga invariably snaps brusquely, "and keep your compliments for some dumb broad who thinks good things about stiff wee-wees, O.K.? As far as I'm concerned, all the stiff wee-wees in the world aren't worth my Mandie's smallest, sweet, swell, subtle smile." Olga sits at a table piled rather terrifyingly high with black spring binders, and asks if anyone remembers the title poem from *Man-Kill.* Mandie's brother, eyes straining, bolts in horror from the poet's vicinity. He may very well know something that no one else does, something about Begone's conviction that the artist has the duty to subvert the canonical conception of phallic mass.

"Man-Kill"

Crowds of man-shit drunk on whiskey,
Crowds of macho snots, all hot,
Crowds of scum-tongues, fingers frisky,
Filthy scab-cocks pushed at twats.

A semen sky! A world of schmucks!
Greasy balls on rapist goons!
Sisters! Let us kill these fucks!
Cut the balls off all the goons!

Slit the testes in sweet fury!
Burn the stiff prongs with our flames!
We need no "just" and "sober" jury
To slaughter beasts! Come, let's to games!

Coincidentally, a much-belated review of *Man-Kill* is appearing today in what is usually referred to as an important literary journal. Mannix Lambert, known to his adoring students and bitterly jealous colleagues as "Mans," is the reviewer, as is only just and right. Who else knows as much, or for that matter, understands as much about contemporary radical lesbian leftist feminist non-penetrant academic poetry as good-old-hip-deeply-caring-hell-of-a-guy "Mans"? This is a rhetorical question, of course. Marpas, the Transformer, who usually appears as a mighty lion but quickly assumes comely human shape when confronted with chocolate or photos of naughty citizens "in," as they say, "action," Marpas himself was once so astonished by Professor Lambert's acumen and sympathy, perception and compassion, and so on, that one dark night he changed him into a woman. For a few hours. Just to see what he'd look like. One of the things that makes Marpas Marpas is his endless and ever-fresh curiosity. The professor doesn't know of this change, lucky for him, given the events of that night, but there are many things that people, especially professors, don't know. As Thomas Ballantyne writes in *'Tis the Thief Is Prejudicial,* "Belike unto an apeish picture out o' wax / Oft men are stumbo'd in drear ignorance." But we digress. Let us see what "Mans" has to say about Ms. Begone's collection.

Hm. Odd.

It seems that the important literary journal has somehow disappeared. It can't be found at the moment, at any rate, but we'll be bringing you the report, the *gist* of the report, just as soon as possible. Or maybe it's the grist. Hot off the wire, so to speak. Or fire. Out of the fire?

"Goddamned slime! Syphilitic hulks!" Olga yells in the general direction of that area in which the important literary journal is *supposed to be.* There, all is warm, inviting, and familiarly depressing. "Macho slime won't even do the dishes!" Olga shouts. It looks like a clear case of *les vapeurs.*

"Right! Right!" Olga shouts again. "Turn righteous fury into female emotional illness, you disgusting cock!" She squats and pisses on a photo of Hugh Hefner.

The news that inquiries are being received from interested females concerning the "looks" of Treadcliffe Marche can no longer be suppressed. There have been more inquiries than is absolutely necessary, and the suspicion is that many girls and women have inquired more than once— an old trick! It is also suspected that the subject's name itself awakens great interest, a phenomenon which Krafft-Ebing has termed *nomenerotism.* To accommodate this flood of morbid queries, the following description of Marche is being furnished to the public:

> Treadcliffe Marche is a young giant, carrying his huge shock of blond hair six feet three inches from the ground, moving his immense limbs, heavy with ropes of muscle, ponderously. His hands are enormous, red, and covered with a fell of stiff yellow hair; they are hard as wooden mallets, strong as vises. His head is square-cut, angular; the jaw salient, like that of a carnivore.

Some Reactions to the Description

"Good heavens!" "Utterly rambunctious!" "Stiff yellow *what?*" "Whoo-ee!" "I can't even *imagine* his picciumiduno!" "I'm all *for* ropy muscles!" "What does he do with those *enchanting* hands!" "I think that really I might swoon!" "What does 'salient' sort of *mean!*" "My entire body is simply on fucking *fire!*" "Sweet Jesus, Mary, and Joseph, give me strength!" And there are other reactions, too many to list here, but available, perhaps, on request. Maybe. We'll see. All are equally admiring, adoring, lustful. So great is the hubbub raised by the crowds of fevered women that Marchosias, the Wolf, of great power in the Order of Dominations, strong in battle, from whose mouth issue gouts of fire, makes a special trip to see Treadcliffe for himself; for beauty, of whatever kind, resident in whatever sex, fills Marchosias with a lively sense of the salacious. To put it more plainly, if Marge "Somebody" is not available, "Mark" (not his real name) will do very nicely. For Marchosias, everything is a sexual object, and friendship often rapidly metamorphoses into that situation which may best be adumbrated in the words of the ancient poet (here left in his own tongue so as not to disturb the sensibilities of the delicate):

> deprendi modo pupulum puellae
> crusantem: hunc ego, si placet Dionae,
> pro telo rigida mea cecidi.

It goes without saying, of course, that Treadcliffe Marche is, to Marchosias's eye, a perfectly wonderful "Mark," one he'd delight in teaching a few amusing tricks to brighten the close of a long day of fruitless literary study.

"Woof!" says Marchosias. "You bet your life, kid! I'd also, to use a phrase I gleaned from the guys at the VFW hall between games of really bush-league straight pool, not kick Marlene out of bed, either, whoever or whatever *he* may be."

No intelligence concerning any Marlene has crossed "the desk," although not much of anything is crossing "the desk" today. It's much too *hot*. Still, professionalism decrees that the persistent rumors which connect a Marlene with a mysterious clubfooted man be made public. So be it.

A late-breaking story from Glen Cove on Lawrence's manuscript reveals that the literary find of the century—some are already calling it "the literary find of the century"—is a collection, or, a "sheaf" of detailed notes for a Laurentian essay on the sexual role played by sugar in the dark, secret blood. The title of the lengthy essay, or so the notes indicate, was to be *Marmalade Eros, Shadowy Imaginations of the Libido,* or *Lace Me Tighter!* More later on this story of the literary find of the century.

Ellen turns the flame under the clam sauce very low and runs to get the phone. The rustlings of her taffeta cocktail dress!

"Ellen Marowitz?" "Well . . . Ellen . . . yes. I'm Ellen Kaufman now, I mean not now. I mean I was Ellen Maro—" "I understand. Ellen Kaufman?" "Yes." "You don't know me, Miss Kaufman, but I'm a friend of Jeff Chandler's, Miner X. Beely?" "Yes, Mr. Beely?" "Uh, well, Jeff asked me to call and tell you that he had to leave suddenly for the, uh, mountains. His brother, little Buddy, is sick, and needs blood, and a lot of other things." "His brother, Buddy? I didn't know about any . . . the mountains? . . . I've got a chicken." "Thanks for being so understanding, I'm sure Jeff will be in touch after little Buddy walks again, or breathes, or whatever he has to do to live, grow, and make the most of his opportunities. Thanks again, Miss Kaufman, you're a brick." "A what? Hello? A *what?* Hello?"

How may we, at this late date, understand the seamy tragedy of Ellen Kaufman Marowitz's life, a life which at this moment discovers her slaving in the kitchen for a man who is even now making smutty overtures to the first wife of her ex-husband? That this is a day for coincidences would seem to be an understatement, indeed. There is no sure method whereby we may see with clarity the incidents which have brought Ellen to this pass, her eyes filled with bewildered pain, her brow beaded with finials of perspiration from the overpowering heat of the kitchen, her cocktail dress grown suddenly and hatefully gauche, her gourmet meal even more uselessly elaborate than it seemed but a moment since —and it was pretty uselessly elaborate even then! However, a brief survey of her immediate family might furnish, as Coleridge may well have written, "clues," or "clews." He was an odd duck, often laboring under the influence of narcotic substances found amid the drenched lichens.

Jacob "Jack" Marowitz, Ellen's elder brother. Large head. Heavy "city" accent. Weakness for white-on-white shirts. Pathological delight in what he has hidden away as his "collections."

Jack "Jacob" Marowitz, Ellen's father. Grey face. Not quite four feet, six inches tall. The butt of many bawdy jokes because of his petite size, these fortunately lost on him, since his only English was a whiningly enunciated "gumballs?"

Sandra Marowitz, Ellen's elder sister. Disappeared near Lebanon while, in the words of a communiqué, "hustling cheap cosmetics kibbutz-to-kibbutz already."

Sheila Marowitz, Ellen's younger sister. At the moment, pitched forward onto the hot sands of Coney Island. A comely woman, changed by the loathsome Lou Henry into a "flesh beast."

Tessie Marowitz, Ellen's mother. Dead from the neck up, as Jack said, of mambos, blue hair, Mah-Jongg, and rum cokes.

So. That Ellen should make a shambles of her life, that she should, at fifty-one, be pathetically enthralled by a slime like Miner X. Beely, that she should—

"Hold it! Hold it just a second, O.K.?"

Who's this?

"I've been listening to this crap and just want to say there are plenty of us who just won't stand still any more for this stuff. This glib 'survey' of yours is filled with racial, ethnic, religious, and sexual stereotypes, slanders, bigotry, the disgusting leer of naked prejudice. No, this won't be tolerated!"

Who *is* this?

"Buddy Cioppetini, if you want to know so bad. I been trying to keep from losing my grip on myself and running amok like your garden-variety lighthouse keeper is wont to do as I search for a missing book I just happen to love. I passed by and heard your, ah, callous bigotry, and had to come and defend my people against this sort of thing."

What people? This is the Marowitz family. More or less.

"The Marowitzes? Lived over the candy store? Oh. I thought you were talking about *Italians*. I'm in, so to speak, the wrong place? As it were?"

As it were, Buddy. There's no missing book here either.

"Sorry, I didn't know you were talking about Polacks. I got it wrong, O.K.? Made a mistake, anybody can make a mistake. I love kielbasa, by the way! Stuffed cabbage with mastiachi peppers? Hey! You gotta hand it to them the way they take advantage."

Right. Say, isn't somebody calling you?

Item: The suggestion, implication, or declaration that Sheila Henry may have been born Sheila Marowitz flies in the face of every scrap of verifiable information presently in hand. Inquiries will be made, however. The identity of the woman who lies on the sands of Coney Island will also be checked, although there is no reason to doubt that she is, indeed, Sheila Henry, whatever her maiden name. But time will tell.

Item: The charming and remarkably attractive receptionist—the sort of woman who makes men bump into trees and lampposts—of Marquis Meetings, Inc. ("Blue-blood Bimbos Do Your Bidding"), calls to remark

Misterioso   433

that the "description" of Treadcliffe Marche, whose name, she confesses with a spicily heuristic chuckle, intrigues her, is uncommonly similar to that of the protagonist of a novel with the unlikely title of *Blix*. Thanks for the literary tip, lovely lady! And thanks also to the others who called in with the same observation: Betty Barker; that awfully attractive vegetarian couple; a Frieda Canool or something like that; a don calling all the way from Cambridge, England, who also asks for your prayers to release him from his unhealthy obsession; and finally, the truly delightful lady—who said that she's happy to be known now simply as the "Queen of Marrakech"—the Empress of the Trembling Golden Gown.

"What makes you think I'm Anne Marshall?" Anne Kaufman says to Miner X. Beely. "A man who would come out with a remark like that to a woman who manages a small religious supplies store, well, strikes one as a man who . . . has plans." Anne is alarmed by Beely, who looks like the sort who might abandon a Chevrolet.

"Why, of course you're Anne Marshall—I mean you *were* Anne Marshall," Beely says, taking a step toward her. "I heard all about you from the fellows over at the Guinness place."

"The what?" Anne says, certain that this unwanted visitor is a psychopath who, without warning, may become unmanageably disheveled. She picks up an enameled-steel spoon rest cunningly cast in the form of the New Testament.

"*The Guinness Book,* you know?" Beely says, "I'm not really Jeff Chandler, I mean *any* Jeff Chandler. My name is Miner X. Beely, Beat-Off Beely? Well, that was a while ago and now, I mean to say that, well, now I really dig chicks."

Anne brains him with the spoon rest and pulls his corpse behind the counter, where she covers it as best she can with the embroidered quadroon. A scream rises in her throat, but she bravely swallows it, a trick she learned while married to Leo. And then it strikes her: This slender madman must have learned about her *from* Leo! She stands straight, flushed with anger, her eyes clear with the knowledge of what she must do. Then she is womanfully striding toward the door, busily smoothing her skirt and adjusting her bonbons, while her jaw performs its wonted and age-old clenching procedures.

Jack Marshall and Tessie Blankenship Marshall look up from the Mah-Jongg game they are "playing" and Jack turns the volume down on their favorite recording of "Mi Amor Pendeja, Chíngame." They "know" that something is amiss with Anne, even though nothing like this has ever happened to them before. Like what? "Egg cream, Pa?" Tessie asks, her eyes, rheumy at best, clouded over with stunned bewilderment. Jack, his face greyer than ever, pretends that he understands what Tessie has said, as he has so pretended for fifty years. Fifty years! Jack smiles, for some reason. He shrugs noncommittally, as he has so shrugged for fifty years. Fifty years! Jack smiles again, and shrugs even more noncommittally. "Perhaps we must go to her!" Tessie cries. "Must we?" She makes a tentative move, as if to rise from her chair, but it is really more like a *rustling*. What is? Jack turns the volume up, and smiles again. "Mambos are excellent," he notes. "Right, dear?" Tessie idly clicks some tiles in her dignified, gnarled fingers, and looks sweetly at him. "My little grey shrimp," she says tenderly, as she has so said for fifty years. Fifty years! Tessie smiles, a smile that—

Is there some kind of a mistake? Who *are* these people?

Let's leave it be, it'll probably sort itself out. Too hot to worry.

Then too: Ex-Hotel Bartender Believes Vodka Martini Cause of Homosexuality; Marvelous Magazine Management Corp. Will Drop Controversial *Professors in Action;* Survey Finds "Mary" Favorite Moslem Name; Minister Decries Mary Janes as "Sin Shoes"; Sister Mary Magdalene, 114, Envisions Protestant Heaven as "Condo Complex"; Mason Jars Occasionally Useful in Sex Therapy, Says Dr. Massa; Massachusetts Evangelist Claims World Created in 1815; Mast Grogan, TV Host, to Change Name to Henri Matisse; Marcus Matz, Expert on Frank Norris, Disappears in California.

A woman signing herself "Maureen, an old pal of April's," writes to suggest that Olga Begone's "Man-Kill" is highly derivative of the early verse of Jean Ingelow, especially the poem, "Divided," in *Poems* (1863). Miss Ingelow, from her thatch-roofed, cuckoo-rife cottage in Kensington, has kindly released the following statement:

Although Maureen, who was once a girl, the very embodiment of Fancy, is now a woman, who is Imagination brooding over what she brings forth, she would do well to remember that the domains of Poetry and of History are represented by two purple peaks. In brief, I am not pleased to have my name linked with that of Olga Begone. As my beloved half-brother, Max, is fond of saying, "Better to starve in England than to be a moiety of the *Mayflower* rout and rabble." I don't know what dear Max means, but there, as they say, it is.

Lips slides *Absalom! Absalom!* into his pocket, despite the stare of a middle-aged woman in a too-short skirt, too-tight blouse, lace-patterned black stockings, and spike heels. She is a bit ridiculous in these things, "desperate" might be the cruelly proper word to use. However, Lips is no less ridiculous than she, and his T-shirt, which bears the message LOVE MAZATLÁN? GET YOUR M.B.A., is no less crass than the woman's ill-fitting clothing. Lips is afraid that she might make a scene, or inform the manager, or otherwise disrupt his plans. He is therefore pleasantly surprised by the sudden intrusion of an outsider into the game of watcher and watched that he and the woman are playing.

"Hello! I'm Thom McAn! I mean the *actual* Thom McAn, the, if you'll pardon the expression, McCoy. Although Marcie Butler, over there by the green beans—it *is* Marcie Butler?—is got up in a devastatingly stunning costume the likes of which is perfect for larking about with lynx and tambourine, pipes and timbers, and oaten reed and thorax, it is not *exactly* what the well-dressed woman wears while shopping! Take it from me, the world-famous designer, manufacturer, and purveyor of affordable ladies' foot stylings for God knows how many years!"

Marcella—for it is she—finishes picking up a few forgotten items and sidles toward a checkout counter as best she can, considering her heels and skirt. Perhaps she doesn't sidle so much as career. Lips pretends to be examining the green peppers. A somewhat embarrassed priest, his physical state the focus of a group of admirers of both sexes, tries, to no avail, to interest his fans in McAn.

"Yes, Marcie," McAn goes on, "I've sold shoes, although flogged is more in keeping with what I did with them, yes, to no less demanding a personage as Charlotte McCoyne, not McCoy, but McCoyne, the true, natural mother of Anne Kaufman, who, at the moment, I feel, is in grave danger, although why I should feel this is a mystery to me. Jayzus McGlade, whom some of you older shoppers (indicates two grey-haired folks who dodder convincingly) may recall as an Irish youth of manly vim and *élan vital,* loved the snappy little ankle-strap number in six fashion shades for fall. By God, they never hurt *his* football playing! And they were no small factor in his all-around locker-room popularity either, take it from his cheerfully brutal pals. Helga McGrath, loving grandmother to a maturely bewitching hearing-seeing-speaking-walking-impaired study in courage with an enlightened interest in painting—don't ask!—was very big on the kind of footwear designed to laugh off the filth and rough going of rural byways. So, when I have an opinion about women's clothing. . . ."

McAn rambles on, while Marcie makes good her escape, and Lips, partially hidden behind a Perrier display, slips *Absalom! Absalom!* out of his pocket to find that it is called *L'Amant et la lune* by Paul de Kock. It also seems to be written in a foreign language, and since Lips knows no language but his own, he can say, with Casca, that it is Greek to him, and be absolutely correct. Lips doesn't say this. Rather, facing the ice-cream freezer, he makes a mincing mow in order to, in his own disturbed words, "pricketh th' ebon Saracen!"

Literary Interlude

> ". . . though I am not enthralled
> To be here in Old Méjico," Melanie said, "land
> Of the homely *taco,* eaten in these parts
> For bread, and the *mastiachi* peppers
> Of great heat, or as the natives say, *calor.*"
> She sat then nervously upon a window seat,
> Like a haunted skylark, and took up again
> Her wretched tatting. Melissa, dark temptress
> And the wife of Baron Darke, felt pain as sharp
> As the sting of the *ñorga* bug for the dear girl!
> Such a golden child, lisping of "fireworkth"
> And "picnicth" and indeed, "hot dogth," too!
>
> "I'm sorry, Melanie, my dearest child,"
> The older woman crooned, sweeping in her

Silken gown like a perfumed typhoon,
Majestically, to sit in ladylike perfection.
"But did I know why the Baron colors crimson
And faints dead away, like a high-school girl,
When e'er you fix him with your eyes as blue
As my forgotten irises beyond the kale,
Perhaps, perhaps I, I might. . . ."

Here the noble beauty paled impeccably,
Then clutched her breasts with trembling hands,
And said, "Perhaps, perhaps I'd know just why
He sent his couriers as swift as Death, toot sweet!
To rainy Nottingham from Eagle House
That fateful and, I understand, ironic afternoon!"

"Oh! How I fondly wish you *did* know, kind Melissa,"
The young maiden whispered softly as a balmy
English breeze upon an English moor. The while
Her gnarled and knotted tatting fluttered weakly
On the brooding, soot-encrusted andirons!

"Just because I am possibly," and here
The girl shuddered like a mast before
A mad simoom, "the unborn child, the baby
Grown to blushing womanhood—dare I ask how?
—The dream-wight of the weird Detectives,
Well! That cuts no ice, whatever that may mean,
Insofar as the dreadful summons in the heat
Of Nottingham's bleak, blazing noon goes!"
Silence fell upon the pair at once.

"Dearest Melanie," Melissa breathed, "as one
Warm, full-blooded woman to another, to a
Puzzled woman, a puzzled virgin given o'er
To primping prettily and blushing, puzzled,
Like the citizens of Thebes, by unanswered
Queries, cunning riddles, and sly tricks
To 'crack the brains like nuts,' as Hesiod said,
I must speak openly and with a heavy heart,
A heart as heavy as the pine log in the hearth."

At this moment, the elder dame was not
The proud and stiffly distant Baroness of
Eagle House! No! But suddenly disclosed
Her steaming, vulnerable soul!

"Dearest Melanie," she said again,
Catching up with her bejeweled hands
The wild folds of richly ornamented
Tulle which ached, or so it seemed,
To detonate themselves in beauty free
So as to make the gloomy welkin sound!
Like, then, was a goddess she.

Settling the massy stuff about her, Melissa
Sighed, "That you may be the unborn child
Of the lugubrious Detectives serves you
No purpose here or there! We welcome you!
As sister, daughter, cousin, niece, or aunt,
As any sprig or twig of femininity, we
Welcome you into the dancing light
Of each night's blazing, merry *fuego!*
And I pray," and here the Baroness heaved
Her splendid bosom toward the heavens,
"That my lord, the Baron, proud scion of
These ancient piles, and plain Bert to me,
His yielding wife, will reveal his chilling
Secret to us twain. And soon," she cried.

At these words, Baron Darke, his doublet
All undone, his hose askew, his boots
All encrusted with the dreadful mud of
El Durango, his blazing eyes wild-staring
In his head like two mad lighthouse keepers
Run amok, entered the great hall of the *hacienda*
And in a voice as sharp and threatening
As a schizophrenic crazy man, he thundered,

"Woman! Or, women! As the case may be!
Good God and blast! I reck not, nor do I wot!
Where is the latest issue of *Men's Action*?
I had begun a hypnotizing tale

Of a comely female anthropologist,
As game as she is desirable in her
Close-fitting khakis, pursued by rabid
Crocodiles, controlled by Moscow! So,
My handsome brace of quails, o-ho! Speak
Quick and bright as popping flashbulbs
And you may avoid my petulance and dump," he spoke.

In the great room, one could hear the soughing
Of the wild *atascaderos,* and the fall
Of a distant pin to the red tile floor,
Tiles red as *hombre's* gore!

"And while I await your female answer,
Which will be, I'll wager my brood Appaloosa,
Soft and sweet as chocolate pudding still a
Little warm, tell me, Melissa," the Baron smiled,
"My bosomy, long-leggèd spouse, dear girl
Who graces lawful bed with flesh so firm the very
Roast beef of the dinner table seems to shrink
In consternation, aye! Tell me, I say, or
I *was* saying, tell me, wife, I will say again,
Why did you, in contradiction of my wishes,
Made *crystal clear* in a hurried, yes, but
Legible and cogent memorandum, invite, and
For *supper,* this next bleak and damnèd Friday night,
The dismal, dastardly, the homely, and the
Hopelessly idiotic Mervishes? Whom all folk swear
To shun?"

Suddenly, a mad gust of desert-hot *viento*
Carried a large cactus in, and past them,
On its blast! Which broke the sullen tension
In the moody room. But not for long.

"I've brought you something to read, Ethan," the slatternly and sullen
Zenobia says, shaking the broken gimp dozing in the homemade wheel-
chair by the fire. "Here." And with that, she furtively jettisons a copy of
The Metal Dress onto her husband's partially collapsed "chest."
    "Thank you, Zeena," the man says courteously, horrible pains

shooting through what was once a recognizable face, but which now resembles a twisted mask of agony. "But, you know, that since my, er, *foe paz,* I've been attracted exclusively to works of non-fiction—such as this marvelous new study of the Everglades and its zesty and informative secrets, entitled *Secrets of the Everglades.* A nice little item."

"Well then," Zenobia snaps cruelly, "if you don't like racy, suggestive fiction now that you're but *half a man,* I reckon that reading up on eyetalian swamps is just about up *your* alley!" She grins dully through dingy, broken teeth, the usual oral equipment of a slattern, at her husband's obvious psychic discomfiture. "There's also—I 'forgot' to tell you—a hamburger, there, on your wizened 'chest.' Best burger in town, or so they claim, danged fools! So go on and *eat up,* while I go and *wake up* Mattie," the harridan concludes, pulling a six-inch hatpin from the shrewish effluvium of her wispy coif.

"Eat?" Ethan furiously croaks. "Eat!? You cruel slatternly virago!" he cries weakly. "How can I eat when you know full well that I am *par'lyzed?*"

Zenobia, happily tucking a brick under her arm, leaves the room, humming. Ethan, shrugging what remains of his once-broad, tanned shoulders, manages to cast both hamburger and "pop" book to the floor, and then, by means of a cleverly designed pulley system imported from the Amazon Basin, turns once again to read in *Metallic Constructions.* This tome, which fascinates and oft bears him away on flights of healthy, manly fantasy, contains a favorite chapter, to which he now directs, once again, his full, if not precisely rapt attention. It is, of course, "How to Build a Strong Sled Out of Scrap Iron," and, reading it, for perhaps the dozenth time, he tries, as best he can, to blot out the vicious oaths and wrenching cries of pain from the coal bin, by placing his wrists deep into the "things" where once his shapely ears had been.

"I will not read *The Metallic Fly* to you again, Zeena!" Mattie's girlish voice quavers. "It's a bad-foul, bad-mean, devil-bad book, and I don't like the strange things you try out when I read it, either! Oh God! If I weren't *par'lyzed,* I'd gather Ethan up in my yearning arms and be gone from this living hell in a moment!"

The sickening crack of brick against shriveled flesh rings clear in the silent household. Ethan, tears coursing from gaunt sockets down his "face," reads on, pitifully. There seems no point anymore in admiring the rude chairs and rough-hewn wooden table placed neatly about.

The quarrel is fast approaching that point at which the closest and most understanding of friendships can be strained almost to the breaking point, even though we may feel, probably mistakenly, as if we have shared, in the best sense, their travails, and followed avidly their "ups and downs"—and how wonderful it is that we have them all together at last!—with a well-nigh hawklike attention to detail. Yet at such moments, little if any decency is shown, and the crystalline highlands often echo with weeping.

"For the last time, Lucy," Tabitha Bramble says, her lips white with anger and her heavy, melonlike breasts straining to burst from her revealing gown, "the Métro is not located in Mexico, thus cannot serve the population of Mexico City. It is, on the contrary, the famous mass-transit system of Miami and Miami Beach. I don't care *what* that vile sexist stud, Mickey, who so enthralls you with his large bologna—how I hate that word!—has to say."

"Mickey's bologna, I trust, is not going to be dragged into this discussion," Lucy Brandon replies, with some asperity, her enormous, girlish bosom heaving with unleashed fury. "Mickey labors under the burden of being a man of the Midwest, a simple man of potatoes and edible roots, an earthy churl of joss and mandrake, a feral galoot, yes, innocently proud of his *machismo,* which he boyishly conflates with baseball caps and cans filled with 'beer.' Yet it is this flaw, if flaw it be, which paradoxically permits Mickey to speak with authority on the Métro. So, in your nose, you painted slut!"

A hollow, ringing silence descends on the room, much like the silence which usually reigns in the Frome household, a silence broken only by the soft ticking of the clock which has, yet again, appeared, and the hoarse panting, or pantings, of Tabitha and Lucy. Their eyes, spiritedly flashing and snapping with full womanly abandon, meet, their hearts race, and without thinking of such trivialities as "Métro" and "bologna," they are suddenly in each other's arms, weeping in joy, relief, and, naturally, excitement. They are not aware—and were they, would they care?—that their surrender to sapphic sensuality and sensational sex, stuffed with superb and socko surprises, will, as usual, pander to the basest of male fantasies.

"Sure. 'Mike in the Morning,' the title story in Mikky Way's run-away success of a collection of superb fictions is just *like* that—really base," Jack Armstrong remarks from deep within the recesses of his comfortable leather-and-tobacco armchair in which he is wont to reflect. "Packs a hell of a sensuous wallop, and though the sex is utterly gratuitous, it's attractively steamy, in a paradigmatic way." He puffs thoughtfully on his richly encrusted meerschaum, his eyes resting for a moment on the papers, most of them of a decidedly cultural nature, scattered on his warmly cluttered desk, with cat. "While some have called 'Mike' a sophomoric display of cynical attitudes toward women, others, despite wide learning and a shithouse full of degrees, have developed respectable erections which have stood them in good stead at social functions and made them decided 'hits' at home. There are," he concludes excitedly, "two schools of thought on, like, broads in bed together. Right? One is about what they're up to and the other focuses on how many of them there are!" Armstrong sinks ever deeper into his chair, pleased that his literary views are finally under consideration. Or whatever it is they're under.

A curse, more than likely.

"Have I ever told you of my trip to Milan?" he says. "Wonderful! Something *about* the Continent. Italy. We'd been, of course, to *Italy*. But the North! So refreshingly non-American, so friendly. Nothing like an Italian! I mean, of course, Italians in Italy! Well, have I? Told you? About? Perhaps next summer we'll. If you've heard this, just, please, just say so, and I'll tell you about my meerschaum. (Indicates smoldering pipe while are heard the panicky sounds of a number of citizens in full flight.)

The Milky Way candy bar is manufactured, as label-readers know, in Hackettstown. Those of you with long memories may recall that just outside this town, on the road to Budd Lake, lies the Bluebird Inn. It has been suggested, and with some vigor, that this is, indeed, a day for coincidence. Had things turned out otherwise, Ellen Kaufman, called, in her youth, Miss Milky Way (!) by those who were put off by her over-powering sweetness, would today have *been* in Hackettstown. Instead, blinded by love, she is, as we know, "bustling about." She is going to get, as the hoary phrase crudely has it, "the shaft," as we may surmise, but that is neither here nor there. In Hackettstown, just about to leave his house and drive to the Bluebird for a few beers and an invigorating, blues-chasing spate of fox-trot delight, is a certain Mr. Mille, a collector, if it can be believed, of 50's trivia, memorabilia, and artifacts, including, most especially, the cocktail dress!

In other words, Ellen had an appointment with this Mille to. . . ?

Precisely. But love, in the grotesque guise of Miner X. Beely, is keeping her at home today. Had she journeyed to Hackettstown, her arms laden with the exotically hued garments coveted by Mille, her life might well have changed utterly.

"If truth be told, I might have waylaid her for some Christian badinage on that little stretch of lonely road what's just beyond the hideously gnarled apple tree," Knute remarks sociably from his hiding place in a dense copse of thornbushes, which are, incidentally, rending his flesh and turning his clothing into tatters, *à la* King Sweeny.

"Rags, actually," Knute says apologetically. " 'Tatters' sounds to me like a fairy word, and as the whole world knows, there are no fairies in the thornbushes!"

How about at the bottom of the garden?

"Well, sure. *There,*" Knute agrees.

Mr. Mille is dancing. In a half-hour or so, besotted by breaks and dips, he will have forgotten all about Ellen's letter, or, as he thinks of it, Miss Milky Way's letter.

"Hi! I'm Karen Millpond! When I'm popping open cans of *really* cold soft drinks, as modern technology, fantastic engineering know-how, and personal savvy whisk us through the heavens, I'm the consumptate professional! But when Milt, my taciturn creative consultant, roars up in his new BM, my nipples get just as stiff as the next girl's. Hi!"

This "Milt" cannot be the same "Milt" who was Sheila's first lover?

"Hi! I'm Karen Minet! An actual professor I met while pouring hot, stimulating coffee and rubbing a few of my female charms up against his tweedy shoulder just *miles* above Denver, told me that 'minet' is French for 'pussy.' When I'm dancing in one of those *hot* new clubs with my sleek fella, cute as can be in my *bitch* of a haircut, I really *feel* like a sexy kitty, or a depraved character in *Misterioso,* the new Broadway hit. Hi!"

"Actually," the actual professor says, interrupting his casual disquisition on his LATEST TRIP TO EUROPE, "the coffee was *not* stimulating, since it was caffeine-free. That's the only kind I drink, else I might die too young to make all the TRIPS TO EUROPE which, I feel, are a scholarly necessity. If you follow me?"

Thanks, Professor, and so long. (Indicates door.)

Léonie Aubois still possesses the three curious fan letters sent from Herbert Hoover to Tom Mix. She has kept them with her for many years, resisting the sharp temptation to sell them time and time again. Indeed (music heard softly in distance), these letters serve, perhaps, as Miss Aubois's anchor to reality (music stronger now, bright with gouts of whipped cream spurting in a major key), perhaps, even, as testaments to *hope.* (The sound is upon us, happily merciless, thick with pseudo-wonderful, Jesus as a regular guy, and death as, sort of, like a better job.) Perhaps we should discover for ourselves the fascination of these letters, sent, no doubt, in remarkable humility and heartfelt egalitarianism, from a Great Statesman, "the Man who whipped Inflation," to an International Western Star. Let's take a look. Léonie surely won't mind, particularly since she's going into seizures as the horrors descend upon her (lush chords softly crash).

Dear Mr. Mix:

I saw you in *Rifles on the Pecos* recently and was quite bowled over by your manly skills, and your American spirit of rugged individualism. Many of the desperadoes who felt the sting of your brand of range justice looked very much like dago anarchists, moustaches and all. "Hanging is too good for them," as you say in the last scene. Well, this is the pass that modernistic nonsense has brought us to, with its kike ideas and sissy foreign pictures. I like a statue you can understand, a manly statue!

I have a lot on my mind right now with the nagging unemployment problem we have, which is caused, as these darn fools around here don't seem to know, by there being so many people out of work. They are *unwilling* to work. But I'd like to tell you that the way you sit on your horse fills me with a manly pride and also reminds me of something.

Yours in prosperity,
Herbert Hoover

Dear Tom Mix:

Thanks for your gracious reply from the ranch and your busy life. I personally don't have a great deal to do right now, what with people crying to me all day long with their hard-luck stories about unemployment and hunger and gosh-all knows what else. If they had any gumption and Christian backbone, they could get a job almost anywhere. Fellows like you and me, self-made men, don't lack for work, but that's because we weren't raised to be mollycoddles expecting everything to be given to us on a silver platter. When I was a boy I walked 22 miles each way to school, usually through six-foot snowdrifts, with only a raw potato for lunch. But it made me into a manly boy and a manly man, if a little thin.

I *thought* that maybe that's what it reminded me of but I didn't really know whether I should think so or not. It seems darn manly to me, in a special, private sort of way, I agree. But you're right that not everyone understands.

Yours in the coming prosperity,
Herbert Hoover

Dear Tom:

Well! Last night was simply the crackerjack event of the year for me. I saw a special screening of *Guns of the Colorado* and never have you acquitted yourself so nobly or bravely along the lines of shooting, fistfighting, strangling, clubbing, and so forth. When you strapped your Colts on in the dry-goods store, I could feel the weight of those "shooting irons" around my own waist. Whew!

As you may have read, I haven't been re-elected. The cabal of communists, socialists, anarchists, and the Eastern kikes and dagos has put me out of office just as I was about to present a plan based on self-reliance, grit, and pluck. There's plenty of money to go around, but people are hoarding it!

Yes, I do have that famous photo of you with your guitar, singing under the live oak with Jackie "Pinto" Moline. But, you bet, I'd sure *love* to see the other one you mention. Believe me, I'd treasure it.

Yours in real Western values,
Herbert Hoover

Many epistolary specialists, political scientists, Depression "buffs," and historians of the cinema feel that these letters, along with the one to

Hoppy, are apocryphal, if not maliciously spurious. The conservative scholar, M. Plaid Soup, writes that his inspection of the letters leads him to believe that they were forged by "a swarthy man, probably Jewish or Italian."

"Hi! I'm Mom! Any Mom at all! Do me a favor, darling, and don't call so often, all right? Keep in touch, sure, nice, but you don't have to be a fanatic about it. Today, for instance, it's so hot that I'm trying to stay as cool as possible by sitting nice and still. I don't, you know? need to be running to answer the phone! Tell your troubles to Jesus for a change, all right, darling?"

Calls have been coming in inquiring whether this day, this ordinary day, is a Monday. It is not, but we are not yet authorized to tell you what day it *is.* Those of you with old calendars or the gifts of an idiot savant know already, of course. That is, if it matters to you.

Gaspard Monge, discovered alone, in the kitchen of a three-room apartment in Bensonhurst: This cannot possibly be *the* Gaspard Monge, the latter having died in 1818. On the other hand, Monge, a Mongol No. 2 pencil in his hand, is excitedly putting the finishing touches on a method which will permit geometrical problems in three dimensions to be solved in the plane. He smiles, puts his pencil down, stretches, yawns, and says, "Voilà! It sims zat I 'ave invent ze descriptive géometrie! Now to calling up a lay-dee frien', Gail Patrick or Deanna Durbin or Freddie Bartholomew, even maybe Marilyn Monroe, to 'elp me zelebrett. Zom wan of zees honey bunches!"

General perplexity. Some *hard questions* must be asked, or so it seems to a clear majority of the Board.

We welcome all interrogations and cannot wait to be persecuted. Names, after all, must be cleared, reputations repaired. Oh, it's easy to *accuse,* yet we ask only that our answers may be given in writing and that we have an undisclosed period of time in which to prepare them. Done?

Done.

1. Does Deanna Durbin buy her tasteful frocks at Namm's of Brooklyn or at Tarnation Emporium of Montana?

2. Is there any truth to the rumor that Gail Patrick and Marilyn Monroe gambled recklessly and also committed several vile acts with persons unknown in Monte Carlo, "sewer of Europe"?

"Eez no wan going to pay a mind to may deezcovérie?"

Quiet, Monge, please!

3. Why has George built a small fire of the pages torn from *Géometrie descriptive*?

4. Is it proper, given the sensitivities of the dizzyingly raised consciousness of our truly enlightened time, to call Freddie Bartholomew a "lay-dee frien'," and to refer to him as a "honey bunch"?

a.) Are *some* men "honey bunches"? Or perhaps "cinnamon buns"? Are they "yentas," "shtarkers," or "gonifs"? Are they, essentially, "obsolete"?

b.) How, then, fare the adventurous, twisted denizens of the quiet suburbs?

5. When Bobby Breen, in the rollicking musical comedy-drama *A New Dimension* (never released), cries, at the climax of the rubber game of Moo Goo Gai Pan he is playing with Gloria Jean (no relation), "Bamboo shoots, four, twelve; bean curd, eight-slam doubled!" what does Miss Jean do? In what key?

"Oo are zees pipple?" Monge asks, understandably. "Bobby Brin? Gloria Jin? Ah weel invite zem too, non?"

Quiet, Monge, please!

6. Anybody? Six? Six, anybody? That's it, then? O.K. The *hard questions* have been asked. We expect full compliance with the agreement?

Absolutely.

The Board stands adjourned.

"Ees Bobby Brin ze fellow wiz ze curlee 'air which makes you cray-zee wiz ennui as he sings a song?"

No one answers Monge, who seems to be more and more representative of the neglected genius. To crown his so-far hopelessly unsatisfying day, his calls to Patrick, Durbin, Bartholomew, and Monroe cannot be completed. However, this cannot be *the* Gaspard Monge, as earlier noted.

"Il n'etait jamais Gaspard Monge," Gil Roulure says. "Il est Théophile Dondey." So he says, but Gil is liable to say anything. We know Gil!

Morax the Bull, a great President and Earl, who knows the virtues of all herbs and precious stones, who imparts skill in astronomy and the liberal sciences, and in all the geometries, especially hermetic, speaks: "It's hot and I won't keep you long. Please forgive me, and accept my apologies. I'm afraid that I must take full responsibility for the sudden and crass appearance of the man who passes himself off as either Gaspard Monge or Théophile Dondey, both of whom, as you know, are dead. *This* man, who has lately embarrassed himself and his unfortunate fellows with his fake French accent and his unfounded gutter allusions to famed film stars of the past, is really a friend of Page Moses, often called, in justifiable denigration and mockery, Doctor Plot. I thought to embarrass Moses by putting *his* "Monge" into a situation too difficult and complicated to be weaseled out of by means of various threadbare devices, e.g., fires and explosions, sudden love or death, trips to strange places, long waits in hospital corridors, boring causes for dull effects, or the bleak knowledge that people are beautiful, after all, even though the air-conditioner is broken and Dad has the shakes. But "Monge," too stupid to realize his danger, embarrassed neither Moses nor himself; rather, he has humiliated me, my staff, and my fellow demons yet again, and I apologize. As a token of my gratitude for your kind attention, here is the solution, on the blackboard behind me, of Fermet's last theorem." (Indicates solution.)

Page Moses, sweltering in the heat like everyone else, and disappointed that the small audience for his impeccably presented summary of *Zuleika Dobson* has drifted silently away, is entertaining himself by working on the plot for a book he means to write. This is a bona fide, absorbing time-passer for the good Doctor, but boring for us, since all that *we* may see of the vaunted "creative process" is Page's face. Luckily, Morax, to make up for his recent gaffe, peers into Plot's head and relays to us the skeletal framework of the planned novel, or so he says.

MOTHER LOVE

Story to be told in the first person by a grizzled Chevrolet dealer and part-time woodsman, Knute, who puts together the pieces of the dark tale of the inhabitants of a grim, hardscrabble farm in the gorse forests which loom. Mother

Church, known throughout the bleak hills as "Ma," drives her hardworking husband, "Pa," almost to despair with her whining complaints about her smoky stove and the crooning scarecrow, despite her knowledge that Pa has all he can manage to put a few, frozen, half-rotted ears of corn on the rude wooden table. Ma's young cousin, Mother Machree, who has been stigmatized since childhood, and is known in the bleak fens as "Sherri," is left penniless, and comes to live with the Churches. Within a month, Pa and Sherri have formed a deep friendship, arousing Ma's bitter jealousy. One day, at Ma's request, Mother Theresa, an old school friend, whom all her previous employers know as "Muffin," appears at the farmhouse door, ostensibly to act both as Ma's amanuensis and Sherri's helper in the bleak and smoky kitchen. In a month or so, however, Muffin and Sherri are locked in furious daily quarrels over the value of Robert Motherwell's "Summer Light" series, with Ma coming down on Muffin's side, and Pa defending Sherri's opinion. Goaded into an uncharacteristic fury by Muffin's and Ma's sneering references to him as "Mister Mouth," and "the world's greatest unknown art critic," Pa cuttingly refers to Muffin's heavy ankles. In the weeks that follow, an uneasy truce is often broken by Ma's vicious attacks on Sherri's current reading—*Mouth of Steel* by Henri Kink—as "pervert trash," and Muffin's almost frantic insults anent the music and sexual tastes of W. A. Mozart, a well-known composer whom Pa and Sherri hold in high esteem. A curious tome entitled *Mrs. Dalloway* also comes in for some alertly savage slander. After a particularly bitter exchange, during which Pa's and Sherri's pleasure in enlightened and serious fiction in a foreign language, and their innocent love for fried nougat are subjected to venomous raillery, Ma insists that Sherri leave. On their way to the bus depot, Pa and Sherri realize that they are in love, and decide to die together rather than part. They zoom down a steep hill on Pa's sled and crash into a brooding bay tree, whose stark, bare branches look like the twisted arms of several maddened lighthouse keepers. However, they are not killed, but are found and carried back to the bleak farmhouse by Mud and Mugg Waldbaum, local cow folk. The drunken village physician, Dr. Johnson Mulloon, is sent for, and, polluted as usual, his surgical attentions leave both Pa and Sherri *par'lyzed* for life, under the cold and cruel eyes of Ma Church and Muffin Theresa, who have become an item amid the bleak hills.

Annette removes the tattered and stained manuscript, entitled "Mademoiselle Mummy," from the book in which it is kept. She unfolds it, and smiles a brilliant, icy smile as she recollects the fate of the man who wrote and then threatened her with it, as if she cares, as if she *could* care!

But the temerity, the vulgarity, the crude *actuality* of the threat! Intolerable, of course. She recalls the expression of awe and terror on his face when he first heard the whispering rustle of the flying rats' wings, an odd, high-pitched sound. Poor man! Now she looks over the manuscript again, for the first time in almost twenty years, and its prose is, indeed, as she remembers it—the dull, sincere, determined monotone of a man with something to expose, something to *say*. How much more delightful the silly excesses of the book in which she keeps the manuscript—*La Dame aux trois corsets*. Annette smiles again, the subtle ochre lighting gleaming dully off her silvery teeth, as she remembers de Kock's delighted laughter when she suggested, with the levity of youth, that he should, by right, call the work *La Dame aux corsets d'acier*. Those were, indeed, the days. Sudden lightning.

Charles "Chuck" Murphy, an Irish-American, who, in his wily manner, often gives his name as "Carlos" or "Chaz" Murphy—the grass doesn't grow under *his* feet—takes his wife, Constanza, grey-haired and with crow's-feet around her eyes, yet still almost as lissome as a young bride (lover, mistress, girlfriend), to the Museum of Modern Art. They've had an amusingly gauche but interesting brunch of canned pork and beans, Jane Parker jelly donuts, mu-shu pork, and Banana Amaze—the dessert which seems to be sweeping the neighborhood, a quiet one in a small suburb, populated, for the most part, by attractive vegetarian couples. Despite their intense if not overtly active dislike for art in all of its unlikely manifestations, the Murphys have heard and read for weeks now about the Modern's exhibition of erotic drawings made for the original, limited, subscription edition of the famous pastoral novel *La Musique et les mauvaises herbes,* known to cognoscenti as "Chords and Swards." Not only has the Modern managed to locate *all* of the original drawings and their numerous preliminary studies as well as a score of unused drawings, but the curator for the exhibition, Mus Musculus, the brash Danish expert on the *fin de siècle,* makes a strong case, in his catalogue essay, for the theory that the hitherto unknown artist can probably be identified as the irrepressible social satirist and society "wit at large," the arrogant dandy known only as Mutt, pronounced "mo͞ot." Charles and Constanza find themselves to be the only people in the wing, and, given this unexpected privacy, the heat of the day, the aphrodisiac effects of the Banana Amaze, Constanza's lissome qualities (already mentioned), and the decidedly arousing drawings to serve as amorous examples, one thing leads to another and then, of course, to another. Ten minutes later, Mr. Mytilene, a Greek shipping magnate with a special interest in cafeteria growth stocks, comes upon the couple, happily engaged in frantically oblivious coupling. Mr. Mytilene stares, and then, perhaps remembering his Catullus, walks quietly toward the writhing Murphys, delightedly muttering, "Ανθρωπος φύσει ζῶον." The cock of cocks, Naberius, who, invisible, has been enjoying the drawings by, it is said, "one who well served the Goëtic Art," instantly comprehends the situation, and, in his hoarse voice, urges Mr. Mytilene on. The Museum of Modern Art often packs a surprising wallop.

Then too: Women Named "Nancy" Liable to Explode, Experts Say; Studies Reveal Nash Favorite Car of Overweight Rabbis; Historian Contends Natchitoches Once Part of Albania; Nathan's Famous Settles Phallic Symbol Suit; The *Nation* May Display "Boss" Tweed's Magic Violin; National Guard to Host Combat Weenie Roast; Directors of National Multiple Orgasm Fund Charged in Office Orgies; Naughtie Nightie Boutique to Market Polyester Lingerie Despite Christian Bowlers' Protests.

Sir Bloom and Lord Bury, idly chatting of things ephemeral, cannot see into the "palais des rideaux," where young Billy Magrino is still twitching and trembling, albeit more rhythmically, on the floor. More importantly for them, they cannot see into the small basement laboratory *cum* sewing room where the prototype of the "Naughty Nurse" costume is getting its final nips and tucks, ruches and gathers. This is not surprising, since the workshop is in a small Nebraska town, Nemo (pop. 49), huddled at the foot of Scotts Bluff, the latter named after Robert Falcon Scott's famed poker hand, 2D3H5C8S10S, which won him monies sufficient to buy the supplies he needed for yet another crackpot jaunt.

"Such ignorance of history surpasseth human understanding," Chet Kendrick says, momentarily setting aside a new collection of essays by his favorite Neo-neo-Humanist, the brilliant if depraved Countess

Nettie, whose extraordinary good fortune in the Nevada casinos is matched only by her breathtaking beauty, a beauty paradoxically enhanced by the raucous bimbos who attend her.

"Actually, the young women so unjustly maligned are not 'raucous bimbos' but a *spirited entourage,*" Chet says. "Two have had *small but important* roles in Academic Playhouse of the Air presentations, three more have served with distinction—*à la* the lady friends of Quintus Horatius Flaccus—at the remodeled New Ecstasy Motor Inn, one was Miss New England Shore Dinner, and another Miss New Jersey Wetlands. Still others have *distinguished themselves* in public service, such as which can be easily checked out with ease and the utmost alacrity. I submit to all fair-minded people the notion that such ladies are *precious adornments* on the body politic, and not 'bimbos,' raucous or otherwise." Just then the phone rings. Or is it the clock that ticks? No, it's the phone. It's Georgene, calling from her bathtub, or so she stoutly maintains. Let's leave her and Chet to their conversation.

"On a day like this a bath is a pretty good idea."

Who said that?

"I did. Me, George."

George seems still to be locked out of the bathroom in which his wife relaxes. He is, too, in the words of the old song, waiting in the lobby of her heart.

It should be said here, and not in a spirit of malice, that most, if not all of the young women who make up the Countess Nettie's "spirited entourage" worked, for a time, at Ofelia's Chateau Joi, where they often found themselves entertaining clients in what Ofelia calls the Newlywed Room. On occasion, they were found by others, usually the police. They are, that is, a bit more, ah, worldly than either the Countess or dear Chet makes them out to be. The Newlywed Room, patterned after a less elaborate model constructed by a gladhanding, clubfooted man in New Mexico, not only imitates, parodies, satirizes, and elaborates upon the fantasies, pleasures, surprises, and disappointments of the usual honeymoon, it most tellingly *invents* specific possibilities of which the honeymoon is most often incapable. The room is equipped with such dazzling appurtenances as a thermostatically controlled blusher- and sweat-machine, a graduated series of rampant pintles, a complete selection, in all sizes, of smooth-bore rustic spheres, a two-way purple-crystal mirror harness, leather pediment straps and velvet-padded snood chains, a perfumed-steam collard vaporizer, a tremble-inducer, and interchangeable mollyprongs of fuchsia, cerise, lavender, chartreuse, strawberry, and lobster plastic, to list but a few. This information is given, as suggested, so that these young women may be fairly judged. It may well be that they *are* "raucous bimbos."

Her father finally asleep, or at least supine in the darkened room, Bunny peers cautiously out of the kitchen window at the woman who still stands in the street, her dress in oafish disarray. Bunny shudders, for the woman unaccountably reminds her of the vicious Nora Avenel, who insulted her *New Mexico Blooze* in art class, then, later, tried to melt her pastels. Bunny wonders where her old painting is, but idly, idly. It *was* a terrible painting, callow, pretentious, arty. That man said, "admirable talents, small but fine," but when she wouldn't. . . . Oh yes, *then* it was, what was it?

He said that it had all the aesthetic excitement of the *New World Dictionary*.

She can't remember what he said. She looks out the window again to see the strange woman heading down the street in the general direction of New York, where most of Bunny's friends no longer live. They've moved away, disappeared, died. Those who are left seem exhilaratingly indistinguishable from each other, especially when they insist on their unique particularity. They like to say things like, "Look, I'm an individul, see?"

"I think I'll burn down the chicken coop," Bunny says. "That's a start." Chances are that nobody will notice the smoke, not today.

"Damn!" Ted Buckie-Moeller blurts, "as I look up from my cluttered desk. If I knew how to get to Joanne's parents' place, and felt like it, and still had my really good Nikon, and *Black Silk Stockings* wasn't coming on in a few minutes, I'd dash out there in the hope that I might add some really fine studies to my 'Conflagrations' series. Hell, I mean it! No, really, I *mean* it." There is *something,* something warm, warm and inviting and familiarly depressing about Ted's false enthusiasm, and his toupee doesn't help much in adding sincerity to his remarks. At least he doesn't say "Wow!"

Nina, whom you may remember, last saw her old friend April propped up, half-comatose, in bed, her peach slip damp with urine. She's thinking, at this moment, of how lucky she is that she isn't April. Here she is, almost fifty, sitting in 99, one of the 687 "best downtown restaurants," sipping a Banana Amaze, and waiting for Josh Cabernet. Josh! Josh! Josh is not quite thirty, a successful lawyer, casual, relaxed, well-dressed, an excellent if hopelessly sane lover, and a man whose "star" is, well, *on the rise!* Look! There it is, right there with those which know the heart and boldly tell of the dynamic pulse and rawness of the ceaseless electricity and dynamics of the harsh urban glamour! You bet. When a mover and shaker like Michelle Caccatanto suggests that a young writer's grit-packed first book may well be the prelude to an eventual Nobel Prize—well! Am I lucky, or am I lucky? Nina thinks, or asks, checking her makeup in her compact mirror. Nina doesn't know that Josh, who is sympathetic and compassionate, yet blessed with an observant, cold, yet not pitiless eye, will not be meeting her today at 99, or anywhere else. A young woman with the cinematic name of Noël is presently tarrying with the dynamic author. As he looks down at her glossy newscaster's hair and her busy junior executive's mouth, he remarks how wonderful it is to be the young and newly famous recipient of a "blow" job in an elegant and expensive hotel room in dynamic, electrically gritty New York. New York! Wow! He adds, thoughtfully, that this is "living." Noël takes a short break—she thinks of it as a "lunette"—from her amorous labors and looks up adoringly at Josh, adoringly and, yes, perhaps saucily, pertly, and impudently. "I love Noo Yawk!" she breathes, and returns to "blow" job tasks. Josh thinks of Nina, and immediately begins humming "No Regrets." But just then a powerful and unexpected *jouissance* that not even *his* notable literary intelligence may detain racks his harshly ceaseless body and puts Noël on her youthful mettle. We are pleased to report that she seems to be acquitting herself as well as or better than the standard, run-of-the-mill, blue-blood whore of the sleepless city. Did we mention that Noël is intelligent, capable, has her Master's in forage-crop communications pathology, is currently working on a novel, two operas, "small ones, really," loves the beach, prefers to kill raccoons with her bare hands, is almost unbearably gorgeous, likes to repair subway cars, and is about to open her own restaurant-supply boutique? We did. Fine. Did we mention that Josh's response to her venereal ministrations is a series of grunts, yelps, pantings, and screams, interspersed with comments which those of a religious bent would term blasphemies? We didn't? Well, so it is.

"I can't, stout Dick, thank you enough for extinguishing the petty inferno which could well have done away with *all* my hair, and, I fear, my skull into the bargain," Buddy said, his deep voice trembling with wonted sincerity, and his knees knocking in the chilly mists that enveloped the sickening mountainside.

"Jiminy, Buddy!" Dick blushed becomingly, " 'twarn't nothing but what you'd or any feller'd do yourself, or himself, or, shucks, even *themselves,* or something of that nature. Fellers just got to stick together and beat out the flames they 'pear to notice on each other's heads—or any darn place *else,* I'd venture, otherwise they'll hang separately! 'Sides, you were prostrated 'count of sick grief and shock."

The boys' relieved and manic laughter quickly echoed from hill to wild ravine, from tarn to smiling cataract, as they stood, sooty, impugned, and weary from their recent adventure, in the small clearing into which the mountain twilight was wildly clambering. Luckily, the fire blazed high and their lorelike meal of boiled junco beans and Dick's by-now legendary big-rock "slagger" simmered tastily in the old black iron pot which Buddy's mother had made for him during one of her numerous tear-stained vigils. Suddenly, a young fellow strode into the circle of firelight, and gratefully stretched his thorn-studded hands toward the blessed warmth.

"I am Manly Normal," the young man said with pleasing candor, "and I feel as if I know Mystery Mountain better than any fellow living. Hurrah!" Then, seating himself, after consigning his attractive Saskatoon to a nearby stand of autumn milkmouth, he looked at the two boys as if seeing them for the first time. "Looks to me," he said to Buddy, "that you almost had your head scorched right off while looking for a *non-existent map."* His eyes blazed strangely as he carefully enunciated this last phrase.

Buddy and Dick almost fell to their respective knees before the incomprehensible stranger, but quickly recovered their dignity, and then sat, relaxed but alert, in the manner prescribed by Cliff Coiffure in

Campfire Manners. "Well, Manly," Buddy ventured finally, "it's without a doubt crackerjack impressive that you should know of our fruitless map search, as fellows call it. Hmm, I'd have to agree that you know the mountain better than any fellow that *I'm* acquainted with!" With this frank admission, the three lads relaxed, and deftly filled their plates with the rejuvenating victuals. They chatted merrily throughout the simple repast, their whoops of comradely laughter sending, for some reason, a rather large avalanche hurtling down upon the University of Chicago and the teeming streets of Chinatown!

"Let me make a long story as short as possible, new friends," Manly sighed contentedly, as he pushed himself away from the fire. The other boys were sprawled insensitively about the leaping flames, and all three had fallen into a digestive reverie, aided by the pungent fluid of the rusk shoots which grew in abundance amid the surrounding faucet-sedge. Manly then quietly continued, his features gleaming in the dancing firelight, a dancing firelight which Buddy, understandably, shied away from jerkily, his usually virile eyes unattractively bloated, and his coat, shirt, shopping bag, and gallus clips cunningly piled upon and wrapped around his sere and shredded "hair."

"I'm what men call," Manly began, "a regular sort of footloose bindlestick, the kind of fellow who tramps about a good bit and sees to it that things, well, that things happen in a certain order of occurrence, more or less."

"Somewhat like the artistic or businesslike sort of experience?" Buddy queried from beneath his protective ziggurat. "In that one seeks a hierarchy of order that one long ago gave up hope of one ever discovering in one's diurnal experience? Or would that be one's occurrence?"

"Gosh all hammock!" Dick marveled frantically, "you are right informed, Buddy, 'bout *ever'thing*. I guess you up and know 'most all the things worth knowing *on!*" As the doughty Witherspoon spoke, he cast more than one surreptitious glance at the shadowy form of the Saskatoon still lying quietly in the weeds.

"You are correct, Buddy!" Manly roared happily, his large face shining moonlike in the mincing firelight. "Presently, for instance, I'm working deuced hard for a strange sort of foreigner named Norman, who owns a genuine oil painting concerning death and perdition and other singularly unhappy ideas, a painting of which he is . . . *inordinately fond,* if you follow my leering innuendo? He hired me pronto, outfitted me with all the abject coolies, rotgut whiskey, and ogives a fellow could ever hope for, and sent me to California's North Bay, supposedly to investigate the role which salad and opera play in cuteness of local thought, word, and deed. From there, I hurriedly departed for Northeast Boise A & M, where the library's collection of primitive treasure maps rivals that of the notorious Ned Blutwurst, the dago, and from th— wh-what's the matter, Buddy? You look as if you've seen a ghost!''

Indeed, Buddy's rib cage was in the distended state usual in such situations of unavoidably horrific manifestation, and he had leaped to his feet to perform a curious "dance" from which even the coarsest forest creatures turned away in embarrassment.

"Is the name 'Ned Blutwurst' somehow responsible for this display of pseudoerotic shenanigans?" Manly whispered to the inured yet plucky Dick, who stood ready to snare, if necessary, his comrade by whatever protuberance presented itself to his grasp.

" 'Pears it's tarnation sure that that's the way it seems likely on being,'' Dick smiled candidly, for there was little or no guile in his plain-as-aprons American character. "The dago's driv poor Buddy plumb crazy with his pert and saucy tricks, just as he drivved Buddy's father, Old Buddy, plumb crazy. On the old feller he used some mighty pert and saucy tricks, including,'' he reflected wanly, "throwing him from a beetling crag hereabouts.''

"But what does all this have to do with Norman, my foreign employer?" Manly cried. His Midwestern politeness, honed to a keen edge by countless lanolin biscuits and hot, noisy kitchens, barely triumphed over the sudden dislike he felt for the blank, placid "face" which looked upon him, its—the "face's"—lips shining with "slagger" and the fugitive halvah shards which had been Manly's tactless but sporting contribution to the rough repast, a repast which was now, he thought bitterly, concluded!

But all—feigned politeness, smoldering dislike, shaky grammar, and .the shenanigans which had brought the usually modest Buddy into scandalous contact with a flowering *bozito*—and a remarkably large one!—*all* was reduced to insignificance as the Northern Lights lit up the icy sky! The three boys stood in silent awe, as the spectacular display of what is often called "Nature's fireworks" spread its attractive colors across the looming vault of heaven.

"Great Scott!" Manly expostulated warmly. "They look like the skyline of North Miami! Or even of Miami Beach, home, as you surely know, of the famous mass-transit system! They are, indeed, spectacular. Hmm, I'd go so far as to call them, let me see . . . 'Nature's fireworks!' Yes, I like that enormously, 'Nature's fireworks.' And so *shall* they be called from this time forth."

Buddy, pleasantly shocked out of his uncharacteristic "manifestation frenzy," nodded in agreement. "An excellent descriptive, Manly, and a metaphor of which, I venture, even Miss Ingelow would be proud," he gaped. "Oddly enough, they remind *me* of the North Shore of Long Island, perhaps because it was there that I first became truly keen on pastel-hued art objects. Somehow, the colors of these noble lights cajole me into a kind of happiness, despite the alarmingly bad luck which Dick and I have been so far fated to endure in this dratted boondock!"

"Goldangit, Buddy!" Dick called softly from the crepuscular weeds, where his dim shape could just barely be made out as it furtively scuttled about on the ground, "you know that things're liable to change for the better. It's a long road that has no silver mining, or something like," he gamely concluded.

"I understand, Normal old man," Buddy said, wisely ignoring the erratic behavior of his somewhat silly friend, "that the Northern Lights are Norwegian in origin. Have you heard or read anything of interest touching on this theory?"

"Indeed I have, friend," Manly nodded queerly, pouring himself and Buddy a generous draught of a hot, nearby beverage. "They appear in the skies only on those occasions when our distant Norwegian friends pay homage to St. Olaf, five days and nights of swinish celebration. The womenfolk cook without surcease, and the fumes of the lūtefiskė, língonbèrries, drammenbëer, koñgsvingér, øddaglög, slágénsláw, and other barbaric delicacies, are said to mix in the atmosphere—just below the notoriously transparent Van Allen belt—with high-speed electrons, photons, protons, neutrons, ions, bions, quarkons, nougats, buicks, and irrefragable gases; this rich mixture instantly producing the breathtaking, luminous extravaganza which I have always called 'Nature's fireworks.' "

"Astonishing!" Buddy inveighed, quickly reddening. "You may find it diverting that in a book recommended to me by my old Dean of Arts and Sciences—a crapulous yet withal droll gentleman—*Nouveau traité des vapeurs,* published in 1770, the Lights are claimed to exert a malign influence on the fair sex, and to cause in them the nervous afflic- tion known as 'the vapors.' Amusingly bully, is it not?" Buddy grinned toothily, glancing toward the thrashing in the weeds which lay beyond the now-forgotten hot-beverage source.

"Amusing? Ha, ha, ha! Why, my young friend, it's more than amusing!" Manly enthused, staring askance at the contents of his cup. "But tell me, precisely what is meant by 'the fair sex'?" He looked up quickly, his expression that of a tired but undefeated Zouave.

"Ha! Ha!" Buddy rejoined, smartly slapping his festoons. Yet his laughter died quickly as, in a trice, he saw Manly flush as deeply scarlet as the Dean of Arts and Sciences, one of the most egregiously flushed men that Buddy, and many others, had ever seen. "I-I-I-I'm sorry, Manly, please forgive my rude laughter. With that phrase I refer, as do most others, to *women,* women and *girls.* I intended you no picayune mental anguish, of that you may be assured. I know only too well how the fellows that one passes on the way up the ladder are the same fellows one passes on the way down the ladder, lest they have passed one on the way up the ladder, or one has not descended the ladder, or certain fellows have jumped or fallen off the ladder, or whatever. Surely, you get my drift."

"Women, eh?" Manly said quietly. "Girls and women? What a crackerjack notion! Hurrah! Is Gloria Jean, for instance, a fair sex?"

"Indeed she is!" Buddy cried delightedly, for he had always thought highly and in the purest way about Miss Jean and her wonderful anklets.

"And then," Manly pursued, "does it mean that Gloria Jean has the vapors? Or did she *have* the vapors, as, for instance, the cult poet Olga Begone did? Or so we read," he added apologetically.

"It's hard to know, Manly," Buddy said in all sincerity, as he poked the fire with a dried bandeaux. "In Hollywood, it is sound business practice for the large studios to guard the privacy of their major stars. For instance, it is rare, indeed, for a star to have his or her advancement barred because of reports concerning said star's incorrect or slipshod speech. The studio moguls simply will not permit such speech to be made public. If, for instance, Gloria Jean or Deanna Durbin or Dolores Délire, in an unguarded moment of excitement or pique, should say, 'It don't make no difference to me, Mac, I ain't eatin' the lousy grub,' the moguls would not countenance the broadcasting of such extemporaneous crudeness."

"This is utterly fascinating," Manly smiled, seating himself next to Buddy on the massive humidoro log which served as a rude banquette. "And what about a girl like Peggy Ann Garner, would it be the same? Would she, too, refuse the lousy grub?"

"Precisely the same," Buddy said, wondering how this conversation had begun. "Speaking of Gloria Jean, I've always had the notion that in the rollicking musical-comedy-drama *A New Dimension* both she and Bobby Breen, her crabbed putz of a co-star, displayed unmistakable and serious signs of the vapors in the climactic game-scene. I strongly suspect that this is why the film was never released. *Much* too powerful and revealing, most pointedly anent the fate of Breen's odiously curled and lacquered hair."

"Hmmm," Manly mused brusquely. "So then, the refusal to release would be an example of the studios' expert business savvy? Much like their expert actions concerning demotic references to dining refusal?"

"Exactly," Buddy said in quiet alarm, his eyes casually fixed on the unbuttoned figure of Dick Witherspoon as he lurched into the firelight, an athletic smile on his sweaty face.

"By the way," Manly urged, "is *A New Dimension* based on *Une Nouvelle dimension* by the great hydrocephalic geometer Gaspard Monge? His only novel, so far as I know, although some putative experts insist that it was written by Théophile Dondey. How incessantly droll! Ha! Ha!"

"I think I've read that it is," Buddy rejoined with cheerful vigor. "Perhaps in *Screen Action,* at one time my favorite periodical. But that was before I began this compulsive, obsessive, and fruitless quest for the blasted, phantom map!" he shouted at last.

"Ah, hello, Witherspoon," Manly said, making room for the weary Dick. "I had an inkling that you were somewhat curious about my retiring Saskatoon. A remarkable example of the *fair sex,* is she not?" he winked at Buddy. Dick smiled, then keeled over to lie prostrate before the fire.

"I've seen Dick once or twice like this in the past," Buddy confessed. "I fear that he occasionally surrenders to the baser passions. Unfortunately, such carnal weakness has proven to be a substantial bar to his advancement in the demanding world of business. Although, in all honesty, I must admit that his divers problems with grammar, syntax, vocabulary, as well as his delight in abrasive slang, have also been a factor. Surely you've noticed?"

"In all candor, I have indeed," Manly quickly agreed, nonchalantly placing his urbane feet on Dick's sated body. "And although my Saskatoon *is* eye-catching, I am always surprised when a young fellow of Dick's caliber is drawn to her. I mean to say, drat it all!, the wench is no Gloria Jean!"

"As long as we're being candid," Buddy sobbed, "I must confess that Dick has always been embarrassingly crass in his manly tastes. It may well be because his father"—and here his voice fell to a whisper—"was a Millinery of the November League."

Manly Normal visibly paled, and for a moment it seemed as if his generous mouth would open wide as prelude to a bout of unrestricted vomiting. But he controlled himself, and spoke earnestly to his new friend.

"Then . . . then the search for the map and for the dago, even the map itself—the entire quest—is but a subterfuge on your part to make rudely healthy in mind, body, and spirit, *if humanly possible,* this pathetic slave to the flesh?"

"You've guessed the bitter truth, comrade," Buddy smiled tightly. "But now, let's turn in, or bed down, for tomorrow may well be a day of impending crisis."

"Good night, Buddy," Manly said throatily, his large eyes clear at last. "I'll see how my young Saskatoon is surviving the night chill—if you don't require my presence?" But Buddy humorously made a crude but universally understood gesture with his fingers, pulled his hale benny around his shoulders, and put another persimmon on the hot coals. The whippoorwills, wise beyond speech, screeched horribly, then all was silent. Nearby, the tree line seemed to lurk nervously.

"There's been some subtle and some not-so-subtle denigration of late of the poet Olga Begone," Michelle Caccatanto says, for some reason, probably literary. "To wit, vulgar remarks about her going on what is ludicrously called an 'acclaimed aluminum diet,' lubricious suggestions concerning her physical attributes and maddening lusts, sneering references to her taste in couture, and excerpts from her works maliciously arranged to depict her as a wild-eyed, radical man-hater with a closetful of ugly shoes and a fear of bananas. Yet how many of these unreconstructed mockers know the delicate poem of nostalgia, lost love, and ineffable longing, 'Still Life with Scotch and Agony,' unaccountably deleted from Ms. Begone's last collection, *Nutless!*? It is, thank heaven, still available to those lucky enough to get their hands on the first and only issue of *Nuts and Bolts,* a journal dedicated to the preservation of true cultural values.in a time of decay and specious 'stardom' in the arts. Permit me to read the opening stanzas of the poem, which is cast in the formal structure called a phantom":

> Though parting with a kiss, a smile—
> I had a funeral in my crotch!
> Her quick touch, her blush, the while
> We slowly sipped our favorite Scotch.
>
> I had a funeral; in my crotch
> There was no love for friends or jobs.
> We slowly sipped our favorite Scotch
> And let our wild tears flow, like slobs.
>
> There was no love! For friends or—

Thank you, thanks, Michelle! Thanks a million. We'll most definitely remember both you and Olga when next we bump into Halpas, Burner of Cities. Now there's a guy who appreciates a phantom!

Eligor still roams about, the increasing heat of the day seemingly exacerbating his desire to intrude upon those things which strike his fancy as open to playful meddling. The inflammatory contents of the latest issue of *Nylon Pussies* are transmuted into photographs of "the friendly cockatoo" and "wonders of the desert," as well as feature articles on "Building Your Own Soup Can Art," "Sleeping under Glass," and "Cherry-Cheese Dip—Boon or Bane?" Clive Oak, abandoning a compliant snake of his acquaintance, is suddenly convinced that he is someone named "Octave," and is then compelled to ask everyone he meets persistent questions about a dinner party of which none of them have ever heard. Anthony Octavio, a translator of precise if meager gifts, in contact with the spirit world, insists that a young woman named "Muffie" served as the model for the character of Ethan Frome in an unreadable coterie novel, *Odd Number* or *Odd Numerals* or *Old Bumbler.* The spirits—known to the "channeling community" as the Official Mouths—cannot be sure of this because of malignant static somewhere over Gnatville. Eligor is immediately interested in Muffie, a young, svelte shopper, and her relationship with what seems to be a *tugboat.* He goes in search of her, halting, at least temporarily, his ludic pastimes. It is a good bet that he—being a demon—is sexually aroused by what are often called "degrading images and depictions." Demons have little interest in social and cultural acceptability, none at all in anybody's dignity, living or dead, and they shit on all flags.

"Hi! I'm Karen O'Grady! When I'm cavorting 'tween cirrus and cumulus, a vicious minority dubs me a French whore, *n'est-ce pas?* But when I've got these spike heels planted on the *la terre,* I know that I'm the hardworking daughter of a hardworking mom, as well as being the hardworking sister of hardworking sisters. Some of *them* are French whores, but heck, we can be whatever we put our minds to being, to be, what we want to be! That's what my guy, an important hotel *hotelier,* says, and he tells me never to forget it. Hi!"

"Hello. Sure an' oi'm the ghost o' Rosie O'Grady, sure an' oi'm be-jayzus sick an' toired, sure an' may all the mavourneens an' cruiskeens be me witness, sick an' toired an' thoroughly banjaxed in me poor owld dead moind, o' hearin' me daughter Karen's name linked wi' that o' Karen O'Grady, the notorious French harlot. Sure, an' me daughter's knees were niver chained togither, but sure, that's a good bit different, bejayzus, than playin' at heathen things loike 'Jello-me-crock' an' 'the egg game,' jist to tink o' which'll send yer sowl to a Protestant hell. Hello." Her voice falters, then ceases.

We are grateful to more people than we can here name for calling to our attention the important information that the "vegetarian couple" who are here, there, and everywhere, are none other than the vivacious Benita O'Hearn, even more delightful with her newly pert breasts and ravishingly inviting lipo-sucked buttocks, and her husband, the pious Charles "Chick" O'Hearn, known to his closest friends as "Momo" and "Cheech," depending on score and inning. "Chick" seems to have had parts of his well-known ears placed to either side of his carefree "nose." Thanks again, heads-up friends!

"The word 'Ohio' is not a palindrome," Oiwin states belligerently, filling his hand with his ever-reliant capstan. He's taken it into his head to guard the cherry-cheese dip woman from possible insult by the outrageous "priest" whom nothing, seemingly, can assuage, save the unthinkable. "Chet and Allen have fled to Fire Island and its vagrant clams, Dwight may, if they're unlucky, join them, others are celebrating in suburb, wood, glade, copse, brake, fen, and atop shale bluff and beetling scarp! Someone, then, must stay on guard!" The cherry-cheese dip woman smiles at him, then looks brightly at Andy, who is writing down certain items of information from suspicious soup-can labels. "Anyway," Oiwin says again, "the word 'Ohio' is *not* a palindrome. To be such an item of linguistic interest as that there, it would have to be 'Oho' or 'Oio.' Get it? You got any questions, just line up in an orderly fashion and as far as this lady's concerned, look don't touch. Right, kid?" She smiles companionably and opens another non-carcinogenic plastic tube of genuine dip.

It's not generally known that Miss Caccatanto—soon to be the wife of Page Moses, the gifted person who is hard at work on a new novel which will, we understand, "blow" the lid "off" New York's glitterati—is interested in the preservation, cataloguing, and study of old films, many of which have not been screened in decades, as well as of more recent cinematic "cult" items. But let's let her speak for herself: "Thanks. It's a pleasure to be here, as you know, and thank God it's air-conditioned. I think you could probably fry an egg on the sidewalk! Really! Anyway, yes, I'm really interested in the old cinema, which I find to be impressively intuitive in its grasp of human affairs, as you know. For instance,

I've just had the good fortune to see *The Old Confederate Dead Man,* a grittily sophisticated look at gays in the Civil War, their travails and triumphs, their crude and fumbling humanity. Incidentally, the film has little to do with the sympathetically gritty poem from which, as you know, it takes its title. Then there's *Old Hoboken,* filmed in Hollywood about 1902, a saga based on *Blix,* a novel of cold despairs and pitiless triumphs, as you know. *Old Hoboken,* by the by, served as the inspiration for the Tin Pan Alley smash, 'I Got the Old Joe in Old Hoboken (and I Don't Want Your Oysters Anymore),' a song that still stands as an amusingly compassionate depiction of early slum life—somewhat like the later 'Old Shep,' with its compassionately amusing refrain, 'Old Shep he daid, / Old Shep he daid, / Old Shep, de maid / Done be afraid.' Of course you remember it! As for contemporary films, I'm extremely interested in rescuing the only extant print of *Lace Me Tighter!,* which uses non-professional actors in all its roles and thereby achieves a kind of impressively grey grittiness, as you know. It was filmed, I believe, in a motel room outside Missoula—speaking of *grit!* Although the characters are not fully realized, their very *humanity* is attractive. Well, it's been marvelous, but I really have to run out to Old Weskit, Page's family's house on the Island, as you know. I foolishly left the proofs of *Too Soon the Loon* there and I *have* to review it this week. It's by *the* Count Olivetti, as you know, and from what I hear around town, it's going to simply blow the lid off the international glitterati—tells absolutely *all.* They say that *some* people won't even be able to hide in Omaha! Well, as Rory the gambler says in *Old Hoboken,* 'the wages of sin is time and a half.' Listen, really, it *has* been marvelous, as you know."

Countess O'Mara is watching, in a kind of senile splendor, *Aini, the Destroyer!* on television. She's already seen it twice this week, and now waits impatiently for her favorite scene, the one in which a middle-aged ex-stewardess prepares lunch for herself in a small efficiency kitchen. The Countess is fascinated because the actress looks, allowing for the passage of time, exactly like a stewardess who was once introduced to her by Lady Bustier at somebody's garden party, long ago. She had been a delightful girl, at once complaisant and demanding, without either false modesty or a penchant for larceny. Countess O'Mara waits patiently, pleased that this ridiculous movie has awakened such a poignant memory. The same sort of possible mistaken identity as the cause of bittersweet pleasure is thoroughly explored in *Le Bousingot* by Théophile Dondey, writing as the anagrammatic Philothée O'Neddy.

Didn't Dondey-O'Neddy also write *Karen, Ma Cherie?*

He did. Now there's a book that *nobody* reads anymore.

The O'Neills, Ed and Kate, are playing gin rummy and drinking iced tea. Ed has lost most of his hair and suffers from mild emphysema, and Kate, although her face still retains traces of a wild Irish beauty, has put on a good deal of weight and has high blood pressure. They are grandparents three times over, and their children think of them as affectionate and loving, though a little too concerned with the petty details of everyday life. Ed and Kate still seek out sex orgies once or twice a month, at which they are vital, inventive, and highly experienced participants. They worry a little about dread diseases, but not enough to keep them at home. They are nominal Catholics, and occasionally go to mass, for sentiment's sake, although neither, understandably, has received the Eucharist in years. All this seems rather strange, almost unbelievable, since this couple— "Pardonnez-moi," Rimbaud interrupts. "Le maître, Monsieur Baudelaire, dit, 'la volupté unique et suprême de l'amour git dans la certitude de faire le mal.' "

Merci, Monsieur Rimbaud.

We have just received word that the woman known as "Onette" is *not* actually Annette Lorpailleur; neither is she Corrie Corriendo or Berthe Delamode, whom you will recall as "colleagues" of Mme. Lorpailleur's. It is, then, clear, that the suggestion to the contrary contained in the Ornamental Sheet-Metal Workers' Union newspaper, *On Their Metal*, is *only* a suggestion. Much more to the point is the revelation that Onette's full name is Onette Oogotz Op, that she is allergic to metal clothing and hosiery, and that she was never taken by surprise in the John Keats Lodge with three dwarfs, a short-order cook, a rope ladder, five gallons of apple sauce, and a home-economics teacher who would not stop singing "Orange-Colored Sky."

"Thank you," Corrie says quietly. "Since I've been looking at the traffic far below, I've realized how small it all seems! Small and virtually *unimportant!"*

"I've got little or nothing to say," Berthe adds, "em nopu era sropav eht ecnis."

Annette turns to stare. Oh oh.

The Orange Dress, at once product and cause of heartache, despair, misery, bankruptcy, dyspepsia, flabby thighs, high cholesterol, asthma, premature ejaculation, and the horror of secondary cigarette smoke, will soon be published, pundits surmise, in a new edition and sporting the new title of *Orange Steel.* Convinced that the quirky novel by Sheila Henry will find its audience this time around, the publisher, Oriental Food Products, is bringing its high-powered marketing strategies, rarely witnessed in the gentlemanly profession of publishing, into play. "We feel that we can sell the book the way one sells cranberries or imbroglios or bean sprouts," Louis Hess, OFP advertising chief, remarks in a recent story published in *Laguna Colony News.* "The whole idea behind modern, or should I say postmodern marketing is to make people lose control of themselves and act in an unseemly yet thrilling manner. We know a little about *that,* don't we?" he smiles at his energetic yet ruthless assistant, the veteran adwoman, "Tits" O'Rourke, known to the "boys on the Avenue" as "Big Tits," an insulting sobriquet which Miss O'Rourke unaccountably cherishes. She looks up brightly from her richly cluttered desk and puffs thought-fully on her delicate meerschaum. Her figure, after all these years, is still trim, although she takes care to wear severe suits in order to conceal her body from the frankly lecherous stares of the lustful beasts in the office, who—

All this is in the *Laguna Colony News* story?

Well. Not exactly. Not *all* of it, exactly.

So stick to the facts, all right?

"Of course," Hess continues, "we're relying on the usual literary prepublication horseshit quotes for use in ads, on the jacket, in store displays, and so on, the works, whatever that means. I flatter myself that I've put together a group of real beauties, by really big book-names, current celebrities, well-known nobodies, the works! The works? Anyway, who said life was fair? Ha! Ha! Anyway, we should definitely sell some big-number *units,* amigo!," he concludes spiritedly, jumping up to pat "Tits" on her bottom, which she has done her level best to conceal, and to make an obscene suggestion concerning egg rolls. "I love this guy!" Miss O'Rourke says, quickly slipping out of her clothes and pressing her voluptuous body—

Come on!

. . . he concludes spiritedly, and jumps up to look frantically out the window, searching for that indefinable something that makes success in a high-powered urban environment worth that thing which it can be worth only if all else is sacrificed to its demands! He thinks, for a moment, of the demands made upon the modern career woman, the insults, the patronization, the humiliation suffered by, for instance, someone like Miss O'Rourke, and chokes back a guilty sob. For he knows, in his heart, that *he,* yes, *he* has been unfair to this beautifully built, irrepressible career woman! He stares unseeingly at the traffic far below. How would I feel if *I* had "big tits"? he agonizes. Then he turns—

All right. Let's see the goddamned quotes!

Here they are, straight from the office, and O.K.'d by the bright young people who are hip and who also know hip when they *see* hip.

"Looks like an Oscar or a Perry bid to this jaded listener."

—Reginald Ose, author of
Turn Your Delusions into Cash

"O'Callaghan and his famous suit of brown paper was never half so much good, clean fun."

—James Joyce

"I like an Oriental girl—and that's what this read delivers!"

—Kate O'Sighle, TV guest

" 'Εν ἀρχῇ ἦν ὁ λόγος, καὶ The Orange Dress ἦ ὁ λογος."

—St. John

"I couldn't put this searing wallop of a page-turner down and finished it on the squash court."

—Rory Blentz, squash devotee

"I'd sure like to meet Sheila Henry or even just look in her window! My goodness, what daring filth!"

—D.D., film buff

"Har! Har! Cutlass me lanyards if it 'twarn't like a-sittin' in a hogshead o' warm apple sauce. Har, har, har!"

—Long John Silver

" 'Tis like a Golden Spiritual Lamp which casts pure Beams that make a House a Home away from Home."

—Ella Weller Wheeler Willis, author of
Crush Rainbows to My Bosom, Please!

Karen Ostrom, tired from the heat and the wet, grimy wind that is beginning to blow up, rings Sylvie Lacruseille's bell. She knows that Sylvie hates to be disturbed, but she has news, or so she believes, of Sheila Henry, or someone who seems to fit Sheila's description. It is not good news. Karen is carrying it to Sylvie because so many of the other people whom she once knew are simply unavailable—disappeared, moved, hiding, insane, living under aliases, or dead: "Our Gang" is no longer even a small group. She rings again, and is about to turn away when she hears a long, high-pitched moan through the door, a sound composed equally of ecstasy, pain, guilt, and loneliness. She stands transfixed, for she recognizes a sound almost exactly like the one she herself occasionally produces. Inside, Sylvie, on her old couch, is lost in the kind of unbearable orgasm that plunders the soul and that she can usually bring about only by playing the "egg game." She feels another orgasm crowding against the one which is slowly subsiding, and begins to sob raggedly in anticipation. The shifty-looking man on the roof of the building across the street has dropped his raincoat, and stares at Sylvie in a kind of religious awe, actually frightened by the holiness of the pleasure he is watching. The movies never prepared him for this! The experience, delicately balanced between the sacred and the profane, may change the course of his shabby, seedy, sexual life. Or not. The time may, indeed, be ripe for such changes, since it is common knowledge that supposed visitations by Our Lady to two local churches —Our Lady of the Bleeding Eyes and Our Lady of Crushing Sorrows— have been testified to by numerous people, none of whom are especially given to religious visions. The shifty-looking man begins to shiver and weep uncontrollably as he watches Sylvie's body being swept by another manic climax. Karen leans against the wall in the hallway and lights a cigarette. She, too, has tears in her eyes.

"Yeah," the big guy in green work clothes says, beginning to sweat, "that's the way it goes. You do what you can and if it comes up a chicken-leg flush, you're all right, hell, halfway home, as they say. The Chevy just burned out its engine getting Alice up to Topeka, or was it Missoula? Anyway, she wanted more than anything to join up with Gladys there, she was convinced Gladys was living the high life. She didn't say anything but I know Alice and the funny way she looks at her housedresses. Gladys would send these picture postcards of the shopping mall and the new glass insurance building downtown and write messages like 'Here's the big story,' and 'I've got it now, honey,' and 'The X marks my window.' Well, after a while, what with the dead grasshoppers in the freezer, and her denims that wouldn't fade, and the way the snow would sort of drift over the pile of empty beer cans in the barbecue pit, and the damn fool baker and his stories, she just took off one night while I was lubeing Jack's pickup for the bear hunt down to the town dump. Yeah, took the Chevy and the Donald Duck insulated ice chest too, and about sixty dollars in cash I'd been saving up for a pool umbrella, because that was kind of our dream. I got a card from her showing the Hotel Pachuco with these two little clouds floating right over the roof, real white they were. They give me a funny feeling, sort of the feeling that you get when you all of a sudden look right into somebody's face in the parking lot. She wrote that she'd be home soon and to lay off the Hershey bars. I always had to hand it to Alice, she had a hell of a sense of humor. Made a nice beef stew too, when she put her mind to it and stayed away from the muscatel. And she fried things from the creek up real tasty too."

It is interesting to listen to these stories of the heartland and its people, who, although inarticulate in their longings and duped by the unheralded courage with which they struggle to evade their humble obligations, are yet the kind of folks who, when they get theirs, keep it, and into whose eyes one longs to stare while the wind blows straight across the gulch, crevasse, or ravine. Many of these stories are collected in the noted pathbreaking anthology *A Pack of Lies,* sometimes characterized as "the Bible of the new, unfrightened American realism," "a Packard to metafiction's ridiculous Edsel," "a gallery of people we can care about in their courageous nullity." Most notably, and coincidentally, one of the stories—"The Paddy in the Brake"—by Bronco Dungaree, inexplicably contains a purported fragment of the purported screenplay for *Lace Me Tighter!* Although there is nothing intrinsically interesting about a piece of shoddy soft-core pornography (and, in our opinion, a spurious piece), a little-known essay on the comparable merits of the film and Dungaree's "germ" story, by Mary Jane Alice Oaktag, points out that the amateur cast was headed by a Gladys and an Alice (!), and was, furthermore, shot entirely in and around a Hotel Pachuco (!) in Missoula (!). Such coincidence leaves us no alternative but to include the suspect fragment. It's right here in the files. (Indicates color-coordinated file cabinets.)

Lace Me Tighter! (Scene 14)

The boodwoire of a very rich French lady, Mme Vermouth. Mme Vermouth enters with her French maid, Fifi. Mme Vermouth slowly lets fall her luxorious penoire which she drops on the bed to reveal her voluptuose body in a cruel whalebone corset. Fifi is also scantily clad in a little short skirt and not much more but a pair of sheer silk hose and high heels. Mme Vermouth gazes sadly at a picture of two poor old tired horses in a meadow, their heads partially hid in thick gorse bushes, then she looks at Fifi.

MME VERMOUTH: It is very warm this evening, eh? (*She glowers strangely.*) Oh God! My bewitching Fifi! Lace me up!

FIFI (*sweating profusely*): It is, to be sure. You bet I will, my lady. How's . . . *this?*

MME VERMOUTH: Oh, my stars! Lace me—tighter!

FIFI: How then is this, my lady? (*Pulling vengefully on the corset strings.*) Is *this* tight enough, Madame?

MME VERMOUTH: No! No! (*In a towering rage:*) I wish greatly to have some trouble with my breathing!

FIFI: Ooff! Phew! That is about as tight as I can lace you up, without splitting you into two pieces, my beloved mistress! Ha! Ha!

MME VERMOUTH: I don't care a thing, my innocent girl! How little you know of the unhealthy sexual desires and practices of the corrupted wealthy class! Tighter! Tighter, I say! *Make* two sections of my trunk . . . if you dare!

FIFI: Sacré blue, Madame! You are laced so tight now that you are panting and pop-eyed, like some sort of wild feral-type animal!

MME VERMOUTH: Pant! Pant! Even . . . tighter . . . than . . . THIS! I feel almost demented, as if I am some kind of a fruit cake!

FIFI: This is quite a formidable performance of womanly pluck!

MME VERMOUTH: It is sweet agony! My well-cared-for body trembles with sharp aches! Now . . . just a little TIGHTER!

FIFI: Puff! Puff! Here we go, Madame! (*Apologetically:*) My arms have not the strength of old since I have damaged them puttering golf balls with the old Earl.

MME VERMOUTH: Yes! Yes! That's it! Oh Fifi! Torture me like a savage redskin of the North American plains and woods! Let me swoon myself to heights of pleasure and fall prostrate on my luxorious couch! (*Falls, sobbing in ecstasy, and almost bent double at the waist.*)

FIFI: Phew! Watch where you are falling in your swoon of passion, Madame! (*She looks at her dazed mistress.*) Hm. Madame has fainted, as usual. All her wealth and power cannot help her to achieve a happy sex life such as is enjoyed by rough miners, neat office clerks, and dedicated schoolteachers much of the time. I am disgusted with her depraved bourjoise lusts—and yet, I feel that she labors under a strange family curse.

Manuscript breaks off.

The Frankenstein girls haven't really given Fred a moment in which to speak to them of his favorite theory concerning the identity of the elusive Baylor Freeq, i.e., that he is actually the bath-and-boudoir-accessories tycoon, Biff Page, currently on his way to an *al fresco* buffet and cocktail party somewhere near Gnatville—but not the buffet and cocktail party in, at present, a jagged shambles. It might, however, give Biff pause to know that the mighty Paimon, obedient to Him who was Drowned in the Depths of His Knowledge, has decided, in demonic irritability, to "annoy and abrade" Gnatville and its environs because of faulty information that this locale is playing delighted host to the false Albanian Lard Goddess.

"Did I ever tell you of my Freeq-Page theory?" Fred asks from beneath an ironing board.

"Did you ever see anything as cute?" one of the girls says, slathering her body with cold cream. "It's something about the way his eyes look when the board falls on those naughty distichs of his," the other giggles, filling her notorious *purge à souffler* with warm chocolate pudding.

"Girls? Just a minute, all right? Girls?" Fred says, scrambling—too late!—to his feet. "Can't we just talk for a minute? Can't we have a little intelligent modernistical conversation like in an interview with Paul West? Where in heck are my pants?"

"Just as cute as a button!" one of the girls screams. "His *pants!*"

It may be helpful to include at this point the information that Dr. Miriam Paimon (no relation to Fred), a Freudian analyst of the "uncanny" school, maintains, in a recent paper, "Hungarian Tendencies in Pseudo-Adolescent Erotic-Games Tableaux in Marin County" (*Erotomagnalephon,* XI, 2, 1982), that such manifestations of antisocietal behavior as may be observed in "the acting-out of prelibidinous Athenic fixations, such as those produced by the clitorally subsumed superego (inversion) in its predictable clashes with masculine id-icons, e.g., the herm, the hot dog, the ironing board, etc., are, rather surprisingly, controlled by the look, feel, odor, and taste of Pall Mall cigarettes."

"And the opposite is also the case," Dr. Paimon says, "despite ill-tempered assaults on the proposal by the few Adlerian nitwits who still have the gall to admit their allegiance to that pompous shrimp. And, of course, there's always the health thing," she muses.

"No, no, no!" one of the girls whoops. "*Bend* the nozzle, silly, *bend* it! Fred, you are *priceless!*"

Corrections of Earlier Errors

Item: Manly Normal erred when comparing the Northern Lights to the skylines of North Miami and/or Miami Beach. The correct comparison is to the skylines of Palm Beach and/or Palm Springs. Normal's error sprang, according to John Crowe Ransom, from an imperfect understanding of the geographical function of the axis of selection.

Item: Panama is not *only* a country; it is also, as Rupert Brooke suggests in the line, "and things are done you'd not believe," a musical composition.

Item: A Panama hat—despite fashion dictates from Paris—is never to be equipped with a string which attaches to the wearer's lapel, even though worn in the *craziest* season.

Item: The Parisian: Dossiers of Longing, by Jean-Claude Rififi, was not employed as the "anchor" by means of which Zuleika Dobson kept herself submerged beneath the cold waters of the fateful flood.

Item: Although Jack Spicer's remark, "None of you bastards / Knows how Charlie Parker died" was once accurate, it is no longer. Time marches right along.

Cox has definitely given up hope of finding any clams on this street of dynamic old bookshops. Yet in one of them he comes across a first paperback edition of *Parts of the Gangs,* a novel by Rajneesh Coney, and a work variously described as "a devastating look at the pleasures and agonies of health worship," "something like a very large, fascinating fish," and "a delightful exercise in today's spurious entelechy." Quite the companion volume to *White Bridges*! Cox thinks. He is not aware that *Parts* is under continuing option to a Major Motion-Picture Studio, and that it may soon start production as *The Party.* This latter is not to be confused with the abortive attempt to film a version of an obscure French novel whose original title we cannot, unfortunately, ascertain. That film was also to be called *The Party,* although we have it on reasonable authority that *The Party* was not the title of the French novel, or, more precisely, the translated title, of course. There is, however, a film still available in videocassette called *The Party,* but it is amateur pornography filmed in and around the bowling alley adjacent to the Naughty Nightie boutique, and has nothing to do with the aborted *The Party,* the potential *The Party,* the French novel, or *Parts of the Gangs.* Or so we have been led to believe. There is, too, the one-act play *The Party,* by Craig Garf, but this is an utterly obscure item.
   "It's a *wonderful* play even though nobody will produce it," Craig whines. "I still feel, however, that craftsmanship is more important than speed or handsome profits. Yet I'll be forever grateful, for it was the writing of *The Party* which permitted me to flee Misty Crag and settle amid the ceaseless pistonings of the thunderous dynamo of the dazzling but heartless metropolis. And there is no business which can compare with the theatre business, or, heck! let me be all-embracing, with *show* business. But is it fair to call show business a business? Is it not closer, in every way, in all its manifestations, both large and small, to the—"
   Thank you! Thank you, Craig! Wonderful. Absolutely wonderful! Even compelling. Certainly heartfelt.
   To recapitulate: The potential *The Party* has nothing to do with the aborted *The Party,* neither of which has anything to do with the

pornographic *The Party,* and none of these three has anything in common with Garf's one-act play (indicates coffee-stained, dog-eared, heavily annotated typescript), *The Party.* However, for our own purposes, which are manifold if obscure, all of the papers, correspondence, notes, memoranda, contracts, photographs, promotional materials, etc., etc., which have to do with or are germane to any or all of the above-named projects, shall be placed, before this day is over, in a group of sturdy cardboard cartons, each of which shall be sealed, and then clearly marked, in dark, permanent ink, with the words, "The Party."

"There's more fuss about all this crap than there is about Passover," Cox says, waxing semi-religious. "I wish to Christ I never bought this stunning companion volume to *White Bridges.* Bibliophilia leads one to strange places. Wouldn't you say so, friend?" he asks Craig Garf. "I didn't do anything!" Craig whimpers. "Get away! Get away! That only *looks* like me in that snapshot! Go on—get away!"

We won't trouble ourselves to discover what has upset the unsuccessful playwright, but allow him to disappear into the maw of the forever-pistoning dynamo, a dynamo which bears ultimate responsibility for *The Party.*

Which one?

Shh.

"Hi! I'm Karen Peachy! Well, I'm not *actually* Karen Peachy, she's out just now, but I'm sort of the next best thing, like, I'm Karen Complexion! You might remember me because of my beautiful grooming and competent grammar. I also know how to handle the tell-tale hair that can do so much to ruin the sheer *fun* of wearing a mini-bikini! That's I! And I know that Karen—the other Karen—is *just* as carefully depilated in the No-No Zone. Oh, hi!"

Albert Pearson definitely does not like what he's just heard from one of his spies concerning Berthe's treatment in flower-glutted Bermuda. Beshary has clearly become—although Pearson has discounted such rumors for years—a ruthless mogul and a heartless tycoon, although some have thought him closer to a ruthless tycoon with a heart of stone. Seating himself at an antique writing table of zither-inlaid mahogany teak, Pearson settles his gold rimless glasses on his face and writes:

Dear old friend and partner,

I know that you mean well, but if the reports I've received today are correct, I feel that you're treating Berthe terribly. He is a very nice man, and I know that you agree with me and Janos that we three are somehow responsible for his "galoot fever" and his penchant for patent leather—often, yes, to the exclusion of really nourishing foods! Be that as it may. I don't understand what pleasure a downright wealthy tycoon, like you, can possibly take in tearing up the poor man's best lace cap, breaking the heels off his black pumps, and taunting him with false stories about fake art works. And stealing his last alimentary strap! Really, Edward, this is beneath even a heartless mogul. In any event, please send Berthe to me as soon as possible! Perhaps a new fall wardrobe from Peck and Peck will brighten his tear-filled eyes. Or some other tasteful store. Whatever, I'm the man to buy such things, as you, to your regret, well know. I'll also replace the collection—Berthe always called it his "pack" —of ceramic Pekes which I know you shattered in a pineapple-induced frenzy some weeks ago. After a time, when the dear man has recovered from your cruelties, I'll introduce him to Pepe—you remember Antonia's Pepe, don't you?—and watch anxiously to see his craggy face light up as Pepe begins to display his flimsy but irresistible repertoire. I *am* disappointed in you, Edward. I will not tell Janos of these things, even though, as you've probably heard, *The Curse* will finally be published and our old friend and colleague is impenetrably euphoric. I will, of course, reimburse you for Berthe's fare. And for goodness' sake, let him take whatever makeup and undies he still has!

Your troubled partner,
Albert

"Hi! I'm Karen Pepsi! Isn't it just *great* how Karen Complexion filled it in, or however you say it, for Karen Peachy, and winged through turbulence and the stray gout of vomit with the best of 'em? Karen Peachy is at a demonstration right now, demanding that nobody call us 'stewardesses' or 'flight attendants' *ever* again! I don't understand it real well, but I do know that I'm all for our demands, which is that we should be called 'stars' or 'bosses' or something like that. Politics isn't my teacup but when I'm amid the snowy billows I smile a whole heck of a bunch! My guy, a weathered, greying exec, thinks they should call us 'honeys.' He's so fun! Hi!"

Diane Drought's daughter, unable to convince her raving mother that she is, indeed, her daughter and not "some Albanian bitch," walks purposefully into Anne Kaufman's shop, just as Anne is striding womanfully out. They meet, bumping into each other softly, yet with an insouciance fit for the virgin bush and its attendant marmosets. Anne steps back, entranced by the pair of ice-blue panties knotted carelessly about her young visitor's alabaster neck. No telling *what* direction fashion will take among the restless young. She smiles carefully, whatever that may suggest!

"May I help you?" Anne asks professionally. "I was just closing, but if there's anything you might need. . . ? A Day-Glo crucifix? Plastic biretta? Mickey Mouse pyx with matching paten. . . ?"

"Aren't you Anne Kaufman, the author of *Perfumes of Arabia*?" the forward minx demands.

"Why yes, I am, but . . ."

"My mother—never mind her identity!—told me about it, and even though you used the pen name 'Anne Leo,' you're a dead ringer for the real tough broad you are, or so it seems, in actuality. The body of Beely, the Whack-Off King, still behind the counter? Or have you, ah, disposed of him?" (Indicates vat of boiling lye.)

"Actually," Anne replies foolishly, "there is a *real* Anne Leo, a well-known barfly. Some maintain that she bears a strange resemblance to the abused heroine of *The Perils of Pauline.* But that was before your time, Miss. . . ?"

"So *this* is Beely," the visitor whispers gutturally, looking down in awe at the grotesque, manly shell of cold fleshly mortality. "He looks like one of the endpaper drawings in the first edition of *Permanent Guests.* By the way," she snaps in the manner of a wily martinet, "why is it that the narrative structure of *Guests,* and its anal-retentive architecture, is so much like that of *your* novel?"

"That's Dr. Perrie's argument precisely!" Anne yelps happily. "That wonderfully warm and famous old geezer! However," and here she smiles and leans quixotically against a fake relic, "the problem is that my book is not a novel but a memoir."

"What have *you* got to remember?" the girl mutters savagely, kicking sharply at Beely's corpse. Suddenly, though, she snaps out of "it." "Wh-what am I doing here?" she complains girlishly. "And wh-who are you? Wh-what and wh-who? I recognize this slumbering figure as Miner X. Beely, sex therapist to the big stars and annual Guinness luminary, b-but h-how are you? I mean wh-who are you?"

"My dear child," Anne gushes profligately, "you are as simple and ingenuous as a corporal in the Peruvian army. As innocent as Dick and April's unborn child, Peter. As chaste as Sister Philomena Veronica, who, in the piss-redolent classrooms of O.L.B.E. Parochial School, taught me the Palmer method and the reasons that Methodists look funny and thus have little chance at heaven."

"So . . . you're Anne Kaufman, my mother's cherished friend!"

"Perhaps I am. But don't interrupt me as I conjure up the past, else you may join the defunct pervert at my still-attractive feet. Yes, Sister Philomena Veronica! So enthralled was I by the sexual mysteries of a chaste sisterhood and the vague, waxy odor of the epicene cloister, by the torturous lusts held in tight control by *women without men,* indeed, so fascinated and psychologically disturbed was I by these carnal puzzles, that just a few years back I played the role of the 'good nun' in a, ah, candid film—whose title I cannot now recall. But I've said too much already. May I make you a nice cup of tea, Miss Drought?"

"But you know my name! How wonderful! But how?" the girl laughs immediately, startling a blasé passerby.

"Who else would disguise herself as the Albanian lady, who, today of all days, haunts the sterile suburbs? And only someone with a knowledge of the summer lard festivals who know of the significance of underwear as outerwear!"

And the two women, one old and marvelous, the other wonderfully vivacious in her obvious bloom, laugh and laugh, forgetting, for a blessed moment, the tell-tale cadaver stiffening, as he so often did in life, beneath a heap of fallen scapulars.

Is that a chapter from *Buddy and His Boys*?
    From what?
    Buddy and His Boys. You know, Buddy, Dick, the mountain?
    A *chapter*?
    A chapter, a chapter, yes, a *chapter!* What are you looking at me like that for?

Hard as it is to believe, Phoenix, who Lispeth as a Child, who Appear-eth as the Bird of His Own Name, singing in dulcet Tones, Phoenix, the excellent Poet of the Seventh Thrones, flies swiftly toward François of Fargo's, in order to avail himself of that establishment's asparagus bread, a bakery product ignored, if not rejected, but a few moments ago by Kirk, known chiefly for his overwhelmingly cheap cologne. How-ever, a recent note states that Kirk has not yet ignored or rejected the asparagus bread, but soon will. It appears that certain things are achronological, insofar as Kirk is concerned. This *is* August 29, 1982. Léonie's calendar is correct, even if *she* is what might be called "wrong." More news: It seems that a number of things may be achronological. Oh well.

"I mean well," Léonie says.

Then too: Scholars Dispute de Kock Influence on Late Picasso Ceramics; Mr. Pimples, Adult Film Star, Claims Sugarless Gum Caused Sudden Sex Change; Biochemists Suggest Some Pistachio-Oval Ice Cream May Be Alive; Pittsburgh to Enter Bid for Leisure Moustache Owned by Pope Pius XII; Murray Baddle Billows, "the Platinum Priestess," Says Most Men Prefer Whores Who Look Like Her Mom; Researchers Fear Famed Plaza May Be Covered with Microscopic Layer of Excrement; Norwegian Methodist Woodsman to Bring Libel Suit against Dr. Plot on Grounds of "Shameless Idiocy"; Donald Plot Charges Joggers Act as "Hosts" to *E. coli* Organism; Studies Reveal Plymouth Favorite Car of "Regular-Guy" Priests; *PMLA* Mulls "Egghead" Comic-Strip Feature; Heart-Shaped Bath-tub Cache Found in Poconos.

"The critic who spoke of Henri Kink's 'Poem' as 'a terse monologue developed amid a welter of illocutionary symbols' clearly based his sincere if specious characterization of the poem on the text as it appears in *Blue Filter,*" Professor Raoul Blinque sniffs. "However, the poem is much more than a simple monologue, and it is not in any way *developed* amid *symbols* of any kind! Among Kink's papers I've discovered a final stanza of 'Poem' which must change the way we think about it—and perhaps about the rest of Kink's oeuvre as well. Kink, for whatever reasons, suppressed the stanza, although it is superior to the conclusion as we now have it, a conclusion, by the way, which has always troubled me because of the essential *nescience* of the *faux-naïf* locution, 'pieces of sky faded blacker.' In any event, here is the 'lost' stanza'':

> Oh! How my case is wrapped
> with the soft basses in the phonograph,
> suddenly, my mommy makes fudge
> from some pieces of pie, and from lacquer!

Would you say, Professor, that the, let us say, macroparatactic strategies of the stanza function as a kind of microcosmic reflection of the larger charnel house motifs found in, for instance, Defoe's fiction?

"Indeed I would!" Professor Blinque says, sitting up straight and joyously whacking his crusty brier against a nearby stand of ivy. "Indeed! Indeed I *would!* Wonderful observation! Yes! Daniel Defoe! Indeed, yes, remarkable, *wonderful!* Acute and perceptive! *Indeed!* Would you care to come over this evening for drinks and little slabs of cheese?"

It might be interesting to note that "Poem" won the annual *Blue Filter* prize, which was, as far as we can recall, a "novelty" Polaroid camera, blessed by the Pope.

Wasn't the camera green, a kind of disgusting green, with some comic-strip character involved? Something... I just can't quite remember.

Right! Right! Loathsome green with a ferocious little Popeye figure on the side. Some kind of promotional deal, a tie-in with frozen spinach. Something.

Henri gave it to Benita and "Chick" O'Hearn, I think. Right?

Maybe, yes. People who were against caffeine, ate hay and seaweed?

"Mr. Congeniality" drags his unspeakably deformed foot over to a sweating member of the group from the Confraternity, and asks him if there really is *nothing* that can be done about the depraved priest who is "knocking" morality into a cocked "shoe."

"And who are you, wiseass?" the weary Catholic says.

"I'm the man who called in to complain," the walking-disabled person replies briskly.

"A Mr. Popeye called us—that's you?"

"Not Popeye, Poppy. Mr. *Poppy*. I called to complain because this display really put the finishing touches on my mood. I'm feeling pretty low, what with the broken toaster and the rust on the motel pool, and how the leaves have been falling on the bears who are up to something funny with Stella, that's my wife, used to be some looker before she started in with the potato chips up to the pool hall in Bozeman."

"What? You got I.D., Buddy?"

"Sorry," Mr. Poppy says. "I got a little—I guess I'm a little confused," he laughs. He turns away and quickly clumps and swishes into an inviting aisle.

"Bears? Stella? Pool?" the bewildered Confraternity brother mutters. "All this because some dumb fake priest bumped into the wrong magazine," he says to the magazine display. And what a display! Have we mentioned it?

Isn't it about time we told the real story about the priest's behavior? No.

Leo, almost paralyzed by now with Old Mr. Boston, sets the needle on the record to play, for the eighteenth time, "My Heart Is Melting (For My Ice-Cream Gal Said No)," by the Ohio Brassy Wamble Aggregate Marching Band. There seems to be a tear, or there seem to be tears, in his eye, or eyes, since he's thinking of one or another of his ex-wives. It must be, aha! Anne, for he sobs, "Oh, Anne! Anne! My sweet Miss Popsicle!" However, it is Ellen who was once called "Miss Popsicle," and not by Leo, but by Anne. So does bittersweet nostalgia falsify the past and make yo-yos of us all, or, in this instance, does it make a yo-yo of Leo.

Dexter Gapoine refuses to be intimidated by the café menu, and, turning to his three companions silhouetted dramatically against the looming pinkish morphemes, he suggests seafood for a welcome change. "I have my Porsche parked on the crumbling hummock of a nearby corduroy. Heck, we can all squeeze in!" he laughs, looking suggestively at Miss Gashe's legs.

"Seafood? Around Misty Crag?" "Hap" Garrett marvels. "But where? Real seafood?"

"Some people know where to get things, 'Hap,'" Berta sneers.

"Am I right, Dexter?" she adds trillingly, directing a powerful simper toward her trim addressee.

"Certainly," Dexter agrees politely, moving as close as he dares to Karen's delightful protuberances, thankful that he is not, after all, what his rather heavyset dad calls "queer." "I'm thinking of a little place that serves the greatest fried clams—oh, not the kind that you can 'tie in to' on the Cape or in Portsmouth, but say! They've got four legs like every other darn clam in the world!"

And with that, the four, with a collective halloo!, begin running wildly toward Dexter's vintage Porsche, their faces registering nothing but contempt for the vetch and thorny snapperweeds which clutch horribly at them.

Edmund Posherde, who, as a respected and rather stuffy insurance executive, no longer remembers that he was, some decades ago, called "Blinky," and, occasionally, "Bunky," by his beautiful mistress, Constanza Murphy, hears some unexpected yet wholly familiar sounds from one of the museum's less-accessible wings. Entering, he discovers a woman and two men, all grey-haired and prosperous-looking, much like himself!—in, surprisingly, various states of undress, and, even more surprisingly, comprising a tableau reminiscent of Catullus's fifty-sixth poem. As he steps back against the wall, he experiences the greatest surprise of all as he catches a glimpse of the woman's rapturous face.

Wasn't Constanza Murphy once known as "Honey" or "Hummy" Potts, or sometimes Pazzo?

No, you're thinking of Berta Garrett.

The Berta Garrett on her way to eat clams?

Yes. Right. That Berta Garrett.

But didn't Mrs. Murphy have *some* sort of alias years ago?

Well, now that you mention it, there have been stories that she was mixed up in some sort of smuggling racket as a "Queenie" Antilles, although some argue that "Queenie" was a wholly different woman and that Mrs. Murphy's alias was "Cunty" Uncles. But nobody knows for sure about any of it.

"Whatever or whoever she is or was," Mr. Mytilene interjects in his Greek-restaurateur accent, "with those legs I don't think she's a good

Christian woman, thanks be to God!" Suddenly, Mr. Posherde makes his considerable presence known to the sweating trio.

"Although I've definitely cast my rather impressive lot with the contemporary," Jack Armstrong says to a group of fawning admirers, "you might be somewhat startled to realize that I sometimes amuse myself by writing in the manner of the minor Elizabethans. For instance, here is a snatch—ha, ha—from the plea of a lovesick swain":

> Dainty darling kinde and free
> fairest maide I ever see,
> deare vouchsafe to look on me,
> listen when I sing to thee,
>   O do not dwelle
>   with that Prell
>   sing fare well to Prelle.
>
> Prettie, wittie, sit mee by,
> feare no cast of anie eye,
> we will plaie so priuilie
> none shall see but you and I,
>   O do not dwelle
>   with that Prell
>   sing fare well to Prelle.

Jack, as is his wont, has neglected to mention a couple of things, the most important being that the greater part of these verses are—how can this be discreetly put?—not his own. Those lines which are his, and which serve as a refrain, a kind of repeated *tornada,* were invented because Jack feels that the inclusion of brand names in a literary work gives said work sensitive wallop. "For instance," Jack likes to say, "take Plumtree's Potted Meat." Everyone smiles, pretending to understand. But who can argue with success?

"Well, it might be good Armstrong, but it's not worth a God damn like real poems like 'The Prelude,' " Leo mumbles, deep in his drunken yo-yo phase, as recently noted. He crawls across the room and pulls a book out of a pile of ghastly "things," then leans against the wall. "Listen you want? Real poetry?"

A cottager leaned whispering by the hives,
   Telling the bees some news, as they lit down,
   And entered one by one their waxen town.
   Larks passioning hung o'er their brooding wives . . .

"See what I mean? This is the fucking President compared to Jack, who is an Assemblyman. This is the stuff!" Leo smiles, bends over the book, and throws up on its yellowed pages. Then he passes out. Just as well, or else we might have been constrained by honesty to tell him that this fragment is not from "The Prelude," but from "The Female Vagrant," a poem much loved by Francis Cardinal Spellman, who always took a copy of it into battle, where, they say, he always fell—and *hard.*

An elucidation: While it is true that Lange's famous treatise on "les vapeurs" is currently creating some excitement, or "stir," in its relation to Father Debris's continuing research into the true meaning of the Décadence, the good priest has asked us to make clear to his admirers that the fortuitous and inspired application of Cardano's formula to Lange's text was made possible only because of his, Debris's, exhaustive study, some years ago, of the curious mathematical patterning of thought in Jean-Baptiste Pressavin's *Nouveau traité des vapeurs,* a book much revered by Buddy and some of his older and more sophisticated Boys. But let's allow Father Debris to tell the story.

"God bless all of you," the wily Jesuit smiles. "I have an old copy of a Spanish primer, *Primer curso de español,* and I'm really pleased that I can tell my story and bring in this bit of fascinating irrelevance. This is a book like where if you hold it and flip the pages very quickly, like you riffle them sort of under your thumb, from the back to the front, holding it right-side up, the pictures go by very fast and they, they sort of, connect. The pictures which are drawings about, say, the present indicative or the subject and object pronouns or the cardinal numbers, sort of tell a story. Not actually a story, but more like a slice of life, an insightful look—yet another one!—into the heartaches and hopes and fears and nobility and all of the people in the drawings and their grappling with, for instance, the subjunctive, which is tricky in Spanish. If you thumb, or riffle, enough times, the little people who go flying by, really *fast,* kind of begin to take on meaning. I don't know how to explain this but they make you feel as if you want to tell your own story, about the little people *you've* known, getting into cars and all, drinking whiskey and playing bingo and talking on Princess telephones, sometimes pink ones or yellow with push-buttons, shampooing with Prell, eating odd treats like Mandy's Mustard Macs and all. Regular people. Anyway, it's called *Primer curso de español,* which means, from what I can gather, well, I really don't know what it means. Prime curse or something. It has these black-and-white drawings. The women's hair looks very glossy."

Thanks, Father, really, thanks a lot. Thanks a million. This way, that's right, no, not that way, just right out that door, watch your step, why don't you lie down for a while when you get home?

Elkins E. Pritchard, whom many claim to be the true author of *Black-jack,* as well as being the founder and prime defender and theorist of Parvanism, a foolish idea, so others claim, of no merit, is waiting in what he *insists* is his "blissfully air-conditioned" apartment for Anne Kaufman, with whom he has arranged an afternoon of carnal dalliance, which he *insists* be called "hijinks." (Indicates apartment and hijinks area therein.) Anne, as we certainly suspect, will probably not be coming because of the adventures of her day, q.v., but Pritchard knows nothing of these. He is doing the crossword puzzle in an old issue of *Genuine Morocco,* or, as it's known to its readers, "the Sin of Creams," perhaps. There are a few blanks left.

 – Procel the Geometer's antique ice-cream bingler. (11 letters)
 – Sheila and Lou ——— - ——— think of Prospect Park with horror. (17 letters)
 – Protestants wear these under their embroidered postulants on Brooklyn Day. (7 letters)
 – Mel Proud and His Melodics made this nauseating song famous. (21 letters)
 – "In Provincetown, the sun cracks deuce and warranty, for ———.": Lamont, *Baltimore Chop.* (6 letters)

From Guy Lewis's window, someone looks down at his broken body on the street below. There may even be some traffic. Then, in a spirit of contempt, defiance, hatred, and scorn, this person hurls Guy's rolled-up

Provincetown Alba out the same window, although this seems to be a much larger, less delicately brushed version than the first. The canvas is followed by a copy of *Psychopathology of Everyday Life*. Although there is no known reason for her to be anywhere near Guy, it is indisputably the case that the hurler is Charlotte Pugh, reputedly the owner, still, of the notorious Naughty Nightie boutique in depraved Kirkwood, Missouri, dubbed by wags "the lucky town that mimes forgot."

"Didn't she get the Pulitzer Prize for that?" Tabitha remarks to Lucy. The two young women are strolling down Renselaree Street, their cocktail dresses, or "frocks," grown suddenly and hatefully gauche, at least to certain passersby. It may, however, be the glare of the sun!

"Who? For what?" Lucy snaps clumsily, wondering if she's going to be quizzed, once again, on the power of the objective correlative. How tired she is of these sudden examinations! She thanks her lucky stars that her cantaloupes are larger than Tabitha's.

"Why, Charlotte Pugh, of course, for *Psychopathology of Everyday Life,*" Tabitha laughs melodically. How she tosses her head and her proud mane of auburn hair!

"Oh, Tabitha! You are my burden and my cross!" Lucy seethes.

"Crosse? Well, she's not much on looks, and she knows less than you do about literary matters, but Delilah has the most *gorgeous* legs," Tabitha admits. "However, I got bigger knockers than she possesses."

"Once again, I must take issue with your feckless knockers boast," Lucy replies reasonably. "Meerschaums put, let's face it, your jugs to shame."

"It's not enough for them two broads to disgrace themselves indoors, no," Rudy says. "Now they're talking that stuff right out on the public streets! Legs, knockers, psychophilogy, Jesus Christ. Soon they'll be writing poems about themselves like my useless fucking brother!"

Harlan Pungoe can hear the faint chiming from Annette Lorpailleur's apartment, even though he is some half-mile away. He is in an electric-blue suit, single-breasted, and quite possibly older than Pungoe. In the August sunlight the bilious brilliance of the fabric has already blinded a horse, two dogs, a sweaty jogger, a militant activist, and a hearty child-molester. If this is indeed Pungoe, how is it that he seems to be in more than one place at the same time? Or times? He *seems* to be Pungoe, and, if so, the years have barely touched him. His pielike face, so malleable in its expressive possibilities and powers that it has driven several men and women mad, is much in evidence. Ditto his rustic twang, store of rural tales, all of which point a homely moral, his camera, twisted tie from wardrobe, and attendant equipment. Sketchy reports are about of children fleeing in dumb terror, of eviscerated cats and strangled dogs, mostly terriers. He is the man with his hand in his pocket! Who takes pictures! Of preadolescent girls! Preferably in their shorts! He's the man who made the phone call at the A & P! And just a little while ago, he was banging on somebody's door! And cursing! Wispy white hair to give him the look of a besotted ham actor playing a besotted ham actor. The clubfoot? Well, of course, there it is, as ugly as, more ugly, we should say, than ever, in a "shoe" of the same blue color as his suit. Good God! He hears the faint, sexual chiming more clearly and his lurching roach-crawl gets faster, something spilling now, something fine spilling from his trouser cuffs, it is sand. Sand from Coney Island. Coney Island? Faster, faster he dips and scuttles, it is Purson, of Bears, Purson, of Glittering Trumpets, who urges him forward. The children run wildly away, and women cover their ears so as to block out his murmured tales of pastoral tragedy, all of which feature stupid homosexuals bashing their heads against trees. The chiming, the chiming, he can see in his boiling mind her spread thighs. Chiming.

Eugenia Hunter, capping her pen, suddenly has an eerie vision of Pungoe and is made to remember her days of shameful debasement as his sexual slave, when she was constrained to answer to the name "Big Mama" Pussie or "Big Mama" Fussy. This servitude quickly effected the destruction of what little self-respect "Sweetums," her first husband, still possessed after his misadventure with the large cardboard object mysteriously "forgotten" at his office door. Soon after, Eugenia began wearing *those* things, and "Sweetums" slowly started thinking of himself as Paul de Kock, even though he didn't know more than three thousand four hundred and twenty-six words of French. From this dementia to his ultimate disappearance in the mists and fogs of Mystery Mountain was but a matter of weeks. Or, let us say, a few short weeks.

Eugenia shakes her head to drive Pungoe's leeringly affable face from her thoughts. Well, her whole story, all of it, everything, will go into her autobiographical memoir, *Qualifications*. In the meantime, Pungoe scrapes and shuffles closer to Madame Lorpailleur, the sweat soaking through the back of his jacket turning it into a mirrorlike surface. Into which no sane creature dare glance.

The Frankenstein girls decide to bid farewell to Fred on this luxurious summer afternoon with a virtuoso ritual which they learned in the crystalline highlands of Cambodia from a priestess of Cetriuolo, "Lord of Carrots." The girls call the ritual "Queen of Sheba," for reasons unknown. Prepared, executed, and concluded properly, "Queen of Sheba" most often leaves its masculine participants unconscious, comatose, psychotic, or dead. Although everything concerning the ritual proper is "veiled in secrecy," to use one of the girls' favorite phrases, we do know some of the materials necessary to its successful execution. They are: a can of Franco-American spaghetti; a spiral-bound 3 x 5 assignment pad; two white candles which have been left overnight in an imported-cheeses store; an aerial photograph of the *Guns of the Colorado* shooting location; a bottle of Dixie Shake; two tablespoons of Frank's Orange Nectar; a copy of Ernest Poole's *His Family;* a bawdy lipogram of at least three hundred words; any page of Faulkner on which Quentin appears; a two-foot length of white silk rope; five white sneakers of different sizes; a small can of *cacahuate* sauce; a pair of badly run white nylon stockings; any fifty words of any poem to an inanimate object, clearly typed, and stained with dried vomit; a pink latex dildo on which is clearly lettered "Live Free or Cheap"; a couple of jiggers of moonlight; a small star. Fred lies naked on the king-sized bed, watching the girls' preparations with what is often called "mounting horror." And yet, his shako is unmistakably bulging.

Guy Lewis's *The Raid* catches, as best it can, the harsh sunlight coming through the window of Ralph's den. Ralph stares at it, pleased that it has been so thoroughly neglected over the years that its crimson and Prussian blue both are now the same greasy, excremental brown. How Ralph, who still despises Guy and Joanne, has come to possess this small painting is a mystery, and why he wishes to display it, more mysterious still. Some of his acquaintances from "the old neighborhood" suspect that his wife, the former Margaret Ramsay, has something to do with it, but since her salacious nature goes hand in glove with "the vapors" as defined by Raulin, and since she, as helpless victim of Ralph's phallocratic beliefs, indeed suffers from that malady, how she could have anything to do with concerns touching on *The Raid* is inexplicable. So far as can be determined, Ralph and Margaret are, as always, at odds. He despises her for her enviably promiscuous past and she him because he compares her, unfavorably, to Joanne. Perhaps. There are certain problems with our received intelligence, given the paucity and quality of questions asked and the contradictory nature of answers received. In any event, Ralph stares at *The Raid* and seems oddly comforted, complacent, almost happy, although he cannot yet know of Guy Lewis's death. Can he?

Isn't that Raum, of the Order of the Thrones, flying, as a crow, from Ralph's neighborhood? Raum, who discerns past, present, and future? Raum, the croaking gossip?

It could be, or it could be, just, you know, a crow. Why?

Well, couldn't he have told Ralph about Guy's death?

Oh, I see. That could well be. That might explain Ralph's—you'll pardon the expression—shit-eating grin.

Item: The recently deceased Sheila Henry's maiden name was neither Ravish nor Ravitch, despite biographical asseverations, public records, and the sworn testimony of a bizarrely accoutered couple representing themselves as her mother and father. Her maiden name was Mulloon, the same as that of the disgraced physician. So she may well have married, in ignorance, her own brother, had Lou's name, that is, been Mulloon, which, fortunately, it was not, and is not now, or so we have been assured.

Item: Antony Lamont's *Rayon Violet* is to be published in Great Britain as *Reams and Reams,* by Dickie St. John-Mouse, a celebrated publisher-raconteur and purchaser of truly fine vintage automobiles. Bertie Crotchlip will star in the thriller as the traditional, implicated thug with pederastic leanings.

At fifty-six, Ann Taylor Redding is one of our loveliest scholars, although "loveliest" may seem a strange word to use in reference to a woman whose masses of shining hair occasionally riot. Although the years have added a few pounds to her generous professorial figure, her straight legs, with their swelling calves and slender ankles, are still beautiful. Dr. Redding's penchant for stack-heeled shoes with small metal buckles, leafy burgs, shady volumes, large fruit pies, and phony Englishmen is, as always, very much in evidence. She also admits, with a blush, that she still has a weakness for "lady soldiers," as she insists on calling the female members of the military, despite feminist frowns. When Evelyn Leonard (who, as Tiffany Cartier in *Black Silk Stockings,* set new standards for the erotic cinema) is mentioned, Dr. Redding speaks, rather too quickly, of lapidary prose, larking about with sphinx and bombazine, and her sister Phyllis, who is, as she assures her listener, often lionized by the little people she identifies only as the "others." No snob Phyllis! Ann crosses her legs, modestly arranges her skirt over her knees, and coolly studies her fingernails, glistening with the shade of polish marketed as Red Moon.

"Red Moon is the favorite of hardworking airline pilots!" a woman who resembles Evelyn Leonard/Tiffany Cartier says. "It doesn't chip or fade, has the color of a California sunset seen through a haze of fresh fruit, and is *all natural!* Good news for you guys—and gals—who bite your nails or suck your thumbs! If you like to pull large combs through your hair with noticeable abandon—it's Red Moon. For the nights of your life, and the life of your lights, uh, nights, life nights, life of night life. Red Moons." She is promptly dropped into a vat of creative directors.

A number of publishing rebels are standing at the bar in Caliph's Walk, speaking of their lives, loves, hopes and fears, those they hate, their careers, and other relevant and revelatory congeries of delimited psychology. For instance: "used to be Chinese . . . chink's Red Silk . . . Red Swan you mean . . . syrinx and flutes and frillies . . . the Red Ink . . . Elizabeth Reese's orgasm . . . O'Nolan . . . in the garden with the fairies . . . Reeve in chains . . . red Chinks at swim . . . swans lutes and pyrex . . . an orgasm of ink . . . Nolan's old bird garden . . . Reeve O'Reese . . . Elizabeth's red frillies . . . *whose* red chink . . . two swans like silk . . ." Someone mentions a book and silence descends like a luff.

"It's interesting to listen to *young* book people speak of things pertinent to their vocation," Sol Blanc wheezes to Saul Blanche, who totters in time to his partner's ragged breaths. "Just from the few snatches of whose conversation we were privileged to hear, it's clear that the pub biz is alive and well, flourishing as never before, energetically killing the weeds of the mast obliquity we like to consider the incriminating speeder who will not accept pap by any beans, but yes! insists, as I have song doted, on being CHALLENGED by the BEST and most COURAGEOUS how shall I say? WORDS!"

"And yet," Saul utters feistily, full of pep and vig despite his corrupt body, while Sol just sort of, well, sits down, "while much space and attention are given rockbuster wallops like *Nouveau traité des vapeurs,* and rightly so, our saloon clientele (indicates youthful rebels), if actually representative of the hip rebels who are *making it all happen,* oddly never mention *Réflexions sur les affections vaporeuses,* the seminal work on the illness which afflicts those who work harder and play harder in sweaty shirts, and the like. Without the *Réflexions,* there would be no *Nouveau,* and although not many care, there would also be no *Regular Guy, Bitch Girl, Buddy on Uncle Ned's Farm, Up Missoula Way, Air-Conditioned Marriage, How Can We Talk about Quietly Calling When We Really Feel Like Buying Tickets?,* and God knows how many other instantly classic masterworks. Ask Michelle Caccatanto! If she hasn't got her nose in a book of short stories what make you feel meaningfully alive, or maybe look like they're alive, or maybe that we're all alive if we only took the time to really be alive, or maybe speak to us of the author's aliveness despite the haunting fact that he was once a drunken short-order cook on a hardscrabble ranch, yowza, well, anyway, why then, she's got a book of short stories on her lap, and she's reading with the avid perspicacity of a thin-skinned muskelonge rising fast and sure for the crappies! *That's* loving books, or I defy you else!"

"Right," Sol agrees. Together they ease toward the air-conditioned ambience which has never ceased to beckon. Perhaps, rather than "ease," their "gait" might be thus described: Together, arms linked, they clumsily amble toward, and et cetera.

May we note here that the crappies abide. Not only abide, but though flustered, flourish, and, flourishing, prevail.

"Hots" Reilly is still more or less contentedly married, so they tell her, and still more or less reconciled to the alias she can't quite remember acquiring, "Humps" Daly, although she vaguely remembers knowing a lot of other women, closely related to her, or so it now seems, with equally improbable names. Her real name is Bárbara, of that she is quite sure. Someone who says that he is her husband is sitting with her at a sticky table in the recreation room. He may well be her husband. These things are clearly a recreation room and a sticky table. They say. Who is this man again? He's astonishingly homely and very old, probably too old to fuck her and that's what she could really appreciate, the hell with the orange juice! Bárbara "Hots" "Humps" asks him again who he is, and he tells her. She wonders why he reminds her of the holy syphilitic in Roberte's poem "Renée Pélagie: The Ecstasy of Her Agony," and he smiles stupidly. She wonders if he ever picks up hot women to fuck in the Reno Tavern and he shakes his intolerable head and offers her a Lifesaver. She asks him to bring her a copy of *La Révocacion de l'Édit de Nantes* by Pierre somebody, find out for Christ's sake, now there's an elegant piece of erotica. She pulls her breasts out of her nightgown and tells him about somebody, Dick Otto or Otto Dick or Ricardo, he loved to suck on them, and why is he staring at her, didn't he ever see a tit before? She reminds him that when she was young and beautiful, *sultry,* he was interested in every *other* skirt but now that she's old and tired and sick all he does is try to undress her and play with her tits and pussy. She reminds him of some friend of his, Richard, or maybe she's thinking of Ricardo Dick, who was always surprised at how cool he was toward her, but not *everybody* was so cool. For instance, Biggs Richard, who was happy to drop in during the week, in the afternoon. And, for instance, the guy who was always talking to anybody who asked about anything, he'd drop in too. And Father Richard, oh yes, she smiles, I imagine it was a sin even though he'd only sit there and stare at me, his pants all bulging, his mouth open, just the way you're staring at me now. She sobs, you're always here, always, with your sticky table and Lifesavers and orange juice and your pop eyes on my old sagging tits, and trying to feel my pussy. Staring the way you stared at those little well-bred tits on Jane Richardson, you remember her, with her clothes and teeth and hair and money. She talked like she had a banana up her ass and a Ping-Pong ball in her mouth. And, she says, she yells, she shouts and screams as two attendants hold her and wrap her robe around her tattered, shredded nightgown, she screams at her husband as he walks toward the door, he's her *what?*, this balding, grey, stooped, addleheaded, drunken syphilitic, this faggot cocksucker, this sticky-table lover, she screams that he was also a goddamned fool for Jane's younger sister Punkie, the one who could have married somebody but ran off with a Cuban or something. "Humps" Bárbara "Hots" is still screaming at her disgusting cruel rotten husband who ruined her life as she's taken back to her room. The Richardson sisters are still a constant source of irritation, although at present their beautifully mannered stupidity poses a threat only to couturiers, sailboats, and high-strung horses.

"Clearly, automatic writing," Florence Claire scoffs. (Indicates transcribed sample of slipshod prose.)

"I reckon it mighty strange that Normal, who seemed such a capital fellow, 'pears to have lit out 'fore dawn," Dick remarked spiritedly to Buddy as the two chums sat shivering in the biting, early-morning mists of the ancient forest.

"Indeed it *is* odd, Dick," Buddy answered with his wonted, almost blunt sincerity. "Our newfound acquaintance seems to have exited with all the speed employed by Richelieu himself during the unspeakable excesses of 4 Germinal, although," and Buddy chuckled good-naturedly, "the famed Cardinal did not have to fret about a comely Saskatoon, eh? Ha, ha, ha."

But despite all, soon a hefty fire was blazing apace, and over mugs of blistering "java" the boys plotted their next move, which seemed to point to a necessary resupplying of their victuals-bags, bread boxes, and miscellaneous airtight containers in varying sizes. "We certainly have the *room* for healthful victuals, and so, away!" Buddy blathered, delightedly quoting the line made famous by Thompson Richie in *The Party.* "Away!" Dick echoed, his knobby fists raised toward the distantly louring sky.

"I loved that moving picture," Buddy mused enthusedly aloud.

"Even when I had no true idea whatsoever of the responsibilities of a key clerical position, Richie, as 'Ridie,' the gallant Lord Ridingcrop, seemed to embody all the manly traits of a titled regular fellow, and yet he never gave the unfortunate impression of being the sort of nance who'd actually *live* in a snobbish town like Riding-on-Alum. Of course, there *were* a few explicit scenes."

"Yes, good pal," Dick interjected loudly, "and I can recollect that the tights he had a mind to doff on almost any pretext showed a powerful lot of his beziques, especially in the dripping-forest scenes, if a fellow is thinking correct."

"Partly true, my astute camerado," Buddy whispered patronizingly, for there was little he didn't know of Thompson Richie's career as a film star, committed naturalist, oenophile, diamond amateur, discreet algolagniac, and best-selling author of walloping good reads. "But if you'll think again, *carefully,* you'll recall, I'm sure, that Richie's beziques are revealed, yes, but not gratuitously. In a word, the aesthetically pleasing exhibition of the excellent fellow's manly equipment serves to further the plot! The actresses are, of course, perfect foils for this masculine display. And Dick," Buddy added waspishly, "please try to remember that an adjective does not perform the adverbial function, all right? One might think that you'd never delivered important papers swiftly and accurately!"

"As always, I'm powerful—powerfully—grateful to you for your seemingly endless corrections, Buddy," Dick hissed neurotically through clenched teeth, his hand fervently gripping a lead pipe he'd come across at the bottom of a tittering rill. "Thanks again."

"What's that in your weary hand, dear ruffiano?" Buddy laughed happily.

"Ha! Ha!" Dick echoed. "Ha! Ha! Ha! That's rich!" The trees bent, whispering, to the sere and yellow grasses of the hummocky glade, bee-drunk in the attar-laced haze.

"Well?" Buddy pursued, refilling their mugs with the caffeine-rich nectar of which the boys had grown weirdly fond.

" 'Pears it seems like a kind of worthless bagatelle given me by the Saskatoon, who I sort of hit it off with last night," Dick fibbed quickly.

"Ah," Buddy sighed in his superior way, "a love token! As Rilke put it, 'give me a garter of thy love, and I will move the world.' Wonderful!"

"I don't recollect I brought any garters with me on this trip, Buddy," Dick blushed deeply. "Charles Rimini-Bates, the fletcherizer representative and rassling coach who took me under his wing at the Holt Rinehart Legion Post, mentioned on garters being, well, right unhealthy to the developing boyish moral fibers. Something about them turning a feller into a fruity-boy. Anyways," he concluded almost smugly, "I threw them away in the degraded trash."

"How unbelievably rich! Garters! Oh, Dick, Dick, you are truly a jocular brick of a fellow," Buddy slathered gaily. "But now let's break camp and see if we can discover a humble thatch-roofed cottage or thatched-roof cottage, at which we may purchase some victuals and other provisionings. As the deathless Alger somewhere writes, 'A fellow needs a stew to speed his stride if he plans to get to Rio.' "

"Rio?" Dick queried ignorantly. "Alger?" he continued in the same vein.

"Don't concern yourself with it," Buddy sighed.

Swiftly the boys began to break camp, and as the last ember was smothered by the fire-resistant branches of the lumbago fronds which stood crookedly about the humid glade, the friends prepared their equipment, and with experienced motions of woodland know-how, *heaved* it in such wise that it landed squarely on their broad backs in an almost welcome involution. Such were their devoted skills.

How many hours they'd walked they did not know, how many rocks, pines, splintered items, quiet falls, and comatose forest denizens they'd passed, they were heartily ignorant of. Just as well! The sun burned down upon their youthfully plucky heads, and visions of their lost companions, of the Saskatoon, of craven Knute, of drear caves and the blubbery lips of the elusive dago, of the maddeningly insubstantial map, and of the comradely jocosity of Manly Normal passed before their fevered eyes.

"This exhausting hike and its exhausting accompanying visions smack of the literary, Dick, don't you think?" Buddy managed to gabble through cracked lips.

"I reckon so, Buddy," Dick rejoined, perspiration soaking his gabardine mashies. Then all was silence once more, save for the sound of the rocks and pebbles which fell from the looming jalousies of polished granite surrounding the boys like so many prison walls, like the ornate facade of the Ritz, like the cold darkness of impure and unmanly thoughts of, for instance, garters! Of a sudden, around a bend in the sylvan track down which they struggled, a small, worn farmhouse appeared, humble in the extreme, yet neat and well-cared for, despite the barren yard's grey dust, and the withered kitchen garden just beyond the sagging back porch.

"Thank Scott!" Buddy ejaculated, halting in his courageously blistered tracks. "This farmhouse, Dick, has appeared as surprisingly and abruptly as a shift in time in the novels of Alain Robbe-Grillet, whose books I've often urged you to read, to no avail."

"I seem to recollect on dipping into one book about the orange chifferobe, but darned if I could tell the men from the women and the furniture and chains and such," Dick laughed stupidly.

"You mean *La Robe orangée,* my thick friend," Buddy gibed gently. "The problem is that you do not read the French language, which makes for a bit of difficulty, n'est-ce pas? Ha! Ha!"

"Let's knock loudly on the blasted door!" Dick uncharacteristically suggested, wondering glumly what a "nezzpah" could be. Although he'd surely be vehement in denial, of late he quietly seethed over his chum's chortling, at his expense. He wasn't interested in those snotty frog books anyway! For a split second he thought, "Loyalty is one thing," yet he pushed the phrase out of his mind before he could think what *another* thing might be. But putting an end to this cultural discussion, both boys stepped boldly to the door and addressed its sturdy oak panels with an imperative tattoo.

After a moment, the door slowly swung open to reveal a furtively bent woman of decidedly unpleasant aspect, her clothes badly soiled with hamburger fat and unrecognizable culinary orts. Screwing her face up into a grotesque grin, she looked at the lads as if seeing them for the first time, and harshly spoke.

"What can I do for you fine boys?" she rasped. "Not much hereabouts a young feller'd be interested in, unless," she paused mysteriously, "he's the sort o' boy who relishes a hanker on sledding!" At this final word, she reeled into a gale of icy laughter, laughter so cold that it seemed almost frigid as it chilled the lads to the quick.

"We're of a mind to find the old blue mill on the other side of yonder Misty Crag if we can," Buddy said soberly, disregarding Dick's bewildered glance, "and we'd be extremely grateful if we might purchase some 'grub' from you. We may look disreputably rough and essentially unlettered, but I assure you that we have some money and are of honest middle-class roots." And with this, he introduced himself and Dick to the tattered scullion.

"My father is a streetcar conductor," Dick interjected proudly. In the strained silence which followed, a loon coughed idly in the bog.

"Well, come on in then, boys," the hag said. "My name is Zenobia, Miz Frome if you prefer, I reckon to be thinking. Don't pay no heed to these two danged fools setting in the parlor—one's my kitchen helper, my pot-walloper, my slop slob," she grinned foully through her shining green teeth. "Roberte, Roberte Ce Soir is her name—or so she fruitlessly wishes!" she cackled gently. "And this other's my husband, Robin, which is what I reckon I pleasure to call him. No need to know his true, Christian name which he give up when the devil crawled inter his overalls, heh, heh. Neither of 'em's good for spit," she laughed, hawking up a sliver of glittering yellow phlegm. "Robin hain't done his duty by me as a *man* for years, an' Roberte—pshaw!—it's all the French tart can do to light a yaw fire with a 'tater match." And with this, the shrew flung herself into a filthy rocker which seemed to shriek quietly with a horrible secret!

The boys stood uncertainly in the middle of the squalid, fetid parlor, thinking that a plunge into a cataract wherein razor-clawed grizzlies gather to bathe would be preferable to this interview, if such it could be called. But by whom? they wondered in unison.

"I-I'm powerfully sorry, Miz Zenobia," Buddy managed hoarsely. "I can see that we've come at an inconvenient time. I notice, for instance, that you're about to 'dig in' to your midday repast," and with this remark he gestured toward a potful of chemises boiling effluviously on the stove. This error occasioned general merriment, as might well be expected. Buddy then gestured to Dick with his eyes, frantically signaling to him like a lighthouse keeper looking for his wave-torn dory, signaling to his chum with winks and blinks that they should leave, and leave apace! But suddenly, a voice issued from the sober and tragic figure of Robin, collapsed, like a large bag, or sack of unidentifiable soft things, in his wheelchair, his hand resting pallidly on the hand of the twisted young woman in the wheelchair which tenderly abutted his own.

The young woman's name, Roberte Ce Soir, had filled Buddy with a curiously "electric" sensation when first Zenobia had blurted it out with her noisome spittle. That, and the way that her eyes melted when she gazed at Robin, seemed somehow important to him—more important, perhaps, than he knew or even dared understand!

In the tense silence, broken only by the buzzing of a fly against the windowpane, Robin's voice, which had, of course, already issued, now issued again. The boys leaned close, listening with rabid attention, for the message might well be an interesting one.

"Stay an' set fer a spell, boys," the disabled man cried weakly but hopefully. "We hain't goin' no whar. We're . . . *par'lyzed!*"

The lads staggered back as if struck by shards of offal.

Questions to Be Entertained

In Betty Barker's collection of "adult musings" on life, *A Batch of Stuff,* o.p., the author states that Sister Rocco Portola "knew a lot of girls very well indeed." Did the female religious in question smoke Gitanes in the privacy of her Spartan room, and, if so, where did she get them?

What did David Rockefeller have to do with offshore oil drilling, if anything, and why do certain neohistoricists link his name with that of John Crowe Ransom?

Why did Berthe leave four complete summerweight uniforms, with extra caps and aprons, behind the bar in Rocky's Tavern, known everywhere as "a hotbed of gender insensitivity"?

How is it that the meter of Theodore Roethke's "My Papa's Waltz" is often blamed for the weak, warm Manhattans served at many wedding receptions?

Why does Professor Brian Rolex, the author of *Illusion and Absurdity: The Uncanny in the Works of Howard R. Garis,* insist that the visiting niblick authority, Fantoine of Brittany, is the "devilfish" of Assyrian mythology?

Whereas a Roman *person* may profoundly involve himself with Roman Catholicism because of its traditionally jewel-encrusted trilbys, garbos, shakos, fedoras, and tatting "sheds," Rome itself devotes much prized leisure time to pasta dishes recently invented in California. What, then, is a "garbo"?

Ronda the Crazy Gypsy (not her real name) sits perspiring in the hot shadows of the small Queens store, known to the local residents as RONDA READINGS AND CONSULTATIONS. Here and there may be seen decks of cards, tea canisters, a crystal ball, and, for atmosphere, some flyblown mystical texts. "I know it's hard to believe," she says, "looking at this ruined face (indicates face, which, while not precisely "ruined," is definitely the worse for wear), that I was once romantically involved with such luminaries and top-drawer people as George the Polack III, the backyard lark, 'Puppo' Chanko, whom I playfully called 'Manny,' and 'Tits' O'Rourke, about whom, as they say, enough said!—as well as with a big guy in green work clothes who had some kind of thing for motels and pool furniture and bears in parking lots—don't ask *me*. Anyway, here I am in Queens, sort of living behind the store with Billy Joe Selma, a barber who thinks he's an Indian brave, Blue Wind. Amazing! How the mighty have fallen, as I sometimes assert, not that I was ever exactly mighty, but there was a time when I called broads like Lady Bustier and the Countess O'Mara my friends. Anyway, Billy Joe just called a minute ago (indicates Princess telephone in popular pink) and said it's important that I tie a pair of my panties around my neck and walk around outside for a while. I may be Ronda the Crazy Gypsy here in Rego Park, but I'm not *that* crazy! Well, I never denied that Billy Joe has his kinks like everybody else, but I always told him fine, just make sure it's in the privacy of the bedroom, not that we actually have a bedroom, and that's just between us, O.K.?, now he wants sexual oddities in the street? No thanks."

Dwight tells Ronnie as the latter is going off his shift that he's goddamned sick and tired of Allen and Chet excluding him like they do, just *excluding* him, when he's normal just like everybody else when it comes to the eternal beauties of nature, the sunlight gleaming on the thatches or whatever they are, the soft breezes sloughing the wild grass, and like that, for Christ's sake. Ronnie surreptitiously picks little bits of licorice off his apron and tries not to stare at Dwight's blackened teeth and lips. He doesn't really want this forced intimacy. Well, he's going to go and see the Eiffel Tower after all, all by himself, maybe he can run into some French boy who won't think that he's an *athama!* But soon, despite these vows, Dwight is calling across Great South Bay from a small hillock in Bay Shore: "Allen!" he calls. "Oh Allen! Chet, Chet, say Chet, you bitch!" State Trooper Kimberley Butz parks her patrol car, gets out, and tells Dwight to get his fucking faggot ass on the sidewalk and keep the noise down, sir. She looks none the worse for her recent ordeal. Just then, a horrendously misshapen man appears out of the mists which forever cloak this small but somehow chic village of the "fog belt." He seems to be trying to smile, twists his hat worriedly in his "hands," then introduces himself as Mr. Ronobe, Master of Rhetoric, the twelfth Marquis of Earl, and asks, or so Trooper Butz records it in her notebook, "if anybody has seen some flying people in the vicinity of Gnatville or Agapa." As Ronnie edges toward a dripping copse of sumac vetch, Trooper Butz takes a step back and places her hand on the grips of her service revolver. As she looks, officially, at Mr. Ronobe, the space which is occupied by his deformed body is suddenly filled with nothing but fog. Ronnie is by now running full tilt toward the Fedora, a small, discreet leather bar catering to putatively straight politicians, wherein his ex-roommate, Guy Ropes, is the waiter-bartender. "Some *flying* people?" Ronnie shudders, and picks up speed. Meanwhile, Ronobe is walking quickly across the bay toward Fire Island, wondering, for the hundredth time, how he, the twelfth Marquis of Earl, managed to get stuck with this shit detail.

But reading *Blackjack* is not soothing to Dick, and he feels a momentary letdown, which he prefers to think of as a "depression." The one positive thing about the book, with whose spine he is idly rubbing his crotch, is that Alice reminds him of Rose Marie, a girl he almost married after he and April went *kaput,* as he likes to say. "April and I, well, *kaput!*" is how he puts it. Occasionally, this remark will inspire someone to throw a chair at him, but for the most part he gets away with such things. He dials Rose Marie and waits.

Isn't Rose Marie's full given name Rose Marie Karen?

Right, of course!

Rose Marie says hello and Dick tells her this and that, *Blackjack,* depressed, thinking of her. So many years and so much water and so many bridges, *kaput!* "Yes," she says. What might have been, his old workshirts, April the bitch and April the cunt, he really tried, well, they really tried, he and she, well. But when he thinks of her wantonly bent over the kitchen table, does she remember that? "No," she says. *Black-jack,* Alice, didn't know her when he wrote it but amazing that she should *be* Alice, doesn't it strike her as strange? "Sure," she says. Rose of Washington Square, he called her if she remembers but does she remember why? "No," she says. Washington Square because they met in the Village, in the Village! She *must* remember. "No," she says. But all the different roses, he means her name and Washington Square and they went to see some play, right, *Odd Number,* in the old Rose Theatre, she must remember? "No," she says. Well then, she might agree that she's a cunt bitch whore cocksucker? Doesn't that sound about right to her? "I'm too old for this, Dick, and so are you," she says, and hangs up. Dick begins to cry, realizes that he is wildly aroused, and goes into the bathroom so that he can watch his face as he masturbates over the sink. "Motherfucking bitches all of them!" he says to the grey-haired old man looking into his eyes.

Horace Rosette sits in an armchair and listens to his joints creak. He pulls a shawl around his shoulders, then continues looking over the typescript of *New and Selected Poems* of Gilberte Brie, from which "Spanning the Azure" has been ruthlessly excluded by Horace, the book's editor. What no one knows, and has never known, is that Gilberte Brie is Horace himself, Horace in, we might say, his Creative Mode, In Touch With A Deeper Reality, etc. Horace is also the Dante Gabriel Rossetti, his little joke, of "Household Tips and Repair Wrinkles," a column syndicated in 137 newspapers, and, too, the Dante Rossini of the Rossini Veggi-Talian restaurant chain. He thinks of himself, however, as an abject failure, for there is no point in being any other kind of failure, or so he thinks, or, in any case, he thinks at this moment that this is what he thinks, although he doesn't actually think the phrase "abject failure." Credit where credit is due. He puts the typescript on the coffee table, leans back in his chair, closes his eyes, and begins to recite, from memory, and with amazingly few mistakes, poems by Rupert Brooke, Wilfrid Owen, Ernest Dowson, Laurence Binyon, Alfred Douglas, Walter de la Mare, A. E. Coppard, Harold Monro, Lascelles Abercrombie, and James Elroy Flecker. On he goes, yet each time he finishes a poem and opens his eyes, he is still alone, wholly bereft of youthful companionship. Alone! Alone! "Alone!" he cries, melodramatically but sincerely, then launches into

> When you have tidied all things in the night,
> And while your thoughts are fading to their sleep,
> La da la da la da la da la light,
> La da la da la sheep.

Well, he never liked Monro anyway, and besides, he can't ever remember this one, ever, he can't remember, well, he can't, it seems that he can't remember what he can't remember, nothing strange about that at his age, he remembers.

Then too: Rostaing's "Vapors" Theory Causes Rift in Decorative-Phallus Sect; Neo-Historical Post-Marxist Deconstructionist Theorist Claims Mark Rothko "Only a Painter"; Round Lake Inn's New Owner Will Revive Lost Glamour of Strip-Tease Contests; Royal Manual to Play Poet Frost in *Natchez-Mobile* Remake; Orthodontist Jack Rube to Change Name to Dr. John Rube, Endodontist.

Rupe stands, arrested, next to the garbage dumpster outside the A & P's sidewalk freight elevator. He is certain—because of (a) the modestly arranged skirt; (b) the Red Moon nail polish; (c) the confessed delight in leafy burgs and shady volumes; and (d) the small metal shoe buckles—that the woman recently "profiled" is his ex-wife, Ann Taylor Redding. "I maintain that Dr. Redding is still one of our loveliest scholars," Rupe blurts deftly, looking shyly away. " 'Loveliest' may be a strange word to use in reference to a woman who's gained a pound or two, but lapidary prose, despite these decayed foodstuffs (indicates shopworn food), symbolic of a degraded urban environment, is my cynosure and flense." He savagely brushes a tear from his rude cheek and disappears, as usual, into echoing nostalgia.

Cornelius A. Ryan sits back in the wicker porch chair and looks out onto the blazing, empty street. He is so wonderfully drunk that he feels cool and softly distant, far away from this wholly unreal Bay Ridge neighborhood. He drinks half of the Tom Collins at his elbow and lights a Camel. His old sister, older than he, is pottering around inside the house, picking up newspapers and muttering about wet garbage. He takes a deep drag and closes his eyes, and within a moment he inadvertently recalls an almost unbelievable night of love he had, some thirty years before, with a woman who fucked him with a wholly abandoned energy, with a girlish hilarity and joy, with tears in her eyes, until he gasped for breath in sobbing passion. Five minutes later, she sat in black, silent depression, and then he dropped her off, at her insistence, at the Kings Highway station. What was her name and where did she live and how did it come about that she picked him up and why did he never see her again? He finishes his Collins, lights another cigarette, pours four ounces of gin into the glass, adds a splash of mixer. The smooth, cool whiteness of her inner thighs, her candidly sexual language, her enthusiasm, her sudden bleakness. What was her name and where did he take her? Where did he meet her? What was her name? Will time tell?

Who should Ronobe meet on Fire Island but Sabnack, Marquis of Wounds and Worms, his battle gear safely hidden away, and his grim visage softened by his decision to—how does he put it?—"give his orders a new interpretation." It is, of course, outright mutiny if not desertion on Sabnack's part, and such reckless conduct reminds Ronobe of the one-time book-review editor of the *Sacramento Bee,* who supposedly recommended, during one holiday season, divers works of the Marquis de Sade's as "stocking stuffers with a festive twist." Suffice it to say that this eccentric editor now calls such notables of the demimonde as Sailor Steve and Patience St. James (aka Ronda the Crazy Gypsy) his dear acquaintances. Thus business "bends its 'frighted glance 'pon the orbèd world," and "mincing mows pricketh th' ebon Saracen!"

"When said yokel book-person was last seen," Sabnack says from his sunny deck, "he was rolling around on the floor of the emergency room at St. Vincent's, chain-smoking Salems and claiming to be Ho Chi Minh. You should have heard his version of the 'Communist Manifesto'!" Sabnack begins laughing so hard that he forgets to infect the wounds he's given a hapless stray dog who has got just a little too close to the beach house which the infernal sprite has occupied. Perhaps "occupied" is not quite the word.

"Wasn't it Saleos, the pander, pimp, and crocodile-fancier, who gave the poor chump the idea back in sleepy, steamy Sacramento?" Ronobe asks. He glances at the dog and sends him flying into the side of the neighbor's house.

"Probably," Sabnack says. "Anybody who'll make the Salvation Army indulge in a nude bebop festival outside Macy's on Christmas Eve—well, *nothing's* too crass for him."

"By the way," Ronobe says, "have you seen a couple of my colleagues, maybe flying around, or disguised as callow high-school boys or middle-aged ladies in cute pink dresses with puffy sleeves? Gusion *and* Glasyalabolas are apparently AWOL after coming over this afternoon to chastise some fake goddess. Don't ask!"

"No. I would have *noticed* two fruits like that," Sabnack says. "Would you look at that dog!" He points his tongue, which has the form of a cancer cell, at the dog, and the animal begins burning brightly within an enveloping sheet of jaundice-yellow flame. "I'm here to, let me see," he says, looking through his notebook, "right, to find some guy who wrote a movie or something, a poem maybe, they're all alike, titled *Two Gentlemen in Bonds.* I'm supposed to get him to collaborate with the guy who wrote *Lace Me Tighter!,* a corset-lovers' extravaganza. Whatever the hell a corset is. Why don't you stay a while?"

"I think I will," Ronobe says. "I'm sick and tired of always pulling the shit details."

"That's how I feel," Sabnack says. "You hungry?"

Let's not even *think* about the dog.

A certain rather familiar Sam rushes out of Crown SuperMart despite, so he claims, a "truly refreshing and enlightening" discussion, to which he has been privy, between two young women about the salutary fantasies of empowerment created by the ingestion of freshly ground peanut butter. (Indicates Crown SuperMart's peanut-butter machine.) "Do you remember one of the questions recently asked?" Sam says. "About Sister Rocco Portola and her Gitanes? Remember? Well, Sister Rocco is now, and has been for some time, Sister San Antonio Rose! She doesn't smoke at all, but is partial to self-flagellation with a cat-o'-nine-tails every Friday night. O.K.? Take it easy," he concludes, and rushes back into the store. This information is, of course, welcome, yet it seems spurious at best, since the Sister San Antonio Rose with whom we are casually acquainted does not know Betty Barker, and has lived at the San Francisco All-Natural Wine Factory and Cute Place for years, as a member of the Order of Sangre de Cristo.

"We of the Order believe in Santa Claus," Sister San Antonio Rose beams, her mouth filled with raw vegetables and nutritious things made of beans and redwood shingles. "And smoking should be punishable by death, of course. Did Christ smoke? No! But Judas did, the nicotine-crazed roustabout!" So long, Sister. Don't take any wooden clappers.

Father Debris, in one of those remarkable accidents which are so often at the root of mathematical innovation and discovery, finds that Girolamo Cardano's formula (q.v.), when applied to texts other than Lange's, yields information which the priest has long desired. For instance, when the formula is applied to Sappho's *Αστερες μὲν ἀμφὶ κάλαν σελάνναν*, the name of the female star of *Blaze over Pago-Pago, The Hot Countess, Tongues at Midnight,* and *December* is revealed, almost miraculously!

"Indeed it is," Father Debris winsomely smiles, looking up from his rumpled desk. "The same wonderfully attractive and vivacious young woman starred in all four films. You quite possibly know her by the name she later made famous, but in the days when films were films and stars were stars, she was the oval-faced, silk-complexioned, flashing-eyed Sarah Lawrence—'America's Mystery Co-Ed.' Subsequently, she starred in *Sargasso Sea* with Douglass B. Satan, as the blind girl crippled for life when her pure love made her zooming sled crash into a tree, and in *Satanism on Saturday,* a film many critics think her best, and in which, as the 'Saucy French Maid,' Fifi, she was required to display her knees in direct contradiction of her religious beliefs. The forever fickle and puritanical public immediately abandoned her, and her career, in a few years, hit rock bottom. Sound familiar? It wasn't until Bill Saunders, a wise, and, I suspect, grizzled press agent, convinced her to star in a small-budget musical under the name Jeanne Popcawne, that Sarah once again tasted some of the sweets of fame. Of course, things would never be the same; her toilets, for instance, would no longer be flushed with champagne. Well. Her last film, *Sazerac,* was a musical version, ironically enough, of her first silent starring role, that of Madame Vermouth in *The Orchid Boat.* This remake is a drab item, wholly uninspired, its only bright spot Sarah's—or Jeanne's—triple-tongue singing of 'Jade Mountain,' which she performs while treading water in a pool filled with giant chartreuse 'lobsters.' After that, she faded into obscurity, yet they say that on still nights in the Hollywood Hills, one can hear her sobbing over rotten scripts." Father Debris falls silent, and sits, bemused, his face a mask of convoluted thoughts on life's bitter mysteries.

Sarah Lawrence? Jeanne Popcawne? *Sappho?!*

It makes him happy. Leave him be.

It's perfectly all right with me! Don't forget, I didn't have a word to say when you decided to tout that rotten short story "Scale Model of Splendide-Malibu in the Lobby of Splendide-New Haven" as one "attuned to how we now live." *Not-one-word.*

Duly noted. Do you think it's getting any cooler?

Hotter.

The disgruntled and footsore Scandinavian, Knute, at length reaches the old Dodge in Scone Canyon and with a great, fearsome oath crawls inside. Although Knute is still defiant, the ceaseless pressure of being a dour woodsman as well as a mysterious Lutheran is beginning to wear down his morale and vaunted pluck.

"Those damned pantywaist sissy-boys, Buddy and Dick, don't help none either!" he says, unhooking his coarse wimple from the heavy granola-canvas apron to which it is attached. "Whew!" he at length bellows. "That old-style wimple, even though it offers mighty fine protection from coochybugs, will *do* for a fellow, and that's for certain. But soon I'll be in Schenectady again and dearest Lars will take me into his brawny, felonious arms!" Then, a smile suspiciously playing about his calloused lips, Knute settles in among the still piles of yellowed newspapers which contain the mute records that speak silently of the quiet desperation of the voiceless throng of dumb humanity.

Lolita Kahane suddenly remembers, standing there on the kitchen sink, that she was once Lolita Schiller, "Dumb Lo" or Lo-Lo, as a few people hatefully addressed her. That seems right to her, although the name of her first husband, Richard Schiller, which comes to her in acute clarity, neither conjures up his face nor anything else about him, save for the memory of his whining voice complaining, as always, about the black grease under his fingernails, oh God, *fuck* his fingernails! "Fuck your fingernails," Lolita says, and is, in the great tradition, "startled by the sound of her own voice." She'd do well, she supposes, to get back to *The Girdle Story,* which is apparently about cold, cruel men doing it *fast* and *hard* to complaisant women, all of whom remind her of Lena Schmidt, white canes or German accents. It's a terrible book, in truth, even though many of "our" most respected journals of literary opinion think otherwise. For instance, some Joe Schmuck writing for, it must have been *Sciacca, Scootch Review* or *Christian Arts Monthly,* had this to say: "Pretty darned good, and even though there is a slight falling-off of narrative ability in the last third of this compelling novel, who else is doing such and knowledgeably writing hauntingly of whatever he is with a courageous power that is politically conscious, sensitively aware, projectively intuitive, and with this and with that passion, too, and also very compassionate and caring? Who indeed?" Lolita climbs down from the sink, showing "a lot of leg," although there is nobody to show this "lot" to. The novel reminds her that Conchita, a hazily familiar name, never wore a girdle in the days when *everybody* wore one. That doesn't mean, however, that Lolita can't remember— not by a long shot!—a few depraved evenings in the Score Motor Inn, Scotch on the rocks or "Scotch," who, although he liked pink on grown women (indicates pink cocktail dress with puff sleeves on attractive mother of three), was, in other ways, well, *all right.* "I'm Scots-Irish," Lolita remembers him saying. "That's *Scots,* not *Scotch,*" he'd say. What a glittering card he then seemed! It is now clear to her that he was yet another boring lout, interested, basically, in doing it *fast* and *hard* to her. At least, *fast.* Despite the banal decor of the usual Scranton motel room, "Scrapple from the Apple" or *The Secrets of the Bottom Drawer,* that was what "Scotch" *really* cared about. That, and the occasional smutty story about the whorish Amelia Sedley and the strange, mesmerizing things that she could do with place settings, cucumbers or wet bath towels. Lolita sits in an easy chair, picks up *The Girdle Story,* and starts reading where she left off on page 92, at a reference to Kansas City, a toy airplane or a perverse Continental gentleman. But before she gets too comfortable, maybe she should climb into the cupboard over the sink. That might be a good idea. Just take care of it now. While it's on her mind.

Not even that mighty prince, Seere's, fellow spirits of the aether know that he is thought to have posed for the famous frontispiece drawing in *Segundo curso de español.* The picture represents a beautiful man on a strong, winged horse. His sharp eyes seem to be ferreting out evil and chicanery, although students, to this day, joke that he's merely trying to conjugate "ir" in all tenses.

"The drawing was done—I remember it as if it were yesterday—in September," Horace Rosette reflects, gently tossing an anthology of Georgian poets to the floor. "I had just finished editing *Set Pieces,* my third collection of Great Short Stories from, ah, Dixie, when I was suddenly transported to Annie Flammard's studio—dear Annie was not yet *acting*—and there, in the most delicious sort of Iberian outfit, with boots and silk shirt and little buttons and fringe and a wide-brimmed hat, oh, *everything,* there was this *beautiful man,* with something really otherworldly about him. I was in Seventh Heaven." Horace picks up his book, and sits in silence, his eyes closed on this memory. He doesn't choose to remember that the model who posed for the textbook drawing was not Seere, but a professional, Greg Purlson.

"Greg Purlson?" Lena Schmidt blathers, stumbling through her apartment, her white cane wreaking its occasional havoc on dishes, glassware, and what look, a little bit, like houseplants. "Greg Purlson was a *beautiful* man! I could see that despite my fast-developing cataracts. He was also a kind man," she continues, thrusting her cane neatly through one of the living-room windows, "in that he introduced me to the knowledge necessary to a young woman's peace of mind by pressing upon me the classic pamphlet, 'Sexology: 100 Facts.' From that day on—thanks to Greg!—I could hold my own with sophisticated sexual beings like Sheila and April. Unfortunately, I soon became vision-impaired, and that precluded a number of ocular-sex thrills which sighted people may take full advantage of, the lousy bastards! But 'a little drop of rain must splash on everybody's face' now and then, as the old song goes."

N.B. Lena Schmidt's remarks are here "translated" and may not precisely correspond with her actual or intended meaning.

Ann Taylor Redding no sooner begins animatedly talking about her dissertation, "Sexual Desire as Evidenced in Selected Phonemic Groupings in Virginia Woolf's *Mrs. Dalloway,*" than her interviewer excuses herself and, as they used to say, takes a powder. Dr. Redding mutters irritably that one would think that she'd offered to read aloud a recent article on the crisis in Israeli morality! Expeditious departure in such an oppressive case would be understandable, surely, she thinks. But what can anybody have against phonemic groupings and the cultural secrets which they often reveal? Especially when well-shaken! The doctor also knows that these groupings may be successfully plumbed only if one understands them to be representative of their maker's attitudes toward his or her contemporaries. In other words, or in other phonemes, as Dr. Redding often says in subtle jest, each grouping presumes a *possible* scene of tension and heartbreak, and *possible* voices from the other side talking a lot of "shit." (Indicates bursts of vocal malarkey.) Dr. Redding, weary now, goes to the window and looks down at Benita and "Chick" O'Hearn munching raw zucchini and strolling hand in hand toward a large assemblage of tofu admirers gathered about the apparently insensate body of Louis Condy, prostrate, and covered over with tar and several layers of feathers. This is life! she thinks, and then decides to take a bath. It may here be of interest to state that Dr. Redding, some years ago, was inspired by her dissertation to write a short work of erotica, rooted in a long-standing and profound phallic obsession which she vehemently denied. One of her admirers, aware of her growing devotion to the literature and cult of the phallus, said:

"It seems to me, Ann, that you're obsessed of late with things, well, phallic."

"What?" Ann replied, then added, "Poppycock! I deny that vehemently!"

Yet she began working on her erotic *récit,* "Shadowie Lumpe," even before her dissertation was approved and her degree granted. Her problem is—and we use the present tense because Dr. Redding is still "at work" on the piece—that she wishes to encapsulate the erotic feminine response to the omnipresent and tyrannical phallus in a language at once enveloping and penetrant, aggressive and passive, lustful and aloof, *non-erotic* yet everywhere vibrant with sexual longing.

This desire, which some hold responsible for the minor disaster which her life has become, is kept alive in her by the demon Shax, Destroyer of the Understanding, who makes her believe, whenever she sets to work on the huge, ragged manuscript comprising notes, notes on notes, bibliographies, false starts, emendations, additions, marginalia, interlinear variants, canceled chapters and sections, pornographic drawings and photographs, etc., etc., that she is a man, possessed of a phantom phallus, the size, weight, rigidity, and very *presence* of which make meaningful work on "Shadowie Lumpe" all but impossible. For how can she create a legitimate work of erotica as true, dark, and brilliantly artificial as sexuality itself, and capable of arousing the deep libido of women, if the imaginary phallus "actually" rooted in her burning crotch drives her to write in the lying pornographic language of lying men? At the same time, such work becomes utterly necessary to Ann if she is ever to speak clearly to women of the lies which men perform in the name of literature, to speak, that is, as *cunt,* to women, as a *cunt* to *cunts.* She often thinks of Maureen Shea, one of April's oldest girlhood friends, whose sexual language is so remarkably childlike and sketchy, and who is so carnally naïve and transparent, that did she, Ann, have *her* sensibility "in reserve," so to speak, she might well compose "Shadowie Lumpe" as the erotically innocent yet anarchic work she can sometimes envision, but not effect. Envision, but not effect! At the moment, Shax is cruelly and gratuitously sporting with her, as she stands naked before the bedroom mirror, cursing and hissing with frustration as she tries, again and again, to roll a Sheik onto the erection which is so stiff that it pains her groin with its urgency. We feel obliged to add that Dr. Redding's sexual complexities have nothing whatever to do with "penis envy," an idea which may well have seen its day. Dr. Redding's complexities cluster around the non-existent phallus which she, at times, truly possesses, and with the fact that she can find no language in which to write either of her own or of masculine eroticism. Suddenly, she gasps and groans as she comes to her hot, spurting orgasm. She falls to her knees.

Lou looks at the picture again, the young woman is more than just familiar. She's a woman who changed his life. Modest, yet not really modest, something about Prospect Park. Long shadows, some big house in Locust Valley. Well, he can still take his car. He gets up, looks for his hat, his fedora, of course, despite the heat it's never really too warm for a fedora! A line from "Sheila Sleeping" unwinds in his brain, then another, then he's remembering huge blocks of the poem, what kind of a poem is it? Somebody in it named Sheila is sleeping. He is completely at home with the poem. He looks again at the young woman in the picture, her shift dress, her good legs, slightly apart, her breasts just suggested beneath the soft fabric. He looks at the picture. He puts it down, picks it up. The way she wears her clothes. "Sheila Sleeping." The memory of all that. Her dress. Sheila. He can't go out now, after all, he has no car, he has no moustache. He hasn't got his fedora! The way she stands. Sheila? Sheila?

Corrections of Earlier Errors

Item: Annie Sheriff, long considered to be no more than a rather unconvincing character in Leo Kaufman's *Isolate Flecks,* is, in "real" "life," Mrs. Balte Brownie. When she is finally tracked down, flushed out, and hauled before Selected Literary Journalists, she will be asked some *hard questions* about her husband's affinity for prepared mayonnaise and his extended absences from home.

Item: Al "Whitey" Shields, recognized in certain quarters of Nuevo Laredo as "Pablito," "Happy," or "the lecherous one," is being sued by the Daughters of Durga International for, long years ago, naming his first wife, Bárbara, "Mrs. Raincoat." A spokeswoman for DDI contends that "the raincoat, as an adjunct to phallocentrism in all its many devious and insidious forms, is akin to the Ship 'n' Shore blouse, a demeaning garment with which women have been, for too long, tragically familiar. The governing board of DDI maintains that the insulting sobriquet was no small factor in Bárbara Shields's ultimate mental collapse."

Item: Gert Shitzvogel has not yet been *officially* informed that, had *The Orange Dress* been published under her name, it would have been reviewed in the *Montclair Co-Op and Lawn News,* the *German-American Family Gazette,* and *Your Art-Fun Weekend!,* and nowhere else.

"Hello! I'm Miss Shredded Wheat, or at least I was, more years ago now than I care to remember. It's terrific to me that my odd friend Sidney still likes to call on me once in a while, and one of these nights I'm going to surprise him by getting into my old Dixie Dugan costume, although I'll probably need a *shoehorn* to do it. Sidney likes twisted little things like that, as I sure found out when he took me last week to see a super-all-hot-action-classic-double-porno bill, *Silk Sighs,* and the sequel, *Silk Thighs,* both of them starring Annie Flammard. The things lubricious that girl could do! Anyway, that's about Sidney's speed, though he's not really a bad guy—a little bald, wears those tacky monogrammed shirts, likes the Boston Pops, and sometimes gets as mad as a Hindu with a raging tooth, but otherwise, he's just about right for me, at present. By the way, my name is, amazingly enough, Karen, *another* one, right?, although between Miss Shredded Wheat and Simone, another name Sidney calls me when we're, you know, being amorous, I barely answer to Karen anymore. Simone is the heroine from a book Sidney admires, *Story of I* or something, but it's a little too French-perverted for me. I mean, like fried eggs and things! Anyway, Sidney says that he knew a woman fifteen or twenty years ago who liked to fantasize herself as this Simone, something that I *don't* do, believe me! I get jealous when Sidney says things about other women but I try not to show it. I'm doing my best and keeping a cheery smile and a good thought and next week I'm starting on that new mineral-oil and lime diet. There's the phone, it's probably Sidney with a halibut or something!"

In this particular suburban neighborhood of small white "dream" houses, parched lawns where late the crabgrass sang, and splintery Adirondack furniture set carefully beneath trees almost totally denuded by the gypsy moth caterpillar, a woman whom her husband calls "Sis" strides purposefully down the street on her way to an assignation with her lover, whom his wife calls "Bro." We may conclude that dopey behavior invades even the most fragile dreams, and that the good life 'mid foliage and flowers is not exempt from the general madness of the day.

Michael Cullinan, who *is* Michael Cullinan, is roused from his disappointment at missing *Black Ladder* by the following question, put to him by an itinerant "populist investigator": "For what or whom do the initials S I S stand?" Such a question is Michael's special meat, or meaty specialty, and, laughing delightedly, the sunny-faced Irish pervert replies, with a gawm and a brogue and a dacent cup of beef tay till further orders, "S I S stands for *Sisters in Satin,* a courageous yet heartwarming film which does not shrink from detailing the secret erotic practices of the convent, high heels and all. Some ignorant film 'experts,' ha ha, continue to make the ludicrous gaffe of identifying the letters with *Sisters in Shame,* a film which, while of some interest because of its fresh use of the lost-brassiere motif, cannot hold a candle, if you'll pardon my ithyphallic figure of speech, to *Sisters in Satin.* The confusion seems to arise from the fact that *Sisters in Satin* is based upon the daily activities of the Sisters of Shame, commonly known as the Order of Sangre de Cristo. Most people wrongly assume that it is *Sisters in Shame* that is so rooted in the actual, but no-no-no!" Mr. Cullinane, excited now, gets up from his hoary desk and moves quickly, for such a small man, to his faded file cabinets, opens one, and begins expertly to scan its contents. "I have detailed descriptions of all the garments worn by the cast of both films, along with those of the garments regularly worn by the nuns of the Order, if you'd care to see them?" But the itinerant interrogator has simply taken his leave, allowing Michael to relax in the safe privacy of his harmless obsessions. No world leader he! He selects two bulging files, for the Sisters of Charity and the Sisters of Misericordia, and takes them to his desk along with a twenty-year-old issue of *Stella's Cellar: Public Wear for Private Occasions,* a biannual catalogue for a specialty business long vanished. To work! he says to himself, rubbing, yes, *actually rubbing* his hands together. Downstairs, May Cullinane is dialing April. It is indeed, yes, a sad old world.

Only Jimmy Blackhead's closest friends know that before he bought the moribund Black Basement he owned the Six of Diamonds, a restaurant famous for its bavette de boeuf chasseur, tomates grillées à la Provençale, poulé sauté beauséjour, and banane étonnement, the last the spectacular dessert of, some maintain, uncanny powers, and which has, of late, been responsible, or so it is rumored, for the sinister deaths of Percival Skeezix, the international bergamot; Cleerone (Slam) McTavishe, the Sneaker King; and "Slick" Jane Whitlock, author of the best-selling smasho courage-packed wallop, *Whores Bleed Red, Mom.* We don't quite know how this legendary dessert (or "sweet") can be held responsible for the demise of three of the people who made our pulsating city the excitingly electric dynamo of a hip thrill that it is, but perhaps M. Rimbaud has a thought or two in his louse-ridden *la tête.* Monsieur?

Rimbaud, clutching a copy of Monge's *Les Constructions métalliques,* momentarily and carelessly half-incarnates himself, his blue-white eye shining. "Sans doute," he says, "la débauche est bête, le vice est bête; il faut jeter la pourriture à l'écart." He smiles ambiguously and his pale image slowly fades. We never *quite* thought of Skeezix, McTavishe, and Whitlock as *pourriture,* but then we are not Arthur Rimbaud. Permit us to note, before angry letters and phone calls begin to come in, that this actual appearance, this *live* appearance by the famed poet whose books sell, year in and year out, in the thousands, was prefigured in Leo Kaufman's justly celebrated "Sleeping with the Lions," his astonishing piece of juvenilia. Jonathan Slug-Smith and Werner Smitts, in their "The Legacy of the Lions: Seminal Imagery in Leo Kaufman's Early Fiction," convincingly argue that the appearance in the story of the Rimbaud figure to a dissolute academic is recapitulated over and again in Kaufman's later fiction as well as in almost all of his mature poetry, finally occurring, in a daring semantic shift, along the cumulative "syntagma plane" as the "lost clam" and "rusted Chevys" of "Leo's Last Poem." Slug-Smith and Smitts also suggest, but far less authoritatively, that the "slime imagery" in Anne Kaufman's poems (see especially "Snails"), usually thought to be inspired by her early devotion to Roethke, is, in fact, a version of her ex-husband's bold employment of a crude yet robust magical realism. The scholarly pair argue that these phenomena suggest that truth is stranger than realism of any kind, and that Anne Kaufman was symbolically correct to enter the retail religious-supplies business.

Leticia Snap, a woman of impure thoughts and proclivities, remarks that "magic realism is like when ghosts and animals, like clams, put on clothes and dance and eat bananas and stuff and talk with real people, isn't that it? It sort of kind of makes you wonder about the meaning of reality in a big way and see like sort of under the surface? I've known a lot of men like that—ghosts, I mean." Miss Snap raises her skirt, and in the best tradition of meat-and-potatoes realism, *unnecessarily* adjusts her garters, showing *a lot of leg* while gazing at the *traffic far below* as if for the *first time*. "Now, for instance, if an exotic cassowary like walked out from under my skirt and started telling me the amazing history of the area in which I presently find myself," Leticia sighs, "that would be magic realism, is that about it?"

Close enough, Leticia, close enough. Nice *pair of shapely gams!*

Harlan Pungoe, still hobbling, scraping, and scuffling through the broiling streets, and dripping with malodorous and toxic sweat, is, according to a secret notebook, or "log," supposedly buried deep within an abandoned tungsten mine on Mystery Mountain, somehow close to the very center of *all* the activities of this summer day. Some citizens, quite recently interviewed, go so far as to insist that without Pungoe, none of the events presented to our rapt attention would even have occurred. That may be going just a little too far, although we have no way of disproving these opinions. It is time, however, now that Pungoe is on his way to what can no longer be disguised as a "casual visit" to Annette Lorpailleur, to indite here those oddities of his weighty presence which make him a figure to be feared even more than reviled, hated, or condemned.

Nota: At an earlier time, and in a very different place, Harlan Pungoe cynically represented himself as "Flem Snopes."

Nota: "The Snorter," a neo-impressionist-radical-pop-performance-feminist-rock-video artist, insists that her recurring bouts with paranoid schizophrenia, appendicitis, heroin dependency, coronary infarction, and chronic hemorrhoidal distress stem from the evening on which she responded coldly and contemptuously to Pungoe's casually "friendly" remark, to wit, "I like the cut of your jib and the lay of your luff."

Nota: Socks of SoHo, the custom-hosiery shop, is considered by the Buildings Department to have been in the process of spontaneous and irreversible self-deconstruction ever since the day that the owner quarreled with "a clubfooted man" over the price of a pair of nickel-plated opera stockings.

Nota: La Soirée intime, the erotic *récit* which figures in *La Bouche métallique,* a marvelous book filled with the subtle tips which literature alone can offer the pressured businessman, is said to exist, *in fact,* as the erotic *récit* entitled *La Soirée intime* by Léonie Aubois, as well as the screenplay (also entitled *La Soirée intime*) by a writer or writers unknown. The latter two "properties" are thought to be early-period creations of Pungoe's.

Nota: The famous Soirée Intime chain of lingerie boutiques is owned by Beshary Contemporary Ventures Inc., of which the principal shareholders are Annette Lorpailleur and Harlan Pungoe.

Nota: It is revealed in the *Thaumaturgic Experiences* of Éliphas Lévi, by means, it is said, of almost impenetrable late-Latin anagrams, that a man who walks with "a dip, stagger, and shuffle" and who favors the mystical color blue will come to be the familiar of Solas of Herbs and Stones, the bleak Raven of Astronomy.

Lincoln Gom is certain that "Some Fun," the translation of "Quelques choses par amusement," by his latest enthusiasm, Paul de Kock, does *precisely* what Ann Taylor Redding has been trying to do in "Shadowie Lumpe." Big talk!

"You'll soon be able to see for yourselves," Lincoln says over the phone, "because the story will appear in the next issue of *Green Sunshine.* Look, I like Dr. Redding, always have, she's got a lot of brains and a drop-dead pair of legs, also her English accent, wherever she picked it up, is charming. But literature is truth and truth is money!" Gom pauses to collect his thoughts, many of which have rolled behind the sofa, then continues. "I'm behind 'Some Fun' one hundred percent and I'm not too jaded or sophisticated, I hope, to admit that I fell in *love* with its nature descriptions, its characters, whose lives we feel we have participated in, and its amazingly sensitive adult scenes. In a word, they all work, gloves in hand, to pertinently wallop a reader! I appreciate Dr. Redding's honest attempt to tell a story from a man's point of view, of course, but de Kock *is,* if you'll pardon the expression, a man. The story may, oddly enough, remind you of *The Sound and the Fury,* or *Abalone! Abalone!,* or even *The Ballad of the Golden Hunter,* and other tales of the South. Or, if you prefer, you may recognize in it the rich gifts of sheer storytelling *just as sheer storytelling,* that we contemplate in

Southern Fiction *just as Southern Fiction,* all made even more stupendously amazing, since de Kock is a French person, a kind of *homme,* I think. Or he *was.* Anyway, one book editor I bruited about with some, a fellow who lunches regularly here and there, remarked that he thinks 'Some Fun' has about it certain of the brooding niceties of the classic fiction of the Southwest, for Christ's sake! He mentioned such classics as the classic *Riders 'Mid the Silver Gorse,* and other classics. In any event," Gom says proudly, "I thought I'd let you know so that you might tell Dr. Redding that she's barking up the wrong lump. Ha! Ha! Ha!"

We are puzzled as to how Lincoln Gom found out about Dr. Redding's project, unless, of course, her frustration and her "block" are common knowledge in the small but intimate world of letters and publishing, a world sometimes honored as "the media business," bless its iron heart. In any event, *we* are not mentioning a word of this to Dr. Redding, and of course, *things* are, for the most part, silent.

Unknown to Berthe, he has this day been befriended by Durga, the Destroyer, the Serene, the Inaccessible. The goddess's benevolent feelings for Berthe are no greater than her ire toward Edward Beshary. She travels swiftly to Bermuda on her lion-dog, where she manifests herself as the Albanian Lard Goddess in her incarnation as the sexually enraptured young woman whose photograph bedevils the priest, and many others, in the A & P. Her plans are to meet Beshary and by the potent magic of her "personality" (indicates awe-inspiring body) and the knowledge that those whom the gods wish to destroy they first infect with greed, to sell the South West Development Company, a bogus corporation, to Beshary Contemporary Ventures, Inc. What will she *not* be able to present to the leering capitalist, as she leans lightly against him at lunch, her pinstriped thigh brushing his? SWD, as she calls it, is in the process of breaking ground for casinos, hotels, spas, brothels, cinemas, boutiques, *everything,* in a desert currently as bleak and barren as central Spain. Guests will be shamelessly pampered and given everything from champagne and caviar to Frank's Orange Nectar and Hooten chocolate bars. The decor, architecture, and landscaping will range from Bauhaus to postmodern to '30s Grand Concourse to fake Spanish moss. Everything will be available to the rich, including, most especially, those things which they don't understand and so must possess. What does he think? Durga asks, sipping her cognac, her hand brushing the big strong handsome virile Arab's big strong handsome virile *batuta.* He looks at her, groggy with cupidity and lust, confusing, how wonderfully! how beautifully! one with the other, a common failing. Durga admires his skull, clearly outlined beneath the sweaty, yellowish skin of his face. "We've thought of calling the complex Nirvanadu," she says breathily, leaning her breasts against his arm. "It has a mysterious but familiar *donnée* to it, we think." Beshary blinks and blinks. He can't stop grinning his death's-head grin. We may be, at this moment, seeing the last of him, but time will tell. (Indicates clock, calendar, and gnomon.)

"Hi! I'm Karen Sperry! When I'm handing out tasty sticks of gum to unpop! the naughty, clogged-up ears of my passengers, my visage is friendly and caring, but hey! when I'm pitching and yawing on the bowjib with my conservative captain in his sassy white cap, I'm all laughter and unbridled admiration. And even though I'm working toward my advanced degree in useless-goods-marketing demographics, I can get with the idea of, like, wet things. Hi!"

Today, as on almost every day, the Splendide-Lincoln, Splendide-Malibu, and Splendide-New Haven are certain to report the disappearance of a number of what disgruntled policemen somewhat euphemistically term "thrillseekers."

And who are, actually. . . ?

Oh, the usual, mostly. Bergamasques, catamounters, thighbinders, mouthstrappées, concrete fans, featherkissers, shoepeople, garterboys, glimpsers, palmfondlers, partyrubbers, and so on.

Among the scores of "regular people, so-called," who have so far disappeared this year are the "Briefs" editor of *Sports Action;* "Jitters" or "Cheesy" Staffel or Stuffit, names employed by the plain Lucía Lewison, who arrived at the Splendide-Malibu still trembling from her modish experiences in the Lido; Myles Standish, an appellate-court judge, given to strange practices in his chambers with *Family Circle;* a fellow known only as Stanley, carnally befriended in his acne-ridden and drooling youth by Joanne Lewis during one of her self-hating frenzies; Stanziani's Neapolitan Restaurant staff, all of whom thought, so the New Haven police report, that they were going on a "boat ride" to Rye Beach, New York; and a man identified only as Star Eyes, so-called from his startling resemblance to a singer who once performed the definitive version of the song of that title, if popular and crisply written tomes speak the truth!

It is an oddity that Guy Lewis's "death by misadventure," among a number of other strange events on this day, was foreshadowed in Elizabeth Reese's undergraduate poem, "Starry Night, Bronxville: With Orgasm." The pertinent lines are:

> Some Guy, sore tempted by the fire escape
> —His dull bedlamite's vulgar patio,—
> Tilts there, then falls, his fall a last coarse jest.

We have so far been unsuccessful in trying to contact Miss Reese, who presently lives in Staten Island and teaches English Composition at a State Teachers' College; we'd very much like to ask her why the word "Guy," in the cited fragment, is capitalized, and how she decided, long years ago, on the "fire escape" as this despairing act's location. We will keep trying. (Indicates women, their sleeves rolled up, at unintelligibly blinking switchboards.)

"Wait a minute!" Cox says, "wait just a minute. That poem was stolen from one of the poems in *White Bridges,* I'd swear to it."

"I am forced to agree with this badly dressed yo-yo," Buddy Cioppetini nods. "The odor of plagiarism hangs over Miss Reese's 'poem' as surely as *E. coli* covers the known world."

"What the hell are you doing following me?" Cox demands. Well, he doesn't actually *demand.*

"I still think that you may know something of my missing *Homo Ludens,* and also you're plenty cute for a guy in real fake honest work clothes and careless coif."

"You noticed?" Cox blushes.

Like the doomed yet really aware polymorphous-perverse lovers in the Paul Whiteman Award-winning opera *Steel Orange,* the eminently singable work based on Wilhelm Stekel's "boot" monographs, Cox and Buddy head quickly toward a known shoe store. Forgotten on the instant are the irritations concerning missing books, sartorial acumen, plagiarism, inspissation theory, etc. As Dr. Johnson Mulloon once drunkenly remarked to Baron Sternhagen on the occasion of that nobleman's tenth-anniversary *hommage* to his miniature Stetson hat collection, "So you see, my dear Baron, that despite a clear and complete index, exemplary notes, and a mercifully brief introduction, no literary intelligence may long detain a yearned-for *jouissance!* Take it from me, I'm a doctor already, I know the agonies to which writers like Robert Louis Stevenson were subject, although I use him as an example only and in no way do I intend to stigmatize him as a mere hunk of fleshly envelope. Right?"

An epiphany from *Treasure Island:*
   "Har! Har! Jim, me lad! Scupper me Stillson jib to yaw the snatch-fathom quadrant, if loose apples don't spile the swabs afore the to'gallants! Har! Har!"

Although a "Stillson" is, indeed, the jib once carried or "flown" on barkenteens, it is, more commonly, the wrench used by meerschaum miners as the favored tool whereby to harvest large blocks of the precious "stuff." Day and night, fog permitting, Daly City is the scene of prodigious efforts as the hardy, stunted folk—whose roots are planted in the medieval mists of Stilton-on-Baskerville—mine the elusive flora, or something. It has always been so, as Tadeusz Creon, one of the world's recognized meerschaum experts, regularly notes.
   "That is true," Creon says, his eyes hideously encased in wrinkles as he looks up from his solitary game of *hrschszt,* an esoteric variation on Big Lotto, and one which is as old as many really old things. "The mining has always been performed according to ritual, for without the pull of continuity, gathering operations always tend to go awry. For instance, you've heard of the Cracow Scandal? Without that pull, it cannot be fully understood." He puffs bestially on his aromatic, crust-encrusted pipe. "Some purists—always there are purists," he spits coldly, "have inquired about Sonny Stitt and his role in the big picture, but to bring music into a discussion of the meerschaum harvest is always a mistake, and sometimes a manifestation of 'love madness,' as defined by Hans Dietrich Stöffel, who, in 1884, recognized and

presented the morphology of the illness in *De praestigiis amoris,* an invaluable work, often incorrectly attributed to Anthony Denim. Hmph!" Creon sniffs, slowly ripping the arm from his noticeable chair. "Denim was but a ne'er-do-well whose only claim to our attention is the role he played in the secular canonization, if that is not too strong a word, of the bulging shakos affected by the *actual* Royal Hussars." Creon lapses into a peaceful silence, his gums calm at last.

It might as well be mentioned, now that Tadeusz Creon has been once again hauled out and dusted off, so to speak, that he is prominently mentioned in April Detective's memoirs, *Strange Coincidences,* as one of the many unsavory men who took advantage of her temporary nymphomania, during what she rather cryptically calls her "Struttin' With Some Barbecue" period. The relevant passage begins, "Mr. Creon—we all called him Teddy—was always waiting for me in the stairwell with his pants off and folded neatly over his arm, in what my mother would have thought of as 'a state'. . . ."

Item: Yolanda Stuzzicadenticcio has not yet been *officially* informed that, had *The Orange Dress* been published under her name, it would have been reviewed in the *Italo-American Banjo News,* the *Scranton Arts Times,* and *Weekend Fox-Trot Hoots,* and nowhere else.

A certain Mr. Suave, which name he pronounces, for his own good reasons, "Sow-EEV," is in the process of "striking up" an "intelligent" conversation with the repulsive Balte Brownie, hoping, in this way, to get an introduction to the towering wreck of a man in thrilling plaids who seems to be his, ah, friend. Eros will stoop, as we know, to anything. "Oh, but certainly!" Mr. Suave says. "Certainly, dear, *dear* boy! 'Suck My Whip,' Sheila Henry's first—and only—short fiction was indeed published, and in *Nougat,* for that matter. But it was *never* included in any anthology." Balte sullenly aligns family-size jars of mayonnaise, wondering what this "fruit," as he quaintly thinks of him, wants. "You may be thinking of Regina Fury's *Suck My Whip,* published by the Sudan Press. Could that be it?" Balte shrugs and begins to straighten out the ketchup shelves. At this moment, in a wild and pulse-throbbing blur of terrifying colors, Bam sidles up to the pair, his large hands just quite naturally *there.*

"I read *Suck My Whip*," he offers, in his best Ivy League fashion, trig, yes, yet a little frayed from psychological aberration. He considers the four eyes which have turned toward him. "I read *Suck My Whip*," he repeats, with the wonderful patience of the elect, and then he drives it home: "I read *Suck My Whip*."

"How marvelous!" Mr. Suave cries, an odd tingle or two carelessly rippling through his once-wiry but now reticent frame. "My name is Sow-EEV," he smiles, his attention momentarily distracted by the sight of a tortured-looking man, in apparent mufti, who crawls swiftly past them on his hands and knees. "Sow-EEV, yes, and I'm delighted to make your acquaintance. My! How very big you are!" At this remark, Balte walks disgustedly to the next aisle.

"You know, of course," Mr. Suave says toothily, "that Regina Fury is the *nom de plume* of Esther Summerson, whose works on obedience, discipline, organic beverages, and the homely virtues of the birch have gained her the affectionate title, 'the simmering spinster.' It's delightful that in *Whip* she gives us a glance at her lighter side, don't you think?" Bam, who long ago laid down the burden of thought, makes the sound of a cork popping, and says, in a friendly but determined way, "Twenty dollars."

We have just been authorized to tell you what day of the week it is. It is Sunday. For the record: This is Sunday, August 29, 1982. It seems to us that certain of the events, occurrences, adventures, conversations, and dramas—bathetic and otherwise—taking place today are more suited to some other day of the week. But we only work here, speaking of bathos, and our occasional suggestions, comments, and complaints are rarely acknowledged, let alone acted upon. However, if we learned one thing at Suntan University, one thing which has allowed us to look at "the human comedy" (indicates breathtaking canvas displaying Comedic Panorama) with an observant, cold, yet not pitiless eye, to inform, that is, the long look with all that is in our power, it is that misogyny recapitulates entelechy. A hard discipline, yes, but one fraught with the morality of shaky ethics and brimming over with food for thought. A hard discipline, yes, but one fraught with . . . oh. Sorry.

Especially forceful and rigorous in this time of namby-pamby folderol when ideas are especially annoying, when people of decent background are considering that maybe history, for instance, never happened or something. You get what I mean.

Wholeheartedly. I mean yes, right.

However, it's also why we're constantly getting yelled at.

"Well, actually, *I'm* the Sun Twin," Saul Blanche says. "Look at my varied illnesses, for Christ's sake."

"No, I'm the Sun Twin," Sol Blanc replies. "You'll notice how I'm limping gamely along, even though my life is practically flashing before my rheumy eyes?"

"Does said 'flashing' include the weekend debacle at Sun Valley when your companion, Miss Languish, glanced at a catered buffet and scarcely a moment later was performing unspeakable acts with Mel Proud and each and every last Melodic?" Saul tragically leans on a handy crutch. "Including the *accordion* player?" He shudders as if for the first time.

"Such a scene, yes, I admit it, also flashed," Sol weeps. "I definitely deserve to be the Sun Twin. We're talking diseases, maladies of the spirit here."

"But I'm the chump of a gazabo whose reckless wager on the Super Bowl lost me my wife of forty years, Susan," Saul groans, looking about for medical solace, none of which, as usual, is in the vicinity.

"I thought the excellent Mrs. Blanche's name was Hettie," Sol remarks.

"You're thinking of the other Mrs. Blanche. You know, the *other* one," Saul smiles. "So, am I the Sun Twin or what?"

"Let's take turns," Sol offers. "I have a hunch that that's what Mr. Beleth and Mr. Halpas intended. God knows, they *looked* serious enough."

Fist's current interview with Lorna Flambeaux reveals that *The Sweat of Love,* her famous book of poems, and a media event of the early '70s which, in Michelle Caccatanto's words, "gave women of all stations, classes, professions, races, and persuasions permission to get proudly and properly 'hot,' " was almost entitled *The Sweet of Love.* "Yes," Flambeaux says, coolly casual in her and with her feet up on the and occasionally sipping from a glass of, "it was definitely going to be 'sweet,' but a dear, dear friend of mine at that time, Sweaty Patsy, seemed deserving of *some* recognition, since it was Patsy who freed my thinking from the prison of bourgeois-liberal phallocentric ideology." Flambeaux frowns for a moment and reaches, yet again, for a. "Patsy, dear Patsy, as Ronda the Crazy Gypsy, now provides spiritual guidance to those currently buffeted by life forces beyond the control of, *perhaps,* generous credit allowances." She toys with her and pushes restlessly the around on the coffee table.

Knute suddenly wakes to the natter of Lorna's voice, amazing though that may seem, and draws his pawlike hand roughly across his deeply weathered lips, muttering "pshaw!" as he performs this essentially masculine act. "Some years back," he says at last, the repressed anger barely detectible in his voice, "I was advised by Ronda the Crazy Gypsy to throw off the insults of those who would impugn my heritage by calling myself 'Swede'—*not* 'Knute the Schmuck,' *not* 'the thick Norwegian,' *not* 'the Scandihoovian tree trunk'—but 'Swede,' an honest and accurate name." Knute shifts about amid the piles of yellowed newspapers, and pulls out his large clasp knife in order to display it to a curious woodland creature, perhaps a beaver. Or a vixen. "So I did, and soon I was married to a woman who read my diary and then refused to perform her lawful conjugal wifely duties, as well as some that seem, now that I think back on it, unlawful," he concludes merrily, his enormous, rumbling laughter —the ruggedly individualistic laughter of a man whom no mere woman can ever tame, a man who, like a great lonely oak, is destined to hurtle off scarps and crash heavily into chasms, and even arroyos!—echoing off the scarps, chasms, and arroyos with which Scone Canyon is so tediously endowed, as geography teaches.

Then too: *Swedish Lust* Producer Denies Film Is "Extravaganza of Lewd Blondes"; Gold Dust Twins Charge Swee'Pea "Ate Things" during White House Performance; Birth-Control Panel to Reveal Contraception-Efficient Findings on Sweet-Orr Overalls; Gstaad's Residents Irked at Government Silence concerning Their Reality; Director Claims *Blushing Nuns* "Symbolist Dialogue" with Church; Publisher Will Publicly Burn "Misogynist" *Synthetic Ink* despite Author's Tearful Apology.

According to possibly specious information proffered in the strictest confidence, Lydia Languish's infamous behavior at picnics, barbecues, cookouts, etc., is *not* the result of her victimization by "the vapors," as has long been supposed. It would seem, on the contrary, that Miss Languish is the special target of Sytry, the Leopard Prince, who assumes among humans a human form, sometimes that of a beautiful man, sometimes that of a handsome woman. This glinting demon's special powers procure love between the sexes and make women show themselves naked. The sexual chaos which results when Lydia strips can only be explained by the intercession of some perverse power remote from the social, ethical, and moral concerns of civilized men and women. This hypothesis is further strengthened by a tape recording, received along with the possibly specious information already mentioned, which allows the listener to make out Lydia's voice, chanting, as she tears off her clothing in the usual way:

> Jussus secreta libenter,
> Fabric razed!
> Detegit feminarum,
> Quim naked!
> Eas ridens ludificansque,
> Wonderful guys!
> Ut se luxorise nudent,
> Use my hot sex!

Lydia, it should be pointed out, knows no Latin, and the syntax of the English "lyric," it will be obvious, can be thought of as strained.

"Actually," Horace Rosette says, "I say as much, about women in general, of course, in my critical introduction to *Tableaux Vivants: Selected Poems of Pamela Ann Clairwil.* Pamela, although certainly not one of our great poets, yet who *is* one of our great poets, or, for that matter, who are two?, certainly has her finger on an important erogenous zone—if I may be forgiven a small *mot*—of women, and understands their concupiscent relationship to outdoor dining. Something about the wheat, or corn, of course. I point out, in my small but scrupulous way, as you'll doubtless remember, that in such poems as the early 'Tahiti,' the remarkable 'Tarot: A Sequence for Waite, Wirth, and Marseilles,' and the fully developed 'Charcoal Drama for Allen Tate,' Pamela clearly suggests the strangely libidinous yet yearningly puritanical tension which develops within those scenes—some quite economically posited—which touch upon the sexually charged politics of contemporary *al fresco* feeding rituals. Oh yes indeed." Horace settles back amid scattered furbelows and tries to remember what Pamela Ann looked like, long years ago. Was she the one who wore the notable pink dresses with the *outrageous* puffed sleeves? Astonishingly bad writer!

Dear Nancy,

I've read in the paper that you are waiting with a sense of tragic heartbreak for the unexpected moment when you might explode. I too live in daily fear of this ever since scientists discovered the idea. Few who know me can sense the horror of what my days have become, especially since I seem to have everything that money can buy including a stockbroker ex-husband who my lawyers took to the cleaners, thank God, he was fooling around with some floozy bimbo tramp slut of a whore stewardess with big knockers, if you'll pardon my frankness, named Karen. For some reason it's always a Karen it seems. Anyway, Nancy, I want to let you know that as a Nancy, when I pray for myself not to suddenly explode, I'll also pray for you even though you are probably not like us, that is, my circle, at all.

> With noblesse oblige,
> Buffie (Nancy) Tate

Lucy Taylor is thinking of Lorzu Fashions and her ex-partner, Lee Jefferson, thoughts she has not had for years. Lucy is very much alone in her little pre-fab house—actually, a bungalow—in Teaneck, and has been very much alone for years, ever since the day that she was ordered to leave town and keep her big dyke mouth shut by Harlan Pungoe and Annette Lorpailleur after the boutique fire. But the story is well known. (Indicates well-thumbed, creased, and dog-eared story.) But *Lee* is still in town! Lucy thinks, bitter again after all this time. *Lee* can still have a drink or dinner or whatever with all the young women she wants to! It is *not fair,* she thinks, erroneously. Sad to say, exile has not improved Lucy, who looks, dresses, and, in general, presents herself in much the same way as she did when young. For instance: baggy cardigan sweater; flat-heeled shoes, badly scuffed; wrinkled, semi-opaque stockings; thin white anklets; hairy legs; pasty complexion; mousy brown hair streaked with piss-yellow grey; and etc., etc. Not even the most fanatic nature fans would, as the phrase goes, "make a move" on the woman. Teaneck may very well be the perfect locale for her, although certain areas of Northern California could easily absorb her without a murmur. The unprepossessing waif can and does blame her lack of feminine society on the fact that she doesn't know a female soul because none is worth knowing. And also because life, as we know, *is not fair.* She walks into the bedroom and lies down on her—but of course!—lumpy bed, and feels the musty, moist heat envelop her. On the dresser she sees "Big Yank" and her Large Economy Family Bruiser-size bottle of Prell. Which? She is sweating a lot, especially under the arms. In this, it will be remarked, she is like Lee. Perhaps I should remove my baggy cardigan sweater, she thinks, as she reaches for, what the hell, "Big Yank," always, when all is said and done, a summer favorite. As she begins to "dig for gold," to use the Mormon phrase, she thinks of Sara Teasdale's lines,

> Oh, beauty, are you not enough?
> Why am I crying after love?

Teddy, a *boulevardier* who occasionally, and without warning, asks pointed questions, wants to know why the Mormons, of all people, use such a phrase, what "beauty" there is in Miss Taylor's life, and what position in the canon is currently occupied by Sara Teasdale. Thanks, Teddy, great questions, really *great* questions. We'll get back to you. By letter. O.K.? How's the wife? Still at it?

"Hi! I'm Karen Teeth! When I'm streaking through thin air, which those in the know sometimes call the 'either,' in a gleaming silver tube, a rhetorical figure which those in the know sometimes call a 'monotony,' I usually do my pseudovirginal best to steal the probably well-off hubbies of 'mature' women who live in fear of sudden explosion, fatty thighs, and bimbo tramps. But when I'm on my hands and knees in an impersonal hotel room, I throw the demure act to the winds—all four of them!—and rely on the burning flesh. Hi!"

It doesn't seem possible, but Frieda Canula, who but recently was "chatting," so to speak, with Bunny Lewis in Gnatville, is reported to be in Tel Aviv. Surely, there is a mistake? Let's listen to a lately unearthed recording of Frieda herself, "talking" about her wanderings, shall we?

"I tears up my close, like bobbykoo people. Good fun but wet! Then, take train, is very nice. Here I am! I look for others of like thinkings and food bents. Here in Tellevauk is the home of many Albanian folk, as so often I shall have had read."

Frieda has reached her destination by train, so she cannot possibly be in Tel Aviv.

"Could be a sinister code about a secret kike weapon we know nothing of," Knute calls from his fastness. "Like the cannonballs of the idlers of Zion."

What, then, does she mean by "Tellevauk"?

"If I may interrupt?" Father Debris interrupts. "I couldn't help but overhear your remarking on the difficulty of 'placing' Miss Canula? I may be able to help?" The priest takes from his soutane a slide rule, a small calculator, a pad, pencil, and a geographical dictionary. "Now," he grins, displaying, by mistake, a small piece of what looks like François of Fargo's asparagus bread, which he swiftly, to his credit, caches. "As Riemann writes, if there are given in a plane a line L and a point P not on L, there are at least two lines through P parallel to L. So far so good?" the canny Jesuit asks. We nod stupidly, a, as they say, gog. "Then," he says, figuring, sliding, jotting, riffling pages, and so on, "I must conclude that Miss Canula is, as you surmise, not in Tel Aviv, but is currently enjoying the activities offered by either Ten Eyck Walk, in historic Brooklyn, or Terre Haute, in fairest Indiana." Father Debris puts his tools back into his soutane and leaves.

What? What did he just do? Ten Eyck Walk? Whoever heard of such a place? In Brooklyn? Just then, the phone rings. It is Joanne Lewis, hoping against hope that the rumor which has put the Albanian woman in Israel is true. We can, unfortunately, but assure her that all we know is that Israel is having a crisis of morality.

"What a refreshing change!" Joanne says.

"So, if we're actually going to get married, Terri," Terry says, chuckling wisely, "you can tell me anything, really, *anything.* We're no spring chickens, and hell, I've been around a little, seen a few things, been in the Navy, by God," he chuckles wisely. "That sojourn of yours, as you call it, and I like that word, in New Mexico? Those parties? Old boyfriends? Hell, don't bother me a damn bit," he chuckles wisely. Terri smiles at him, or, to be more precise, her shimmering, snowy plates do, leans back in her porch rocker of chaste Shaker design, clasps her arthritic hands in her still-attractive lap, and begins to speak, remembering. "Biff and Harlan and Teddy and Joanie and Marlene and Sam and Georgette and Dolores and Liz and Chester and Max and José and Ed and Kate O'Neill and Ricardo and George and Connie and Louie and April and Johnny. And me. And, oh yes, Terry, like *your* Terry is spelled. I almost forgot him because he'd only come every couple of weeks, you know, when he could get ahold of some really *big* pooches." She picks up her crocheting. "Is that all right, dear?" she smiles. Terry seems to be rigid, his eyes wide beneath his Coors baseball cap, his wise chuckle stuck somewhere in his throat, his eyes frantically signaling "amok! amok!"

Billy Joe Selma is telling Ronda this and that, the injustice, the misery that his people have suffered. His Indian accoutrements, or what he thinks are Indian accoutrements, lie on the table before them, wet from the sweating beer bottles clustered there. There is no justice. The asshole son of a bitch insulted him. Nobody cares about the wily buffalo or the great flame or the holy spirit or the wampum pipe or the smoking coup stick. The swift sun dance! Ronda is laying out the Tarot deck and not really listening to what she privately thinks of as Act Two, Scene One. Barnett Tete, senile old bastard, he's behind the damn movie with its crass remarks and shitty script, just like he backed that turkey *Thames,* who was in it? That old idiot-faced fuck with the jet-black hair and the wrinkled neck, should have put him in the old ham's home years ago? That's the one where the Sioux chief turns out to be some faggot child molester? Disgusting. And he also produced the one about the halfbreed Kiowa who spits on the flag, what's the matter with the fucking swine? And if truth were known, he's behind this disgusting freak film *Lace Me Tighter!,* where a dirty rich broad asks some other filthy bitch to treat her like a savage Indian brave would and, like, torture her, you dig? It's always the same old shit! Ronda sees herself in the Tarot with surpassing clarity, dead at last, wishful thinking. Billy Joe says that we should never have let the bastards know a word, not word fucking one, about Thanksgiving, Indians have always been the goddamnedest fools. He looks over at Ronda then and asks her if, hey, she went out today like he asked, with her panties around her neck, he has his reasons, and Ronda turns over The Tower and says that of course she did. What was he saying about some rich broad with jet-black hair?

" 'That's for Me' is thought of, with a kind of enervating regularity, as Our Song, by Janet and Tom Thebus, although in the midst of the sweetness and light which is their life together, Janet occasionally has unexpected visions of Tom's body, bloody, broken, and quite satisfactorily dead at last, at the bottom of one of the ravines which crisscross Mystery Mountain, upon which their living-room windows mercilessly look. Oh well. Tom, to give the devil his due, is often startled awake by a recurring dream in which a young woman sits, naked, on a large flat rock in the middle of a field. She looks at him as he passes in the coach of a commuter train, and smiles ambiguously. Sometimes he sees the title of the book she holds so tantalizingly in front of her private parts, *There's a New Sun in the Sky,* but he can never make out the author's name. As the girl begins to raise the book, he eagerly brings his face closer to the window, in order to see her sex, then knows, with a shocking certainty, that she is his mother. At this point, he wakes, sweating, fearful, terrified of sin and yearning for grace. At such times, Janet touches him tenderly with her knees, puts her hand on his shoulder. After all, well, after all. He's a good old wagon. The one thing she cannot abide, however, is his craven praying, after which come his altar-boy stories, followed closely by a detailed accounting of how he broke his parents' hearts and crushed their spirits, and all because of— oh God!—a married temptress who forced him to—oh God! Janet thought, and thinks still of Tom's parents as two vicious, greedy hypocrites, but has not mentioned this for some nineteen years now. However, in moments of overwhelming ennui, usually when Tom tearfully gets his battered Baltimore Catechism out, she accuses him of wallowing in his own stupid and impossible gloom, and says that *his* song should be 'They Can't Take That Away from Me.' Or is it they *won't* because he won't let them? Or is it, they can't, *thank God*? He looks at her, at such times, with the sort of pitying understanding which fills her heart with rage and her eyes with stinging tears. I know these things," Fred concludes, "because Thebus often confided in me during the many hours we spent as fellow commuters, oh, years and years ago now. Also, I drew a few conclusions on my own. I was in accounting then, as I may have mentioned, and some think that when I went into the re-insurance game, I died. But no. Here I am!" The old man attempts what gifted authors call a brave smile, despite the ultra-casual leather straps which embrace his head. It would seem, contrary to all expectations, that Fred has survived, intact, the "Queen of Sheba," much to the Frankenstein girls' amazement and delight. And there's *still* some zip in the old coot yet!

"Wooo!" one of the girls gasps. "I'm pretty much all enthused again! Loosen his ropes, will you sweetie?" she says to her sister. "It's that *dream* he told got me!" Her sister nods, clucks uncharacteristically, and tests the consistency of the hot fudge sauce, then adds another spoonful of cayenne pepper. She is startlingly and vulgarly provocative in a black lace version of an SS uniform. "Slide the *cannoli* over it right *now*," she laughs. "This fresh old guy is ready *again!*"

"SS?" Himmler barks. "Who are dese people? I vant to zee dair paperss! Black lace? It zounts like mongrelized Choo corruption. DAIR PAPERSS!" he screams. The redoubtable chicken-fucker is lucky that he is, so to speak, "on the outside looking in."

The wind, stronger now, as if taking its tragic cue from the mood of tension and heartbreak which grips the humble agricultural area (indicates "farm"), is bending the tender young burgeon almost to the ground, yet its force can do nothing to set the demoralized cow on her feet again. Troy cradles boss's great, cockeyed head, trying not to look after his Helene, oddly dwarfed by her considerable luggage, as her feet kick up the choking, clayey dust formed by the effects of sun and drought upon the brick-red clay which covers the bleak, clay roads and offers shelter to naught but the papery cloche-bug, summer scourge of the alfalfa gin. Troy stares sightlessly into his cow's huge, liquid eyes, and croons, in an untrained but pleasant alto, his heart wild with pain, "Thinking of You," the show-stopper from *Thoreau*, the last musical that he and Helen "took in," or was it "took to"? Durned if he could ever get fancy city-talk right! But that was in happier days, before tragedy fell heavily, like a large, drunken boondocker, on the simple family of the rich alluvial bottomland. From a flask, then, he pours an ounce or two of Three Feathers, one of our finest blended whiskies, "smooth," as testimonials confess, "as silk," down the gentle Guernsey's big throat, which Troy, despite a year of college and a proud stint in the National Guard, humbly persists in thinking of as a "thote" or "thoat." So, one never knows! Boss is coming around, and is, in fact, scrambling to her feet! An unfettered cry of bitter joy rises from Troy's own distended "thote" as he understands, and completely, again, yet again, that certain things have actually happened after all! And despite everything! And then, in his reverie, he hears Helen's voice calling him from the sun-blasted porch, calling, calling out the news that a Three Stooges film, one of their very best, is about to begin. When *was* it that Troy first realized that the zanies were brilliantly surrealistic? God! he thinks, what a strange maze life can be, in all of its odd occurrences, and even adventures. Supporting the youthfully lovely cow with a perhaps overly solicitous hand, Troy leads her toward the house and Helen's reassuring, matronly presence. He refuses to glance, even insouciantly, toward the road, where now the only sign of his lost daughter—O lost! and by the lost wind lost, lost!—is a thin puff of reddish "whiffle" dust on the trembling horizon. He cannot see, as he reaches gratefully for the icy tumbler of Thunderbird proffered him by his wife, his wife and Helene's mother—O lost! lost!—the big guy, sad and portly in his green work clothes, who awaits his daughter. Nor can he know that just two weeks from this coming Thursday, his slightly built and sadly undernourished girl will realize that there is no money to repair the large crack in a motel swimming pool, that certain patio umbrellas are torn and quite disreputable, and that Tillie, a cruel cashier who hates the dusty heat of a small town, will fill herself to bursting with cynical doubts about a number of fairly important statements. It seems that *everyone* knows how things are.

We have on hand the *Times* of London and the *Times* of New York, or, correctly, *The Times* and *The New York Times;* we subscribe to and read both newspapers. This information, while of a private nature, is here tendered in order to lay to rest certain objections of which we are currently in receipt—obviously the concerted effort of a vulgar cabal—as to the accuracy of some of our statements concerning, among other things, literature, the plastic arts, theatre and cinema, music, science, mathematics, philosophy, psychology, medicine, horticulture, cuisine, linguistics, and sexuality. All of our statements are checked and double-checked with *the facts* as these two "newspapers of record" possess them. Any errors are, of course, our own, but we do make every effort, really, to verify all remarks. We are, of course, wholly responsible for our opinions concerning events and "personalities," but we insist, over and over again, that said opinions are scrupulously objective. For instance, and briefly: We still maintain that Emmanuel Chanko, quite possibly the leading authority on the life and art of Jeff Chandler, is wrong in his blanket condemnation of *Tin Pig,* the novel on which *Chorus Orgy,* a pioneering film of the "montage-dialogue" school, is based. We believe that *Tin Pig,* rather than being the "literary equivalent of faeces," is a sensitive, delicate treatment of the impact of marital spats on a gourmet cook and real-estate "whiz." Mr. Chanko holds that we really know nothing of California, but he is not only a morphodite who likes to wear half-slips, he is also a *cetriol'.* (Indicates large specimen of the latter.)

"On the other hand," Knute says, wiping great tears of bitter laughter from his exophthalmic eyes, "I also despise those names given me by others, mostly wiseacre city kikes, who are always trying to ravage sweet Christian girls so that they can put their blood in matzels—everybody knows that. Names like 'Shambling Galoot,' 'Two-Bit Hitler,' 'Boy Scouts' Revenge,' and 'Tin Woodman.' I was even called the last name in print, for gosh sakes, by that mockie drunk pervert, Leo Kaufman. Yes indeed! In his 'Tit Poem Number Five,' which is supposed to be, or so I've heard from talk bandied around by the Cambridge 'Rowdies,' a disgusting gloating over how many sweet, clean, Christian sorority girls in pink dresses and cotton underpants this Jew befouled! 'Course, the 'Rowdies' is all namby-pamby English sissies, but they talk good sense." Knute suddenly stretches his arm out the car window and signals wildly to a lurking Scandinavian silhouetted against the eastern sky. "Lars! Lars!" he calls hoarsely, his weathered brow abruptly wrinkled with creases of wilderness wisdom, yet not, be it said, *unhappy* creases. "Lars!" he calls again, floundering helplessly amid the shifting piles of yellowed newspapers. But it seems as if the distant figure in filthy parka and fur-trimmed chockablocks hears nothing, nothing save the wind through the sere leaves of the towering ouzels. But Knute will not, he *cannot* give up, it has been too long, too long since that careworn moment when he first set out on what he now knows is a fruitless quest for his lost Zuleika! Clawing his way to the window, he places his rawhidelike mouth as close to it as he dares! Then he cries, piercingly, keeningly, hoarsingly desperate, "Tommy! Tommy! Over HERE, Tommy! In the old DODGE!" But the silhouetted figure moves implacably on, somewhat like Fate, or Time, toward the "tree line." (Indicates some half-dozen representative citations in Southern fiction.) Finally, his gumption at its lowest ebb since the morning, years ago, when he realized that his beloved Invisible Scarlet O'Neil was, quite probably, a Roman Catholic, he makes one last effort, so-called, to attract the plodding Northman's attention. "Tonia!" he screams bodaciously. "Tonia! Tonia!" But the distant hiker, of whatever identity, has disappeared into the sulky forest. So it ever is at such times.

Questions to Be Entertained

John Hicks, while writing a weekly column for *Toujours Gai,* fell in love with Jackson "Jack" Towne, who had, at the time, something to do with the Buildings Department, wherein Hicks was then also employed. John, as we know, is now Adelaide Hester's "guy." Is this current amorous attachment an indication that the Homosexual Rehabilitation and Behavior Modification Society program which he was "urged" to participate in by Dr. Mona Girls, "the Turkish scourge," was successful in terminating, or at least, abating certain vicious practices, e.g., pumpkin-beating, scrimmaging, horsing around?

The *Tractatus,* a difficult and demanding wallop of a reading thrill, on which Berthe Delamode patterned the specialities offered by her spectacular brothel, Creations Tastefully Designed, Inc., boldly asserts that one picture is like one word, or any word, or that a word is like seeing things, or *something,* or some *things,* or something like that. Why is it, then, that the once marvelously trim and handsomely coiffed Mme Delamode currently suffers from a "maladie nerveuse," one which is exacerbated by the sound of galloping horses?

Raulin's *Traités des affections nerveuses du sexe* and Lange's *Traité des vapeurs* are, of course, two of a mere handful of classic medical texts upon which all modern knowledge of "the vapors" rests. Yet Professor Solomon Traxy claims, in the current issue of *Science Fads,* that "Raulin and Lange were a pair of perverted nances, given to unnatural practices, and, as my research reveals, they were also culturally misogynistic." But can Professor Traxy be called an *authority* in Vapors Studies, given his admittedly superficial familiarity with the "neurasthenia papers" of Jean Ingelow?

Dexter Gapoine, Karen Gash, and Berta Garrett are laughingly speeding toward Misty Crag's only clam house, but Berta's husband, "Hap," is nowhere to be seen. Why has the technique, by judicious use of which Mr. Garrett has been excluded from the party, been called the "Tremont Avenue Toodle-oo"?

The shifty-looking man finally controls his quivering and weeping, and decides to destroy his raincoat, disturbing as this may be to the unwritten code which binds the large, and for the most part, nameless as well as tortured band of American perverts together in a rigorous camaraderie of need. Need and desire. And hope. Need, desire, and paralyzing fear. Fear of discovery and the wish to be helped. The fear of being helped. The wish to be paralyzed. The paralyzing desire to—

What code is that? Hello? Hello?

Now the raincoat is finally blazing, and two charming Consciousness Scouts from the Tribade Conspiracie converge on the subject on the roof, the scene of painfully joyous confession, and the need to be discovered. Trixie, one of the Scouts, is speaking. Hard to keep one's eyes off Trixie! The other Scout simpers a little.

"The subject is filled with remorse for his debauched deeds, and here, on this rough-hewn, semidesolate roof, a roof as anonymous as a Trojan condom, or, to those of you who have more than a few grey hairs, a Trommer's beer, we are privileged to witness what attractive, body-conscious, slender, college-educated couples who feel that keeping up with current fiction is essential, call an 'extravaganza of wholesome despair.' But here's State Trooper Kimberley Butz to share some of her thoughts with us, despite all. Trooper Butz?"

"Thank you," Trooper Butz asserts, a mysterious smile playing lethargically about the full pout of the lips which have, in the past, been known to cause the toughest male troopers to spill their large glasses of

Three Feathers whiskey—a *man's* drink if ever there *was* a man's drink, and there was! "Thank you again," Trooper Butz smiles again. "I've been involved in pervert arrests before. Not pretty, I can vouch for that. When they begin to tear up their decks of obscene playing cards, well, it's not too much to say that there's a kind of rapier pertinence about it, and it almost attains the indefinable perfection which is at the heart of all great dining experiences, an unexpected analogy, I agree. My sister, Karen, however, insists on staying in the back room, mostly, of the Tropical Bible Aids Shoppe in North Miami. Touch of neurasthenia. She wanted, of course, *so* much to be a stewardess, serving mankind and all, then, one day, she had a vision which she now rather deftly describes as being like 'an editorial hand guiding clumsy prose to a lapidary finish.' Whew! Now there's a turn of phrase, and with women like that about, it makes one feel that the perverts *will not win!*"

"Hi! I'm Karen Butz! When I'm in the back room of the shoppe, I dream of terrible men burning their raincoats on rough-hewn wooden roofs, the rain pelting down on their pasty, look-at-me faces. It's then that I understand how articles like 'They Lived by the Bible—But Wallowed in Lust!' can actually appear in magazines of quality like *True Action.* Although little if any decency is shown, even if requested politely, I've come to realize that there really *are* people like Elmont Truro, who talked to his own sister's pantyhose, and 'Legs' Tubetti, who, when possessed by his depraved other self, 'Sucks' Tortoni, described morally offensive movies to helpless vagrants to whom he'd promise cigarettes and fortified wine for their attention. How many saintlike bums he enflamed and doomed to perdition I can't even begin to imagine! Here in North Miami we don't have anything *like* that, and some old-timers say it may be because of our rather famous skyline, which *is* a wonder. Of course, there's a man who lives nearby, by the name of Tucci, or Tuccio, or Tucco, an Italian film mogul, but he seems very nice, loves children, food, wine in moderation, games of chance, and noise. I don't think that *he* can be held responsible for those other dagos who sully the very name of strictly private individualistic interpersonal intimacy with real emotional attachment thrown in. Which is *our* middle name."

Thanks! Karen, is it? Thanks a lot, Karen!

"Just a minute! A good friend of mine, a lovely woman who has a really nice parking space, tells me that Tucson, in Arizona?, is just *filled* with dagos, but according to the hotline columns of *True Action, Actionworld,* and *Action Monthly,* there are very few incidents where, for instance, undies are stolen from clotheslines for Satanic rituals, or regular, manly guys go bowling in their wives' high heels, or porno kings laugh in the face of the law which is helpless before them and their sleazy, big-shot lawyers filled with talk about free speech and the rights of these inhuman flesh-beasts! who desire to make us want to jump all over each other and *do* things! It's one thing to talk about the power of the objective correlative and the current needs of the business world, and quite another, *I* think, for drooling perverts to be able to ogle gorgeous gams and shapely jugs wherever they turn, be it here or be it there! So you really can't blame the honest dagos, can you, whatever people say?"

Not at all! No indeed! And thanks! See you soon, Karen, is it?

"That's Karen for you," Trooper Butz laughs sincerely. "If you ask me, she's got a crush on Delilah Crosse, even though she's never met her. Has had for twenty years. Well, it's all in what the dissolute painter in *Hellions in Hosiery* calls the 'spirit of Arthur Rimbaud.' "

Rimbaud? *Hellions in Hosiery*? What?

Shh. It's not important. And it's getting late.

"My heart fell instantly into a fairly disturbing irregularity of rhythm," Buddy expostulated thoughtfully, "when I realized the misery and horror permeating that wretched cabin. Or perhaps bungalow. As far as I'm concerned, I'm only too dratted happy to put plenty of rough trail between it—and *us.* " And so saying, he began to take even longer strides into the hushed, dripping forest. Dick needed no inducement to keep up with his doughty chum, and, at times, even rudely elbowed Buddy out of the way in order to demonstrate his own virile disgust, coupled with wise compassion.

Soon, huddled together on a barren plat of fenestrated moraine, the lads watched the dawn rise, their arms linked, their differences, such as they were, settled for the moment. "I 'low that what burrowed deep into my quick," Dick said, the morning mists almost totally engulfing his awed face, "was when the terr'ble hag asked us what 'grub' was, and was it some type of 'flywheel tool.' My blood just about up and give a curdling yell then," the boy remarked.

"I agree, ingenuous pal," Buddy nodded, disturbingly squeezing one of Dick's tumid biceps. "But what, too, of the addiction the trio obviously shared—that to Tudor beer? There were moments when one could virtually see their chances for meaningful, productive lives frittering themselves away into some sort of bad Janus-like paste of shame!" With this odd remark, Buddy helped himself to one of the stale biscuits which Zenobia had finally been prevailed upon to relinquish for what Buddy would later call "a beautiful cent."

"Is this Tuesday, Buddy?" Dick nonchalantly asked with a sadly fleeting smile. But then, quickly recovering, he said, "Forget Tuesday! How is it that you've gone and locked up the food lard? A small biscuit and some sparkling stream water'd, I powerful 'low, go down pretty fine about now with *this* feller! How come only your mouth is stretched gluttonously out of kilter with victuals? Amn't I too made of red flesh, or blood?" At the conclusion of this uncharacteristic speech, Dick fell into a sullen dump, the sparkling moraine silt flying up about him in nervous clumps.

"Oho!" Buddy exclaimed, almost unpleasantly, his hands, filled with biscuit, held high above his head, out of his friend's reach. "First of all, and although I expect the question was only the badinage of smoke-screen on your part, as you rather lamely admitted yourself, this is not Tuesday, according to my pocket astrolabe, an ingenious navigational surd made in the manner of the common tachometer. Are you listening? *This is not Tuesday."* But Dick was rolling about on the ground in a semblance of Protestant anguish, his web belt and cordovan brogans creaking with their superbly wonted dash.

"Secondly," Buddy continued, as his eyes amusedly searched the skies, "I reject the term 'food lard,' even though certain linguistic trend-setters claim that since it once appeared in the *Tulane Drama Review* when drama was drama, it smacks heavily of the permissible." Buddy paused to sneer freely. "Perhaps such a barbarism is allowable in *Tunisia,* where the poppies encarnadine and the enervating heat prevent fellows from doing hardheaded and productive business. But it is not so *here,* I vow to you, where traffic hums far below busy hotel windows and communication is the life's blood of important executive messages! Where, by gosh, nylon was invented, as I've related!" His eyes were moist with excitement, and his back twitched against a spiny bung, whose half-eaten crown seemed almost labile in the matutinal haze.

"Buddy, dear comrade!" Dick blurted wetly. "Forgive me, please, if'n I got you on a worry, for, darn it to tarnation, I sure as thunder warn't a-fixing to. It was just a hunger pang what fixed to make me want to feel like fixing to rile you. Are we all square now?" With this, he and Buddy shook hands like two half-frozen Mounties meeting unexpectedly while strolling in the Yukon tundra wastes.

"Great Scott!" Buddy presently screamed, "what can I have been thinking of, heartlessly to deny you food, you, my hiking buddy, my assistant in arcane yet practical chemistry experiments, my farm companion when adventure takes us to the lands of wheat, corn, puling hogs, and scattered outbuildings?" The lad, with a muted cry of youthful exuberance, opened the padlock on the bulging food bag, and handed Dick a small biscuit. The latter's hand closed on the homely morsel, so redolent of grease spots and linoleum, and suddenly the sun burst through the haze to reveal what seemed like Roman candles joyfully streaming in the sky!

When the youths awoke, the sun was high in that same sky, and the chichi beetles were drumming madly in the hollow logs which seemed to yearn almost hospitably. How absurd! And yet, it *was* time to leave, and suiting action to a few obligatory words, late morning found the boys crashing, as always, through silent acres of bitter vetch.

"Oddly," Buddy panted loquaciously, "I dreamed just now of Joe Billy Tupelo, a young file clerk I was acquainted with some years since. He wore wonderfully knotted bow ties in crackerjack patterns and muted colors, but was, I fear, fated to a brutally demeaning career in lower management because of his ruffian nickname, which was 'Texie' or 'Taxi,' I can't quite remember. That, and, of course, the fact that he recklessly, and in despite of his starched white shirt, exposed himself one afternoon, and during *inventory!,* to Elisa Hess, the department-supervisor's wife. It was a full-blown scandal, and mortifying to all parties concerned," Buddy concluded, veering slightly to his left so as to trample a nest of tarantula eggs cunningly attached to a discarded fender. "Nature's camouflage," he marveled, as he did a practiced "jig of decimation."

"What does 'expose himself' mean, Buddy?" Dick queried, joining in the spirited assault on the potential monsters. "Is it kin to, say, a gal showing off her attractive legs in creamcake poses, kind of like Lana Turner? Or the current Miss Tutti-Frutti?"

"Ha! Ha!" Buddy roared wordlessly. "How wondrously amusing a companion you truly are, Dick, dear, clumsy dope! Showing off one's attractive legs and exposing oneself are not precisely alike, even," and Buddy began quivering beneath a new wave of barely repressed mirth, "when taking *creamcake* poses into account! Creamcake!" And with this, the husky youth fell to his knees, his body helplessly twisted in abandoned hilarity, his eyes dropping tears as rapidly as if he had just consumed a handful of mastiachi peppers.

"I'm obliged to you, Buddy," Dick grumbled quietly, racking his brains to remember the correct word for partially clad, leggy women in indecent poses. Goldurned if he hadn't *seen* enough of 'em! The problem, as the churl well knew, lay in his avoidance of reading those items useful to a young man intent on wearing a crisp white shirt and quiet tie each day, a young man entrusted with bills of lading, rubber stamps, a desk calendar, and various pens and pencils. What *had* he read, really *read,* recently? He twitched in shame! *Twilights,* a best-seller, which, while being a staggering wallop of a riveting read, was light and frothy and, well, *cheap* in its libidinously candid descriptions of the degradation of more than one female body. He buried a violent fist in his open palm so loudly that he startled the surrounding chirps. That, yes, and "Two Guys from Hackensack," which—but at the memory of this story, the boy blushed and fought free of the wild, dark temptations which often seemed to come along lately, usually *without warning.*

"By Cecil Tyrell, am I correct?" It was Buddy's voice, calm and quiet as a batwinged cat's paw among the legendary magnolia and honeysuckle of the South, O lost! Lost amid the red clay roads, O forever lost! lost!

"Wh-wh-what in tarnation, B-Buddy?" Dick said, taking a step backward into a small churn of viscid bonito. "Y-y-y-you. . . ?"

"Yes, I've read your mind," Buddy mouthed demurely. "I've been waiting for the right moment to try out this newfound wrinkle of mine. I hope I didn't give you too much of a turn, sock of a chum," the large-boned lad glowed fervently. "I feel that it's on the same intellectual level as sight-reading difficult piano music." He colored fetchingly.

"Tarnation take all! Lord a-mighty Goshen's sake!" Dick rejoined hysterically. "It's a blasted wonderment! To think that you're sort of two different classes of friend—a regular American fellow and a mysterious mind reader, sort of foreign and pizenlike. Pshoo!"

"Whooff!" Buddy tittered into a quickly waiting handkerchief. "I've never thought of it that way, possibly because I've never read anybody's mind before. Hmm. *Two* Buddies, you say? Or at least, imply? Rather like, if I may rapidly construct the classic analogy, two totally unlike and sternly opposed Janus faces on two otherwise identical coins!" He reddened uncomfortably, and fidgeted. "Ha! Ha! I should say, of course, rather like one Janus face, bisected on the lateral plane, on two coins of different size and value." Blushing ferociously now, the durable fellow fell to his hands and knees once again, and pressed his face to the dewy mallow, limp in the insipid sunlight. "Drat," he whispered to a leaf bud, "it is exactly, again, as if I've been listening to, as Dick has said, Nick Maggie, or is it Magger? When I entertain the difficult concept of the Janus face, I become a nattering fool, much like the effete Prince Poniatowski, his breeches tight as a bongo skin, in Chicharrón's *La Última despedida.* Dick *must* not cotton to this bookish likeness." With that, he scrambled massively to his feet.

Dick, a true-blue friend, ignored Buddy's outburst of gibbering idiocy, as always, and soon an efficient and seductive campfire had chased the grey chill which always descended from Misty Crag at this hour, and the delicious aroma of the biscuit stew which bubbled cheerily in the old rude blackened pot of seasoned oak filled the boys with renewed hope. The trees soughed implacably, the clouds heaved themselves into semi-recognizable shapes at times, the plashing waters made the comrades consider their departed friends, even now, perhaps, part of the great food chain. Time seemed to pass as slowly as if it were a thick, viscous liquid, like syrup or honey, or, perhaps, like molasses, yes, *molasses.* Time passes slow as molasses, they thought.

Sighing, some time later, in slothlike contentment, the boys fell into a discussion about the wisdom, or at least, the *conventional* wisdom, of leaving Mystery Mountain in order to return to the variegated panoply of urban life and the modernistic responsibilities which awaited them, the "humming electricity of the clerical," as someone had so neatly put it. Perhaps Abbagnano. At this point, Buddy softly said, his eyes darting toward the verdant screen surrounding, "I've been thinking, Dick, of your old Uncle Johnny, 'Mr. Tuxedo,' and what advice he might now have for us in our dilemma, outside, that is, the connubial," he gaily blushed.

"Uncle Johnny?" Dick almost perspired, yet gulped. "I reckon that I haven't thought on him for a month of Sundays' blue moons. Uncle Johnny," he uttered pensively. "You know, dear pal, that he passed away some five years ago?"

"Yes!" Buddy snapped genially. "You *told* me! Somehow, he was tragically struck in the temple at a wedding reception, as I recall. He was always the life of the party, the swell old chump!"

"He held a patent, you know, on the recipe for the Warm Manhattan," Dick weakly enthused, "and, even at his powerf'ly advanced age, keeping up his book of wedding-and-honeymoon jokes, stories, observations, and tips was a reg'lar daily task of his." He looked toward the verdant screen, heaving in the wind as slow as molasses. "There's a story, uh, banded about, you know," he muttered ruefully, his fingers nervously filling his mouth, "that his passing on warn't exactly an accident. That the bride was sort of, well, that the girl, that she was fighting the old feller off, and. . . ." The boy reddened profusely and hid his steaming face in his "java."

"Fighting him *off?*" Buddy queried relentlessly, his eyes, despite themselves, popping like a demented lighthouse keeper's clogged ears. "Then you mean that the dirty little rumor. . . ?"

"Correct in all partic'lars, I'm afraid," Dick confessed. "The *coupé da grace* blow to his wrinkled temple came from a violently snapped garter which he'd, in some kind of mad fashion, got his old face tangled up in."

"Lord!" Buddy breathed in horror. "And here, I've been sitting and thinking of the old fellow with mingled feelings of warmth and patronization. Yet, he died a common pervert, exactly like the fellows in the raincoats."

"I reckon so," Dick said in a whisper. "His funeral," he shuddered, "was picketed by the Porno-Death Kommando of the Daughters of Durga International." He paused, then passed a sweaty hand over his wiry stubble. "So, as far as *advice* goes, why, pshaw!, I 'low that any request, even if the duffer was still with us, why it'd be replied to with a risky story, that's what I 'low!"

"Live and learn," Buddy had a chance to say before a stranger burst quietly through the verdant screen. "How fine to see you young fellows," he said with robust simplicity. "My name is de Kock, novelist and correspondent. I trust that you lads are not unfamiliar with good letters?" And with this provocative remark, the gentleman made himself at "home."

"Hello! I'm Miss Tutti-Frutti of 1982. I just have a minute to say that this idea that Dick Witherspoon has that my creamcake poses are somehow who *I* am is just all wrong! As Miss Tutti-Frutti, I visit military bases, hospitals, battleships, wonderful and caring homeless kitchens, county fairs, amusement parks, mortuaries, and car dealerships. All right, so I show some attractive leg now and then, but it's for a good cause. In real life, my name is, for the record, Karen, and I'm interested in a career in theatre, movies, cinema, or television, in stagecraft, you know? And, of course, being a responsible anchorperson. Because the news is important to everybody, not just to people who never ever look at creamcake glossies. I've never actually heard that expression, 'creamcake,' by the way. Is that a business word?"

"Hello! I'm Miss Understand. Karen, if you like. My current enthusiasms, even though I'm what many call middle-aged but I like to think of as 'older but wiser,' as in 'if you don't want my peaches climb my tree anyway,' include unashamedly revealing my attractive, hard-won body to the *right* man, and he doesn't have to be handsome, just caring and sensitive and with a sense of humor and a few bucks. I also right now just love the marvelous sequel, finally!, to *Unicorn Crimson, Unicorn Grey—The Duke of the Golden Prong*—and, let's see, Civil War Songs of the Union Army, and the poems of Rupert Brooks, especially the one beginning 'O little friend, your nose is ready.' The oddest thing about poetry, Rupert Brooks's or anybody's, is that I first got interested in the stuff after reading an article on it, in, of all places, my ex-fiancé's favorite magazine, *Universe of Action.* Really! I remember being so surprised that I called Fred's, that was his name, Fred's attention to it.

Fred, as usual, just grunted and went on doing some of that darn research of his on some movie something or other. Thank God we never got married! You don't think this skirt is too short for me, do you?"

What's this note here? U.P. What's this mean?
  No idea. U.P.? Up?
  Well, yes. But.
  No idea then. Sounds familiar, though. U.P. Up.

April finishes another bottle of the elixir which, in its wonted role as a "changer of reality," is indeed changing the semi-comatose woman's liver into something very like pumice stone. She thinks to get up, but is peremptorily arrested by a vision, one so powerful as to seem, as she may later phrase it, "trust Mike Smit's fuzz-hair" ["just like it was there"]. April's vision is of herself twenty-five years earlier, her hair jet black, her eyes clear, her figure slender in a miniskirt, sleeveless crocheted sweater, and close-fitting suede boots, her lipstick a pale pink-white. She is on the landing just outside the emergency-exit door of the small company for which she works as a clerk-typist, engaged in certain sexual activities with a tall, mustachioed UPS driver. Perhaps Catullus may, once again, be called upon to describe the nature of April's current adventures, of which this present one is fairly representative:

> nunc in quadriviis et angiportis
> glubit magnanimos Remi nepotes.

As the grinning UPS man, resplendent in his crisp chocolate-brown uniform, reaches his climax, his eyes starting forth with surprise and delight, and wait till he gets back to tell the guys in the garage!, April, rigid in her sweated bed, a knuckle in her mouth, stares in terror at the tiny, motile penises wriggling blindly in their thousands on the walls, ceiling, floor, and bed. "Oh! oh!" she gasps, meaning "No! no!" Or is it that she gasps "No! no!" meaning "Oh! oh!"? Whatever, the miniature phalloi pay her no heed.

We are finally in possession of certain information which may serve to clarify the occasional difficulties, ambiguities, problems, contradictions, and paradoxes of the matters here under "review," as we prefer to say. There is, of course, given the shifting nature of information, the possibility that the aforementioned difficulties, ambiguities, problems, contradictions, and paradoxes may be compounded. With this caveat firmly in mind, the information follows.

Nota: Valefor, Mentor of Thieves, who appears to man as a thief, and who leads those with whom he is familiar into theft, is the fiend ultimately responsible for Norman's possession of Guy Lewis's painting *The Valley of the Shadow of Death,* sometimes called the "Moon River" of Abstract Expressionism. Valefor has told of the particulars of the theft—carried out, apparently, by Bart Kahane in return for a little black dress with matching shoes, hat, and bag—to Vassago, a mighty prince, "good" by nature. Vassago immediately visited Norman and told him the seamy story behind Bart's sudden offer of the painting. Norman was not especially pleased by the visit, since it was Vassago's fancy that evening to appear dressed in a suit of an eerie, shifting, shimmeringly iridescent blue of a shade "to look upon which," so declares Antoine de la Mothe Cadillac in his study of the *Grand Grimoire, Ventriloquists' Dummies,* "is to feel the wind of madness pass across one's face." Norman has since placed the painting in storage.

Nota: Vepar, Duke of Storms and Tempests, appeared quite recently to Mamie Morsett, the celebrated prizewinning poet of "meticulously exact traditional forms with a crisp modern punch!" as Michelle Caccatanto has, perhaps justifiably, often written. The demon, incarnate as a fetching mermaid, swam up to Ms. Morsett on her beloved wind-strewn, tempest-clogged beach ("the sea, the sun, and the quiet peace always seem to rejuvenate me," the poet has repeatedly claimed) to warn her to "lay off," as he carefully put it, his friends, the clams, and to find herself another subject, "like Vermont," the sprite reportedly said, "or potatoes," before heading back to sea. Ms. Morsett, in an admittedly stultifying telephone conversation, threatens that she'll be "in close touch" with prizewinner Peter Viereck concerning "new subject matter" and the ever-handy iambic pentameter, "the breath of heroes," sometime after Labor Day. Good news at last! In the meantime, she and her husband, a prizewinning instructor of Creative Writing and a fine poet in his own right, are having some repairs made on their little

gale-buffeted cottage, or "shack," built in 1682 by the Puritan eccle-
siastic and mystic Geoffroy Chandeler.

Nota: Vine, Monster of Witches, who is fond of making calm waters
stormy, is the diabolical force behind the producer Virginia Vivaldi's
suspiciously megalomaniacal plans to film, over the next ten years, a
series of "operals" based on old Tom Mix classics—*Rifles on the
Pecos, Rio Grande Leather Man, Guns of the Colorado, Claw Sky,
Dude Chump!,* and others not so well known. In a tumultuous press
conference marked by senseless violence and sexual innuendo, Ms.
Vivaldi, pressed on her decision to commit hundreds of millions of
dollars to an admittedly quixotic project fraught with risk, angrily
denounced the legacy of economic frugality passed on by the late
president of Jayvee Studios, Jerrold "Jambo" Vizard, calling him "a
man with a mind like a Volvo owner's." The conference broke up soon
after in a melee of angry shouts, threats, screams, wild punches, and
indecent gropings, when Ms. Vivaldi's husband and business manager,
Quirt Bimbeau, suggested that Mr. Vizard had been "a sexual slave and
dupe of Minna von Hattiesburg," characterized by Mr. Bimbeau as
"a big whore, like."

Nota: A long-awaited letter from an actual professor whom we occasionally employ to do scutwork informs us that *The Voyage Out,*
attributed by some scholars to Jack London, was "probably" written
by Guillaume Apollinaire under the pseudonym "Virginia Stephen."
The professor also takes the opportunity to give us some excruciatingly
complete details and academic anecdotes concerning his latest TRIP
TO EUROPE, which, as far as we can discover, was "wonderful" and
"exciting." He notes that he "hated to come back" and that there is
"nothing like Europe." He is a heck of a guy, and let's indeed hope that
he "got *some* work done."

Nota: Vual, the Camel, he who speaks Egyptian, he who excites
friendship even between enemies, he who arouses the love of women for
each other, was, in the early '40s, the original choice for the Women's
Army Corps' (WAC) tutelary patron and guiding spirit. After revelations
concerning the deity's true nature had rocked the youthful WAC to its
very foundations, most of which were, in accordance with government
specifications, lightly boned, a new spiritual leader, Lord Ridingcrop,
the twelfth Earl of Terraplane, was named. Soon after the feisty

nobleman's extraordinary recreational tastes became known to the Army, he was supplanted by the city of Waco, "Wedge of Paradise," for what the Joint Chiefs of Staff termed "obvious reasons."

"You could get a nice tattoo in Waco years ago," Walt says, strolling into the A & P. He's wearing plaid trousers, which, in a civilized society, would lead to his arrest and imprisonment. "A very nice tattoo, nothing gauche or fey, but redolent of the values of the Southwest. Fairly *smacking* of them. A lone star, a rattler, a scorpion rampant. . . ."

Walt? Who is Walt? What *is* this?

"Instead of being rude and making a fool of yourself into the bargain," Walt says, "you might tell me if the A & P has any copies of *Absalom! Absalom!* left amid the crisp, tangy apples."

Look for yourself. Whoever you are.

"And these trousers are not, believe you me, *my* idea," Walt grumbles.

Myrtle Wandajajiecowicz has not yet been *officially* informed that had *The Orange Dress* been published under her name, it would have been reviewed in the *Sheetmetal Patio Gazette,* the *Polish-American Accordion Intelligencer,* and the *Platform Workers' Crafts Weekly,* and nowhere else.

Item: War Action, the original and still *top* magazine for *nonstop combat thrills,* announces its intention to expand its coverage. Beginning with the BIG October issue, *War Action* will include stories of the WAR on CRIME, featuring a regular monthly "Crime Tips" column by State Trooper Kimberley Butz, author of *I Maimed a Rapist—And Learned to Laugh Again!,* and some hunk of woman!

But the strange foreign woman seems to have returned, and is standing again in front of the house, while Bunny peers at her from behind a yellowed lace curtain. She is at her wit's end, because as far as she can tell, her father has decided to stop trembling, quivering, shaking, gasping, and, for that matter, breathing. There is an excellent chance that he is dead. And now this stupid, ugly woman is back, she is not in Israel or Brooklyn, but here! And, oh God! What's happened to the chicken coop? It's smoldering, yes, but there are no flames! "Oh Jesus!

Oh Jesus!" Bunny says, "what good is *smoldering?*" She runs to the door, sobbing, as they occasionally say, "uncontrollably." Frieda looks up and stops feeling the sweat-soaked areas of her shatteringly homely dress, smiles in her friendly American way, and raises her smutty hand in imbecile salute.

"Go away!" Bunny screams. "I'm *not* Bunny Lewis! I'm *not!* I never went to the Art Students' League! My name is Joanne Ward! My father is, of course, Mr. Ward, one of the neighborhood's great barbecuers and machine-shop teachers, currently retired and perhaps deceased. My mother, *Mrs.* Ward, died some years ago of a sudden unexpected outpouring of bile, hatred, and despair centered on the celebration of the holidays, especially those 'robust' holidays having to do with colorful dried leaves, objects of warm earth tones, wrapping paper, and bushels of savage food! Especially defunct birds! My ex-husband, Guy, will come and tell you *bar stories* if I just give him a call, that's all it takes. *One call,* and he'll tell you movingly funny anecdotes of gin-mill life for a solid week! Now, get out! Get out! Go away! I can't stand it anymore." Frieda looks at her and begins, once again, to walk away, while Joanne sinks to her knees at the door, directly under the place where Mrs. Ward was wont, each fall, to hang sprays of Indian corn, dried leaves, deformed gourds, and other impedimenta of the harvest. This scene may represent, if we are not careful, that which is meant by the hoary phrase, "there's no escaping the past." But suddenly, a noise is heard from within the house. It seems to be, it is! Mr. Ward calling hoarsely for his barbecue implements! Apparently he is alive, after all. Time will tell. There's no escaping the past. Let a smile be your umbrella.

Item: Despite his odd method of "reasoning," Blow is correct in his assumption that he was conceived behind the bandstand of the Bluebird Inn. His father, Dave Warren, one of New Jersey's legendary fox-trot instructors and egg-seekers, speaks on his deathbed in Netcong: "Hello there, nice of you to come and see an old man. I'm on my deathbed in beautiful Netcong, New Jersey, a place in which the late Alexander B. Davis was once served an absurd mixed drink which he dryly dubbed a 'Brooklyn.' It is also the birthplace of Andy Warhol, who got his start in the exciting art business right here, as well as the architectural paradigm for much that is good and real and spiritual in our nation's capital, Washington, D.C. I thought I'd come clean and confess that I'm Blow's dad all right, although I'm afraid that I don't know *who* his mom is. Sniff. (Indicates eyes brimming with tears.) I'd guess it's either Sailor Steve or Werner Smitts. Whew! What a load off my mind! It's also kind of nice to cash in my chips wearing these really cool and comfortable all-cotton pajamas. It's a real killer-diller, gate!" In the background can be heard the familiar strains of "String of Pearls." Or is it "Skylark" or "Deep Purple"?

Duke Washington sits in his furnished room in front of a fan, drinking beer and listening to old bebop records. He's snapping his fingers, oop! He's tapping his foot, bop! He's scatting along with the solos, sh-bam! After all these years, Duke is the same boring lout. Though bald and sadly gone to seed, yet hath he his hipness entire. He wants to go out and sit in an air-conditioned bar, but there's a chance, a very *slim* chance, that Henri Kink, that goddam square jive-ass Jew mother-fucking turkey faggot, the producer of, among other hit shows, the long-time ratings leader among daytime soaps, *A Waste of Shame,* might call with an offer of a small part in *Mickey's Bologna,* the new comedy smash series. Duke hates Henri as he hates almost everything, for he is much too perfect, too hip, too smooth, too knowing, too well-dressed, too *streetwise* for all this poke-lip ugliness, too canny, collected, wary. He opens another can of beer. Smooth, wary, collected, canny. Oop-bop-sh-bam!

"What?" Fred says, struggling against his restraints. "There's no *real* Duke Washington! Duke Washington's a role once played by none other than the shadowy Baylor Freeq, one of my many interests, as you know. Remember, girls? Remember I told you in the restaurant of my research?"

"You are a funny cute geezer and a big old baby," one of the girls says, watching her sister begin the notorious *cannoli tremolo* on Fred's painfully alert body.

"Oh sweet Jesus," Fred gasps. Or utters hoarsely. "What in the heck is *that?*"

"You are just as *darling* as a ten-cent button!" his ministering angel laughs.

We were asked last month by an editor of our acquaintance if we'd be good enough to help in the "difficult yet rewarding" task of bringing a first book by "an unknown author" to the attention of the "reading public," *those* feckless sons of bitches! Well. We have tried to, how shall we say?, "put it off" in the hope that the unknown author might die, or that the editor might forget the essentially innocent ski weekend he delights in perversely recalling our reluctant participation in. (Indicates pile of incriminating photographs.) We insist now as we insisted then that *no one* was drugged or hypnotized or blackmailed (indicates pile of screenplays in which the line "blackmail is an ugly word" is underlined in each) into "doing" anything! Not the blind Scoutmaster, the Rosicrucian dental technician, the truss model, the thrill-hungry housewife whose lips were starved for soul-searing kisses of abandon, and certainly not the hook-and-ladder company captain with the big family and happy dogs! However, friendship worth keeping is friendship worth working for, or at. So, the following contribution to the life of modern letters. (Indicates wave of nausea.)

FOR IMMEDIATE RELEASE

Esther Waters, the dynamic author of *Odd Ends,* who humorously describes herself as being no more than a "fed-up housewife" just five years ago, tells, in her compelling book of personal and personalized essays, of her abandonment of her boring husband and restrictive family in order to "feel things I'd always wanted to feel right down to my shoes." Feel she did, as *Odd Ends* testifies. More than merely one sprightly, cool, intelligent, amused, and spirited woman's look at the strange, surprising, fascinating backwaters of American life, *Odd Ends* presents us with wholly possible and viable alternatives to what Ms. Waters calls "the rat race" of modern life, the "wasting of our natural powers through getting and spending." As she so eloquently puts it in her Introduction, "I wanted to be free, to fly again, to know what it was to make great discoveries in the laboratory and studio, as well as to star in the boardroom and the bedroom!" In this compelling and often shocking book, you will discover:

THE LITTLE TOWN of Webster Groves, Missouri, whose *entire population* learned conversational Greek in three days, and was soon chatting of *delissos, massgrevvi, soss, aybol,* and *spigtami* like the sons and daughters of Ulysses.

BILL WEEPERS, a highly respected tennis spectator, who unabashedly tells of his love for Adolf Hitler—the Man, the Moustache, the Myth behind the Meerschaum pipe.

THE DOOMED PATIENT who feels that the courteous yet hollow slogan "Welcome to Kansas City" is no substitute for the daily Popsicle now denied him.

THE SUBWAY MOTORMAN, Benjamin Welles, who disappeared in the Amazon Basin during a vacation jaunt and was rescued by a tribe of gentle ostriches.

EDGAR GRAHAM WEN, who speaks with startling candor of his horror of culottes.

RESPECTED APPELLATE JUSTICE Harold Wenj, who reveals the shocking practice of sexual self-abuse throughout the judiciary; "It's the robes," he says sadly.

THE WEST VILLAGE "character," J. Bartholomew Whammo, who has lived for three years in a tent set up in the kitchen of New York's finest *cabochon* restaurant.

AND MUCH MORE * Including * the sickening truth behind the steamy luncheon scene in the box-office gold mine *What a Girl!* * the hilarious story of how "Vomit and Die!" became the award-winning docudrama *What's for Supper?* * the "rodeo marriage" of "Giggles" Whinge and "Gallie" Bilge, judged by *Today's Genetics* to be the stupidest women in the world * the inspirational and touching story of E.B. White's invention of English grammar *

Odd Ends by Esther Waters. Available soon at your bookstore.

"As if Pascal's *Pensées* were written by St. Augustine and Sheila Graham."

—*Tamara Shicksa-Rabinowitzowicjiez*

His unseasonably heavy tweed jacket reeking of dried sweat, a despairingly seedy Vance Whitestone hesitates before entering his shop, The Good Company. The place depresses him, the costumes and uniforms depress him. His *bored salesclerks* depress him. The Florence Nightingale Camisole. Oh God. The Stern Stepmother Bathrobe. Oh God. The Ilse Koch Whip-and-Garter Combo. Oh God. He stands, smelling himself, fresh sweat soaking the rank, threadbare fabric. "Is it possible that I once wrote interoffice memos?" he says to his tie. (Indicates proverbially grease-stained tie.) "Is it really true that I once gave orders to Lee Jefferson, undressed Karen Ostrom, even unto her silken flesh, was a business partner of Lincoln Gom's?" He steps back from the shop and stands in an adjoining doorway. "Lincstone Productions was once half mine?" Vance starts to cry, then begins a pained, maddened dance, bringing his knees, in exaggerated prancing, almost to his chin, hurling his hands into the air, fingers opening and closing spasmodically as if in an attempt to catch flies. "Weird Widow Corset-Mask Set," he sobs. "Oh God, oh God." He would, quite possibly, whistle in his dementia, except that, as we know, he is a stranger to the art of whistling.

White Sun Talent Associates is, for all practical purposes, run by the scheming and cold-hearted mogul Edward Beshary. Janos Kooba, one of Beshary's partners, has been for some years now engaged almost exclusively in his literary pursuits, and Albert Pearson, the third partner, has privately disclosed that he is not averse to selling his shares to Beshary. "Who needs the aggravation?" he often says, slapping his knee, or, when at home, ogling his still-attractive wife of thirty-eight years, Ruthie. Beshary has ruthlessly, cruelly, and coldly stepped up his efforts to absorb those companies "ripened up well for a simple plucking," as he puts it in his still-uncertain English. So, besides being a trifle, ah, *tapette,* he also scorns the language of the great nation that has made him rich! As we know. Among his recent acquisitions are Contemporary Ventures Inc., White Sun Village, White Sun Cabanaland, the Black Basement, Crescent and Chattaway, Marvelous Magazine Management Corporation, *Scranton Arts Times,* and Daughters of Durga International. Yet, for all his success, soon the dear, stubbly face of Berthe—as well as his hairy gams, calloused feet, bloodshot eyes— will be gone from his life forever. Of course, if Durga, the Serene, the Relentless, the Unknowable, has her way, *everything* will be gone from his life forever. *Telex bunt impetigo, trio gator.*

At precisely 4:00 P.M., Whitey enters Village Victuals to spell Bud. It is not too much to say that this hapless young man despises his emotional problems and is also getting sick and tired of the severe beatings administered to him by enraged and insulted women shoppers. "I can't help it," he says at times to a pal with whom he likes to share an orange-colored "drink" and a bag of crunchy things. "I'm not like, you know, a *sex* fiend. I don't even have a big one like Bud! I *really* hate it when the ladies laugh and call me 'Teeny Peeny' before they beat the shit out of me. What a life being a despised pervert!"

"Hello! I'm Miss Whole-Grains, although I don't feel too darn healthy standing in this dirty, drafty hallway listening to Sylvie howl in what the English language, rising to the occasion, calls 'exquisite pleasure.' Well, I don't know about exquisite, but more power to her! And let's hope the poor horny creep with the raincoat looking in the window is having a little fun too. I'm *actually* Karen Ostrom, *really,* and it wasn't *my* body they found twenty years ago at The Red Swan. My God, was that twenty years ago? Anyway, I heard it was Sheila Henry they found there, but Sheila just died *today.* At the beach, I hear, that's what I'm here to tell Sylvie. Oh hell, who cares about us anyway? Incidentally, I've been looking for Vance to see if I might borrow some money from him, but people—well, *people*—say that he's just disappeared. I could use a decent winter coat, I mean that's why. God, I don't know why I'm sniffling. Something's wrong with me."

Then too: *Whores in Heels* Picketed by American Fellatio League as "Demeaning to Working Women"; Rupert "Roger" Whytte-Blorenge to Open First Shoefreex Store in Wichita Falls; Mme Marguerite Wig Denies Ties to Wilkes-Barre Banana Orgies; Scholar Suggests "Sheldon Feinstein" William the Conqueror's True Name; Freddie Willingmouth to Direct "Win a Bundle" Great-Fiction Promo Drive; Latest Research Shows Windsor Knot Cause of Unwanted Body Hair; Newly Discovered Papers Reveal Yvor Winters May Have Thought Wittgenstein Author of *Tender Buttons;* Marie Louise "Chinks" Wong to Star in *A Different Slant to Love;* Emma Woodhouse, 58, "Beach Babe" of '60s, Dies of Lust; Furor in GOP as Senator Katie Woodward Claims Husband "Wears the Skirts"; Leonard Woolf Invented "for Lark" by Virginia Woolf, Experts Argue.

"You'll excuse our startled appearance and unfriendly demonstrations of a perhaps boorish nature, I trust," Buddy said, flushing hotly with the memory of the crude language and shocking bodily contortions with which he and Dick somewhat unfairly greeted the distinguished author Paul de Kock. "We've had a number of right unpleasant surprises these past few days, or weeks, or so, here in the merciless brush, eh Dick?" the sincere lad softly queried of his friend.

"Tarnation o' sakes!" Dick shouted in an excess of nervous

prostration. "You say 'a number'? Pshaw! Seems like onto more'n a zillion on 'em, tol'able more and then some, or so, to me!"

"Pay my staunch companion Witherspoon's somewhat disabled language skills little or no heed, Mr. de Kock," Buddy inveigled desperately, the firelight leaping still toward the soft black sky studded with numberless, shivering astro-quarks. How far away they seemed!

"I understand completely," de Kock pensively grimaced, "being an author with profound insights into human nature and all. I half suspect," he laughed richly, suddenly helping himself to some more biscuit stew and "jamoke," "that you fellows may be feeling the effects of *mountain fever,* caused by rarefied, ozonified air, half-raw chuck, voracious hicks, the frustration of one's dearest plans, and the absence of the gentling abilities of female companionship. Sound familiar?" the scribe added, uncannily.

"I *say,* old man!" Buddy spat in surprise. "That's extraordinary! It's almost as if you've been dogging our steps, listening to our chats, fair undermining, I might say, our varietal impetuosity, at least performatively, for days on end!"

"Tut-tut," the wise author imperiously choughed. "It's simply that I've seen many cases of the ailment. One of my dearest friends, Lord Woppie of Azania, almost lost his *gules sinister* because of the devilish malady. Incidentally, old Woppie served as the model for Hubert, eleventh Earl of Worcestershire, in my *Gus Takes on the Mauve Sachet*—perhaps the most popular of the 'Gus de Toite' series. You've read it, of course? Or perhaps you've read *Georgette,* which, I dare say, would be more to *your* liking," de Kock smirked.

"I'm afraid not, old man," Buddy remarked, his eyes apologetically agog. "I find modern literature much too *drastic.*"

"We kind of cotton onto classical authors with uplift messages of the caliber of your Jean Ingelow, whose clean, muscle-toned verses helped us considerable just a day or two yonder back to search out a powerful cool and laughing freshet rill!" Dick proudly breathed.

"Jean Ingelow?" de Kock blustered, inadvertently kicking a glowing ember into a nearby primitive potting shed hulking darkly in sad disrepair. "You're better served reading Wordsworth and his leech-besotted doggerel of nostalgic blubbering! Better served with *World of Signs* by Derek Tights, 'the housewife's tamale.' Why, boys, *nobody* has read Jean Ingelow since before World War I. She's thought of as a large cardboard object, no more!" The embittered author heatedly spat into the blazing shed, meanwhile flinging his arms about in an excess of literary ambition gone to seed, and envy unfettered. Unpleasantness was manifestly palpable!

"So," Buddy lightly declared some time later, "you're on your way to the village of Misty Crag for some seafood, eh? Isn't it odd, Dick, that *we* thought Misty Crag but the *nom de forêt* of a beetling scarp, as shown on reputable, up-to-date maps?"

" 'Odd' is the gimcrack, gewgaw, tin-plate word for it, Buddy," Dick concurred in a subtly moronic voice, baring his teeth at their arrogant guest. Although the boy could not countenance the notion, the truth of the matter is that he had been sorely smitten by Miss Ingelow's poems, and, through them, by the poet herself. Goodness only knows what the lad would have done had Buddy shown him the frontispiece engraving of the poet in a lace snood! But the future tormentor of a number of resentful clerks took care not to let the well-fingered tome out of his sight or his hands!

"This stupid, wayward conversation follows closely on the feet of the dialogue between Mary Siffay and Thoresen Gossard in my *Lamond and the Loony.* You've surely read it!" de Kock hissed malevolently, his eyes gleaming in the firelight that danced as lightly as do slightly demented lighthouse beams. But Buddy and Dick pretended to whisper to each other, tittering vapidly, a surefire tactic, which, most often, drove craven adversaries into the blind bewilderment of the beaver trapped in the rude basement of his woodland home by a sudden watery onslaught of spring bilboes. Finally, after what seemed an eternity of fake confidences, Buddy remarked, "No, my literary friend, we haven't read *Lamondada Loony. Write and Be Happy,* the premier handbook for the budding author who longs to tap into the vibrant electrodynamics which inform the sizzling world of the pulsing media business, places your book in the DONT'S section, I'm happily forced to admit. Your *My Voice in Raymond* also languishes there," he boyishly whooped in triumph.

" 'Pears a feller might be 'lowed as how a certain *other* feller maybe won his own self the booby prize in the world of big-money *power* literature," Dick snapped, flinging a rock at a group of curious ferrets that just then shambled swiftly by.

"Why, you impudent, nondescript rubes!" de Kock exploded shame-lessly, his avid muscles straining toward a nameless lost—O lost!—perfection of once-glowing youth, now gone, gone! Gone forever! "What can you two petty clerks, shambling about like those ferrets who just passed by, know about this pathetic mountain, owned, yes, *owned,* I say, in proud manumission by the University of Chicago, huddled there below? What, I say, also, can you know of the agony of creative-prose composition, its blank pages, its typos, its faithful clichés?" Suddenly, the excited author was on his feet, and in his gnarled right hand, his typing hand, a hand as powerful as the arm from which it naturally protruded, Buddy and Dick glimpsed, with some alarm, the flash of a clasplock-switch lamprey!

As the boys prepared to flee in terror into the saturnine, fog-choked bosk, an attractive young woman, in some sort of figure-flattering uniform, strode proudly into the clearing on lustrous pumps. The boys paused in their potential career, and de Kock, thoroughly chastened, smashed his weapon with a slab of calcimine. As all three goggled, the woman spoke.

"Hi! I'm Karen Wyoming! I'm *really* sorry to impinge so unex-pectedly on your rugged, manly interlude, but this secluded site happens, like, to be on the path to Chinatown, whither I'm headed, to convince our Oriental compadres that the delirious skies would be, like, *moreso* if they'd just sort of *fly* more! They seem to prefer to poke around with their mu-shus and gai-goos and noodle things. Anyway, I want to get down there *sometime* before the Year of the Snail, for gosh sakes! I know that you fellas suspect that I'm all business because of the really intense sales-persuasion mode I'm in, but believe me, when I'm closeted with my guy, a frozen-dessert engineer, we really *work* at having an imaginative, fulfilling, pleasantly kinky, and guilt-free sex life, despite the odd chancre now and again. We also love good histor-ical novels like *The Dame from Troy's Corsets.* Hi!"

Then she was gone, and with her intelligent and winsome "Hi!" echoing in the miasmic mists, the lash and sting of the trio's late dis-agreement seemed to dissipate like a lightning bolt. The three embraced fondly, and the boys loudly proclaimed that rarely had such a fine fellow as the noted author stumbled upon their camp. Or even camps! For his part, de Kock, in an explosion of stunning humility, passed up the golden opportunity to call attention to the obvious fact that *he* had authored the novel spoken of with undimmed praise by the comely airline employee. He was proud, and rightly so, of his virile modesty, as were the boys. They were, in a manner of speaking, *all* proud.

"We're deuced proud of your enchanting modesty, de Kock, old cruller," Buddy confessed sheepishly, as the three set out in a cold drizzle. "Such silence, as my dad, Old Buddy, once put it, is 'golden chaff that gilds the chinks of paupers' cells.' " The lad wept bitterly into his faded tallboy for a moment, then recovered his storied aplomb.

"Thank you, dear boy," the portly author blushed innocuously, draping his neckerchief over his abashed face. Some time briskly passed, and then came the inevitable moment for the boys and de Kock to part company. A rustic signpost at a gale-whipped crossroads proclaimed that MISTY CRAG lay some few miles to the north. With a furtive display of snots and half-hidden tears, there were embraces, embraces and kisses, yes!, rough, manly, stubbly, crude, brutal, painful, and effluvious embraces, and wet, hairy kisses all 'round! Then, almost oneirically, Buddy and Dick watched de Kock plunge, at first lurchingly, then "ass" over teakettle, down the steep, mud-clogged road which led to the secluded town's legendary clam house, hidden, as devotees discover, to their peril, amid mounds of aromatic furze. The boys, crying openly now, blindly adjusted their moocher-pack websling straps and walked on in silence, their garments merrily steaming in what was surely the blazing sun!

"I reckon how that de Kock feller is at bottom *all right,* Buddy," Dick carefully enthused, "though for a spell I plumb thought on right walloping his head something fierce to learn him to get on with plain folks."

"Hm," Buddy noted with thoughtful alacrity, "I agree, Dick. A capital fellow, yet I too had a bad moment or two during which I rather basely thought of assault and battery and imagined his crushed body at the bottom of a yawning gravel pit, many of which, as you can quite easily see, hereabouts hazardously abound." Buddy paused, his eyes fixed on his steadily tramping feet. "I'm half-persuaded that much of his choler and imbroglionic actions are directly related to his unfortunately suggestive surname. A fellow comes in for a deuced hazing when he has to bear the burden of a depressing monicker like that, don't you agree, Dick?"

"I . . . I guess . . . so," Dick said uncertainly. "Sure. I . . . reckon so."

Buddy stared at his companion in amazement, and was impatiently about to recall to him, as an analogy and reminder, the tragic, depraved fate of their schoolmate, Herbert Shitface, when Dick spoke again.

"Say, Buddy," he blushingly droned, apparently dismissing de Kock's appellative problems summarily, "is there a picture of some sort or type of, uh, Miss Ingelow, uh, somewhere in her poem book of verses? It seems I reckon I thought once to have got a flitting glance at summat like," he shrieked at last, in barely controllable passion.

"Ha! Ha!" Buddy cackled nervously. "I fear not, Dick." The last thing he wished, now that they were well-nigh home, saving, of course, a brief detour at the great university, beetling quietly in the shale bluffs and devastating sunlight at the foot of the precipitous yaw of scuppered hills, was a lovesick gangle of a chum, panting and sighing and grappling with unbecoming and repeated tumescences, instead of keeping a sharp eye out for flash stook-blazes and psychotic carnivores. "No indeed, Dick," he lied expertly, his handsome face taking on the unforgettable qualities of a mass of dampened, unresponsive cheesecloth. "That's a steel engraving of Yasmine Danscul, Miss Ingelow's constant, ah, her constant, ah, let me not say companion, rather, as the French so suavely put it, her *femme entretenue,* or 'entertaining lady friend.' "

"Oh," Dick pouted sullenly, and in a flagrant excess of venereal pique he threw away his lightweight aluminum mess kit. Clang! it went. At that moment, they topped a crude rise, and before them, dazzling white in the sun, hulked Ye Olde Red Swanne Inne, empty now save for the bygone glories of half-stifled memories, still barely flickering in the hearts of older folks, the vast majority of whom were probably dead.

"What's thet?" Dick said ungraciously, lapsing clumsily into the rube-like twang which Buddy well knew would doubtless preclude a chief clerkship for his stubborn friend.

"*That,* old man," Buddy trilled fruitily, "*that* means that we've somehow come down on the other, some might say the 'wrong' side of the mountain, and now stand at the border of Yonkers!"

"Do you mean to tell a feller that, that, that. . . ?" Dick burbled stupidly, lowering his suddenly heavy torso to the cracked concrete, or asphalt, of the attractive city's outermost street. Perhaps he remembered that in Yonkers, "jewel beyond the Bronx," all streets lead implacably to what the townspeople dub "urban life."

"Yes!" Buddy said, joining his comrade on the ground. "The great university has apparently been, in some remarkable manner, moved to Yonkers! This is indeed Yonkers, for that ancient pile is the world-famed Red Swanne! This is the sort of capital suspension of the laws of nature which gives pause even to hard-driving chief executive officers who brook no nonsense and work twice as hard as their underlings! Great Scott! On the other hand, now that I am somewhat calmer, I realize that neither the university *or* Chinatown, its exotic neighbor, is visible. Hm, perhaps I err in my loose and easy, not to say glib talk of miracles," the boy concluded, thoughtfully placing his knuckles into his mouth, which seemed quietly to await them.

And so they wonderingly sat, drinking in the sight of the friendly town, birthplace of Andy Warhol; warmly dopey in the enervating sunshine, each knew, in his quietly pounding heart, the strong, somehow good feeling that would not leave, that would perhaps *never* leave; each knew the wonderful feeling of having confronted the strange secret of Mystery Mountain, and the even more wonderful feeling that the fog-enshrouded nights of the mountain no longer held their wonted fear, their wonted Janus-faced dichotomy of both fear and excitement at the same time, and in, of course, the same place, or two places at once! Soon, the boys would probably rise and attempt to find their way home, home, where a hot supper waited on the groaning table of a cozy kitchen. Home! they thought as one.

Yet somewhere, somewhere amid the clammy winds of the highest peaklike tors and crevasses, Ned Blutwurst, his altered features shockingly like those of the aging Elizabeth Barrett Browning *couchant,* was, even now, in the macabre process of destroying, without leaving a trace, Knute and the damaging knowledge he possessed of the Cambridge regatta scandal. *Whooshhh!* the mere shell of a car roared, as obliterating flames engulfed it.

We have been, in a word, *besieged* by informants complaining of and correcting certain errors in the foregoing episode—apparently the final one—of *Buddy and His Boys on Mystery Mountain.* Although we doubt the importance of such complaints and corrections, much as we doubt the importance of the narrative itself, let alone its necessity, several brutal threats persuade us to include the received data, without, we hasten to say, any commentary of our own to temper their inconsequentiality.

(a.) None of Paul de Kock's novels has ever been translated into English, although certain sections of *La Dame aux trois corsets* were included, in translation, in the anthology, *Modern Midwestern Sex*, edited by Horace Rosette.

(b.) Paul de Kock's "breakthrough" stories, which caught the attention of Virginia Woolf, "the overbred scribbler," are, unaccountably, not mentioned in the episode. They are "Mon Hochepot, hein?" (trans. "You're the Top") and "Je suis bien content d'avoir terminé cette dissertation d'anglais" (trans. "Yours for No Down Payment Easy Terms").

(c.) Yasmine Danscul was not yet born when Jean Ingelow died. She is, in fact, an old friend of the boys' florid and debauched Dean and a sometime lecturer on "Odd Costumes and Business Success."

YoYo seems to have lost control of herself and is calling for her father, whoever he might be, to come out of the saloon in which, drunk or sober, he cuts something of a "fine-figured job of a man." After some half-hour of tears, threats, and pleading, John Greene Czcu, staggering slightly, emerges from the New Rensselaer Bar and Grill.

"Where is the Chief?" he unexpectedly asks. "My great, noble, redskinned savage of a blue chief?"

"You ain't my pa!" YoYo screams, falling quickly into a sodden heap of out-of-style garments. Czcu reenters the saloon to sporadic, albeit somewhat drunken applause.

Janos Kooba, noting this sidewalk playlet from the limousine which is speeding him toward the airport, whence he will depart this evening for a fete in his native Yugoslavia, shakes his grizzled head. "And the fools thought for long and exceedingly difficult years that *The Curse* was too melodramatic! It is enough to make a lesser man than I threaten to sough interminably." With this, he sinks back into the plush upholstery, his eyes, which but a moment before had darted about like the demented lighthouse-keeper father of a jilted daughter with Heinrich Himmler's baby in her womb, peaceful at last.

"Vot? Vot? Fair iss hiss paperss?"

Despite the fact that Fred's mind is curdled, if not devastated, by the
indefatigable ministrations of the Frankenstein girls, it appears that he
is correct in his opinion concerning Duke Washington's "actuality."
The proof may be found in the small bedroom of an apartment situated
somewhere in the midst of the semipulsing borough of Queens, where
sits Chico Zeek, raconteur, experimental filmmaker, director, dogged
admirer of *The Orange Dress,* and borrower of trifling sums. He turns
the volume down on his radio so that he may hear his neighbors, Gladys
and Angelo Zeno, go to it like the wren and small gilded fly. As he settles
back to listen to the shouts, screams, splintering furniture, breaking
glass, threats, curses, and wild laughter of the rutting couple, his eyes
fall on the photo of Barry Gatto, who, as Baylor Freeq, played Duke
Washington in *Hellions in Hosiery.* Those were the days! Chico
thinks. When he could afford to live next door to svelte, educated,
attractive vegetarian couples with numerous interests, rather than these
two Yahoos. Suddenly, an enormous crash is heard—surely the dresser
again! "I love you! *Darling! Baby!* PUSSY! WHORE!" follows, a
predictable coda. He doesn't know whether to laugh, cry, get drunk,
masturbate, or kill himself. Such, such are the joys.

Zet arrives at the A & P and walks directly to the melons, not that he
wants to be anywhere near the melons. He doesn't particularly care for
melons, and wonders, in his rattling brain, why the store doesn't have a
Thomas Wyatt section, or at least a John Crowe Ransom section. He
stands sullenly yet dutifully next to a giant bin of honeydews, and as
Marcella Butler, who has returned to the A & P for her own good
reasons, passes him, he looks at her and says, somewhat rudely, "Me
lusteth no longer rotten boughs to climb." Marcie cracks him sharply
across the face and continues on. It is apparent that Zet, an unpleasant,
unemployable youth who recognizes an objective correlative when it's
pointed out to him and is wholly aware that cocktail dresses have suddenly become hatefully gauche, has been "assigned" to the A & P. This
has probably been done, for ineffable reasons, by Baal, the Cat, who
has an unseemly interest in the retail-foods business; certainly not by
Zepar, whom some have incriminated. Zepar, the Crimson Duke, who
drives women mad with lust, has other fish to fry. At this very moment,
with the shades of night threatening to fall, and soon, Zepar, in black tie,

is rushing about city and suburb, looking for small parties to enliven with his presence. Enliven and, shall we say, *surprise?*

"Absolutely!" Zepar says. "I have no interest in *melons,* and have no wish to meet the crude fellow who seemingly *lives* for them. My word!"

Exhausted by the bourgeois, phallocentric attention paid her new aluminum diet ("Fat Poetess Hopes Metal Regimen No Fad"), Olga Begone decides, in her anger and ennui, to read her old, never-mentioned, and almost forgotten novel *Zeppelin Days.* She takes it from its hiding place behind the bathtub and beneath layers of dried polygonum and dense, thickly wadded clusters of greisen and shards of raw meerschaum. It must be thirty years since she's even *seen* the typescript. She sits by the window and begins to read, amazed, after a time, to discover that the novel is quite possibly the worst thing in the language, after *The Duke of the Golden Prong,* of course, that puerile exercise in penis worship. Perhaps worse! How wonderful that it was Sister Rose Zeppole, of all people, who saw with such clarity that Olga's true talents lay in poetry. Dear Rose. The soft night she came directly from the set of, what was it?, *Sisters in Shame?*, her face flushed and her eyes bright with love, still in her habit and wimple. God! She was beautiful, even if she was a little overweight from all those Hershey bars. She wanted to be thin, like Olga. "Like you." Ha and ha. Dear, dear Rose. Who was it who recently told Olga that Rose is now the companion of that insufferable bitch Tania Crosse? Well, she has to eat. Olga puts the typescript into a brown paper bag and places the bag in her garbage can. That is that.

There's a Zippo lighter in Zippy's hand. The latter is a young psychopathic delinquent with a special interest in arson, and his tool of choice, the Zippo lighter, has given him his nickname. At present, he is setting the paper-goods products in the A & P's basement afire, after which he will torch, in probable order, Crown SuperMart, Rudy's Superette, and Village Victuals. He thinks, as he watches a carton of Scott tissue catch nicely, that he can't really help it if these stores happen to be in the "Zone," *his* "Zone." Nobody has ever been able to discover what Zippy means by this, but it seems that it changes, sometimes from day to day. Whatever or wherever it means or is, Zippy obeys its call to action unquestioningly. There go the Bounty paper towels.

As this cruelly hot Sunday draws to a close, the fact is not lost upon us that many other curious and noteworthy things have happened today, involving people whose lives are, perhaps, as interesting or bland as those to which we have been constrained to pay heed, however superficially. Some of the other arresting and even intriguing incidents so far reported have been made so, perhaps, by the very paucity and sketchiness of the information surrounding them; for instance, we know of the reprehensible actions performed by Deirdre Angelica, a glittering zipper opened by George Zaremias, divers benisons conferred on Melissa Butte, the weathered yacht scuttled by Jurgens Yurplatt, unusual consternations caused by Sydelle Cooze, the robust xylophone sounded for Morton Xenon, the huge debts incurred by Monica Delizioso, a venal wit joking with McDonald Webfoote, restless energies expended by Prudence Echevarría, a muscular vagina clasping Smitty Vandoosian, various frivolities indulged in by Charlotte Funze, the despairing ululation heard by Barry Ugh, spectacular gaucheries committed by Zoe Guitarra, the concupiscent tootsie provided for Caspar Tittlenose, juvenile hilarities perpetrated upon Wanita Hutchins, the weird string bean eaten by J.J. Stinsonberg, assorted imbecilities retailed by Lona Iacozzo, the impudent rodeo attended by Edwin Rodgers-Wales, sophomoric japes pulled off by Ella Jacaranda, an appalling queue waited on by Jeremiah Quentin, licentious kudos lavished on Olivia Kincannon, a svelte pannier woven for Marcus Peterpeak, the jocular lectures delivered by Mary Ellen Lemonade, a paper oil well sketched by Teddy O'Mara, scandalous memories treasured by Dolores Melanzana, the aloof nylons gift-wrapped by Bill Nemo, eschatological nuances suggested by Betty Newport, the curious machine invented by Guido McMac, gloomy orisons offered by Norma Okeechobee, the filmy lingerie stolen by Bert LaLane, troublesome psychoses suffered by Shauna Psaltery, a blustering knight dressed down by Ingemar Knauss, facetious queries asked of Ella Queynte, a loose jib secured by Ralph Jocelyn, querulous ripostes aimed at Mimi Ragazza, the crippled iguana nursed by Emil Ippolito, amusing situations stumbled upon by Agatha San Remo, an enormous ham carved by Moise Al-Raschid

Hillel, improper transactions made by Dorothea Trigridd, the new gymnasium buffed for Jamie Georgeton, vainglorious undertakings undertaken by Jennifer Ulalume, a bloodthirsty fly smashed by David Farquhar, startling visions encountered by Angelique Vanilla, a stuffed eagle ogled by Jackie Endicott, hollow welcomes extended to Jane Weir, the unabridged dictionary perused by Cecil Densmore, the crippling xenogamies endured by Eileen Xanthos, a gigantic cucumber sliced by Jerry Corfu, stultifying yearnings hidden by Berta Margolies, the sacred broom plied by Welles Banjo, illegal zealotries championed by Marjorie Sciszek, and the toy airplane dropped on Robert Armbrister, but that is all we know.

Lee Jefferson, whom we have been reminded is sometimes called "Zooz" or "ZuZu," nicknames given her years ago by one of her lovers, is exhausted. She beats some of the dust from the files off her skirt and blouse, wipes her sweaty, streaked face with a tissue, and sits, sprawled, at the crammed and cluttered desk. This anthology business has awakened a lot of memories, most of them unwelcome. Lee lights a cigarette, and realizes how desperately, how completely, how deeply tired she is of all these "contributors," of, really, hell, everybody. Old friends, lovers, acquaintances, all the fools, all the enemies, the darlings, the dears, the predators, the manipulators and the manipulated, the victims, the sweethearts, the mad, the disappeared, and the dead. Tired of all of them. Herself as well. There's been a lot of laughs, anyway. Usually at somebody's expense. Well. A job is a job. Life is life. And life, as they say—and *say*—goes on. The office is very dim now. The sun is low over New Jersey. Twilight is approaching, yet another twilight. Soon it will again grow dark.

DALKEY ARCHIVE PAPERBACKS

DALKEY ARCHIVE PAPERBACKS

STEPHENS, MICHAEL. *Season at Coole*   7.95
WOOLF, DOUGLAS. *Wall to Wall*   7.95
YOUNG, MARGUERITE. *Miss MacIntosh, My Darling*   2-vol. set, 30.00
ZUKOFSKY, LOUIS. *Collected Fiction*   13.50
ZWIREN, SCOTT. *God Head*   10.95

FICTION: BRITISH

BROOKE-ROSE, CHRISTINE. *Amalgamemnon*   9.95
CHARTERIS, HUGO. *The Tide Is Right*   9.95
FIRBANK, RONALD. *Complete Short Stories*   9.95
GALLOWAY, JANICE. *Foreign Parts*   12.95
GALLOWAY, JANICE. *The Trick Is to Keep Breathing*   11.95
HUXLEY, ALDOUS. *Antic Hay*   12.50
HUXLEY, ALDOUS. *Point Counter Point*   13.95
MOORE, OLIVE. *Spleen*   10.95
MOSLEY, NICHOLAS. *Accident*   9.95
MOSLEY, NICHOLAS. *Assassins*   12.95
MOSLEY, NICHOLAS. *Children of Darkness and Light*   13.95
MOSLEY, NICHOLAS. *Impossible Object*   9.95
MOSLEY, NICHOLAS. *Judith*   10.95
MOSLEY, NICHOLAS. *Natalie Natalia*   12.95

FICTION: FRENCH

BUTOR, MICHEL. *Portrait of the Artist as a Young Ape*   10.95
CÉLINE, LOUIS-FERDINAND. *Castle to Castle*   13.95
CÉLINE, LOUIS-FERDINAND. *North*   13.95
CREVEL, RENÉ. *Putting My Foot in It*   9.95
ERNAUX, ANNIE. *Cleaned Out*   10.95
GRAINVILLE, PATRICK. *The Cave of Heaven*   10.95
NAVARRE, YVES. *Our Share of Time*   9.95
QUENEAU, RAYMOND. *The Last Days*   11.95
QUENEAU, RAYMOND. *Pierrot Mon Ami*   9.95
ROUBAUD, JACQUES. *The Great Fire of London*   12.95
ROUBAUD, JACQUES. *The Princess Hoppy*   9.95
SIMON, CLAUDE. *The Invitation*   9.95

FICTION: GERMAN

SCHMIDT, ARNO. *Collected Stories*   13.50
SCHMIDT, ARNO. *Nobodaddy's Children*   13.95

DALKEY ARCHIVE PAPERBACKS

FICTION: IRISH

CUSACK, RALPH. *Cadenza*	7.95
MAC LOCHLAINN, ALF. *The Corpus in the Library*	11.95
MACLOCHLAINN, ALF. *Out of Focus*	7.95
O'BRIEN, FLANN. *The Dalkey Archive*	9.95
O'BRIEN, FLANN. *The Hard Life*	11.95
O'BRIEN, FLANN. *The Poor Mouth*	10.95

FICTION: LATIN AMERICAN AND SPANISH

CAMPOS, JULIETA. *The Fear of Losing Eurydice*	8.95
LINS, OSMAN. *The Queen of the Prisons of Greece*	12.95
PASO, FERNANDO DEL. *Palinuro of Mexico*	14.95
RÍOS, JULIÁN. *Poundemonium*	13.50
SARDUY, SEVERO. *Cobra* and *Maitreya*	13.95
TUSQUETS, ESTHER. *Stranded*	9.95
VALENZUELA, LUISA. *He Who Searches*	8.00

POETRY

ALFAU, FELIPE. *Sentimental Songs*	9.95
ANSEN, ALAN. *Contact Highs: Selected Poems 1957-1987*	11.95
BURNS, GERALD. *Shorter Poems*	9.95
FAIRBANKS, LAUREN. *Muzzle Thyself*	9.95
GISCOMBE, C. S. *Here*	9.95
MARKSON, DAVID. *Collected Poems*	9.95
ROUBAUD, JACQUES. *The Plurality of Worlds of Lewis*	9.95
THEROUX, ALEXANDER. *The Lollipop Trollops*	10.95

NONFICTION

FORD, FORD MADOX. *The March of Literature*	16.95
GREEN, GEOFFREY, ET AL. *The Vineland Papers*	14.95
MATHEWS, HARRY. *20 Lines a Day*	8.95
MOORE, STEVEN. *Ronald Firbank: An Annotated Bibliography*	30.00
ROUDIEZ, LEON S. *French Fiction Revisited*	14.95
SHKLOVSKY, VIKTOR. *Theory of Prose*	14.95
WEST, PAUL. *Words for a Deaf Daughter* and *Gala*	12.95
WYLIE, PHILIP. *Generation of Vipers*	13.95
YOUNG, MARGUERITE. *Angel in the Forest*	13.95

Dalkey Archive Press, ISU Box 4241, Normal, IL 61790-4241
fax (309) 438-7422
Visit our website at http://www.cas.ilstu.edu/english/dalkey/dalkey.html